Sudetenland

George T. Chronis

AUTHOR'S NOTE

My association with Czechoslovakia began many years ago as a teenager with the help of a pen pal living in Prague. Through the exchange of letters, magazines and books I developed a fondness for the land of my friend from Central Europe. As often happens in such cases, one gets a look at history from another perspective and that instilled a desire in me to discover more about that part of the world.

In my later studies I took the opportunity to learn more about the First Czechoslovak Republic whenever I could. Classes in 20th Century history here in the United States diligently discuss the events leading up to the Munich Conference in 1938 where Great Britain, France and Italy agreed to cede large swaths of Western Czechoslovakia to Germany. The discussion is usually devoted to the consequences of appeasing dictators, but very little was ever said about the nation this diktat was perpetrated upon. Many of my classmates would have been surprised to learn that Czechoslovakia in those days was a thriving and prosperous country with a capable armed forces and strong defences that could have put up a tough fight against Germany.

The political crisis over the status of the Sudetendeutsche minority in Czechoslovakia during the fall of 1938 could have exploded into conflict any number of times. The historical record shows that Adolph Hitler was intent on taking what he wanted by force yet was cajoled otherwise as a result of continued British diplomacy. This novel plays on the possibility that an unintended mistake provides Hitler with the provocation necessary for him to do what he wanted to do anyway... invade. Had that occurred, our world would be a very different place today.

As the Czechoslovaks were once part of the Austro-Hungarian Empire, city names can often be confusing. English speakers call the capital Prague, the Czechs call it Praha and the German name is Prag. This is especially confusing for the ethnic German cities within Bohemia. Rather than constantly switch between Eger and Cheb, or Karlsbad and Karlovy Vary, I have relied on German city names where the population was predominantly German in 1938.

Similarly, characters will often say the name for many terms in their own native languages. While I provide the English name in descriptions, readers can find handy cheat sheets online at the web address below:

I have included many real people within these pages in the roles they carried out historically. In doing so I have tried to stay as sincere as possible to each of them based on the factual record. For my own characters it was immensely satisfying to throw them into the boiling cauldron and watch this historical "what-if" unfold through their eyes.

www.sudetenland.georgetchronis.com

FOR BOŘIVOJ
& DR. RADA

A Czechoslovak Fokker F.VIIb transport

JULY 14, 1932
PRAHA-KBELY AIRFIELD, ČESKOSLOVENSKO

The new hangar was going up ahead of schedule. Out in the countryside far from the capital it was easy for the workmen high up on their scaffolding to hear the droning of aircraft engines heading toward the field. One of the new civil airliners was coming in – a big one at that – a Fokker F.VIIb Tri-motor with silver wings was approaching fast at low altitude. Dangerously low. The laborers were far too high up to jump, and there was not enough time to climb down. Their only option was to watch nervously as the Fokker flew straight at them, and then roared overhead with only a few meters to spare. The stream of air from the three big propellers rattled the scaffolding so severely several workers were almost knocked over the side. They all cursed the bastard pilot – raising their fists and hammers as punctuation – while the aircraft banked to the left over the field to cast its shadow on the vehicles lined up nearby on the grass landing strip.

The surge of air flowing behind the low-flying airliner sent dust billowing over six men in dark suits standing near the line of automobiles. Four of that number – bookish men unaccustomed to aeroplanes – huddled uncomfortably together. Buffeted by the blast of air, they fidgeted nervously in their ill-fitting suits while struggling to hold onto their hats. The remaining two men – taller and more commanding – made a point of standing away from the nervous ones. They were well accustomed to aerodromes and stared calmly at the arriving plane. They also had better tailors. Their suits were conservative in cut, yet the material and fit were above average. The one concession to vanity was their fedoras worn at a rakish tilt. A workman's hammer thudded hard into the ground at their feet, yet neither of the men flinched.

Furst looked up to see the owner of the hammer on the construction scaffolding still brandishing his fist at the aircraft. This amused Furst. He could have had the fool arrested. That too would have been amusing but there was no time for such indulgences. Hearing the Fokker gun its engines, Furst shot a sideways glance at his companion.

"It's about time. The damned dust and this accursed heat are a bitch," Furst blew off steam. Next he gestured rudely at the tense quartet nearby. "And when did baby-sitting bureaucrats get added to our duties?"

Burda had grown to enjoy the short fuse of his junior partner, although as a matter of respect he had to work hard at not grinning when Furst grew annoyed at one perceived infraction or another. There were so many such misdemeanors that Burda had lost count. It took all of his control not to laugh when Furst was so serious.

"Perhaps a useless piece of slime is not so useless after all," Burda remembered how Furst had described bureaucrats before.

The comment aroused Furst's curiosity, "Jan, what do you know?"

"Not as much as I suspect," Burda chose to be vague.

The Fokker's pilot throttled back the engines coming in for the landing. The tri-motor's main undercarriage tires touched and then planted themselves firmly upon the hard surface. The tail wheel came down quickly and the pilot applied his brakes. The Fokker slowed as it approached the cars, then U-turned in front of the vehicles before coming to a stop. A ground crew ran up to place wedges under the aircraft tires, then signaled the pilot to cut the engines of the high-winged monoplane.

Burda was scarcely twenty-nine yet was learning that the closer you got to real power the more years it took off of your account. Case in point, the man stepping out of the fuselage door was Edvard Beneš, the first and only foreign minister in the Czechoslovak state's brief fourteen years of existence. The forty-eight year-old was a small man but his imprint on the nation was huge. It was his diplomacy that had secured international support for the creation of a free Czechoslovakia in 1918. And by the looks of it, the foreign minister was not a happy man today. Beneš handed off a number of diplomatic satchels to his waiting junior ministers, whom Beneš swiftly dismissed before moving quickly on to Burda, and ignoring Furst completely.

"I've met you before?" Beneš addressed the intelligence officer.

"Yes, foreign minister. I was present at your last intelligence briefing before you left for Paris," Burda replied.

Beneš was pleased at having remembered the man, who had never had reason to speak during that briefing, or a reason to move out of the shadow of his master. But this was not who Beneš had wanted to see, and that displeased him. "Forgive the rudeness. I am very tired and there is much yet to accomplish today. Where is your chief?"

"Unavoidably detained, foreign minister," was all Burda could answer in return.

"Enlighten me, please," Beneš," was growing weary.

"Mister Moravec is away from Praha, near the border. We got your message to him, and he is returning immediately, but he won't make it back into the capital before late tonight," Burda was not at liberty to discuss why the boss had gone to Eger as state security was at stake and it was a sensitive matter.

The insufficient explanation came as one more in a long string of recent annoyances for Beneš. It was obvious pursuing the matter would be a waste of time. "Unfortunately, what I have to report cannot wait. In his absence you will have to do. I've called an emergency meeting with Syrový and the chiefs of staff. Your section must be included. Be at the Foreign Ministry in four hours."

FOREIGN MINISTRY – HRADČANY, PRAHA

Furst swerved the dark blue Praga-Piccolo coupe to a screeching stop near the front entrance. The car had barely come to a standstill when the passenger door swung open and Burda jumped out of the car in a rush. Rather than drive on to find a legal parking spot, Furst switched off the ignition and casually got out of the car to follow along.

"I'm not writing the paperwork if you forget to show the identification again," Burda pointed at the windshield.

Furst reached back into the car and put a wide band with a military crest around the inside of the sun visor as Burda sprinted up the steps to the main entrance of the Hapsburg-era building. Burda could feel the first wisps of a cool breeze toying with the back of his neck and at this hour he would have much preferred sipping a coffee at an outdoor cafe. But the foreign minister believed what he had to report was of major importance and there frankly was no one else more senior available from the Second Department to send than Burda. His superiors in the army's military intelligence wing had all gone to the western border to finalize plans to set up financial institutions that would cater to Germans with bad credit. The whole undertaking was an elaborate front to ensnare potential agents in government employment across the border and was so hush-hush that no one outside of the department was to know about the operation. Not the foreign minister, or the army generáls that Beneš had summoned, could know why Colonel Moravec was out of Praha.

Inside the building, Burda stopped to gather his thoughts and straighten his tie. Furst pulled out his cigarette case and offered Burda one of its contents. Unfortunately, it wasn't one of the French brands Burda favored. "Thank you, but not now. Save me one for later."

"Guaranteed. I'll save the last bullet for you, as well," Furst replied sardonically – lighting up a cigarette for himself from a matchbook and taking a long drag. "Alright then, go in there and get it over with. I'm hungry after all of this running around today, and waiting around up here won't make it any better. Steaks are on you."

"That's negotiable," Burda checked his wristwatch. "Damn, I've got to get upstairs or I will be late."

As Burda's steps echoed down the hall Furst found a wall to lean against. His partner could be detained for a considerable amount of time and he would need to find ways to entertain himself. Before Furst could ponder further on the possibilities, a young woman left one of the nearby offices and walked in his direction. The curvaceous redhead made eye contact and smiled. Since Furst had the good sense to hold her gaze, she stopped beside him.

"May I have a cigarette?" the redhead flirted as she sized him up. Her conclusion was the body underneath the suit was taught and firm by the way the wool fabric draped his features.

Furst reached into his coat for the cigarette case and smoothly pushed off from the wall. "Of course you may."

Burda entered the meeting room believing he had a few minutes to spare, but discovered to his embarrassment that Beneš had already begun his briefing. Seated around the sturdy mahogany table, with its matching padded leather seats, were the old foxes from the Great War that made up the general staff. These were the men who bolted from their units in the Austro-Hungarian army and raised the Czechoslovak Legion in Russia to fight the Hapsburgs... and they were all staring at Burda.

Apologies my young kapitán," Beneš saved him, "but I began the briefing early."

As there were no available chairs Burda backed himself as inauspiciously as possible against the nearby wall next to Beneš' aide.

"Podplukovník Moravec has obligations outside of Praha and is not able to attend. Kapitán Burda here will represent the Second Department in his absence," Beneš explained.

Generál Syrový tapped the tabletop with his finger. He was curious to know why the Second Department chief was unavailable, but thought it impolite to further interrupt Beneš' report. "Please proceed foreign minister."

"As I was saying," Beneš continued, "Earlier today I briefed President Masaryk on what I am about to share with you, and he has given me his approval on my recommendations."

Beneš opened up his leather satchel and took out a set of typed notes. His aide was immediately at his side to begin handing copies of the document out to the generals.

"As you are aware, I have been at the World Disarmament Conference in Geneva. In my estimation, this was the last opportunity for the

European powers to prevent another conflagration. For ten years, Czechoslovakia has worked closely with our partner states to get this conference off the ground. The centerpiece of the conference was a proposal by President Hoover of the United States. If accepted, the major powers would have agreed to qualitatively disarm – to progressively eliminate offensive weapons in favor of defensive weapons over time. But the French, British, Italians and Japanese repeatedly gutted the plan with provisos eliminating any concrete reductions. The proposal has become a list of principles without any teeth," Beneš concluded.

The generáls accepted the politicians had to make the attempt but the possibility of success was nil. The fascists were expanding their power, the democracies were fearful of the fascists and the communists lurked in the gutters waiting for an opportunity to strike. How could there be progress toward disarmament?

Beneš leaned back in his chair, considering his next words carefully. "Our allies and our enemies are mentally preparing for war. They may not profess as much openly, but those are the facts. Everything I have witnessed inclines me to believe that a grave crisis in Europe is unavoidable. The national socialists in Germany and the fascists in Italy will precipitate it. As I have just recommended to President Masaryk, we have four years. The crisis will likely overtake us in 1936 or 1937. By then, the republic must be prepared for war."

JULY 18, 1932
SPECIAL TO CONSOLIDATED NEWS
BY WALTER HAUTH

BERLIN – With less than two weeks remaining before parliamentary elections, the German nation convulsed in yet another spasm of violence within the city of Hamburg. Yesterday, only two days after chancellor von Papen rescinded a federal decree outlawing the private armies of the Nazi Party, national socialist storm troopers marched through working class neighborhoods of this blue-collar city. Despite a police escort, local members of the Social Democratic Party came to blows with the brown-shirted national socialists. Local authorities estimate that nineteen people were killed, and as many as three hundred more were injured on both sides.

In the capital, Berlin, chancellor von Papen responded to the violence by accusing the Prussian state government of being incapable of maintaining law and order. Sources within the German national government say von Papen is likely to capitalize on the rioting to push for a dismissal of the elected social democrats running the Prussian state – political rivals of von Papen's Centre Party. In response, social democratic officials within the Ministry of the Interior threatened to call up the labor movement's independent defense auxiliary, the *Reichsbanner*, to defend the elected government in Prussia. The *Reichsbanner* is reported to have at least four hundred thousand well-trained irregulars, and rumored to possess as many as three million reservists throughout Germany.

National socialist leader Adolph Hitler condemned the street violence and accused social democrats and communists of inciting the disturbance as uniformed Nazis were *peaceably* attempting to exercise their right to parade without molestation.

The bloody clash between rival political parties in Hamburg is but one more example of the deterioration of conditions in Germany. The Great Depression has hit this country hard, with the number of unemployed swelling from two and a quarter million in 1930, to more than five million today. As ordinary Germans grapple with the worsening conditions, the national government has been unable to shore up the faltering economy. Only two months ago, president von Hindenburg demanded the resignation of Heinrich Bruening of the Centre Party, who held the chancellorship since March 1930, and who was replaced by von Papen.

Neither has the worsening economy left von Hindenburg, a hero from the Great War and president since 1925, untouched. In the March elections this year, von Hindenburg was forced into a run-off when he could muster only forty-nine percent of the vote, just short of the majority needed to win outright. In the April 10 run-off elections, von Hindenburg garnered fifty-three percent of the vote, thanks in large part to support from social democrats fearful of a win by Mister Hitler. Hitler himself received thirty-seven percent of the run-off vote, while Communist Party candidate Erich Thaelmann came in third with ten percent.

Concerned about further rioting prior to the parliamentary elections scheduled for July 31, the chancellor's office told members of the press that von Papen would likely sign a decree tomorrow banning political parades until after the voting.

FEBRUARY 5, 1933
OTTENSEN DISTRICT, HAMBURG

The Magirus heavy lorry rumbled down the pitch-dark avenue like an angry pachyderm – exhaust snorting loudly from the exhaust as the driver shifted gears to pick up speed. The slab-sided beast of metal had been *liberated* from the city yard precisely for the huge chevron-like plow mounted to the front for winter road clearance. Following close behind the Magirus was a convoy of eight smaller freight-hauling trucks, each packed solid with indomitable men brandishing a variety of clubs, wrenches and other heavy tools. Cutting right around a corner too tightly for how fast the Magirus was hurtling forward, the cell leader behind the wheel struggled to keep control of the mass of metal. In a spray of sparks and loose gravel, an edge of the snow plow dug into the street, braking and steadying the Magirus sufficiently to keep the lorry from rolling over.

By sheer luck the cell leader's life had thusly been saved. If not from the crash that should have resulted from his rashness, then from his cohorts following close behind who would have reacted harshly had their plans for that night been dashed.

The Reichsbanner company commander rested one hand on the wooden pistol holster attached to his belt, while grasped tightly in his other hand was a rolled up party flyer wielded like a saber. The joint rally had completely filled the warehouse and he had the rapt attention of every soul before him.

"Look around you! In factory and workshop, in town and country, the will for a united front against the fascists exists. Social democrats and kommunists must jointly defend the Deutsche state," he fought to be heard above the cheers. "Make no mistake, we are under siege. Social democrats must say to kommunists: the policies of our parties may be irreconcilably opposed, but if the fascists come tonight to wreck your organization's hall we will come running, arms in hand, to help you. Kommunists must promise us that if our people are threatened they will rush to our aid--"

--An explosion interrupted the rally as the corrugated metal side of the warehouse imploded – forced inward by the snowplow mounted on a Magirus heavy lorry. Unsuspecting factory workers and longshoremen tumbled under each other as the force of the breach knocked them down like dominoes. As the Magirus reversed out of the gash, dozens of Sturmabteilung brawlers poured in swinging pipes and clubs as they spread out into the interior.

The Reichsbanner commander gathered his composure and turned in the direction of the flood of Nazi street punks. He pulled the Mauser C96 pistol from its holster, took aim and dropped one of the lead attackers. "Workers! Beat them back!"

Shouts of defiance rang out as the socialists and communist party members leapt into action with whatever blunt instruments they could lay their hands on. In the front line of the SA brown shirts was a burly, barrel-chested brute, fiendishly wielding a long pipefitting. He was picking stunned targets up off the floor then hitting them square against the head to drop the victims back upon the wood planks. A bullet sped close past the big man's head, drilling a hole through the temple of the brown shirt beside him. The SA brawler fell alertly to one knee in a defensive crouch to confirm his comrade was dead as three compatriots rushed the platform to take down the shooter. Satisfied, the SA leader leapt back up to his feet with weapon ready. Nearby a young red was unlucky enough to be picking himself up off the floor – easy prey.

All the stunned Krisch saw was a big blur forcefully pulling him the rest of the way onto his feet. Before Krisch could bring his arm up to swing a fist, the brown shirt cursed, then head butted him. Somewhere close to unconsciousness Krisch felt himself slung over the shoulder of the bear and carried outside in the frigid winter air.

Confident that he had gone far enough not to be followed down the back alley, the brown shirt plopped the inert socialist down against the wet brick wall of a shuttered shop. Distant echoes of violence and death drifted up through the alley while the bear glared at the limp form at his feet.

"Anton Krisch. I would never had taken you for a leftist agitator when you dated my sister."

The distantly familiar voice roused Krisch from his stupor. Looking up, he focused on the big round face with recognition. "Morgen, why are you in my nightmare?"

Krisch made an attempt to stand but Morgen pushed him square in the chest with the business end of the pipe, forcing Krisch back against the brick wall.

"Saving your skin for old times sake," Morgen wanted the notion to sink in. "Listen, I liked you back then, kid. You and Kristina were good together and would have made a decent pair if we had not been forced to pick up and leave."

A flood of pleasant memories flowed through Krisch's mind. He pushed the pipe aside and looked up at the big brother of his first real love. "What happened? Your whole family just disappeared. No good-byes, no letters, no reason... just gone."

Morgen's arm tensed as he raised the business end of the pipe and then slammed it against a cobblestone. "My father wasn't so lucky as yours. No trade union contract, no strike fund, no union aid for the unemployed. He was a clerk, just a clerk. And when all the banks closed, there were no jobs for clerks, no rent for the house. When the landlord put us out we had to sell off most everything we owned to pay our debts. We went to live with my uncle in Wilhelmshaven and were forbidden to talk about it to protect the last shred of my father's pride. She wanted to tell you but father forbade it."

Slowly, and never breaking eye contact with Morgen, Krisch picked himself up. "How is Kristina?"

A fleeting expression of softness crossed Morgen's face. "Dead. She died from influenza the first winter in Wilhelmshaven."

Krisch's eyelids stayed shut for a long time. When they opened he wiped the blood away from his forehead to better focus on Morgen.

"And this is how we honor her sweet memory," Krisch's blood stained hand gestured at the SA badges pinned to Morgen's chest. "We are a nation of dead people! The good ones who have already been taken and all of the rest our comrades will soon send to the grave. Morgen, is there no bottom to this well of hate?"

If Krisch was hoping to touch something sympathetic in Morgen, he had failed. "I do what I have to do. When everything you ever had was taken away, and the rest of the world doesn't give a damn, it changes you. If this is the only way for me to crawl back out of that pit, to get my fair share, so be it."

Morgen reached over and ripped the SPD pin from Krisch's lapel then threw it over a nearby fence. "That's better, now get your ass out of here," Morgen advised. "You were a good kid once and you meant a lot to my sister. That's how I honor her memory."

Done with sentimentality. Morgen's giant hand fell heavily on Krisch's upper arm to shove the younger man in the direction of the alley exit. "Move. If you are smart, stop running with these reds, you'll live longer."

MARCH 23, 1933
CONSOLIDATED NEWS SYNDICATE HQ
FULLER BUILDING, NEW YORK CITY

Another thrilling assignment on New York City nightlife: who was there, who came with whom, what they wore, who they left with... nothing more than glorified gossip. It never failed to amaze her that with so many people down and out in the depression, folks still wanted to read tripe about so-and-sos who still lived conspicuously high. Well, it kept Hollywood in business. Hell it kept her in business, too. At least that's what she reminded herself as she weaved through a line of decrepit wood desks to drop off her copy with her assignment editor.

Ros burned for the chance to cover a great murder mystery or a city hall scandal. She was wasting her time with all this frilly stuff. But try and convince the editors that a woman should be getting those jobs and you'd get a laugh... a big laugh. They didn't care, good assignments went to reporters who'd been around awhile and earned the right. And face it, how many women stuck around in broken down old buildings like this one watching typewriter ribbon ink seep in through their pores. And as she looked around at the choice examples of reporters on the floor – their rumpled shirts, coats and slacks that may not have been washed in months – how many women could put up with the odor? How did she put up with the stink?

At least Ros looked and could talk a good game. Some of her male colleagues even said she was easy on the eyes thanks to the raven black hair plus the long legs – and that was before they got drunk at Callahan's down the street.

"Hey Des," Ros approached the grizzled old executive editor. "Here's the Carter Party story all clean and ready to go."

"Yeah, thanks Ros. I'm sure it's fine," Des kept checking his galleys without even looking up at her.

"I can tell you're overjoyed. Look, maybe one day you guys will learn to appreciate that it takes skills to make this rubbish you hand me

interesting," she tried to get some respect while dropping the pages into a wire tray on his desk.

Des didn't look up from his proofing. It would have betrayed a mischievous glint. "Take it someplace else, angel. We all pay our dues."

Yeah, maybe she *should* take it someplace else, at least out of this joint, Ros Talmadge told herself. Malloy over at AP had challenged her to a round of billiards and she didn't want to keep him waiting for the pasting she was going to give him tonight.

"You're gonna miss me when I'm gone," Ros vowed as she turned to leave.

"I'm crying already," Des threw the threat back at her. But the reporter wasn't sticking around for more punishment since he could hear her shoes tapping against the marble floors with authority on the way out. Too bad Des had to bring her back. "Hey, Ros, the boss wants to see you."

Ros pivoted around, but didn't stop backpedaling in the opposite direction. Chatting with Harry Lasky was the last thing she wanted to endure on this earth "Sure, Des, I'll catch him tomorrow."

"Not tomorrow... now," he raised his voice. "You know how the boss is when he doesn't get what he wants."

"Like a three year-old... I know," Ros said it loud enough for everyone in the vicinity to hear. "What does he want... fashion advice? Does Harry have a date or something? It's only been six months since the divorce."

Ros was unaware of who she was backing into – a wiry man standing with his arms folded over his chest, and a resolute expression plastered on his face. Harry Lasky was listening to it all and was not amused.

"Ah, Des don't get all bent out of--," Ros stopped abruptly as her backside bumped into something. She turned around slowly to find herself eyeball-to-eyeball with the seen everything, heard it all owner of the Consolidated News Service. "--Harry, there you are. Did I tell you that Mrs. Randall Carter was asking *all* about you at her party last night?"

"Can it, Talmadge," Lasky pointed toward the corner office with glass walls. "In there, now."

This was one occasion where a smile and turning on the charm would not save Ros' skin. She sighed and marched off in the direction indicated. Unfortunately, the trip took her right past the jockey-sized McCoy and a bunch of other amused reporters who whistled and cheered in their best racetrack form.

"Sweet talking won't get you out of this one, Ros," McCoy jeered.

Ros ignored the taunt and continued on her way. The chortling stopped when McCoy turned around to discover Lasky staring him down.

"Everyone has an opinion, huh McCoy?" Lasky reproached the reporter. "You have so much to say, great. An Independent Subway construction crew just busted a sewer main around sixty-third in Queens. Go out and write it up... in person."

"Ah, chief," McCoy pleaded.

One day he was going to clean out this bunch of comedians and hire real reporters. And to add emphasis to how much he thought of McCoy, Lasky took a swing with his leg to kick the suddenly swift-moving reporter in the rear. That put the fear of Lasky into the suddenly quiet newsroom. "Hop to it, wise guy."

Ros strutted into Lasky's office, coming to a dead end in front of the wood desk that was as long as Rhode Island. She tapped the sole of her shoe on the floor impatiently while Lasky bellowed at someone else in the newsroom. At least the afternoon view over Manhattan was pleasing. Blowing in like a foul wind, Lasky slammed the door and walked right past her.

"Boss, I'm sorry to run a little fast with your image back there," Ros offered up in appeasement.

Still rounding his desk, Lasky shook her off with a wave of his hand. "Forget it. That's not why you're here. I have a job for you."

Wondering whether she should be concerned or happy, Ros decided to play along. "What kind of job?"

Sitting down, Lasky rifled through some paperwork until he found the document he was looking for.

"Yeah, go find this guy Lester downstairs, he'll get you all set up. Lodging, fares, advances, the whole low-down," Lasky finished, handing her the form.

"Who's Lester? What are you talking about? Where am I going?" she blurted out before taking a wild glance at the paperwork.

Lasky thought if he could keep Ros distracted, maybe he could get the problem child on the boat before she could cry about needing a raise. He reached out and grabbed the form back. Throwing it on the desktop, Lasky signed the paper with his fountain pen.

Done, he thrust the page back at Ros. "Paris. I'm sending you to Paris."

Ros looked down at the form, then at Lasky, then back at the form. "I'm going to Paris? When did someone around here start liking me?"

"Stop dreaming, no one around here likes you," Lasky taunted her while he walked back around to the front of his desk. "That screwy Miranda just stabbed me in the back. She found herself some guy over there, got married, and now she's running off to some French island in the Caribbean. I need someone to pick up the pieces in Paris. That's you."

"Just slow down. Miranda got hitched?" all of the angles weren't coming together in Ros' head.

"Yeah, nice announcement: *Hi Harry, I got married, and I quit,*" Lasky mimicked a feminine voice. These damn ditzy broads were always letting him down. But Ros showed promise. Pointing his finger repeatedly at her nose, he continued his rant. "Miranda left me high and dry, so I'm sending you to pick up the pieces. You, I don't have to worry about. With that mouth, no one is going to be marrying you."

"Harry!" Ros yelled indignantly. "You're not painting a very enticing picture for me here. What if I don't want to go to Paris?"

Lasky stared at her incredulously. "Who doesn't want to go to Paris? Any one of those stooges out there would kill to go to Paris but none of them have what you've got."

With her natural skepticism starting to boil over, Ros leaned in closer and started jabbing Lasky in the shoulder with two fingers, slowly backing him up against the desk.

"I know what you're up to Harry," her tone low and threatening. "Miranda was on a fashion beat. That means to you the only thing I got that those mugs out there don't have, is boobs. It's another glorified gossip beat, you rat!"

"It's Paris! C'mon, every woman wants to go to Paris," Lasky shouted in his defense.

"That's not the point," Ros continued poking him. "I'm tired of going to county fairs. I'm tired of the only labor unrest stories coming my way having to be in washing machine factories. I'm tired of reporting on this ditzy socialite, and that boring dolt of a millionaire. I want a real beat like a real reporter, Harry. I can do the job just as good, or better, as those guys out there and I cost less."

"Stop trying to get on my good side," Lasky retorted, readying his counter attack. He hadn't expected *this* much of a fight. But he needed her and he couldn't run the risk of her bolting. "Listen, give me a chance here. You're the only person I've got who can jump in and take over for Miranda. But you're also a hell of a lot better than she is... err, was. You won't have to work as hard to cover her beat. In case you haven't noticed, between the Nazis and Mussolini, there's one crisis after another going on over in Europe. I'm sure there's going to be *some* important stories Walter and our boys won't be able to get to. What you do with your free time is up to you."

Somewhere in there were a couple of compliments, but she wasn't going to let him twist free that easily. Paris did sound kind of nice, and he was throwing her a bone in the way of real work, but Ros was sure the beat would take up more time than Lasky was promising, and she wanted something else from him... for pride, and because she could. So Ros just silently stared Lasky down, daring him to add one more carrot to get her to sign on.

"Okay, and I'll throw in a raise," Lasky conceded after a long standoff.

"Done!" Ros threw her arm out to shake hands and seal the deal.

MAY 8, 1933
ÉCOLE SPÉCIALE MILITAIRE DE SAINT-CYR

The three Czechoslovak junior officers were almost done with the military academy Napoleon himself had founded one hundred and twenty-five years before. These competitive young lieutenants had been lucky to make it to Saint-Cyr – usually a privilege reserved for older graduates from the Staff College in Praha. But the army was expanding swiftly and the generals would never satisfy the demand for new officers if all of the old traditions were followed. As the Czech military had been patterned after France's following the Great War, it made sense to send the most promising candidates to Saint-Cyr to train in advanced tactics and military history.

"Well boys, soak it in while you can," Kopecky and his compatriots cut their usual path between buildings. "In a month they're going to toss us out of here."

"Maybe sooner if Capka doesn't stop arguing with Dieudonne about practically everything that comes out of the old man's mouth," Bozik pointed accusingly at Capka.

"Keep it up, Bozik. Some of us can't get by on our good looks," the balding Capka backhanded his friend's shoulder. "Besides, you think the same way I do: move fast, hit hard, and get out. The only difference is that you want to risk your hide in a stitched together airplane."

"Sneer if you will, my obstinate and stocky friend," Bozik adjusted his cap to a more rakish tilt, "but sometimes it's safer to keep what we know to ourselves. Remember how Dieudonne dressed you down last week?"

"The Army of France does not train bandits," Kopecky adjusted his voice and manner to mimic the dignified, upper class antiquarian.

"I'm surrounded by cowards," Capka spit into the grass.

"Slow down," another cadet in a French uniform was running up behind them.

Distracted from Kopecky's comical imitation of their instructor, Bozik recognized the Frenchman, "It's Darzal."

Darzal liked the Czechs. They were fresh, friendly and damn handy to have around in a pick-up football match. They reminded him a lot of his old schoolmates in Cherbourg, and he felt much closer to them, at times than the stuffy louts from old families that mostly attended Saint-Cyr.

"Gentleman, did you hear the news?" Darzal joined their ranks. "Marshal Dieudonne has a surprise for us."

Capka hated when the French cadets elevated the old war-horse to such a lofty rank, even facetiously. Darzal probably was trying to needle him.

"Surprise? I doubt the old man has it in him," Capka scoffed.

Capka's attitude drew a smile from Darzal. "Nevertheless, I have just discovered that today we are being treated to a guest lecturer."

The lecture hall may have started off as part of a regal chateau, but five generations of youthful subalterns had left their mark on the musty high-ceilinged chamber. The room went quiet as Dieudonne and another officer walked past the tall, soot-tinged windows to the front of the hall that was occupied by two huge maps: one of Europe, the other of the world.

Dieudonne was by far the older of the two. His wispy white hair and moustache, together with a suit that was twenty years out of date, gave him a grandfatherly manner. The old man proudly wore his many service medals on the breast of his suit jacket as he escorted his guest forward. The other fellow was an army major full of pride and attitude in a perfectly pressed uniform, and as tall as a great tree.

"Good morning, gentlemen," Dieudonne stepped up to his lectern while the tall major stood at stoic attention behind him. "As you are well aware, there has been a small vocal minority among you who are critical of the established theorems of the Army of France."

Old Dieudonne stared directly at Capka so there was no doubt where that artillery round had been targeted.

"Never let it be said," Dieudonne continued, "that an examination of battle logistics and strategy at my hands, would be so suspect as to ignore opposing theories. The remaining weeks of this course will be dedicated to the mobile application of armored vehicles in battle. But to properly introduce these themes to you, I have called on an old friend, a former instructor here at Saint-Cyr, and one of the most gifted minds serving our nation today. Major Charles de Gaulle.

"Thank you Colonel Dieudonne," de Gaulle stepped forward as the instructor seated himself near the windows. "And thank you cadets. I graduated from this institution in 1912, served in the Great War and fought at Verdun. I was a member of General Weygand's staff in 1920 when the Bolsheviks were turned back at Warsaw. I taught history here in 1921. In 1925 I was appointed to the staff of the Conseil Supérieur de la Guerre. Between 1927 and 1929, I was part of French forces occupying the Rhineland. Until recently, I was posted for two years with our military mission in Lebanon. If my career has taught me an intrinsic lesson, it is the need for strategies based on preventive intervention. Of a mechanized professional army ready to move onto the offensive at the onset of a crisis, rather than depending on the hurried massing of ill-train conscripts to be thrown by the thousands at the invading enemy, hoping to stem the onslaught.

"One sees the French army of today constructing its doctrines, its plans and its systems in accordance with the lessons of the last war, when we must instead seek inspiration in the operations of the great cavalry of the olden days. The army of the future, thanks to its engines and caterpillars, will be able to come into the open as well as to disappear with great speed. In short, these tanks and mechanized lorries will change their position, their direction and their dispositions almost instantaneously; and will do so independently."

"You finally got your wish," Kopecky punched Capka playfully on the arm. "Someone who thinks like you do."

"The amount of destruction caused by modern war, the effect on civilian populations and the loss of critical resources, have restored the utmost importance to the seizing of territory, not the ceding of it," de

Gaulle pressed on. "To lose Thionville and Briey would be to surrender half our steel production. To accept a temporary withdrawal from Strasbourg would mean that we would have to raze it to the ground in order to retake it. If the Germans cross the Meuse, the battle is brought to the gates of Lille. If they capture Antwerp and install their airplanes and submarines there, our communications with England become seriously affected.

"Now, consider the alternative," de Gaulle moved over to the map of Europe. "If we were to get possession of the Sarre Valley, it would give us ten thousand tons of coal a year. Were we to reach the Swabian Danube, we would be cutting Austria off from Germany. By seizing Treves and the Eifel plateau, we would cover at the same time Lorraine, Belgium and Luxembourg. Whoever holds Dusseldorf, paralyses the Ruhr. If Lyon is threatened across Swiss territory, its defense is in Geneva. Whoever controls Sardinia is in the best position to dominate the Western Mediterranean."

Before Kopecky could drag him down from behind, Capka rose to address the French major. "Pardon me, sir," Capka interrupted. "What is the exact tool you would use to take Dusseldorf or occupy the Sarre?"

De Gaulle's boots cracked sharply upon the old wood floors as he moved away from the map toward his questioner. "Whom am I addressing?"

"Lieutenant Ladislaw Capka, Československé armády, sir," Capka announced proudly.

"Very well, Lieutenant Capka," de Gaulle stepped close enough to impose his height advantage over the young Czechoslovak. "A weapon based on the internal combustion engine that can exert extreme strength, and can hold the enemy in chronic surprise. A tool of ruthlessness and suddenness that will take whatever is required, wherever it is needed, with all speed. Six divisions of the line completely motorized, caterpillared and armored will constitute the army necessary for carrying out such a campaign. Each one of these six divisions will be provided with all that is needed to carry on the battle independently from beginning to end, without resupply, even if it is encircled by the enemy."

"Does France have such divisions, major?" Capka was skeptical.

The reality tore at de Gaulle's heart but he was honor-bound to answer truthfully. "No, not yet."

SEPTEMBER 17, 1934
SUDETENDEUTSCHER VOLKSBANK
AUSSIG, SUDETENLAND

If his supervisor found out, he would appear weak and unreliable, which had led Platen to travel far from Berlin to get the funds that were needed. No one would know, not with a loan from a legally charted bank on the

Czech side of the frontier. There would be no way for his superiors to discover Platen's financial distress. The twins were unexpected and his salary at the Interior Ministry was not enough to pay all of the bills. The country was still in a depression and he was lucky to have a job as it was. *Oskar*, his wife whined... *Oskar, ask for a raise*. There were four other men of his grade competing for promotions, which meant the chances of success were not good. So Platen was here, far from prying eyes, walking into the small, modest bank office. The national socialists were hell-bent to build ties with Germans on this side of the border so they had officially sanctioned this bank to do business in Germany. At least Platen wasn't doing anything illegal. Ahead of him was a desk where a be-spectacled man with a receding hairline sat behind a placard proclaiming *Loans*.

"How can I help you sir?" the banker asked.

"I'd like to inquire about one of the small one-thousand Reichsmark family loans you advertised," Platen produced the clipping he had saved.

The banker motioned to a chair. "Excellent, sir. Please have a seat."

As the young German clerk sat down, the banker pulled a form and a pen out of a desk drawer. "What is your name and city of residence?" the banker inquired.

"Oskar Platen, Berlin," he looked about to see if anyone was listening.

Prague's Vinohrady district

AUGUST 16, 1937
APARTMENT – VINOHRADY DISTRICT, PRAHA

The view was stunning. Dawn breaking over the old city. He could get to like this fourth-floor apartment – big open window behind the bed, warm, sultry weather... gorgeous. Perhaps the apartment owner not letting him get any sleep the previous night had additional merits.

"Naaathan," was the playful and plaintive plea that came from below the window line.

He was paying too much attention to the sunrise and not enough attention to his hostess. The American stray in Prague lowered his eyes to gaze at the stunning woman whose bed he was sharing.

"The view is very pretty," he assured her as their rhythm connected fully again.

"Then why don't you get closer," she growled hungrily, pulling him toward her.

"Damn, no comb," Bulloch thought to himself as he slid his fingers through his wavy brown hair. The sun was higher now as he left the apartment building, but it was still early. Looking at his cheap watch, he figured he had just enough time to get back to his place, clean up, and get to the embassy at an acceptable hour. An attempt at appearances still had to be made. Hurrying down the stairs to street level, the new kid at the legation buttoned up his shirt and managed a lazy knot for the embarrassingly wrinkled tie. He vaguely remembered waking up with his wrists tied behind his back with the same tie – and smiled.

Thankfully, there weren't many people he knew out this early who would see his one cocktail party suit in such a ruffled condition. What a night... what a girl? How she managed that flat at her age on a foreign ministry salary was questionable. The oriental rugs, fancy furniture, paintings – must be a well-to-do family. She didn't say, and Bulloch didn't need to ask. As long as there were no angry husband, father or fiancée to contend with, he'd be happy to visit her often. Bulloch stopped for a moment, pleasantly recalling her perfumed skin, soft hair and curvy small frame.

While sprinting through the small park to reach the correct municipal streetcar line he needed, a smartly dressed fellow wearing a black fedora heading in the opposite direction got in the way.

"Dobrý rano," Bulloch greeted the man politely as he moved to get past him.

"Good morning to you... Captain Bulloch," Jan Burda returned the greeting.

Bulloch did not recognize the man. Was this someone he had met at a state mixer? Or worse... was this someone who had no business knowing Bulloch at all. Intrigued, the American military attaché turned with as much dignity a man in a rumpled suit could muster, and faced the fellow he did not recognize.

Burda's poker face didn't betray his enjoyment of the puzzled look on the American's face, or the anticipation of what he was about tell the attache next. "I trust last night was an enjoyable one for you?"

Bulloch's hands tugged at his jacket hem as he considered how to buy some time to figure out who this guy was and what the man wanted.

"Have we met?" was the best Bulloch chose the direct approach.

"We have not been formally introduced, but I have been aware of you for some time," Burda paused a long moment for the admission to register before extending his hand to the American. "Jan Burda, staff captain, Czechoslovak army."

Bulloch started to connect the dots together in his head. The Czech's mannered English, his familiarity with Bulloch, a Czech army captain out of uniform, the nicely tailored suit, plus the smirking insinuation that he knew where Bulloch had been the night before sealed the deal. He might be new in Prague, yet Bulloch had made a point of knowing who applied the heat in these parts.

"A pleasure to meet you Mister Burda," Bulloch let their handshake demonstrate the confidence he was feeling. "How are things in the Second Department?"

Burda was impressed. Perhaps the American military attaché *was* more than the leisure-seeking lout he so readily aspired to. That could make the man a potential ally, which would prove Colonel Moravec right once again. The boss was uncannily accurate in judging people. Time to bait the hook.

Gesturing with his thumb over his shoulder at the apartment building, Burda dug his hook in deeper. "Captain Bulloch, you must be aware that Miss Chábera is employed at our Foreign Ministry."

"So that is her last name. Thanks, the two of us never got around to exchanging business cards," Bulloch's tone displayed some annoyance. "But yes, I was aware of her employer... it definitely was a point in her favor. Jirina's English is much better than my Czech. But our interest in each other is strictly... personal, not professional."

That was the obvious truth yet there was always the chance the woman had been a set-up to entrap Bulloch in some way. The attaché brashly put his left arm around Burda's shoulder and roughly yanked the Czech close – forcing them to walk side-by-side through the little park. The move would feed the European stereotype of Americans, and might get him killed, but Bulloch needed to go on the offensive.

"Hey listen... we can talk, buddy-to-buddy, can't we," Bulloch intimated in an overly familiar fashion.

Burda looked nervously at the unwanted arm wrapped along his shoulder, but the American did not give him a chance to protest.

"Were Jirina and I *supposed* to meet at that reception last night?" Bulloch continued. You can be straight with me.

The American was either very good, or he was an oafish pain in the ass. Either way, Burda was growing amused that the man was wiggling off his hook. With Bulloch's tall build and boyish face, no wonder the girl fell for his exotic charms. Burda stepped out from Bulloch's grasp and brushed the left shoulder of his jacket with the back of his hand like brushing unwanted dust away.

"No, no collusion or ensnarement, Captain Bulloch," Burda confided sincerely. "But given the nature of our work, any relationship between Foreign Ministry staff and another government's military attaché, draws attention."

Better yet, such a relationship gave Burda the perfect opportunity, and pretext, to seek out a foreign national.

Bulloch pondered his options for a moment before replying. "Does that mean you would prefer Jirina and I stop seeing each other?"

"No, you can screw her every night of the week, if that's what she wants," Burda coldly attempted to regain control of the conversation. "As long as you're not prodding her for classified information, it's up to her what compromising positions she places herself in."

Bulloch could see the start of a smile weeding its way across Burda's face, and couldn't stop from chuckling himself. "And your boys will be watching, of course?"

"Of course," Burda conceded jovially.

"Watching how close?" Bulloch

"Fine, have it your way," Bulloch was relieved to be out of immediate danger as the subject for a scandal. "So what do you really want?"

"Call it a professional courtesy, but I would appreciate an opportunity to discuss some issues that concern us both," Burda edged closer to his real agenda.

"Now? It's kind of early," Bulloch answered, rubbing the back of his head. "Long night, you understand."

"Indeed, I do," Burda needled the attaché again. "Please, let me make amends. May I buy you some coffee, captain? I know a fine kavarna not far from here that will not be terribly busy.

"I'll take you up on that offer," Bulloch agreed, curious what professional issues this odd Czech fellow wanted to talk about. "Which way?"

Burda gestured in the direction of the old city. "Follow me."

Sure enough, Burda led him to a small cafe on Slezska. One of those little neighborhood hole-in-the walls that makes up for lack of space by annexing large swaths of sidewalk for tables and chairs – a few of them already occupied by businessmen reading their morning newspaper. Burda chose a table furthest from the other patrons.

"This will be relatively private," Burda still looked around to be sure. Passing autos, and the ample number of pedestrians going about their business, would drown out the conversation from their table. A waiter walked outside, delivered an order, and then approached the two new customers.

"Dobrý den," the waiter called out, more as an inquiry than a greeting.

"Dve turecka kava," Burda ordered.

"Well, that will wake us up for sure," Bulloch grimaced at the thought of one of the strong Turkish coffees they served in Prague.

"No, no, no, don't worry, they're good here," Burda assured. "Sweet *and* dark, almost like chocolate."

Leaning back in his chair, Bulloch examined Burda critically for a while before speaking. "So what kind of business would you like to transact?"

"An exchange of information," Burda was all cool seriousness. "We would like to share with your government some of the provocative data we have collected recently. If you find it as useful as we think you will, then we would propose an on-going relationship of such sharing."

Bulloch quickly concluded he needed to be very careful with this guy. Burda could be a rogue looking to turn a quick buck, or a good stiff doing his job? There also was a possibility that the man might not be Czechoslovak at all and Bulloch could get caught in a diplomatic provocation.

"Forgive me for being discerning this early in the morning," Bulloch raised a hand to rub his aching right temple. "Who exactly is making this offer, and *whose* data is being offered?"

"Colonel František Moravec, chief of military intelligence for the Czechoslovak general staff is making the offer. The data is German." Burda answered concisely.

Should Burda be on the up-and-up, the brass back in Washington would be interested. But Bulloch would not get involved with anything other than an official overture.

"I hope you're not looking for any financial rewards? Trust me, the U.S. Army doesn't give military attachés much of a budget," Bulloch lamented.

Burda smiled. The American was concerned about subterfuge. His instincts were good, despite his lack of experience. Burda knew their army provided little practical intelligence training for its attachés. They were sent out to observe foreign military deployments, report what they saw, and little else. That made them jokes as far as intelligence officers go. But this captain was smart, if nothing else. He had potential. Burda could see another round of questions forming behind the man's eyes, so he decided to cut to the next act. Reaching into his inside jacket pocket, he took out a fat envelope, and handed it to the American.

Bulloch turned the envelope over and over, examining both sides for a title or description, finding none. "What's this?"

"Fall Grün," Burda acted as if Bulloch should know what the title meant.

That sounded like German to Bulloch. Unsure of himself, the attaché took his best swing at a guess. "File Green?"

"Close. Case Green," Burda filled in the correct title. "You are holding in your hand a draft of the German high command's strategic plan for the invasion of Czechoslovakia. It was approved in June, but came into our possession only recently. In fact, the war games the Germans just conducted were based upon that document."

The gravity of what Burda has just described caught Bulloch by surprise. His eyes darted quickly between Burda's face and the envelope.

"That sounds serious," was all Bulloch had time to say before the waiter returned with their coffee.

"Dekuji," Burda thanked the waiter without breaking eye contact with Bulloch.

When the waiter was out of earshot, Bulloch pulled the envelope across the table closer to him.

"Very serious, I assure you," Burda sipped his beverage. "To restrain Germany from launching the offensive described in those pages will take pressure, the kind of pressure only a few nations such as the United States can apply."

What was waiting inside the envelope could be a complete fabrication, yet Bulloch felt the guy wasn't snookering him.

"Okay, I believe you, but this is bigger than anything I have ever dealt with before. Hell, the only reason I am in your country is that my predecessor got transferred and they had to dredge the bottom of the barrel for a quick replacement. I don't have the experience to adequately evaluate the credibility of a document like this," Bulloch would not send anything back to the Military Intelligence Division in D.C. unless he was sure of its authenticity.

Burda stayed focused on his coffee, taking a long sip, and savoring the flavor. "You really should try this. It's quite good."

Having forgotten about the coffee entirely, Bulloch took the advice. The dark brew was definitely strong, but much smoother in taste than he had anticipated.

"In the abstract, you are quiet correct," Burda continued. "Without a frame of reference, personally verifying the authenticity of this battle plan would prove difficult. All we ask is that you pass it along to your superiors. They will seek confirmation from other sources of course, but my department is certain those confirmations will be forthcoming,"

Burda knew full well the Americans would check with their people in Paris and London where the French and British services had been on the receiving end of such documents for a long time.

"How often do you people lay your hands on such information?" Bulloch had to think about his future. Washington might like hot goods like this and want more.

"With greater frequency than you might suspect. We would like our relationship to be an ongoing one, captain. There is every reason to expect we would share additional intelligence of this nature in the future," Burda trusted his intuition regarding the motivation behind the American's last question.

Bulloch felt confronted with a decision of significance. Truth was he was a poor man's son who got lucky with a free pass into West Point and his intention was to ride that train for all it was worth. Experiencing as much of the world as possible was what interested Bulloch, not leading the charge for God and country. That's why becoming an attaché had appealed to him. The assignment was a fairly smart way to stay an observer, not a participant. Now this man had deposited something very serious right onto his lap and Bulloch felt strangely compelled to accept it. There was every chance what was in the envelope before him might boost Bulloch's career very nicely. The attaché downed the last of his coffee then rose from his chair. Casually straightening his jacket, he picked the envelope up off the table.

"After I read this Fall Grün of yours, I might want to check out a few things before sending the material back to Washington. How do I reach you?" Bulloch rubbed his thumb and forefinger together.

Burda produced a small silver case from his jacket pocket, extracted a card and handed it to Bulloch. "Call that number, they will find me."

"You were right, the coffee was good," was Bulloch's final words as he walked off.

Burda watched Bulloch continue in the direction of the old city. As soon as the American had turned a corner and was out of sight, Furst ambled up and plopped down onto the seat Bulloch had just vacated. His suit was easily as rumpled as the American's had been.

"You look like shit," Burda volunteered.

"And you didn't spend all night watching an apartment block. I told you the bitch wouldn't throw him out until morning," Furst reminded his partner.

Furst examined Bulloch's cup, but there was nothing left to drink. Burda's cup still had something left, however.

"A shame to waste a perfectly good cup of kava," Furst reached over and downed the contents of the cup without asking.

Noticing the waiter nearby, Burda motioned to him to bring two more cups of coffee.

"Did the American bite?" Furst inquired.

"I will wager he'll play with us. It's too big an opportunity for him to walk away from. You could see it in his eyes," Burda remembered.

"Fine," Furst scoffed. "But what does cutting the Americans in really do for us? They're not going to go to war if Czechoslovakia is attacked."

"The Boss is worried about the French," Burda reminded his partner. "The more hard information we give them, the less they want to know. Everything hinges on Paris if war comes. The Soviets are not obligated to commit unless the French come in first. We have no treaty with the British. The idea is that if we can get the Americans more involved, and supportive of our situation, that will have a positive affect on the French. The new American envoy will arrive soon and he is not your typical political appointee. This fellow is influential, a powerful assistant secretary of state that Roosevelt handpicked to take the post in Praha. We'll never have a better opportunity to impress upon the Americans the seriousness of our situation."

"Does President Beneš know that we're meddling in diplomacy?" Furst rubbed his chin still finding it difficult to think of the former foreign minister as head of state despite two years having gone by since President Masaryk had stepped down.

"No, he does not," Burda reacted sharply. "So keep this to yourself otherwise we might all end up cleaning latrines."

BULLOCH'S FLAT
MALA STRANA DISTRICT, PRAHA

Resisting the urge to examine the documents in his possession Bulloch threw the envelope into his leather portfolio case and locked down the flap. It could wait for a hot shower, shave and a change of clothes. Donning his dark olive army uniform gave Bulloch a sense of added control. He adjusted the Sam Browne shoulder belt over his duty jacket then donned the peaked cap. Too late, Bulloch became aware of the whine of electric motors approaching outside and realized he'd never make it to the streetcar in time. Luckily, Bulloch's apartment wasn't far from the embassy.

Every time Bulloch turned the corner that put him onto tiny Trziste street, he was reminded how peculiar a place this city was. A short walk uphill on the cobblestone steps was Prague Castle, home to the Czechoslovak president. Close by were most of the major Czechoslovak government ministries. Many of the buildings below the castle were hundreds of years old like the U.S. legation directly in front of him: Schoenborn Palace. The ornate building dated back to the early 1700s and lived up to its palatial description with more than one hundred rooms, thirty-foot high ceilings, and seven acres of orchard and park land out back. There even was a rumor that Kafka had lived there for a time during the Great War before the U.S. government bought the property in the 1920s.

The funny thing was there was no grand yard, fences or gates protecting these palaces from the streets. Even though many of them were embassies there usually were just two big wooden doors anyone could walk up to. Bulloch had grown up in a rural community and was well familiar with the peace of mind of knowing the neighbors and leaving your doors unlocked. But when it came to government buildings, especially those owned by foreign governments, he was used to huge, symbolic architectural edifices you had to walk a mile around just to *get* to the entrance. Prague operated like no big city he had ever been in.

The gate was open, and Bulloch entered the compound. Sitting on a stool just inside the arch was one of the Czech civilian guards employed by the embassy to make sure no one strolled in unattended. Petr always had a book on him, and loved to chat about politics and philosophy. Bulloch had liked the guy straight off because the man was so full of life. Petr was in his forties, and walked away from World War I with a limp. But one of the reasons Bulloch had taken to Petr was the man could care less about old war stories and was much more interested in introducing Bulloch to local breweries and pubs.

"Good morning kapitán," Petr greeted Bulloch in his accented English. Then he pointed at Bulloch's portfolio case. "Busy day already?"

"Oh yes... sometimes the work just finds you whether you like it or not," Bulloch patted the case.

Petr understood that dictum, and both men laughed as Bulloch headed into the office quarter of the embassy.

As Bulloch reached the top of the stairs leading to the upper offices, he ran into the embassy's second secretary, Geoffrey Billings, who was all smiles for a change. Both men were about the same age, but as different as two contemporaries could be. Billings was career foreign service and had been born to the privilege and resources of a well-heeled Philadelphia family. It seemed to Bulloch that Billings was always trying to undercut him. Over what, or why, he didn't know. Most days Bulloch endured the man's caustic banter by imagining a right hook landing upon the secretary's nose that knocked those expensive little wire-frame spectacles into another room.

"Hey, Bulloch. I lost sight of you last night. One minute you're chatting with that lovely young woman, the next minute you both disappeared," Billings fished for details.

"Probably just a coincidence, Geoff," Bulloch suggested.

Not dissuaded, the secretary glanced at his wristwatch and smirked. "I don't know, this is kind of late for you to be getting here. What kept you?"

If Bulloch was going to be forced into playing this game, he might as well give the secretary what the man wanted to get rid of him. "Just doing my job: examining Czechoslovak national assets."

In the time it took Billings to digest the line Bulloch walked right on by. At the end of the hall Bulloch came to a door identified by a plaque reading *Attaché*. He entered the small room and closed the door softly. Jammed inside the confined space were two roll-top desks, their wooden swivel chairs, several file cabinets, one window overlooking the gardens, and a large map of Czechoslovakia on the wall. A previous occupant had squeezed in a goodly-sized worktable right in the middle of the room. Bulloch thanked that person every day. The table gave him a place to spread out documents before filing a report, and also gave the embassy staff someplace central to drop off memos, mail and other materials.

Bulloch glanced briefly at the new mail, and decided that it could wait. Unlocking the desk, he pulled open the cover and placed his portfolio on top of the desk. Next, he unlocked the case and retrieved the envelope that Burda had given him. After staring at it for a few moments, he sat down, pulled out the pages within, and began to read.

Pulling his eyes away from the German battle plan several hours later, Bulloch rubbed his forehead. Having to constantly refer to the German-English dictionary had made studying the pages a real chore. He looked to the sunlight streaming in through the window and realized that it was long into the afternoon. A glance at the clock above the door confirmed it was just shy of three o-clock. Putting the last pages down, he walked over to the file cabinet where there was a water jug and clean glasses face down on top of a tray. Bulloch poured himself a glass of water, downed it, and then returned the glass to where he found it. Next he unlocked one of the cabinets to retrieve a folded map.

Smoothing the map onto the table Bulloch closely examined the detailed view of Germany. Going back to his desk, he picked up a notepad where he had made notes while translating. Back at the map Bulloch grabbed one of the pencils that resided in the cracked and chipped coffee mug on the table and started making notations.

Finished, he folded the map back up, collected the pages Burda had provided, and then placed everything into his portfolio case. Bulloch locked the case, took it over to the file cabinet where he deposited it into the bottom drawer. After making sure all the drawers are securely closed, he locked the cabinet.

Bess Flynn was checking over an outgoing cable, searching for coding errors before handing it over to one of her two teletype operators. My how she enjoyed giving orders to these headstrong young male children. She had worked switchboards too many years with no respect not to enjoy her circumstances. Once she was a lieutenant in the Signal Corps, heeding a plea from General Pershing for volunteers who spoke French to sign up and go to the front lines to handle communications during the Great War... and almost got killed too. What was her reward when she came home? The Army said she and the other women volunteers weren't veterans – *The Army didn't swear in women* – was the lame argument of the bureaucrats. As she remembered it sure looked like an army officer who swore her in. Guess those really had not been lieutenant's bars on her collar.

Now Bess was a little older, a little grayer, and a little wider... but she still carried the fire from those days. Lucky thing she married a foreign service man. He was good for her, and the adventure of overseas postings kept her soul alive. But after a while she needed to feel useful and was happy when her husband mentioned they had communications work available.

"Here, this looks good," she said before handing the message to the closest operator. "Get this off as soon as you can, hon."

As Bess turned around, who should she see walking down the steps into her radio-teletype section but that handsome young thing: Bulloch. Being forty-five didn't bother her. If she hadn't been a married woman Bess, would have loved to teach that youngster a few things. For now, she'd just gaze approvingly at that firm young body heading her way.

"Captain! What are you doing in my section?" she called out.

Bulloch didn't know what gave Bess her edge. He would ask her out for a drink to learn why but figured the old girl could likely drink him under the table. No matter, Bulloch liked her too much not to play along. "Permission to pass, ma'am."

"Permission granted. What can I do for you, Nathan?" Bess pointed a pencil at the attaché.

"Bess, I have a cable I'd like you to slip into the outgoing pile as soon as you can," Bulloch requested.

"We can manage that, traffic is light today," she hoped the message would be juicy after a boring day. "What have you got?"

Bulloch pulled out a cable request form from his pocket and handed it to her. "It's short. Address it to Major Truman Smith, U.S. Embassy, Berlin. Go ahead and use the normal code."

SMITH. NEED TO SEE YOU. IMPORTANT. COMING TO BERLIN TOMORROW ON THE EARLY TRAIN. ARRIVING CHARLOTTENBURG STATION. BULLOCH.

"Short and sweet." Bess winked at him.

"Thanks, Bess," Before Bulloch could turn to leave, Bess got up from her chair to stare him down. "You keep yourself out of trouble up there. You hear me, captain?"

"Yes, ma'am," Bulloch promised, tipping his cap to her.

AUGUST 17, 1937
PROVING GROUNDS
1ST ARMORED REGIMENT, MILOVICE

After asking Kopecky to drop everything to trek here to the countryside on a *matter of urgency* that balding pain in the ass had four companies out on dawn exercises. Friendship or not, Kopecky should have got back in the car and left, or made life miserable for someone back at regimental headquarters as only a major from the Ministry of National Defence could. Instead, Kopecky decided to drive out into this muck to see what Capka was up to.

The unavoidable ruts cut into the dirt road were spine wrenching and convinced Kopecky that he was pushing the Tatra staff car too fast. After downshifting for better traction, he reached into his jacket for a pack of cigarettes. While fumbling around the dash for the lighter, three Škoda PA-III armored cars crested the rise directly ahead of him at speed. Kopecky looked up and realized it was time to be somewhere else. He gunned the engine and swerved off the road where he caught a glimpse of the armored car commander's worried face sticking out above the turret. Coming to a stop at the base of the small incline, Kopecky threw open the car door and got out to walk off the adrenaline filling his veins. One day, the combination of cigarettes and Capka would get him killed.

The armored car he had almost collided with had come to stop down the road. When Kopecky relaxed enough to take notice he saw the crew commander climbing down the side. Kopecky waved him off. There was no damage to himself or the Tatra. Better for the reconnaissance platoon to be on their way before their compatriots arrived fast from behind. With the din of additional engines fast approaching the wait would not be long. Pulling the Tatra back onto the road would be pointless so Kopecky reached back into the car to find the lighter. By the time he had taken a long draw on the cigarette, three OA-30 armored cars catapulted over the rise signaling the rest of the parade had arrived. Several T27 trucks laden with troops were next, escorted by several two-man machine-gun tankettes. The thinly armored vehicles were good for little else than training, and Kopecky hated that the worthless contraptions were still in service. But in the rearmament race with the Germans the army needed every tracked machine it could lay its hands on.

The soldiers in the rear of the trucks were taking off their helmets and wiping their brows, Kopecky noticed. Capka was working his own tankers, plus the infantry and recon platoons he had laid his paws on, rather hard. Kopecky's friend was a rising star, a staff kapitán in the tank corps. The rush to build an army of more than thirty divisions nearly overnight, four of them armored, had created many opportunities. In the old Austro-Hungarian service, it might take twenty years for a lieutenant to make major. Yet the need to build and train Czechoslovak armored divisions from scratch also demanded officers to lead them. Capka was close to making major within six years.

Kopecky could also feel pleased with himself. As the units in the field had needed to grow, so too had the organization supporting it. Earlier this year, the Ministry of National Defence had created a Seventh Department dedicated specifically to mechanized armor strategy and organization. When the new Department was formed, Kopecky had moved up from junior staff officer to a newly minted major.

The last of the troop trucks and tankettes filed past. The noise of their engines was replaced by a deeper rumble, accompanied by the clatter that tank treads made while tearing up soil. The tanks were not using the road, he realized. Kopecky dropped the cigarette and ground it to ash with his boot as he felt the earth rumble under his feet. It would be prudent to move, Kopecky thought, but he was already too late. A Škoda LT-35 tank broke into view above Kopecky – finally lurching to a stop in a cloud of dust, rocks and debris. The tank's commander, riding exposed through his top turret hatch, barked some order into his radio microphone. Done with his message the tanker climbed out of the turret to stand on the deck of his mount. The dust cleared enough for Kopecky to recognize Capka removing his leather helmet.

Kopecky trudged up to where the Škoda had come to rest. Capka was content to let his friend come to him, but did have the courtesy to jump the rest of the way down to the ground. The remainder of Capka's tanks fanned out on either side of their leader before heading down the hill – neatly avoiding Kopecky's staff car.

"Forgive me for thinking I would find you on base after you dragged me out here," Kopecky," tried to disengage mud from his boot with little success.

"You're early," Capka backhanded Kopecky's shoulder. "I am impressed."

"Cocky bastard," Kopecky grumbled. "I just polished these boots."

"A little mud is good for headquarters staff on occasion," Capka surveyed his flock passing by.

"Looks like you have a battalion out here at your beck and call," Kopecky changed the subject. "How did you manage that?"

"It was decided that I required further training as well. The rest are a short-term loan," Capka knew a battalion command was in the offing once the army had received more new tanks from the factories.

"How are these crews shaping up?" Kopecky found Capka's brutal appraisals useful back at headquarters in Praha.

"Much improved since the last time we spoke," Capka admitted. "The cavalry graduates coming out of the war college understand the concepts but with all the rest it's breaking them of bad habits. Armor, mechanized infantry, artillery... it doesn't matter. When you first take them out on maneuvers, they all spread out along a wide front. Like placing a drop of ink in a glass of water. I break as many of them of that as I can get my hands on, but it takes time. The biggest hurdle is giving these cubs an instinct for coordinated attacks where we mass armor and mechanized infantry at specific choke points. But we'll be ready when the Germans come.

"My friend, why did you drag me out here?" Kopecky wondered whether it was just to show off.

Capka grabbed Kopecky firmly by the arm and pulled him behind the tank as the rest of Capka's crew popped their hatches to get some air.

"Last week, that French military attaché, Faucher, was out here again," Capka swept his arm at the proving grounds. "It is obvious what kind of preparations we are making for the next war. So I ask him, what options are the French general staff considering for advancing into Germany in case of hostilities? I could understand if he was under orders not to reveal this. I could understand if he did not know himself and therefore could not tell me. Tomáš, Faucher told me nothing because there was nothing to tell."

Kopecky rubbed his brow wearily. "I have had similar misgivings. Since late spring, different departments at the ministry have attempted to set up protocols for joint military action with our French counterparts. Those requests have been... *deferred*. I had hoped it was typical French bureaucratic inertia that could be overcome. Lately, I fear otherwise."

"That is why I wanted to talk to you. I had hoped I was wrong after speaking to Faucher," Capka kicked a rock far down the hill in disgust. "You know, and I know, that our entire strategic doctrine is predicated on us holding the Germans in Bohemia and Moravia, while the French open up a new front in the West. We *will* stop the damn Germans but what happens if French divisions stay put behind the Maginot Line? What then?"

Capka was barging into a sensitive topic where Kopecky worked. Few in the army dared to question Czechoslovakia's alliance structure. As with any article of faith, questioning negates the faith. So few questioned. "Damn you... what would you have me do?"

"Grow some balls," Capka motioned for his crew to take a walk. "If the French dally we have to have a method of grabbing the Nazis by the throat and compelling them to surrender."

"I know how you think, Ladislaw, but it is not that simple," Kopecky was being drawn into the same old argument. "Even if we rout the Germans at the border, and thrust inland, we don't have the manpower to hold very much territory."

"That is what you always say but I have been considering the matter in greater detail. What if we went after something strategic, a target of importance that would collapse the German government if it were lost? Berlin is less than 300 kilometers from the border. Think what would happen if we took Berlin from them?" Capka pointed north.

"Occupy Berlin? To punch through Brandenburg would take every motorized unit we have," Kopecky appreciated his friend's tactical mind yet he also knew the general staff had too long a border to defend to commit everything to only one sector.

"Stop giving up so easily," Capka stabbed a forefinger repeatedly at Kopecky's chest. "A bunch of us out here in the field are up to our necks in grief trying to train these new troops to think and fight differently. We need your bunch in Praha do the same."

Neither man wanted to budge from his position so they stood facing each other stoically with arms crossed over their chests.

"My only regret is that you're insufferable when you are right," Kopecky was tired of standing in the muck. "I will see what can be done."

"Now you are talking sense," Capka's friend was always good as his word once a pledge had finally been extracted from him. "For the record, I am neither cocky nor insufferable, but I will buy you lunch."

"Don't you mean breakfast?" Kopecky tapped his wristwatch.

"Perhaps for you lazy louts in the capital. But out here where the work gets done, it is lunch time," Capka corrected him.

"Whatever you call it, I accept. It is the least you can do for almost getting me killed out here," Kopecky hoped the base kitchen was decent.

U.S. EMBASSY
MALA STRANA DISTRICT, PRAHA

It was still fairly early in the morning when Bulloch opened the door to his office. He unlocked the file cabinet and retrieved the portfolio case, then relocked the cabinet. Bulloch placed the case on the center table. Bulloch felt a little silly locking everything in sight but he wasn't taking any chances. Pulling out the middle drawer of his desk Bulloch retrieved a holster with *U.S.* burnished on the side. Easing the M1911A1 Colt pistol out of the holster, Bulloch double-checked to make sure that the clip was loaded, the chamber was empty and the safety was on. With this cannon it was well advised to get into the habit of engaging the safety at all times regardless of whether a bullet was sitting at ready in the barrel. Satisfied, he slipped the handgun back into the holster, locked the desk and walked back to the table.

Next, Bulloch checked inside the satchel to make sure the German attack plans were still safe in their nondescript envelope. With nothing amiss he placed the holster next to the gift from the Czechoslovak captain.

Securing the case for travel, Bulloch picked up the telephone and dialed an internal embassy number.

"Hi, this is Bulloch. Is Otto spoken for this morning? I have to courier something up to Berlin and I could use a ride to the train station... great, I'll meet him down in the courtyard in fifteen minutes. Thanks."

Burke Elbrick was hard at work getting his day started. Prague was a small legation and there was plenty of work to go around, especially for a third secretary like himself still fresh at his post. So it was with some surprise when his door opened unexpectedly and Bulloch walked in dressed in a sharply starched uniform as if ready for a military review. Elbrick had learned to be suspicious when the normal routine around the embassy was broken and Bulloch was never routinely on station this early in the morning.

"What can I do for you, captain?" Elbrick asked, looking up from his reports.

Bulloch deposited his portfolio case on the third secretary's desk with a thud. "I'm couriering documents up to Truman Smith at the embassy in Berlin, and need tags."

Elbrick got up from his chair, looked at the case, and then in Bulloch's eyes. "Sensitive?"

"Very," Bulloch replied with more seriousness that Elbrick had ever observed in the man. A serious Bulloch was also out of the ordinary.

"Are you making the trip today?" Elbrick asked.

"Y'up, morning train," Bulloch supplied as few details as necessary. He didn't much like Elbrick. The feeling was mutual.

Elbrick checked the lock on the case to make sure it was secure. From a desk drawer he found the appropriate pouch tag, and wrote in the necessary information. Next he grabbed a clipboard hanging from the side of the desk – filling in the top form, denoting the courier, addressee and destination embassy. When done, he handed the clipboard and pen to Bulloch.

"Please sign in the spaces I've marked," Elbrick requested.

Although unnecessary given Elbrick's penchant for accuracy, Bulloch scanned the form for errors before signing since it was always good to keep junior foreign service officers honest. Finished, Bulloch handed the clipboard and pen back to Elbrick, who then attached the pouch tag to the case in such a way that the case could not be opened without removing the tag.

"Do you have your diplomatic passport and courier letter on you?" Elbrick didn't want to give the German border guards any reason to make trouble for the captain. The concern was mostly for the documents, not Bulloch himself.

Bulloch grabbed the case and smiled. "Triple-checked before I came over. All are up to date and in order. There shouldn't be a problem."

"In case Vinton asks, when do you think you'll be back in Prague?" Elbrick wondered.

Bulloch hadn't had time to speak with the chargé d'affaires, Vinton Chapin. In fact, Bulloch was heading out so early in a concerted effort to avoid Chapin before conferring with Smith in Berlin. The documents Bulloch possessed were sensitive, and the Prague legation was without a chief of mission. Chapin wasn't a bad fellow, but he was the interim chief at the embassy until the new minister arrived. Bulloch did not want to share what he had just yet, and Chapin may feel duty bound to transmit the documents up the ladder to one of the senior U.S. ambassadors in Europe, or direct to Washington. That would be dangerously premature, and would steal too much of Bulloch's thunder.

"I should be back in a couple of days," Bulloch did not expect any problems.

"Fine, have a good trip, captain," Elbrick knew attachés had different responsibilities from everyone else at an embassy, so he was in no place to judge.

WILSONOVO STATION – PRAHA

The black four-door Škoda 640 pulled up alongside the ornate Nineteenth Century building that was Prague's main rail station. Although a bit smaller than comparable America luxury automobiles, such a car was considered a limousine in Czechoslovakia and drew enquiring glances from passersby. Several women made a point of watching this unknown in a foreign uniform get out of the Škoda.

Bulloch closed the door and thanked the legation's friendly Czech driver. "I'll cable ahead before I leave Berlin so you will know what train I'll be on."

Riding to Wilsonovo was an advisable precaution when couriering sensitive documents to limit exposure in crowded public places. The car was actually a luxury few American embassies enjoyed, as the State Department didn't pay for fancy automobiles. This Škoda had been a gift from a local business group and former minister Wright had found room in the budget for a domestic driver.

The train station was built in the Art Nouveau style. It definitely was flamboyant by American standards, and would fit in with the ritziest architecture Manhattan could offer. No matter how many times Bulloch walked in he couldn't help staring at the finely curved wrought ironwork above the entrance, or the curvaceous figures sculpted everywhere into the masonry. There definitely was some pride in the fact that such a grand structure had been renamed after Woodrow Wilson, for the part the president played in helping Czechoslovakia become an independent nation after the World War. Bulloch entered the west wing of the station and headed for a ticket station. Thankfully, the lines were short and he was soon facing a smiling young woman at ticket window.

"Jednoduchna jizdenka, Berlin-Charlottenburg," Bulloch's request for a one-way ticket to the German capital erased her smile and replaced it with a pout.

"Round-trip, yes?" she asked in a heavy accent, concerned that Bulloch was making a mistake.

She was worried about him. That was sweet, and typical of the people he had met in Prague.

"One-way, for now," Bulloch put a reassuring emphasis on the, *for now*. "I will return soon, dekuji."

That seemed to put her at ease, and Bulloch pulled some koruna notes from his wallet to pay her. Transaction done, he waved, smiled and walked back around to the stairs leading down to the tunnel leading to the passenger platforms. Looking at the departure board, Bulloch found what platform he needed for his train.

Unbeknownst to Bulloch, Furst had been watching the American from a distance. The light through the steel lattice and glass ceiling was good making it easy to track the attaché. An insistent whistle blew from the steam locomotive at Bulloch's platform. Furst watched as the train came to a stop and conductors lowered carriage steps for passengers to board. Observing Bulloch step onto a carriage, Furst moved down along his platform until arriving at a rail agent's post. Keeping the train in view, he picked up the telephone handset as if he owned it, drawing a disapproving gaze from the agent.

"Prosim," Furst displayed his Ministry of Defence identification before the agent had a chance to protest. The agent nodded his head in approval and went back to filling out forms. Furst put his credentials back into his jacket pocket, dialed a number, and waited.

"Burda. Our friend is taking a trip to Berlin," Furst reported calmly. This seemed like an odd choice of destination for the American considering what had been placed in his possession, but Furst would leave it up to his partner to worry about what to do about it.

2ND DEPT.
MINISTRY OF NATIONAL DEFENCE, DEJVICE

Burda stuck his head into the office belonging to Colonel Moravec. The head of Czechoslovak military intelligence was leaning back in his desk chair contemplating a recent report from the western border. It was a small office with an abundance of books and documentation neatly stacked everywhere one looked. Burda always thought the master of spies looked more like a kindly university professor than a man charged with managing the deadly game of espionage.

"Bulloch is on the move," Burda rapped lightly on the door.

"Where to?" Moravec remained focused on the report .

"Furst is down at Wilsonovo and says our American just boarded the morning express train to Berlin-Charlottenburg carrying a diplomatic case," Burda stuck to the details the way his boss preferred.

Moravec leaned forward, intrigued. "Did Štefan see the courier tags?"

"Yes sir, I made sure to confirm that," Burda stepped closer to his superior.

"There may be no connection," Moravec stroked his chin for a long time before he got up from the chair. "That rail station is reasonably close to the American embassy there, and would draw less *official* attention than the main station at the zoological gardens. All features you would want in an embassy courier run. This trip could have been previously scheduled."

"I don't like coincidences," Burda tapped a pencil against the keys in his pants pocket. "Yesterday Bulloch is given Fall Grün, today he is on a trip to Berlin."

Burda's instincts were usually good, and there was ample reason to be cautious since Kirinovic had been retrieved from German captivity. Kirinovic... whose mind was so far gone the man was now a cowering lump of flesh thanks to the drugs and interrogation the Germans applied on him. Then there was Salm, Agent 52, who had been beheaded in German custody.

"If I have misjudged Captain Bulloch, then we will know soon enough," Moravec walked around to face his young pupil. "The Gestapo will start looking under rocks we don't want them to, and our agents will report soon enough that they have been compromised. But while our young American is a habitual philanderer, I don't picture him a fascist sympathizer."

Burda knew it was fruitless to argue the point without supporting evidence. Moravec's genial disposition was sincere, but those eyes of his were steel. "Then we wait, watch, and see how Bulloch plays out?"

"Exactly," Moravec said, patting Burda on the shoulder. "Now, as long as you won't be dealing with Bulloch for a few days I require you and Furst to get down to Eger on another matter."

BERLIN TRAIN, CZECH/GERMAN FRONTIER

Bulloch's uniform was as good as mothballs on the northbound train. No one wanted to be seen next to him going into Germany so the attaché had the window seat and bench all to himself during the journey. It had been weeks since Bulloch had made the Berlin courier run, and looking out the window was not a bad way to evaluate Germany's transportation network. But he wasn't seeing much of anything at the moment due to the usual delays as the train crept up to German territory. Then the German border police would hold the train up further as they methodically checked passports and other travel documents.

Nearing the frontier crossing, Bulloch noticed additional roadway obstructions on the Czechoslovak side. For years now, he had learned, you couldn't just drive straight into Czechoslovakia. The roads zigzagged through concrete emplacements that also doubled as tank traps. Bulloch also knew that not far away in the surrounding hillsides was a growing network of camouflaged concrete forts. He hadn't been invited inside one yet, but from he could pull out of a happy, and drunk, Czech artillery officer one night, these fortifications were more advanced than their French cousins on the Maginot line in the West. Apparently the Czechoslovaks had access to all of the latest designs that had taken the French years to refine and made additional upgrades of their own.

The reverse was not true on the German side: no forts or engines of war in view from the main rail line. Bulloch expected there were goodly numbers of troops and artillery hidden not far away but you couldn't see them. What he did see on the German side of the frontier were the gentlemen dressed in black watching the train... and watching their own frontier police.

Bulloch heard the precise steps of military boots coming toward him: three frontier police in uniform with their old-fashioned shako caps. Despite the traditional uniforms, ever since internal police authority had been turned over to Himmler's SS a few years before the constabularies were being filled with party men. Bulloch didn't like the type, and decided to ignore the odd looking little squad until they got closer. Casual indifference usually got the border troops worked up. Too bad the view out the window was so boring.

The feldwebel in the lead reached Bulloch's bench, expecting the foreigner in uniform to respectfully hand over his papers, and not much liking that the man was paying him no attention whatsoever.

"Pass, bitte?" the policeman growled, more of an order than a request.

Bulloch finally acknowledged the sergeant by calmly turning from the window and grinning like he had a royal flush in poker. The attaché reached into his uniform jacket, extracted his diplomatic passport and courier credentials, and handed them to the self-important German who snatched them abruptly.

American, diplomatic staff, courier... everything checked as the feldwebel read threw the documents. He looked the American over again and then focused on the case at his feet. It had the proper tags. For good measure the Grenzpolizei officer picked through passport again – intently looking for something to be out of order.

"Why are you entering Germany?" the sergeant demanded of the insolent foreigner in reasonably good English.

"Official business of the U.S. government," Bulloch held out an upturned hand in anticipation of receiving his papers.

If his shift had not been close to finishing the border guard would have enjoyed removing the smile from the American's face. But he had better things to do with his time so it wasn't worth the trouble to detain the American. The feldwebel ignored the attaché's outstretched hand to let the documents drop to the floor while he moved off to concern himself with other passengers.

COUNTER-INTELLIGENCE OFFICE
REICH MINISTRY OF WAR – 72-76 TIRPITZUFER, BERLIN

Abwehr headquarters was reminiscent of a maze requiring keen senses to find one's way out the same way one came in. The facility was actually a block of graceful old houses on a tree-lined street near the Landwehr canal that had been connected long ago. The interior passageways were narrow making it difficult to avoid fellow officers and administrative staff. All of the old bedrooms, hallways, maid's quarters, kitchens, living rooms and staircases were still much as they had been originally. The only difference now was each room was home to different sections of the counter-intelligence branch. Admiral Canaris and Colonel Ottke were forming and staffing new departments at a frenzied pace. All of these departments were secret naturally although some of them were so secret they did not have names, staff rosters or official budgets. Heiden's was one of those departments.

The Counter-Intelligence Office was organized into three divisions. Group I carried out espionage and collected intelligence. Group II was devoted to performing acts of sabotage. Group III was charged with conducting counterespionage activities. As Heiden had carried out missions in each category he was never really sure which group his small sub-department fell under. No one had told him and Heiden had deemed it better not to ask. The former kommando, who looked out of place in such comfortable surroundings, arrived at the door he wanted: Obertsleutnant Ottke. Listening briefly for sounds of conversation or activity, and hearing none, Heiden rapped the door sharply three times with the back of his hand, as was his fashion.

"Enter," was the curt reply that arrived through the door.

Ottke finished a notation as his visitor closed the door securely. Placing the ink pen back into its well, the Lt. Colonel closed the journal and addressed the field operative.

"Major Heiden, what have you for me today?" the man in the musty room been in anticipation of this report for days.

With his superior in a good mood Heiden allowed his posture to relax. "It is done. We have a man on the inside."

This news pleased Ottke immensely. The admiral may have personally recruited Heiden, but Ottke soon discovered this forty year-old *recruit* thought much the same way as he did. Heiden was one of those professional types who would die rather than let an assignment left undone. Ottke could appreciate that quality in a man.

"Excellent. I want this treated like any other deep penetration. No direct communication unless faced with an emergency. We can't let proximity lull us into a false sense of security. Coded drop-offs and invisible ink as well," Ottke ran through the list.

"Understood. There will be no lapses in procedure," Heiden knew exactly how Ottke preferred such matters to be handled.

CHARLOTTENBURG RAIL STATION, BERLIN

The whole place was crawling with Gestapo. Charlottenburg wasn't that big a station to begin with, so adding this much heat was rather noticeable. Not that the secret police in Germany really cared about being noticed – they hadn't cared about high visibility for years – they actually thrived on it. Sure enough, a Gestapo man bumped him in a rush to the platforms.

"Good evening, Major Smith," that man tipped his black hat in greeting.

Smith never got a chance to return the gesture before the gauntly tall was out of sight. He didn't know the guy personally, but it was obvious the fellow knew him. Smith had ceased to be bothered by such encounters. That was life in Berlin for an American military attaché. They always wanted to let you know they were watching. No problem there. The question was, what had the man with the unsavory occupation been in such a rush?

As soon as Smith reached the platform, he understood immediately and was angry with himself for not remembering. Before him was a raucous group of foreign correspondents hooting and hollering up a storm – not caring that there was a crowd of Gestapo men taking pictures and taking down names. The Nazis were expelling Ebbutt of the *London Times* from Germany. Nice guy but he was one of the harshest critics of the Hitler regime. Ebbutt also had contacts deep within the government. Smith had been told once by one of the American press corps that Ebbutt's superiors only ran a fraction of his stories. What a pity.

Smith counted more than twenty correspondents with more still arriving to send off one of their own in style. Reporters... had to love them. Given that he was there on legitimate business Smith was happy Bulloch's train was arriving a bit further away from the show. They'd be noticed in their uniforms, but left alone with all of the press commotion.

As he reached the correct side of the platform Smith could see the inbound train drawing closer. He loved these big steam engines. Too bad he didn't get a chance to ride them as far as he would have liked. Berlin and Paris were the two big postings in Continental Europe. More often than not, the couriers came to you from smaller U.S. legations. But this wasn't a normal courier run. Bulloch appeared to have something out of the ordinary to discuss. At least that's what Smith gathered from the cryptic cable he had received. Smith didn't know Bulloch well since the younger man had only recently been posted to Prague after Winslow was reassigned. This was Bulloch's first assignment as an attaché and Smith hadn't expected much out of him. Smith had asked around regarding how Bulloch got into the program during a freeze on new attachés. The rumor was the kid had someone on his side in Congress so Smith expected even less out of the youngster. The funny thing was, Bulloch hadn't seemed liked a spoiled rich kid the one time they had met.

The train from Prague slowed to a stop in a hiss of steam and blowing of whistles. Down came the carriage steps and passengers hurried off to whatever their business was in Berlin. Smith scanned up and down the train until he spotted the olive drab and khaki army uniform he was looking for. Moving in that direction Smith wondered whether he was getting long of tooth for the job. This was Smith's second tour as an attaché in Berlin – the first had been during the twenties. Berlin was a posting that took a lot of effort to pull off. Getting the Nazi brass to invite Lindbergh over like it was their idea was Smith's latest coup. There had been grumbling back home that the trip would be turned into a propaganda stunt, yet Smith knew Lindbergh would report back on everything he saw at those new aircraft factories and airfields the Germans showed off.

"Bulloch, welcome to Berlin," Smith extended his hand. "Good trip, I take it?"

"No complications, but disappointing. Except for a flight of Dorniers I saw flying low nothing interesting presented itself the whole damn trip," Bulloch shook hands with his Berlin counterpart.

"Yeah, the Germans have that travel corridor pretty well buttoned down," Smith confirmed. "C'mon, let's get you back to the embassy so we can talk about what brought you up here."

As the two officers joined the stream of passengers leaving the station, Bulloch noticed the commotion outside the carriage of the nearby train. "What's going on with that bunch? I thought public assemblies had been banned. There are fifty people over there having a party and that's not counting the Gestapo chaperons."

"A British journalist is getting evicted. Tit-for-tat in return for a few expulsions the Brits just laid on the Germans. The local tribe of correspondents is giving him a send-off," Smith tried not to show too much interest.

Continuing to stare at the journalists, Bulloch spotted a woman in their midst: tall brunette with great legs... even from a distance. "Hey, who's the skirt?"

The question caught Smith's attention because there hadn't been a woman with the group earlier. So he paused to see if he could recognize her. "Don't know her name. She's new, wire service, based in Paris. That's all I know.

"Hey, maybe I can have some fun on this trip," Bulloch adjusted his tie.

"Don't go stirring up trouble, captain," Smith pointed his finger in the junior officer's direction. "The last few weeks have been blissfully quiet around here, and I'd like to see it stay that way for a while."

Losing the smile, and taking on a much more serious disposition, Bulloch glanced down at the portfolio case he was holding. "That may change."

"Hey, Talmadge... wave goodbye to Norman." a slightly tipsy Canadian reporter from Toronto bumped into Ros.

She didn't even know Ebbutt except by reputation and reading his byline. The only reason she was here was because Hauth thought he might need help covering the Nazi party congress next month in Nürnberg and he wanted her to get acquainted with the territory and personalities. Ros was glad she was posted in Paris because after only a couple of days in town, Berlin was getting under her skin. She was definitely sure she didn't like the way the closest Gestapo goon was leering at her. After a few nights boozing it up with the local press corps Ros had learned Berlin may be where the action was but what good did it do most of these reporters to wade through all of the official hostility when the editors back home were too scared to run their sauciest material. Lucky for her, saucy wasn't a problem for Harry Lasky.

U.S. EMBASSY
TIERGARTEN DISTRICT, BERLIN

What passed for Smith's office was crammed full with equipment and journals. Bulloch admired the orderly stowing of the accumulated material but was stunned at how little space was available in a primary legation like Berlin. Then again, he had never been in this particular building before. The Embassy, strangely, worked out of several buildings near Berlin's oldest public park the Tiergarten.

"Apologies for the cramped space." Smith closed the door behind them. "When I got here in 1935, they told me these were temporary accommodations until we could move into the new facility over on Pariser Platz. Lately, I've grown used to the idea that these digs are permanent"

Bulloch took off his cap and hung it on a coat rack next to Smith's. "What's holding up the move? I thought Washington bought the new property a long time ago?"

"Back in 1931, to be exact. But the damned building burned down and Congress has taken its good sweet time allocating funds to build a new structure," Smith pulled two swivel chairs closer to Bulloch. "So captain what brought you up here in such a hurry?"

Bulloch took a seat and unlocked the flap of his case. "Yesterday I was the unsolicited recipient of an overture from Czech military intelligence."

The wet-behind-the-ears U.S. military attaché from Prague had Smith's full attention as he sat down in his chair.

"Don't know that I buy it," Bulloch continued, "but the general idea was they wanted to cooperate by sharing useful data about the Germans from the goodness of their hearts."

"Who contacted you?" Smith asked.

"A fellow named Burda, a captain in their army. Never laid eyes on him before he approached me on the street yesterday morning," Bulloch stretched open the case.

Smith tapped his temple with a pencil eraser while thinking. "I don't recognize the name. No reason I should, since those guys rarely come out into the open when they work up here. What makes you think this Burda guy is legitimate?"

"This." Bulloch reached into his case and pulled out the envelope, handing it to Smith.

"Definitely some heft here," Smith turned the fat envelope over in his hands.

"The documents are billed as a battle plan code-named Fall Grün that supposedly was issued around two months ago. My German is rotten, but from what I can decipher, those pages do read like the invasion of Czechoslovakia the way a German would write them. The signatures and seals also look genuine despite the quality of the photocopy," Bulloch drew attention to the features.

Smith hurriedly scanned pages – picking out intriguing tidbits, then moving on. "There is a lot of detail in here, right down to the battalion level."

"Yeah, that was my reaction," Bullock stood up to make use of a wall map of Germany. "The strategy calls for an attack from Lower Silesia near Grulich," Bulloch pointed out on the map. "Right between Bohemia and Moravia. The object is to drive a wedge south to the Austrian border – cutting Czechoslovakia in half. There are no timetables, so I can't tell whether this plan is a theoretical exercise, or something more substantial. But it is very thorough in most other departments. Burda says the Germans are using this Fall Grün as a basis for military exercises. You're a lot more knowledgeable about the composition of German units than I am. To me it all looks genuine, but you'd be better able to pick out a Czech fabrication. That's why I wanted to get your opinion before passing those documents along to Washington."

"Let's consider for the moment, that this document is on the up-and-up," Smith joined Bulloch at the map. "I'm envious... it means Czech intelligence has deeper hooks into the Germans than anyone suspected."

"And now they want to share it all with me," Bulloch tapped the pages in Smith's hands with his finger.

"The only reason for the Czechs to put this little gem into our hands is that they want to get our attention. You couldn't possibly reciprocate with anything this valuable so my bet is that someone in Prague wants to get the U.S. more involved in what's going on over here. Does this captain want to get paid?" Smith knew cash greased a lot of these transactions.

"No, Mister Burda would rather give than receive. If he is playing me it is not about money," Bulloch was still unsure of his Czechoslovak benefactor.

"When does your new chief of mission arrive?" Smith switched topics.

"Sometime early next month," was all Bulloch knew.

Smith scratched his head in thought for a moment. "It may be coincidental, or this document came your way timed to give your new minister something to chew on right off the train. I think you owe it to him to keep this under wraps until he arrives. Ambassador Dodd here would love to get his hands on a German invasion plan of Czechoslovakia. It would confirm his arguments about the regime but he's back in the States for a few months. If I turn this over to our chargé he'll eventually send it on to Ambassador Bullitt in Paris, which means it will get buried so deep no one will ever see it again. No, best you keep this safe for a couple of weeks. I would appreciate going over these pages in detail, and photograph a copy for myself before you head back to Prague, if you approve?"

"Of course, I intended as much when I decided to cable you," Bulloch was pleased they saw things the same way.

"Hey, why don't you get cleaned up, and relax for a couple of hours until I'm done with this gift of yours," Smith slapped the pages on his desk. "Then we'll see if I can talk my wife into joining us for a late dinner."

2. PROMOTIONS

**German chancellor Adolph Hitler at the
National Socialist Party Congress in Nürnberg**

SEPTEMBER 8, 1937
SPECIAL TO CONSOLIDATED NEWS
BY WALTER HAUTH

NÜRNBERG – Tens of thousands of Germans have descended again upon this historic Bavarian city, home to the annual Reichsparteitag: the party congress of the ruling national socialists. The eight-day rally began last Monday, and runs through Sept. 13. This assemblage of pageantry, military might, adulation, fiery oratory, party propaganda, and choreographed masses of human beings the world has not seen since the days of the Roman Empire. Not even Il Duce, the Italian firebrand Benito Mussolini who compares himself to those powerful Roman forbearers, can whip up this many ardent followers into such a display of devotion and political passion.

In a speech yesterday in front of thousands of followers standing in a seemingly infinite number of orderly uniformed rows upon the massive parade grounds here, the German führer Adolf Hitler addressed the powerful display of humanity before him.

"Not by bayonets did we compel the people, but by the force of limitless idealism we won the German people and led them under our banners," Hitler reminded the world.

Herr Hitler had less kind remarks for the peaceful democracies bordering on Germany, especially those such as Czechoslovakia that have large ethnic German communities. But he saved his most blistering oratory for followers of the Communist International, and Josef Stalin in Moscow.

"Today who will refuse to see or even deny that we find ourselves in the midst of a struggle which is not concerned merely with problems of frontiers between peoples or states but rather with the question of the maintenance or the annihilation of the whole inherited human order of society and its civilizations?" Hitler implored. "The revolution of society which has been the work of Bolshevism means nothing else than the destruction of those intelligences which are native to a people... Germany will not be overrun either from within or from without! And this fact, I believe, is a very great contribution towards peace for it will serve as a warning to all those who, starting from Moscow, are seeking to set the world ablaze."

The fight between national socialists, and communists is an old feud in Germany. Before the Nazis came to power, pitched street battles between both sides were a common occurrence in big industrial cities such as Hamburg and Bremen. But after Herr Hitler became chancellor in 1933 he pushed through numerous decrees abolishing opposition political parties, accusing thousands of communist and social democratic party members as being agents of terror and imprisoning them in *preventive detention* to ensure the security of the state.

Despite such harsh measures, it appears the national socialists have become accepted within the international community. In a dramatic change from previous Nazi party rallies, diplomatic representatives from the United States, France and Great Britain have chosen to attend for the first time in an official capacity. But the attendance of American chargé d'affaires Prentiss Gilbert has created something of a row within U.S. diplomatic circles. His superior, ambassador to Germany William Dodd is currently home on vacation but on the record as vehemently opposed to the State Department's decision to permit Gilbert to accept the German invitation. According to a letter from Dodd to Secretary of State Cordell Hull published in the *New York Herald Tribune* on Sept. 4, Dodd has opposed attending the Reichsparteitag event for four years on the basis of a one-hundred and fifty year-old U.S. diplomatic tradition prohibiting participation in official political party celebrations within foreign countries. Dodd has also been a longstanding critic of the Nazi regime during his tenure in Berlin.

ESTERWEGEN CONCENTRATION CAMP
EMSLAND, DEUTSCHLAND

He hoped the camp commandant was having a good time at the Reichsparteitag in Nürnberg. Ah, the privileges of rank. For SS obersturmführer – or should he be honest and say SS jailers – the parties and camaraderie of an expense-paid week of reveling in Nürnberg was a ways off. No, his part was to sit here at this desk and process paperwork. Always more paperwork when the damn leftists died, the young officer thought to himself. Why did he have to be here saddled with this burden? This wasn't the glorious service to the Fatherland and the party that he had expected. At least it was still warm, as he looked out the barrack window at the afternoon sun starting to set. Soon it would be uncomfortably damp, thanks to the boggy wasteland the camp had been built on. A few weeks after that, the real cold would set in. Then there would be more dead reds, and more damned paperwork.

After signing off and rubber-stamping the last form, Achtziger smacked the files closed then stood. At least he could smoke with the commandant away. The lieutenant found his cigarettes straight away but had to pat several jacket pockets down before locating any matches to light one with. It was time to get rid of today's paperwork.

"Clerk! Clerk! Get in here," Achtziger called to the outer office. An inmate in the customary dark uniform with the big white number patch sewn onto his jacket walked in and stood at a respectful attention. Achtziger liked this red. The man was a bit older than him, but not nearly as olden as most of the socialist and kommunist party leaders that made it to the camp. But this prisoner was different. He was an efficient worker and neither his eyes nor his manner suggested revenge or disobedience.

"There's another stack to be filed," Achtziger pointed at the files on the desk.

The prisoner scooped them up and was about to leave when his jailer stopped him. "Wait a moment," Achtziger saw no reason to be callous to a good worker. He popped another cigarette from the pack, lit it with his own, and handed the treat to the prisoner. "What is your name again?"

"Krisch, sir," the inmate didn't really enjoy smoking but after three years in the camps he knew acts of charity were a rarity you didn't refuse. The important thing was not to grovel over the offering, which would admit that the SS had total power over you, but accept the token with honor.

"Why are you here, Krisch?" Achtziger was sincerely curious. "You're not a rabble rouser, party leader, street brawler, or even an important trade unionist. Whom did you piss off?"

Krisch thought over his response very carefully before answering. "My father was a shipyard foreman in Hamburg, very active in the union, and in the local SPD. It was expected that I joined the union, and the party. I imagine it was a case of *like father, like son*, sir."

The SS man nodded his head in agreement. The Gestapo was very efficient in their background checks, family history and personal affiliations. "What happened to your father?"

"Heart attack. Died in 1933," Krisch chose not to reveal how wires had been attached to his father's fingers and the fierce electrical shock they carried had caused his father's heart to seize.

"Maybe that was best," Achtziger acknowledged, feeling uncomfortable for the first time – his own fault for asking personal questions. But he had wanted to know, and what's done was done. "Listen, don't spend too much time on those files tonight. I want to close the place down early. As long as the senior officers are away having a good time there is no reason I cannot enjoy a few extra hours."

"Understood, obersturmführer. I'll get these ready for tomorrow, tidy up my area and go for the evening. Thank you, again, sir," Krisch held the cigarette up.

"You do good work and I appreciate it," Achtziger waved him off.

Krisch could feel the weight of the unsaid, *dismissed*, and quickly made his way with the files back out to the austere outer office. As much as Krisch would have preferred to put out the cigarette to save what was left for a deserving comrade who would better enjoy the tobacco, to do so was dangerous. Achtziger would be offended.

Before putting the files into a wood basket on top of the well-worn desk, Krisch quickly scanned them for the names of the newly deceased, and the *official* causes of death. There were two files, two names. Loritz... gunshot wound. Fool, he was a hothead and you couldn't tell him differently. The guards loved tormenting him, and threw Loritz on the toughest labor details. No matter how much weight the once burly toolmaker lost, or the daily beatings, he wouldn't stop mixing it up with the guards. This time a guard ended it with a bullet.

Krisch examined the next file and felt his heart sink. Faulhaber... why did it have to be Faulhaber? Cause of death: tuberculosis... and being one of the most prominent newspaper editors in Germany. As one of the most influential social democrats Faulhaber had been among the first political arrestees in early 1933. Never a militant he had the kind of intellectual and moral presence that made him a threat to the regime. Faulhaber had not fled the country like most of the other prominent Jewish editors had done. For no reason Faulhaber would be locked away for weeks on end, stripped naked and left in a dark, cold cell with no furniture, no toilet and very little to eat. Eventually tuberculosis began doing the work for the guards.

When Krisch was transferred to Esterwegen from Oranienburg in 1935, he was lucky enough to meet Faulhaber during one of the editor's longer reprieves from isolation. A true leader, Krisch could think of no one else who could have managed to convince that many angry socialists and kommunists to forget their ideological differences, channel their hate, and work together to survive. It was Faulhaber who had had convinced Krisch to work for the SS in the camp. Krisch had no reputation so there was no reason to pick him out humiliation. For prisoners they did not care about there was work close to the SS as orderlies and clerks where Krisch could learn more of what they knew. He would be working for his fellow inmates and no one would utter an ill word in Krisch's direction if he did what Faulhaber asked.

So Krisch became a clerk for the SS. He reported what he overheard and what he read in the many dockets that passed through his hands. For two years, Krisch watched Faulhaber, only in his forties, slowly waste away from the inside while Krisch operated in conditions that were soft by comparison. Now Faulhaber was gone.

After he had closed the file and stamped out the cigarette, Krisch returned pencils and papers to their proper spots on the desk. The obersturmführer always waited for him to leave first before locking up so Krisch walked outside and closed the door behind him.

Dusk was approaching so the work gangs sent outside daily to till soil for farmers, and build roads for new enterprises, were returning through the cheap corrugated metal facade that made up the main gate. Hard, brutal work it was. But when a few of the men saw Krisch, they slowly straightened their bent backs. Krisch nodded in silent acknowledgement and forced himself to walk in the opposite direction past the SS barracks to the long rows of cheaply constructed prisoner's barracks.

Krisch felt a chill in the air. Esterwegen was built on barren land close to Holland and not all that far from the cold winds of the North Sea. As he was a *trusted* prisoner with important duties, Krisch could meander around the camp without being bothered by the guards.

The gaunt and shrunken inmates of Barracks 14 busied themselves in animated conversation. Only the watchers who kept vigil for guards at the windows were silent. As word of Faulhaber's death had spread through the camp, the same scene was played out again and again as members of work gangs returned to their barracks for the night. But Barracks 14 was different. When Faulhaber was not in solitary confinement, Barracks 14 was his base of operations, and where his leadership committee resided. With their leader gone, the men in dark uniforms argued on how to respond to his death.

"He's here! He's here!" one of the watchers yelled suddenly from his post, and all was deathly quiet within the room in an instant. All eyes were on Krisch when the door squeaked open and he stepped inside. The attention so surprised Krisch he paused uncomfortably at the entrance long enough that the closest watcher was forced to swing over and shut the door.

Scholl, one of the senior members of the leadership committee hurried over to speak with Krisch. "Klaus died in confinement today. What I want to know is how did he die?

"His lungs finally gave out," Krisch was surrounded by dozens of anxious faces." This last trip to confinement was too much for his lungs."

Scholl, the graying former shop foreman, stood tall like the old days when he addressed tradesmen on the floor of his factory. "So, they finished what they started: a slow, cruel death by cold and starvation. He was the best of us, and now he is gone."

"So what will we do about it?" Frail Albers directed his makeshift cane at Scholl.

"We carry on in Faulhaber's name to finish what he started," Gohler, a committee member like Scholl, edged past his barracks mates.

"The first thing we do is send messengers to the other barracks, make sure they know the truth so they can calm down any hotheads," Scholl knew they could not afford a camp-wide riot.

"Next, we strengthen our leadership," added Gohler, who once had been influential in the SPD and one of the more eloquent Reichstag members. "Faulhaber cannot be replaced, but we can choose someone who will work tirelessly to carry on his work. The committee has voted to add Anton Krisch to its ranks."

"Me?" Krisch's head snapped up sharply. "You cannot possibly believe I'm qualified for such a responsibility."

"Why not you?" Scholl stepped closer to rest his hand on Krisch's shoulder. For two years who has operated under our jailer's noses, returning with information of the outside world, helping us to focus on something beyond our imprisonment? Who has always been ready to lend a supportive voice and a strong arm? Don't discount yourself, Anton, for we have not. Faulhaber, liked you, and wanted you to play a fuller role. The committee has no reason to disagree."

"Thank you for recognizing my minor contributions but I have never been the leader of anything," Krisch was not convinced.

"Oh, but I disagree," Gohler countered. "Sometimes destiny chooses those who least expect to carry the load, but are best able to do so. This is a camp full of recognizable leaders. That's why most of us are here. You are in a most enviable position. You have the respect of your fellows and the Nazis believe Anton Krisch is a nobody. Should they eliminate the rest of us the way they eliminated Klaus, who carries on? Accept your duty and let us get to work."

"Damn you, I will accept," Krisch decided surrendering was the only way to shut the old bastards up.

SEPTEMBER 9, 1937
BULLOCH'S FLAT
MALA STRANA DISTRICT, PRAHA

The two weeks since he had returned from Berlin had been restive for Bulloch. He was sitting on an intelligence gold mine and he couldn't do anything with it due to protocol. Technically, his direct day-to-day superior was the chief of his diplomatic mission. Bulloch had an obligation to share the German battle plan with the Prague chief after forwarding it home. Trouble was, there had been no chief of mission in Prague since May and Bulloch wasn't sure what chargé d'affaires Chapin would do with the documents. That had led Bulloch to delay sending the

German documents to his military superiors so that he would not have to share them with Chapin.

Another concern was that Bulloch was pretty sure he was being followed. By whom he didn't know but they were good enough to stay out of sight. The Czechoslovaks were the obvious culprits and Bulloch was of a mind to question Burda on the subject, but the intelligence officer was staying scarce despite Bulloch having left the fellow a message a few days before.

Then there was Jirina. She was feeling neglected and didn't take well to not being the center of his attention. The probing questions had already started. Jirina was circling around the subjects of infidelity, a change of heart, and immaturity. She would draw some conclusion... the wrong conclusion, then Jirina would dump him because he couldn't tell her what was really occupying his thoughts.

All of these issues could have been solved with the arrival of the embassy's new minister. Wilbur Carr was supposed to have arrived by now. His ship had landed in Hamburg more than a week previously. Carr had taken a few days to visit the embassy staff in Berlin while Chapin had sent Otto up with the car to bring the minister and his wife down to Prague. They had left Monday, yet here it was Thursday and they still had not shown up.

Bulloch had tried to study up on Carr to have an idea who he was working for. One of the first bits of information Bulloch discovered was that Czechoslovakia was Carr's first diplomatic mission abroad. Further digging revealed Carr was an institution at the State Department. The guy was sixty-six and had been on the payroll since 1892! Think of all of those years in administrative work. He had been an assistant secretary of state for over a decade and was a firebrand behind reforming the Foreign Service into a more professional outfit. What puzzled Bulloch was why Carr, someone who should have retired already, was being given his first diplomatic job in an important foreign capital? Wasn't it a little late to be starting a new career tack? What's more, word was that it was Roosevelt's idea but no one seemed to know why Roosevelt wanted Carr for the job.

When Carr still hadn't turned up by three-o'clock, Bulloch gave into his growling stomach and ventured out for a late lunch. Walking back to the embassy Bulloch was thinking over how he was going to manage an immediate audience with Carr when everyone else on the staff would have the same idea.

Turning a corner within a few hundred yards of the embassy Bulloch noticed the gates leading to the interior compound were open and the legation's Škoda was sitting inside the yard where a small but growing crowd of embassy employees were surrounding a well-dressed older couple standing near the Škoda. Otto was back at the boot retrieving suitcases with the help of Petr. The Carrs must have just arrived. Bulloch adjusted his uniform jacket as he joined the welcoming committee.

"Bulloch, get yourself over here this moment and meet Mister and Mrs. Carr," Bess waved him closer.

Bess was his own special angel, Bulloch was sure of it. From the corner of his eye he saw Chapin and Billings exit the office quarter in a hurry to reach their new chief. Bulloch would have a few moments with Carr before the minister's primary deputies could whisk him away.

"Minister Carr, Mrs. Carr, this is our military attaché, Captain Nathaniel Bulloch," Bess thrived on social introductions. She was all smiles and took special effort to stretch out the *Nathaniel*. She knew it annoyed her favorite captain.

Bulloch found himself receiving a firmer handshake from this older gentleman than he had expected. "Nathan, sir," Bulloch held off a reproachful stare at Bess. Next it was his turn to take Mrs. Carr's hand. "Welcome to Prague, ma'am. I trust your trip down from Berlin was a pleasant one."

"Very enjoyable, thank you, captain," Edith Carr, replied, sure this young officer was a rapscallion charmer but nothing a capable woman couldn't manage with a little dedication and firmness. "But we're quite relieved to finally be here."

"Actually, we're even more relieved the Germans hadn't already overrun Czechoslovakia before we arrived," Carr jumped into the conversation.

Bulloch returned his attention to the their bespectacled new minister, and realized the man was completely serious. That much was clear to Bulloch as Carr's steady, intelligent gaze was measuring up the attaché.

"That's a refreshing point of view, sir. Not everyone sees the situation down here that way," Bulloch was pleased Carr already had a good grasp of the neighborhood.

"Then they either have their eyes closed or they don't get out much," Carr huffed.

Chapin and Billings added themselves to the group and didn't waste any time busting up the conversation.

"Minister Carr, Mrs. Carr... welcome to the legation. I am Vinton Chapin, chargé d'affaires, and this is second secretary Geoffrey Billings," Chapin announced. "We're very glad to have you with us."

"Sir, Madam," Billings bowed respectfully as Otto and Petr came forward with luggage in tow, waiting for instructions.

"Very good. Otto and Petr will take your personal belongings to your residence. I'm sure you're tired and wish to rest up after your long trip," Chapin continued.

"Actually, I want to get a head start on tomorrow," Carr interrupted. "Where's my office, gentleman?"

Billings managed a puzzled glance at Chapin before gesturing back at the office quarter. "Right over there, minister."

"Good, good... let's have a look," Carr accepted enthusiastically. Before walking off Carr looked over at his wife with his warmest smile that he saved only for her. "My dear, can you spare me for a while?"

"Of course, I can manage just fine," she responded just as warmly.

Carr returned his attention to the chargé d'affaires. "Mister Chapin, I want you to present me with a schedule of who I need to see in Prague after I present President Beneš with my credentials, as well as in what order I will need to see them."

"I will be honored to assist you, sir," Chapin had already assembled the list.

"One more thing," Carr paused, adjusting his spectacles, then looking back at Bulloch. "At the earliest opportunity I want you to reserve a good chunk of time with young Captain Bulloch here. Our journey through Germany has left me with many questions that are best suited to his skills and jurisdiction. Can I count on you both to arrange this?"

Although Chapin wasn't completely sure he liked Minister Carr's early recognition of the legation's attaché, what he asked for would be done without question. "The captain and I will confer this evening and schedule a time as soon as possible."

"Excellent, then please show me to my desk," Carr prodded.

The circle around the Škoda broke up. Chapin and Billings led the minister to his new office, while Mrs. Carr was shown the way to the ambassador's residence. Before Bulloch could feel smug about his good fortune Bess poked him in the ribs with her elbow as she moved off after Mrs. Carr. When she glanced over her shoulder at him there was a huge grin on her face.

SEPTEMBER 10, 1937
OUTSKIRTS OF ASCH, SUDETENLAND

It was supposed to be a quiet, low-profile trip to the far western tip of the republic to see first-hand what the ethnic Germans were up to as the Nazi party rally across the border was building to a climax. This part of the country on the border was more German than Czech in its ways and architecture. Despite years of trying to get the Czech names for these towns accepted, the local population stubbornly refused to use anything but the German names. Czech government officials were openly scorned here, local policemen often felt as if they were under siege in their stations, and a number of careless intelligence agents had been abducted in recent years by Gestapo teams to be tortured and imprisoned in Germany.

Much of the economy in the shadow of the Sudeten Mountains was industrial and the working population here had taken a terrible toll with the start of the depression. Never happy with the 1919 treaty that made them full citizens of Czechoslovakia, bad economic times brought out the worst in many ethnic Germans at the same time Hitler was coming to power across the border where he was promising an economic miracle and delivering on that vow. Most Sudeten Germans, the democrats excepted, didn't care to see the costs of Nazi administration, however. The Sudetens saw the Nazis as saviors to their *second-class* citizenship in Czechoslovakia, as well as their economic woes. By 1935, Konrad Henlein's Sudetendeutsche Partei had taken root. Henlein called for general autonomy for the region at first yet his full agenda was nothing less than union with Germany. Things soon started getting ugly. Add in the stupidity of a few insensitive local Czech administrators and a testy situation had grown into a slow burn. Moravec had sent Burda and Furst west to help monitor the Sudeten districts while the crescendo of Nazi agitation overflowed from across the border in Bavaria.

To their surprise, it had been quiet in Asch – deathly quiet. Walking around the town there had been the usual polite greetings in passing, but from afar, angry stares reserved for outsiders. Speaking German exclusively did not help much. Many people in the country spoke German. Furst and Burda were outsiders and therefore under suspicion. The stillness on the streets was tense. Like the hammer on a revolver held tautly above the shell casing, waiting to strike... waiting for someone to pull the trigger.

But nothing happened. After a couple of days, the intelligence officers decided to set back on the long drive back to Praha. Furst didn't mind the dusty country roads or the hot summer air blasting in the open windows. He could finally relax behind the steering wheel of their new Praga-Baby coupe – well at least new to Furst and his partner. Their old Piccolo had been a dependable workhorse but the Baby had a curvy shape that was much easier to look at and responded much better to Furst's instructions. But paramount in Furst's thoughts was heading back to more hospitable parts of the country where he could take a long shower, change into clean clothes and enjoy his fill of cold Pilsner. That last thought inspired Furst to whistle up a pub tune from his old neighborhood. But one glance at his partner cut his musical endeavor short.

"Just why are you so sour?" Furst was perturbed at Burda's mood. "Nothing happened. No problems. The damn town was quiet. No one knifed us while we slept."

"You slept?" Burda was surprised.

"I always sleep," Furst negotiated a hole in the road. " Don't change the subject. Why are you so vexed? Would you prefer that one of these local Nazis blew up the tax collector's office in your honor?"

"Frankly... yes, I would have," Burda admitted. "Something is not right out here. Hell, Asch might as well be in Germany. The Reichsparteitag is in full bloom with stirring speeches about Grossdeutsches, Czech villainy, the right of self-determination and *none* of the local riff-raff gets caught up in the moment? Doesn't that strike you as odd?"

"You are hopeless. Maybe these Sudetens can only chew over one notion at a time, and they are too concerned about listening to Herr Hitler's bluster to care about other mischief," Furst brought the vehicle around a curve in the road leading to a narrow stone bridge ran over a stream. "There doesn't have to be a *reason* behind everything."

"Yes, there does. The challenge is being able to see the reasons," Burda slapped the dashboard.

"Oh, so I am not so bright, is that it partner?" Furst shot back as he slowed the Praga to cross the narrow bridge.

"Look, I was referring to myself, not you --" Burda was interrupted by the loud *pop* a blown tire made.

"Damn! Must have lost a tire," Furst was preoccupied with the car lurching to the left and his struggle to keep the coupe from bashing into bridge's low wall. Successful, he guided the difficult Praga off to a stop on the edge of a grass field.

"Did you see what we ran over?" Burda had looked out his window but had seen nothing that would have caused the blowout.

Furst was already opening his door. "No, didn't see a thing. Let's check it out."

The agents climbed out of the wounded Praga – Burda getting a look at the bad tire as Furst circled around the front of the vehicle.

"Completely flat," Burda figured they would have to cross to the other side of the bridge to retrace the path of the car to see what they had run over.

Furst kneeled down beside the tire for a closer look. Examining the tread he found no evidence they had caught a nail or glass. Next, he ran his hand along the tire's side. At the bottom, where the deflated rubber was flapped over itself, Furst ran his fingertips over the area. His body tensed at finding the round puncture hole.

"Shit," Furst hissed, jumping to his feet to look for his partner.

Burda was already a few yards over the bridge when his eye caught Furst burst into a run toward him and gesturing to the ground.

"Jan!" Furst yelled as he ran. "Bullet!"

A rifle shot ricocheted off the wall next to Burda as Furst dived for cover. On instinct, Burda quickly dropped to a defensive crouch, tucking his body close to the base of the foundation. More shots zipped over their heads. A better-aimed bullet chipped off a section of the stone above Furst, who carefully eased himself to a sitting position with his back against the wall.

"The tire was shot clean through," Furst caught his breath long enough to pull his vz.24 pistol from its shoulder holster and chamber a round. "Well, you wanted some excitement."

Burda ignored the taunt and slipped his own service pistol. "Did you see where they are firing from?"

"No, they're out of sight," Furst responded as particles of stone showered down on him from another bullet impact. "I bet they are on the other side of the field along the tree line. That is where I would be shooting from."

"If we can flank them, we have the advantage," Burda concluded.

"How did you arrive at that conclusion, professor?" Furst was skeptical.

"If they are firing from across the field, we're dealing with rifles, not side arms. We can shoot faster with our pistols if we get close enough to surprise them," Burda was already thinking about how to close the distance with their ambushers.

"Unless someone is really fast," Furst pointed out. "Remember Janouch? That bastard should have been a sniper. He was damn quick with a bolt-action rifle."

"Are you going to disagree with everything I say today?" Burda gestured with his pistol.

"I don't know. What are you going to say next?" Furst teased him.

"I'm going to check our position," Burda proposed.

"There you have it, I am in full agreement with that course of action," Furst prodded his partner on.

Burda stayed low while he shifted fifteen meters to the right. After taking a deep breath Burda raised his head just high enough to peer over the top of the wall toward the trees on the other side of the field. As he dropped back down to safety, a bullet cut through the air where his head was a second before. He inched back to Furst.

"They are staying out of sight," Burda reported. "From that position, they can easily hit anything on either side of the bridge."

Furst looked from one side of the bridge to the other, evaluating their location, then pointed in the direction away from the shooters. "Did you see where this stream bed leads to?"

"North... doesn't matter. We aren't leaving the car," Burda checked his coat pocket for spare magazines. "Do you know how long it took me to get that car? How much paperwork had to be submitted before the purchase order was issued? I'm not giving it to some Nazi stooge. We are not leaving the car."

"Fine... we are not leaving the car," Furst chimed in. "Then what are we..."

Furst stopped himself and signaled to Burda to say nothing. He wanted to listen. It was too quiet.

"Our friends out there are up to something," Furst whispered.

Working back along the base of their stone protection in the direction of the Praga, Furst peeked around the edge far enough to spot four men carrying Mauser rifles cautiously fanning out onto the field.

Furst cursed as he pulled his body back out of sight.

"How many?" Burda crawled over to join him.

"Four... with Mauser rifles," Furst held up four fingers.

"Four, that's not so bad," Burda could not figure out what was bothering his partner.

"No, this is bad. If they are breaking cover this early, they must think we are unarmed. That means that scum thinks we are bureaucrats. I won't be insulted that way," Furst raised his weapon and tensed like a big cat ready to pounce on its prey. "I am going to drill a hole through the forehead of the first one of those bastards that comes in range."

"No, I have another idea," Burda chose to ignore his friend's strange sense of humor. "Let's try not to *drill* anyone today if we can help it. The headlines would be bad: *Riots, Anarchy, Czech Oppression.* We sneak along the base of stone guard to the far side so we can drop down into the stream bed unseen. Once we are down below the bridge, we hug the embankment as it fans away from our pursuers. Maybe then we can get behind them."

Furst considered the plan, looked down the length of the bridge, and nodded his head in assent. "Not as much fun as my idea, but sound. Let's go."

Crawling on their stomachs like lizards the Czech agents slithered as quickly as possible to the other side of the bridge. The worst was dropping into the wet muck below like dead bodies tossed into a grave. Pausing to listen, and hearing nothing, Burda motioned them forward along the embankment.

After moving some distance from the bridge, Burda and Furst stopped to listen again. The four riflemen had reached the car by the sound of it. The car doors opened and closed, and they could hear their possessions being thrown to the ground.

"Common bandits," Furst spit out the words like a bad piece of meat. No incriminating documentation was in cars while in the field, but the thought of this bunch rifling through his gear made Furst cross. He climbed up the embankment wall in slow methodical increments until he could just peer over the top. All four were milling about the Praga – arguing and looking around until a decision was made. Furst let himself drop back down next to Burda. "Two are crossing the bridge, two are looking for us underneath."

"How fast can you run?" Burda challenged his partner.

"Faster than you," Furst was already crouched like a sprinter.

Burda waved his arm in the direction of the stream ahead of them. "That tree line on both sides of the embankment extends all the way to the shooter's hiding spot, yes?

"Affirmative," Furst was itching to move.

"Follow me, that is where we are going," Burda ran off for the trees before waiting for a reply.

The Czechs had cautiously made their way through the trees until they had found the makeshift camp of the ambushers. It pained Burda to watch the four manhandle the Praga off to a secluded corner off the road. Luckily, Furst had taken the ignition key with him. From their vantage point the intelligence agents got their first chance to properly observe their adversaries. By the way the four carried themselves they were young. Like many Sudeten militiamen they were dressed in German SA cast-offs: brown tunics, blue-gray pants, black jackboots. The rifles looked new – Mauser Standard Model – the short-barreled commercial version of Germany's standard-issue infantry weapon. It took a while, but the four eventually decided to return to their nest as Burda had counted on. Having lost their targets, the militiamen would want to move onto a new location. Their missing prey might come back with Czechoslovak police.

As the four Sudetens neared, Burda and Furst each found a wide tree to position themselves behind. When the ambushers were less than twenty meters away, Burda slipped the safety off his pistol and glanced at Furst who gestured an *okay* signal in return. Burda took aim at the point between the third and fourth riflemen. Satisfied, he depressed the trigger. The explosion from the 9mm weapon shattered the pastoral summer air and sent the young militiamen diving for the dirt.

"The next shot will take one of your heads off," Burda barked as he stepped away from cover. "Who is going to volunteer?"

One of the men pushed his rifle away from his body and slowly locked his hands behind his head. Believing their comrade had the right idea the other three did the same.

"Very good," Burda extolled. "That was very smart. You may yet live beyond this day. Do not move, gentlemen."

The four men did as they were told while Burda collected the rifles under Furst's watchful gaze. Once the Mausers were safely out of reach, Burda checked each man closely. There were bayonet knives and rope coils on their uniform belts, but thankfully no side arms or grenades stuffed in the boots.

Now... unbuckle those belts," Burda ordered as he stepped back a few paces. "Slowly gentlemen. When you have finished, clasp your hands tightly behind your heads again."

When the command was carried out to his satisfaction, Burda used his pistol to cue Furst to gather the belts.

"That's fine. Let's have a look at the four of you. I want each of you to sit up. And once again, hands behind the heads if you do not want a hole drilled between the eyes," Burda gestured with the pistol for emphasis. "I am a very competent shot at this range."

"That is no exaggeration," Furst confirmed in perfect German.

Burda grew angry looking at the faces. They were four baby-faced teenagers – eyes full of frustration... and fear – just four stupid kids.

"What mischief you boys have been up to today," Burda mocked them like a reproachful schoolmaster. One of the youngsters, a tall boy with wavy hair and freckles didn't appreciate the condescending tone, but Burda could care less.

"Are you going to execute us now?" the boy with freckles demanded.

"No, I haven't beaten you senseless yet," Furst stepped closer to the teenager. "Shut your mouth."

Freckles backed down while his comrades remained mum.

"Excellent," Burda continued. "We are making progress."

Furst took coils of rope from the belts on the ground. There was enough to securely bind the hands of their prisoners behind their backs. Burda noticed and nodded his approval. Furst moved behind Freckles with rope and one of the bayonets. He cut the right amount of rope, pulled the boy's arms tight behind the back, and secured the wrists, as Burda kept guard. Done, Furst moved to the next boy to do the same.

Furst finished lashing the last of the four bound teenagers to the trunk of a separate tree. They were going to be that way for a long time, so Burda had wanted them sitting while lashed. Something else Burda had wanted was for the lads to have their backs to each other distant enough so that they could not reach one another. His partner was a sly one on occasion and Furst would look forward to seeing how this played out. Until then, he tied each teenager's boots tightly together to make it more difficult for them to escape their bounds. After double-checking every knot, Furst emptied the pockets of each of the kids for identification and other paperwork.

"I have all of their papers. What now?" Furst dropped the documents onto the ground.

"Take that stuff back to the car. Also, collect the weapons. I think everything will fit in the back," Burda estimated."

"No problem there," Furst was sure the Praga would hold it all. "It won't take me long to get the tire changed, and then we can get back on our way."

"So you're going to leave us out here to rot?" Freckles demanded indignantly.

Burda kneeled down close to the boy, letting his pistol sway back and forth menacingly not far from the prisoner's nose. "Considering that you and your friends ambushed us with the intent to kill, I don't have a problem leaving you all here for the wolves to nibble on."

Such a fate was not very popular with the other boys, who squirmed in their bindings. That brought a smile to Burda's face, but Freckles was trying hard not to be intimidated.

"Then lets try this again. Who is your commanding officer? Who sent you out here to shoot at us?" Burda continued.

"No one!" the lad refused to oblige. "We don't need orders to shoot at Czech villains who oppress us."

Burda mulled over the boast for a few moments before going on. "Fine then. If you will not be cooperative, perhaps I should listen to the advice of my associate and shoot you four where you sit. That way we can be done with you."

Freckles struggled in his bounds to no avail. "Go ahead! But one day our people will be part of the Reich, and *everything* will be different."

Burda stood again, looking down at the boy very sadly. "Perhaps. But this is not that day. You are not making a very good case in your defense, boy."

Burda gagged Freckles securely with a rag so he could not make any noise. Done, Burda fired a shot into the earth next to the tree. Not being able to see what was going on, combined with the gunshot, alarmed the other three teenagers. They squirmed in their bounds and began to cry out.

"Your turn," Burda's kneeled beside the youngest boy. "Who sent you?'

"Dreschler! Helmut Dreschler," the scared boy spilled the answer. "He is ortsgruppenleiter in district four. Please do not kill me."

"Very good. You will live, boy," Burda stood up and walked away without another word.

SEPTEMBER 13, 1937
MINISTER'S OFFICE – U.S. EMBASSY
MALA STRANA DISTRICT, PRAHA

Wilbur Carr could not officially represent the U.S. government until his diplomatic credentials were officially accepted by President Beneš. But Beneš had taken a long weekend to relax at his country home in Slovakia. In the interim, Carr had busied himself with picking the brains of his senior staff during the day. During the evenings, Carr had himself introduced within Prague's diplomatic and social community. He didn't necessarily agree with everything that he was told in these conversations, but Carr was keenly interested in ferreting out the human dimension of how people would react during the unavoidable crisis that was coming.

This morning Carr was sitting down with his eager young military attaché, Bulloch. Chapin had been neither enthusiastic nor critical of Bulloch when briefing Carr on the legation staff – suggesting that Bulloch had not been on station long enough for Chapin to form a judgment. It was obvious neither man possessed a working relationship with the other. That would change immediately, Carr decided. On the most militarized front line in Europe, he couldn't do without the insight of a military mind, even a newly minted one such as Bulloch's.

A polite knock on the door broke the silence. Carr pushed his spectacles higher up on his nose. "Come in."

The door opened enough for Bulloch's head to peer inside. He had never been in this office and was unsure of the layout.

"Please come in, captain," Carr rose from the desk chair and extending his hand.

"Minister Carr... thank you for seeing me," Bulloch shook his hand. "How are you settling in?"

Bulloch had a good, firm handshake, which Carr approved of. The captain was also dressed in a neatly ironed uniform, another a good point in the young man's favor. Carr also noticed that Bulloch carried a portfolio, indicating the captain was prepared and intended to work.

"Marvelously well. Please take a seat," Carr directed the attaché to one of the guest chairs. "As I listened to some of the broadcasts from Nürnberg this week I can't see how the Czechs can escape the war being forced upon them. That means I will depend a great deal on your advice."

"Honestly sir, I haven't been here much longer than yourself. I don't know how much help I can be to you," Bulloch did not want Carr's expectations of him to be too high.

"In my long years of service I have often found the measure of a man is how he responds to a challenge, not necessarily how many challenges he has faced," Carr clarified what his expectations would be.

"I appreciate your trust in me, Minister Carr," Bulloch saw there would be little room for slacking off on this post. "Have you had a chance to meet with President Beneš, sir?"

"Not yet," Carr removed his spectacles. "He's been away from Prague since I arrived. As long as we're on the subject, what do you think I should know before I speak with the president?"

"Perhaps this," Bulloch reached into his case. "Minister Carr, recently I was approached by a Czechoslovak army officer assigned to their military intelligence division. Since then I have confirmed he is who he says he is. The man gave me a very provocative document, which I have also verified."

Carr found was handed a thick envelope, and could not resist extracting its contents. "What have we here?"

"Its German title is Fall Grün, which translates to Case Green. After careful examination, this is a provisional plan for the invasion of Czechoslovakia," Bulloch Watched carefully for Carr's reaction.

The weight of the envelope seemed to grow magnitudes heavier in Carr's hands. After leafing silently through many pages, the minister put the pages down on his desk and rubbed his eyes.

"How did you verify its authenticity?" Carr thought this might be a difficult task for a new attaché.

"I took it to Major Truman Smith, our attaché in Berlin. He's the most experienced American officer on the Continent, plus he's done several tours in Germany," Bulloch thought one day he would like to have that job.

"I've met Smith. He's a good man and very thoughtful. Have you shown this document to anyone else?" Carr flipped through the pages.

"Although I have submitted the originals of these documents to the Military Intelligence Division back in Washington, Smith and I both agreed to keep this matter quiet until you arrived on station," Bulloch wondered if Carr knew that most attachés were convinced the intelligence division never read their reports.

"I appreciate that, son," Carr thanked providence this youngster had a head on his shoulders. How many times had he had to go before

Congress, knowing the only way to win allocations was to keep his cards close to the vest until it was time to reveal them. "You've had an opportunity to review this document. What are we dealing with here?"

"As I said, sir, it is provisional – an early go-around with no timetables for execution. Think of it as an answer to a series of *what if* questions. If France should be paralyzed by internal turmoil, how could Czechoslovakia be neutralized? 'If France threatens war, how many German divisions massed at what locations would be needed to break through Czech defenses quickly before the French can mobilize and attack in the west? After the breaching the Czech border, what are the strategic objectives of the army? What's alarming is how much organizational detail is already present at this early stage," Bulloch ran down the list.

"Then it is your evaluation that this exercise was written as the result of a policy decision by the German government, not just a routine series of contingency assessments?" Carr lifted the document up in his hand.

"Minister Carr, a response to policy is the way the transcript reads. The presumption is that Czechoslovakia will be attacked. The questions are under what circumstances. The answers are by what means," Smith and Bulloch had both agreed on this.

Carr sighed, put the pages back down on the desktop, and thumped them slowly with the fingers of his writing hand. Chapin and the rest of the diplomatic secretaries were optimistic Czech/German relations would not deteriorate into war. The Berlin chargé d'affaires, Gilbert, was of the same mind when Carr had sat down with him last week. They reasoned Hitler was all bravado and posturing for the gallery but that he wasn't so foolhardy as to plunge Europe into another world war. Certainly this was the message Mister Roosevelt wished to hear. Prague may be Carr's first mission abroad, and while he may lack certain diplomatic experience, one thing he knew all too well was the politics of power. His instincts told him that Hitler would move on the Czechs. He wanted to believe otherwise, as his more seasoned subordinates counseled, but Bulloch had just brought him round full circle. Carr stood up to look out the window at the gardens outside window.

"Why did the Czech army officer give you this information?" Carr was curious to know.

"Honestly sir, I believe they are looking to jumpstart a political response back home via the War Department. It is the only angle that makes sense," Bulloch took the liberty of standing next to Carr at the window.

"This may be an attempt to recruit you into some kind of espionage against Germany," Carr lectured Bulloch like a concerned headmaster. "Under no circumstances are you to allow yourself to be encouraged or coerced into any illegal activities on German soil."

"I quite agree, sir," Bulloch had no desire to play the fool. "Although I got the impression there would be more of these *presents* in the future."

Espionage was not what Carr expected to be confronted with on his second full day on the job. Part of him fiercely disliked the whole concept. Yet Carr knew that to give good counsel a professional needed solid facts. He may regret the decision later but he was inclined to allow Bulloch to proceed.

"Captain, you may not accept currency from foreign nationals, nor agree to pay any foreign nationals for any sensitive information," Carr turned to look the attaché in the eye. "You will honor the law of the Czechoslovak Republic, and the laws of any countries you may be traveling through. You will under no circumstances besmirch the honor of the United States, or the uniform you wear. You may not divulge sensitive information about the United States, or her armed forces. However, I leave it up to you to use your best judgment regarding how to employ European military facts acquired through your own observations. Abide by these instructions, Mister Bulloch, and I will condone this *relationship* of yours."

"Yes, sir. I'll see how this plays out, and keep you posted," Bulloch admired the piercing clarity of those sixty-six year-old eyes.

"Fine, I'll look forward to seeing what you turn up," Carr encouraged him. "Just remember you're not working alone. Find me if you need me."

2ND ARMORED REGIMENT, VYŠKOV

Too many of *his* tanks were out of commission. Worse, there wasn't a damn thing he could do about it. He had mechanics and repair garages, what he didn't have were spare parts, towing cables and field transport. It was an absurd ritual. When he marched into the maintenance shed to learn why more of his precious Škodas were on blocks, the četařs held up their wrenches in surrender: *No sir, sorry sir. We have no parts. The tanks have to go back to the factory for repair.* How many memorandums had to be written to the general staff and the politicians urging them to recognize that prosecuting mobile warfare demanded mobile field support? Having one or two platoons of tanks stranded at the plant in Plzen for repair was unbearable.

"Podplukovník Srom," an unfamiliar voice behind him announced itself.

The lieutenant colonel whirled around to find a well-pressed and annoyingly young major standing before him. The man's collar bore the badge of the armored corps over cavalry yellow, but no regiment number. Odds were good the young cub was one of the bright *wonders* the generals, in their infinite wisdom, had whisked out of advanced officer training and into a comfortable desk job. This one never sweated a summer day locked down inside the steel walls of a tank, Srom was sure of it.

"What brings you out into the trees and fields of Moravia, major? Tell me that you have come all the way from comfortable Praha to assure me that someone at the general staff is listening and my mechanics will be getting the replacement parts for my tanks that were promised months ago? While you're at it, tell me your name," Srom barked.

"Kopecky, sir. Seventh Department," he saluted. "Apologies, sir I wasn't aware your logistical shortage was so acute. But that's not why I am--".

"--Every fortnight for the last three months I've submitted an urgent requisition for materials that should rightfully be on hand to keep my tanks on the field," Srom stepped closer to leave an uncomfortably small space between the two officers. "Three times I have called on General Vaněk and asked for his intercession in the matter. You are going to stand there and claim you are unaware of our legitimate needs, major? What exactly do you and your compatriots do in Praha while we here prepare to fight a war?"

"Podplukovník, these deficiencies are well understood," Kopecky had not travelled all the way from Praha to get a dressing-down over the likes of faulty gears, electrical systems and ball bearings. He had to find a way to get the colonel off the subject. Srom was one of the most forward-thinking officers in the army. Two years before he had published a book, *Tanks In Combat: Their Tactical Use*. While the general staff had long endorsed mechanized armor, infantry and artillery as the best means to quickly adjust to incursions along Czechoslovakia's long borders, Srom was one of a group of officers that argued for the republic's mechanized units to be used as a weapon to open holes in battle, not just plugging them.

"Raising three tank divisions from nothing has taught us volumes about equipment and procedures no one knew we needed let alone procure in abundance. If I pledge to go back to headquarters and personally look into the problem, will you hear me out on another matter of the utmost importance?" Kopecky tried to cut a deal.

Srom was intrigued... this pup had brass balls. It was worth hearing him out, especially if doing so might keep his Škodas from being trucked back to Plzen.

"That's a fair bargain, major. I accept. Now, what can I do for you?" Srom sat down on a nearby wood stool and folded his arms in anticipation.

Kopecky glanced at several of the mechanics nearby and decided what he had to say was better said in private. "Perhaps there is a better place where we can discuss things?"

"Of course, major," Srom understood immediately. "I have the perfect spot in mind. I trust you have not forgotten how to ride a steed while posted in the capital?"

"No, podplukovník, I have not forgotten," although Kopecky did not admit it had been a very long time.

"Very well, follow me," Srom got up and led the way out of the shed.

Kopecky was reminded how much the Moravian countryside looked like a scene out of a children's tale with small, picturesque villages nestled into green hillsides full of trees. Especially when one got off the local roads as Srom and he were doing now on horseback. Horses were one of the benefits of being posted to a field unit. Many artillery divisions, while mobile, were not yet motorized. So there were some magnificent horses available to be *borrowed*.

Srom led them to a small hill topped by several large boulders amid a sparse stand of trees. Dismounting, the lieutenant colonel walked his horse close to a boulder with a natural platform eroded out of it. He took several flasks out of his saddlebag, handing one to Kopecky.

"Ah, you like getting out, my friend," Srom affectionately stroked the brow of the horse with his gloved hands. "Rest and enjoy the grass."

Srom released his grip on the leads, letting them dangle. The horse drifted off a few paces to graze.

"Fine mare," Kopecky released the hold on his own animal. "I do miss riding in my job."

Srom opened his flask and took a discreet sip of the whiskey within. "And just what is your job, Mister Kopecky?"

"Mostly evaluating new mechanized design proposals from heavy industry – to determine whether they comply with the army's specifications, or can exceed those specifications. Or pretty much anything the generals tell me to do," Kopecky saluted Srom with the flask.

"Sounds boring," Srom took another sip. "Is that why you came so far to see me? Are you searching for some excitement?"

"In a fashion," Kopecky raised one of his boots to balance against the boulder. "I am in search of someone to lead a revolution within the army."

Srom slowly screwed the lid on the flask and slipped the container back into his tunic pocket. "You don't strike me as a mutineer, major. Humor aside, what are you really all about?"

"There are a few of us within the departments, more in field units, who all harbor the same concern. If the French do not mobilize when war comes we want to have a strategy in place to win decisively," Kopecky hoped that Capka was happy now.

"You a presumptuous young bastard, Mister Kopecky," Srom allowed the major to roast on the spit for a time. "Do you honestly have so little faith in intelligence of your superiors? Let me share a revelation with you. You are not the first person to travel this road and you might be surprised to learn just who has arrived as the same destination before you."

SEPTEMBER 14, 1937
CNS HEADQUARTERS, NEW YORK CITY

The boss wasn't going to like this... not one bit. That's what Des told himself when he tore the wire dispatch off the teletype. Worse, most of the night crew hadn't made it in yet. Des would be the one who would have to tell the boss. Resigned, he loosened his tie and pointed himself in the direction of Lasky's office.

"Look, pal, I need a table for four, tonight, in the Zebra Room. What part of that do you not get? I spend a lot of money in your joint and I could use a little consideration," Lasky stretched the telephone cable to reach the window so he could look at the busy street below. "No, I don't care that this is short notice. This is Harry Lasky you are talking to."

Des stopped himself in the open doorway, waiting for the boss to get what he wanted. In all of the years he had worked for him, Des had never known Lasky to make a reservation a few days ahead. The boss enjoyed making a fuss way too much for that. Fact was, kicking up dust outside the building was his way of relaxing.

"Hey, you want me to talk to Rudy?" Lasky tugged at the taut cable with no success. "No, I didn't think so. Yeah, I know you'll have the table ready at ten. Thank you!"

Lasky crashed the telephone handset down on its cradle as he turned away from the window. That's when he noticed Des was in the vicinity. "How long have you been there? You have that look on your face. I hate that look. That looks means I'm going to lose my last meal and not leave this floor for the next two days."

"Sorry, Boss. This just came in over the wires and I thought you should have a look," Des closed the distance between them to hand over the page. "Old man Masaryk died."

Lasky snatched the paper from Des' grasp to read the dispatch. "This is huge. His funeral will draw some of the biggest names in Europe. We've got to get Walter going on this now that the damned Nazi party congress is over with."

"Yeah, but didn't you tell Walter to handle the run up to Mussolini's state visit to Berlin?" Des braced himself for the storm.

"You're right, Mussolini brown-nosing Adolf is bigger news. Why couldn't that old Czech wait a couple of weeks to croak? No we can't pull Walter off the Musso visit, and Clarence is still in Rome. That means... damn. Why does God hate me?" Lasky gazed skyward. "Never mind, we know why. Find Talmadge."

SEPTEMBER 15, 1937
U.S. EMBASSY
MALA STRANA DISTRICT, PRAHA

Rereading the cable he was about to transmit to Cordell Hull in Washington. Fate had presented Carr with an opportunity and he dare not ignore such providence. Tomáš Masaryk was the father of Czechoslovakia, the first president of the republic, and the personification of Czech independence. Something like George Washington and Thomas Jefferson all rolled into one person. His funeral would draw the most influential statesmen in Central Europe. It was essential that Carr be assigned as FDR's special representative to the funeral. There would be no better way for Carr to establish himself as the voice of the United States, and to immediately cement relationships with dignitaries from allied states pivotal to the Czechs.

The language of the cable was clear, concise and to the point. Carr was satisfied he had set the correct tone as he hurried down the hallway. Before he could descend the stairs to the lower level, Chapin intercepted him.

"Minister Carr, we just received a note from Beneš via messenger," Chapin was out of breath. President Beneš is back in Prague, and requests that you meet with him tomorrow to present your credentials, and to discuss *other issues*."

"Excellent," Carr took the note from the chargé to read. "Thank you, Vinton. Come with me while I take this cable to Bess downstairs to send off to Secretary Hull."

SEPTEMBER 16, 1937
LES TERNES DISTRICT, PARIS

She hated the long flight of steps to her third floor apartment. Especially following a week chasing after self-important bureaucrats. Her feet were killing her so much she had taken off her shoes and stashed them in her shoulder bag right after getting out of the cab. Lugging two suitcases was no joy either. What was she drinking to think that Lasky was ever going to pay her enough to afford a flat in a building with a doorman... or an elevator? Next time she'd have to remember to cut down to one piece of luggage

Struggling up the last few steps, Ros noticed some kid sitting outside her door. Too tired and disheveled to be alarmed, she dropped the suitcases to the floor with a thud loud enough to startle the napping teenager to his feet.

"Hey, what do you want? The rent is paid up," Ros was too tired to remember to ask the question in French. Now that she could see his face Ros recognized the youngster. It was Armand the runner for the CNS Paris bureau.

"Miss Talmadge... sorry, I fall asleep," the boy apologized in his slow English.

Now she felt like a mean hag as well as sleep deprived. "Armand, what are you doing here?"

"They told me to wait for you," he managed, rubbing his still sleepy eyes.

"For what? How long have you been sitting here?" now she was concerned about the kid.

He pulled out a cable from his pocket, waiting for her to take it. "Since yesterday, the chief said you had to read this."

Forcing the poor child to hang around past midnight waiting to deliver a cable meant one thing: someone, and she had a good idea who, wanted something and right now Ros wasn't in the mood. "You read it."

"But it is for you," Armand was confused.

"Yeah, that is what's worrying me," Ros turned around to gather her luggage. "You've already had a look, haven't you, kid?"

Afraid now that she had guessed he had read the cable, he decided his best course was to be honest. "Yes, but only because --"

"-- Then go on and read it for me," Ros was too tired to wait for the explanation.

Armand wasn't happy having to stretch his English this way, but she was pretty and very different from the French women he was used to so he did as she asked:

LASKY, 14 SEPTEMBER, CNS NEW YORK CITY. START. TALMADGE. DUTY CALLS. FIRST CZECH PRESIDENT, MASARYK... DEAD. FUNERAL SET FOR 21ST. BIG DEAL. HAUTH STUCK IN BERLIN. ALL YOUR SHOW. TURN AROUND, DESTINATION PRAGUE. LEAVE IMMEDIATELY. RAIL ALREADY BOOKED. TICKETS & DOCUMENTATION AT BUREAU. CONFIRM UPON RECEIPT. HARRY. STOP.

Ros opened her door and deposited the luggage within while leaving Armand waiting for some type of acknowledgement regarding the cable. When she reappeared, she was fingering through her pocket book pulling out a cross-section of Franc notes.

"Thanks for waiting, Armand," Ros startled the boy when she shoved the bills into his hand. "Here's the deal, you waited here until morning. Got that?"

"You want me to wait for you?" he wasn't sure what she was asking him to do.

"No hon," Ros assured him sweetly. "You go somewhere and have a good time. Just stay as far away from the bureau as possible. Don't you go back there until after ten o'clock in the morning. When they ask, you had to wait here until nine o'clock in the morning for me to show up. Comprends?"

Armand smiled as he realized the ruse she was after. "Oui! À demain."

As the boy scurried off to spend his unexpected fortune, Ros shut the door focused on one thought: drawing a long hot bath.

3. COMMITMENTS

**Former Czechoslovak president T.G. Masaryk's
funeral procession along the Vltava River in Prague**

*SEPTEMBER 20, 1937
NOVE MESTO, PRAHA*

The Czechs were in a solemn mood. Masaryk was dead, and they could
sense their future would be a good deal different without him. There had
been no greater proponent or defender of Czech independence than the
old man. Despite advanced years, and ill health this larger-than-life figure
was his nation's sturdy oak. Not a trivial matter in a country surrounded
by hostile neighbors. For the funeral, Minister Carr and a small group of
other foreign VIPs would walk slowly behind the carriage bearing
Masaryk's coffin. All of them would be easy targets. To ease his mind,
Bulloch traversed the entire five miles that the funeral procession would
take the following day as it meandered through the city. He found
nothing amiss, yet felt better having made the effort. The late hike had left
him damn thirsty, however. There was a cozy place he knew of called U
Pinkasu down in the "New Town" district of the city that would do nicely.

Descending the stairs to the room he liked the best, the one with a
vaulted ceiling, Bulloch was disappointed that there wasn't an obvious
place to sit. The regulars may be glum, but they were out in force.
Searching the room again, he noticed an open spot at the end of a table
and headed in that direction. As Bulloch got within a few feet of the
crowded table a muscular man in a transit authority uniform raised his
head. The bleary eyes grew confused, trying to place the vaguely familiar
cut of the military uniform with the completely unfamiliar emblems sewn

onto it. Thinking that it mattered little at such a time as this the transit man motioned the soldier to sit down next to him.

"Dekuji," Bulloch thanked the man as he sat down. The word of thanks went unnoticed as the fellow promptly returned his attention to a conversation with a colleague seated at the table. Bulloch turned over a coaster in anticipation of a waiter. Thankfully, he didn't have long to wait before a Pilsner was put down in front of him, followed by the ubiquitous slip of white paper with the first tick mark of what Bulloch intended would be many more. Reflecting on that first deep, refreshing sip Bulloch realized how serious life had gotten. There was a lot of fun to be had in playing the dashing young American captain, which was appealing to a dirt-poor California farmer's kid. He was still poor, but the uniform hid a lot. When he had signed on as an attaché, Bulloch hadn't given a rat's ass about Europe, ideology or what big fish swallowed small fish. Europeans killed Europeans and they were good at it. Maybe these Czechs were getting to him.

With impeccable timing, another full glass of beer appeared, but the arm delivering the Pilsner was not the waiter's. Bulloch glanced upward to notice the arm belonged to a smiling Czechoslovak Army Air Force officer he didn't know.

"Would you be the American attaché?" the air force staff captain's English decent.

Being easily identified went with the brass *U.S.* pinned to his lapel. "Quite right. The name is Bulloch.

"Bozik, 44th Fighter Flight, 4th Air Regiment," the staff captain replied, lifting his pint of Pilsner. "Na zdravi. To your health, Mister Bulloch."

"And to yours, Mister Bozik," Bullock stood, raised his glass in a toast. "Are you posted near Prague?"

"Close enough, so a few of us were able to get away to pay our respects to President Masaryk," Bozik pointed out the seven other pilots seated at another table.

"Yes, I'll be paying my respects tomorrow, as well," Bulloch raised his glass again.

After both captains downed the remaining contents of their glasses, Bozik continued. "I understand your minister will walk in the procession tomorrow. He honors us greatly."

Bozik looked forlornly at his empty glass, then back to his table, then back at Bulloch.

"Do you speak Czech?" Bozik inquired slyly.

"A little," Bulloch wondered where this forward fellow was going with such a question.

"That will do. Please join my cohorts and I," Bozik motioning for the American to follow him. Bulloch grabbed his white slip of tick marks and followed happy for the chance to let the world's problems sink away for a little while in the company of other soldiers.

The transit man scowled at the two captains as they left, thinking once again how army types always thought themselves too good to drink with working men.

The intoxicated little troop negotiated the confines of the narrow street in a jagged yet jolly formation. Bulloch began to wonder whether the city father's had bestowed each neighborhood with so many public clocks just for this sort of circumstance – to remind legions of sauced citizens to get their butts home. The clock he was passing under confirmed the opinion of the one a block before that it was long after midnight and tomorrow would start far too early. As they came upon the bridge west to the Mala Strana district Bulloch stopped and saluted sloppily at the zigzagging airmen. "Gentlemen, this is my fork in the road. Good night."

Bozik disengaged from the rest of his companions, motioning them to go on. "I'll catch up with you later."

"Thank you for inviting me to join your party," Bulloch offered his hand. "I hope one day to return the favor."

"Soldiers should drink together, and you looked like you needed someplace to belong," Bozik slapped Bulloch solidly on the shoulder.

Neither man noticed a figure stepping out of the shadows across the street.

"Is this a fraternal order of kapitáns?" Burda walked into the light of the street lamp.

"You don't write, you don't call... I was getting worried it was over between us," Bulloch felt himself sobering at the sight of the intelligence officer.

"Ah, you missed me. That's touching Captain Bulloch," Burda insinuated, waving his cigarette once for dramatic emphasis.

"A friend of yours?" Bozik inquired, not recognizing the man in the business suit.

"Štábní Kapitán Ondřej Bozik of the 4th Air Regiment, meet Kapitán Burda of the Second Department," Bulloch made the introduction loudly despite the hour.

The introduction did little to impress Bozik as he looked back and forth between the two men. "Spies... I feel dirty. Here I thought you were an honest soldier, Bulloch."

"You meet all kinds in my line of work," Bulloch sounded as happy as someone tasting a bitter lemon.

"Have you been drinking, kapitán," Burda directed at Bozik.

"Obviously, not enough," Bozik was going to tire quickly of this general staff fellow if he stayed. "Gentlemen. You obviously have business to conduct, and I should not let my pilots wander off unattended. Bulloch, I'm glad you could join our little assembly."

"Thanks for taking me in. Next time I'm buying," Bulloch waved goodbye.

"Very well, stay out of trouble. I intend on collecting, kapitán," Bozik stared disapprovingly at Burda before heading off after his men.

"Did you enjoy your evening?" Burda asked as he stepped closer to Bulloch. "I'm impressed you held your own and remain standing."

"There you go lurking again. You could very well have joined us back at U Pinkasu," Bulloch admonished the Czech.

"You were having such a good time, I didn't have the heart to interrupt," Burda offering a cigarette from his pack.

Bulloch waved him off. "No thanks... nasty habit. It'll kill you, almost as quickly as sentimentality."

"Do most Americans have so little respect for manners," Burda pocketed the cigarettes.

"Ouch. I deserved that," Bulloch confessed. "Hey, I don't like standing in one spot too long. Let's walk. Why have you been so scarce lately? I never got the chance to properly thank you for passing along those German war plans. That document definitely raised a few eyebrows."

Burda nodded his head in agreement as the two men walked toward the bridge, their footsteps echoing through the damp night.

"Very good. There were a few matters to attend to on the western border," Burda thought of the recent ambush by the schoolboys that led to the capture of the Sudeten Nazi cell leader." Have you visited our Sudeten territories yet?"

"Only in the north. Your Interior Ministry does not recommend that foreign nationals visit the western districts. Something about not being able to guarantee the safety of visitors," Bulloch goaded.

"Quite true. That's why I'd like to offer you an armed escort," Burda had something new he wanted to show the attaché.

"In uniform or out?" Bulloch wanted to get a better feel for what kind of trip the Czech had in mind.

"Out. Less conspicuous is advisable." Burda made the recommendation from personal experience.

Bulloch pondered the possibilities as they crossed the bridge onto the Mala Strana side near his apartment. "Do you get shot at much?"

"With regularity," Burda mused.

"Sounds like the bad guys have poor aim," Bulloch was reminded of B movies back home.

"Their aim is getting better," Burda reached into his jacket pocket with his free hand to pull out a spent 7.92mm rifle cartridge, which he handed to the American. "Luckily the bullet that used to be attached to that shell casing missed."

"Sounds serious," Bulloch decided to play along.

"Warnings from the Interior Ministry aside, my department believes you would benefit from a fact finding trip to our frontier with Germany," Burda had the agenda all worked out.

"Feeling the sting of that Himmler propaganda, are you?" the constant accusations in German newspapers and radio broadcasts were fresh in Bulloch's mind.

"The truth is the most powerful tool in our arsenal, captain," Burda made a mental note that this American was not naive.

"Fine, when do you want to take this trip to the country?" Bulloch already had plans to journey to the border towns but had waited on Carr to arrive in Prague. Now that the minister was on the job the timing couldn't be better for a guided tour.

"As soon after the funeral as possible," Better the Americans see how conditions in the German areas were decent so that they could report it to his superiors.

"I'll have to make sure my superiors have no plans for me, but I think I can clear my schedule a couple of days from now," Bulloch did not see a conflict in his schedule.

"Excellent," Burda stamped out the cigarette on the ground. "You have my permission to carry a sidearm."

"Does that mean I get to fire it?" Bulloch paused in front of his building.

"Anything is possible," Burda was pleased at the prospect of having an additional friendly weapon backing them up on the trip.

SEPTEMBER 21, 1937
PRAŽSKÝ HRAD, PRAHA

Although they called it a castle, Bulloch always thought that description was overly generous. Yes it was on a strategic hill overlooking the entire city but this was a palace that a battle-trained garrison would have a hard time defending for very long in any era. The compound was big, however, with many wings and numerous stone courtyards. In the outermost courtyard Bulloch waded through a sea of dignitaries and bureaucrats from many nations. He already knew that Minister Carr would follow the funeral carriage this way out the main gate while Bulloch would attempt to follow the slow moving procession as close behind as he could.

For a moment, the area in the center of the courtyard cleared, and Bulloch noticed a tall brunette in a stylish form-fitting dark blue suit, heels and hat. She was looking around as if she was searching for someone in particular. Her height, and something about the cavalier way she had that small purse slung over her shoulder, told him that he was staring at an American. European women never showed you that kind of pent-up energy looking for a reason to explode. The question was whether she was the wife or daughter of a diplomat or businessman. He'd prefer she were someone's daughter. Pondering the possibilities was an agreeable diversion that Bulloch was happy to distract himself with until woman locked eyes on him and marched in his direction.

Ros had found what she was looking for: an American who worked at the embassy. They were scarce and she needed to nail down an interview with the new big-name diplomat in town, that old codger Carr. Already past retirement age and Roosevelt sends him on his first foreign assignment to a crisis zone. There was a story there and she wasn't going to be brushed aside. That was a U.S. Army uniform a few yards off, and he just had to be on the embassy staff. Cute too, she thought. That would just make it easier.

"Hey handsome," Ros called out as she approached Bulloch.

Feeling cornered, Bulloch said nothing and stared as she stopped a few feet in front of him. Up close, something about this woman was nagging at him, but damned if he could figure out what.

Ros thought the poor boy couldn't be that tongue-tied. Officers were never that innocent. Something else had to be wrong, and she began to panic wondering whether something was wrong with her outfit. As Ros adjusted her jacket and quick-checked her clothes, there was nothing else left to do but ask, "What's wrong, I spill something on myself?"

"No, sorry. I just haven't seen an American woman in months," Bulloch had not seen a looker from back home in a long time. "You new in town?"

"Y'up, here to see the old Czech off, but then it's back to Paris."

Bulloch saw he had been hasty in pegging her as diplomatic family. "Reporter, eh? Newspaper or syndicate?"

"Good boy. Syndicate. Consolidated News Service," Ros saw the guy quick on the uptake.

"Sorry, angel. You'll have to go through channels before you can pester Minister Carr," Bulloch saw the whole set-up coming together and decided to wiggle out of it.

Damn, this guy wasn't going to fall for a pretty face as easily as she had thought so she switched to the sympathy approach instead. "Ah, c'mon... help a girl out."

"Would if I could, sister. But I'm not your man," Bulloch suggested smugly.

"But you work at the embassy, right?" she pleaded.

"Correct, but I'm not diplomatic staff," Bulloch pointed at the emblems on his uniform. "Now if you want to talk tanks and airplanes, I'm your guy."

She knew she was getting the run around, but she was enjoying herself for one last change of tactic: putting her hands on her hips and leaning forward close enough for him to smell her perfume. "I don't suppose there's any weak spots in that armor plating of yours, champ?"

"Not a chance," he chuckled. Spotting Chapin not far away in the crowd, Bulloch decided he might as well have a bit more fun, and pointed at the chargé d'affaires. "See that little man over there by the wall in the suit from 1925?"

"Oh, give me a break, the joint is full of them," looked in the exact direction the captain was pointing at. That's when she saw a man fidgeting by the stone foundation. "Yeah, got him."

"His name's Chapin. He's your ticket," Bulloch was delighted to send the dame chargé 's way. "Go easy on him."

"Thanks, doll, I owe 'ya," Ros leaned over, kissed him quickly on the cheek, winked, then sashayed off after her next target.

Bulloch admired the view as she left – convinced the show was as good going as it had been coming.

HRADČANY CASTLE, SOUTH WING

Carr fussed with his uncomfortable old-fashioned stiff collar in one of the staterooms full of dignitaries. Billings stood by the older gentleman's coat and top hat. The young embassy second secretary didn't see why most of these elderly relics had never bought a new suit since 1918 but looking around the ornate room at least his boss wasn't alone in this peculiar sense of diplomatic fashion.

"Damn collar," Carr grumbled. "I should have selected another one before leaving the legation. This one will have to do though."

"Minister, are you sure you are up to this? It's a very long procession: five miles or more," Billings thought now was the proper time for one last inquiry about the day ahead.

"Stop coddling me, son. It's unbecoming to both of us," Carr brushed him off. "Thank you but I am no stranger to long walks as my wife will attest. This is a great honor for our mission, and for me personally. If you wish to have a long career in the Foreign Service you must embrace such opportunities."

Carr reached for his coat and pulled it on with vigor. Next he took his top hat from Billings. "Let's get on with it," Carr donned the hat with a jaunty tap to the brim.

OUTER COURTYARD
PRAŽSKÝ HRAD, PRAHA,

Bulloch knew it was impolite being there for a funeral and all, but he was too amused watching Chapin arguing in exasperation with the leggy reporter. But the show came to an abrupt end as the bell in the nearby cathedral tower began to toll. Prague had as many or more cathedrals than any European city he had been to. But this one sat directly within the castle walls so the bell was especially loud. Bulloch didn't notice a trim uniformed man in his fifties navigate through the crowd and up behind him.

"Delightfully tall isn't she?" General Louis-Eugene Faucher, the French military attaché in Prague, observed with the kind of delight a hungry man reserved for a big meal.

"Rather out of your league don't you think, general?" Bulloch was not at all sure he liked that this prehistoric buzzard was circling already.

Faucher was disappointed in the American. "Nathan, one day I *will* have you living like a Frenchman."

"You're an old man, Louis. Amazingly well preserved, I'll give you that. But you don't have a shot," Bulloch was duty bound to burst his bubble.

"She's American yes? Then she will find me exotic," Faucher countered.

"She's already been to Paris. More likely she will think you smell bad," Bulloch indulged himself as cruelly as possible.

"Nonsense. I bathe every day," Faucher was barely ruffled by the insult.

"Correction... you smell French," Bulloch pinched his nostrils together.

"A shocking lack of respect for a senior officer," Faucher finally showed some annoyance.

"Perhaps, but not in my army, friend," Bulloch was content that he had finally made a small dent in the Frenchman's ego.

Faucher put his hand on Bulloch's shoulder in a brotherly way. "I will forgive you if you introduce me to her."

"Sorry pal, I don't even know her name," Bulloch acted as cool as Cagney might in a flick.

"Nathan, I have no more time for your questionable wit," Faucher took his hand back in a huff. "Neither will I be deterred by your paltry attempts at obstruction. Adieu."

As Faucher made to squeeze through the crowd in Ros' direction the cathedral bells begin tolling continuously indicating the start of the procession. What little open space in the courtyard vanished as Czechoslovak legionnaires worked at clearing a path for the funeral carriage.

"Damn you," the stymied general made his way back to Bulloch. "This is your fault for delaying me. Now I will have to follow that fool Blum for the rest of the day."

"All part of the service... say, what's your beef with Blum? I thought you were a Popular Front man," Bulloch tossed out the untruth as a little extra salt on the wound.

"You are insufferable, Nathaniel. Interfering with my dalliances is one thing. Insulting my politics is uncalled for... very impolite. We will discuss it later," Faucher adjusted the tilt of his kepi. "For now follow me. I've already arranged it with the authorities. We'll pick up the procession after the dignitaries clear the main gate. Let's hope they fed those damn horses something solid yesterday."

Bulloch could see the army honor guard leading the three teams of horses pulling the slow-moving funeral carriage out from the inner courtyard. But Chapin and the leggy reporter were nowhere to be seen. He wondered whether she got her interview with Carr.

MOST LEGIÍ, PRAHA

Capka had never seen this many men, women and children on the bridge before. Even the Sokol athletic rallies never drew this many bystanders. The people adored Masaryk. There would never be another like him. He had liberated them all, and now the tall, principled and determined old gentleman was finally free of his burdens. Capka felt the weight of those burdens keenly, something he was sure he shared with the citizens on the bridge as the gun carriage bearing Masaryk's body passed slowly by.

He had not recognized the foreign politicians respectfully behind the carriage. For Capka politicians were a necessary evil and the best that could be hoped for was that they possessed a sense of duty and pragmatism that overcame their natural penchant for corruption and mischief. Still it was an honor that the procession following the carriage stretched as far as he could see.

A long time after the cortege thinned out Capka continued to lean against the bridge railing and watched. It seemed like all of Praha was out in the streets doing the same thing. He didn't think he had ever witnessed such a powerful expression of mass solidarity. Capka was moved. He doubted that Hitler, Mussolini, Stalin or Franco would receive such a warm public display without a few bayonets prodding them in the rear.

"You're late again," Capka grumbled as Kopecky finally turned up at his side.

"You're insufferable," Kopecky leaned back against the railing.

"Tough getting through the crowds?" Capka decided to let his friend off easy in Masaryk's memory.

"Impossible. I found a good place to stand and watched the carriage and the marchers go by. I was stunned, the line of dignitaries went on forever," Kopecky swept his arm in a wide arc.

"I don't think I will ever forget this day," Capka confided. But now it was time for business. "What did you want to tell me?"

"Progress, my friend. Srom is working with us. Or perhaps we are working for him. I am no longer sure. It's a small working group. But it's started. For now we are calling it Doctrine R," Kopecky whispered.

"R as in Rychlá?" Capka was not impressed. "How unimaginative."

"Double meaning actually: rapid strategy, produced rapidly. Srom was adamant that we avoid getting cute and remain focused on the objective," Kopecky saw he had Capka's full attention.

SEPTEMBER 23, 1937
SLEZSKA CAFE VINOHRADY DISTRICT, PRAHA

Bulloch found himself sitting outside of the same café that Burda had introduced him to almost six weeks before. The downside was this happened to be Jirina's neighborhood she had dumped him the week before. During the funeral march Faucher had gotten even for the abuse Bulloch had dished out by revealing that Jirina had dumped him for a Brit. The Frenchman prodded Bulloch for miles trying to discover what he had done to the girl to make her want to insult him so. Bulloch would change the subject, and the Faucher would detour back to Jirina a few minutes later – payment in full for distracting him from the leggy reporter.

To be Burda to their meeting place Bulloch had roused himself for the infrequent luxury of relaxing with a coffee and enough time to skim the Herald Tribune. If the sport jacket, slacks and golf cap he was wearing said anything it was that this was a man on vacation. So Bulloch wanted to feel that way for a moment despite the Colt nestled in its shoulder holster under his jacket. That's when Bulloch noticed a silhouette blocking his sun, and it wasn't Burda.

"You're out of uniform, fella," Ros was dishing out the flirt. "It's my lucky day. Yes I'll join you. Thanks for asking."

Bulloch had been caught of guard and recognized the voice too late to protest.

"C'mon. Cheer up," she continued. "Too early for you? I don't bite. Actually, yes I do bite but not too hard."

"Why aren't you on a train to Paris?" The last thing he needed was a reporter on hand when a Czech military intelligence officer showed up.

"Well good morning to you too," Ros gave up trying to be nice to the jerk. When the waiter attempted to slide by the table, she reached out to grab his jacket and pull him back. "Pardon. The gentleman is buying me a cup of coffee."

Resigning himself to the inevitable, Bulloch ordered his new companion a Turkish coffee of her own.

"That's better," Ros wagged a finger at him.

"Don't mention it," Bulloch decided his best chance at damage control was to change the subject with a question he already knew the answer to. "Did you get the story you were looking for?"

"I got my interview with Wilbur Carr yesterday so I guess I owe you some small thanks for pointing me in the right direction," Ros was trying to keep the guy talking in the hopes his manners might improve.

"Chapin never had a chance," Bulloch was still delighted at pulling that prank. "I'm glad you got everything you needed."

"There was one bit of information I wasn't able to get," Ros took the captain at his word.

"Like I said before," Bulloch raised his arm to object. "I'm not the right guy--"

"-- Your name," she interrupted.

Feeling a bit embarrassed, Bulloch eased back in his chair in retreat. "Off the record… Nathan Bulloch."

The waiter arrived with the additional coffee. Ros took a sip while savoring her victory. "That's a good Virginia name but you don't have an accent."

Bulloch tipped his cap in mock gentlemanly fashion. "I'm from California, ma'am. Father never was too specific about the family history."

He had just lied. His grandfather had lost everything in the Civil War – wife, house, farmland – so he packed up what little was left and had headed west. But Bulloch had no intention of going near that subject with her.

"Good to meet you Mister Bulloch. Ros... Ros Talmadge," she reached across the in anticipation of a firm handshake. "Paris, by way of New York City."

Neither of them noticed Burda approach their table.

"Isn't it rather early to be granting interviews?" Burda addressed the question to both Americans.

Without showing the slightest surprise, Ros looked the Czech up and down and decided on a good offense. "Why Nathan. You never said you had your own valet. Does the War Department know what you're doing with our tax dollars?"

"I wouldn't go quite that far," maybe Bulloch liked this skirt after all. He took another sip of coffee and decided to run with her lead at Burda's expense. "But in my line of work, engaging a local driver is a smart move."

"I think he knows a bit too much about me though," Ros was suspicious of the overly serious fellow she had never met who happened to know she was a reporter.

"I happen to be acquainted with a Frenchman in particular who is very curious about journalists. He happened to mention you the other day." It was something of a lie. The French attaché had made inquiries, but not to Burda.

"Oh really," Ros perked up. "French did you say?"

"I know this Frenchman," Bulloch coughed while swallowing. "*That* kind of curiosity you don't want."

"Don't be jealous, hon," Ros flirted back. "I can take care of myself Captain Nathan.

"Of that I am sure," Burda had no doubt the woman was very enterprising. "Mister Bulloch, did you wish to make your appointment on time?"

Taking the hint, Bulloch gulped down the rest of his coffee and stood. After throwing down enough Czech crowns to cover the bill he handed the paper to Ros. "Here you go, check out the competition. The man is right we must be going. Miss Talmadge it was a pleasure. Do you know when you will be back in this part of the world?"

"Not yet. But the way things are heating up around these parts you can bet I'll be back," the look she gave him was more of a threat than a promise.

"You know where to find me. And if you give a fella some advance warning he'll buy you a drink," Bulloch didn't like the way this reporter just popped up unannounced.

"We'll see soldier boy," Ros played hard to get.

"Don't talk to strangers, doll. They might get hurt," Bulloch warned as he walked off.

"Good day Miss Talmadge," Burda tipped his hat on the way out.

"Something is fishy with that pair," Ros trusted her reporter's intuition. "And I think I am going to find out what."

OPERATIONS DIRECTORATE
COUNTER-INTELLIGENCE OFFICE
REICH MINISTRY OF WAR – 72-76 TIRPITZUFER, BERLIN

He was tired of this accursed room. Cramped, dark and impossible to keep neat. There was no place left to securely store the new equipment and gadgets the labs were coming up with. Some officer would take him to task for lax security he was sure. At least for now he could just squeeze in the last shipment of invisible inks into a space within Cabinet Four. Unfortunately, the effort left him unawares that Obertsleutnant Ottke had snuck up behind him.

"Leutnant, when you have a moment," Ottke inquired in a tone that was more demanding than polite.

Resisting the urge to react hastily the junior officer calmly completed his organizing and securely closed the locker before facing the chief of operations. There were rumors about Ottke's past exploits but no one dared to ask. "What can I do for you today, obertsleutnant?"

The kid did not rattle easily Ottke noted. "How many of those new field wireless sets do we have available?"

"Approximately a half-dozen, sir. That is not counting the defective units awaiting repair," the lieutenant was not surprised the item the colonel wanted was both in short supply and prone to not working.

"How long before you can procure thirty reliable sets?" these continuing procurement and reliability problems annoyed Ottke.

"At the rate we're getting new sets... probably three months, sir," the lieutenant was exaggerating somewhat but he wanted the colonel to appreciate their supply constraints.

Catching the last part of the exchange as he entered the room was Hauptmann Wolff the duty officer. "The leutnant's estimate is correct under current conditions. However, I believe the manufacturer can be *persuaded* to provide that many sets within six weeks. Would that be sufficient, obertsleutnant?"

"That sounds promising. What would need to be done?" Ottke was impressed with Wolff's show of initiative. That one would go far.

"The manufacturer is the brother-in-law of a high-ranking party member," Wolff seized the opportunity. "So the manufacturer has no sense of urgency. If the importance of our requirements could be made clear to this party official, I believe that could have the desired effect."

Ottke stroked his chin while he considered the proposal. "So we need to blow steam up this manufacturer's trousers? I believe I can arrange that. Have all of the names on my desk in an hour and I will take care of the rest. Good thinking, hauptmann."

"You will have them, sir," Wolff had been looking for a means to kick some respect into that slug of a factory owner for months.

EAST OF RAKOVNIK, BOHEMIA

The journey westward had been a wild ride. The driver had a penchant for driving too fast and testing tire adhesion on every curve as the tiny Praga careened through a hilly, forested area. Pretty scenery but Bulloch had no chance to enjoy the view. He was too busy being thrown about the cramped back seat like a badly jostled parcel. Burda though seemed completely unruffled by his colleague's risky driving – swaying back and forth in his seat without a care. After one vicious blind curve too many Bulloch decided he was done keeping quiet.

"Hey! Can you give the accelerator pedal a rest up there, buddy?" Bulloch leaned forward.

Furst half glanced at the American via the rear-view mirror without comment. His reply was to take the next turn hard enough to toss Bulloch forcefully back in his seat.

"I guess not," Bulloch was beginning to dislike this guy more than Burda. "Is there a reason you're treating me like a pinball?"

"It's safer," Furst had no idea what a pinball was, but was pleased if the American was discomforted like one.

"He can talk?" Bulloch leaned forward again. "I didn't know trained monkeys could do that."

Amused, Burda looked over his shoulder at the American. "You'll find my friend here has a lot to say when he chooses to."

"Does he have a name, or should I just call him Cheetah?" Bulloch pressed on.

"Furst," was the sharp, authoritative response from the driver.

"Pleased to meet you, pal," Bulloch didn't sound very sincere.

While he worked out the next nasty thing to say, Bulloch looked out the side window. A train in the distance was making its way up a ravine. That is when it hit him full on... the answer to the question that had been bugging him for days.

"It was the train... got it!" Bulloch snapped his finger next to Burda's ear.

The odd gesture startled Burda. "Got what?"

"That reporter, Talmadge. I knew I had seen her before the funeral. Now I remember where," Bulloch was proud of himself.

"I didn't realize you had met her before Tuesday," Burda was growing curious.

"Yeah, she was on the platform at the train station," Bulloch recalled the moment in his mind.

"Would that be Wilsonovo or Charlottenburg station?" Furst decided to get even for the trained monkey remark.

"Hey. I only just met you and you know a hell of a lot about my business, mister," Bulloch protested.

Furst smiled for the first time during the trip. "I get around."

"So I *was* being tailed. You're good. I never spotted you, fella," most of Bulloch's knowledge of undercover work came from the pages of *Black Mask*. There might be a job for you yet with Pinkerton's."

"What?" The American's constant string of strange references was confusing to Furst.

"Never mind," Burda broke in. "I have been meaning to ask you about your trip to Berlin. Why did you go there so soon after I provided you the Fall Grün copy?"

"I have to have some secrets, bud," Bulloch saw no reason to spill everything these Czechs wanted to know. "Listen, you dropped a huge gift into my hands. For that I am appreciative so let's leave it at that."

"We do have a vested interest in knowing what you are doing with that document," especially since there had been no evidence that the American government had seen the German plans.

"Fair point. You will be happy to know, you passed," Bulloch decided that was all he was going to say on the matter and Burda would just have to chew on that.

As the American was set on speaking in riddles, Burda decided to drop the subject for the moment.

"What about the woman reporter?" Furst returned to the more interesting topic. "Where did you see her?"

"At Charlottenburg station," Bulloch saw no downside in confirming what the intelligence officer already knew. "She was on the other platform with a bunch of drunk news hounds saying so long to some Brit who had pissed off the Germans in print. Have to say... nice legs though."

"On the Brit?" Furst teased.

"Funny, pal. No on the dame," Bulloch wondered who did this guy think he was, William Powell?

"Brits... Jirina, your girl from the foreign ministry... she has found quite a lot to impress her in a Brit," Furst twisted that particular knife deeply, and enjoyed doing so.

"That shot was below the belt, brother, this gunsel was starting to wear real thin with Bulloch.

Burda slowly but firmly pushed Bulloch back to his seat. "We're here."

Bulloch had been too preoccupied with the verbal jousting and had not paid enough attention to where they were. The car was dropping into a valley occupied by a small city. Staring them in the face was an industrial plant.

"That looks like a soap factory," Bulloch guessed since he had seen a few of those before.

"Exactly right. I am impressed, captain," Burda glanced back at him.

"You brought me all the way out here to show me a soap factory? Well, maybe we will come away with some free samples," Bulloch thought they had something a bit more exciting planned than an industrial tour.

Furst stopped the Praga at the guard gate and showed an I.D. to one of the guards on station. The guard waved them through and Furst maneuvered the car to a loading dock area of a warehouse with a row of metal doors.

"We came here to see what is inside," Furst told the anxious American as he parked the Praga.

"Sometimes we need to store large seizures of evidence in a safe location," Burda added some detail as he got out of the car.

The large metal warehouse door rolled upwards to the whine of electric motors. Burda led them inside while Furst found the switch for the interior lights. The harsh tungsten bulbs revealed a large storeroom filled with dozens of mortars and World War I-vintage water-cooled machine guns. Stacked high were boxes of ammunition and German stick hand grenades. Close by were rifle crates stamped with *Mauser* on the side.

Burda walked over and glided his hand slowly along a portable mortar's smooth barrel. "We confiscated this ordinance earlier this week near Karlsbad. The largest cache of weapons we have ever impounded."

Bulloch stepped closer to inspect the stash, then whistled loudly. "There's enough here to outfit a regiment. What tipped your people off?"

"We got lucky. A Sudeten separatist leader fell into our hands and talked," the interrogation of Dreschler was fresh in Burda's memory.

"Why store all of these munitions here," Bulloch spotted a crowbar he could use.

"Not so many ethnic Germans here in this area to cause trouble while we decide how to dispose of all of this material," Burda thought this soap plant was quite a good temporary hiding place.

Bulloch pried open the top of one of the Mauser crates. Putting the crowbar down, he picked up one of the rifles and examined it carefully from stock to barrel tip. He repeated the process with two more crates before venturing an opinion.

"These 98ks are all new manufacture… straight from the factory in Germany," Bulloch opened the bolt on one of the rifles. "The mortars are new too. The machine guns, grenades and the rest all look like original Reichswehr issue. It's obvious where this stuff is coming from and no one seems too concerned about hiding where it's coming from. The next question is who's paying for all of this firepower?"

Burda stepped over to where Bulloch stood adjusting the Mauser's targeting sight. "There is not a price tag attached. In fact, the arrangement is reversed. The ordinance comes *with* money."

Bulloch whistled loudly. "You do have a problem on your hands."

"Perhaps it is not just our problem," Furst countered.

"Yeah, I've heard that pitch once or twice," Bulloch as he carefully returned the rifle to its crate.

"What concerns us is these arms shipments are getting larger and are crossing the border in greater frequency," Burda kneeled to pick up a jagged piece of wood crating from the floor.

"How many guns and shells do you confiscate in a month?" Bulloch wanted to come up with some totals.

Furst took an envelope out of his jacket pocket and handed it to the American.

Bulloch pulled out the folded manifest and pointed to the numbers on the paper. "Yikes, that's enough to start a war."

SEPTEMBER 24, 1937
STATE, WAR, & NAVY BUILDING
WASHINGTON, D.C.

That old dog Carr didn't waste any time. While he respected Carr and the counsel the State Department veteran provided, the man was something of an apolitical reformer who could be troublesome. Rather than risk such complications President Roosevelt saw an opportunity to ease Carr out of State at the same time he needed someone in Prague who would counterbalance Dodd's dire conclusions from Berlin, and Bullitt's generally rosy reports from Paris. That was good enough for Sumner Welles, State Department undersecretary and the president's man within these halls. But this status often put him at odds with the man who's office was around the corner: Secretary of State Cordell Hull.

Without a word the administrative aide guarding the inner sanctum looked up, registered Welles had arrived, then motioned over his shoulder with a pencil in the direction of Hull's door. Welles never broke stride as he marched on through the door.

"What do you have for me?" was the curt greeting from the silver-haired old lawmaker from Tennessee sitting behind his desk composing a memo.

"Wilbur Carr's first full assessment report from Prague," Welles answered as he hovered a comfortable distance from Hull.

"How's it read?" Hull prodded like the practicing lawyer he once was.

"Our new minister has been busy," Welles checked his hand-written notes before continuing. "He's already had a full meeting with Beneš, plus regional dignitaries that were in Prague for the Masaryk funeral. He says Beneš is amazingly upbeat and believes that the worst German provocations are already behind them."

"Really now," Hull's curiosity was aroused. "That's surprisingly optimistic for Beneš. What about the Czechoslovak legislators and business leaders? I'll bet Carr has already slipped into the social set over there."

"You know your man," Welles returned his attention to the report. "He says the Prague upper crust is plenty worried that the worst is still ahead. Center-left politicians are generally cautious as well, but conservative elements believe distasteful but necessary accommodations with Hitler will be made."

"Roosevelt will be happy that Beneš is optimistic," Hull was intrigued that someone in Central Europe was optimistic. "What is Carr's personal evaluation?"

"That's where it gets good, Mister Secretary," Welles paused long enough for Hull to catch on something serious was coming. "Carr says conditions on the ground point to a German invasion and to expect it before 1940."

Hull slammed his pencil down on his desktop calendar. "Why? Based on what?"

"Apparently he has had the opportunity to examine what he views as an authentic order of battle prepared for the German high command," Welles paraphrased. "Invasion plans to be exact. Preliminary but very detailed, he writes."

Hull shot up from his chair to grab the report from Welles to see for himself. "How the hell did he get his hands on something like that? Did he get it from Beneš? "

"No. Apparently Carr got the document from his own military attaché," Welles filled in while Hull rifled through the decoded pages.

"Startling, if true. Who does the army have assigned to Prague again?" Hull continued to flip through pages.

"Someone new. A captain named Bulloch on his first posting," Welles had already checked.

"Eager young captains will buy anything," Hull had seen it happen before. "Why would Carr believe the document is accurate? Who is the source?"

"The young attaché does not name names but the conduit is through the Czechoslovak military," Welles added fuel to the fire.

"This is preposterous," Hull threw the report down on his desk. "Beneš is all roses while his generals telegraph the opposite message. There is every chance these *plans* are fabrications. Carr should know better."

"Pretty much what I thought too at first. But if you look closely, there's a note attached from Truman Smith in Berlin," Welles indicated the location of the addendum. "Young Bulloch took what he had to him for an appraisal and Smith believes the plans are authentic."

"I'll be damned. Smith thinks this kid hit gold, huh?" Hull paused to consider the implications. "The president won't like this one bit. Spain is barely contained. The Japanese are bombing Shanghai into rubble and gobbling up more of China. We have our hands full. If hostilities break out between the Germany and the Czechoslovakia the whole of Europe will go straight to hell. Cable Carr. Ask for clarification. I want more meat on the platter before I take any of this to Roosevelt."

CONSOLIDATED NEWS SERVICE BUREAU
QUARTIER DE L'OPERA DISTRICT, PARIS

Every time Ros visited the Paris Bureau she was sure Harry Lasky had never been there himself. There was no way in hell that Harry would ever foot the bill for an office around the corner from an opera house in an area full of picturesque cafes and theaters unless Lasky worked in Paris himself. The CNS bureau on Boulevard des Italiens probably predated Harry's ownership he probably thought all Paris real estate was dreadfully overpriced. For that reason Lasky could never be allowed to visit Paris. She'd have to talk to the bureau chief about that. She loved this area of town too much for Harry to barge in and take it away for cheaper digs.

Bounding up the last few stairs to the second floor of the Nineteenth Century office building, Ros rushed in through the bureau's main entrance and waved at the receptionist as she went by. The space was small by American newsroom standards but with so many correspondents on assignment in Spain and elsewhere it was rare when more than a few of them were here at the same time. So Ros was happy to see that Clarence was in today. The old guy was a real pro and she liked him. Clarence was fifty-something but would never tell his exact age. The hair might be silver but it was a full head of silver and he kept himself trim and dapper despite the rich food you couldn't escape here in the city.

"Welcome back, kid," Clarence greeted her as he put down the collection of wires he had been reading. "Great job on that Masaryk dispatch."

"Thanks," Ros said as she perched herself on the edge of the writing desk he was sitting at. "What brings you back to town?"

"With Musso in Berlin there was nothing happening in Rome so I came back here to run down a couple of local stories," Clarence took advantage of the moment to lean the old leather chair back a few degrees. "Shouldn't you be taking the weekend off?"

"Ha! No rest for this girl. I'm plotting," she rubbed her hands together.

"Thanks for the warning. I'll keep my head down," it was obvious to Clarence the girl had plenty of moxie.

"You don't have to worry about me," Ros assured him. "Now Harry, that's another story altogether. Which reminds me. I have a cable to send back to the Loud One."

"Don't let me stop you. Harry Lasky deserves as much indigestion as the law allows," Clarence urged her on.

"If he doesn't fire me, let's grab dinner while you're in town," Ros wanted to pick his brains.

"That's a date, sister," Clarence picked up his paperwork.

Ros laughed, patted him on the shoulder and moved off in the direction of Jerry at the copy desk. Jerry was another good guy. He never mangled her articles, and he never treated her any different than the other guys around the bureau. She owed him a drink.

"Hey, Ros," Jerry drawled in his laconic Southwestern way. His version of French had a strain of Creole to it that annoyed Parisians no end. "Nice work back there in Prague. I think it went over pretty well with the boys back in New York. They didn't change a thing."

"That's what I like to hear," Ros thumped his desk with her hand. "Thanks for sticking around late to get the second half."

"Just let me know when you have more words coming and I'll take care of 'ya," Jerry promised.

"Be careful. I don't want your wife getting mad at us both." Ros always thought Jerry must have been a cutie before his hair started to go. But it had been going for a long time and the poor fella wasn't much older than she was. He didn't seem to care though and his pretty French wife Marguerite liked him just fine.

"Don't worry. She has to work late too so she understands," Jerry was making it easy on here as always. "What can I help you with today, Ros?"

"Do you have time to send a wire back to our pal Harry in New York?" Ros wanted to see if Jerry would cringe.

Instead Jerry eagerly pulled a pencil from the old mug he used for a pencil holder then grabbed a note pad. "I'm ready, shoot."

Ros thought about her composition one last time then handed the page to him.

HARRY. BACK IN PARIS. QUESTION? SOMETHING DOES NOT SMELL RIGHT IN PRAGUE. BUT NOT SURE WHY THE SOMETHING DOESN'T SMELL RIGHT. WANT TO GO BACK SOON TO DIG UP SOME BONES. CAN WE WORK IT IN?

Czechoslovakia as it appeared in 1938

DECEMBER 8, 1937
SPECIAL TO CONSOLIDATED NEWS
BY WALTER HAUTH

BERLIN – A mild winter descended upon Europe with a carpet of newly fallen snow blanketing major capitals across the continent. Nervous Europeans gave thanks that another twelve months has almost past without the civil war in Spain overflowing into the rest of Europe. But there is worry for 1938 as the pounding of war drums continues here in Berlin and in Rome. Yet October and November were calm with few violent incidents within ethnic German communities in countries bordering Germany. Even propaganda, the language of provocation, has been muted. With Christmas only two weeks away ordinary people speak of hope that international disputes can be negotiated away. German foreign minister von Neurath has signaled Germany's willingness to come to the bargaining table with Europe's democracies. As Christmas approaches it truly is all quiet on the Western Front.

DECEMBER 9, 1937
MAIN SQUARE, PLZEN

Early in the day this part of the old city was always crowded. The more the better for he preferred not be noticed. Especially since he had no choice but to stay here for the better part of a week if his goal was to be fulfilled. It could not be helped. Today was Thursday and agent expected it would take his letter until Monday to arrive at its destination in Prag via post. He could pass in this part of the country as a traveling businessman. His favorite ruse was to play himself off as an Alsacian in the employ of a French conglomerate. France was an ally of Czechoslovakia and the cover story explained his French, Czech and German language skills. Although not uncommon to find men of German heritage in this region of Central Europe, originating from Alsace alleviated most suspicions about his sharp Prussian chin. That and the selection of ill-fitting French suits he had brought along.

A local bumped his shoulder unintentionally but rudely while passing in the opposite direction. A curt, *pardon,* from the older man was the only acknowledgement as was custom. This was excellent as people only collided with those they didn't notice. The Czechs had designated him A-54. He preferred Karl. The name was fictitious of course but the addressee on the envelope would know the name. A few paces ahead stood the mail receptacle and the letter was soon deposited.

DECEMBER 13, 1937
U.S. EMBASSY GARDEN
MALA STRANA DISTRICT, PRAHA

Chapin wasn't going to be satisfied with a little blood. After a few chilly turns through the hibernating shrubs with Minister Carr, Bulloch was sure the chargé was after a whole chunk of flesh. The invitation to join the two diplomats on their morning ritual was a surprise. Neither had said much to him in weeks. Not since he filed his report on the German small arms the Czechs had interdicted coming through the border. Chapin had a lot to say now.

"Are you satisfied, captain?" Chapin's hot breath escaped skyward as he started in again on the attaché. "Based on your recommendations Minister Carr reported to Washington his gravest concerns regarding the deteriorating conditions between Czechoslovakia and Germany. The reality has been far from it."

"Those conclusions were fair based on what I observed," Bulloch might have thrown a fist if the minister had not been between them.

"Face it you were duped by provocateurs using you to stir up trouble at this legation's expense," Chapin clenched a critical cable from Washington in his hands.

"Vinton. You are being too harsh on Captain Bulloch," Carr raised a hand above his head to stop the procession in its tracks. "Yes, perhaps I should have exercised more restraint in managing his reports. But it was my decision to report what I did to Secretary Hull. I myself saw the preparations for war on both sides of the border when I came to Prague and I remain convinced hostilities are inevitable."

"A state of mind this, *novice*, shamelessly took advantage of to further his own career," Chapin was not done casting stones at the attaché.

"You disagree with my work, fine," Bulloch jabbed his gloved hand in Chapin's direction. "But you're dead wrong if you think I was doing anything else but my job, pal."

"The fact remains you are responsible for this legation raising an alarm that has proven unfounded," Chapin refused to give ground. "Invasion plans, a flood of covert munitions shipments to ethnic German reactionaries… all very dramatic. The truth remains that there have been no provocations in three months. Our credibility in Washington has been ruined because you were played by your sources, captain."

"Cease this squabbling, both of you." This encounter was getting woefully out of hand and Carr decided he had to put a stop to it immediately. "If we reported hastily the fault lies with me. The responsibility is mine and mine alone. Vinton, we will be more cautious with our official assessments in the future. Captain, I ask you to show the same restraint in the direct reports you file to your superiors in the army. That's the last I want to hear about it. I don't like to be wrong. But if I have to be wrong, I'd rather it was because war did not break out."

HEADQUARTERS
SERVICE DE RENSEIGNEMENT, PARIS

A part of him knew to be suspicious when his world went quiet. Quiet wasn't a natural human condition. If there was quiet it was because someone had decided quiet was required to further his own purposes. Then there were the politicians from Premier Chautemps on down. They liked the quiet, and did not appreciate the chiefs of their intelligence services creating doubt in the nature of the quiet. So Colonel Thollon sat at his desk, sifting through the reports from his agents contemplating what conclusions he would provide for the politicians.

A firm rap at the door didn't prevent him from taking a long drag from his cigarette. There was a hierarchy to door rapping. Firm and repetitive meant urgent. Light indicated a curiosity approaching. But firm by itself signaled importance. He had to accept the unavoidable. "Enter."

The young captain from the operations group, Constantin, opened the door and approached confidently with a folder under his arm. Thollon remembered what it was like to be full of such self-assurance. It was before the gray set in around his temples and the good food in the neighborhood had set in around his gut. He put out his smoke and looked up at the man. "What have you for me today?"

"There's been an unexpected development on the Czechoslovak front, sir," Constantin replied as he handed over the folder.

Suddenly fatigued, Thollon rubbed his eyes before taking the documents. "What now?"

"The Americans have continue making inquiries into the disposition of German units on the Czech frontier," Constantin placed the file on Thollon's desk.

"That is odd," Thollon observed as he pondered the information. "Do we know what departments are involved?"

"We are seeing activity from both diplomatic and military intelligence channels. Very intriguing," Constantin was sure Thollon would want to know more. "You can check the references for yourself, sir. But by the nature of the inquiries we gather the Americans have knowledge of, or access to Case Green and seek to validate their assets."

"Ha! Characteristically late to the party," Thollon slapped the dossier. "It would be just like some of our British friends to share that document as a means of circumventing Chamberlain."

"There is no evidence of a British connection in what we have although nothing precludes it either. We do know that Ambassador Bullitt lunched privately with Chautemps last week, and our man on the premier's personal staff overheard Bullitt refer to some *alarming evidence out of Czechoslovakia*," Constantin added.

Thollon laughed at the picture that came to his mind. "I bet that news soured the premier's soup. *Out of Czechoslovakia...* Beneš knows better than to stir the pot diplomatically with the Americans. They can do nothing and it serves no one to antagonize Hitler when Hitler is perfectly able to accomplish that on his own. So the diplomats are chattering away. How much do you want to wager that all of this can be traced back to Moravec?"

"Prague is not my section, sir," the captain reminded his boss. "Why would you suspect Moravec?"

Thollon rose from his chair and walked around the desk. "My counterpart in Prague may have a great many reasons to do so if only to put more pressure on us to sign onto his own presumptions. Very well, let's find out what is going on. I believe it is time we stepped up our activities in Prague."

DEJVICE DISTRICT, PRAHA

Getting an opportunity to eat lunch out was rare luck. Burda was not used to such pampering. Luckily there were a number of good hospody near the general staff headquarters for a quick meal and a beer. The place he had in mind today was a bit fancier than most, but the better furnishings would help keep the warmth inside on a cold day. Besides, two of the owner's nieces worked there and they were easy to look at.

While crossing the street Burda felt a more familiar chill and hazarded a subtle glance over his shoulder. Nothing out of the ordinary greeted his gaze – just the normal mid-day collection of locals rushing from the warmth of one shop to the next. Yet the feeling didn't go away while passing the small stores as he proceeded down the block. Reaching the other corner Burda had to wait for traffic to pass, which gave him another opportunity to check around. Still nothing was amiss. Soon after crossing to the next block he was at his destination and was greeted by a blast of warm air as he went inside.

The bar wasn't crowded so Burda went straight for a stool after hanging his coat and hat on the wall hooks near the entrance.

"Pivo," he ordered when the bartender looked in his direction.

"You having lunch today?" the bartender asked as he drew the beer.

"Yes, I've got a good appetite," Burda knew exactly what he wanted to order.

"Then I'll send a server round," the bartender promised as he set the beer down.

Burda had only managed a few gulps from the pint glass when he noticed a man had sat next to him and was asking him about what was good from the kitchen. The voice was familiar.

"Co nam doporucujete?" Bulloch queried.

Distracted from his drink Burda turned his head to confirm the owner of the voice, who was back in civilian clothes it seemed. "The potatoes and pork are excellent."

"Sounds good for this weather," Bulloch noticed the intelligence officer's expression betrayed the slightest bit of irritation.

One of the owner's nieces, the one with the short-cropped hair, appeared next to Burda looking for his lunch order. He felt cheated that he could not appreciate her properly now with the American around. When she had gone, he directed his attentions back to his beer. "I didn't see you out there."

"Yeah, that has to hurt... my being an amateur and all," Bulloch sensed he should not take the mocking approach too much further.

"I don't like surprises," Burda wagged a forefinger at the American.

"Sure you do, pal. You just aren't used to being on the receiving end," Bulloch decided he had exacted enough abuse. "Forget it for now. We need to talk."

"About what?" Burda downed the last of his beer and motioned to the bartender for two more.

"Careers... mine to be exact," Bulloch took a long swig from his glass before putting his cards on the table. 'Listen, getting tagged as Chicken Little doesn't lead to a promotion, at least not in my army. Sorry if this seems ungrateful but I'm not in this for you, I'm in this for me. If your side gets something out of the whole arrangement, that is perfectly fine. I have no grand illusions about doing my part to save Europe from itself. So when I start taking it on the chin from passing along your goods... that concerns me. The next time you have something to share you had better be one hundred percent sure that that our friends across the border will actually do something despicable, understood?"

"Completely," Burda was resigned to Bulloch's pragmatic self-serving attitude. It was understandable under the circumstances.

Unnoticed by either man, Furst appeared in the entrance and began scanning the interior without taking off his hat and coat. Furst had not told what local pub his partner was heading for but knew this hospoda was a favorite. When he spotted Burda at the bar next to the American, Furst was intrigued. Then again, his partner didn't always tell him when and where he was meeting a contact. After thinking it over Furst decided he couldn't wait for the conversation to run its course and ambled over to interrupt it. The niece delivered Burda's lunch just as Furst arrived. Furst let his eyes follow her as she marched off but Burda and Bulloch didn't seem to notice. A shame he thought... all the more reason to break them away from whatever topic they were so absorbed with.

"Jan. The boss wants to see you now," Furst butted in between them.

Bulloch exchanged glares with Furst as Burda sighed. It was sadly obvious he would not get to enjoy his lunch. Burda got off his stool and reached for his billfold. After taking a few crown notes and laying them on the bar, Burda turned to Bulloch.

"Lunch is on me. We will talk again soon, captain. "

2ND DEPT.
MINISTRY OF NATIONAL DEFENCE, DEJVICE

Moravec was pacing the halls of the Second Department like an escaped lion. Suddenly the lieutenant sorting incoming reports sensed the intelligence chief by his side, clipboard in hand, checking something off a list.

"Please pull together the latest border reports, plus whatever else has been filed in and around Plzen," Moravec tapped the clipboard with the pencil.

"Yes sir, immediately sir," the lieutenant was curious what had the boss worried. Every station was reporting quiet in their area. "Should I bring the results to you directly or to one of the senior staff?"

"To me directly. I must prepare," Moravec wanted no delay in receiving the data.

"Prepare for what?" Burda had caught the last of the chief's instruction.

Moravec looked up from his clipboard long enough to make eye contact with Burda and Furst but stomped off down the hall without answering the question. The two captains had to run to keep up with him.

"Plzen. I am going to Plzen, and you both are going with me," Moravec consulted his clipboard again. "Sorry to interrupt your lunch, Jan, but we have received a note from A-54. He requests an immediate meeting in Plzen."

"Tomorrow?" Burda now understood the urgency.

"No, tonight," Moravec turned down a hallway in the direction of his office.

"Why Plzen?" Furst well knew A-54s ways. "He has never ventured so far east for a meeting with us."

"Yes this is unusual... and dangerous. You might be noticed by German or Hungarian agents, " Burda did not want Moravec walking into a trap.

"That is true, but the risk is acceptable," Moravec stopped abruptly to continue the explanation. "I was there for our previous rendezvous with Karl and he did not disappoint me. And if you do your usually efficient job at obfuscation, as far as the rest of the world is concerned, I'll be on the road to Slovakia."

"It's not that simple," Burda protested. "We cannot guarantee--"

"--Enough, I am going," Moravec raised his hand to make the point.

"I'll set that Slovakia cover story up straight away, sir," Furst saw there was no changing the boss' mind on this one. A-54 was their most valuable source of information out of Germany.

"Good," Moravec had no time for such arguments. "Next, contact our people in Plzen and have them prepare the safe house down there. Lastly, I'll need both of you to help me go over the latest border reports. You never know with the Germans. If we've missed something, I want to find it out what before leaving Praha."

BRASSERIE
QUARTIER DE L'OPERA DISTRICT, PARIS

Clarence had picked the joint. One of those cheerful 19th Century-era places with nice big windows to watch the world outside, plus high ceilings possessing a traffic jam of globed light fixtures above dozens of little round tables like the one she was sitting at. Ros had really grown to enjoy these little mid-day sessions with Clarence. He was a character all right – someone who had been in Paris forever, with a ton of stories to show for it. Acclimating to the continental beat had been so much easier thanks to him. Ros had just decided she would have to do something nice for the guy when she noticed the veteran journalist was walking in her direction.

"Hello, kid," Clarence wrapped his jacket over the back of a spare chair.

"Thanks for coming out in this chill, friend," Ros reached to pour him some wine.

"A pleasure. I enjoy our rendezvous'," Clarence dropped into his chair. "What's on the agenda today?"

"This is my first Christmas in Paris, what does a person do?" Ros got straight to the point.

"You could go home and visit your folks," the silver-haired reporter advised in a fatherly tone.

Ros thought about the advice as she sipped some wine. "Maybe next year. This is my first holidays in Europe and I don't want to miss a thing."

He leaned across the table for emphasis. "What's to miss? If you haven't heard, it's pretty quiet out there. Our esteemed colleague Walter said so, so it must me true."

Clarence just didn't give a damn about pecking order, and she loved that about him. "Careful! Mustn't make fun of a *living legend* of journalism."

"If you only knew half the legend, sweetheart. Curl your ears it would," Clarence leaned back in his chair to look for a server. "Say, what does a man have to do to get a drink around here?"

"I like you, Clarence. You have the scoop on everyone," and better yet he shared with her.

"Except on you," Clarence steered back to the prior subject like a good reporter should. "Why do you want to stick around this damp, dreary town?"

"Only you would call Paris dreary," she laughed. "But you know the score. As soon as I was half way across the Atlantic Hitler might sneeze and I would be stuck interviewing passengers in the boat's casino. Too late anyway, I already sold Harry on a piece about how Christmas will be celebrated in the major capitals of Europe."

"Fair enough," Clarence got a new idea. "Say, why don't you spend the holidays with Lena and I? We do our own thing on Christmas Eve and have lunch with her family the next day. Tag along."

"Oh I couldn't impose like that," Ros did not want to butt in on them.

Clarence stared her down before continuing with his pitch. "Sure you can. I won't hear anything else, and Lena will back me up on that. Trust me, you don't want to cross her when it comes to taking in orphaned reporters."

Ros could imagine why *he* wouldn't, and that too brought a smile to her face. Seeing that he was serious she decided to accept the invitation. "Alright then. Thank you very much for helping out a pal."

"You're okay, kid. We'll have a grand time," Clarence poured some more wine for them both.

"Hey, what else is good here?" Ros asked seeing a server heading in their direction.

"Too late for the shellfish, which is wonderful. The lamb is excellent too. Try that," Clarence recommended.

"Deal!" Ros would check with the server. Until then, she had something else to run past him. "Sorry to pile on but I have another favor to ask," Ros coyly shifted topics.

"No. Sorry. I can't get Harry to sign off on a raise for you. Hell, Harry doesn't sign off on raises for anyone so I really can't help you there," Clarence once again went for the joke.

"You're bad," she leveled a forefinger at him. "I've known for a long time that Harry's a cheapskate, so you're not getting off so easy. No, I wanted to ask you about an odd comment I got while on that X-mas story I just mentioned."

"Shoot," Clarence was curious what could possibly be odd about a Christmas interview.

"So I go to Rome and get the story there. Next up was Vienna. Here I am chatting away with this ancient culture minister fella who has been at this job for years. Nice guy. I asked him the standard questions: What's the traditional way the holidays are celebrated? What will be different this year? What would he like to change for next year? This is where it got odd. He put on this queer expression and said he wouldn't be around next year. So I figure the old guy is retiring. But he says no, he has no plans to retire. He would not say another word about it. What do you make of that? He was saying something but I wasn't getting it," Ros concluded.

For the first time ever she saw Clarence' go all serious on her. "Let me tell you a few things about Austria."

2ND ARMORED REGIMENT, VYŠKOV

The regiment was far from being up to strength and would not be so for months. More than enough time for Srom to commandeer this particular structure for his purposes. He had a large table set up in the middle of the austere barrack's open area. Sitting on top sat a three-dimensional relief map of Czechoslovakia.

Srom had been quietly assembling the working group for weeks when Kopecky volunteered of his own accord. That was unexpected yet good fortune nonetheless. Kopecky brought with him a young guard of officers to complement the lieutenant colonels and generals Srom had already drafted. Five of Srom's enlistees were invited to this first meeting. Srom did not have to ask them to consider the possible tactical conditions under which war with Hitler may have to be fought. That was a mental process they conducted endlessly on their own. But tonight was the first time they would all meet together to chisel out a more adventurous counter strategy all could agree to. He expected an impassioned debate.

Vrana, Kucera, Janouch, Hanus and Plzak understood that tonight they were leaving their senior ranks at the door. All were innate competitors and Srom wondered how would Kopecky perform amidst these wolves? That was if the young major got there. Kopecky was late and Srom seriously considered starting without him until a chilled blast of air announced the major was finally making an entrance.

"Good evening, gentlemen. Sorry to be the last one here," Kopecky lugged his supporting materials inside. "Have you started?"

"Not yet. The slick roads delayed everyone," Srom gave the younger man some cover.

"I'll take some small comfort in that," Kopecky racked his military coat and cap.

"Tomáš, is there anyone here you have not met?" Srom asked.

Kopecky had the advantage of access to each man's personal dossier, which he had consulted when Srom had confirmed the composition of the working group. While he was not friendly with any of the five, Kopecky had at least met three of them before. As he had the luxury of examining the photographs in each man's dossier Kopecky was able to engage the remaining two officers by name.

"Plukovník Kucera, good to finally meet you," Kopecky extended his hand to the colonel.

"Mister Kopecky," Kucera was impressed at being recognized by a man he had never met. "Excellent to make your acquaintance."

Kopecky turned next to the muscular Hanus to repeat the performance. "Podplukovník. We've never met, but a good friend, Ladislaw Capka, serves under you."

The lieutenant colonel gripped Kopecky's hand tightly and nearly lifted him off the ground when they shook hands.

"So you know that pain in the ass bastard. That explains your involvement in our little cabal." Upon finally releasing Kopecky's hand to the junior officer's relief, Hanus coarsely addressed the rest. "Mark my words, that damn lightning rod Capka will be the first Czech in front of the first column entering Germany whether anyone orders him there or not."

"I have no argument with that assessment, sir," Kopecky was still examining his right hand for bone damage.

Srom made a mental note to inquire further into this man Capka. Kopecky had mentioned him before and Srom liked what he was hearing about the fellow tonight.

"Speaking of assessments, what did the intelligence boys in Praha have to say?" Janouch butted in, hoping to spur the group to their stated business.

"Something else has them all astir at the moment, and no, they wouldn't tell me what," Kopecky explained as he moved closer to the relief map to illustrate his report. "As for the Germans the Second Department has no alterations to make to their evaluation of last summer. Based on their sources they still expect German attacks in force here in the north of Moravia that drive south to cut the Republic in two while Slovakia is squeezed into submission with the help of the Hungarians. With that accomplished, they plan to punch through with a third attack from the west to push us east into the trap."

"They still want to attack our strongest fortifications? That is both arrogant *and* stupid," Plzak disbelieved he was hearing the same rubbish yet again.

"Yes, that strategy does sound quite a lot like what the French taught us at Saint-Cyr," Vrana's depreciation of their ally drew laughter. "No, think like Guderian: *What you can't go through, go around*."

"I hardly think the enemy believes his own factory output propaganda, nor should we," Hanus did not accept Guderian had the quality of equipment for such a strategy. "Neither their squadrons of shiny bombers or available ground artillery is sufficient to break our lines in the north. I suspect their main attack will come somewhere in the mountains opposite Dresden, and south of Asch, if they attack at all."

"That would better fit their tactical doctrine," Srom consulted the map.

"Exactly," Hanus moved close to Srom's side. "Guderian's best chance is to penetrate through the Erzegebirge passes. He won't get far before his divisions extend themselves recklessly and we close in from all sides to strangle them. After that, we counter-attack north through the same passes."

"Right idea but with a twist," Kopecky jumped in. "Hitler will want to invade where he has the most Sudeten separatists available to stir up trouble: Asch, Eger, Karlsbad, etc. If they want to avoid our strongest fortifications they very well might combine the bulk of their forces for one primary attack in the west."

"But the attraction of an attack through the Erzegebirge range is the direct line of approach to Praha." Srom defended Hanus. "They will want to force our government to fall swiftly. From the west there is no direct route to Praha."

"No, no... the kid has a point," Janouch cut in. "The deepest belt of ethnic Germans is in the west. Hitler is political to a fault and will put far too much trust in his Sudeten paramilitaries. He might reason these traitors can surprise us with sufficient chaos and sabotage for German divisions to get into the open to reach Praha before we can react. As long as we deploy enough units to bog them down in the west, we could position the rest between Aussig and Reichenberg where there would be precious little to stop us from breaking out through the Erzegebirge ourselves to drive on Dresden."

"Exactly," Kopecky was encouraged the other officers were reacting positively to his observation on tactics.

"This is promising, gentlemen," Srom could tell they would end up with many potential options from this first meeting.

HOSPODA – DEJVICE DISTRICT, PRAHA

She stole a glance at him again while serving a new group at a table across the room. He had been sitting at the bar for hours since lunch, which was very unusual behavior for a foreigner. He even held his liquor well – minding himself politely the whole time. His Czech was good, but the accent was odd: American or Canadian perhaps. Her aunt had spoke often of Americans and their odd accents. Auntie would know. Twenty years before there were plenty of Americans around helping to build public institutions after independence. She'd seen pictures of her aunt taken back then and she was beautiful, although not shy. Her aunt always said those American boys were cute and usually said it with a naughty smile. From a little girl, Petra always wanted to be like her aunt – stylish and sophisticated. That's why she kept her hair a little on the short, *independent* side. It was tough keeping her grades up at the university while working at the hospoda to afford her tiny little flat and the current outfits from Paris. Petra could take home any man she wanted, and looking at this American now, she had made up her mind she wanted to take this cute one home tonight. Auntie would approve.

The urge for Bulloch to return to joint with the great food in Burda's back yard had been impulsive. Staking a claim in the other man's territory made him feel better and maybe Bulloch could drown out some of the seriousness he was feeling in good pilsner. He had worked too hard to finagle an attaché career where the worst hazard was a bad martini if you played your cards right. Now Chapin wanted him gone and was still looking for any ammunition to tarnish Bulloch's reputation despite Carr's support. This was more complication than he had bargained for.

Bulloch noticed someone orbiting close behind him, which caused his muscles to tense up despite all of the liquor in him. Ignoring the lurker had no effect so he put on his best salesman's smile and turned around on the stool. To his surprise, standing there was the barmaid – prettier than he recalled – a barmaid with mischievous eyes.

"I get off soon," she declared. "Why don't you tell me about it."

RADECKEHO SQUARE, PLZEN

Timing was everything. A-54 would appear precisely at a certain time – no earlier, no later. Suddenly, given up by the darkness, there he would be. Moravec had met him once before and knew the man would not show himself until he was sure he would not be recognized. The man's real name, Moravec did not know. *Karl* was the only moniker the fellow would provide. But by his thorough ways and the amazing quality of the information he had provided to date, of which the Fall Grün plans were the most incredible, the Czech spy chief had pegged Karl as Abwehr and likely not an inconsequential member of that intelligence service at that.

The Second Department had cultivated many Germans in the years since Moravec took command and reorganized operations. Most of those turned to his needs had been mid-rank Wehrmacht officers with a gripe to pursue and a bank account to fill. Pound sterling or dollars tended to be the currencies of choice, which were deposited into Swiss accounts. Contributions from these agents had been useful but Karl was different. What he had delivered was priceless and it was the German who had cultivated Moravec directly by post. If this fellow Moravec had designated A-54 felt the necessity to come out into the open he felt an equal necessity to meet him personally.

So began Moravec's third slow loop through the large square ringed by art nouveau architectures. The electric globes atop the street lamps cast a pretty glow in the crisp air as Moravec passed in front of the theater at the center of the square with plenty of light for Karl to watch by. At close to midnight, there were no streetcars running that he could see and the winter cold was enough to keep sensible folk indoors. Moravec felt the numbness seeping into his bones through the heavy trench coat. His wife would be angry with him. There would be no hiding the reddish burns on his face from the cold. It could not be avoided.

Furst had been correct Plzen was an unusual choice for a face-to-face meeting such as this. Although much more convenient for Moravec, choosing one of the small German towns on the German border had been A-54's prior preference. Crossing back and forth was much easier for a German agent concerned about being missed. That his star agent had the latitude to travel this deep into Czechoslovakia also suggested the man was Abwehr. Moravec glimpsed a shadowy figure ahead wearing an Ivy cap and bundled under a heavy coat stepping out from under the theater's rotunda. They met midway between street lamps.

"Thank you for meeting me on such short notice and on such a cold night," Karl had naturally planned the rendezvous in this way to add a sense of urgency and to test how valuable the Czech considered their relationship.

"Business has been slow lately, and I enjoy the diversion," Moravec had no intention of appearing desperate to this man. Moravec was still evaluating the man and how much he could be trusted. "This way, I have a car waiting."

Karl and Moravec warmed their hands by the fire as Burda hovered near the front door. The safe house was a modest country-style home on a large plot ringed by trees that was secluded but still close to Plzen. At this late hour seclusion would be essential. What they needed to do tonight would take hours. The warmth from the fire eventually penetrated far enough under his coat for the German to consider taking it off. Looking about the room, A-54 decided to drape the heavy garment over the back of a sofa, then placed his cap on top of the coat.

"Much better," Karl ran his fingers through a mane of thick, dark hair.

"Can I get you some cognac?" Burda felt sure the libation might help with the cold.

"No, thank you. Coffee would be nice though," Karl wasn't going to let this junior spy runner get him drunk.

"There is a pot warming now," Burda preferred having most contingencies covered.

"Excellent. A cup for me too when the pot is ready," Moravec was pleased his team always thought through such details without being instructed to do so.

Burda walked over to an interior door where he swung it open far enough to show two fingers to a colleague inside the kitchen. Satisfied, he leaned up against the wall – close enough to hear what his boss and the German had to say, yet far enough to give them a small sense of solitude.

"I am somewhat embarrassed to ask for your assistance," Karl had a very unusual proposal to make. "However, I see no other way to carry out my mission."

"Indeed," Moravec rubbed his chin. "How may we assist you?"

An older man arrived from the kitchen carrying a tray with two cups of coffee, a small cream jar and sugar bowl. He placed them on the table by the sofa then returned to the kitchen. Karl sat down on the firm sofa where he added sugar and cream to his coffee. Preferring his black, Moravec picked up the other cup and saucer and sipped the warm beverage where he stood.

"My orders are to establish five clandestine radio transmitters between Moravia and Slovakia. Despite being quite familiar with Bohemia, both Moravia and Slovakia are out of my experience. With some good recommendations on the best locations to place these transmitters, my superiors will be very pleased with me," Karl lifted the coffee cup to his lips.

"I understand completely," Moravec was tantalized by the intelligence advantage the German was offering. There was no longer any doubt, A-54 was Abwehr. "There are exceptional sites near important installations in both states that we can introduce you to. We can even monitor them for you later to insure that they are not accidentally disrupted by local authorities."

"You are most generous," Karl noted as he relaxed back onto the sofa, pleased to see Moravec respond as he had hoped.

Despite the urbane banter between the two men, it was obvious to Burda how his boss would exploit such an arrangement. It was almost unbelievable that they would get the opportunity. Still his critical nature restrained his enthusiasm. The Germans had invested large sums into mobile radio technology. This his department had substantiated from several other agents. But what Karl was describing was a step ahead in capability. While he did not like to interrupt Moravec, Burda had to clarify what equipment they were dealing with. "But aren't Moravia and Slovakia beyond the range of your transmitters?"

"No," Karl replied matter-of-factly, putting down his cup. "These sets are new, smaller, easier to conceal, with much longer range."

"A closer examination of an example would be useful in deciding where to place these transmitters," Moravec gambled in the hope of inspecting the technology.

"True, but sadly that will not be possible," Karl reached over to his coat to pull out an envelope for Moravec. "However, I can give you some time to examine the technical specifications. Also inside you will find a complete set of cipher codes and frequencies that the transmitter operators will use to file their reports."

Impressed by the enormity of the windfall he had just been presented, Moravec immediately turned to Burda to hand off the envelope to him. "Have the boys start on these documents straight away."

"Yes, sir," Burda took the envelope through the door to the formal dining room were a half-dozen Second Department men waited to photograph just such a trove of information.

Moravec sat next to the German agent on the sofa and poured himself more coffee. "A most generous gift."

"But of course. You are doing me a very great favor. I would have been of mediocre effectiveness on my own selecting sites in Moravia and Slovakia," Karl was enjoying this game immensely.

"Are your five the only transmitters being positioned?" Burda returned from the other room wondering about other agents, and other transmitters.

"There might be others but none that I am aware of," Karl lied. There were no more of these new models yet available but better to keep the Czechs on their toes.

"No matter. Now that we are in possession of the frequencies and cipher codes we soon will know whether there are more of these new sets operating," Moravec was unable to suppress a smile. His people would now be able to monitor all German agents in the country reporting on older model radios, as well. Karl had presented them with a tremendous gift indeed."

DECEMBER 14, 1937
DEJVICE DISTRICT, PRAHA

The temperature outside the covers was frosty. Naturally she stayed warm underneath, but Bulloch's backside was turning to ice. A flat this small should have held the heat better. There was barely enough room for the bed and wardrobe. Bulloch learned her name was Petra and she was having too much fun at his expense – laughing every time he had to stop what he was doing to pull the blanket back up. At least she had run Chapin completely out of his head. But this business with the blankets was getting old. Bulloch grabbed her firmly about the hips and maneuvered her on top so suddenly that Petra squealed in delight. Taking it as a challenge, she squeezed herself tightly around him and rocked back and forth trying to drive Bulloch a little crazy.

"It's cold!" Petra complained when she got winded enough to notice.

"Let's see how much you like it," Bulloch tossed the covers further away.

"Oh, I see how you are," Petra could not reach the blanket. "Fine, keep me warm then."

She relaxed her body and slid down next to him so their bodies cupped together perfectly. Not sure he was ready for a lull in their lovemaking, Bulloch lightly kissed her bare shoulders. She expressed her approval by pressing her bottom firmly against him.

"Don't worry, I'll keep you warm," Bulloch entered her again.

"Is that a promise?" Petra matched the rhythm of her body to his.

"You bet," Bulloch snuck his arm around so he could cup her breast and pull her body closer to his.

Petra was intoxicated with this handsome American. She reached back to stroke his neck while he made love to her. "I've never done it with a spy before."

"I told you... I am not a spy," Bulloch whispered in her ear.

"Be quiet. A spy is much more romantic," Petra turned her head to bring their lips close enough to kiss. Hungry for him, she playfully teased his lips closer with her moist tongue.

Christmas had come early this year was the last thing Bulloch thought before losing himself completely in her.

**Support for Austrian chancellor
Kurt von Schuschnigg in a Vienna neighborhood**

JANUARY 4, 1938
VON NEURATH RESIDENCE, BERLIN

Predators and prey were finally all in attendance, the German foreign minister noted to himself as he walked through the entry lobby into the main parlor. This pleased him for he had chosen the guest list very carefully. Good drink, strong personalities and contrary ideologies were an excellent mix to loosen tongues. Too bad the chancellor had gotten fed up with Ambassador Dodd and had sent him packing back to the United States. Dodd was wily, quick witted and always a challenge. No matter. The Italian, Hungarian, British, Austrian, French, Yugoslav, Polish, Spanish and Swiss legations were all well represented. For effect he had sprinkled in just the right mix of party members in possession of a modicum of social grace to help stir up competitive conversation. As the host it would be undignified for him to cause his guests significant discomfort. Foreign diplomats well understood what these social affairs were all about. In fact, they got quite testy when they weren't invited.

Herr Göring intercepted a waiter circulating with a platter full of champagne glasses as he stepped into the parlor. After taking a sip the commander-in-chief of the Luftwaffe located von Neurath, grabbed an extra glass and swiftly made to intercept him as well.

"Constantin. Did you hear that fool Schuschnigg on the wireless?" Göring handed the full champagne glass to von Neurath.

"Yes, a most unfortunate display of bravado by the Austrian chancellor. *We remain ourselves alone.* What was he thinking?" von Neurath Perhaps because he was now in his sixties, and less tolerant of such frivolity, von Neurath wondered how many formal suits could one man actually own. "There will be no hope for peace at all if he continues with such rhetoric."

"The Führer was not pleased," Göring confirmed what von Neurath already knew. "He took it as a personal affront. He wants to put a boot up Schuschnigg's rear."

It was the same problem the foreign minister had faced constantly since Hitler came to power in 1933 – the man's fragile ego. "We are not yet ready should he choose to move on Vienna. A rash undertaking before our diplomatic program takes hold could cause unnecessary friction with the French and British. And there still are the Italians, who continue to claim they are the guarantors of Austrian independence."

"Forget all that," Göring barked, jabbing a stubby forefinger at von Neurath, "I suggest you move up the timetable."

Von Neurath sipped the champagne while considering how to respond. He loathed that his well-formulated plans were so abruptly brushed aside. But Göring had a point. Time to salvage what was possible. "Moving up the timetable may be the best course, Hermann. Schuschnigg must be warned off. What do you think about a face-to-face meeting? Find some pretense to bring Schuschnigg to visit Herr Hitler so that the Führer may explain reality to him. "

"Schuschnigg must come to heel, one way or another," Göring salivated at the idea of that little man locked in a room with an angry Hitler. "And I believe you will find the Italians will now be supportive since Senor Mussolini's last visit to Berlin."

The German foreign minister hated when Göring knew more than he did on such matters. But Hitler did not always share everything discussed in private with von Neurath.

"Excellent, I will cable von Papen in Vienna tomorrow," the foreign minister would once more adjust to the situation. "See if you can persuade the Führer how useful it will be to our needs if he can keep his well-founded anger out of the press while I set von Papen to work on Herr Schuschnigg. We want this to appear to be a timely and friendly status conference on German-Austrian relations."

"Agreed," Göring was relatively sure he could prevail upon Hitler as long as he did so quickly. "But understand if that damned Austrian court convicts any local party members down there between now and then, it's out of my hands. In that eventuality there might be a panzer division outside Schuschnigg's chancellery within forty-eight hours."

"Don't remind me. I have an appointment with the Austrian envoy to discuss that very subject," von Neurath was sure he had never seen this particular suit on Göring before.

JANUARY 6, 1938
LES TERNES DISTRICT, PARIS

Clarence arrived at the flat he was looking for. He hoped it was the correct door not wanting to tackle another flight of stairs if he didn't have to. The hour was early and many Parisians did not take well to having their doorbell rung at such an hour. He would throttle the kid who had given him the address if it was wrong. Clarence rapped soundly on the wood door. A minute later Ros answered looking like she had just pulled on her robe. The girl was a little rumpled, but still happy at his surprise visit.

"Clarence. What brings you to my door? Come in," she beckoned, closing the door behind him.

"I have a hot tip for you, sweetheart," Clarence confided, looking around as he walked into the tiny apartment. "Remember our conversation last month? Looks like things are heating up in Vienna. The Austrians just convicted a bunch of national socialist cronies, and the high muckety mucks in Berlin are hopping mad. What's more, I have it on good account that the Italians are going to put pressure on the Austrian chancellor with the help of the Hungarians. There's going to be a big pow wow in Budapest next Monday. Schuschnigg either gets religion or he'll get his rear end kicked. That will be the message since Musso is not going to protect him."

This wasn't a tip Clarence was laying a feast at her feet. The byline exposure could be huge, but there was one problem. "What about Walter? Isn't he already running with this?"

"Probably, sweets," Clarence casually flipped his favorite silver dollar. "But he will be chasing down the trail in Berlin... not Vienna."

"What are you suggesting?" Ros stared the old fox in the eye.

"You know what I am suggesting. It's cold, Walter hates the cold and we don't have a bureau in Vienna," Clarence laid the scheme out for her.

"What if Harry won't go for it? Vienna will cost extra bucks. Talking dollars out of Harry Lasky is like getting blood out of a rock," Ros figured should know better.

"Don't ask Harry... just go," Clarence prodded her. "My guess is that Walter won't break anything until after the Italians get back from Budapest. That gives you four days to get yourself set up in Vienna. As long as you can deliver the Austrian angle, Harry will be stuck. He'll need your copy, and just have to pay the bills if he wants to keep getting what he wants."

"You're amazing Clarence," Ros laid a big kiss on his cheek. "Now who was your source on this again?"

Clarence chuckled. "Nice try, but I didn't say. Not going to either. My source will remain anonymous. You can bank on the fact that this is a person I trust. I guarantee you there's going to be plenty happening down in Vienna, and soon."

"You're that sure?" Ros had to ask before going out on a limb.

"Absolutely positive," Clarence caught the coin and shoved it into a pocket. "This is your shot, kid."

"Okay then," Ros twirled around. "I'm going to Vienna!"

REICH FOREIGN MINISTRY, BERLIN

Von Neurath slammed a Vienna newspaper down on the desk in front of Austrian ambassador Stefan Tauschitz. This was no show. The German foreign minister was genuinely livid as he circled around the envoy seated in his office.

"Twenty-seven Austrian national socialists tried, convicted and sentenced! What's wrong with you people?" von Neurath did not expect an answer. "Do you fathom the abyss you are jumping into?"

Tauschitz understood all too well how the previous day's convictions would be received yet pressed on.

"Herr foreign minister. These malcontents were lawfully found guilty of attempts to subvert the legal government of the Austrian republic. This is an internal matter. For the Reich government to have any legitimate interest in these people would suggest that their orders to carry out these vile provocations originated in Germany," Tauschitz tried to turn the matter around on the accuser. "Is that what you are suggesting, sir?"

"I suggest nothing of the sort, Herr Ambassador. Such allegations are as unfounded as they are contemptible," von Neurath knew Tauschitz spoke the truth and that complicated matters.

"Would you prefer that we unsealed the court documents for all to see?" Tauschitz was angry enough to rise from his chair to embellish the point. "No, I do not think Herr Hitler would like those headlines in the London or Paris dailies, would he? Forgive me, for I have always respected you but I must be blunt. What more exactly do you wish from us? We pledged to tie ourselves to your destiny last July. Why bully us? Why send these provocateurs to destabilize us? You have already won. Austria is honor bound to walk side-by-side with Germany, to support your foreign policy, and to integrate our economies. What is served by fomenting chaos?"

"You do not understand, Tauschitz." This Austrian simply did not appreciate the constraints under which von Neurath had to work. No the ambassador didn't comprehend at all. "The wind is blowing from Berlin and it is moving with a force much greater than last July. Interfering with national socialist aspirations, of any kind, will lead to an explosion. The continued internment of party members is bad enough. These new convictions must be overturned or the result will be ruinous for your government.

"You demand too much," Tauschitz objected.

"No ambassador, you protest too much!" von Neurath showed him the door.

JANUARY 7, 1938
COUNTER-INTELLIGENCE OFFICE
REICH MINISTRY OF WAR – 72-76 TIRPITZUFER, BERLIN

The winter of 1938 was heating up unlike anything Hans Gisevius had witnessed since Hitler ordered the Rhineland reoccupied in '34. As he hurried down the narrow hallway to catch up with Director Ottke, Gisevius knew the job was about to get very interesting.

"Sir, I have news," Gisevius caught Ottke's attention.

"There is too much going on for seclusion so tell me what you learned." Before the admiral had recruited Gisevius to the Abwehr the man had been a member of the Gestapo. Now he was instrumental in keeping Ottke informed on what their rivals in the SS were up to.

"Our source on Himmler's staff has confirmed a new cycle of subversive activity is planned against Austria." Gisevius summarized how the SS had been given task of executing Herr Hitler's displeasure with Schuschnigg's recent act of defiance.

"As I expected. This is too big an opportunity for Himmler to show what he can do on his own," Ottke had few illusions about the politics at work. Such a response should have been channeled through his Abwehr directorate. A pity, but their operation would just have to adapt. "We had better start assessing how the border states will respond. I don't foresee any resistance from the Czechoslovaks or the Italians but anything is possible. We should also re-evaluate the British and French. Based on the most recent reports from Paris, I'll wager that the current French government will fall in the next month of its own accord. The timing is perfect for Hitler to press his agenda."

"Really, Chautemps is out?" Gisevius had yet to hear this news.

"Oh yes," Ottke assured him. "The socialists will never give him the blank check to bankroll favored factory owners, even for rearmament."

"If the French are in disarray, I doubt the British will protest much," Gisevius could see all of the chess pieces coming into play.

"If Signor Mussolini got his feathers ruffled like four years ago, maybe the rest would make some noise. But Austria will not be saved by Italy this time. We still need to monitor these government's closely as the crisis develops, however. Come with me. We must talk to the admiral about funding further operations in Austria of our own to keep up with the SS," Ottke quickened his pace.

JANUARY 10, 1938
2ND DEPT. – MINISTRY OF NATIONAL DEFENCE, DEJVICE

Moravec felt a bit guilty. It was an incredibly cold morning and he had summoned his senior staff members to an unscheduled meeting before dawn. They were all representative of the particular type of man he felt was best suited to intelligence work: unmarried, not too young, not too old, fit but not possessing a military bearing, and flexible when it came to the needs of the profession.

Moravec could not sleep the night before, so he excused himself to his wife and arrived in the early hours of Monday to see if anything noteworthy was brewing. Perhaps his wife was correct and he did possess an intuitive sense about such things. True enough, there on his desk was a disquieting report that had just arrived from one of their lower-level agents in Berlin. After re-reading the document several times, Moravec had the duty officer drum up several pots of coffee. They would need the caffeine. His director of espionage within Germany, Major Strankmueller, already was well acquainted with the report having been the first to lay eyes upon it upon arrival. But Moravec's deputy Lieutenant-Colonel Tichy needed to be informed, as well as his primary lieutenants: captains Burda, Frye and Furst.

"Gentlemen," Moravec perched himself on the corner of the desk. "A56 has just submitted a most rousing report claiming with a high degree of certainty that German/Austrian relations are entering a new phase. Chancellor Schuschnigg's attempt to illuminate interference in Austrian sovereignty by local national socialists will not result in the resignations of Nazis within the Austrian government. Specifically councilor of state Dr. Seyss-Inquart and state minister Glaise von Horstenau. Fifty-six is positive these men will not resign in protest following last week's court convictions in Vienna as was expected. Göring personally ordered that neither Seyss-Inquart nor von Horstenau were to give up their mandates without conferring with him first."

Tichy leaned forward to leaf through the report pages. "Fifty-Six is usually reliable. You realize the implications of Göring telling Seyss-Inquart and Glaise-Horstenau to tough it out?"

"All too well. Berlin does not intend to back down this time," Moravec had hoped otherwise. "The struggle for control of Austria will accelerate to a new level of volume and violence. We will need to divert additional resources to better monitor events on both sides of the border. Dr. Beneš may desire to intervene if it can be done jointly with our allies, and should the Italians decide to show some backbone. But the chances of that are slim. Gentlemen, we have a crisis on our hands.

HOTEL GRANBEL – INNERE STADT, WIEN

Too bad the budget wouldn't take The Ambassador. But Ros could afford the old, well kept, conservative and a little drafty Granbel. She'd survive of course although her Paris coat was a little light for this weather. There probably wasn't a way to expense a new winter coat and get it past Lasky, at least not until she had an exclusive to extort him with. Clarence was sure the local Austrian Nazis wouldn't take the recent convictions of their people lying down. That was her trump card. Once she had the first byline in when all hell broke loose the story would be hers and no one else would be able to muscle in on the Austrian angle.

As soon as Ros hit the lobby she realized she had completely forgotten the name of the joint that Clarence told her to visit straight off. It was some old café where most of the foreign press hung out. It was a French name at that. According to Clarence, Bill Best with United Press had sat at the same table every night for the last ten years. With no time to spare Ros needed to get a leg up from one of these hacks. It was rough dropping into a new beat with no clue who pulled the strings around town. Ros was drawing attention pacing the middle of the lobby when the right name finally popped into her head. Ros marched over to the young man in the stiffly pressed uniform standing behind the front desk.

"Good day. What is the best way to get to Café Louvre?" Ros hoped he spoke English.

"You're in luck," he wished all guest queries were so simple. "That café is very near the hotel."

BULLOCH'S FLAT
MALA STRANA DISTRICT, PRAHA

He was going to be late. Nobody else's fault but his own for running out of clean shirts and not making a trip down to the laundry. Luckily he had a few new dress shirts stashed away. The problem had been finding them. Bulloch's flat wasn't a model of neatness befitting a U.S. Army officer and he liked it that way until moments like this when he was racing the clock. He had finagled a prized pair of tickets to a charity ball that night knowing Petra would leap at the opportunity. That girl was made to dance – every step a suggestion, every dip an invitation. Bulloch locked the door knowing he wouldn't be home before dawn.

When Bulloch got off the trolley near the embassy the French attaché Faucher was lurking with an undistinguished male companion. The latter's overcoat and derby hat were damp from the weather. Faucher's uniform somehow managed to remain starched despite the moisture.

"There he is," Faucher pointed out Bulloch. "I don't see why you wish to speak with this novice – especially here where he can easily escape. I doubt Bulloch has spent much time fulfilling his intelligence duties. Now, his romantic conquests, which I admire, are quite respectable."

The field officer had already gone over the American's slim dossier before arriving just before Christmas. Faucher was correct the good captain did appear to be the perfect lout and wholly unremarkable. Yet Thollon was positive that the Americans were up to mischief in Prague and there was no other stone left to look under. That meant this Bulloch was either very good or a waste of time as Faucher advised. Following the man had turned up nothing so the only way to settle the issue was face-to-face.

While he considered walking off in the opposite direction, Bulloch resigned himself to checking what silly French diversion Faucher had ready for him today.

"Looks like I have an audience this morning," Bulloch called out to the two men. "What brings you to my place of business, general? And who is your friend here?"

"A colleague of mine," Faucher exaggerated of course. Faucher had never seen the man until the day before but his credentials were in order and there was no reason to deny a representative of military intelligence the introduction he sought. "We were hoping to exchange notes, as you Americans say, on the Czechoslovak military build up."

"Would love to talk shop, but not today. I have a full docket," Bulloch adjusted his coat and tie. "A shame I can't help you boys out."

"There always tonight," Faucher's companion preferred working after dark.

"Sorry, no can do. I have a date tonight," Bulloch enjoyed the opportunity to taunt Faucher.

"He has the most amazing luck for someone possessing such unremarkable features," Faucher took a friendly swipe at Bulloch. "The university student or someone new?"

"The university student. Don't take it too hard, old man," Bulloch gave as good as he got.

"See what arrogance I must suffer with," Faucher waved dismissively at the American.

"Just so I am not accused of being impolite, let me introduce myself," Bulloch extended his hand to the unknown Frenchman. "Nathan Bulloch... pleased to meet you."

"Didier," the field officer went through the niceties. It was the name on the passport. The name would change when he left Prague. "My apologies for the short notice and arriving unannounced. I only just arrived and looked up General Faucher."

"Are you military?" Bulloch inquired.

"Armaments actually. We have many contracts with the Czechs that bring me here to Prague," the field officer supplied a cover story, but a very plausible one.

"Then we probably should have a talk before you leave town," Bulloch did not want to punt a perfectly legitimate opportunity. "I'd be curious to hear your opinion on how the Czechs make use of the ordinance they purchase from your company. Are you in town long?"

"A while. I would enjoy learning some of your impressions on the same subject," the field officer was making progress.

"Personally, I would rather hear about the university student," Faucher had different priorities. "I'll phone you about an agreeable time for us all. Don't let us keep you, captain."

"Until another day, gents," Bulloch hurried off.

"Another day indeed," the field officer agreed.

CAFÉ LOUVRE – INNERE STADT, WIEN

The place was spacious with tall windows and a high ceiling but the interior was not as bright as the Paris cafes she was accustomed. Rather than staking out one of the marble topped tables she decided to meander about first in search of targets. Not knowing who she was looking for was a slight problem but reporters were odd ducks and she'd recognize them if she heard them. Moving across the crowded length of the establishment Ros heard what she was searching for: English. At the far end of the café was a booth table inhabited by three wildly animated rascals who could only be members of the press. She could make out a couple of Brits with the third person possibly an American. All of them were men, which would make her entrance easier.

"Hello boys," Ros slinked up to their table.

It took longer for the din of their argument to die down than Ros thought she deserved. Must be the coat so she took it off. The fluid way the coat slid from her shoulders, and the shapely form revealed underneath, encouraged Roland to pay attention. He put down his pint glass with a thud and rose from his chair.

"Chaps. The Times of London calls a recess to these deliberations, and recognizes a new emissary to these proceedings," Roland busted up the conversation. "And to whom do we have the honor of addressing, dear lady?"

"Talmadge. Consolidated News," Ros set down some roots by throwing her coat on the bench seat.

The pudgy balding little man at the table reacted strongly to the mentioning of her employer. "Oh really, Hauth afraid to leave Berlin these days? Maybe Goebbels won't let him back in if Walter leaves town. Is that it?"

The three men chuckled loudly at the thought that Consolidated's senior European correspondent might be frightened to travel. Ros found the idea funny as well and joined in. The pudgy little guy definitely was an American.

"Endicott, with Hearst," he raised his glass.

"Pleased to meet you but you've got it all wrong. Forget Hauth this is my show. I smelled fireworks all the way back in Paris and decided to hit town in time for the show," Ros rested her hands on her hips

The third man at the table took his time looker Ros over from head to toe before joining in with the banter. "Your nose is good, and the rest of you is not bad either. Why don't you join us?"

"Now you're talking, mister," Ros sat down with tem. "And who might you be?"

"Sanderson, Daily Telegraph," the third reporter answered. He was the youngest of the group and Ros noticed he had a stronger chin and better complexion than most Brits she had met.

"How long have you been in town, angel?" Endicott wanted to know more about who was wiggling her way into their business.

"Just blew in today and looking for a tip or two from you hounds," Ros stuck with the truth to ease their suspicions.

"There it is gentlemen, the lady is looking to charm her way into our hearts and notebooks," Roland accused playfully. "Tell us girl, you've looked around the city, what do you see?"

Ros saw the challenge for what it was and got serious. She'd have to show them that she had skills. "I see a lot of poor angry saps looking to take their troubles out on someone. Reminds me of Brooklyn only prettier architecture."

"Not bad for your first day on the ground," Endicott appreciated the way the dame saw things.

"Fellas, I might as well be honest with you," Ros put both of her hands on the table. "I was here six weeks ago and got a good look around. This teapot is going to explode. I know it and you know it. I just didn't expect the place to boil over so quickly. So I have to play catch up, which I don't like to do. I also have to ask for help, which I like doing even less. But I'm stuck. I need to know what it was like around here after those local Nazis were convicted last week."

The three reporters looked at each other, and despite the sure knowledge that they were being conned, nodded their consensus. This kid had moxie and they enjoyed the game too much to send her packing yet.

"More confused than I expected," Roland was again the first to speak up. "Seyss-Inquart and that bunch seemed genuinely shocked and at a loss how to respond."

"I expected civil unrest," Sanderson chimed in. "At least in Graz. Adolph's step-children are strong up there but it didn't happen."

"You watch. They'll act up as soon as they get their marching orders from across the border. I bet it won't take long either," Endicott didn't have much respect for these local Nazis.

Roland took another gulp from his glass and shook his head in disagreement. "Maybe not. Schuschnigg always seems to stay a step ahead of the goose-steppers. The constabulary is in the habit of nabbing the disagreeable types before they can get into much trouble."

"Not for long," Sanderson scooted a bit closer to Ros. "I say Schuschnigg is getting too cocky and Adolph will soon slap him silly. One more incident is all it will take."

"So where do we go look?" Ros leaned in before any more observations could be offered.

The three veterans were not sure what the new kid was talking about and were caught off guard.

"Look for what?" Sanderson was sure he had missed something.

"The incident. Where is this *incident* going to happen?" Ros couldn't believe the blank stares she was getting. "Hey, I am counting on this bunch of yours to be ahead of the game. Surely someone in the government is dropping clues."

Endicott laughed loudly and leaned back in his chair. Then he raised his tumbler in toast to Ros. "Watch your backs, gentleman."

JANUARY 11, 1938
CNS HEADQUARTERS, NEW YORK CITY

McCoy nervously hovered over Des as the editor meticulously scrutinized a collection of typewritten pages. Des could have eased the reporter's nerves with a quick read of the copy but McCoy was a wise guy who deserved a few turns on the spit once in a while. Outright torture Des left to Lasky who he noticed was heading full steam up the aisle in their direction.

"C'mon Des," McCoy could no longer contain himself. "Throw a pal a line. What do you think?"

"That's actually a good lead you have in their, fruitcake," Des looked up from the pages and smiled. "I'm not sure you wrote it but I like what I'm reading."

"I get no respect at all around here," McCoy lamented. "One day you jokers are going to appreciate me."

McCoy felt the disturbance as Lasky stormed by the desk onto parts unknown. Harry looked all worked up about something. Usually Harry didn't miss an opportunity to vent steam at Des when something work related was needling him. Could be the ex-wife or her lawyer getting his goat again. If so, they were all doomed.

"Hey boss, hold up I have a tip for you," McCoy called after Lasky inviting the torture he was about to receive.

Lasky pivoted around to close back in upon the reporter. "Oh really, McCoy. It's a slow day. What have you dredged up?"

"That out of town story you have me on," McCoy had hit some pay dirt finally.

"Yeah, Factories for Freedom. I remember. Why ain't it done?" Lasky edged closer to the reporter.

"Almost done, boss," McCoy backed up against Des' desk. "The British and French war orders are upping employment here stateside. Airplanes mostly."

"What else is new?" Lasky had better things to do than this regurgitation.

"I'm just getting to that part, chief. There's this guy I know at Curtiss-Wright who called with a tip. He says the French purchasing delegation is stalling on the next contract. They're balking at the contract prices and won't sign the paperwork. So I called another fella I know over at Martin and he said they're having the same problem. Looks like the procurement types back in Paris have a case of indigestion," McCoy was sure this was a hot tip.

"Based on some of the stuff I've read coming in from our folks over there it sounds to me like Chautemps is losing his grip," Des felt charitable enough to help pull McCoy's butt out of the fire. "Could be we'll see a new government."

"It could at that," Lasky was pleasantly surprised at something useful coming from McCoy's pea brain. "Thanks for passing that along, McCoy. This will be perfect for Talmadge to run down. Ambassador Bullitt is really chummy with the damn French. Bullitt would be the perfect politico for our girl to sweet-talk the goods out of. The day is looking up, gentlemen."

JANUARY 12, 1938
INTERIOR MINISTRY, WIEN

His subject was a precise man who left for lunch at precisely the same time each day, and returned exactly an hour later without fail. A professional learned to observe a target to learn his ways, his rhythms and his soft spots. The formula did not change even for the minister of Federal Internal Administration. The watcher glanced at his pocket watch. When he looked up there was the minister ascending the main steps. The official would be late from lunch today.

"Minister Baar-Baarenfeld," the watcher came up behind the older man and placed a restraining hand on his shoulder. "I must speak with you on a most serious matter."

The minister was startled and swiftly grew annoyed as he recognized who had detained him. "Skubl, in the year you worked for me how many times did I implore you never to do that?"

"Countless times, sir. But as you will recall, I don't work for you any longer," Skubl enjoyed playing this game.

"I have just enough influence left to fix that small deficiency my annoying young friend," the minister threatened.

Only a few years before Baar-Baarenfeld had controlled both of the Interior Ministry's prime departments. Skubl had been his director of security. To politically appease the national socialists, Baar-Baarenfeld had been stripped of authority as minister of public security, which chancellor Schuschnigg had shamelessly handed over to Glaise-Horstenau. The chancellor sincerely believed von Horstenau was an Austrian first, and that would outweigh the man's sympathies toward Hitler. Baar-Baarenfeld held no such illusions.

"I am of better use to you where I am, which is why we need to speak," Skubl proposed.

"Very well, then come upstairs," Baar-Baarenfeld had work to accomplish."

"No, sir. My office would be more appropriate," Skubl motioned back to the street.

Skubl had an arrangement with numerous taxi cab drivers. In return for fixing certain traffic infractions, the drivers would abandon their parked cabs for as long as he needed to grill a suspect in the back. Skubl had come to consider these cabs his private offices and he could choose any district in the city for the random seclusion he required away from prying eyes. This was how Baar-Baarenfeld found himself parked several kilometers away from his ministry.

"And you are sure the source is reliable? There is great personal risk for both of us if your information is incorrect," Baar-Baarenfeld was too old to take such risks.

"I am confident in my information, sir. These Nazis are not particular about the riff-raff they attract. This source has many prior vices of long acquaintance. He's up to his neck in trouble and he knows my price for keeping his neck. If he were to be inaccurate with me he soon would be sent back to his new fascist friends with a big note pinned to his coat: *Informer,* " Skubl had promised the small weasel.

"An effective deterrent, I'm sure," the minister missed this aspect of security work.

"Very. But this whole affair is delicate business," Skubl un-holstered his service revolver to check the cylinder. "The chancellor is incensed with Tavs and what the man said in a newspaper interview. I will have the authority I need for the raid. I have reliable men already selected for the job who understand discretion. What I don't have are the means of isolating Glaise-Horstenau from causing mischief for the chancellor or myself after the fact. That is where I need you, Eduard."

"We'll either save Austria, or doom her, but that we will leave to history," Baar-Baarenfeld was tired of all of the Nazi machinations. "What is the timetable?"

"Berlin has placed Tavs at the center of the coup in his capacity as the party gauleiter here in Vienna so that Seyss-Inquart and Glaise-Horstenau are shielded from suspicion. Tavs' orders are to orchestrate a new putsch within weeks. We must move on him quickly," Skubl clicked the cylinder back into place and holstered the revolver.

KARTNERSTRASSE – INNERE STADT, WIEN

The route leading to the old opera house through the middle of the city was one of the narrowest metropolitan streets Ros had ever come upon. She was suddenly sorry that there wasn't enough time for her to explore the area better during her quick visit in December. The extra detail would have added more color to her story.

What she saw a few steps later caused the reporter to stop dead in her tracks. Without a picture the folks back home would never have believed it if Ros had described the sight in front of her. Adorning the building directly across the street from the opera house was a huge portrait of Adolph Hitler. The eyes stared at you no matter the angle in a very unsettling way. Checking the street address confirmed this was the right building, which got Ros wondering whether the hounds down at Café Louvre had put her up to this as a way to test her mettle. Ros hadn't been able to arrange for an interview with Seyss-Inquart as she had hoped so the gang had suggested she come down here. They only said that it was important and she would have to see for herself. The building with the huge portrait of Hitler was the Official German Tourist Bureau. Squaring her shoulders, Ros marched up into the main entrance.

Once inside there were more surprises. The interior reminded her more of a union hall than an establishment to encourage tourism – heated conversations, printed tabloids and political-looking handbills everywhere she turned and not a vacation brochure in sight. Ros could kick herself for not spending more time as a kid with her odd ball German uncle. Maybe Ros would have picked up some of the lingo. That would have been useful now with these publications she was running her eyes over while meandering through the crowd in the foyer. At best her German was spotty yet the snippets of conversation Ros was picking up on were angry and political.

Her exploration brought Ros close to a desk where a determined and sour fellow of college age was seated. He had been eying her for a while but the feeling she got suggested the guy wasn't watching her because he found her attractive. The demanding way he challenged her with *Fräulein* confirmed that ogling wasn't on his mind.

"Oh... hi there, handsome," Ros threw her big city charms at him. "Could you help me throw together a list of all the perfect places to visit in Munich?"

His perturbed glare was as chilly as the rest of the building. "Deutsch, please?" he demanded in pidgin English/German.

"Sorry hon, no can do," Ros tried to appear hapless. "Please be a sweetheart and go find someone who can help me."

The goon seemed inclined to throw Ros out the door when an older, clerkish-looking runt grabbed a nearby clipboard and approached the desk. "Forgive us, mesdame. We don't get many English speakers here. How can I help you?"

"Why thank you for eavesdropping, mister. My husband and I will be visiting Munich in a few weeks and I wanted to find out what the city has to offer. You know, night life, museums and theatre," Ros improvised as she went along.

"Ah yes, we'll be happy to help but we'll have to schedule an appointment," the clerk handed her the clipboard and a pencil. "Please provide your name and where you are staying in Vienna and we will contact you at the earliest opportunity."

"Aren't you a doll," Ros took the clipboard and showed no hesitation in writing down: *Mrs. Monica Claybourne, Hotel Bristol.*

CONSOLIDATED NEWS SERVICE BUREAU
QUARTIER DE L'OPERA DISTRICT, PARIS

Clarence could still fling an ascot with the best of them – landing the hat squarely on the small bust of Plato that he kept on the edge of his desk from eight feet away. The newsman found the statuary years ago in a corner shop and always enjoyed his ritual of pulling the wool over old Plato's eyes. He settled into his chair and placed a mug of tea on its cradle. Clarence had just set fingers to attacking the nearby typewriter keys when he sensed his bureau chief fidgeting next to him. The reporter didn't need to look to know the man had a pained expression on his face.

"What's eating you, Tuck?" Clarence continued typing without looking over his shoulder at his colleague.

"You seen Talmadge lately?" Tucker was getting grief from New York.

"Not lately, boss," Clarence replied truthfully, but that wasn't going to be enough to get the Tucker to go away. Clarence had always found the man to be an admirable correspondent who should have stayed on that side of the business. The guy was happier back then. Once Tuck acquired the wife and the extra expenses that went along with her heading a bureau was the only route up to higher pay within the syndicate. Trouble was Tucker found riding herd on the rest of them distasteful. He never liked being ridden when he was a reporter and hated turning arbitrary screws on anyone else. If Tucker was nosing around now it meant Lasky wanted something bad.

"Harry is looking for her, insistent like. Know what I'm saying?" Tucker wanted New York off his back.

"Oh indubitably. You have my condolences," Clarence was not going to give Ros up.

Tucker thrust a handful of cables down on the desk next to the typewriter. "I could use some help here. Any idea where I can track her down?"

"Last I heard she was nailing down some lead. Don't know the particulars," Clarence offered up a morsel to get rid of him.

"Just great," Tucker headed back toward his office. "If you lay eyes on her, send her my way on a bullet."

"Will do, boss," Clarence kept droning away at the typewriter keys.

SCHWARZENBERG CAFÉ
SCHWARZENBERG PLATZ, WIEN

Her visit to the *tourist bureau* had left her feeling so chilled that she had ordered up two hot brandies. The new café had caught Ros' attention on the way up to the opera house. With nothing else on the schedule, Ros stopped on the way back and grabbed a corner table. Street hoods and union bosses had nothing on these Nazi creeps. She wanted her back to the wall since her gut told her these local Nazis would be checking her out and may even try to tail her. On that depressing thought Ros sipped deeply of the first of the two brandy glasses. Feeling a bit more steady Ros diligently started writing down quotes and descriptions in her notebook while the memories were fresh. After a while Ros sensed someone casting a shadow over her shoulder and she prepared to bolt from the table.

"Is one of those glasses for me?" the shadow broke the silence. "Quite straight of you to think ahead."

Ros relaxed, recognizing the voice belonged to the guy from the Daily Telegraph she had met at Café Louvre. Ros continued writing in her notebook rather than look up. "Not so fast hot shot. That brandy is already spoken for. But you're welcome to sit down and join me."

"I'll claim that as a partial victory," Sanderson draped his sport coat over the back of the free chair and sat down. "You realize you are quite remarkable at discovering our favorite haunts for someone who only has been in town for two days."

"I'll take that as a compliment," Ros put down her pen and reached for the brandy glass for another sip.

"Forgive me for prying... but two brandies? "Habit or purely medicinal?" Sanderson jested with her.

"Medicinal," Ros downed the rest of the brandy. "I'm still trying to disinfect myself after that official German tourist bureau you boys roped me into visiting."

Sanderson savored a chuckle at her misfortune. "Yes, I see. That sorry collection of sour bastards will put the scare into anyone."

"I've walked into some of the unfriendliest establishments that New York City has to offer hunting down a story. Never have I been on the receiving end of such hostility in a place where they didn't even know me," Ros still had the jitters.

"The sad truth is that a sense of humor is not part of Herr Hitler's program. But you can't really take that all in until you face it up close," Sanderson felt it was a lesson she had to experience on her own.

Ros gestured to a waiter nearby for two more brandies. "Yeah, that bunch added a whole new meaning to deadly serious. I'm glad I gave them a false address when they started asking too many questions."

"Smart move," Sanderson leaned back in his chair. "Say, why don't you simply drop the pretenses and come along with me tomorrow."

"Oh really," Ros was a little weary to have to deal with a lecher right now. "And if I come along with you, what then, sweets?"

"Don't tease me this is a completely professional proposition." Her defences were up and Sanderson would have to dance around them skillfully. "I am taking the train over to Graz for a story and I could use the company. Consider the trip additional grounding in Austrian politics. Graz is a city full of dreadfully serious fascists like those you encountered at the tourist bureau."

"You sure know how to treat a girl," Ros felt like decking the clown for picking on her. "I'm not sure I'm ready for that kind of excitement just yet."

"You'll do fine," Sanderson leaned forward to reassure her. "Besides, it's all set. I have interviews lined up with the local party leaders. They're making a lot of noise about *national socialist aspirations*. They're literally begging for attention, and will be on their best behavior. Say yes."

Ros emptied the second brandy glass before answering. "Hell, why not. I'm not getting any interviews around here."

DEJVICE DISTRICT, PRAHA

Another late night rifling through reports, cross checking between German, Austrian and Swiss operatives. They were looking for similarities or coincidences to stand out and few did. Furst much preferred the purity of field work. The sense of excitement plus the element of uncertainty kept the mind sharp. Until they were through with this tyranny of paperwork, lack of seniority had its privileges. Burda knew how keyed up Furst could get and would send him out to fetch sandwiches... or *svickova na smetane* if there was time to wait for the beef sirloin to be cooked properly. Escaping out of the building into the crisp air with time enough for a quick pint of pilsner is what kept Furst from going crazy.

But what he observed upon approaching Burda's favorite hospoda torpedoed Furst's good mood. He didn't much like the American attaché but now Furst wanted to pummel the man and dump him into the Vltava. From across the street Furst saw Bulloch leave the hospoda arm-in-arm with one of the owner's nieces. Worse, they were both giddy as they ran along together. Off goes Bulloch for a night on the town with one of the nieces while Furst stayed locked up in the department for nights on end reading and re-reading stale descriptions of overheard conversations. As much as he wanted to convey Bulloch unconscious and bruised onto a slow freight train to Bulgaria, Furst shoved his fists deep into his overcoat pockets and entered the pub to fulfill his mission. There would be time for Bulloch later.

JANUARY 13, 1938
HOTEL GRANBEL – INNERE STADT, WIEN

Three days and the tiny hotel room was already a disaster. The proportionally tiny armoire wouldn't hold her road wardrobe without a fight and she wasn't sure whether it was worth it given the armoire's peculiar scent. So clothes were strewn in every direction, which was why Ros was running from one corner of the room to the other in her stocking feet looking under blouses, skirts and lingerie for her shoes. She finally spotted the tip of a shoe peeking out from under a covered chair. How they got under there she didn't know. There wasn't time to worry about it as Ros dug the comfortable low-heeled shoes out into the daylight and onto her feet. Grabbing her coat, hat and purse Ros was finally out the door just in time to catch the creaky old elevator down to the lobby.

This guy Sanderson seemed all right – about as regular a guy as a Brit was going to get. Not hard to look at either she reminded herself... and then quickly chased that idea out of her head since it would only lead to trouble she couldn't afford. Especially since he was throwing her a meaty bone. She didn't want to feel both obligated *and* attracted to this guy. The favor would have to be repaid. How it got repaid was still undecided.

The lift finally creaked to a noisy stop ending with a jarring bounce and a thud. At least she was still in one piece. Ros rushed out of the elevator with the other guests into the lobby. Glancing at her wristwatch revealed she had a few moments to spare so Ros dashed to the front desk to check for messages.

"Any messages for room four-ten?" Ros asked the rotund desk clerk, a well-dressed man somewhere past forty.

After checking the array of boxes behind him, the clerk returned with a folded cable. "Yes, one message mesdame."

"Thank you," Ros replied as she accepted the paper from him. Turning around, she walked back into the lobby to read the message. It was from Clarence:

> *KID. LASKY IS ON THE WAR PATH. CAN SEE THE SMOKE ALL THE WAY FROM HERE. HE'S LOOKING FOR YOU AND NOT TAKING NO FOR AN ANSWER. IF YOU'RE ONTO ANYTHING, NOW MIGHT BE A GOOD TIME TO REEL IT IN OR START THINKING ABOUT FINDING OUT WHAT PAPA WANTS. WILL COVER FOR YOU AS LONG AS POSSIBLE.*

"Damn Lasky," she cursed under her breath. He couldn't bother someone else right now. No, he had to tear up the boards looking for her. What now? There was always something with that man. Wadding up the cable into a little ball, Ros deposited it into her coat pocket and headed for the front door.

Sanderson leaned against the waiting taxi checking his notes. He was still considering how much of the Graz interviews he was going to turn over to his new American lady friend. Yes, it was an altruistic move on his part but also woefully transparent and self-serving. He fancied her and wondered how far he could go in this direction before he made a fool out of himself. Before he could dally more with that thought the object of his attention burst out of the hotel entrance and rushed in his direction.

"No worries, Rosalind," Sanderson believed the woman thought she was tardy. "We're right on schedule."

Ros strutted right by him and into the cab. "Stop jabbering and get in the car."

Sanderson peered inside the door. "Tough night?"

"I said, get in!" Ros grabbed his coat and yanked.

HOTEL BRISTOL – INNERE STADT, WIEN

The morning front desk clerk was hand dusting the counter top when he noticed a rather serious customer in a dark overcoat with a head topped by a black homburg materialize suddenly. The hotel got all types, some stranger than others.

"Looking for a room, sir?" the clerk inquired.

"Not today," the man answered, sliding a folded schilling note of high denomination across the polished wood. "However, I would like to visit with one of your guests on business. Mrs. Monica Claybourne. Which room may I find her in?"

The clerk thought about the bribe, his minuscule salary, and how useful the extra funds would be for a university student on a budget. Perhaps the odd fellow was a police investigator and who was a clerk to stand on hotel protocol. The clerk happily palmed the note with a clear conscious. "None, sir. We have no person staying here by that name."

The man slid a twin to the first bill across to the clerk. "Please confirm that for me."

The student, pleased at his good fortune, took the second note. Examining the bound register thoroughly left no doubt. " I'm sorry, no Claybourne... Monica or otherwise. You're welcome to check the register for yourself."

"You have no tall American woman staying here?" the man's voice showed no emotion, annoyance or displeasure.

"A guest like that I would have remembered and I have been working every day this week," the clerk closed the register.

"Thank you for your time," the man in black left without further comment.

VOLKSPOLITISCHE REFERATE
TEINFALTSTRASSE – INNERE STADT, WIEN

Events were finally in motion. All that was required were the final decisions regarding prominent targets on the approved list. The murder of chancellor Dolfuss four years earlier turned out to be a disaster. Mussolini was fond of him and ended up complicating matters tragically for the cause. They wouldn't make the same mistake again. Leopold Tavs had everything required for success at his fingertips in this fine old baroque structure that served as the headquarters for the movement in Vienna. They would be smarter this time and they would turn Austria to their needs. Not that Tavs had any great love of tiny Austria as he was Sudeten by birth. He loathed how the allies had carved up the empire after the Great War. That Czechs controlled his ancestral lands perpetually gnawed at him. But the Czechs were too strong to deal with at the moment. Their time would come later when there would be a new empire, an all-German empire this time. Tavs would wear a uniform again and discard these tailored business suits for good. But the genesis would begin here in the humiliated capital of the Hapsburgs. But the purposeful way one of his adjutants was approaching him in the main hallway meant something pressing needed dealt with.

"Dr. Tavs. A special courier has just arrived from Berlin," the adjutant was carrying a thick envelope, which he placed in the gauleiter's care.

"Excellent, I have been awaiting this." Tavs opened the envelope and examined the document in approving silence. Upon finishing his perusal he folded the pages and returned them into the pouch. "Remarkable."

GRAZ TRAIN, NIEDEROSTERREICH PROVINCE

Sanderson and Ros faced each other in the comfortable coach car. The trip went through a good portion of Lower Austria and Styria before arriving in Graz so Sanderson wanted their seating to be relaxing through the entire journey. Women could get so crabby about such things. Little good the effort had done him as Ros had ignored Sanderson most of the trip.

"You're not you're brilliant self today," Sanderson broke the silence again.

The comment drew an impertinent stare from Ros as she preferred to look out the window in silence. Giving him the silent treatment hadn't been Ros' intention she just wasn't in the mood for witty banter. Ros had to give him credit though, for the couple hours they had been rolling south Sanderson had not whined about being ignored. She decided to change the subject. "Do you have a first name, Sanderson?"

"Ah, it would be Robin," Sanderson was unsure why she had responded with a query about his given name.

"Really? That's such a shame. I think I'll just keep calling you Sanderson," Ros let her mean side get away from her.

"Well then," Sanderson buried the urge to reprimand the woman for a lack of manners. "Now that we have that settled let me forewarn you that I am not readily distracted nor confused by such misdirections. You're not being good company and I would appreciate knowing why."

This fella was good, Ros was impressed enough not to toy with him further. "I've got home office problems. I need to rustle up a story with some teeth, and soon. Otherwise the head fruitcake is going to kick me back down to covering women's shoes for the fashion pages."

"No wonder you've been such a frightful companion," Sanderson dished a little unkindness back. "I know that particular form of desperation well."

"Do you now?" Ros was not in a mood to be patronized. "Who would have guessed you had slogged through column inches full of hemlines, stockings and shoulder pads."

"True, I don't have keen experience in the area of women's footwear and intimate apparel but I do know what it is like to have the London morgue held over my head as an incentive." Sanderson could still recall the dreadful smells.

Ros had to agree that everyone paid their dues in this business. "Okay, you're forgiven."

"Note to self," Sanderson touched a forefinger to his right temple "Never impugn the lady's hard road to success."

"You'll live longer," Ros let a laugh slip out. "What high muckety mucks are we going to dance with on this trip?"

"Topping the list is professor Armin Dadieu," Sanderson savored his win in cheering up the American. "A chemistry savant extraordinaire and leader of all things national socialist in Styria. Perhaps the good burgermeister of Graz, Dr. Schmidt, as well."

"Does everyone in this postage stamp of a country have a doctorate?" Ros had been keeping score. "Hell, even the barkeeps are doctors."

The woman had a point, Sanderson noted. "Honestly, that's an observation I have never considered before. But you're dead on, this part of the world does have more than its share of the woefully well educated."

"Don't you find that creepy?" Ros still had a ways to go to understand these people. "The professors I know are all old, lovable and wear loafers not jack boots."

"Quite true, but goose-steppers do make for infinitely more, as you put it, column inches," Sanderson was making a career out of covering fascist provocateurs.

"As long as you put it that way, let me ask you flat out," Ros needed to circle back to her own pickle. "Any chance I can ride your coattails with this Dadieu guy? I could use a lucky break."

Sanderson decided to let a few seconds tick off to build some suspense before answering. "Not that I would characterize this as an exclusive but the professor is not known for giving interviews."

"Hey, no problem. I get the picture. This is your show," Ros backed off.

"Not so fast, Miss Talmadge. I'm not that selfish. I've had a few bountiful weeks in a row and could be persuaded to give you a portion of the interview," Sanderson held out a morsel.

"That's awful swell of you," Ros perked up. "But what is this going to cost me?"

Sanderson put his hands behind his head and leaned back into the bench cushions. "I'm sure you'll find something appropriate to the occasion."

"We'll negotiate later," Ros was strictly business. "Right now, tell me more about this Dadieu guy."

CAFÉ LOURVRE – INNERE STADT, WIEN

The foreign correspondents had staked out their usual table for the evening's banter and boozing. As far back as any of the regular members of this little ritual could remember there had never been a night when there had not been at least two of their number on hand. Tonight there were three.

"Where's your shifty countryman, Sanderson? He hasn't missed a night in weeks," Endicott thrust an accusing finger at Roland.

"He finally got his audience with Dadieu in Graz," Roland had yet to be so lucky.

"Oh, yeah, Sanderson has been hanging on the wire for weeks waiting on that one," Sylvie sipped her scotch. She was a regular stringer for Associated Press. "Dadieu is a good show and worth the wait. Hey guys... change of subject. Have either of you seen our new arrival? I haven't run into her yet and I want to see who the competition is for myself."

Sylvie had worked too long to get an international beat and liked being the only girl in their tidy little association. Sharing wasn't something she swallowed well. Especially since this Talmadge woman was a little younger and, from eyewitness descriptions, easy on the eyes.

"The way I heard it Sanderson took her along to Graz," Roland winked at Sylvie to get the message across and her blood pressure up.

"That rat bastard isn't wasting any time," Endicott figured the Brit was in for a fall.

"Are we sure it was even his idea," Sylvie settled back in her chair to enjoy a cigarette. No, she didn't like that this little tart was already messing with her boys.

"Oh, our pal Sanderson isn't *that* impressionable, sweetheart," Endicott had seen worse. "But if the lovely Miss Talmadge plays him for a chump you can have first crack at her. I promise."

DADIEU RESIDENCE, GRAZ

The neighborhood was neat, tidy and close to the university, which was about what Ros expected. The books said Graz was one of Austria's major metropolises yet that description was relative. Where Ros came from the good professor's abode would be considered more of a cottage than a house. It was definitely a modest affair yet extremely well kept despite the ravages of winter. As they reached the front door, Sanderson straightened his tie and Ros adjusted her coat.

"Ready?" Sanderson checked.

"Ready as I'm ever going to be, sport," Ros rapped the door solidly. "This is all new. I've never put a Nazi on the spot before."

"Picture a mobster without a sense of humor," Sanderson proposed.

Ros' laughter was cut short by the forceful opening of the door by a dour-faced housekeeper of considerable years.

"Do you have business here?" the housekeeper disliked outsiders.

"Herr Dadieu is expecting us," Sanderson switched to his official voice. "We have an appointment. Mister Sanderson and Miss Talmadge."

"Yes, the press," the old woman hissed contemptuously. "You may enter."

They stepped past the housekeeper to enter the house. The interior was just as modest and tidy as Ros had expected. Before she could get much of a chance to look around the housekeeper had closed the front door and was already prodding them into the parlor. Ros was sure the rush treatment was on purpose to keep then away from the family silver.

"Dr. Dadieu will be with you in a few moments. Sit down," the housekeeper commanded. "I have coffee prepared."

"Yes, thank you," Sanderson could tell Ros was starting to chafe under fire and wanted to get rid of the sour employee as soon as possible.

"Your coats," the woman held her arm out straight.

The reporters took off their winter coats and surrendered them to the housekeeper who left for parts unknown. Sanderson sat in one of the available chairs while Ros took one side of the settee, which she immediately thought could have benefited from a softer cushion.

"Frosty," Ros took her notebook from the purse to write down the nickname.

"You are new around here. The old girl is positively effervescent compared to most her age," Sanderson had been hustled out many a residence by worse offenders.

"And here I thought Parisians had the market on unfriendly dispositions." Ros' quip got a laugh out of Sanderson.

Right on time the front door opened and closed loudly. A hardy man with strong, attractive features removed his winter coat and hung it on a hook in the hall. "Welcome. I am Armin Dadieu," he approached the two reporters to shake hands with them.

Ros could barely restrain herself from staring. The guy was drop-dead gorgeous. She stood and willed herself to speak. "Ros Talmadge, Consolidated News."

Sanderson waited his turn and hoped his American friend would not go weak at the knees. "Robin Sanderson, Daily Telegraph. Thank you for having us."

"My pleasure," Dadieu held Ros' hand for a while longer before releasing it. "Although I do not recall mention of Miss Talmadge during our prior communications."

"The impression I got was that you wished to get your side of the story out to the wider world. Miss Talmadge has just arrived in Austria to better inform the citizens of the United States. I took the liberty of asking her to join us. I trust you will not object."

"No, of course not," Dadieu conceded graciously. Although he was wary of last-minute alterations to plans and would be on guard for any mischief. "Let's get started. Please sit down. Well then, where do we begin?"

That he sat close to her on the settee was uncomfortable in a number of embarrassing ways so Ros instinctively starting talking. "You seem very young for a man in possession of your many responsibilities."

"Really... is thirty-six considered unduly young in the United States, madam?" Dadieu was unsure whether she was being laudatory or critical.

"Well, you've been director of the Physical Chemistry Department for six years already," Sanderson broke in to steer control of the interview back his way. "When did you receive your doctorate and what drove you to accomplish so much so quickly in life?"

"In 1926 here at the University of Technology," Dadieu was curious that these two were not lunging for the usual political agenda. "We all have a purpose. I respond well to challenges. If others view the results as accomplishments, I am honored."

What a charming bastard this professor was, Sanderson decided. "What about chemistry fascinates you?"

"Reactions," Dadieu had not discarded his passion for science. "Discovering what elements will cause reactions that we can harness to facilitate the needs of man and the state."

That was a mouthful worthy of a good little party boy, Sanderson noted as the housekeeper was back carrying a coffee set on a tray. Putting the tray down on the table in front of the settee she poured and served the coffee – starting with Dadieu and intentionally ending with Ros.

"Thank you, Charlotte," Dadieu expressed his appreciation as the housekeeper left the room.

Ros marveled that *it* actually had a name. Like the rest she sipped her coffee and decided the lull provided as good a time as any to ask a few questions. "So when do you find time for politics?"

Finally the pleasantries were melting away as Dadieu had expected. "You assume that civic involvement is a distraction, Miss Talmadge. On the contrary, Austria is facing great challenges that all conscientious citizens must address."

"Why national socialism?" Sanderson narrowed the focus. "Why not work with chancellor Schuschnigg?"

"The United Kingdom is still a great empire, so I will forgive you the naiveté underlying that question," Dadieu felt it obvious the Englishman had not prepared sufficiently. "Austria today is a minor shadow of its former self. We are a people accustomed to greatness who are now reduced to insignificance. In 1918 our territories were stripped from us. We attempted to join with our ethnic German brothers in a natural pan-Germanic union yet the allies forbade it. Our former national purpose and identity were taken from us and it is only natural that Austrians look to a future in which they can replace what was lost. The Nationalsozialistische Deutsche Arbeiterpartei understands these yearnings and supports our aspirations. Herr Schuschnigg is a petty totalitarian content to keep Austria in the shadows. We deserve more."

"But you lost the war," Ros reminded the professor.

"Many countries have not won the day on the battlefield yet they retained their territorial integrity as nations. Austria was sliced into little pieces with your President Wilson leading the way. Why is Austria alone denied the opportunity to better herself, to build something greater?" Dadieu shot back saw the matter as simple justice.

"Today Austria, tomorrow…" Sanderson slyly suggested the obvious. "Many Europeans worry that a greater Germany is provocative and a threat to peace. Can we trust Herr Hitler?"

"Your question is misplaced, Mister Sanderson," Dadieu could see this was just another biased undertaking by the British press. "The pervasive poverty caused as a direct result of economic sanctions since 1919 has been the ruination of millions of innocent people – that my friend is the greater provocation. When any people has suffered as much as the German people have suffered since the Great War they must stand taller and speak louder simply to be heard by those who oppress them. From that perspective Herr Hitler and national socialism are not the threat so many make them out to be."

Ros sensed the building hostility in the room and decided to shift gears to defuse the tension. "So why is a handsome, successful fellow such as yourself still single?"

JANUARY 14, 1938
CNS HEADQUARTERS, NEW YORK CITY

If that dizzy dame had run off to some Adriatic villa to escape the cold weather he was going to send her skulking off to Alaska to write about the bears. No one left Harry Lasky in the lurch. But he would have to find Talmadge first. The problem was no one *responsible* had a clue where she had run off to and the rest weren't saying. That's what he got for being nice to a dame. They always took advantage. If he couldn't yell at her he'd yell at Des because his right hand man couldn't track her down either.

The cable had only been in Des' hands a moment when he saw the boss approaching fast in a full lather. "Hey chief, good news."

"Can it, Des. I want to talk about Talmadge," Lasky was running so hot his necktie was loose.

"So do I, boss," Des was trying to show him the cable with no success.

"You tell me... do I need to have the French cops dredge the Seine or can I just fire her now for dereliction of duty?" Lasky started pacing.

"I don't know if you want to fire Ros just yet since it could lead to a lawsuit," Des thought the *L* word my break Lasky's concentration.

"I have enough of that to worry about with my wife," Lasky was too frustrated to get on that subject. "Can I at least have the river dredged?"

"No need, Talmadge isn't in Paris," Des pointed to the cable.

"So you're holding out on me too. Where the hell is she?" Lasky wasn't getting it.

"I am not holding out on you, boss. I've been trying to tell you I just found out Ros is in Vienna," Des was ready to quit.

"Who sent her there?" Did you send her there? Tucker sure as hell didn't send her there and I know I didn't send her to Austria. I'm running this circus and no one tells me a damn thing," Lasky clenched his fists tight.

"Because you're always too busy talking, chief. However she got there, Talmadge just sent this story in," Des shoved the cable into Lasky's hands. "A pretty good story too, I might add. You should read it."

Lasky furiously skimmed through the cable pages. "Give me a synopsis while I read."

"A huge interview with one of the more prominent Austrian Nazis. I don't remember seeing this guy give an interview to the American press before," Des had made a point to check.

"Any idea how she came by this?" Lasky wondered aloud, still skimming.

"Nah, not a clue. Looks like she pulled the story in on her own," Des tried to give Ros an assist to shut Harry up. "Good leg work by the kid."

"She's still in hot water," Lasky pushed the pages back at Des. "But this ain't bad work. Clean it up and get it out on the wire. When that is done get that wayward child on the phone. I don't care how you manage it or how much it costs. Talmadge has to tell me when she's onto something. She's giving me an ulcer I tell you."

"You already have an ulcer," Des reminded Harry.

"Shut up!" Lasky stormed off back in the direction of his office. "And find me Talmadge!"

6. DISPATCHES

Journalists and writers at a Vienna cafe

JANUARY 16, 1938
SPECIAL TO CONSOLIDATED NEWS
BY ROSALIND TALMADGE

GRAZ – Most Americans don't think of the quaint and picturesque nation of Austria as a hotbed of political struggle. If Americans think of Austria at all this country at the crossroads of Europe is remembered as the seat of power of the old Austro-Hungarian Empire, which was dismantled by the Allies in 1919 following the Great War. No longer an important nation in Europe many Americans could be forgiven if they didn't realize an independent Austria existed at all.

Yet the truth is that growing forces of discontent and hardship are fueling extremist movements dedicated to the politics of hatred and revenge. At the center of the storm is the province of Styria where the people are steadfast supporters of the same national socialist principles at the heart of Adolph Hitler's government across the border in Germany. Their party may be banned under the administration of chancellor Kurt Schuschnigg in Vienna yet here in the provincial capital of Graz the people do have a leader in professor Armin Dadieu. A brilliant chemist gifted with charm, good looks, and a command of oration not often seen in an academic, the youthful Dadieu has ideas that could rock the stability of Europe and shock many Americans.

Granted a rare interview, I sat down with professor Dadieu in his home in Graz a few days ago to better understand the man and his politics. This reporter learned why he believes German people throughout the continent of Europe are oppressed, why he believes in a future when Austria is united with Germany as one nation, and how he responds to the challenge that his beliefs are putting this war-weary continent a step closer to open conflict.

CAFÉ LOUVRE – INNERE STADT, WIEN

Sequestered at their usual evening table in the café, Sylvie, Sanderson, Roland and Endicott raised champagne glasses in the direction of an embarrassed Ros. She saw no reason for toasts after being thrown an easy home run ball. Ros couldn't tell whether they were making fun of her, or truly liked her.

"C'mon fellas," Ros hated these reporter's rituals and the hangovers that came with them. "Give it a rest. This is not a big deal."

"No, we won't hear of it," Endicott raised his glass. "You're one of us now and this tight little group has rules. To your first bagging of big game on this beat."

"Rules are rules," Sylvie poured herself another shot.

Sanderson joined Endicott, "Cheers."

"You are in the big leagues now without a doubt," Roland made it unanimous.

Figuring the best way to get the ritual over with was to accept it, Ros downed half of her glass of sparking wine.

"Thank you. I appreciate this," Ros urged the men to sit down. "But I was only tagging along, folks."

"That doesn't matter. You got an important byline out of the deal," Sanderson took another sip of champagne. "And I *will* get repaid for services rendered."

"Ah, that's the sleazy little man I know and love," Sylvie blew him a kiss.

"Don't be mean, Sylvie," Roland teased.

Sylvie leaned over and pinched Roland fiercely under the arm. "You want to see mean, dear?"

"Ow! That hurts you evil witch," Roland shied away from Sylvie as the others laughed at his discomfort.

"Have some more of this, it'll help," Endicott refilled Roland's glass.

"I believe I will," Roland moved a bit farther from Sylvie.

"Aren't you pleased to be a full voting member of our little club?" Sanderson changed the subject.

"Pleased doesn't come close to describing how I feel about this bunch," Ros pushed her empty goblet toward the middle of the table. "Could someone fill this thing up, I'm dying over here."

The serious stranger in the dark overcoat was playing a hunch. He was sure Mrs. Monica Claybourne was a fictitious creation. Which begged the question, whom was this woman and what was her business spying on the party front office? There were only so many English-speaking women in Vienna of her youth and physical features. So he determined his best strategy was to observe the establishments that foreigners frequented. The Americans had no interest in placing a skilled intelligence agent in a minor capital such as Vienna. So he doubted he was tracking a professional. However, there was always the possibility the woman was a British agent posing as an American. The serious stranger in the dark overcoat would have to be discrete just in case.

Seating in the crowded cafe was scarce but he was fortunate to find a small inauspicious table with a good view of the entire floor and ordered a cognac to fit in. His hunch was that a self-assure American woman playing games in Vienna probably was a reporter and a recent arrival at that. Foreign reporters frequented this cafe and so he was here. The odds rolled in his favor again as he spied a table with five English speakers toasting one another.

JANUARY 18, 1938
BULLOCH'S FLAT
MALA STRANA DISTRICT, PRAHA

Petra had neither classes nor a shift at work to distract her this morning so there was no reason for her to rush out at dawn like usual. But Bulloch still had to make an appearance at the embassy and Petra was doing her best at distracting him as he finished washing up. It didn't help that he was easily distracted and she was hard to ignore – prancing around with nothing on but one of his dress shirts barely buttoned at the middle.

"You realize I only have so many of those ironed and ready to go in case I need to wear my dress uniform?" Bulloch knew it was a lost cause.

"Of course that makes wearing them more fun," she giggled. Next Petra slinked up to him, leaned up on her toes and kissed Bulloch sweetly on the lips. "You could always take the shirt back."

The woman was torturing him. And parts of him were responding enthusiastically to the torture. Bulloch pulled on his pants and an undershirt. Not to be ignored, Petra ran over to the bed, picked up a pillow and jumped up and down on the mattress.

"Do I do this to you when you have to go to work or class?" Bulloch considered reclaiming the shirt she was wearing.

"Maybe you should," Petra backed up on the bed a bit.

The standoff was interrupted by a loud knock at his apartment door.

"What now?" Bulloch brought his forefinger to his lips and pleaded for silence. All he needed was for her to waltz out from the small bedroom while he was dealing with the unexpected visitor. The look he got from her in return translated into a whimsical *maybe*. Maybe would have to do as Bulloch hurried to the front room to get the door. Facing him was one of the embassy couriers looking a little contrite.

"Sorry to bother you, captain," the courier handed him a note. "Minister Carr wants to see you."

"Thank you very much. Let them know I'm heading in straight away as soon as I pull the rest of my uniform on," Bulloch was sure he heard a muffled giggle from the bedroom yet the courier showed no hint of noticing her.

"Will do, captain," the courier mercifully left.

Bulloch closed the door wondering what was up with Minister Carr that required an off-the-schedule meeting.

U.S. EMBASSY
MALA STRANA DISTRICT, PRAHA

Bulloch dashed down the hall leading to Minister Carr's office in a rush. He had left Petra in the bedroom reading a textbook on the bed. Today she was wearing his dress shirt and tomorrow she might start walking off with his clothes. If that happened he'd never get them back. There would be a discussion about this, one he knew he was going to lose... in bed, with a smile on his face.

Bess Flynn approached Bulloch as he rounded the corner near Carr's office. She had her on *duty face* on and a collection of cables in her hand. That meant something was definitely brewing.

"Glad you could make it, captain," Bess knew something the young captain did not.

"Have I ever let you down, Bess?" Bulloch figured she was going to spring something on him by the devilish look in her eye but he could not figure out what.

"Not yet, son. Then again you're not assigned to my unit. You'd be working your sweet buns off then you can bet on it. Case in point..." Bess reached up to fiddle with his shirt buttons. "No way in hell would I let you show up with your buttons in the wrong holes."

"For crying out loud," Bulloch went after the buttons Bess wasn't working on.

"You have fun last night, captain?" Bess had heard about his new lady friend and by his guilty reaction she had him dead to rights.

"Can we keep this our secret, Bess?" All of the buttons were now where they were supposed to be.

Bess looked Bulloch up and down and then winked at him. "Keep your nose clean and I will think about it. Now that you look presentable get your butt in there to see Mister Carr, he's waiting on you."

"Yes ma'am," Bulloch felt like saluting as they went their separate ways. Entering the outer office, Carr's assistant gestured for Bulloch to continue on in.

"Minister," Bulloch found Carr seated behind his desk.

"Good morning, captain," Carr rose to greet him. "Please have a seat."

"Did you and Mrs. Carr have a good weekend?" Bulloch placed the cap on his lap.

"Fabulous, thank you. The Fodors had a dinner party. There was all kinds of hob-knobbing with Czechs in-the-know plus members of the foreign business community," Carr had found it a wonderful *and* productive evening.

"Did you learn anything interesting, sir?" Bulloch knew the minister usually got great tips from these affairs.

"Nothing much in your field, son. Much the same as I've been hearing since I got here: orders to the armament factories are up, output per week continues to increase and the percentage of defects is declining. No difficulty yet in getting raw materials into the country from abroad. But they are nervous, very nervous about the future," Carr's tone betrayed some concern.

"Did they tell you why, sir?" Bulloch wished to compare notes.

"Austria," Carr leaned back in his chair. "The people I spoke with this weekend are concerned about Austria. The government in Vienna is on a collision course with Hitler, which leads them to feel everything is going to boil over down there. That's why I want you to head south on the sly and have a look."

The proposal had caught Bulloch off guard. "Wouldn't that be something better explored with our legation in Vienna? I don't want to violate any protocols and my German isn't the best."

"I want no filters, son," Carr knew what he had in mind was something of a risk for both of them. "I need an eyewitness account from someone I can trust and that someone is you, captain. You have a good eye for detail and you have no problem talking with the local people. What happens in Austria is going to impact Czechoslovakia directly. That's why I want an appraisal from someone on my staff. And I have it on good authority that your German language skills are getting pretty good."

"When do you want me to go, minister?" Carr obviously had his mind set on the matter so Bulloch wasn't going to argue with him. Besides, he had not been to Austria yet and wanted to go.

"Immediately. Get a feel for what's going on down there. I also want your appraisal on whether we have the potential of a refugee problem if the worst happens and there is a fight for power between the national socialists and Schuschnigg. If there is a stream of people coming over the border the United States will be duty bound to lend assistance and I want to have a better idea of what assistance to ask for. I probably don't need to tell you this but while you're down there, look things over from the military side of things. I want the Army to get fair value from their man," Carr was ready to send the attaché on his way.

"No worries there, minister. I will get us everything we need," Bulloch stood up and donned his cap.

OLD ROOFTOP – BRNO-VENKOV

Furst's shoe slipped on a shake. He managed to regain a firm grip, but cursed himself as he felt the sting of a wood splinter that had punctured his finger through the glove. The roof hadn't changed since he was a kid. It was the same dilapidated mess of wood and metal as it always was, only worse. But it was a mess that Burda and he could use. They had set up the German radio set for Karl across the street in a good location with a fine view of the city. Now he and Burda were crawling around in workman's uniforms laying antenna wire for their own monitoring station where Czech agents would spy on the German agent that would be sent to take up residence across the street. The cluttered rooftop would hide their work well. The outrageousness of the whole farce took Furst's mind off of the splinter.

"Too bad your grandmother is no longer around, I could do with a snack," Burda joked as he bent a nail over with pliers to wedge in a section of wire.

"Not really. If my grandmother was still around she would be in the attic screaming at us and firing my grandfather's old hunting rifle through the roof," Furst's grandparents would have never permitted such an *uncivil* use of their property. But one of his uncles owned the empty house now.

"Ah! I see now where you get your sunny disposition," Burda worked another nail.

"Go ahead, laugh it up," Furst hoped to see his partner's family one day.

"Almost done here," Burda changed the subject. "We can go downstairs in a minute to finish up. Too bad you don't have relatives in Slovakia."

"Trust me, the world doesn't need any more of my relatives," Furst laid the last of the wire.

U.S. EMBASSY
MALA STRANA DISTRICT, PRAHA

Geoffrey Billings walked briskly down the hall to the front reception desk to drop off a parcel for pick up. He had a lot more to do before he finished up for the day and didn't want to waste any time. Billings didn't care who the middle-aged man in the frumpy suit chatting with the receptionist was. He just wanted to drop off the package and go.

"Carter, someone from the Czech Finance Ministry will be by to pick this up before close. Thank you," Billings did not require an acknowledgement.

"Mister Billings, one moment," the receptionist pulled Billings back as he tried to leave.

"What is it, Carter?" Billings had pressing matters to attend to.

"This man is looking for Captain Bulloch," Carter gestured toward the fellow at the desk. "Yet I can't find him anywhere and the staff list says he's in the embassy today. Do you know where he is?"

Billings looked the stranger up and down. Definitely French but no one that he recognized. That meant this was someone who could be gotten rid of.

"Do you have an appointment with the captain?" Billings looked for a way to send the Frenchman away.

"Didier Lerrault," the man introduced himself politely and proffered a card. "No, I did not have an appointment. I was in the neighborhood and I thought I would follow up on an earlier conversation I had with Captain Bulloch."

Examining the card, Billings recognized the logo of the aircraft manufacturer employing the fellow and was smugly satisfied that he had rightly pegged the man as French.

"Sorry, Mister Bulloch is away from the embassy on business," Billings would say no more.

"Do you know when he might return?" Didier tried for one more shred of useful information.

"No, I'm sorry, I do not. You may leave your card here at Reception with a note where you may be contacted while you're in Prague. I'm sure the captain will contact you at the earliest opportunity," Billings did not wait for answer.

The field officer watched the departing embassy functionary with the conviction that he despised all diplomats regardless of their flag.

WILSONOVO STATION – PRAHA

Once again Bulloch found himself walking through the tunnel leading to the train platforms. Only this time he was heading south. He had packed lightly into one small leather satchel. While he'd be in civilian clothes during the trip Bulloch decided not to leave the Colt behind. He had bought up all of the recent newspapers and the consensus of the reporting was anything could happen in Austria at the moment. So the pistol was stashed not far away from the diplomatic courier credentials on the satchel.

Dark shapes passed by Bulloch as he climbed the steps out of the tunnel. This late in the day the low light reaching the platforms was diffused and unflattering. Ice and snow still clung to the exterior glass of the steel lattice ceiling while steam from the locomotives condensed on the inside of the glasswork. Bulloch surveyed the platforms as best he could for trouble yet saw none. At the top of the carriage steps to his train Bulloch took one last look around. The only thing that caught his attention was the train conductor on the platform looking up at him impatiently. With nothing amiss Bulloch stepped inside the carriage to look for a seat.

7. COMBUSTION

**An Austrian army ADGZ armored car
moves into position in Vienna**

JANUARY 26, 1938
HOTEL GRANBEL – INNERE STADT, WIEN

Sanderson banged on the door a third time. This was embarrassing.
Sleepy hotel guests were opening their doors to stare at him in the hall.
Damn, lazy yanks, he thought to himself. He should just leave her. That
would teach Ros a lesson. But no, he had to fancy the woman. So he
rapped the door a fourth time.

"Rosalind!" Sanderson yelled for the last time.

He almost fell inside as the door was jerked open. Ros glared at
Sanderson as she stood in her doorway in a bathrobe, hair pinned up,
taking a plug out of her ear.

"This had better be good, Brit boy," Ros crossed her arms over her
chest.

"You can thank me later," Sanderson rushed by her to get away from
the crowd gathering in the hall. "Get dressed. All hell is breaking loose."

2ND DEPT.
MINISTRY OF NATIONAL DEFENCE, DEJVICE

The teletype specialist reviewed the text of the latest message as it came
off the machine. As soon as the wire transmission had completed he
would change the ribbon and paper roll a little early. He'd seen days like
this before. Soon the machine would be churning out messages without a

break. Luckily for him it was not his job to get the higher ups out of bed early to read the wires that passed through his hands. Tearing the cable off the machine he turned to the duty officer.

"Urgent report from Vienna, sir," he handed over message.

HOTEL GRANBEL – INNERE STADT, WIEN

Sanderson burst out of the hotel entrance, catching the doorman unawares. The hotel employee was fast enough to catch hold for Ros, who hopped out on one foot trying to adjust a recalcitrant shoe to fit correctly on the other. In rushing to get the shoe right she dropped her winter coat on the wet ground.

"Damn," she looked at the stained coat. "Hold up Sanderson!"

The doorman bended down to pick up Ros' coat, patted it down, and handed it to her.

"Thanks, sweets," Ros managed a smile on the run.

With no taxi out front, Sanderson jumped into the street to flag one down. The startled driver who finally pulled over had almost hit the reporter. The near miss didn't ruffle Sanderson in the least. Instead, he proudly claimed the automobile like a captured beast by standing on the running board.

"Hurry up woman," he waved his arm at Ros.

As Ros ran up to the cab, Sanderson leaned down to speak to the driver through the open window. "Teinfalstrasse."

"Teinfalstrasse," Ros stopped next to him. "Why the hell are we going down there? It's too early for even the Nazis to be causing trouble."

"Oh shut up and get in the cab," Sanderson was this close to leaving her behind. "I got a tip. The police are shutting the place down."

LEIPZIGER PLATZ 11, BERLIN

What he wanted to know was how that solicitous bastard von Papen had gotten his private phone number. Like most parasites the man found new ways to hang on. He was already one of the few politicians to survive from Hindenburg's government. Wily he was... always concocting some new need that only he could fill. The last time Göring thought Papen's days were numbered the leech convinced Hitler that only Papen could ease the Austrians into anschluss. *Schuschnigg would trust a fellow Catholic,* he cajoled Hitler. Now look at matters down there... a complete mess with Schuschnigg posturing for the world press about Austrian independence. Göring hoped that Hitler would follow through on his threats and finally sack Papen so Göring could finally be rid of him. But no, Papen couldn't fade away quietly in failure. He had awakened Göring from a sound sleep. The last person Göring wished to talk to while standing by the night table in his silk bedclothes was an unsettled Papen.

"What? You say what?" Göring could barely hear the pest. "Impossible, they wouldn't dare. Who else have you contacted?"

Göring's face went red as a familiar voice broke in.

"I'm sorry the line has gone dead, sir," his private operator announced.

"Get that miserable worm back on the phone. But first connect me with the Führer's personal secretary." If Papen was right, Göring had to speak with the chancellor.

TEINFALSTRASSE, WIEN

The cab driver took the corner too swiftly not expecting the traffic jam confronting him. Ros and Sanderson braced themselves in the back seat of the cab as the driver applied a heavy foot to the break pedal to stop the vehicle in time. The avenue ahead was completely blocked with other vehicles. Uniformed police officers had closed the avenue ahead with wood barriers and were preventing cars and pedestrians from getting by on the sidewalks.

"End of the line," the driver looked over his shoulder at his passengers.

Sanderson checked the fare on the meter then took out his wallet to pay the driver as Ros opened her door to step out. A small group of agitated young toughs brushed by her heading in the opposite direction.

"They arrested our lawful representatives," one of the boys yelled out angrily as he pointed back at the police.

Sanderson got out of the cab and hurried around to stand beside her.

"C'mon... soon we'll never get close," he tugged on her arm.

The two reporters sprinted up to the barrier, pulling press passes out of their pockets as they ran.

"It's all done here, nothing more to see," The two nearest police officers had their hands full attempting to push the crowd back.

As Sanderson's paused to assess the next best course of action, Ros followed her instincts and launched herself forward into the growing gap between the policemen. It wouldn't have been the first time she slipped past a preoccupied cop. Back in New York it was all part of the job. She had done it a hundred times. When Sanderson realized what Ros was up to, he was already too far behind to catch her. The nearest policeman stopped what he was doing and jumped back to place himself squarely in front of Ros.

"Nein! Verboten," the officer demanded with a raised hand.

Ros sighed and displayed her press pass for the cop as Sanderson squeezed through.

"No reporters. Please go on your way," the unimpressed policeman shook his head.

"Then tell us what we aren't allowed to see," Ros goaded the officer.

"No comment, state business." Anything dealing with the Nazis was sensitive. His orders were clear: no reporters were to be permitted past the line. The pretty foreigner wouldn't like it, but this was as far as she and her friend got. The truth was the officer hadn't been told why the national socialist leadership was being arrested and their files confiscated. That wasn't part of his job. Crowd control was his job.

"Who *can* tell us what is going on?" Ros persisted, while standing on her toes to look over and past the cop's shoulder.

"The proper authorities will make the proper announcements at the proper time," the policeman knew the lecture by heart.

While Ros kept peppering the officer, Sanderson carefully scanned the scene outside the headquarters building. No one was bound or being escorted out of the structure. They were too late for that, obviously. What he could see was a covered lorry waiting in front of the entrance guarded by uniformed police as a procession of plainclothes men were depositing boxes taken from the inside. There wasn't more to be seen so he turned to Ros. "We should go."

Taking the cue Ros looked at the cop and flirted. "Never could argue with a man in uniform. Thanks, hon."

"This better be good I could have worked him," Ros argued with Sanderson as they walked away from the barriers.

"Oh be quiet, we're too late by far. You and your bloody ear plugs," Sanderson mimicked putting plugs into his ears.

"Hey, don't lay this on me. Name any other gal who could get out the door any faster on no notice. Besides, I told you I'd stop wearing them. You ungrateful jerk," Ros backhanded his arm.

"Very well... you could have got past the policeman," Sanderson shrugged off the hit. "It would have been a waste of time. I took a long look down the road while you kept the good officer busy. The arrests had already been made. The only vehicles out front were collecting records not people. That means the person we needed to chat up is on the inside and we weren't getting inside despite your flirty charms."

"Don't be so sure, mister know-it-all," Ros knew she could win that dare. "You haven't seen my best stuff yet."

"Very true, when are you going to pay up on that threat?" Sanderson saw an opportunity for sly facetiousness.

Ros slugged his shoulder with her fist. "Back to business, fella. Now that we're done here, what's our next step?"

"I'm glad you asked. I have an idea," Sanderson rubbed his shoulder.

REICH FOREIGN MINISTRY, BERLIN

Early mornings suited von Neurath. He relished the solitude that permitted him to prioritize his thoughts without interruption. It was the only time of the day he could thoroughly peruse ambassadorial reports while sipping tea. Yet serenity was not sufficient today. The antique teacup shaking in his hand was evidence enough of that.

The career diplomat had been alerted. Quietly, discreetly... but warned. His days of service were to be terminated soon. He could only hope that nothing more was to be terminated. Pride and duty would keep him planted in his chair, in this office. Just as pride and duty had led him to presume that he could play a part in managing the political wildfire that had swept the country six years before. Instead the flames would consume him.

A nervous knock at the door drew von Neurath's eyes up from the document in his hand. "Enter."

The door swung open. The foreign minister could not say that he had ever spoken to the man wearing the sheepish face though he was sure he had passed the young fellow on the lower floors. If one such as this was knocking on his door there must be an emergency.

"What have you?" von Neurath noticed folded sheet of paper in the man's hand.

The balding clerk puffed out his chest knowing full well that he may never have another opportunity to be noticed by the top man in the ministry. "Urgent cable from ambassador von Papen in Vienna."

Von Neurath took the cable and read it carefully several times.

> *"CONSTANTIN. EMBASSY PHONES DOWN. TAVS AND, LEOPOLD ARRESTED BY FEDERAL POLICE. NO PUBLIC DISCLOSURE. SHALL I PRESSURE SCHUSCHNIGG FOR THEIR RELEASE, OR WAIT FOR INSTRUCTIONS? –PAPEN."*

"This is bad," von Neurath focused on the staffer before him. "What is your name?"

"Oskar Platen," the man replied dutifully.

"Well, Herr Platen, you and I have a lot of work to do. I need you to make sure that the ambassador gets my reply immediately. I cannot underestimate the importance of getting this transmission through in a timely manner. Understood?" von Neurath could suffer no misunderstanding on this matter.

"Understood," Platen took a deep breath.

The foreign minister swiftly wrote a reply on the cable.

> *FRANZ. SCHEDULE MEETING WITH SCHUSCHNIGG IN ANTICIPATION OF FURTHER INSTRUCTIONS. –NEURATH.*

INTERIOR MINISTRY, WIEN

Sanderson and Ros hurried into the main lobby of the handsome old building. She looked over the interior as discretely as possible looking for guards or any other watchers that might pop up at the wrong moment to stop them from getting close to the official Sanderson wanted to hit up for information.

"Hey, do you know where you are going?" Ros asked again in a hushed voice.

"Oh yes, been here dozens of times. Follow me we'll go straight up the stairs to the very spot. Just try to look like an underpaid civil servant," Sanderson suggested as the reporters ascended the stairs to the upper floors.

"Don't know if I can play that," Ros shook her head. "Underpaid reporter, no problem. Underpaid show girl, I can manage. Underpaid office worker, no sweat. But I don't think I can put on a sourpuss long enough to pass as a civil servant."

"Please don't start me chuckling, dear woman," Sanderson reached the floor he wanted. "You'll ruin everything."

"Okay, I'll leave the sour face to you. You Brits are used to putting those on," Ros was happy to give him some of his own medicine.

"Oh I see how it is. This is you're way of getting even for getting you out of your slumber this morning," Sanderson speculated.

"Buddy, you haven't begun to see me get even with you for that," Ros hit him hard on the same shoulder as before.

"Evil woman," Sanderson massaged the tender area. When you fancied them too much is when women inflicted the most pain on a man. There was no time for such thoughts now as they were at the right spot. He opened the door to the interior minister's outer office and stormed inside with Ros.

"We'd like to see the minister," Sanderson inquired politely of the dour older woman seated behind the desk guarding the inner office.

She took a moment to size up the two new arrivals and frowned. They were definitely foreigners, and by their attire, most likely unsavory tabloid writers.

"I'm sorry the minister is unavailable," the guardian refused them.

"When might we make an appointment?" Ros asked sweetly as she stepped forward to the desk.

"The minister is very busy. There are no appointments available," the guardian dismissed them curtly.

Minister Baar-Baarenfeld opened the door from the main hall and paused while trying to figure who these two visitors were.

"Herr Baar-Baarenfeld, what can you tell us of the arrests on the Teinfalstrasse today?" Sanderson had his notebook and pencil out immediately.

Baar-Baarenfeld had expected a visit from the press, just not so soon. He recognized this one as a British subject he had granted interviews to before.

"You work for the Telegraph, correct young man?" Baar-Baarenfeld set upon forcing the fellow to adhere to the civility.

"Yes sir. Good to see you again. We're trying to get the facts behind this morning's arrest of prominent Nazi party members," Sanderson pushed the point while he had the opportunity.

"And who is your companion?" Baar-Baarenfeld stalled further turning his attention to Ros. "I do not believe we have had the pleasure of meeting before."

"Ros Talmadge, sir," Ros walked over to shake hands with the minister. "Consolidated News Service."

"Very good to make your acquaintance, Miss Talmadge. Are you new to Vienna?" Baar-Baarenfeld continued with the formalities.

"Not so new now, sir, but still finding my way around," Ros was trying to get on the old codger's good side.

"Minister Baar-Baarenfeld... the arrests this morning?" Sanderson grew impatient with the polite banter.

"Oh yes," Baar-Baarenfeld had been pleasant with the reporters but now it was time to escape from their clutches. "I really couldn't help you with that. I haven't been in charge of internal security matters for some time."

"Surely you are aware of these arrests?" Sanderson was incredulous.

"Honestly, I really have nothing to say. You'll have to wait for responsible parties to comment directly," the minister would stand on protocol regardless of what he knew.

To punctuate the minister's last word, the reporters felt the cold presence of the guardian directly behind them.

"That is all the minister has to say to you, please leave," the dour woman commanded.

Baar-Baarenfeld had used the diversion to slip away to the sanctity of his private office, leaving Sanderson and Ros no other option but to depart.

"Thank you so much for all of your *help*," Ros got in the last word as the door thwacked shut behind them.

"He knows alright," Sanderson stood in the middle of the hallway and fumed.

VOLKSPOLITISCHE REFERATE
TEINFALTSTRASSE – INNERE STADT, WIEN

Skubl took a certain satisfaction sitting in Tavs' padded leather chair perusing the cache of incriminating documents that his crew was dredging up throughout the building. The Nazis had never seriously considered the government bold enough to raid them. The volumes of evidence turning up betrayed that arrogance. Technically, the building remained the property of the state, which had been provided for lawful political activities. What he saw before him now confirmed all that he suspected and more – that lawful political discourse was the last thing on the minds of these traitors. As one of his trusted police lieutenants brought in another box of papers considered to be more incriminating than most, Skubl's only concern was how well this evidence would be used.

"We're still sealing up more records and correspondence from all over the building. The place is stuffed full with it. It will take us at least another hour to empty it all out," the policeman put the box on the desk.

"There's no rush. Get it all," Skubl looked into the box. "What do we have here?"

"More operational and recruitment lists with hundreds of names plus notations on assignments. If you give the order we'll be rounding them up for weeks," Skubl's man was anxious to get started rounding up such riff-raff.

"That is the question of the day, isn't it?" Skubl only hoped Schuschnigg would give the order.

MOUNTAIN ROAD
NIEDERÖSTERREICH PROVINCE

The old fella driving was growing on Bulloch. This was their third day motoring around this incredibly scenic area. He'd hired the unassuming man based on the recommendation of a local innkeeper. Bulloch had gotten what he had wanted. Frederich was friendly and talkative, which meant the tour was both enjoyable and more informative.

"I'm surprised there are not more roads around here. Either for real estate development or enterprise," Bulloch saw plenty of commercial opportunity around him.

"Don't need them." The American was full of questions but Frederich didn't mind. The man was paying well and was a pleasant passenger. And even in these ugly times Frederich had not lost his sense of hospitality.

"What about trade? Doesn't a lot of cargo have to go to and from Czechoslovakia?" Bulloch tried to draw out the older man.

"I guess so, but all of that goes by train or river barge. No one uses trucks to move it. Not here. Most of those heavy loads get transported north through Germany or south through Hungary today, not Czechoslovakia. Things were a little different when we were one big country before the war," Frederich recalled fondly.

"I imagine that's still hard to get used to. Being a smaller country now," Bulloch was curious what the driver's politics were.

"But of course," Frederich took another corner on the road. "A lot of people don't like being a small nation. They feel we don't matter anymore and we are almost as inconsequential as Liechtenstein. They miss the old days."

"Do you miss the old days?" Bulloch caught a glimpse of another beautifully green valley ahead.

"Me? Heaven's no," Frederich laughed loudly. "Too many people, too many problems back then. My family was not important so what good was an empire to us. Other than I ended up as a lorry driver during the war. Best thing that ever happened to me. I liked it. That's why I'm still driving now. Why are you so curious about roads and transport?"

"We're always building things in America," Bulloch had been expecting that question for days. "If we're not building things, we're tearing something down to build something else. America is a big country but my bosses don't think America is big enough. So they sent me here to see what may need to be built around this part of the world."

"Like roads? That might be nice but I would not get your hopes up," Frederich felt bad he had to disappoint the young traveler.

"Why not?" Bulloch anticipated a negative comment on bureaucracy.

"The way things are going you wouldn't get one road project finished before everything goes to hell," Frederich shifted to a lower gear as casually as before.

CAFÉ LOURVRE – INNERE STADT, WIEN

Endicott fed up with the runaround he had been getting all day, but he finally had got someone in the government to talk with him off the record. It wasn't much, but it was a start. This could be the biggest story of the year and he knew the only way to ride it was to share with the others to find out what extra puzzle pieces they had. The editors wouldn't like it if they knew, but they would like being scooped even less. He was pleased to see that Sanderson, Roland, Sylvie and Ros were already in the joint waiting for him.

"Listen up folks," Endicott spread his arms wide like a carnival barker. "Looks like the government shut down the entire Nazi operation. That bunch is locked down tighter than a barrel of Texas crude. The government won't even admit that they have Tavs and Leopold on ice. This is big!"

"Big as the space between your ears," Sylvie had no patience for another session of *Tales of the Great Endicott*. "Sit down and shut up. We're way past that, sweetheart."

PRESIDENTIAL CHAMBERS
PRAŽSKÝ HRAD, PRAHA

Moravec closed the door securely behind him. It was late, and he hoped the president had taken his afternoon walk. Beneš was always more amiable to unscheduled briefings if he had cleared his mind.

"František, good to see you," The second president of the Czechoslovak Republic rose from his chair and came around the desk to receive his director of military intelligence.

"Mister President thank you for meeting with me on short notice," Moravec raised the dossier he had brought with him.

"What concerns you?" It was obvious to Beneš by the spymaster's manner that something of urgency was behind his visit.

"Sir, the situation has changed in Vienna." The Austrians were barring their teeth in a way that Moravec estimated would force Hitler's hand.

8. MISDIRECTION

**German Generals (L-R) von Rundstedt,
von Fritsch, and von Blomberg**

FEBRUARY 4, 1938
SPECIAL TO CONSOLIDATED NEWS
BY WALTER HAUTH

BERLIN – For nearly two weeks Europe has tensed awaiting an explosive response from Berlin to the Jan. 26 arrest of high-ranking Austrian national socialist party members in Vienna. In a stunning development, Adolph Hitler's government instead lashed out at dozens of Germany's highest-ranking government ministers and generals.

Those sacked at the top were foreign minister, Constantin von Neurath; minister of war, field marshal Werner von Blomberg; and commander-in-chief of the army, Colonel General Werner von Fritsch. In the most shocking revelations of all, von Blomberg and von Fritsch were dismissed following serious allegations of sexual scandal. First it was revealed that von Blomberg had recently married a former prostitute then charges were leveled upon von Fritsch accusing the career military man of being a homosexual. Both of the military men were forced to resign their positions awaiting investigations by civil authorities. Rather than announce replacements for these top military men, Hitler announced that he would personally assume supreme command of the German war machine.

As for Minister von Neurath the German government provided no explanation for his dismissal. Replacing the long-serving diplomat was as foreign minister is Joachim von Ribbentrop who was most recently the ambassador to Great Britain.

Reports continue to surface that dozens more high-ranking officials have been replaced by Hitler. Whether the chancellor, in power since 1932, is merely reshuffling his government or consolidating his power is yet to be seen. The Nazi party here has often shown brutal efficiency at stifling dissent as well as political opponents. Regardless of the intent the government shake-up has chilled discourse between civil servants here in the capital.

FEBRUARY 5, 1938
DEJVICE DISTRICT, PRAHA

The sparsely furnished loft above the small store did not qualify as a safe house. The space was a convenience – one of many Moravec had arranged throughout the city. He had been at the head of intelligence long enough to place his own trusted men close around him. Yet there was always the possibility an enemy agent had burrowed in elsewhere within the department. Too many high-level meetings held too closely together, especially on a weekend, drew unwanted attention. So Moravec had these hideaways tucked away across the capital for his senior staff to meet unnoticed.

Burda entered the loft from the hallway and immediately set himself to checking that the window shades and curtains were tightly drawn before joining the rest. Moravec was sure the man would check the state of the curtains several times more before they were done. It was Burda's way of relieving nervous energy.

"Furst says we're secure outside," Burda sat down with the rest.

"Then we can begin," Moravec started. "What do we know of Hitler's purge?"

Strankmueller, Moravec's director of espionage within Germany lit a cigarette and settled back against the settee's faded fabric. "We know that in addition to von Neurath, von Blomberg and von Fritsch, sixteen conservative generals were sacked outright. Forty-four others were transferred to trivial postings of no consequence."

"When do you believe the decision to clean house was made?" Moravec's deputy, Tichy, thought it valuable to know whether the purge was a spontaneous decision.

"I'd wager their fates were sealed back in November, 1936. As you will remember, Hitler called together his senior ministers to outline his ambitions for annexation of Austria and Czechoslovakia. Blomberg, Fritsch and Neurath all argued with Hitler. They dismissed his strategy as imprudent since Germany was nowhere ready for war, and risked drawing France and Britain into taking military action that Germany could not defend against. Our sources report that Hitler has stewed over this affront ever since," Strankmueller had numerous confirmations to support the analysis.

"So he is clearing the deck of all opposition in one huge swoop," Burda lit a cigarette. "That suggests the bastard is on a timetable?"

"That and something more," Tichy had a hunch. "Forced resignations and reassignments should have been sufficient for Hitler to get his way let alone these dramatic and titillating sex scandals. Hitler does not trust his officer corps to get the job done. Note that he is not appointing yes-men replacements to run the war ministry – not even Göring. No he is vesting all of that authority in himself. So many disgruntled generals could be an opportunity for us"

"Agreed, and we will pursue that opportunity, but Jan is correct regarding timetables. We must first look at the immediate threats posed by this purge," the scenario was clear to Moravec. As I see it the purge is a direct response to Schuschnigg's arrest of Tavs and Leopold. Hitler is clearing house for the direct purpose of moving on Austria without opposition. Even von Papen was recalled to Berlin at the same time and he was always a vocal proponent of an evolutionary approach to Austrian annexation."

"The status of von Papen is unclear," Strankmueller had new information he ruffled through his notes for to confirm. "We thought he was cast out with the rest but suddenly Hitler is sending him back to Vienna with a memorandum for Schuschnigg."

"An ultimatum?" Moravec leaned forward with interest.

"The contents are unknown. Our source has not seen the memorandum," the purge was causing difficulties for Strankmueller's operatives. "If the ultimatum threatens war there has been no change in deployment of Wehrmacht armored or infantry divisions to support such an incursion."

"Neither have we seen any extraordinary provocations from Heinlein's Sudeten thugs to divert our attention," Burda stepped away to check the curtains.

My sense is we are now dealing with events that will move much more swiftly than we have prepared for," Moravec got up from the settee to stretch his legs. "I suspect we will see major redeployments of the enemy's forces as soon as Hitler's new command structure settles in.

FEBRUARY 9, 1938
CHANCELLERY, WIEN

A representative of *The Telegraph* was not cancelled upon without notice. Sanderson was standing in the study that Schuschnigg used for press interviews arguing with the government press secretary.

"What do you mean the chancellor has called off my appointment?" the timbre of his voice was rising. "Do you know how long it took me to arrange this interview?"

"Of course I know, Herr Sanderson. All interview requests are vetted by me personally," Colonel Adam was growing impatient with the reporter. "The chancellor sends his regrets but important affairs of state have regretfully forced him to cancel your interview at the last minute."

Sanderson wasn't mollified in the least by the explanation and was decreasingly concerned about showing his displeasure.

"Very well then. If Chancellor Schuschnigg is not available today how soon can we reschedule the interview?" Sanderson tried to salvage the affair.

"The appointment cannot be rescheduled at this time. The chancellor's schedule will not permit it," Adam was of a mind to deny the Englishman what he wanted.

Sanderson had always found Schuschnigg to be the utmost in civility. If the chancellor made a promise he kept it. The reporter in him had to know whether there was a story to pounce on.

"So, Colonel Adam... am I quoting you correctly that matters of extreme state urgency have led Chancellor Schuschnigg to cancel long-standing obligations?" Sanderson had whipped out his notebook and pencil from his jacket pocket.

"I said no such thing," Adam was growing exasperated with such antics.

"And you can confirm that the chancellor has made the decision to extend the period of military service to meet growing regional threats?" Sanderson leveraged a tip he had received from a reliable source that morning.

"This audience is over," Adam not only found the Englishman inconvenient but he knew too much. Further discussion would only exacerbate the problem. "You will be contacted when your interview with the chancellor can be rescheduled. Good day."

Without waiting for a reply, Adam turned his back on Sanderson and walked out of the room. Internal security officers would soon follow to insure that he had left so Sanderson pocketed his notebook and pencil on the way out. There was something going on after all. Adam's quick retreat at the military service extension question was all the proof Sanderson needed.

REICH FOREIGN MINISTRY, BERLIN

The door to the foreign minister's office lay directly in front of him. Their new leader was calling in everyone for private meetings. Many of those called had been summarily fired from their jobs to make room for von Ribbentrop's favorites. Platen took a deep breath before knocking. He was sure his short career was about to end. Everything was changing and he had no connections in high places to protect him. Deciding to get the encounter over and done with as soon as possible he rapped on the door and was met with a confident voice instructing him to enter.

"Yes, come in," von Ribbentrop jovially rose to meet his visitor. "Oskar, is it not?"

"Yes sir, Oskar Platen," the low level clerk took the seat offered to him.

There was quite a bit one could discern from such a simple introduction, von Ribbentrop knew. All successful diplomacy depended on applying pressure to a man's personality strengths or weaknesses. This ministry peon was ready to shit his pants. There could be many reasons for that and he would know why.

"Why are you so tense, Platen?" von Ribbentrop played the caring elder.

"Am I to be relieved of my duties, sir?" the personable attention had helped Platen to subdue his anxiety.

He had heard the same question dozens of times since taking over as foreign minister and found hearing it once again amusing. So much fear... that was good, von Ribbentrop could use that fear to further his needs.

"No, far from it. Everything in your file suggests you have provided dedicated service. Relax, you are being promoted Platen," von Ribbentrop assured him.

And Platen did relax. "That is wonderful news. Thank you very much, Herr von Ribbentrop."

Convinced that he had the man's attention, von Ribbentrop went on with his agenda. "My personal secretary and staff are still in transit from the London embassy. You will report directly to them when they arrive. I realize the recent changes in the ministry have caused much uncertainty with many of the professional staff here in Berlin and I wanted to clear up as much of that uncertainty as possible. I would have had you in earlier to see me, but as you can well imagine, the Führer has had much for me to do."

"You are showing me a great honor, sir," Platen was awestruck to be treated so well by his new superior. "I will do everything I can to assist them upon their arrival."

"Very good," the fellow's reaction was just as von Ribbentrop had intended. "Back to your duties now, Platen."

FEBRUARY 11, 1938
U.S. EMBASSY
MALA STRANA DISTRICT, PRAHA

The report had been coming together in his head for days. Writing it would not be a problem. Feeding the sheet of paper into the typewriter on his desk, Bulloch spied the wall clock. It was closing in on two-thirty, which was sufficient time to pound out the assessment with plenty of cushion to meet up with Petra later. Friday nights just didn't have the same meaning here that they did back home. She didn't understand why he never wanted to miss a Friday night out with her but she liked the attention, especially after he had been away in Austria. Her curiosity about the trip had been intense and Bulloch grinned while reflecting on the ways she had tried to cajole answers out of him. Who needed a full night's sleep anyway?

The report would have to play well with both the State and War departments so Bulloch worked himself into that frame of mind and reread what he had so far.

Crisis Assessment

Summary: Austria's northern border with Czechoslovakia lacks adequate road and rail networks. This fact significantly restricts the freedom of civilian and military movement. The constraints on mechanized transport are severe. To move heavy armor, artillery and infantry units to the Czechoslovak border swiftly is out of the question. The roads are narrow with transit by motorized divisions slow and vulnerable to air attack or sabotage. Railroad transport is even more vulnerable since there is only one rail line into the area, with a hub in Linz.

Conclusion: Given the wide support within the Austrian populace for union with Germany, the potential for refugees flowing into Czechoslovakia is low and the lack of road and rail options further reduce that potential should Germany coerce union by invasion. Further assuming a German occupation and control of Austria the Wehrmacht would have great difficulty in moving units close to the Czechoslovak border and would not be able to do so with any secrecy. Worse, the Germans would not be able to resupply its forces adequately. The advantage would rest with the Czechoslovaks. In addition to advantages in unit strength and transport networks on the Czech side of the frontier, border defenses and deft use of difficult terrain would also stymie any German incursion. Should the Czechoslovak Army Air Force be deployed to forward air bases as called for in mobilization plans these pilots would have a high likelihood of destroying Austrian rail links...

Bulloch grew aware of a knock at his office door. He looked up from the typewriter toward the door. "What?"

The door opened slowly revealing the Frenchman that Faucher had in tow a while back – hat in hand, and his coat draped over his arm. Bulloch was positive that the man was wearing the same wrinkled suit as before.

"Captain Bulloch. I hope I am not disturbing you," the intelligence officer had finally caught up with the American.

How the fellow had gotten this far into the embassy without a warning or an escort annoyed Bulloch. And he couldn't quite remember the man's name.

"Hello, ah, Mister Deed... Diid," Bulloch stammered.

"Didier," the operative filled in the rest. "General Faucher introduced us."

"Yeah, pal," Bulloch recalled, rising from his chair to greet the man. "Sorry, it's been a while. How did you get up here anyway?"

"I had other business here at the embassy and one of your colleagues was kind enough to point me in the direction of your office," Didier had been forced to fake a visa interview.

"Thanks for dropping by," Bulloch was not very pleased at all. "What can I do for you?"

"I still would enjoy speaking with you to get a fresh perspective on Czech rearmament so I might better market our new products here," Didier picked up on the same raison d'être used when both men had first met.

"Doesn't your industry already have enough of a problem supplying French orders? At least that's the word I get from back home from people working at factories filling expedited French contracts," Bulloch shot a few holes in the Frenchman's reasoning.

"Sadly true, I am afraid." The Frenchman smiled. This American was not stupid... so much the better. "But this will not always be the case. We are making great strides in production efficiency, and until production levels are raised, there are always licensed production agreements."

"You folks are always looking for a profit," Bulloch checked the wall clock. French design influences were an aspect of the Czech armed forces that he had not spent much time on.

"Tell you what," Bulloch decided he could gleam some insights from the guy. "I have to meet my lady friend a little later tonight and I have some work to finish to get out of here on time. Why don't you meet me at the same place I am meeting her: U Pinkasu down in Nove Mesto. Say five-o'clock. That will give us about an hour to chat. How's your expense account?"

"Paltry, yet sufficient," Didier could finally get this mission over with.

CAFÉ LOURVRE – INNERE STADT, WIEN

Endicott blew through the cafe in a huff. He'd been trying to get a straight answer all day to a very simple question and was blown off at every turn. If someone else hadn't scooped him by now it would be a miracle. Endicott was so intent on making tracks he accidentally bumped into William Shirer who was getting up from his chair.

"Charles," Shirer brushed off the collision. "Still running over people, I see."

"Yeah, Bill, I'm under my quota for the week," Endicott pausing to chat. "You could have put me over the top if I had seen you sooner."

The two old pros shook hands. Shirer had just moved over to CBS to work on radio broadcasts. That was one way to get ahead in the money game, yet Endicott considered radio as way too prissy. Then again, having a kid in the oven as Shirer did changed a man's priorities.

"How do you like working for Murrow?" Endicott had known Shirer long enough to be blunt.

"Ed is great but radio takes some getting used to," Shirer tapped the back of the chair fitfully with his fingertips. "It's hard getting comfortable with reporting live."

"You'll do fine," Endicott stifled an urge to ask his competitor if he had the answer the Endicott was looking for. If Shirer played coy and jumped on the story he could have it out on his next studio broadcast long before Endicott would have time to file.

"Thank you for the good wishes, Charles. Although I'd have a good bet that you're simply plain happy to see me out of print and want to keep it that way you competitive bastard," Shirer was very close to the truth.

"You were good I'll give you that, Bill. Too bad you're out to pasture," Endicott patted him on the back.

"We'll have to continue this banter later," Shirer looked at his pocket watch. "I'm already running late."

"You're on. I'll buy the first round," Endicott promised as both men went their separate ways.

"Hey! Does anyone know where the chancellor of this postage stamp of a nation is?" Endicott directed at Sanderson, Sylvie, and Roland when he reached their table."

"We were just discussing that very subject," Sanderson looked up at Endicott. "My interview with the good Mister Schuschnigg, the one I have been finessing for weeks, was cancelled at the last moment with no explanation."

"I smell a rat," Endicott hung up his coat and hat on nearby wall hooks.

"Probably a big fat German rat. There are plenty of them walking around out there," Sylvie gestured at the nearest window.

"How can you tell?" Roland happily fed her the straight line.

"Besides the smell? That look of utter contempt they put on for every one and every thing," Sylvie had spent the whole day tracking down leads.

"I can't for the life of me understand what is holding the socialists back from starting a row in the streets," Sanderson could not understand their restraint.

"And I suppose you are one of those who thinks it's always the left that starts trouble?" Sylvie pounded her shot glass onto the marble top.

"Oh please," Sanderson pushed himself away from the naive tart.

"Folks! Let's concentrate," Endicott had better fish to fry. "Where the hell is Schuschnigg?"

"Well, if you can believe it, the good chancellor has chosen this very moment as the perfect time to relax and take a ski vacation," no one had noticed Ros arrive at the table. "And I don't believe that tripe for a moment."

U PINKASU – NOVE MESTO, PRAHA

With superficial pleasantries and several drained beer glasses behind them, Bulloch and Didier were finally circling around meatier conversation. The French salesman's questions always had a little twist to trick Bulloch into saying more than he should. This gave the attaché the distinct feeling that he was being played.

"Why me, pal?" Bulloch was tired of answering questions. "Why are you so interested in my opinion?"

"You are American, not French or British. French and British perspectives are easy to find. So I think perhaps you see something different that can benefit me," Didier repeated his rationale.

"That's a bunch of horseshit," Bulloch took another gulp from his glass. "In my line of work there isn't much more to say than strength of numbers, quality of training, and reading some colonel's book on tactics... approved by the high command, of course. So my *perspective* won't be much different from Faucher's."

"Why do you assume I am captivated with such pedestrian observations as those? People don't buy weapons based on doctrine they buy arms based on fear," Didier tried another tack with the attaché. The American constantly remained distant, refusing Didier's subtle attempts to draw him into revealing any deeper knowledge of German war aims. The question was whether Bulloch was difficult by nature, or by design. "Fearful politicians buy more goods from people like me. What do the Czechoslovak military officers tell you? Do the Czechs honestly fear that the Germans will attack them?"

"I feel bad since you're buying the beer, and all, but there is only one answer to that question: *Ask Adolph,*" Bulloch laughed off the inquiry.

"You are insufferable, captain," the Frenchman would not get a chance for a follow-up question as Petra romped up, sat down next to Bulloch and draped her arm around his shoulder. The military discussion was over.

"Dobrý den," Petra broke in, laying a lingering kiss on Bulloch's cheek. "Who is your friend here?"

"A lonely businessman from Paris in search of some conversation," Bulloch perked up knowing he would finally be rid of the guy.

"There are lots of those in Praha these days," Petra turned her attention to Didier. "Did my Nathaniel help you feel better?"

Knowing the opportunity had passed, the intelligence officer admired her lithe form and the American's good fortune. "Very much. Will you join us mademoiselle?"

"Sorry friend," Bulloch possessively wrapped his arm around Petra's waist and raised her off the bench with him. "The lady and I have a date. Have a good trip home and au revoir."

INNERE STADT, WIEN

The stroll from the cafe had been pleasant yet Sanderson's could not let go of the disappearance of the Austrian chancellor. The group had broken up late and he had insisted on walking Ros back to her hotel. Sanderson was so worked up that he had ended up being a dreadful companion, and knew it. For her part Ros nodded in solidarity as he went off the handle but she was not as bothered by the phony ski trip story the government was circulating as he was.

"This is all so very frustrating." They had just passed a wall with a political stencil supporting Schuschnigg that promptly set Sanderson off again.

"What? That you can't fit the pieces together or that I'm not properly mystified?" Ros teased him.

Sanderson stopped in his tracks to point an accusing finger at her.

"Where are your priorities, woman?" Sanderson was aghast she was making fun of him at such a critical moment.

"Feminine or professional?" Ros saw no reason to let up if he was going to be a goof.

"Either, or both," Sanderson threw his arms into the air. "Something is going on and we're missing out on a major story. Doesn't that bother you in the least?"

Instead of answering Ros continued onto her hotel – forcing him to follow. "More than you know, Robin."

He hated when she used his first name. It always meant she was going to tell him something he didn't want to hear.

"If I don't keep the copy flowing back to New York, Harry is going to pull me out of here."

"That would be catastrophic for my current mental state," Sanderson was confronted with something that worried him more than Schuschnigg's disappearance.

Ros appreciated the admission. It was nice to be chased by a good egg for a change so she stopped for a moment to look him in the eye.

"Oh, I think you'd survive, pal," Ros planted a lingering kiss on his cheek. "But I am grateful for the sentiment. See you tomorrow."

Not giving him a chance to respond Ros walked the rest of the way to her hotel and went inside. Sanderson put his hand up to where she had kissed him. It was a morsel, a throwaway to be sure. But it was the first time Ros had given him any sign that he had a chance with her. And he no longer had a care about the Austrian chancellor.

KOPECKY'S FLAT
VINOHRADY DISTRICT, PRAHA

The question on his mind as he unlocked the door to his apartment was whether he'd sit down with a bottle of cognac, or collapse on his mattress. Either way it was late and Kopecky was happy for his short respite from his general staff duties. He found the floor lamp waiting in the dark and switched on the bulb, which cast long shadows through the small apartment. The flat was expensive but he was supremely fond of the cosmopolitan district. While depositing his coat and service cap on their respective wall hooks Kopecky's nose caught a slight odor that meant it was time for the maid to come through the place again to tackle the dust.

Loosening his collar, Kopecky decided on the cognac. He walked into the kitchen and went straight for the second cupboard. Kopecky knew the route like a blind man and didn't need a light. The glass was right where it should be but his hand didn't find the bottle. Annoyed, Kopecky reached back to switch on the kitchen light but there was no bottle where it should be. Where had he left it now?

"You always had good taste in cognac," a familiar voice called to him from the front room.

Startled, Kopecky whirled around to search through the dim light. What he could not see from the kitchen was Capka sitting in one of Kopecky's high-backed chairs drinking liberally from the cognac bottle.

"I had forgotten your affinity for locksmithing," Kopecky followed Capka's voice from the kitchen with a clean glass in hand.

"You forget far too many things, my friend," Capka sounded a bit drunk.

"That's a dreary state you're in. Mind if I join you?" Kopecky pulled a chair closer.

"Please do," Capka held up the bottle.

Kopecky sat down in front of Capka and held out the tumbler. At least Capka's motor control was still adequate. No cognac spilled to the floor and his friend's grip around the bottle was firm. Kopecky was heartened as Capka was intolerable when he past his limit... not to mention dangerous. For now there was room to reason with him.

"Did I forget our date?" Kopecky sipped his drink.

"I prefer the element of surprise," Capka drank again from the bottle.

"Ah, then this must be an important visit," Kopecky concluded. "What brings you in from the cold, my friend?"

"I have a problem," Capka mumbled softly.

"When was the last time you had a woman?" Leaned closer in the dim light.

"Is that your answer for everything?" Capka straightened up in the chair.

"Frankly, yes," Kopecky continued to draw him out. "Yet since your need far outstrips the likelihood of fulfillment, I admit it is a limited strategy."

"I'd like to stick you in one of my tanks for a while to give you some honest work to chew on. You wouldn't be so flippant then," Capka raised the bottle to his lips.

"There it is then, this is a professional discussion," Kopecky was making progress.

"I hear talk of splitting off portions of our motorized divisions into quick-reaction teams for use against Sudeten insurgents. You thought I wouldn't find out about that, did you?"

"Now I understand the source of your poor disposition--" Kopecky did not get a chance to complete the sentence.

"--How the hell am I supposed to be combat ready to take on the Germans if you fools at staff start carving off tanks and armored cars from my brigade?" Capka strangled the neck of the cognac bottle tightly.

"You have not been paying attention." Kopecky worried the bottle might shatter. "Look how the Nazis are disrupting Styria and other Austrian provinces. Long before the panzers cross our border we will have our own insurgencies to put down."

"You should have told me what was going on," Capka pressed the issue.

"Give me some credit. Have you lost any men from your brigade? Srom and I are working hard to insure the best trained of our brigades remain intact. It isn't easy, you know. Do I come to bother you about it? No I do not since you have enough to deal with. But you need to get something through that thick skull of yours. These quick-reaction units are an opportunity," Kopecky took the cognac away from him.

"Opportunity? You are turning us into policemen. We will be like mice attacking a tiger when the German divisions come," Capka made a poor attempt at swatting Kopecky away.

"You of all people know how hard it is to train large motorized divisions to coordinate well. By creating these quick-reaction units a whole lot of our people will get comfortable in the execution of the same concepts. Yes it will be on a smaller scale but the training will still be there," Kopecky hoped his argument had sunk in.

"I only half believe you," Capka was a little wobbly standing up. "But if I find you have fed me a line of crap I will chain you to the back of my Škoda and drag your hide back and forth over the proving grounds until your mother will not recognize you."

9. IGNITION

Berlin's Potsdamer Platz during the 1930s

FEBRUARY 13, 1938
WILHELMSTRASSE, BERLIN

Heiden leaned his shoulder comfortably against a lamppost to consider the irony that a lifelong indoctrination on what constituted proper posture meant nothing in the intelligence service. It was necessary to beat the military bearing out of a man otherwise wearing a civilian suit was a useless and obvious farce. So Heiden learned how to blend in with the crowd, to move with them without drawing attention, and to unlearn a lifetime of his father's stern lectures. But the watchers had to be ever vigilant to be sure they were not being watched themselves. For that reason Heiden never liked staying in one place too long. His subject, a likely traitor with a loose grasp on his obligations to the state, had returned to his ministry building. If all went to plan, his ride would appear in moments to spirit Heiden out of the area. On cue, the weathered Daimler sedan rounded the corner and pulled up to the curb. Heiden opened the back door and got in. To his surprise he was seated next to the director.

"Nothing is wrong, I can see the question in your eyes," Ottke motioned to the driver to speed off. "Although I shouldn't be able to read your eyes after how long you have been at this work."

Both men had been cut from the same *politically unreliable* cloth. Despite distinguished service each had been drummed out of military service for minor indiscretions. Their common link was Canaris who had a habit of throwing a lifeline to those he knew could be of use to him. Ottke's long experience in field espionage was a major asset to the admiral. Heiden had led elite shock troops successfully in missions too tenuous for regular regiments – a necessary skill when the admiral required a precise use of force. Both professional soldiers shared additional Canaris virtues: loyalty and courage. Ottke was the right hand to the Head of Abwehr headquarters and Heiden reported directly to Ottke.

"Forgive me, I did not expect to find you waiting for me in my own vehicle, director," Heiden had little patience for surprises.

"I like to get out once in a while myself and I thought you would appreciate hearing the latest on the Austrian situation. Hitler lowered the boom on Schuschnigg last night," Ottke handed a large envelope to Heiden. "The fool Austrian actually thought he was being invited to the Berghof for a discussion."

"I see, that's where Schuschnigg disappeared to," Heiden turned the envelope over in his hands.

"Perfectly pulled off by the SS. They stopped Schuschnigg's automobile on our side of the border and substituted his guards and driver with members of the Austrian Legion – men that Schuschnigg had exiled," Ottke marveled at how much effort Hitler expended on annoy and demoralize his enemies.

Heiden reached into the envelope and pulled out several telephoto black-and-white pictures showing the Austrian chancellor exiting his vehicle and walking up and into Hitler's den.

"Pitiful really," Heiden finished with the photos. "No one knew he was in Germany. They could have killed Schuschnigg right there and only a handful of people would have known. I can imagine his mental state when they delivered him to Hitler."

"That pied piper Papen earned his lease on life for a while longer. I don't know anyone else that could have convinced Schuschnigg to embark on a secret meeting in Germany and have him thinking that unmasking of the Tavs putsch would provide leverage over Hitler. Brilliant work," Ottke regretted Abwehr could only watch the show from a distance.

"Never underestimate politicians and diplomats when their necks are on the line," Heiden trusted none of them. "What were Hitler's demands?"

"Schuschnigg must appoint Seyss-Inquart and other prominent national socialists to the cabinet. Amnesty must be granted to all party members imprisoned in Austria. Political rights must be restored to the party. If Schuschnigg accedes to these demands by February fifteenth, Hitler will accept expulsion of Tavs and Leopold to the Reich and Austrian independence will be guaranteed as long as economic and foreign policy is tied to Germany's." It was obvious to Ottke that Hitler had lowered the hammer on the Austrian.

"And if Schuschnigg refuses?" Heiden had a good idea how the Führer would encourage compliance.

"Austria would be invaded immediately. Hitler even trotted out General Keitel to explain the finer points of the current invasion plan. It must have been quite the show. But I am quite dumbfounded that they allowed Schuschnigg to return to Vienna without first capitulating." That was how Ottke would have run the operation.

"I suspect they let Schuschnigg go because more time is required. Even Hitler has to know the army isn't ready to invade anyone," Heiden knew the Wehrmacht was a mess, and not the finely oiled machine championed in the newsreels.

"Doesn't matter," Ottke had seen the latest directives. "They're accelerating the timetable for anschluss to cover up last month's purges. This whole Austrian affair is going to move very quickly. We must be ready when we are called upon to do our part. That's why I came after you this afternoon. I need you to start working up operational objectives at once.

PRIVATE DINNER PARTY, WIEN

The bottle of champagne uncorked with the dramatic pop the financier's guests were anticipating. He enjoyed these socials as his wife Lola referred to them. Many a business deal had its inceptions in this drawing room. Then there was the pleasure of mixing intriguing and intelligent members of the community and standing back to watch what resulted. Which was one reason he had invited the British reporter and his American wife. The apartment was large by Vienna standards, which made it perfect for regular entertaining. Especially since Lola had a flair for the refined without sacrificing comfort. Guests always fell over themselves to remark how welcome they felt. Ludwig Frum would miss these socials and this home.

"Drink up my friends. I want to empty the cabinet before some brown shirt comes to claim it," Frum played to a round of nervous laughter.

"Why do you go on so?" complained Raoul Steiner, a dealer of fine books in the city for more than twenty-five years. "This last week was marvelously quiet."

"You are so right, Raoul," Lola did not see why her husband had to ruin the mood. "Such a relief to have no demonstrations or street brawls."

"The quiet worries me," Roland extended his empty champagne glass in Frum's direction.

"You reporter people are always looking for an altercation to sensationalize. Fine, your newspaper has less to print, but why should a peaceful week bother you?" the gray-haired little book dealer insisted.

Roland sipped from his newly flush glass of sparkling wine before explaining. "Think about it. The two top Nazis in the country are locked up tight, their headquarters raided, their files confiscated and *nothing* happens. The government doesn't say a word, the Austrian Nazis are not crying foul, Berlin doesn't protest... does that sound like the way things usually work in this part of the world? Of course I am worried."

"Don't jinx it dear. Be optimistic for a change," Sylvie tugged parentally at his jacket sleeve. "We don't want to make a bad impression in front of such generous guests."

"No it should bother him, my dear," Frum solemnly filled more glasses. "As much as it pains me to say this I recommend that you all leave Vienna soon."

"Why are you saying that?" Lola demanded from across the room. "That's not funny."

"I was being quite serious, darling," Frum felt the entire room riveted upon him. "I learned something this afternoon that was very disturbing."

Sylvie knew that when the bankers got rattled that usually meant trouble was not far around the corner. Always follow the money if you wanted a lead, which is why she agreed to masquerade as Roland's wife. And she smelled a big lead here.

"And what might that be?" Roland did not wish to give their lovely hostess time to intervene.

"Chancellor Schuschnigg did not take a vacation as was announced by the Chancellery. He held a secret meeting with Hitler in Germany. It did not go well," Frum was still aghast that Schuschnigg would have thought otherwise.

"That's news my friend," Roland pulled his notebook and pencil out from his jacket pocket. "Off the record, of course, what did old Adolph demand?"

Lola stepped closer to her husband, concerned for what he was about to disclose, and angry that he had not spoken to her about it first. "Ludwig. This is not wise."

"But necessary," Frum assured her in a tone that made it clear he had no intention of being dissuaded. "The same old demands were made. I don't have much in the way of details. My friend in the cabinet was unfortunately short of time. The thrust of the matter is that either Schuschnigg brings Nazis into the government or Germany invades Austria within two weeks."

"That is very un-neighborly," Roland quipped while scrawling the final details down.

"This is not humorous, sir," Steiner found the Englishman appalling.

"Behave," Sylvie pinched Roland's earlobe to raise his awareness. They needed this bunch to keep talking. "Don't mind him... please go on. "What did Schuschnigg tell Hitler?"

"I wish I knew the details. What I do know is that the chancellor did not refuse the demands," Frum added with some sadness.

"Stalling for time," Steiner hoped for a positive outcome in the news. "Schuschnigg needs time to contact Mussolini for support as in thirty-four."

Lola would have preferred not to speak of such things at all but there was so much all of them would all have to do and there was no time to nurture false hopes.

"No, that won't happen, Herr Steiner." Lola moved closer to place a hand on his shoulder. "Il Duce adored chancellor Dolfuss and was angered by his assassination. My cousin in Milan says Mussolini does not feel that way about Schuschnigg and won't order the Italian army to the Brenner Pass again in support of Austria. All the state newspapers there are neutral or cold when they write about Schuschnigg."

"My apologies for such an unpleasant choice of conversation," Frum went to his wife's side and put his arm around her." "But this has weighed heavily on me all afternoon. As a friend, I thought you all should have as much time as possible to act prudently. My advice is that we should start thinking about leaving Austria."

FEBRUARY 14, 1938
HOTEL GRANBEL – INNERE STADT, WIEN

The argument Ros had always made as kid to her mother was that if you couldn't see the sunlight then a person was under no obligation to get up early. Despite having never won that argument Ros had never gave up on the philosophy. No matter the scarcity of sunlight in winter-bound Vienna, rules were rules and she always pulled the drapes before turning in. Unfortunately, the black phone clanging on the nightstand was violating several important subcategories. Resigned that the caller was not going to give up, Ros lowered the heavy bed covers far enough to reach for the phone.

"Yeah," she saw no reason to hide her anger.

The voice on the other end of the line confirmed she was having the worst kind of nightmare.

"Oh brother. Harry, do you know what time it is?" Ros sat straight up in bed. "Give a girl a break... no that is not true. I am not stringing you along... You're pushing it, Harry... How do you know about him? Listen, if I was ditching you for the Telegraph, which at this point sounds pretty appealing, you'd be the *first* person I'd call. No way would I pass up that kind of joy... give it a rest, boss. I'm following up on a lead – maybe something, maybe nothing. If it's nothing I'm heading back to Paris with my tail between my legs... Yes, that's the *only* thing between my legs as if that's any of your business you rat! Good night, Harry!"

That miserable man was worse than her mother. Why couldn't she have gotten an old-fashioned room without a phone? Here she was a half a world away and already Harry had heard about Sanderson. Ros retreated back into the bed and dragged the covers over her head. Less than a minute later the phone rumbled alive again on the nightstand. The smart choice was ignoring the call but the urge to dress Harry down won out. Ros' arm shot out and grabbed the receiver. "Shut up, Harry! Leave me the hell alone."

As Ros was about to slam the phone back on its cradle it dawned on her that the voice she heard wasn't Harry's. Ros pulled the phone closer to her ear to figure out who else had the nerve to disrupt her slumber. "Oh, Sanderson. Sorry. I thought it was... never mind. Why are *you* calling me at this hour?"

After listening to him for a few moments, Ros threw back the covers.

"You're damn right I want to be there!" she hung up on him and leapt out of bed.

ROLAND'S FLAT – 2ND DISTRICT, WIEN

The tiny apartment was claustrophobic as the reporters squeezed around the table in the front room. Sylvie and Ros had cornered the compact settee through intimidation. Endicott could care less about polite manners and niceties... this was business. Special treatment wasn't part of the deal but he was outnumbered and they both were insufferable in the morning. So Endicott took one of the kitchen chairs that had been provided knowing he'd get even later. As for Sanderson in the chair next to him, Endicott wondered if the Brit really knew what he was getting into with the dame.

Roland was pouring hot breakfast tea into cups next to the fresh biscuits on the table before he hurried to the next room for something.

"Since when do you play favorites, pal?" Endicott was peeved at Roland asking Sylvie to the dinner party.

"Don't be a loon," Roland was still busy in the other room. "I never play favorites."

"Then why did you take along the skirt," Endicott pointed at Sylvie.

"My dull friend," Roland returned from the kitchen. "This was a social event for couples. Having sent my Margaret back home I needed a stand-in."

"And you lack the equipment, sweetie," Sylvie stuck out her tongue at him.

"Will the three of you give this a rest I want to hear why Roland brought us together," Sanderson picked up a teacup.

"Right," Roland took his cue, teapot still in hand. "This whole country is going to come off the hinges."

"Uncle Adolph somehow got Schuschnigg to his mountain chateau and personally put the screws to the poor duffer," Sylvie went straight for the good part.

"Quite, the panzers are revving their engines," Roland added the punctuation.

"Hey! What was your headline, little man?" Ros tugged on Roland's shirtsleeve.

"Berghof Blackmail," Roland puffed out his chest proudly.

"That is quite good," Sanderson snatched a biscuit from the tray.

"Don't encourage him," Endicott dismissed the praise with a wave of his arm." Roland is terrible at headlines. I bet Sylvie gave it to him."

"Why yes, I did." Sylvie's smirking admission got the crowd laughing and broke the tension in the room.

"Roland, you are shameless," Ros sipped her tea.

"I never ignore a good suggestion, and neither should you," Roland wagged a finger at the other three. "This scoop comes from a reliable source in the banking community with government connections. Now I want my mates to get the jump on all the other riff-raff in town. You watch, everything is going to move fast."

Ros gulped down the rest of her tea then abruptly jumped up from the couch. "Later chumps I've got work to do. Thanks for the tip Roland."

"Wait. You're not thinking of going it alone are you?" Sanderson put the teacup on the table and stood up to block her way.

"Not thinking about it... doing it, love," Ros walked right past him to the rack in the hall to grab her coat and hat. Harry's accusation earlier that morning had been irking her. It was time she cut out on her own to send a different message back to New York.

"Wait." Sanderson called after her. This was not the time to venture out by one's self. He'd never forgive himself if anything happened to her but Ros was already through the door.

CNS HEADQUARTERS, NEW YORK

These damn reporters would kill him yet. If he could he'd hire a private dick to tail each and every one of them not in New York. Not a one of them could give a straight answer to a straight question anymore, especially the wayward children overseas. Like crossing an ocean gave them extra license to ignore Harry Lasky. He had a syndicate to run, copy to deliver and competitors to beat. A pile of paperwork was sitting on his desk and could he get to it? No, here he was pacing behind his desk on the phone arguing with Walter of all people. Good old reliable Walter was giving him grief. Lasky was so worked up he did not notice the phone cord from the cradle was tangled up with his chair and about to cause a crash

"Yeah, Walter," Lasky clutched the phone tightly. "What, you positive about that tip? Three sources, good... An ultimatum on Austrian annexation by Germany you say? That's golden... Don't tell me you don't know when it's going to happen. There can't be an ultimatum without a deadline. Dig deeper. Get me a date. The whole story rides on that God damned date! Fine... listen, Ros is still in Vienna. I'll get her moving on the angle down there. Now you call me tomorrow, you hear."

Lasky turned to slam the receiver into its cradle but tipped the chair over as the cord went taut. Throwing the telephone to the floor in disgust,

Lasky marched out into the newsroom. "Des! What the hell is that number for Talmadge in Vienna again?"

FLORIDSDORF DISTRICT, WIEN

They would have preferred to meet openly and defiantly on the factory floor but there were too many ears and not all of them could be trusted. What came next was crucial to the movement and he would not put that at risk. This aisle between stacked pallets in the warehouse would have to do for the decision Späth and the other two union leaders were about to make. His authority came after a twenty years journey from shop apprentice to foreman. If fate ordained it was they who would stand firm for the workers, then stand they would.

"Then it is agreed. We will strike in support of the government. There will be no fascist putsch." Späth raised a weathered hand to cast his vote yes, followed in kind by his two comrades who also voted aye.

"And the militia," Drau pressed to the core of the matter. "Do we issue firearms?"

"Yes, call up the special units and issue the guns. Let's see how the Nazis deal with bullets." Späth agreed... violence was best checked by violence.

REICH FOREIGN MINISTRY, BERLIN

Taking charge of a major ministry of government in the middle of a regional crisis was not the debut von Ribbentrop would have chosen for himself. Yet Hitler saw him as a man who could get things done without needing steam shot up his pants and von Ribbentrop had no intention of contradicting the Führer's assessment. Glancing at the dossier he had just pulled from the file cabinet von Ribbentrop became aware that his secretary was speaking with a sense of urgency.

"Herr foreign minister, the London embassy is holding. They say they must speak with you immediately," the man held up his phone.

All von Ribbentrop needed was another emergency. The situation in Austria was delicate and evolving. The British weren't interested in making a fuss over the Austrians. What other mischief was afoot? But London had been his station and he trusted them. Best to find out. He walked over the secretary's desk and gestured for the phone.

"This is von Ribbentrop, what is the problem?" von Ribbentrop sat on the edge of the desk. "Slow down... what about the afternoon edition? *Berghof Blackmail!* The damned British press... no, you were right to alert me. Protest this most vehemently as soon as you can get an appointment, and keep me informed."

Von Ribbentrop sighed as he handed the phone back over to his secretary. "More excitement I am afraid. Please get me Herr Goebbels. I'll take the call in my office.

FLORIDSDORF DISTRICT, WIEN

This intersection was as far as Skubl was going to get. His Steyr sat hastily parked at the curb and they were now on foot. He hoped the procession of workers would be so kind as to not to scratch the paint on the vehicle as they marched by with their banners and placards. There it was, a general strike supporting Schuschnigg and the Fatherland Front. Skubl wasn't sure whether he should kiss them or shoot them. The chancellor would need the workers in his back pocket yet the unions taking to the streets was adding fuel to the fire. The whole rotten house might go up in flames. He looked over to Glanz – one of his most trusted precinct captains – standing beside him. Both men had too many years behind them to possess illusions about what they were facing.

"I was afraid of this," Skubl gestured at the marchers with a sweep of his arm. "We can only hope they don't march into any of the Nazi neighborhoods."

"They can't be that stupid, sir," Glanz saw workers as far down the road as he could see. "They are sending a message but I don't think they plan on provoking a riot. Not yet."

"Unfortunately, we can't depend on their continued discretion, my friend. Some punk throws a brick and we're all cooked. We have to keep them separated. Get to a phone and relay the direction of the marchers so our boys can get in position and set up cordons. Let them head into the Ring but keep them away from the Nazis," Skubl struggled to be heard over the slogans shouted by the workers.

CNS HEADQUARTERS, NEW YORK

This was going to be good. Des had to hand it to Talmadge, she was nailing the Vienna angle. The copy she was phoning in was going to make the boss happy. Better yet, it would shut him up for a while. Des checked over the text he had just scrawled on a pad. He wanted to be sure he got it right while the memory was fresh. Ros always read well so this report wouldn't take much cleaning up. "Okay, let's get this finished. Here's that last graph back at you:"

Finally, faced with sure imprisonment in special concentration camps in Germany constructed for trade unionists and leftist political leaders, Austrian workers fearful of a Nazi party takeover here have taken to the streets shouting: Nein to Hitler. The fate of Austrian

independence may hang in the balance depending on what transpires
in Vienna's industrial districts during the next forty-eight hours.

"Great material, doll. I'll type it up and get it out. I love 'ya. The boss will love 'ya. Well, at least he'll really like you for a couple of days. Keep this up I'm proud of you.... bye."

Des hung up the phone and jumped up from his chair. He'd put a bullet behind getting Ros' story out. Picking up the phone he pressed a button to another internal line. After no answer ten rings later he slammed the receiver back down. "Okay, who knows where Harry is?"

10. DUETS

**The Berghof. Adolph Hitler's personal estate
in the Bavarian Alps near Berchtesgaden**

FEBRUARY 15, 1938
CHANCELLERY, WEIN

Austrian and international reporters crowded into the reception room. The crisis was drawing newsreel teams too. If the number of correspondents kept growing Colonel Adam might be forced to hold future briefings out to the courtyard. There was nowhere else to hold this many newspaper people. Crammed together tightly like this they were more surly than usual. Adam decided to start press conference before there was a riot.

"Decorum please," Adam outstretched his arms like a priest commanding his flock. "Decorum, thank you. Your news organizations will receive information as it becomes available. I can confirm that chancellor Schuschnigg has convened the Council of Ministers to fully discuss his private meeting with Herr Hitler at Berchesgarden."

Endicott muscled his way to the front and interrupted the Austrian press secretary. "What did old Adolph want this time?"

This American never failed to annoy Adam. All reporters were needy and self-absorbed but this man approached every encounter with an air of entitlement beyond rudeness. Given the circumstances, Adam gleefully considered the possibility of deporting the rude American.

"Mister Endicott. The substance of the chancellor's negotiations are still confidential and will remain so until he has had an opportunity to seek guidance from the ministers," Adam dressed down the unruly child.

"C'mon, give us the goods for a change. What about you personally? Will you at least get to stay on after the Nazis take over? From what I hear they pay their front men pretty good," Endicott needled the spokesman to the approving chortle of his fellow hacks.

"Sir, I would appreciate it greatly if you would take this proceeding seriously," Adam knew the American was attempting to pry loose some unintended admission by intentionally irritating him. Luckily one of the reporters from a French left-of-center paper was cutting in.

"Is it true that chancellor Schuschnigg is under a one-day deadline to annex Austria to Germany or face immediate invasion? Will Austria fight if invaded?" the Frenchman's sources had been very specific.

"Anschluss is not an issue of the discussion during the chancellor's negotiations in Germany. There is no deadline on this question. The Austrian Republic will always defend its interests," Adam parsed the facts to avoid answering the question.

Ros wasn't satisfied with Adam's response and decided on a different approach to draw the spokesman out.

"Colonel Adam. What of the popular front workers striking in support of Austrian independence?" Ros nudged to the front. "Will the chancellor heed their wishes? Will Herr Schuschnigg meet with the social democrats before answering Hitler?"

These Americans were everywhere like flies. Adam cursed under his breath as he counted still more Americans in addition to these first two. They were almost as thick as the British press.

"The government respects the interests of all of its citizens, but as you well know, the social democrats and the national socialists are not a part of the Fatherland Front. The chancellor is not required to consult with either group on state business." Adam was relieved to notice a correspondent from one of Mussolini's party-approved newspapers and called on the man.

"Is it true that the chancellor has ignored the advice of signor Mussolini to smooth relations with Germany?" The Italian reporter had been instructed to press Adam on Schuschnigg's intransigence.

Adam had hoped for a more congenial question, and didn't appreciate the attempt at lecturing. "I have no knowledge of any such communications."

Sanderson had been to enough of Adam's briefings to know the man wouldn't take much abuse before closing down the event.

"Colonel Adam, sir. Has chancellor Schuschnigg requested support from the British or French governments? And if so, what kind of support was requested?" Sanderson struggled to be heard over the other reporters.

"As I said before I am not at liberty to discuss sensitive communications between governments." Sanderson was another fly on Adam's list. The Americans and British were going to usurp the briefing despite his best efforts. Adam would instruct his staff to assemble the Austrian correspondents privately and end this circus. "Thank you, that is all for now. My office will have updates available to you later in the day. Please make your requests directly with them."

Adam turned his back and left the room – ignoring the rising rancor of the reporters who were not able to pose their questions. In the center of the storm Sanderson, Endicott, Ros, Sylvie and Roland huddled up together close to where Adam had stood.

"Damn. I didn't get a chance to ask my question thanks to you three," Sylvie tossed her notebook into her purse.

"That blowhard wouldn't have answered you anyway," Endicott spit on the floor.

"He might have if I had bedded the repulsive little frog when I had the chance." Despite the admission the press secretary was definitely not her type though.

"Oh no. Nothing would be worth that, sister," Ros grabbed Sylvie's arm.

"Well, if you are determined to pass out your womanly favors, my dear..." Roland leaned closer to Sylvie to play along.

"Roland you dog! I am going to tell your wife," Sylvie pinched his earlobe with her fingers and tugged. "You listen to me, mister... behave!"

"Very well, have it your way you heartless woman. I'll behave," Roland capitulated and Sylvie released her grip on his ear.

"Shall we talk business," Sanderson proposed, hoping to steer his compatriots back to business. "I detest waiting on that Adam fellow to parcel out slim morsels about what Schuschnigg is discussing behind ministry doors."

"Not much else we can do," Endicott raised his arms in exasperation. "No one else is talking, not even the pro-German crowd."

"You boys go ahead and be sensible. I have a different idea," Ros pulled Sylvie by the arm toward the exit. "Come with me, gal."

"Hell 'ya. I'm game," Sylvie signed on based on moxie alone.

"Where are you off to?" Sanderson called after them.

"You'll find out," Ros was still putting together her plan and did not notice the serious little man in a black coat staring at her on the way out.

2ND DEPT.
MINISTRY OF NATIONAL DEFENCE, DEJVICE

New tactical maps of the Austrian border with Czechoslovakia and Germany in deep detail adorned the operations room. This relatively quiet frontier had turned hot as valuable information was pouring over the radio frequencies that Karl had provided them. The swiftest way to illustrate the details for the command team was visually.

"Our monitoring of the German frequencies provided by A-54 have netted a huge amount of signals to and from this area here,"

Strankmueller updated them on fruits of their eavesdropping. "So far the wireless traffic has not been coded. In the last week OKW has put its armored and motorized divisions on alert and has begun moving support units up to positions closer to the Austrian border at these points. The signals have been phrased as new directives and not part of a pre-existing training maneuver."

"How do you interpret the signal traffic?" Moravec was always keen to track how well the analytical skills of his team were developing. All of them had come to the spy game fresh and had to learn intelligence work from the ground up. That handicap hadn't stopped them from setting up perhaps the strongest network of operatives within Germany.

"Two scenarios as we see it, sir," Strankmueller turned to face the group. "Hitler sacked the senior leadership of the Wehrmacht only ten days ago. These alerts and unit movements could be a way of giving the army something to occupy itself as the party's handpicked replacement generals get an opportunity to access their commands and junior officers. Or, as we suspect, Hitler is ratcheting up the pressure on Schuschnigg in the most direct way available."

"Which scenario should we bet on?" Moravec opened the issue up to the rest of the team.

"I would lean toward a combination of both scenarios with an emphasis on rattling Schuschnigg," Tichy did not see why they should choose only one when both fit.

"Agreed," Strankmueller thought the same way as Tichy. "As far as we can tell there has been very little dissension or drop in morale within army ranks as a result of he purge. If they are moving their pieces on the board now my conclusion is there is a distinct strategic purpose at work."

Moravec moved closer to the display maps to illustrate a point. "Yet none of their main combat unit placement looks like invasion readiness to me. If we believe our sources, Schuschnigg's deadline to comply is tomorrow. Did we misread something?"

"I can say with complete confidence that there is no urgency whatsoever to the German signal traffic from German agents within our borders," Burda gave some extra weight to Moravec's position.

"All that is true yet I am sure the diktat is real," Strankmueller went back to the reports. "All of our various operatives and sources corroborate each other even if that may not fully seem to be the case on the ground. Hitler has no reason to doubt he can achieve his demands without being compelled to use military force. Our sources also tell us he has every expectation that the Wehrmacht can achieve a swift victory without much preparation. On these counts there is no contradiction in the data. Hitler is playing the bully and he fully expects to extract the political concessions he desires."

"Gentlemen. The president does not believe he has options to respond militarily to German aggression in Austria," Moravec shared the latest guidance from the castle. "France and Britain have already accepted the concept of Austrian anschluss as a *fait accompli*. President Beneš also rightly surmises that under the circumstances if we took any overt military action Czechoslovakia might be judged the aggressor in German internal affairs. We require more time to extend our frontier defenses along the border with Austria. Therefore, it is our job to find ways to slow down events in Austria behind the scenes. Hitler will not turn on us as long as he's fully engaged in subduing Herr Schuschnigg. Find me more options to buy us that time."

Moravec's edict signaled the end of the meeting. All but one of the officers collected their notes and files to leave.

"Sir, there are reactionary cells within the German officer corps that are hostile to Hitler and the party," Strankmueller moved closer to Moravec. "We know of them but none of my agents has violated your orders not to make direct contact. Our posture toward such opposition groups could become more active now that German provocations are on the rise."

Moravec smiled knowing Strankmueller had likely already made contact so he could deliver on his proposal.

"Can we insert an agent in their midst without being blatantly obvious?" Moravec wanted more control over the relationship if he chose to pursue the option.

"More difficult but possible," Strankmueller already had several operatives he could rely on.

"Draw up a list of candidates and I will review it." Moravec had previously resisted sponsoring internal subversion inside Germany but events were moving much too swiftly to dismiss the opportunity.

Burda raised an eyebrow at the discussion but didn't comment. It was a very dangerous game. The Germans had already kidnapped Second Department agents on the Czechoslovak side of the border. Given the excuse he was sure they were capable of far worse. He hoped the boss would not seek his counsel on the subject.

"Where is our American friend?" Moravec changed the subject.

"Mister Bulloch has returned to Praha," Burda was happy to expand on that topic. "None of our people have discovered where he went although we suspect it was Austria."

"Intriguing. I'd like to think the captain is taking his job more seriously," Moravec felt some vindication at the news. "One day the Americans will again have a pivotal role to play in Central Europe. Captain Bulloch is going to help make that happen. So don't let him get himself killed in the meantime, I still have use of him."

BARRACKS, SS-DEUTSCHLAND – MUNICH

Morgen faced down the SS-Verfügungstruppe enlisted men standing at attention in front of their bunks. Intimidation of these pups was easy to accomplish. The street riots and brawls of his youth had left scars much more daunting than the scharführer badges on his tunic. Morgen loved giving these *true believers* a reason to piss their pants. They were all ideologically pure volunteers from rich families and he would teach them fear. If they survived this old brown shirt each would be strong and each would be feared.

"Your life of luxury is over you lazy bastards," Morgen stalked the line of men. "Now you get to feel what it's like to get wet and cold in full view of the enemy. I'd rather drink with an old red on the factory line in Hamburg than any of you. Those guys knew how to fight. Soon you might get a chance to show me whether any of you can do more than talk. Suit up for combat and be ready to move out tomorrow at zero-six hundred hours. And that includes field packs. Any questions?"

Schlosser hated Morgen's endless reservoir of self-important diatribes. It had not been enough for the party to eliminate the SA leadership. One day Schlosser would enjoy getting rid of the rest like Morgen.

"How long will the exercise last this time, sturmscharführer?" Schlosser's tone betrayed little respect for the squad leader.

"Who said this was an exercise, party boy," Morgen closed in on him. "Oh no. You're going to get your hands dirty this time that's a promise. Start picturing those hands around the throat of a communist apparatchik. I guarantee you there's a red out there who has a bullet with your name on it. If you are unlucky your executioner will cave your skull in with a hammer behind a barricade in an unfamiliar industrial district. There will be no long-range kills for you. This is the SS. You get to kill up close... or die up close."

Morgen ran his forefinger slowly down the deepest of his facial scars. "If you paid attention to what I've tried to teach you maybe you will be lucky enough to walk away with one of these."

"Where are we going, sturmscharführer?" another private was eager to change the subject.

"Where you are told," Morgen never took his gaze off Schlosser. None of you be late tomorrow or this boot will be so far up your asses you won't need a truck to get where you're going."

U.S. EMBASSY
MALA STRANA DISTRICT, PRAHA

Bulloch had to sprint to catch up with Minister Carr who was making his circuit around the garden. The attaché had an idea he wanted to run by him... an idea that was scary since Bulloch generally wasn't keen on sticking his neck out.

"Good afternoon, minister," Bulloch finally caught up with the older man.

Carr calmly stopped to see who was hailing him. "Oh, hello captain."

"I hope I am not intruding," Bulloch knew Carr didn't get much time to himself.

"Heavens no. Mrs. Carr is busy on one of her projects. I'm happy for the company on such a fine day. Please join me," Carr continued walking.

"Thank you, sir," Bulloch took his place beside the minister.

"Actually, it is I who should thank you for that fine report, captain," Carr had found the analysis very useful.

"You're welcome sir." The minister's approval would work in Bulloch's favor. "That's one of the reasons I came out here to see you."

"How so, son?" Carr was intrigued with what the attaché had on his mind.

"I want to go back to Austria, sir." The proposal had been on Bulloch's mind for days.

"For what purpose, captain?" Carr wanted to pursue this request carefully.

"You've read the dispatches... looks like Austria is heating up pretty fast. If I could actually watch the German army on the move that would be extremely useful information to have." Bulloch just had to not get shot in the process.

"Such an expedition put your life in great danger and I will not have you injured unnecessarily," Carr reached out and gripped his arm tightly.

The minister had not said no. An eyewitness account of German aggression would be priceless. But Carr wouldn't approve of the mission if it were done recklessly. "Are you sure you can make your observations amidst all that turmoil without getting caught?"

"Trust me, sir. I have a strong sense of self-preservation and no intention of getting myself compromised. But seeing how it all plays out if the Germans invade is the chance of a lifetime," Bulloch could not let it slip that skulking about over the border had been one huge rush of adrenaline. "Without your approval, however, I won't go minister."

"If you promise me that you'll take no unnecessary chances, I'll approve your request off the record, captain," Carr already felt a bit guilty for endorsing the adventure.

"Thank you, sir. I promise to stay out of trouble," Bulloch realized it had been a long time since someone was genuinely concerned for his wellbeing.

"When will you leave for Austria, son?" Carr released his grip on the youngster.

"In a few days. There are several loose ends I need to tie up first," Bulloch was mostly thinking of Petra.

WIEDEN DISTRICT, WIEN

Reading from the list they had prepared Ros was pleased at how many individuals they had come up with on such short notice over coffee at a small cafe. Getting the home addresses to go along with the names had taken a few phone calls but Sylvie knew just who to ring up. Sylvie was definitely a resourceful co-conspirator. As they climbed the steps leading up to the first address on the list, Ros patted her new partner on the back.

"Listen sister, you did a great job digging up all of the details," Ros complimented her one last time for luck.

"Thanks kid," Sylvie nibbled at the eraser on her pencil. "But this still seems like a long shot. These old bats aren't going to spill the goods. At least not to us foreigners."

"You've been off the society pages a long time, haven't you?" Ros chuckled.

"With no regrets," Sylvie shivered at the memory.

Ros reached out with a gloved hand and drew Sylvie close. "Follow my lead. We're going in asking about Vienna high society and we're coming out with the dirt on what their husbands are up to."

"These girls are pretty sharp and suspicious. They're not the dizzy types you're used to," Sylvie gestured over her shoulder with the pencil.

"Perhaps, but they also will be worried and anxious. These are crazy days and they'll die for the chance to share their feelings as long as we can ease them onto the subject." Ros used her hands to illustrate a broadsheet headline. "*Brave Women of Vienna Hold Up Noble Traditions in Time of Crisis.* Besides, do you have any better ideas?"

"Nope." Sylvie put the pencil over her ear. "What do we have to lose."

"That's the spirit," Ros stopped to check the address on the notepad one more time. "Frau von Gloustenau, straight ahead."

CNS BUREAU
QUARTIER DE L'OPERA DISTRICT, PARIS

Clarence's typewriter was reaching a staccato climax as his fingers pounded the keys faster to finish the last graph in the article. New York was waiting on the copy and he needed to get it cabled back post haste. Clarence noticed Tucker was strolling by and wondered what the little man wanted now? Despite the curiosity, Clarence did his best not to show interest in his bureau chief's approach until Tucker was unavoidably standing before him.

"Have you been reading Ros' stuff?" Clarence stayed focused on typing.

"Y'up," Tucker was mostly lonely with so many of his reporters out of town.

"Looks like this Austrian dust-up is building into a real page-turner," Clarence decided to tweak the poor boy.

"Don't you get any ideas about heading for Vienna, Clarence. I need you here," Tucker positioned himself over Clarence's typewriter.

Clarence looked up for the first time in the conversation. "I have no intention of running off to Vienna."

"That's right," Tucker puffed out his chest.

"Naw, I'll be off to Rome now that I have this assignment done for Harry," Clarence pulled the last sheet of paper from the typewriter roller and stood up.

"What?" If all his reporters were gone, Tucker would be forced to pick up the slack himself. That's not why he became a bureau chief.

"My Italian contacts are all nervous and wanting to talk. I'll be riding down to Rome on the next train. We'll need the Musso angle. You know how much Harry likes Musso... comic relief," Clarence reached for his ascot.

"No, I won't have it," Tucker tried to stall Clarence's departure. "Listen, you'll need to clear this whole wild goose chase with Harry first. Otherwise, I need you here."

Clarence snatched a cable from the far side of the desk, which he shoved into Tucker's hand on the way out. "Done deal. Got Harry's okay right here, Tuck."

PROVINCIAL HOUSE, GRAZ

Professor Dadieu strode purposely up to the front doors with two aides following close behind him. The next few days would be crucial and there was much preparation to be done if they were to consolidate power. In the satchels he and his men carried was information to be shared with the good city burgher. Why in these days of action there had to be so much paperwork bewildered Dadieu. He was a man of science and was no stranger to documentation. Yet every moment he devoted to forms and communiqués were moments stolen from the cause. Someone inside the building was observant since the pudgy, well-fed burgher rushed out of the doors to greet him.

"Professor, I heard the news from Vienna," the burgher called out. "Our people are in the cabinet at last."

"Not quite, my friend," Dadieu cautioned with an upraised hand. "Schuschnigg might yet be so obstinate as to refuse the Führer's demands. In that case I have received instructions. If we are not included in the cabinet as we are due then our people must be ready to act decisively."

The burgher shuddered visibly at the implications of acting decisively. "I want no part of violence. I am a civil servant!"

Dadieu patted the older man on the shoulder in a patronizing way. "Don't fret. My people will take care of everything. All that is required of you is to make sure at the proper time there is no official interference with what must be done."

"How will I know when is proper time?" the Burgher had never participated in such a thing before.

"That's why I am here." The hand that had patted the burgher's shoulder now turned the official back toward the building.

"What if Schuschnigg declares martial law and sends the army? Have you thought about that?" the burgher had only so much faith in radical academics.

"The chancellor doesn't have the will," Dadieu explained with complete confidence. "If I am not mistaken, there will be plenty of time before Schuschnigg can get enough troops here to hinder us. We will declare Styria national socialist and appeal directly to Berlin for support. It's all planned out."

"The plans that will stymie Schuschnigg are in there," the little politician pointed at Dadieu's case.

"Of course, of course... we have accounted for everything," Dadieu needed the burgher to be calm and to play his role without disruption. "Rest assured, our people will be in power. The only variable is how soon."

CAFÉ LOUVRE – INNERE STADT, WIEN

There was little more for Endicott and Roland to do but sit and wait at their little table. Schuschnigg and his ministers had been at it all day and into the night. If no one was spilling their guts then matters had to be serious. Being kept in the dark was eating at Endicott but the mannered little Brit was taking it all in stride despite the unusually tense crowd in cafe that night. Endicott took a deep gulp from his pint of beer and checked his wristwatch again. The only consolation was he saw Sanderson walking up with a full bottle of scotch and three small glasses.

"A completely useless day," Sanderson dropped the bottle to the tabletop with a thud.

"A completely useless day," Roland chimed in.

"Finally give up, did you?" Endicott wondered what had taken him so long.

"They're still in there debating. It was after nine o'clock and they were no where close to a resolution," Sanderson sank into a chair.

"The last rumor that flew through here is that there is an open phone line between the ministers and Berlin. Schuschnigg proposes, old Adolph refuses," Roland thought that one rang fairly true.

"An hour before that someone ran through and said old Kurt had told Hitler to stuff it," Endicott should have laid a bet on that one.

Sanderson poured himself a stiff shot of scotch. "Appears as if I've been in the wrong place. Our tidy little group heard none of this while waiting outside the Chancellery."

Deciding to switch libations Endicott poured some scotch. "Damn I wish I knew what cards were on the table."

"Anyone hear from the girls?" Sanderson looked around the cafe.

"I was about to ask you that myself," Roland checked the label on the scotch bottle. "I'm starting to worry about our intrepid femmes."

"Don't bother, little man," Sylvie's voice came at them from not far away. "Now if you want to buy two hard-working dames a drink, that's different."

Sylvie and Ros hurried up to the table in high spirits as they tossed their coats on nearby hooks and sat themselves down at the table.

"Allow me, ladies," Sanderson happily leaned over to the bar for fresh. "Sounds like you might have good news to share."

"That we do," Sylvie confirmed while settling into her chair. "And you can thank the kid for coming up with the caper."

"What caper? What have you two been up to all day?" Endicott wasn't sure he was going to like the answer.

"Getting the story my grizzled friend," Ros raised her fist victoriously. "Roland's tip about Hitler putting the screws to Schuschnigg was right on the money. It's real. Berlin wants Nazis added to all the major cabinet ministries, pardons for all convicted agitators, economic concessions – pretty much complete capitulation or the tanks roll."

"Holy crap," Endicott pounded the table. "What else did you two get?"

"Schuschnigg is trying to dodge and wiggle his way out of the noose – calling Mussolini for support, cabling Britain, you name it – but no help is coming. This could go on all night but that's what's on the table. You can read in print tomorrow morning," Ros leaned back in her chair as Sanderson poured scotch into her glass.

"And what *sources* did you ladies get on record for confirmation?" Roland posed the crucial question.

"The wives. We went out and visited with the good fraus of government officials. Ros thought it up," Sylvie raised her class to the kid.

Endicott confiscated the half-drained bottle of scotch as he rose to his feet to retrieve his coat and hat. "I'll be damned. Wish I had thought of that. Folks, I'm going back to my hole to lick my wounds."

11. THREATS

A national socialist rally in the streets of Vienna

FEBRUARY 19, 1938
SPECIAL TO CONSOLIDATED NEWS
BY ROSALIND TALMADGE

VIENNA – The delicate balance in Europe shifted this week as Austrian chancellor Kurt Schuschnigg was forced into making serious concessions to Germany's Adolph Hitler. Three days ago the Austrian head-of-state gave into demands made by Hitler during a secret meeting on Feb. 12 at the German leader's Berchesgarden retreat. Under threat of invasion Austria's council of ministers deliberated all day on Wednesday until the wee hours of Thursday before finally agreeing to add members of the previously banned Austrian Nazi Party to plum cabinet posts, including the interior and foreign ministries.

Now in charge of the Vienna police and internal security forces as interior minister is Dr. Seyss-Inquart, previously councilor of state. Seyss-Inquart's first official action in office was to order police not to interfere with national socialist political activities. His second official action was to take the night train to Berlin to receive instructions from his German masters.

Chancellor Schuschnigg also agreed to grant amnesty to more than three thousand local Nazi party members – seven hundred of them in jail and twenty-five hundred awaiting trial on various charges including everything from civil disorder to treason. Two of the most prominent of these jailed party members include Dr. Tavs and Dr. Leopold, both arrested last month on charges of planning to overthrow the government. Both men are to be expelled to Germany.

In a public statement yesterday German ambassador Franz von Papen called the February *agreement* between Austria and Germany the first step to the establishment of a Central European Commonwealth of Nations under Germany's leadership.

The mood here in the capital following the announcement of the concessions is mixed. National socialist supporters are jubilant while middle-of-the-road citizens fret over what will happen next and trade unionists openly speak of armed resistance. While the streets of Austria's major cities remain calm, it is the calm before the storm in anticipation of Hitler's speech before the Reichstag scheduled for tomorrow.

CNS HEADQUARTERS, NEW YORK

Lasky poured Des and himself a stiff shot of bourbon... and why not? He was happy. Lasky could count on his fingers and toes the times his reporters made him happy during the last ten years. And here was that pain-in-the-rear Talmadge showing get-up-and-go he hadn't seen in years. Lasky had been sure she was all talk but the gal was giving Walter a run for the money on the Continent. She'd demand a raise, and he would give her one later after a fight, but he was paying her dirt anyway so who cared.

"Damn if Talmadge didn't come through," Lasky toasted his good fortune.

"I told you she was good, chief." Lasky would take too much of the credit if Des didn't pull him back to earth on occasion.

"You've been soft on her all along," Lasky dunked his hand at Des. "I wasn't so sure she could pull it off. But now we have a rising star on our hands so let's keep her busy. Let's get her to play up the street angle big. If there's going to be an explosion, that's where it will go off. Somebody's thug is going to break someone else's thug's head. That kind of copy will sell newsprint. And see if you can arrange for some on-the-scene camera action. Photos will help when Vienna blows up."

"There's something you're forgetting, boss," Des had only the best interests of the syndicate in mind.

"What?" Lasky refilled his glass because he could see what was coming.

"Now is the time to sign off on a raise for our girl. Do you want to lose her to UP or CBS?" Des had seen it happen before.

"Not yet! I don't want to spoil her," Lasky slammed the bourbon bottle onto the desk. "We have to keep her hungry. Just tell her I'm pushing through the paperwork as fast as I can but that you're increasing her expense account immediately."

"You never gave Ros an expense account, boss." Des found Harry was consistent that way.

"Even better! Give her one – standard starting balance. That should keep Talmadge happy for a while." No way Lasky was going to spoil his new star until he was sure she could keep the scoops coming.

"You're a real peach, Harry," Des muttered as he finished off his bourbon. He would see to it that Ros' expense account was a little sweeter than Harry's usual skinflint rate.

FEBRUARY 20, 1938
SCHWARZENBERGPLATZ, WIEN

The stunned expression on people's faces is what struck Ros the most. Like they were watching some unexpectedly wretched theater performance – too fascinated to go, too horrified to stay. Just normal people gawking at the chanting national socialists marching by: *One people, one Reich, one leader.* Mixed in the crowd was a stoic bunch casting angry stares yet none of them threw a fist or a stone at the noisy Nazis parading down the avenue.

"A lot more peaceful than I expected," Ros tapped a pencil against her notebook.

"It won't be Hamburg in thirty-two but these sods will get ugly soon," Sanderson had gotten fairly familiar with the fascist playbook by now.

"How soon?" As long as the oracle was dispensing predictions Ros figured she might as well ask.

"After old Adolph's speech tonight. None them want to upstage the top man. No, they're going to wait to hear how Hitler sets the stage. Then look out," Sanderson was sure the windowpanes of many merchants would be shattered during the next twenty-four hours.

"So this is a pep rally," Ros finally felt she was catching on.

"What are you going on about?" She had him confused again with still another odd reference.

For people who shared the same language Ros was learning there was plenty these Brits were clueless about. "I'm sure you have a much more charming name for them but back in school, right before a big athletic event, a pep rally is when the whole student body turns out to pump up the home team."

"Oh quite. I for one would like to see you all pumped up," Sanderson flirted shamelessly.

In return Ros directed the business end of her pencil at him. "Down boy. You and I have work to do."

"You are a hard woman," Sanderson regretted not saying *nasty* instead.

"Cheer up, brother. I'll buy you a drink later," Ros tried to cheer up the boy since he looked so sad. "Right now let's pull some of these people aside for a few questions."

ALTSTADT, LINZ

After a few days Bulloch felt comfortable in getting around the city on foot and by tram. Despite being the third-largest metropolis in Austria, Linz didn't feel all that big. The Danube cut right through the city and the industrial east side seemed like an entirely different community. The old town he was walking through now had its own separate charm distinct from the rest of the neighborhoods. None of the districts hit you as connected. Someone at the embassy had once said that Linz was a lot like Chicago. That was a laugh though. Linz may be a big commercial hub for these parts but it had nothing on Chicago in the *big* department.

What he confirmed from his last trip to the country was that all rail traffic heading to Czechoslovakia through Austria came straight through Linz. A few well-placed aerial bombs and no panzers would be taking the easy route to the border on railroad cars. A regular visitation by Czech bombers could keep the rail lines out of commission indefinitely.

The avenues were full of people cheering the recent Nazi-friendly changes in government. Bulloch knew from old newsreel reports that Linz was Hitler's hometown but this was ridiculous. Brandishing the swastika and singing these political songs was still illegal. Bulloch was sure these demonstrations would only get worse after Hitler's radio speech. That's when he remembered what that old Austrian fellow had to say while driving Bulloch around. *The whole country was going to hell.*

Bulloch had been reading the local papers and noted how the unions had pledged their support for Schuschnigg three days ago. The chancellor was fighting to counter-balance his concessions to Hitler by bringing in the banned Social Democratic Party on an equal footing with the Austrian Nazis. That was political dynamite that could turn Austria into another Spain. If enough of the workers were armed they might hold off the Germans long enough for Stalin to intervene with military aid. Hell, the Czechs might even make it easy for the Soviets to get more guns in. That would be one hell of a mess.

SCHWARZENBERGPLATZ, WIEN

Another street demonstration, another nondescript taxi parked nearby just inside an alley. This time they were observing Nazi marchers but at least they could do so in obscurity from the shadows. Glanz still did not know why Skubl had dragged him out into the middle of this street theater. He had a mind to resign due to the installment of their new interior minister and getting stuck out here only intensified the desire to pack it in.

"What good are we doing out here? This is a waste of time." Glanz had seen his fill of national socialists.

"I appreciate the relative privacy, my friend. Did you know our phones are tapped?" Skubl wasn't supposed to know.

"No. When did that happen?" Glanz had expected such insults but not so swiftly.

"Associates of Seyss-Inquart... yesterday," Skubl had learned form one of his informants. "The orders came from a branch office of the German secret police that was just opened here in Vienna. Every conversation is being recorded on gramophone records."

"I don't suppose you would allow me to smash those records," Glanz knew exactly where the equipment was housed. "I could be quite discreet."

His lieutenant's zeal pleased Skubl but Schuschnigg had forbidden any such action. The chancellor still believed in a political solution. "Starting immediately you and I answer directly to the chancellor but unofficially. Our orders for now are not to interfere with Seyss-Inquart or national socialist activities."

"Does the chancellor know about these taps?" Glanz was not ready to let the matter go.

"Yes, I told him myself. He has his own plan for dealing with the situation and no he did not confide in me the details," Skubl paused to hand Glanz an envelope with names. "For now we watch the watchers – trusted men only. Use discretion but build a record of their activities. Perhaps one day we can use it as evidence of illegal activity."

"Understood. You realize it won't be long before they get their people close enough to make such work difficult," and Glanz guessed would necessitate many more rendezvous in Skubl's cab network.

"Keep your group off the books. There is enough lunacy going on in the streets to supply sufficient alibis to answer questions about what our people are up to." Skubl would embrace the dictum: *in chaos there is opportunity*.

"Speaking of which, the intersection choke points you requested have been set up and manned. We can break up and separate opposing groups of marchers if they get too close," and break in a few skulls, Glanz anticipated.

Excellent but do not disrupt the demonstrations. Let them fly their swastikas and banners. Only shut them down if they turn violent of their own accord. If they overreach too quickly we can use that to our advantage," Skubl ordered, hoping the Nazis would be that stupid.

CAFÉ LOURVRE – INNERE STADT, WIEN

This was the first occasion that they could remember where the establishment was wholly vacant. Perhaps the locals knew more about what Hitler was about to say in his speech than the learned foreign correspondents huddling at the bar close to the radio. It was obvious the citizenry didn't feel inclined to share the experience in public or at the cafe.

"Appears the good Viennese prefer to listen from home," Roland gathered Hitler's children were few in this neighborhood.

"Who but us wants to be in a crowded theater when everyone knows someone is going to set a fire?" Endicott sounded like a country jurist.

"You boys are going soft," Sylvie teased the lazy louts. "I know some partisan beer gardens in particular neighborhoods that will be full of loud angry people. I thought about joining in but realized I'd never hear what Hitler was barking about."

"Who's going to translate the loud little man for us tonight? I can never keep up with him when he gets rolling," Ros wasn't sure the German chancellor understood good grammar.

"I'll do the honors," Sanderson reckoned it was his turn.

"Don't edit out the nasty parts like you did last time, pal," Endicott had gotten into a fix with an editor over that translation.

"You caught onto that, did you?" Sanderson chuckled. "I was only smoothing out the rough edges."

"Yeah... I catch you smoothing again and you'll wake up in the back alley with a headache and it won't be from a hangover," Endicott brandished a fist.

"Testy, aren't we?" Sanderson wouldn't mind some fisticuffs withe American.

Roaring applause rose from the radio speaker. The proprietor behind the counter calmly walked over to the radio and turned up the volume. Despite the occasional static Hitler's voice boomed out from the speaker.

"The usual opening platitudes, assertions and running on about German uniqueness and greatness," Sanderson leaned in over the bar to listen. "Oh but this is new!"

"What?" Ros hated his dramatic pauses.

"The fellow just pledged to defend all ten million ethnic Germans in Europe," Sanderson had to concentrate harder on the broadcast as Roland whistled loudly.

"There went the line in the sand," Endicott gulped down a shot of whiskey.

"Schuschnigg and Beneš are toast," Sylvie had not expected the Czechs to get the Adolph treatment so soon.

"Wait, wait..." Sanderson requested as he strained to hear. "It gets better, or rather worse. He just declared that every German in Austria and Czechoslovakia must have self-determination."

"I was wondering when he would finally get around to the Czechs," Ros realized Austria must be a done deal to Hitler now."

Sanderson was having trouble keeping up with the translation. "It is in the long run intolerable... for a self-respecting world power to know that fellow countrymen across the frontier... are continually undergoing the greatest hardship because of their sympathy, their feeling for union...

their common experience… their point of view… which they share with the whole people."

"Look out Prague and Warsaw," Endicott imagined that being on the receiving end of that threat was like knowing some crazy bastard coming for your throat.

FEBRUARY 21, 1938
INNERE STADT, WIEN

Shattering glass ripped the early morning quiet, replacing calm with the sharp tonality of aggression. The window of the antiquarian bookstore collapsed into hundreds of jagged shards around the Fatherland Front placard propped up in the main display. That the hated symbol of Schuschnigg remained standing left the two teenage provocateurs furious. There were more Schuschnigg loyalists to visit and limited time before the streets filled with citizens who could identify them. With a nod both reached into the sacks slung over the shoulders of their long coats to grab additional rocks to hurl. This time the Fatherland Front placard crumpled with a direct hit from the volley and went down. Satisfied, the boys turned to run up the street – swastika armbands on their sleeves.

HOTEL GRANBEL – INNERE STADT, WIEN

Ros bolted upright in bed. The boom that awakened her sounded like it had exploded right there in the room. Leaping from the bed, she rushed to the window and pulled the curtains. Ros saw the jewelry store just down the street going up in flames.

"That's getting a little close." The day was getting off to a much earlier start than she had planned but it went with the job. Ros ran to the wardrobe and began yanking out clothes to wear.

ALTSTADT, LINZ

Bulloch luckily had planned an early checkout from his modest hotel. Traveling out of a light duffle bag was a must for quick departures. Not ten minutes after paying his bill and selecting a route Bulloch was dodging out of the way of an angry mob. The streets were full like the night before but the mood had gone from jubilant to ugly. Seeing crowds surging down the street yelling *Heil Hitler* didn't surprise him anymore. But the number of German-issue SA-style uniforms blatantly worn out in the open was new. Bulloch had listened to Hitler's speech on a tavern radio. Whatever disenchantment these people felt at the world and their government, Hitler had tapped into that well of anger and lit a match. These folks were looking for trouble.

The attaché watched helpless as some of the uniformed types roughed up an old shopkeeper inside his store. Bulloch had to fight the urge to jump to the old man's aid. Busting a few heads would be a pleasure but for now Bulloch had to circle around the mob and get to the train station. Hopefully the line to Graz was still running.

TROLLEY STATION, WIEN

Hurrying the last few steps to street level, Ros found herself smack in the middle of a street brawl. Popular front supporters and Nazi party members were at each other's throats. The clash was spilling out from the middle of the street onto the sidewalk at her feet. At least on this day, on this block, the Nazis were outnumbered for once. Taking notes she realized the pro-Nazi marchers had been confronted by the larger mob of workers who were making a point of pulling down every Nazi flag, banner and armband they could get their hands on. The street was strewn with the trampled regalia. Ros didn't see any guns or knives but there were plenty of clubs and fists flying. Lucky for her, Ros looked up just in time to duck a bottle thrown in her direction.

CHANCELLERY, WEIN

At least there was one place in the city the police were defending in force. Good thing too given the size of the pro-Hitler crowd pressing up against the cordon. Getting to the seat of government had been a major chore for Sanderson. Vienna was a mess: no taxis, public transportation blocked... thank goodness his shoes were sensible. All along the way he had seen scant evidence of the police. Either they were overloaded or they had been told to stay home. These were the first government barricades he had seen. Showing his press credentials to the nearest officer netted Sanderson nothing more than an indifferent grunt. Looking past the uniformed man, Sanderson recognized a police district inspector and waved. The inspector called to the officer and instructed that Sanderson pass behind the line.

"Thank you. I'm glad to see a friendly face," Sanderson felt a little lucky for the first time that day.

"You won't find many," the revierinspektor continued observing the barricades for trouble.

"You brought a lot of friends today. Expecting trouble?" Sanderson focused on where the inspector was looking.

The revierinspektor found the question amusing. "Not from this lot. They are loud but they are not stupid. The chancellery is off limits. We lost Dolfuss that way. This time no one gets close to the chancellor."

"What are your orders?" Every detail would help Sanderson with his report.

"Which ones?" the revierinspektor had half a mind to discuss the conflicting instructions they were working under.

"How about the orders you plan to follow," Sanderson could tell the man wanted to speak his mind.

"Oh those. Don't interfere with lawful demonstrations. Ignore illegal brandishing of outlawed political symbols... for now. Ignore incidental personal assaults... for now. Do what is necessary to keep all crowds away from Federal buildings," the revierinspektor thumbed in the direction of the chancellery behind him.

Sanderson penciled the comments into his notes. "And what would *you* like to do?"

The revierinspektor began rapping the business end of his nightstick against his free palm. "Teach this trash some manners. Then retire."

CHANCELLOR'S OFFICE
CHANCELLERY, WIEN

The view through the window was dreadful. All his efforts to bring stability and diffuse tension were being ripped to shreds in the streets. The Nazis were forcing him to react in one of two ways. He could call in federal troops, rule as a dictator and risk invasion. Or he could open up the matter to a vote of the people, risk civil war *and* risk invasion. The problem was Schuschnigg was neither a dictator nor a democrat. Standing there watching the demonstrations he found neither option palatable

"The violence is not subsiding," Schuschnigg looked to the dutiful Skubl for advice.

"No sir, it is accelerating," Skubl needed an answer now. " Minister Seyss-Inquart has forbidden the police to interfere with these demonstrations except in the most outlandish of circumstances. We will lose control of the streets unless the handcuffs are removed from our hands."

Skubl was correct and Schuschnigg heard a resounding – *enough* – speak to him from somewhere, which led the chancellor to make a decision for good or for ill.

"These people go too far," Schuschnigg slammed a fist into his palm. "I won't see them abuse the nation any further. I'll sign a decree, effective tomorrow: all meetings and parades are forbidden except for certified members of the Vaterlandich Front. How long do you estimate it will take to cool these hot heads down?"

"Three to four weeks should do," Skubl added several weeks for good measure.

"Then the decree will run for four weeks," Schuschnigg ordered with satisfaction.

PRATERSTRASSE, WIEN

New York City had its nasty side but Ros had never felt this close to her own mortality. The raw excitement of kneeling behind an impromptu barricade and interviewing a young unionist holding his block against Hitler's hordes was intoxicating. All she knew of him was that his name was Dieter, his breathing was fast and his durable work clothes were marked with blood, grease and dirt.

"The damned Nazis think they own the streets but not this street," Dieter lifted a fist.

"How many of your people have been injured?" Ros estimated in the dozens.

"Too many for me to count," Dieter was too busy with the fight to know.

The lull was shattered when several shots rang out. Dieter instinctively pushed Ros to the pavement as the bullets overshot them. "Stay down!"

Without further hesitation Dieter ran off along the barricade to rally his comrades. Feeling too exposed on the front line Ros crawled to a safer vantage point at the entrance to an alley nearby. Ros made it to the alley, rose upon her knees and leaned back against the brick wall. Although safe, Ros looked down at her outfit and realized the oil stains were never coming out. Next to her in the alley were several workers armed with clubs and heavy tools. A woman clutching a blunt hammer slowly edged to the alley entrance to peer out onto the street. The woman satisfied her curiosity just long enough for a bullet to cleave a nasty wound along her forehead. She collapsed back into the alley as another bullet kicked up debris next to her limp body. Horrified, Ros rushed over to drag the fallen woman back into the alley. The wound was bleeding profusely and Ros figured she had to act swiftly or the woman would bleed to death. Ros shed her coat and tore off her blouse sleeve to use as a bandage to the woman's forehead. "Ah hell, I need help here!"

FOREIGN MINISTRY, ROMA

The pushy American wasn't taking no for answer. This was the third time he had presented himself to her. The reporter had some connections or else he would never have made it as far as her desk, which meant she had to be somewhat polite. But he had gone too far so she stood to accentuate her authority.

"Senor, your persistence is commendable, but the answer is unchanged. Count Ciano is not taking interviews on any subjects. If or when that changes you will be contacted," Carlotta delivered the rejection out as diplomatically as possible.

Clarence had to chuckle. He hadn't gotten a brush-off like this since his first wife. This lady would take some deft tenderizing.

"Oh the count will *want* to talk with me," Clarence was playing the big shot.

"And why would that be?" Carlotta could see no reason why the foreign minister would waste his time on this pudgy newsman?

"I almost married his cousin," Clarence played the lie with a straight face.

"The claim caught her completely off guard. What had been an annoyance had now grown into a problem. The wrong decision could mean her job and a lot worse. Then Carlotta noticed the man was wearing a wedding ring and her confidence returned.

"Oh really," she pointed at the marriage band. "What does your wife say about that?"

"She's French. Need I say more?" Clarence had to admire the tenacity of this gatekeeper. Most women he had met in such positions were not the loveliest of specimens but this lady wore her years well. Maybe he could use that. "Tell you what, let me take you to dinner so I can explain it to you."

Carlotta considered the proposal carefully. Agreement would give her more time to check the man's credentials, which would dictate how best to deal with him. Turning to her desk she grabbed a pencil and scribbled down the name and address of a discreet and charming bistro not far away. "Very well. Meet me at this place at seven o'clock."

HOTEL GRANBEL – INNERE STADT, WIEN

Sanderson paced up and down the small lobby. He had stopped caring about drawing the attention of the staff and hotel patrons because Ros was late… very late. She was two hours overdue and not in her room. Every time someone came through the entrance he looked up with hope only to see some frumpy little businessman or visiting scholar. Feeling a burst of cool air from the entrance he almost didn't turn to look but turn he did. There Ros was… looking positively bedraggled. Her blouse was streaked with blood and oil, a sleeve was torn off and her face was smudged with grease.

"Ros, what happened?" Sanderson rushed over to her to help.

She greeted him with a blank stare. Then without a word Ros slowly wrapped her arms around Sanderson, lowered her head on his shoulder and began to weep.

12. DIGGING IN

German sympathizers take over the city of Graz

FEBRUARY 24, 1938
JOSEFSTADT DISTRICT, WIEN

He would be scolded by London for calling the barren and tattered second-floor apartment the Vienna Bureau of the Daily Telegraph had they known. Sanderson needed an outpost closer to the government where he could crank out dispatches. This location was also fairly central to the inner city and the outlining districts. A plus was the proximity to the university where he could find bi-lingual students to hire for quick translations or as stringers. If he brought the students in they all required a base to operate from so his tiny flat had to go. Sealing the deal on this new space was the abundant window area facing the intersection below. The extra light was a blessing should the electricity fail and he was on deadline.

Furniture was something Sanderson would have to work on. All there was time to buy was the well-used yet still comfortable settee, a couple of wood chairs, a bed, plus the pock marked yet solid old dining table he was using for a variety of purposes. If nothing else it was long and solid – his command center he chuckled while pounding the keys on his portable typewriter.

Austrian chancellor Kurt Schuschnigg finally stood firm this week to the radical political elements bedeviling his administration. In addition to prohibiting all public political activity by groups other than his own Fatherland Front, Herr Schuschnigg forced his new interior minister Dr. Seyss-Inquart, with close ties to Berlin, to address the country on national radio to urge Austrian national socialists to cool down the violence of the last weeks. Seyss-Inquart ordered everything from the singing of Nazi bar songs, to flouting heil Hitler salutes, barred from display in public...

The insistent rapping on the door finally grabbed his attention. Sanderson got up from his chair to attend to source of the interruption. Wrenching open the door he found himself face-to-face with Sylvie who did not wait for an invitation to enter.

"Sorry to bother 'ya," she tossed her coat at him while passing on the way to the sofa.

"Not at all. Always glad for a diversion," he responded politely to her fait accompli.

"A little sparse in here don't you think?" Sylvie looked the large apartment over and sat down on the sofa.

Pulling up a chair to the settee, Sanderson sat down facing the seat back. "Rather hard to get a decorator in these days. Can you recommend someone?"

"Oh behave," Sylvie settled back on the uneven cushion as best she could. "How's your girlfriend? No one has seen her in days."

"First time Ros has ever had someone die in her arms. She took it hard," Sanderson had first hand experience in that regard.

"Didn't stop her from filing a story," Sylvie didn't think the girl was that poor off.

"That was before the adrenaline wore off. You could ask her yourself," Sanderson wondered what Sylvie was really up to.

"If I could find the girl I would. She's gotten scarce. Why do you think I came here to ask you?" He was a smart boy and she bet he could figure it out.

"Why indeed?" Sanderson had seen many of Sylvie's double entendre interrogations.

"Aren't you two an item yet?" Sylvie jumped to the point.

"Is that a professional or personal query?" Sanderson played obtuse for fun.

"Entirely professional," Sylvie found him insufferable at this game.

"My arse!" Sanderson laughed in her face. "And if you must pry the answer is no."

Sylvie's lips betrayed a discreet smile of satisfaction. She got to her feet, wrapped her fingers gently around his arm and pulled him up. "Oh hon. C'mon, take me to dinner and tell me all about it. I know a couple of places around here that should be open."

MARCH 1, 1938
GRAZ

He found it hard to believe that anywhere in Austria could be worse than Linz. Then Bulloch spent his first few days in Graz. The city felt like it had already seceded and joined with Germany. Thinking back on his family tree, Bulloch knew something of secession and saw some resemblances. The good citizens had been told to put away their swastika armbands, flags and cherished photographs of Adolph Hitler and now they were ready to lynch somebody.

A group of male university students caught his eye as he strolled by them. They were huddled outside a bakery shop like a football team discussing their next play. Bulloch easily figured out which one was the leader of this squad – an imposing youngster with a receding hairline who held the rapt attention of his teammates.

"Trust me, it won't be long," the ring leader assured his men.

A lanky companion argued his opinion passionately. "With a few more hours we could have completely taken over the province."

From a quiet and stout looking fellow came a sensible comment. "No, Berlin is not ready. There are no forces on the border yet to assist us. We could take all of Styria but Schuschnigg would have sent in the army. I'm not ready to be a martyr yet."

"Exactly," the leader added. "We will have our day. A few weeks won't matter. Austria will be joined with Germany. There is no reason to act rashly."

"You are all soft, worse than the old conservative bastards who lost the Great War. You don't know how to fight," the lanky fellow accused his comrades.

That was when the group grew aware of Bulloch and stared at him menacingly. Bulloch could have taken the bunch in short order but he wasn't done in Graz quite yet and couldn't afford trouble. So he raised his right arm in a truncated Nazi party salute for as long as he could stomach. The gestured defused the moment. The students laughed boldly and patted themselves on the back. Bulloch felt dirty and walked on.

CITY JAIL, ROMA

First a hot bath was in order... then several bottles of red wine with some kick. Ten days in a cell had left Clarence incredibly parched, rumpled, and smelling like a hobo from Hoboken. Even his new best friend, the Italian ambulance chaser escorting him out of the jail building, was keeping a respectful distance. Clarence couldn't blame him. What concerned the reporter most was how the hell his little caper had gone so wrong. Maybe his wife was right about no other woman wanting him but her.

"Senore, what took so long to get me out?" Clarence looked over to his patron.

"Be pleased you got out at all Mister Clarence," Ansoldi scolded the reckless American. "I don't believe they knew what they wanted to charge you with. Although attempting to influence a state official is a very serious--

"--She's a secretary," Clarence pointed out in his defense.

"Yes, but the secretary to the foreign minister, my friend. You could have disappeared for a very long time. Luckily you have many friends in Rome," Ansoldi's contribution to the man's release had been filing paperwork.

"Thank God," Clarence counted his blessings. "What's next?"

"That's the good news. The possible charges have gone from espionage, diminishing to bribery of a state official and finally now have been explained away as an ill-considered romantic overture. This is Italia after all so the latter is not sanctionable. However, you must produce a formal written letter of apology to the lady and another to Count Ciano. Then you must leave the country immediately," Ansoldi implored him.

"That all?" Clarence grumbled... Italy was getting much too serious for his taste.

"You most behave," Ansoldi added sternly as they reached the bottom of the steps.

"I've always hated that last one," Clarence observed honestly.

The sidewalk newsstand caught the reporter's attention. He'd been out of touch for too long and was hungry for news. Stacks of local broadsheets sucked Clarence closer like metal to a magnet. The headlines were all pretty much the same: *Italian Ambassador Warns Vienna to Ease Tensions.*

"Damn!" He had a lot of catching up to do.

"What?" Ansoldi asked, wondering what the American was going on about now.

Ignoring his Italian attorney, Clarence fumbled in his pockets for change, paid the newsstand owner and grabbed the three most prominent newspapers. Thrusting the papers under his left arm, Clarence looked up at Ansoldi. "Thank you from the bottom of my heart for all of your help, senore. I know what I have to do and I hope I won't be needing your services anytime soon... and send the bill to that address in New York I gave you."

Before Ansoldi could comment, Clarence shook his hand and hurried off. "Stay out of trouble, Mister Clarence... and don't forget those letters."

The newsstand owner looked up and shrugged his shoulders as he went back to organizing his newspaper stacks.

"Americano," Ansoldi raised both hands upward in dismay.

MARCH 3, 1938
JOSEFSTADT DISTRICT, WIEN

Sanderson patted down his jacket pockets in performing his regular ritual when leaving the building: notebook, check; pencils, check; billfold, check; keys, check. He was a third of a block away when he thought he heard a familiar voice. Glancing over his shoulder Sanderson saw Ros running up behind him. Some of the old cheer was back on her face, and that pleased him.

"What are you working on?" She had to hold onto her hat as a breeze blew through.

"Ready for another go, are we?" Sanderson was happy his yank was back. Not everyone could handle fatal carnage but what he saw on her face said that she could.

"Yes, I need to get working again... desperately," Ros wrapped her arm inside his.

"Well then I'm your man," Sanderson started on again with Ros alongside.

"I never doubted that," Ros felt lucky she had someone to lean on. "Thanks for checking in on me and for not pushing me. I needed a few days to get myself right."

"Good to see you worked through your demons." The strong grip she had on his arm suggested some more time was needed but Sanderson wasn't of a mind to complain.

"More like they worked through me," Ros went for the joke to get them off the subject. "But that's done and I'm back in the game."

"Excellent, you can tag along if you'd like," Sanderson had been off to corral an army colonel he had interviewed before.

Ros tugged him to a stop on the sidewalk. "Actually, I have a better idea."

"Oh really... let's here it, my dear," Sanderson trusted her instincts as she had been getting fabulous results.

"Remember our trade union friends?" They had visited Ros while she was taking time off.

"Who could forget that terribly intense lot," Sanderson smelled a lead approaching.

"They have ears all over the place and passed along a fat tip to me. Seyss-Inquart is going to stir the pot again. He's going to disobey Schuschnigg and allow Nazi symbols to be brandished in public. He'll do this in a pro-German address during the next few days. Want to go to Linz with me to hear a speech?" Ros terribly wanted company on the long trip.

"Aren't you full of surprises." How could Sanderson say no to an adventure with his private yank. "Of course, that sounds like a marvelous expedition."

SUBURBAN NEIGHBORHOOD, BRNO

Few of the neighbors would notice the military police escorting the uniformed officer from the modest home to a waiting Škoda sedan right after dawn. An arrest and trial were enough shame. There was no need to parade the man in handcuffs before his neighbors in full daylight. Neither did the Second Department need an audience asking delicate questions. Thankfully, there were few accused traitors to arrest. Burda could not convince the boss there was no need for him to personally attend such arrests. Yet because there were so few cases of treason, Moravec was determined that he *had* to look such men in the eyes.

"I wish you wouldn't expose yourself when we make these arrests, sir," Burda returned to an old disagreement.

"You concern is appreciated," Moravec could not argue with the logic behind the request. "But I *need* to see them for myself, to speak with them. I must know what makes a man betray his oath, his uniform, his country."

"He is Hungarian," Burda thought that fact was reason enough.

Moravec would not succumb to that frame of mind. "We do not have the luxury of thinking in such a cause-and-effect manner. He is a Czechoslovak citizen. The man has an admirable service record. What caused him to throw away loyalty to the service he served so well? We have millions of ethnic minorities in this country. If we can't trust any of them based on their heritage the republic is doomed."

"Respectfully, ethnicity has to be a factor along with financial need and everything else we look for," Burda saw a different truth. "It will take generations before the bonds to the nation are stronger than bonds to blood. But ethnic Hungarians and Poles are not what I lose sleep over. Not with Hitler giving speeches openly promising to unite ethnic German everywhere in Europe."

"I wonder whether that pledge includes the many thousands of oppressed Germans in Pennsylvania?" Moravec had been told on good authority that this American state was indeed full of people of German heritage.

Damn the old man. He always diffused a good argument with that dry humor of his. Yet behind the absurdity of the question was a cold reality. That was a Czech for you. "Give Hitler time. Austria today, us tomorrow, who knows in a couple of years."

Moravec tugged on Burda's coat sleeve and pulled him outside the house. He needed to tell the captain something important without being overheard as well as change the subject.

"I've learned that British ambassador Henderson has just delivered a discrete offer to Hitler from Prime Minister Chamberlain," Moravec lowered his voice. "Britain promises to cede territory in Africa to Germany should Hitler reduce its re-armament programs, and disavow further territorial expansion in Europe."

"Seriously?" Burda was not used to Great Britain actually making an effort to reduce tensions in Europe.

"Yes, the memorandum was delivered yesterday, and sadly, rejected by Herr Hitler immediately. Sometime today or tomorrow President Beneš will issue a statement that we will defend ourselves if attacked by Germany," Moravec had spoken with Beneš.

"Well then," Burda watched as the Škoda pulled away down the road. "The more of these traitors we root out the better."

MARCH 4, 1938
SIDEWALK CAFE, ROMA

He was done. There was no more wiggle room left... no more stalling. He was using that train ticket in his pocket tonight, Clarence reminded himself as he sipped an espresso and nibbled at his morning toast and fruit. During the past few days he had tried to get something tangible on record about what it would take for Italy to stand up for Austria but his old pals in town had gotten scarce. There was nothing more he could do but return to Paris. A portly man in a business suit sat at the next table and ordered a light breakfast from the waiter. A few minutes later Clarence realized the man was saying something while skimming through his magazine.

"Senor," the man whispered while turning a page. "No questions, do not speak. I will say this but once. A friend does not want you to leave Italia empty-handed. You can follow what I am about to tell you to its logical conclusion from Paris. The Austrian chancellor is planning a surprise. Whether he succeeds, or fails, the attempt will complicate his position severely."

CNS HEADQUARTERS, NEW YORK CITY

He liked the kid a lot. That's why Des had run interference a couple of days for her with Harry. Her story on the union worker dying in the alley had been a tearjerker... and great copy. Stuff like that took a toll the first time around and he had told Ros to take it easy for a few days. But doing so turned Des into the middleman courier between them. Harry could never just accept the message. No, he'd have a dozen questions or orders to bellow back at Des to take care of.

"Hey Boss, you wanted to hear when Ros checked in," Des gritted his teeth and poked his head inside Lasky's door.

"Well, well, well... it's about time she got back to work."

"Have a heart, chief. You read her story that wasn't an easy situation to deal with." Harry needed a remedial course in becoming a human being, Des was sure of it.

"Old news, my friend. What has Talmadge dug up for us?" Lasky was always hungry for more.

"Remember that new Austrian interior minister taking his marching orders from Berlin?" Des always had to set the stage for Harry.

"Yeah, that Size Quart guy," Lasky struggled with these goofy Austrian names.

"Seyss-Inquart," Des gently corrected, always the copy man. "Ros says he's about to let the local Nazis out of the closet. Very hush-hush but she got a good tip. She plans to be right on top of the story should the guy actually challenge the chancellor and allow swastikas to fly openly and silent Hitler salutes to be given in public."

"Silent?" Lasky wasn't sure he had heard that right.

"Without saying the heil Hitler part," Des painted the picture for him.

"Sheesh! What's wrong with these people? Why hold back now when the whole damn camel is in the tent? What else do they have planned?" Lasky thought these Nazis were too queer for words.

Des checked his notes. "Let's see, it will be kosher to sing the German national anthem in public and to sell pictures of Adolph."

"What is this guy, a cabinet minister or a publicist?" Lasky ridiculed the Austrian minister. "Hell, he should have worked for Louis B. Mayer. I'm sure Mayer would pay better. Okay, that sounds good. You tell Talmadge to keep it up. We could use more of the labor angle, and it wouldn't hurt to get some people in the Jewish community to speak up. They have to be worried. And tell her not to forget to get some more Nazis on record. I like the impact when we get wide-eyed true believers talking."

"She's already on it, Boss. Some kind of surprise Nazi rally tomorrow in Linz: Hitler's hometown," Des had laid out the full agenda.

"I like it! Keep me posted." That Kid Talmadge was turning into gold for Lasky.

MARCH 5, 1938
HAUPTPLATZ, LINZ

If one more fat, bespectacled little fart crashed into her, Ros swore she was going to deck the bastard. Austrians were supposed to be polite and orderly but these folks were out of hand. Even the little old ladies were swinging their handbags like truncheons. Sure, the narrow little streets Sanderson was leading her along couldn't handle the flood of people pushing their way through. She understood that. But these locals were acting like they were late for a hanging. The next time she left the states Ros decided she was bringing her baseball bat along.

"Are you sure you have a clue on how to get where we're going or are we just following the crowd?" Ros was sure they were lost and he would not admit it.

"We're positively heading the correct way," Sanderson replied with total confidence as he dodged an elderly man shoved in his direction by someone else.

"You did not answer my question," Ros was sure they were following the other salmon.

"Have I yet led you astray, my dear?" She was onto him but Sanderson loathed to admit it... and would not have to now that he saw what he was searching for ahead.

"Oh brother, you're this side of J. Wellington Wimpy," Ros elbowed him on the arm.

"Another one of your daft public servants, I presume. Spare me the insults please. This street leads to the main city square – the only place big enough to contain an assembly this size," Sanderson made it sound like he had known all along.

"Fine," Ros wasn't going to apologize. "You'd think that someone would have widened the streets after all these years. What good is a city hall if you can't get there?"

"This is Europe. Unlike your pubescent confederation Europeans did not have the benefit of starting from scratch one-hundred and fifty years ago," Sanderson pointed out condescendingly."

"Lots of stuff gets knocked down with as many wars as you people inflict on each other. You'd think you folks would be smart enough to add a little progress when it came time to pick up the bricks. But no, everyone on this crazy continent builds everything back to look exactly the way it was," Ros had a dim view of European snobbery.

Sanderson had to admit that she had a point. "Does it make any difference that the first railway in Europe was built here in Linz?"

"No. Not when I can't see a thing because the streets are too small and too full of clods," Ros stiff-arming a student attempting to step in front of her.

The main square was flooded with raucous Nazi supporters as they squeezed their way in. Students had climbed upon the statue in the center of the square waving Nazi flags and banners. On a second-floor balcony a man stood pausing for the crowd to quiet down.

"Wow... there must be thousands of people here," Ros struggled to make headway.

"Tens of thousands, I'd wager," Sanderson had never seen a rally this big in Vienna.

"Look at that," Ros pointed at the tiny balcony. "That must be Seyss-Inquart."

"Yes, must be. That's the Rothaus – the city hall. Only official oratory is allowed from that balcony," Sanderson drew on his history courses at Cambridge.

Seyss-Inquart implored the crowd to quiet themselves as the interior minister leaned forward to the microphone stand.

To outsiders we say we are Germans, and we are Austrians too, and stand on Austrian soil," Seyss-Inquart raised his arms. What is Austria? The eastern march of the German nation in the Alpine and Danubian region. Austria is German, and only German!

The partisan crowd erupted in approval. They were too loud for Ros to hear enough of what Seyss-Inquart was saying so she decided a better vantage point was required.

"C'mon, we need to get closer," Ros did not wait for an answer before setting off.

"That might be a challenge," Sanderson attempted to stay close to her as she bullied her way through the surging sea of people.

"Nah. Not much different than the subway after five o'clock," Ros was meeting some resistance as she cut between the faithful. To get closer to Seyss-Inquart's second-floor perch, Ros decided raise her arm and go native. "One ruler, one Reich!"

Sanderson watched as the seas parted through the riff-raff. "My word that was a good idea."

In the minds of men, the national German Reich is already a fact. And not only a fact of cultural significance, but a fact of political significance.

Accepting that they weren't going to get any closer the reporters jotted down Seyss-Inquart's latest words while the Austrians around them shouted encouragement.

"My Lord, he's declaring Austria a German state," Sanderson finished making his notation. "This is major... an outright challenge to Schuschnigg from his own minister of the interior. The cheeky git."

The independence of Austria could only be endangered if forces should arise which sought to divert Austria from the German course, and set her against the Reich.

Ros tapped her pencil atop her notepad while digesting what she had just heard. "That's more than a challenge to old Kurt. That was a declaration of war."

13. EXPLOSION

Supporters of Chancellor Schuschnigg take to the streets

MARCH 6, 1938
SPECIAL TO THE DAILY TELEGRAPH
BY ROBIN SANDERSON

LINZ – Austria careened into violence and near civil war yesterday as the country's interior minister used a speech here before fifty thousand national socialist supporters to openly call for unification with Germany.

With Adolph Hitler's home town as a backdrop, Dr. Seyss-Inquart spoke from the city hall balcony and openly defied chancellor Kurt Schuschnigg by issuing orders legalizing the display of Nazi salutes, banners and symbols including the swastika twisted cross. Seyss-Inquart also made singing the Austrian national anthem a footnote, issuing new rules that the German national anthem may be sung in full as long as a single verse of the Austrian hymn is sung first.

Before opposing political factions in the country could raise objections Nazi stalwarts fanned out throughout the cities in mass demonstrations in support of Seyss-Inquart and union with Germany. At first the demonstrations were loud but peaceful. In Vienna, Nazi marchers avoided bastions of popular front groups opposed to Hitler as they moved along the inner city streets to the outlining districts of Mariahilferstrasse, Waehringerstrasse, Alserstrasse, Praterstrasse and Landstrasse. But as the day wore on, and the marchers grew bolder, there were violent clashes with trade unionists.

As Austria waited on an official response from chancellor Schuschnigg, local police under the authority of Seyss-Inquart seemed unable or unwilling to quell the disturbances. At least for now there were no reports of direct violence against Austrian Jews as was the pattern in upheavals in Germany in recent years. However, accounts from Graz, the second-largest city in Austria, indicate a much higher level of violence than seen elsewhere.

MARCH 8, 1938
GRAZ

The joint was coming apart. Seyss-Inquart had been bold and these Nazis in Graz were out of control. They couldn't wait for the panzers to roll in over the border and were in open revolt on their own. Dadieu and his shadow government had marched in, kicked out the legal provincial government and declared themselves German citizens. What was it with Nazis, beer halls and putsches anyway? To fit in Bulloch had *liberated* a swastika armband from a guy who wouldn't wake up for a while. The fellow had stumbled out of a bar without witnesses and Bulloch had blind-sided him with a brick. That armband was pretty close to a passport to anywhere he had wanted to go: smile, stiff arm a Nazi salute and walk on by.

All over the city Bulloch had watched the organized rounding up of political opposition: shop keepers and workers mostly. This bunch had made up their lists ahead of time. Where the people on the lists were taken to cool their heels he wasn't sure yet. All of a sudden Bulloch felt very uncomfortable hanging around watching these monkeys play. He realized it was only a matter of time before some goon started looking over the hotel ledger and asking questions in the search for spies. Radicals were always looking for spies. Bulloch figured he had better forget the play-acting and start thinking like a spy, which meant getting the hell out of town.

CHANCELLERY, WIEN

Skubl respected the chancellor's desire to find a peaceful solution but he could see no peaceful resolution to the problem facing them. The Nazis were taking over any streets not protected by barricaded workers. Seyss-Inquart had ordered the police to leave the Nazis alone and the chancellor would not call out the army worried about what Hitler would do. Schuschnigg's head was in a vise and had been since his audience with Hitler.

"Sir, we either take control of the situation soon or else we completely lose control of the country," Skubl was sympathetic, however both men had taken an oath to the nation.

"I have had enough," Schuschnigg picked up the telephone and dialed an internal number. "Send in General Jansa." After slamming the telephone back down on its cradle, Schuschnigg lifted himself up from the desk chair. "These provocations cannot be tolerated but we cannot rely on force alone. We must counter the national socialists politically as well. Their special status within the Fatherland Front is a cancer. First, I intend to elevate the social democrats to the same status."

The Germans were scared of an open fight, Skubl was sure of that. But politics was the Nazis' forte. They relished a political brawl. He wasn't sure it was wise to give them the opportunity. "That is dangerous, chancellor. Berlin will bellow that you have formed a people's front with the communists. They'll blare it out over the radio and in the newspapers."

"Let them bellow, it will avail them nothing," Schuschnigg reached for some statistical reports on his desk. "I plan to call a national plebiscite on independence. That will settle it. The estimate is that there are four-point-four million eligible voters. The social democrats can deliver one-point-four million votes, we'll carry the rural vote of one-point-five million people and the Jews are another three hundred thousand we can count on. That's more than three million votes. We'll win the referendum."

"If we can hold the country together long enough to hold a vote, sir," Skubl was pleased to see his leader baring some teeth. Schuschnigg had been thrust into power after the death of Dolfuss so wielding power was not his calling.

The door opened and Field Marshal Jansa walked in. "What is your decision, Chancellor Schuschnigg?" A few days before the Germans had called for the marshal's resignation. Someone had leaked his plan to defend the border opposite the German town of Kieferstrict and Jansa relished the thought of putting the Nazis back in their place.

" Feldmarschalleutnant, we must restore order but we must do so with a minimum show of force," Schuschnigg's plan was to measure his punches. "The boil that is festering the worst is Graz. Dadieu and his cohorts are in open rebellion. If we put them down I believe it will cow the rest of their fellow scum around the country. These Nazis are bold but they are not brave."

Skubl saw the bigger picture and smiled. No one but the Germans would argue whether the use of force to put down an open rebellion was justified. Following that up with bringing the social democrats back into government, plus the referendum on independence, should throw the pro-German movement on its heels.

"What troops have we available to send to Graz, Jansa?" Schuschnigg wanted the size of the force to be proportionate to the situation.

"It is my pleasure to report that one troop battalion, an armored car unit and a squadron of aircraft stand ready to restore peace and order to Graz, sir," Jansa had already assembled the force in anticipation of this purpose.

"Then send them immediately, feldmarschalleutnant," Schuschnigg now considered his next step. "I want Graz taken care of for I go to Tyrol tomorrow. Dr. Seyss-Inquart is not the only man who can give a speech."

MARCH 9, 1938
ROAD FROM GRAZ

Bulloch sat in the open back of a beer truck leaving Graz. He had spotted the truck making its last delivery that morning and the driver had been kind enough to accept some currency notes for the ride. Bulloch hadn't actually checked out of his hotel room not wanting to draw attention to himself. Instead he left cash behind to cover the bill. Low-flying aircraft caught Bulloch's attention as was leaning against his overnight bag. Looking up he saw a gaggle of silver Austrian Air Force Fiat CR.32 fighters roar overhead toward Graz. As the local Nazis would have more important things to worry about than him, Bulloch happily rolled the armband off his jacket.

AUSTRO-CZECH BORDER

Damn these things were fast... cramped too. There was hardly room in the nose for him to sit down. The twin-engined bomber was one of the first Tupolevs in the air force's inventory. Kopecky's senses told him the Soviet-built bomber was moving close to three hundred miles per hour. The ones built under Czech license-production would be even faster. He couldn't fathom how the communists managed to come up with such a modern design. Soviet workers were not up to the talents of their comrade aero designers, however. The ill-fitting welds and panels Kopecky saw around him would not be allowed in Czechoslovak factories – improvements that should reduce the plane's proclivity for shaking and rattling. The countryside zoomed by under the bomber's glass nose as the plane careened low through the hilly terrain at top speed. No fighter in the air force was faster, nor any pursuit plane in the inventories of Hungary, Poland or Italy. Only Germany had a sleek monoplane fighter entering service that could catch the B-71 as his friends in the air force had designated the Tupolev. While that knowledge was cause for concern, Kopecky also knew that aircraft designers at Avia were working on a low-wing fighter of their own that would balance the scales.

The prospect of the Germans crossing the border in force and annexing Austria presented the army with major concerns. As a precaution, the frontier with Austria was only now starting to be fortified. Neither were these new defenses intended to be as deep as those constructed to the north or west. The prospect of Guderian's tanks attacking the republic in force from the south as well would put a severe strain on their available tank regiments. There might not be enough men and machines to spare for the kind of retaliatory counterstrike Srom had been planning. Regardless, before Srom's tactical group met again to discuss these new challenges, Kopecky needed to survey the Austrian frontier for himself. Capka was correct... the geography was on their side. The ground below was not made for tanks.

As Kopecky thought about their options the droning of the French-designed inline engines a few feet away from his head was reassuring. It would be up to bombers like this one to control the battle of supply lines here and elsewhere. Would they have enough of them was the question.

DEJVICE DISTRICT, PRAHA

The boss had chosen a terrible time to be out of the country. From every report coming in it looked like Schuschnigg was paralyzed and Austria was falling apart. Graz was in open revolt and the streets of every major Austrian city were awash in turf battles between Nazi and leftist gangs. Burda had lost count of how many hours he and Tichy had poured into incoming reports. Moravec's network was working beautifully. Burda hoped they had not missed some critical observation or follow-up that would be obvious to Moravec. Soon he and Tichy would need to brief the president and the general staff on those observations.

With some time to spare all Burda wanted was some sausage and cabbage in some quiet corner. Tichy had told him to take a long break as nothing had changed much for hours. Twenty minutes after leaving the compound screeching tires behind him broke Burda away from his stroll. Fellow pedestrians were jumping out of the path of a vehicle as its mad man driver hard braked to the curb. Alarm turned to annoyance when Burda recognized the automobile was his own Praga with Furst at the wheel. Furst leaned over to pop open the passenger-side door.

"Scaring old women and young children is not in the duty manual," Burda was really more upset at not getting the sausage.

"I have better things to do than chase after you," Furst had heard it all before. "Get in the car, please. It's important."

"It had better be. I haven't eaten since yesterday," Burda stepped into the car and slammed the door.

Furst pushed a wrapped sandwich into Burda's chest, put the Praga in gear and sped off. "Listen. Schuschnigg has some backbone after all. He sent the army into Graz to put down the putsch."

"Are Dadieu's student brigades resisting?" Burda hoped they had.

"Who knows? Tichy sent me out after you as soon as the news came in," Furst was too busy driving to speculate.

Burda remembered his hunger and unwrapped the sandwich. "Where did this come from?"

"I'm always prepared," Furst reminded him.

"Thank God for that." Burda took a bite out of the sausage on rye.

CAFÉ LOUVRE – INNERE STADT, WIEN

The civil strife had taken a further toll on regular patrons. Sanderson admired the proprietor his tenacity for keeping the doors open during it all. The reporter also knew there was a weathered iron mallet on the other side of the bar. That small detail was enough to convince Ros the effort to get here would not be wasted. Women, he sighed to himself. One moment she was wading into the fray, the next she was worried about getting her shoes scuffed. During his time in Vienna the Café Louvre had always been an apolitical establishment. That didn't mean there wasn't an interest in events. The radio was on loud reporting on the army's progress in Graz.

"Sounds like the army has wrested back control of the city," Sanderson picked up the end of the report.

"I wonder whether our friend Dr. Dadieu is behind bars or in a hospital. He's much too pretty to die for the cause. A jailhouse follow-up would make a great Page One," Ros hoped she would get the chance.

"I see... catch them on the way up *and* on the way down," Sanderson saw she had the predator instincts of a tabloid staffer.

"Some folks just get what's coming to them," Ros had no regrets about torpedoing Nazis. Spotting Roland coming in by himself she pulled Sanderson by the jacket sleeve in that direction. "Hey Roland, you look lonely. Have you seen the rest of the gang?"

"Don't know exactly," Roland met them half way. "Endicott got a tip yesterday that old Kurt was leaving town unannounced. No one knew or would say why so he decided to sleuth it out. Sylvie went with him."

"Is the good chancellor jumping ship or hunkering down, that's the question?" Ros worked through the possibilities.

"Hunkering? That sounds positively scandalous," Sanderson teased her.

His reward was her poking him in the chest with an elbow. "Quit joking, junior. This is serious."

PROVINCIAL GOVERNMENT HOUSE
INNSBRUCK

Just what he needed... the woman of substantial girth to his side had suddenly slammed into him as she jumped up and down like a mad cow.

The Schuschnigg supporter almost knocked Endicott over, which drew a snicker from Sylvie at his expense.

"Watch it, sister. If I go down, you're going down with me," Endicott promised while regaining his balance.

"Why can't you just enjoy the moment? Isn't it nice to know someone in this country actually likes the guy?" Sylvie was going to use that angle in her story.

They had pulled every trick in the book to get into Tyrol in time to hear Schuschnigg give this speech. Endicott had rolled the dice on a suggestion from one of his government sources. Luck was with him as they arrived to find a local crowd chomping at the bit to see their leader. Endicott didn't think Schuschnigg had gotten as big an audience as Seyss-Inquart had in Linz but the city square was jammed full of people who were going wild over his speech.

"Then again, maybe you can put anyone on a balcony and folks around here will applaud," Sylvie continued on. "Want to give it a try, old pal. If they cheer for an old sourpuss like you they'll cheer for anyone."

His mind registered that she was babbling on about something but Endicott really wasn't paying attention. "What?"

"Never mind," Sylvie gave up as Schuschnigg started in again.

> *Now I want to know, and must know, whether the Austrian people want this free, German, independent, social, Christian, and united country to be free from the suffering of party divisions.*

The Tyroleans approvingly interrupted the chancellor again. "What do you think? Twenty thousand... thirty thousand?" To Sylvie It seemed like more people had swelled into the square..

"Who cares, anything over ten thousand is news," Endicott cut her off as Schuschnigg leaned forward to the microphone.

> *Now I must know whether the motto, bread and peace in the land, can bring together our countrymen, and their Front, which is invincible. And whether the idea of equality for all men in the country, so far as they stand by the people and the Fatherland, is for all men without exception?*

Endicott and Sylvie listened as the Austrian chancellor challenged his Nazi opposition openly and outlined a plan to force a national vote to decide whether the people wanted independence, or union with Germany. If that wasn't bold enough, Schuschnigg planned to hold the vote in only four days on Sunday, March 13.

"Wow, the old duffer has some fight left in him after all," Sylvie was excited that this was becoming a real fight. "A no vote on German annexation would stop Hitler in his tracks."

"Don't be pie-eyed. The brown shirts will just move in and bash enough heads to keep people from voting," Endicott remember that's how in played out in Germany.

"No, no, no, this could work," Sylvie disagreed. "If he can keep the socialists and the communists together, Schuschnigg could pull it off."

"The Germans know that too. They killed Dolfuss in thirty-four and they'll knock off Schuschnigg too. These guys play to win," Endicott would bet on it.

"Whose side are you on anyway?" Sylvie hated spoilsports

"My side toots," Endicott had his priorities straight. "This story is already written. Schuschnigg is in a gang war but he doesn't have a clue. You don't bring a ballot box to a rumble. Old Kurt here is no Capone... he doesn't know how to fight dirty."

"You don't know everything, fella. You've been wrong before," Sylvie called him out.

"When was that, sweetheart?" Endicott challenged her.

Sylvie's hands dropped to her hips as she leaned in closer to him. "I distinctly remember a story with your byline about how the French were going to toss Hitler right out of the Rhineland."

"My source led me wrong. It happens," Endicott had been broadsided on that one.

"Then there was that time you wrote up how sweet Stalin was to the Republicans in Spain – sending them all that military gear free of charge to fight Franco. Turned out the Soviets were charging their fraternal comrades in Madrid and draining all the gold out of the Spanish treasury," Sylvie could think of a few more occasions Before she could recite her next example Schuschnigg's tone grew menacing.

> Threats and attempts at intimidation, which are being made here and there under the cloak of patriotic sentiment, will not be tolerated.

"Okay mister know-it-all, will a big stick be enough for your gang war?" Sylvie so wanted Endicott to eat crow.

MARCH 10, 1938
TROLLEY – NEUBAU DISTRICT, WIEN

Schuschnigg's speech had been a shocker. The chancellor had grabbed the momentum from the national socialists and it felt like a pause had set in by this morning as all sides rethought their strategies. Ros didn't have the stomach to get caught in another street battle just yet so she decided to take advantage of the calmed neighborhoods to head across town to interview Jewish civic leaders on their reactions to the upcoming vote. But after a time she looked out the window and noticed small bands of pro-Nazi thugs breaking into stores with Fatherland Front posters or banners.

The further past Josefstadt the more violence she saw on the streets. Old men and women were randomly beaten or chased off. What Ros saw made her sick.

The trolley suddenly lurched to a stop. Ros stomped her heel on the floor because she should have paid more attention to the road ahead. Autos, trucks... everything had come to a complete stop on both sides of the street. Ros joined in with the rest of the passengers to try and get a better look at what was snarling traffic. Dozens of thugs had flooded into the street – weaving between stopped vehicles. Right outside the trolley window she saw a couple pulled out of their modest sedan by four toughs wearing swastika armbands. The poor people were beaten with sticks by their attackers.

"Stop that! Stop hurting them!" Ros banged futilely on the glass.

A crash behind her announced someone was hitting the side of the trolley with something blunt. Several angry, middle-aged men forced open the side door and boarded the trolley with clubs. Working up the aisle they set about identifying who might be workers or Jews. She immediately sat down to appear inconspicuous. It didn't work. One of the brutes pointed her out.

"You! Who are you?" the man brandished a club at the woman.

Ros got a grip on her fear as while considering alternatives. "A tourist."

"What business has a tourist in this district? There's nothing to see here. Are you a Jew?" the brawler looming over her demanded.

"No, I guess I got on the wrong train. I think I am lost. I don't know where we are," Ros pleaded innocently. If he smelled out that she was lying she was done for.

The thug looked Ros up and down several times without a word. The clothes were wrong. So was the haircut. Her German was simplified and odd. The woman wasn't Austrian that much was true. He didn't have instructions about foreigners so dealing with her would only cost him precious time he didn't have. .

"Go home woman!" he decided to pass over her.

"I will. I will. I promise," Ros acceded timidly. It was for show but she had to play it that way. Ros forced herself to look straight down as the man turned his attention to the passengers ahead of her. She watched and could do nothing as most of the people on the trolley were roughly pulled outside. Harry would howl with joy if she got out of this mess and filed an eyewitness account. But for now Ros could barely fight off retching in the aisle.

OBERKOMMANDO DES HEERES
ZOSSEN, SOUTH OF BERLIN

Austria was out of control. In a best-case scenario his people would be the guiding hand directing the efforts of the Austrian Nazi militias to a purpose. But right now everything down there was a mess with too much was happening too quickly. His teams had barely gotten into the country and were still setting up. Adding to Ottke's irritation, General Beck had called him in privately to go over the status of counter-intelligence operations in Austria. The status was a joke and Ottke told Beck exactly that. He was about to detail their minimal available options when the office door flew open and Hitler's most dutiful general, Wilhelm Keitel, strode in unannounced.

Ottke made eye contact with Keitel and saluted. Beck ignored the intrusion in favor of the tactical dossier in his hands. Ottke could feel the army chief-of-staff beside him bristle at the entrance of the recently appointed commander-in-chief of the Oberkommando der Wehrmacht – the new army high command Hitler created after the February purges. The chancellor may have put himself in charge of the armed forces but it was Keitel who carried out the chancellor's directives. Keitel was an officer driven by strategy, tactics, battlefield execution and full loyalty to Hitler. Ottke knew Beck considered Keitel a yes-man.

"Gentlemen. Excellent that I find you both here," Keitel often was not treated with the necessary priority. "Der Führer orders that all Wehrmacht commanders assigned to Plan Otto report their readiness... immediately and in detail."

As he thought, Hitler wasn't going to sit still for an Austrian plebiscite. Ottke knew the very suggestion was an affront to his leader's pride and ego. Which meant there was no limit to the force he would bring to bear on Schuschnigg.

"Has the Führer ordered the invasion," Beck inquired coldly without looking up from his reading material.

"Not yet, but he is furious at the Austrian chancellor and will invade rather than let a vote on independence be held," Keitel dutifully sat through the hour-long harangue.

"That vote is only three days off. Impossible," Beck slapped the paperwork down onto the table.

"Are you sure you want me to relay that opinion to Herr Hitler, general?" Keitel no longer would sugarcoat intransigence from his colleagues.

"Otto is a bare sketch as you well know," Beck rose from his chair slowly. "The chancellor told us, you told us, that anschluss by force was not expected this year. From the chancellor's own lips we were informed that Schuschnigg had been brought to heel at the Berghof, that we had what we required from Austria without a fight and that the focus was now on the Czechs. Are you telling me the Führer was mistaken?"

"General Beck. While I can appreciate your position the chancellor will not," Keitel could sympathize on the circumstances yet acknowledging reason was of little use. "Do not dissuade yourself. If he meets resistance on this matter, Herr Hitler will rage that the army is stalling and he will call in the SS to invade instead. I doubt any of us would appreciate the consequences of that eventuality."

"Nevertheless, I cannot lie to the chancellor," Beck was too fatigued with Hitler's constant vicissitudes to budge on the matter.

"I'm sure your sincerity will be received in the way it was intended, general," Keitel concluded having decided it was fruitless to argue the point further. Beck would have to face the outcome of his own stubbornness. Where Ottke stood, Keitel did not know. He would confer with the counter-intelligence director directly some other time. "Good day, gentlemen."

Keitel left as authoritatively as he entered, neglecting to close the door on his way out. Beck was relieved the man was gone. He simply was not in the mood to play Hitler's reckless game any longer... not with the army and the nation, at stake.

"We should talk more later on that other matter," Beck proposed in a low voice.

PRATERSTRASSE, WIEN

Getting out of Innsbruck had been a chore. Regular train schedules were still out of whack and any seats available in the direction of Vienna had been sold out already. When they happened upon an entrepreneurial fellow in a local beer hall they hired him and his Daimler sedan to make the trip. It wasn't cheap but Endicott and Sylvie both agreed that whatever important that was going to happen in the days leading up to the vote was going to happen in the capital. Most of the trip had been pleasant. The villages the car owner had chosen for food and fuel had been calm and agreeable. They had made good time until nearing Vienna. That's when traffic had slowed. Obviously, the city was still smoldering.

"Yeah, waiting for the train would have been slower," Sylvie stared out the window.

"Cut it out already," Endicott was getting tired of her constant complaining. "You know damn well the next available train wasn't going to show up for days."

"Forgive me. The torture of being cooped up with you for hours plays tricks on the mind," Sylvie had reached her Endicott limit.

"You're no peach either, sister," Endicott felt himself pushed back into the seat cushion as their tit-for-tat bantering was interrupted by the abrupt braking of the sedan. "See, our driver is tired of listening to you whine, too."

"No, look out the window... everyone is stopped: cars, trucks, everything." Sylvie rolled down her window and poked her head out to look down the road. What Sylvie saw had her swiftly dropping back into her seat and tearing into her purse.

"What? What did you see?" Endicott had his hand on the door handle ready to bolt.

"We have a street fight right up front that you can't see unless you look between the cars," Sylvie yanked a notebook and pencil from the purse.

Endicott opened his passenger door to step out on the running board to get a better look for himself. Hearing the door unlatch the car owner looked back with a horrified expression. "Nein!"

The warning was too late. Endicott had opened his door just as the riot up ahead was surging back in their direction. What Endicott took for a factory worker was knocked to the ground at his feet – moaning incoherently from the fall and a nasty gash to the forehead. The wrench that had delivered the wounds was in the hand of a man wearing a black coat with a swastika armband on the sleeve. By the expression on his face the fellow wielding the wrench wasn't pleased with the fool getting out of the Daimler. Without a word between them, Endicott was thrown forcibly to the pavement, after which he felt the dull thud of the wrench connecting with his shoulder and ribs. From what sounded far away Endicott heard what sounded like Sylvie screaming.

JOSEFSTADT DISTRICT, WIEN

Sanderson paced in near the telephone stand. The cost of that little luxury had earned him a nasty wire from London but with all the chaos in the city the past few weeks the outlay for a working line had been invaluable. When the phone rang he thought it might have been Ros – she was late again. To his excitement it was a tip all wrapped up and presenting itself at his feet. That's why he could not be bothered when there was a knock at the door. It would have to wait... then again, perhaps not. Sanderson noticed the door opening slowly and he cursed himself for forgetting to lock the door earlier. Ros peeked in and he felt absolved of the need to pay further attention when he had the incoming tip to deal with. Ros waved then quietly closed the door.

"Sorry I'm late," she whispered.

"Right. Got it. Thanks again," Sanderson concluded the call and put the receiver back on its cradle.

"It's rough out there," Ros added, somewhat miffed that Sanderson wasn't paying much attention to her.

"Glad you made it! We're leaving," Sanderson rose to his feet suddenly and announced.

"What? Do you have any idea what's going on out there and what it took for me to get back here?" she watched him run off unconcerned.

"Of course! The workers are marching on The Ring," Sanderson collected those items they would need on the streets. "Several thousand at least."

They could have an argument about his insensitivity and Ros could get the horrors she had just witnessed off her chest. But Ros was angry with these Nazis and what they were doing to honest people. Watching the workers crack some heads would feel a good deal better than talking.

"*Vigilante Justice Sweeps Austrian Capital,*" Ros tested the headline. "About time if you ask me. This baby is going to write itself."

CHANCELLERY, WIEN

The continuing unrest had taken a toll on Schuschnigg since returning from Tyrol. It was obvious that that the Germans would not stand idly by while he held his plebiscite. They continued fomenting the most vile provocations throughout the country, which kept Schuschnigg locked up within the chancellery for his own safety. Neither could he relax with Skubl's watchmen constantly escorting him around the premises. *Two of my most trusted men*, Skubl had promised – more of an order than a reassurance. Schuschnigg appreciated that his security chief had vowed never again would a chancellor be gunned down on government property but Schuschnigg was weary of it all. Restlessly patrolling the halls did little to alleviate his mood, especially when bad news would follow him regardless.

"Forgive me, chancellor. A message for you from Herr Skubl," a senior aide named Werner approached.

"What now?" an irritable Schuschnigg demanded.

"Several thousand social democratic workers are marching on the city center. Since the interior minister has ordered the police not to interfere with Nazi demonstrators the workers intend to restore order themselves," Werner caught his breath. "He also says Seyss-Inquart has ordered the police to use rubber truncheons and drawn sabers to disperse workers who make it to The Ring. Herr Skubl requests orders, sir."

Schuschnigg felt his body shudder at the further bloodshed approaching. "Send word that I will send him instructions presently." When Werner had failed to leave, Schuschnigg gathered there was still more bad news to dispense. "What else?"

"Dr. Wilhelm Keppler is in the chancellery," Werner kept the unwelcome announcement short. "He carries a diplomatic note."

More annoyances, Schuschnigg thought. Keppler was another lapdog for Berlin's pleasure. He considered leaving Herr Keppler to cool his heels for several hours in some tiny storeroom. That would bring some small pleasure but that was a luxury he could not afford. "Where is Dr. Keppler?"

"I left him downstairs in the custody of a guard until I could locate you, sir," Werner did not trust the man to be left alone.

"Go and fetch him," Schuschnigg dismissed the young man.

"To your office, Herr Chancellor?" Werner was puzzled by the incomplete command.

"No Werner. Right here will do just fine. I don't expect this to take long," Schuschnigg was of no mind to afford Keppler's appearance any status.

The chancellor turned to stare out a nearby window while Werner went off to retrieve Keppler. There was black smoke hanging over parts of the city. He never had felt such sadness and anger before. Four years of holding the country together and all of his efforts were coming unraveled. If there was a special place in Hell he hoped Hitler, and his ilk, would be delivered there one day by someone more powerful than him. Schuschnigg heard the approaching footsteps of Hitler's sycophant stop behind him.

"Chancellor Schuschnigg," Keppler broke the uncomfortable silence. "I have a personal communiqué for you from Herr Hitler."

"Do you now. And why isn't this communiqué not being presented by Ambassador von Papen?" Schuschnigg stressed the proper protocol with his back turned to Keppler.

"I was informed that telephone and wire communication into the capital are disrupted sir. Von Papen could not be reached. Given the urgency I was called upon as an intermediary," Keppler spoke the fiction he had been supplied.

"Promoted to the German embassy staff, have you Keppler?" Schuschnigg turned on the man to taunt him. "Very well, let me see this communiqué."

Keppler handed Schuschnigg an envelope. Upon reading the contents Schuschnigg grew visibly angrier. "Another ultimatum, eh? So I am to call off the plebiscite for six weeks and I am to resign as chancellor in favor of Seyss-Inquart?"

"Yes sir," Keppler began to fidget under the chancellor's gaze.

"That I comply with these demands or two-hundred thousand German troops will cross the border immediately," Schuschnigg lowered the document.

"Yes sir," Keppler looked down at his shoes in submission.

"You may convey the following to Herr Hitler," Schuschnigg drew himself up as if to pounce on an inferior prey. "So confident am I in the Austrian people that he can have his six week delay. But this public disorder most stop immediately and stay halted. Oh, express in the strongest terms that I decline to resign."

"Do you think that is wise?" Keppler braved, hoping to give Schuschnigg an opportunity to submit a more favorable response.

"That is all Dr. Keppler," Schuschnigg dismissed the lapdog. "Herr Werner, take the guard and escort the good doctor from the building."

When they had moved a sufficient distance away, Schuschnigg turned to Skubl's men. "I have a message for Herr Skubl. Tell him by tomorrow I intend to call out the reservists, arm the workers and order troops to the border."

HOSPITAL, WIEN

The police may not be doing much to prevent the violence in the streets but they had proved superbly adept at keeping anyone else from getting into the affected districts. The barricades were all up and manned and there wasn't an obvious way to skirt them. Sanderson was still peeved at being blocked from exploiting his on-the-money tip. Peeved enough to contemplate the feeling of satisfaction that throwing a right fist to the policeman's jaw would bring. Luckily his pretty yank companion made the rightly sensible suggestion that they investigate some of the major hospitals. She had seen first-hand how many serious injuries these street battles produced, and if they couldn't see the action for themselves, why not chat with the poor sods who had survived it.

In the commotion of an ambulance crew arriving with more wounded citizens, Sanderson and Ros snuck into the hospital behind them. They found there were at least a dozen people with broken limbs or light wounds sitting in the aisles waiting for attention. Too many of them old people who happened to be in the wrong place, Sanderson speculated. Down at the far end of the hall Sanderson saw a doctor loitering for a bit. Not wanting to lose the opportunity he pointed the man out to Ros and nodded. Sanderson figured the man would be more inclined to postulate for a delightfully pretty creature than some other man wasting his time. Ros scampered off down the hall while adjusting her clothing in the odd way that women do. He never saw how it made them any more presentable but it was enjoyable to watch all the same. He'd get the report from her later. For now he threw on his most charming demeanor and made for some of the traumatized little old ladies nearby.

The doctor was taking a quick break for a cigarette, Ros noticed. If a medicine man was lighting up he must be having a bad day. Ros wasn't sure if she wanted to interview him or bum a cigarette and share the moment. He was somewhere around fifty with tasteful strands of silver cutting through a thick mane of disheveled dark hair. She could tell he was very tired and decided it would be best to take the straightforward approach. Out of the purse came her notebook, pencil and press pass.

"Excuse me," Ros intruded upon the physician. "How many people have been seriously injured?"

"Are you looking for anyone in particular?" he answered, still focused on somewhere else far, far away.

"No, just in general. I'm trying to get a sense for how many people have been badly hurt," she clarified for him.

"Too many," the doctor focused on her finally. "There is no official total. No time for that. At this facility I'd say around seventy have been gravely wounded: gunshots or blunt instruments to the head. Many more with broken bones, lacerations and other maladies we haven't had an opportunity to address. Look around for yourself."

"I noticed and I know you are doing the best you can," Ros tried a little sympathy to keep him talking. "Have you seen anything like this before?"

"No. Never. It is disgusting. I am ashamed for my nation," the doctor confessed.

Ros sensed movement behind her and heard the sound of women's shoes closing in on her and the doctor. She concluded it must be a nurse who would surely pull the physician away for some emergency. Ros knew her next question would likely be her last so it had better be a good one. Before she could blurt it out, Ros felt a hand rudely grab her arm above the elbow and whirl her around. But instead of facing a head nurse out to protect her flock, Ros found herself face-to-face with Sylvie. From the state of her hair and clothes she was having a rotten day too.

"Ros! Thank God. I need you sister," Sylvie tugged her arm.

Seeing an opportunity to politely slip away from more intrusive questions the doctor cut his cigarette break short. "Pardon me. I have more patients arriving that require care. Good day."

"Sorry kid," Sylvie apologized as the doctor walked off.

"No. Don't worry about it. You look like something is terribly wrong," Ros' mind feared the worst. "The last we heard you and Endicott were off chasing down Schuschnigg before his speech."

"It's Endicott, he's hurt bad. We were on our way back into Vienna when everything on the road stopped moving and he was dragged out of the car and beaten up something terrible. I tell you if there had been a gun in my purse I would have used it," Sylvie's father had taught all the kids to be good shots... skills she felt like using.

"Slow down, hon. Where is he? Where's Charles?" Ros grabbed Sylvie by both arms.

"Down the hall. Follow me," Sylvie broke away to rush to the room.

SIGNALS ROOM – 2ND DEPT.
MINISTRY OF NATIONAL DEFENCE, DEJVICE

The sergeant leaned back in his chair contemplating the clock on the wall and the impending completion of another boring shift. He could almost taste the lager on his lips. For now he adjusted the radio dial to be sure it didn't drift off of the German frequency. Nothing had happened on this frequency for weeks. Then he remembered what winter maneuvers had been like in his old infantry battalion and thought boring wasn't so bad. The frequency suddenly came alive in his headphones and the sergeant sat up straight in the chair. The lager would wait. The Germans were using code on this frequency for the first time. After getting it all down he checked his cipher book to begin decoding the signal.

Tichy had just made his afternoon check of Moravec's office for anything that may have been mistakenly delivered there during the colonel's absence. They never talked openly about Moravec's trips abroad and Tichy always made a point to make sure general staff reports were not accumulating on his desk to make it obvious the boss was away.

"You have to get the boss back from the Netherlands," Burda burst in.

"What happened?" Tichy turned around and knocked a decorative clock off the desk.

"We've just intercepted signals to SS units in code. They have been ordered to positions on the Austrian border," Burda showed him the intercept. "We must report this to the chief-of-staff and the president."

STATE, WAR, & NAVY BUILDING
WASHINGTON, D.C.

There was too much on his plate. The world was coming apart at the seams and there was little in his control to make any difference. The United States still had too many of its own problems, which gave him and Roosevelt few options. They could only plead reason to European and Asian governments in the hope memories of the stink of death from the Great War were still fresh. The perfunctory rap at the door broke his concentration and meant Wells was letting himself in. Hull had sent the undersecretary to check with his British friends and was anxious to learn what they could add to the reports from U.S. embassy staff.

"Success Mister Secretary," Wells entered in a good mood.

"What did you learn?" Hull prodded, happy to put down the dreary reports he held.

"Schuschnigg cabled Chamberlain this morning seeking *advice*," Wells had been told.

"Seeking a handout is more likely," Hull knew better

"Very true. Turns out Schuschnigg is facing multiple German ultimatums promising invasion unless he steps down and makes sure the cabinet is aligned two-thirds Nazi before he leaves the building," Wells put the memo down before the secretary of state.

"I don't need this on top of China and Spain," a weary Hull took a moment to lean back in his old leather chair. "Any idea how the Brits plan on responding?"

"Oh yes. Mister Chamberlain will respectfully reply that the British government is in no position to guarantee protection from the dangers Austria faces, so no aid or advice will be forthcoming. It's all there," Wells pointed at the memo.

"Do me a favor," Hull rubbed his forehead. "Call the White House and let them know that I am coming over to see the president."

**An anti-Nazi banner of the Social Democratic Party's
Iron Front paramilitary organization**

MARCH 11, 1938
JOSEFSTADT DISTRICT, WIEN

That morning they had woken up early to sirens and news that Schuschnigg had called up the 1915 reservists for army service. Unfortunately, there had not been much time for sleep before the alarms sounded. By the time the two reporters had left the hospital the hour had been dreadfully late. At least Endicott was out of immediate danger. Sanderson was still shocked at the barbarity of the assault upon him. But the crusty old fart was eventually going to make a full recovery, according to the doctor. Endicott would likely make the hospital staff miserable waiting for those broken limbs in traction to heal but heal he would and that was a relief. Life would never be the same if the jammy git had died on them.

The downside of prevailing upon Ros to stay put at his flat for the night was that he lost possession of the only cot and was thereby consigned to the sofa. Sanderson didn't want her going off on her own at night the way the streets were. Especially after Ros' own close call on the trolley. Sanderson made a note to himself to pay greater attention to his yank in the future. The way he found out about Ros' perilous trolley ride was overhearing her tell Sylvie at the hospital. Bungled that one he had. So he had informed Ros firmly that she had to stay... period. She didn't like the *paternal treatment*, as she dubbed it, but the argument that his tawdry office was much closer to the international phone and wire offices persuaded her in the end.

Trying to make the best of it, Sanderson got up and set about working up some tea and biscuits and Ros joined him soon after. Sanderson rather liked the way they looked as she stood by his side at the window sipping tea. His mind pondered what it would take to make the occasion a regular arrangement. She wasn't smitten with him, unfortunately, yet Sanderson sensed Ros had warmed to him over the weeks and there was room for hope. Standing there at the window his free arm rose to find a cozy resting spot on her shoulder and for once the girl did not shrug him off. The moment evaporated when a nattily dressed old duffer rounded the corner down at the intersection to post an official looking bill. That quickly led to a command for Sanderson to venture forth to investigate what was on the bill. That's how they had learned of the reservist call up.

There was probably much more going on but they both agreed it was more important to write up their reports from the previous day. Sanderson dredged up his spare portable typewriter for her and their fingers had been tapping away at the keys for close to an hour.

"Damn. Perhaps we should have used carbon paper. We may not get outgoing cable or phone lines for a while and could be forced to use couriers," Sanderson wished he had thought of that earlier.

"Oh great. You want me to hand over my copy to a complete stranger." There were some aspects of civil wars Ros was still getting used to.

"We may not have a choice. I was in Madrid when that one started. Lots of things change in the middle of war," Sanderson pulled a page from the typewriter.

"Stop bragging," Ros had noticed how the guy was always talking up his past exploits. "Honestly though, how long can we ride out this brawl?"

"That is a question you will have to answer for yourself," Sanderson found some people did not do well without electricity or water. "This could all be over in a couple of weeks or we may be stuck here for months without the normal pleasantries."

"Listen fella, I won't be the one jumping ship. I've waited too long for an opportunity to be indispensable in this business and no way am I checking out early," Ros was not going to let anything or anyone get in her way.

The fist pounding at the door ended the discussion. Sanderson was glad he had remembered to latch the door for once, and hoped it was good news and not a squad of Nazis looking for victims.

"Hey Brit! Open up," a woman's voice yelled from the other side of the door.

"That sounds like Sylvie," Ros motioned for Sanderson to let her in.

"That it does," Sanderson was already out of his chair.

Sanderson barely had the door unbolted when Sylvie pushed her way in. She was dressed in the same outfit he had seen her in the previous night at the hospital.

"What's the hurry?" Sanderson ducked out of the way to secure the door.

"There are goons all over town," Sylvie went to the window to check if she was followed. "I couldn't even get back to my place for a change of clothes."

Ros got up to stand by Sylvie. "You might as well ride it out with us, hon."

One night on the cot and she ran the establishment, Sanderson marveled to himself a tad indignant. He wasn't sure whether the presumption resulted from Ros' nationality or gender. What was a poor bloke to do?

Sylvie looked at the way the ridge above Sanderson's nose was all crumpled up and figured it would be wise if someone asked him if she could stay at his place. "What do you say, old buddy... can you take in another refugee?"

"That would be the most sensible course," he agreed. "But you birds are going to have to procure you own clothes. You can share my flat, you can share my food, you can share my typewriters but you cannot share my knickers."

"I've seen your knickers. You don't have to worry." It wasn't the truth but Sylvie liked teasing him that way in front of Ros.

"Hey, we heard about the reservists being called up," Ros noted the odd knickers references for later and changed the subject. "What's happening out there?"

"A bunch. Schuschnigg has express trains moving troops up to Kufstein," Sylvie was proud the way Schuschnigg wasn't giving up.

"Where's that?" Ros wasn't familiar with that town.

"Western border with Germany. About a ten hour train ride from here," Sanderson went to look for a map.

"That's not all... old Kurt is arming the workers," Sylvie saved the juiciest part for last.

REICH FOREIGN MINISTRY, BERLIN

The army may be dragging its heels but his Luftwaffe had responded splendidly when Hitler had ordered Fall Otto initiated. What was Beck thinking? Such obstinacy was unsustainable and the man was smart enough to know better. It would be his undoing, Göring was certain. The old guard had lost its chance to restrain or oust Hitler. It wasn't going to happen. If war was necessary neither Beck nor any of his generation could stop it. Regardless, Göring held hope that Austria could still be joined to Germany without bloodshed. The material and social disruption would be a vile waste. Germany required access to Austria's resources now and did not need to be saddled with the costs of subduing a foe and the cost of reconstructing destroyed infrastructure.

Göring hadn't seen this much physical activity at the Foreign Ministry in years. Ribbentrop had everyone worked up into a lather. Even Göring had lost track of how many diplomatic initiatives were in play. That's why he had decided to be courteous and pay the foreign minister a visit. He did not want to pry von Ribbentrop away at such a delicate juncture.

"Thank you for accommodating me," Göring was pleased when an obviously weary foreign minister met him personally.

"My pleasure, Herr generalfeldmarschall," von Ribbentrop was still courting allies in the cabinet. "This way please, we have much to discuss."

"Namely, what the hell is happening down there?" Göring intoned by the foreign minister's side. "Can't anyone get the message through to that obstinate little man, Schuschnigg?"

"Not from a lack of trying. Our third ultimatum was delivered at two-thirty this morning... and rejected," von Ribbentrop had concluded another method was needed.

"That fool. He can't bluff Hitler. This will lead to war by tomorrow," Göring lamented the waste.

"Agreed, but I am doubtful Schuschnigg is bluffing," von Ribbentrop did not underestimate the Austrian chancellor. He pulled Göring into a nearby reception room and continued. "Seyss-Inquart is in a panic. We've already received several cables from him asking us to calm the situation."

"That willow!" Göring wanted to lash a stout beam to that pliable spine. What is upsetting him now?"

"Schuschnigg ordered the federal armories opened and the trade unionists given weapons. Seyss-Inquart reports the process is progressing at an alarming rate and he fears Austria will soon devolve into civil war like Spain," von Ribbentrop assumed Göring had known.

"Insanity," Göring was caught off guard by this news but did not want to show it.

"We would have something to pressure him with if the Wehrmacht was already over the frontier in force--" von Ribbentrop began.

"--No time for that," Göring grew excited and abruptly made to leave. "There still may be a way. I'll explain later."

RAILROAD SIDING, AUSTRIAN COUNTRYSIDE

Too bad he had no clue where he was. The train had been moved off the main line. None of the conductors would say why and he doubted any of them even knew the reason the way the schedules had been disrupted. Bulloch had no one to blame but himself. He craved sleep and the supple chair he had claimed in the passenger coach had seemed such a safe place that he had nodded off. When he awoke the train was already on the siding and no passengers were being allowed off the overcrowded carriages. One of the porters had identified the village nearest to them but

Bulloch didn't recognize the name and would have to locate it on a map later.

The incessant tooting of a steam whistle grabbed Bulloch's attention. He lowered his passenger window all of the way and leaned out to look in the direction of the whistle. It wasn't long before Bulloch saw another passenger train zoom by heading in the opposite direction on the main tracks. But the passengers he saw had helmets and rifles and military gear. At the rear was a flat car holding artillery pieces in front of a livestock car carrying horses. In a matter of moments the other train had sped past them. The government was sending troops to the border. Bulloch began to second-guess his decision to head toward Vienna.

FLORIDSDORF DISTRICT, WIEN

The last of his boys were climbing into the back of the old Steyr factory lorry. The unions had been imploring Schuschnigg for weeks to accept reality and arm the workers. The old dog had finally thrown open the armory doors that morning and Späth's people had been ready. No Nazi had been seen anywhere near them and Späth was sure they had been caught with their pants down – never believing Schuschnigg would actually embrace the unions. Späth hadn't believed it either but no matter. The armories were opened for them. The only hindrance had been persuading the army types to distribute additional ammunition. Späth could be very persuasive considering he knew the quartermaster's family and where they lived. Now it was time to go. With the last of his people and ordinance up on the truck Späth raised the rear gate up and locked it into place. They were done here. Späth patted the loaded army-issue pistol on his belt then jumped up into the passenger seat as his driver put the truck in gear.

ESTERWEGEN CONCENTRATION CAMP
EMSLAND, DEUTSCHLAND

The communiqué meant a change was coming, perhaps an important change. That's what a message delivered to the camp by motorcycle courier meant. Nothing mundane ever arrived by motorcycle. Achtziger was digesting the contents personally in the privacy of his office as the standartenführer would want a digest of the communiqué before deciding whether to read it for himself.

Krisch proceeded with his daily filing chores without showing any interest in the communiqué. It was an acquired skill. He actually was very curious but even a hint of inquisitiveness would breed the kind of suspicion that would swiftly put him on a work detail, or worse. His position, such as it was, depended on appearing unconcerned. Krisch had sustained the charade for more than a year now. Well enough that he often thought the lieutenant felt sorry for his dutiful, apolitical clerk who wished nothing more than to make the best his unfortunate incarceration. Once, that characterization may not have been far from the truth but a concentration camp changes a man.

Despite what bits of news he overheard in conversations, or gleamed from some of the documents he read, Krisch felt uncomfortably cut off from the world outside the camp. Few new political prisoners, their best source of news, had been sent to Esterwegen in recent months. So his comrades put more pressure on Krisch for information. He was sure that Hitler had consolidated control over the leadership of the army back in February. The SS officers in the camp had joked about certain generals they had hoped to see added to the inmate roster. Except for some other talk about Franco's forces pushing east to the Mediterranean coast from the Basque territories the winter had offered up little more than long, cold, uneventful days. Hence his burning interest in the communiqué.

Krisch heard the leather soles of Achtziger's boot's striking the wood floors behind him in their familiar precise fashion. He ignored Achtziger and remained focused on the slow routine of his filing – another part of the charade.

"Krisch, are you Catholic?" the lieutenant inquired thoughtfully.

Of all of the personal questions the obersturmführer had asked over the years, Krisch realized the jailer had never before gotten around to the subject of religion. Why now, Krisch wondered? "No sir, Lutheran."

"Ah, a shame. Looks we'll be having some new company for you soon," Achtziger teased, folding the communiqué and inserting it back into its envelope. "A lot of them... Catholics from Austria."

HOSPODA – DEJVICE DISTRICT, PRAHA

Furst draped his coat over one of the hooks inside the front door then looked around. His luck was good. She was working this evening. Next he paused long enough to determine which tables she was serving and whether there was an open seat on a bench at one of those tables. Furst sat down and waited for her to present herself. Propriety dictated that he couldn't stare at her despite how much staring at her would please him. But he could enjoy her scent as she drew closer.

"Sausage again" Petra teased playfully? The tall, quiet man had been in a lot lately. But was it the food or something else that kept him coming back?

"Sure," Furst noted that the niece had remembered him. "That and a pint of pilsner."

"Anything else?" Petra decided to see what the tall man was really interested in.

"Perhaps. Are you a free woman again? I haven't seen your boyfriend around in a long time," Furst looked around the hospoda.

Another aspiring suitor... at least this one was handsome and somewhat more polite than Petra was accustomed to. So many of them were neither. But there was something dangerous in the way he looked into her eyes that intrigued her. She would have to be careful with him. "How sweet of you to ask. He is away on business but will be back soon."

"Between us," Furst lowered his voice and leaned closer to her. "What do you see in that American?"

"I'll never tell," Petra winked at him. She ended discussion on the topic by spinning away to head back to the kitchen with his order.

Furst was satisfied. He had gotten what he came for.

SIGNALS ROOM, CHANCELLERY, WIEN

The clerk's hands shook as she read the telegram again. She desperately wanted the contents to read differently. No matter how hard she tried the same sentences stared back at her every time she read them. Part of her wanted to put the piece of paper down and slip away – far, far away. The clerk had not noticed her shift supervisor meander up behind her.

"What's the problem, Maria?" he had noticed her odd behavior. The last weeks had worn heavily on his crews. Some handled the burdens better than others. Maria had not been a problem but he had never seen her simply stop before or fail to respond to a direct question. The supervisor gently reached in to take the telegram from her hand. The message looked official. He sensed that she had turned to look up at him while he read. Then the words hit him like a stone and he understood. The supervisor placed a hand on her shoulder to steady him as well as her. "Maria, I can't wait. The chancellor has to see this immediately. While I'm gone I need you to authenticate this transmission – now. Understood?"

The urgency in his voice overrode her fear and Maria felt in control again. "Yes sir. I'll double-check the sender immediately."

The supervisor was already through the department's door.

CAFÉ LOUVRE – INNERE STADT, WIEN

Sanderson returned to the table with three clean glasses and a bottle of local white wine. Tonight it was only the ladies and him on hand. Endicott was still in traction and no one quite knew what Roland was up to. As for the majority of local clientele he could only surmise that they preferred to huddle up next to their radios at home waiting for the next shoe to drop. It was going to be a long night for everyone.

"Ladies, I bear good tidings," Sanderson announced as he set the bottle and glasses on the table. "The proprietor says he's staying open, war be damned. He won't have hooligans steal his stock tomorrow. As he appreciates our still showing up the nectar is on the house tonight."

Sylvie grabbed the bottle to check the label. "What a sweet odd duck he is, this is a decent vintage."

"Aren't we the lucky ones," Ros could use some lighter moments for a change.

"Speaking of luck," Sanderson saw an opening for a matter weighing on his mind.

"Ah crap, I sense a lecture coming our way," Sylvie filled their glasses.

"Must you ridicule every honest impulse?" Babysitting both of these tarts was wearing thin on him.

"We're reporters, hon. It goes with the territory," Sylvie had to remind him again.

"Why do I even try?" Sanderson leaned back to sip the wine.

Ros reached over to touch him on the arm and get his attention. "It's okay, tell us what's on your mind."

"You're not going to like it," Sylvie had been down this road before with Sanderson.

"That' okay, let's hear him out," Ros wanted to hear what he had to say.

"It's nice to see at least one of you are sensible," Sanderson appreciated Ros' efforts. "I think we have to think about contingencies if hostilities break out."

"What he's really saying is when do we women run out of town with our tails between our legs," Sylvie provided her own translation.

"You really should listen to reason once and a while," Sanderson admonished her. "With civil order breaking down, it could get very ugly here. All manner of atrocities could happen, and do happen."

"No, you listen, I stay. I do my job. I was in China and Spain. I've seen the worst first-hand. What about you, sister?" Sylvie turned to Ros.

"You people are a pill. This is not a decision I want to make tonight. This is not a decision we have to make tonight. What I want most is to get a shower, some sleep, and some fresh clothes," Ros tabled the subject.

MARCH 12, 1938
CHARLOTTENBURG RAIL STATION, BERLIN

How much would the Germans pay to know that the chief of Czechoslovak military intelligence was traveling home through their territory? A substantial premium he imagined. Moravec doubted he would ever see home again if his adversaries did learn of his train itinerary. There wasn't a German operative in custody important enough to trade for Moravec's release. Changing trains in the middle of Berlin was as brazen as it was foolhardy. Tichy and Strankmueller would be livid with him when they learned of it. Next time he went abroad they would send Furst to mind him. Moravec was sure Furst would simply knock his chief unconscious rather than argue the merits of the risk.

Moravec had to return to Praha immediately. Matters in Austria were advancing much more swiftly than their estimates, which is why he had cut short his business in the Netherlands. The problem was all flights through German airspace had been cancelled. Weighing the options, Moravec wagered he had a better chance of drawing attention to himself flying through hostile Hungary or Poland than taking the train through Germany. Despite their poor relations a majority of Czech goods and businessmen traveled through Germany so there was a good chance he could blend in. Would the chief of the Second Department be so stupid as to take the train through Berlin? Moravec had to believe his counterparts would scoff at the possibility and would neglect to instruct their border units to check for him specifically.

His train from Holland had been punctual so there was just enough time for Moravec to peruse the newsstand for the afternoon papers before boarding the connecting train to Praha. He was starved for some news on what was happening and would just have to sift through the obvious propaganda. The headlines announced the Wehrmacht had crossed the frontier in the morning on request of the new Austrian government to calm the crisis. Hitler was leaving immediately for Linz. Moravec purchased two broadsheets from the vendor plus a pack of cigarettes. The latter as an affectation to draw attention away from any obvious anxiety he might exhibit closer to the border later. Moravec stuffed the purchases into an outside pocket of his overnight bag and returned to the crowded platform leading to his train.

JOSEFSTADT DISTRICT, WIEN

Another day, another cacophony of screaming sirens at daybreak, Sanderson pondered groggily from the settee. Did the racket outside signal a change or just more of the same? He was sadly lacking in motivation to answer the question. Then the sharp crackle of a bullet round leaving some gun barrel nearby compelled Sanderson upright in bed – eyes open, and very awake. The bed sheet he had hung for the modesty of the women curtly furled up and Sanderson watched as a pair of his silk pajamas rushed by to the big window in the room – the pair Ros had recently requisitioned. He had a decidedly sinking premonition: *What would be an outrageously stupid course of action with gunfire going off in the neighborhood?* Sure enough, his very own Pandora threw back the curtains in the most conspicuous manner possible. Just as he was about to admonish his daft comrade in newsprint, Sanderson was buoyed by the site of his favorite nightshirt – which Sylvie had greedily liberated the night before – making haste for the window.

"What are you doing, sister? You want to get a bullet between the eyes?" Sylvie tried to pull Ros from the window.

Ros pointed to the street below where a squad of Nazi militia were chasing someone clutching a large, rolled up canvas or poster. The fleeing man was soon out of view down the street as one of the militiaman fired a shot on the run that missed its mark.

"Don't worry, mother, that near-sighted bunch couldn't hit a bus," Ros shrugged loose from Sylvie's grasp. Something else caught her eye outside. From the same direction that the chase had come from, Ros pointed out a crew posting announcements on lamp poles and walls. "Hey! Look at that."

Sylvie drew up close to Ros to see for herself. "Certainly look official don't they."

"That might be worth a look," Sanderson finally swung his feet off the bed.

Ros ran back to her side of the partition gesturing dismissively at him as she passed. "You're about as audacious as McClellan in 1862."

"Who?" It was too early for Sanderson to decipher her daft references.

"Never mind," Ros ran back out having hastily thrown on a robe. "I'll be right back."

He was fixated on whether he knew whom this McClellan fellow was until Sylvie walked over and slugged him on the shoulder. "Why did you let her get out the door in a bath robe, Poindexter?"

"Ow!" Sanderson rubbed the sore spot. "You birds are taking just a bit too much advantage of my good nature."

"That's bird, papa. You let one get away," she reminded him.

"Oh hell," Sanderson finally caught on.

Sanderson was out the door in his bare feet, cursing the knotty wood stairs as he ran down to the street after Ros. He found her at the corner, reading the just-papered notice on the trunk of the light pole. "Why must you persist in dashing off into danger at every opportunity? I have a right mind to leave you to your own devices, madam."

"Oh hush," Ros dismissed his chiding without taking her eyes off the poster. "We snooze, we lose. Put some clothes on, we have work to do." Ros walked back to the building leaving Sanderson to read the bill alone.

SCHUSCHNIGG RESIGNS
MIKLAS ORDERS ARMY BACK FROM BORDER
SEYSS-INQUART APPOINTED CHANCELLOR.

LUFTWAFFE AIRSTRIP, MUNICH

Not that he was unappreciative for the quick flight from Berlin but Ottke was not a fan of the Junkers 86 he was a passenger on. The narrow, inward retracting landing gear always seemed like the most abominable of engineering choices to him. They were always one wrong bounce on the runway away from collapse. As the Luftwaffe pilot brought the Junkers in fast for a landing, Ottke's body stiffened in his chair, bracing for the inevitable crash. Two hard bounces later the tail wheel was safely down on the ground and Ottke relaxed. Looking out the small window he watched as the pilot maneuvered the plane to a parking space. He was pleased to see that at least the Luftwaffe was taking matters seriously and parking the planes a good distance from each other. Austria may not be much of a military threat but one good bomb hit could do immense damage if wartime procedures were ignored.

The Junkers rolled to a stop and Ottke felt power to the engines cut. A crewman walked down the aisle to the back door, opened the hatch, lowered the folding stairs and stepped down to assist anyone who needed help off the plane. When it was Ottke's turn to descend down the narrow stairs he got a crisp salute. These were the occasions he enjoyed wearing his full uniform and Ottke returned the salute to the young officer. He didn't have long to wait for the Horch staff car to arrive. The vehicle pulled up beside him and Heiden had the top down. Ottke was pleased to see a wireless set in the back seat. That would be most useful during the next several days.

"Director," Heiden reached over to open the passenger door.

"Prompt as always, major," Ottke seated himself as Heiden put the Horch in gear and drove off. "What's changed since I left Berlin?"

"Our operatives report no resistance to Wehrmacht or SS units moving south. Good thing too. Like we thought, Guderian's tanks aren't the most reliable of beasts," Heiden had seen the first estimates of mechanical breakdowns.

FARMHOUSE, NIEDERÖSTERREICH PROVINCE

Who was knocking at his front door was a mystery. No one was expected, especially with all of the excitement. Politics would be the death of the country he groused to himself while slowly ambling to the front of the house. Radio reception was unreliable out here but he got enough of the news to know people should stay put in their homes until the damn mess blew through. His well-oiled Mauser from the last war was stored nearby so the prospect of mischief-makers didn't bother Frederich much. A quick peek out one of the front windows would tell him whether he needed to retrieve the rifle or not. Peeling back the curtain he saw a squad of troops. Even if he didn't read the papers these last few years, Frederich would always recognize the rank badges on the uniform collars. An officer, feldwebel and two soldats were waiting on him. Germans. What were they were doing so far out here? Frederich suspected the whole lot was probably lost. He had no qualms with soldiers doing their duty. Frederich drew himself a tad up and threw open the door as the young leutnant was in mid-knock.

"Excuse me sir," the leutnant stammered a bit. "I understand that you have a heavy truck in good working order. Is this correct?"

"Yes, that is correct, leutnant," Frederich answered politely. He could tell the officer was freshly minted and not all that sure of himself. "Why do you ask?"

"We have official need of the vehicle, sir," the leutnant stood his ground, barely.

"Do you now. And when do you intend to return my truck, leutnant?" Frederich wished to measure how these boys were trained. There was etiquette involved in civilian requisitions and he wondered whether officer schools still taught such things.

"Sir, I cannot guarantee when the vehicle will be returned, or if it will be returned at all," the leutnant answered honestly. "If the truck should not be returned, or returned with damage, you will be compensated properly."

Frederich was satisfied, and decided that it was time to give the youngster what he came for. "Well, we'll see if you still want the old bucket after you have seen her. She's not fast, but I maintain her myself so she is reliable. You'll find her around back behind the house. If you still want her after that, leave me with a signed receipt and good luck to you, son."

"Thank you, sir," the leutnant saluted crisply, very happy there would not be an argument. So many things were going wrong that day and he was glad there was nothing else to add to the list. "We'll go have a look at your truck."

Frederich thought about returning the salute then decided against it. He wasn't that arrogant. "Very well, go on then."

The soldiers veered off to circle round the back of the house. Frederich could see lots of German army traffic out on the road, which intrigued him. He shut the front door and started walking towards the road where a very small tank was parked off to the near side. By the look of the open toolbox resting on the back compartment it was a broken down tank. Not much of a tank he thought to himself. It was so tiny with a light cannon – probably 20mm. Good enough for little Austria but no match for a French Hotchkiss he wagered. The French were fools, he concluded. If *this* was what the Germans were riding nothing would have stopped the French from marching on the Rhineland in 1936. Nearing the tank he stopped to watch. A crewman pulled himself out of the engine compartment, threw a wrench back into the toolbox and swore loudly. Frederich knew such frustration well.

"You boys stuck here a while? Thirsty? If so, I could get you something to drink," Frederich felt bad for the boy.

"Careful, we might be here a long time and could drink you dry," the frustrated tanker warned.

"I'm not worried," Frederich had plenty of food to share. "Can't you fix it?"

"I only wish. When these damn Mark IIs break down we have to wait for someone to come in with a lorry to truck them back to the factory. That's the only place that can make the repairs. Who knows how long that will take," the sergeant explained as he took a rag to wipe his oily hands before walking around closer to Frederich. "So yes, some drinks would be wonderful, sir. Thank you for your hospitality."

"My pleasure," Frederich liked these boys. "I'll go fetch some beer and then maybe you can tell me more about your vehicle here. I drove lorries during the Great War and your tank looks a lot faster than the crawling barns we had back then."

CAFÉ LOUVRE – INNERE STADT, WIEN

Ros found Roland all in one piece sitting on a bench outside the cafe sipping a hot tea from a thermos cup and happily unruffled as usual. The streets may be in chaos, with glass breaking all around and people running for their lives, but dear Roland was an island of calm. Ros wondered what he may have added to his tea but didn't smell anything alcoholic as she strode up to the bench.

"Hey Fella. Glad to see you holding down the fort," she sat down next to him.

"Not much else to do, really. The owner didn't open today and I can't say that I blame him," Roland finished his tea.

"We thought that might happen so there's a new meeting place. When Sanderson gets here we'll be off," Ros was glad the little guy had better luck than Endicott.

"Very sensible," Roland screwed the cup back onto the thermos bottle.

"What have you heard today?" Ros wondered what Roland had snooped out.

"Darn little, I'm afraid. And what I did hear was quite disconcerting," he still wasn't fully sure what to believe yet. "A policeman, a nice chap too, told me the Germans crossed the border this morning at the request of Seyss-Inquart."

"That's what I heard too. What's odd about that?" Ros didn't see the problem.

"Well, a highly placed fellow I know, under the strictest confidence, told me yesterday afternoon that the Gerries moved across the border *yesterday* before the Austrian troops could make it to the frontier in strength. That's why old Karl called off the plebiscite and resigned," Roland gathered she hadn't heard that one yet.

"Schuschnigg believed the Germans invaded yesterday?" Ros got nose-to-nose close. "Are you sure about that?"

"That's the rub. I can't get any corroboration though. The phones are all static and there are so many blasted Nazi revelers blocking the streets that it's hard to get around to anyone who might know for sure," Roland disliked being stymied so thoroughly.

"We can't let that stop us," Ros jumped up. "We have to track your lead down and get that information out to the rest of the world."

"That might be difficult," Sanderson tossed in as he approached. She was going on at the top of her lungs and could be heard a half a block away. "The new administration is suspending our communications privileges and won't say for how long. That's the least of it. More dictates are blowing in from Berlin hourly."

"There you are!" Ros yanked Roland forcibly off the bench. "There has to be a way. Roland knows for a fact that Schuschnigg believed the Germans invaded yesterday."

"Well, not for a fact, really," Roland did not want to give the wrong impression. "But it seems that this fellow--"

"--Quiet!" Ros shut him up. "This is the best tip we've had in days. We have to track it down... now."

"No argument there," Sanderson knew better to get in Ros' way when she was on a roll. " Just understand that regardless of what we learn leaving the country may be the only way to get a dispatch out."

"Fine, if that's what it takes, " Ros pushed the two Brits down the sidewalk.

FLORIDSDORF DISTRICT, WIEN

Broken glass and bricks lay strewn all about the roads and sidewalks throughout the suburb and damp blood stains were easy to spot mixed in with the debris strewn about the now abandoned barricades. The unionists had put up a fight here, Glanz noted while navigating his way to his rendezvous. With the Wehrmacht racing for Vienna the workers had pulled back from the outer barricades. There might still be a battle for this working class district if the rank-and-file did not decide it more sensible to blend in with relatives back in the countryside, or slip over the Czech border. There were lists and the arrests would start soon. Excluding the occasional set of suspicious eyes lurking behind curtains, or an alley corner, Glanz had never felt so alone in the district. He was sure there wasn't another uniformed policeman for kilometers around. Rounding a corner, Glanz saw his target, a well-weathered Daimler cab parked between two battered sedans unlucky enough to have been caught in the middle of the street fights the day before. With one last look around for possible threats, Glanz opened a rear passenger door and sat next Skubl.

"Learn anything, sir?" Glanz doubted there would be any surprises.

"I have made the appropriate inquiries." Of those few reliable sources Skubl could locate. "Some will no doubt fight stubbornly for their neighborhoods but there will be no organized resistance from the left. Vienna will not be like Paris in 1871."

"That's the feeling on the streets. I'm still not sure if it's better this way or not," Glanz was still itching for a fight.

"Perhaps Austria is not worth fighting for. We'll know soon enough. What's the situation in the Jewish neighborhoods?" Skubl went onto his next agenda item.

"Tragic really. The shop owners are being assaulted and their establishments looted. Some of the well-to-do families are being dragged out of their homes, beaten and left to bleed in the street. No one from our ranks has violated Seyss-Inquart's decree not to interfere in these humiliations," Glanz felt dirty again.

The report sickened Skubl. His men were professionals and would not hesitate to step in and stop such wanton pillaging under normal circumstances. Skubl was sure the Jews would see worse deprivations, and soon. "Tell the old hands to assist citizens where they think they can without drawing suspicion, or to resign. The situation is disgusting but it is only going to get worse. Hitler will be in the city today or tomorrow. Before then, Seyss-Inquart's new government will have passed a resolution approving anschluss. That will be it for local control. Everything will come down from our new masters in Berlin. I won't have any of our men endanger themselves or their families."

"They'll arrest us anyway," Glanz was sure a noose was waiting for them.

"Perhaps, perhaps not, my friend," Skubl tapped his walking stick on the window between them and the driver to signal it was time to move on. "If so, remind them you are a good German who follows orders. They'll make us sign an oath, we will do as we are told, and all of us will live with the stain for the rest of our lives."

RADIO-TELETYPE SECTION
U.S. EMBASSY
MALA STRANA DISTRICT, PRAHA

It seemed to Bess that if Minister Carr was making a personal visit down here in the basement he must be terribly troubled by something. He always sent Chapin or someone else for the routine stuff. She recognized the cable in his hands as the important one she had just delivered to the minister. It was the latest report from Austria. Bess respected Carr immensely... liked him too. There were few people she would rise from her chair to greet here on her territory. "What can I do for you, minister?"

"Bess, are you holding out on me?" Carr knew there was little or nothing regarding the embassy that she did not know about or make a point of knowing about.

The question caught Bess off guard, and while Carr's tone was not threatening, she honestly had no clue what he was getting at.

"Now sir, what on this green Earth would I keep from you?" Bess turned on the sweetness. "If Mrs. Carr is planning a surprise birthday party, I don't know a thing about it I assure you."

"No, Bess, my birthday isn't for a while yet," Carr had to respect this disarming woman who could bring a smile to his face at such an urgent moment. "But I am concerned for our young Mister Bulloch. These reports about Austria are distressing. You are one of the few people who knows where the captain is. He is overdue and I am worried. Have you heard anything from him?"

"No sir. Trust me I'd let you know if I had. Now remember, that young'un has a strong sense of self-preservation, and he ain't stupid. It's a mess down there but he'll turn up," Bess got the minister feeling better about things.

"Thank you for saying that, Bess. I'm still worried though," Carr felt like he had lost track of a child.

"When our young captain does drag himself through the front door, I'll tan his backside for being out past curfew and not calling home. I promise, sir," Bess meant every word.

JOSEFSTADT DISTRICT, WIEN

He saw now that he had a promising career as an innkeeper. His editor back in London who was paying for the flat wouldn't be pleased if he knew reporters from four competitors were lodging with Sanderson – so much for the rulebook during war. Sanderson's neighborhood had not been hit as hard by the civil strife consuming the city and Sanderson would feel wretched if something terrible happened to any of his mates. Although he might have to modify that judgment shortly if the recently arrived Endicott continued to complain so loudly. The unappreciative git still hadn't thanked Sylvie for braving the trip to collect him from the hospital steps.

"They tossed me out I tell you. Do I look healed to you?" Endicott gestured as best he could to his bandaged head and leg cast."

"Why couldn't you get wounded in the jaw you ungrateful stooge?" Sylvie was fed up with him already. "They needed the beds for people in far worse shape than you. Get over it."

"Aren't doctors supposed to take a Hippocratic oath over here?" If I had a good lawyer I'd sue them for sure," Endicott wasn't listening to her.

Sylvie threw up her hands and walked away from the sofa Endicott was perched on to stop briefly next to Sanderson. "Do you think we could get the Gestapo to take him? I don't think there is any capital in Europe our boy hasn't offended."

"Well ain't she something. Let's see how you are when you get mugged, sister," Endicott didn't get an answer as Sylvie marched off to the solitude of the tiny kitchen.

Ros had an idea on how to cool Endicott down as she approached him.

"What, you want to jump on too?" Endicott wasn't going to take any guff from Ros either.

"Heavens no," Ros treated him like his best friend. "I was just wondering when was the last time you had a good shot of scotch?"

"A lifetime," Endicott's mood perked up. "You know where we can get some?"

"I have a good idea. Stay put, I'll be right back," Ros went to join Sylvie in the kitchen.

"You're a life saver, kid... unlike the rest of this crowd," Endicott discovered his sore ribs ached more when he got too loud.

Sanderson was not mollified as Ros slinked by and winked at him. "You realize there are some things around here that require the permission of the proprietor, dear lady."

"A little scotch would be delightful," Roland lent his support.

"There you go, mister proprietor. The customer is always right," Ros considered the matter settled.

"The lot of you are going to eat me out of house and home," Sanderson offered for the record, already accepting defeat on the subject.

"What are we dealing with out there since I've been laid up?" Endicott changed the subject. "I can't move very well but I can still type. Nothing is going to stop me from writing up what those Nazi goons did to me."

"Type away but getting a dispatch out of the country has gotten rather dicey. The telephone and teletype exchanges are down or unreliable. The situation will only get worse once the censors get up to speed," Sanderson had now informed everyone.

"Quite right. Uncle Adolph is expected to march victoriously into Vienna tomorrow. The new boffins managing the machines at the telegraph office might take a dim view of forwarding unflattering reports," Roland was doubly suspicious of whether the lines were actually down or simply turned off for that very reason.

"Nothing a generous bribe can't handle," Endicott was already working an angle to circumvent the censors.

"True, greed knows no politics," Roland found the American's proposal meritorious.

"Then it's agreed," Endicott pounded his good fist on the armrest.

"What's agreed?" Ros had talked Sylvie back out of the kitchen with an odd set of four not-too-dirty glasses and a depleted bottle of scotch.

"Yeah, what are you three plotting behind our backs?" Sylvie could smell a con a mile away.

"Charles here has a proposal that will get us all arrested," Sanderson thought the bribery idea was completely daft.

"You worry too much. If we grease the wheel a little with some up-front money then we can get our wires sent. No big deal," Endicott wasn't budging.

"You know full well what needs to be done," Sanderson raised his voice to make the point. "One of us has to get out of the country tonight with everyone's reports before the Hun marches in. It is the only sure and safe way to get our dispatches to their destinations."

"Oh that again. You do have a one-track mind. Let's just draw straws and get it over with," Ros was tired of hearing the same speech. She put the glasses down on the table in front of the sofa and Sylvie poured.

"That's much better," Endicott savored the alcohol then rummaged around in his pocket to retrieve his lucky silver dollar. "I still say bribery is easier but if this means so much to you, let's flip for it. The way I see it, I'm too gimped to be the courier but I can still manage to toss a coin to see who goes."

Sylvie was within striking distance of the coin in a second. "Let me see that silver dollar, gimp?" Sylvie snatched the silver dollar from Endicott's hand, checked both sides then bit it with her teeth before returning the coin to him. "Just wanted to make sure it was legit government-issue. Not everyone likes gambling with you."

Endicott didn't like getting knocked when he was down. "One of these days I won't be laid up like this and you'll regret those words, doll."

"Like I'm worried. Let's get on with the coin flip," Sylvie nudged Endicott close to a fractured rib.

"Ow! You did that on purpose, you witch," Endicott decided to go along because the woman had talked to his doctors and knew every defenseless wound and bruise he had. "The way I see it we'll do this in three parts. Lose the call and you go onto the next round. But lose the final round and you leave town. First up, Ros and Roland. Ladies first. What's your call, Ros?"

"Tails," she watched as Endicott tossed the coin in the air. It fell to the floor, bounced and came up heads.

"Heads it is," Roland bent over to look at the result of the flip. He picked up the silver dollar and handed it back to Endicott.

"Next up, Sylvie and Sanderson," Endicott set up the second coin toss. "Not that she qualifies as a lady but to stay consistent we'll have the pit viper call it. What's it going to be?"

"Heads," Sylvie was watching for a pattern to develop.

Endicott tossed the coin a second time and it came up heads a second time.

"Maybe that silver dollar is rigged after all," Sylvie picked up the coin and slapped it hard into Endicott's palm.

"Shut up, you won," Endicott dismissed her. "Okay, that leaves Ros and Sanderson for the last flip."

"You call it," Ros ordered Sanderson. She didn't appreciate the whole ladies first rule and didn't need any handicapping.

"If that is the way you want it. Let's test Sylvie's hypothesis. I call tails," Sanderson would have Ros out of the country for her own good if Sylvie's suspicions about the coin were incorrect.

"Endicott flipped the silver dollar for the last time. Everyone watched the coin ascend and then fall to the floor with one solid, authoritative clang – tails. The reporters paused as they stared at the result.

"Looks like I have packing to do," Ros broke the silence.

MARCH 13, 1938
SIGNALS ROOM – 2ND DEPT.
MINISTRY OF NATIONAL DEFENCE, DEJVICE

The volume of German wireless intercepts during the previous two days had been staggering. Their radio crews had worked double shifts without breaks to keep up. Burda had sat down to help on Thursday and had never left. During the last three days he had not read of anything but token resistance to Guderian's two invading tank divisions. Having swallowed Austria so easily, what other adventures might Hitler attempt and how soon? The thought hung over Burda like the dull blade of a well-used guillotine as he pulled another intercept from the pile to decode.

There was a silver lining, however. The latest German transmissions were describing resistance of a different sort. Burda had seen a status report from XVI Panzer Corps. Thirty percent of Guderian's tanks and vehicles had either broken down or run out fuel. Lack of organization, logistics shortfalls and crew inexperience were all were being blamed for the embarrassing state of affairs. The roads were so clogged with disabled vehicles between Linz and Vienna that Hitler had been forced to postpone his triumphal arrival in the Austrian capital for a day. Burda felt reassured knowing that his adversary was so unprepared for launching this invasion.

NORDBAHNHOF PRATERSTERN, WIEN

The streets had been quieter this morning. Calm enough for Sanderson to cajole a cab driver to dash Ros and him to the rail station. The trip had proven rather surreal. Amidst the looted storefronts and avenues littered with riot debris were old ladies placing flowers all about to pretty things up. Having made it to the station without molestation, Sanderson left Ros with the cab to hold the driver while he made sure trains were still running to Hungary. They were, luckily, yet the station was a mad house and he was glad that he had secured a ticket the day before. Sanderson had intended to see Ros onto the train but she was insistent that he would lose the cab and a safe trip back to Josefstadt by doing so. When Ros put her hands on her hips for emphasis, Sanderson realized the argument was over.

"Thanks, you're a peach for wanting to look after me like this but I am a big girl and I can get myself on a train," Ros hugged him goodbye.

"I'd never suggest that you could not, my dear, but I'll feel like a heel if I don't personally see you on that carriage," Sanderson protested one last time.

Ros stared into his eyes long enough to make her point. "No, really, I'm okay. Get yourself back to your lair. I don't want to worry about what might happen to you if you have to walk all of the way back."

"Very well," Sanderson found it difficult to argue as she was being sensible for a change. "Let's make sure you have everything. Passport?"

"Check," Ros confirmed.

"Ticket," Sanderson continued.

"Check," Ros patted her jacket pocket.

"Dispatches?" Sanderson moved on.

"Check," Ros squeezed her purse tight to her side.

"Cash?" Sanderson worked further down the list.

"Check," Ros had stashed the bills in multiple compartments.

"Addresses of mates in Budapest?" Sanderson continued.

"Check," Ros pointed to the inside jacket pocket.

"Extra pairs of shocking undies?" Sanderson threw that one out to break the tension.

"That's all, we're done," Ros was un-amused. "Take care of yourself and I want to talk with you one way or another as soon as possible. You hear?"

"Agreed. Safe trip now," Sanderson urged her on.

Ros knew he had feelings for her. She, on the other hand, wasn't sure what she was feeling for him. But she owed Sanderson for so much and wanted to leave him something he'd appreciate. So Ros grabbed him by the tie – he always wore a tie – and drew his lips close to hers. After a sweet, light embrace, she drew her lips away and walked off with her one travel bag. Despite herself she was going to miss the guy and she could picture the befuddled look on his face as Sanderson watched her disappear into the crowd. When he couldn't see her anymore, Sanderson climbed into the front passenger seat of the cab and the very relieved cabbie put the vehicle in gear and made for home territory.

Navigating her way through the throng of anxious Viennese desperately pushing and shoving their way into the station was a chore. Ros fretted that every sideswipe by a set of luggage, or each sudden bump from someone bulling their way past, meant her pocket was being picked. When she made it to the customs checkpoint, Ros was actually relieved to see police were on hand to maintain order. She observed that the barrier she was waiting in line to pass had been hastily thrown up, allowing too much crowding, but Ros eventually made her way to the front. After handing her passport to the customs man he meticulously perused its pages and then handed it to a nearby policeman, instead of back to Ros.

Before Ros could argue the policeman gestured for her to move off to the side.

Why wasn't she let through to the platform when everyone else ahead of her was allowed to pass? Was it because she was an American? Did they know she was a reporter? A little man in a dark coat and hat approached her. The policemen gave the fellow her passport then left them alone. Honestly, Ros found most Austrian men were rather odd but not in a dangerous way. This little wart was different. Not only was this guy odd, he oozed oddness in a way that made her very uncomfortable. Kind of like the way she felt when she bumped into the undertaker once as a kid: creepy. Only this guy was worse. His skin looked like it had been embalmed. Finally, after thoroughly going over her passport several times the fellow finally looked up at her.

"Leaving Vienna so soon, Miss Talmadge?" he asked with a voice just as creepy as his skin. "Or is it Frau Claybourne?"

Ros tensed. That was the name she had given the goons when she had paid a visit to the Nazi tourist bureau three months ago. "It's Talmadge. Is there a problem?"

"Oh no, everything is now quite in order," the undertaker assured her.

"Then may I have my passport, please?" Ros held out her hand. "I have a train to catch."

"My apologies. There are some questions that must be answered before I can return this to you. The use of false identities, espionage and other matters that must be dealt with," the little man noted while slipping her passport into his coat pocket.

"Listen, you must have me mixed up with someone else. I am a reporter with the Consolidated News Syndicate. I have a valid press pass that I would be happy to show you," Ros hoped a brave front might cause him to back down.

"Yes, your repeated publishing of scandalous lies is another matter that we need to discuss," the undertaker licked his lips in anticipation.

Telling Sanderson to go home was looking like a very bad decision. Then again, no reason the both of them had to get locked up. Somehow, she didn't think feminine charm would have any effect on this walking corpse. So Ros chose a different approach. "Listen, I'm sure you'll understand. My employer is a total rat and a complete pain in the ass. If I don't turn up where I am supposed to, when I am supposed to, he'll start making a lot noise with all kinds of important people between here and Berlin. Eventually you'll have to explain what you did with me and you don't want that kind of paperwork. So why don't you be a good boy and let me catch my train?"

Holding out her hand again didn't result in the return of her passport as Ros had gambled. Instead he suddenly reached out and grabbed her securely by the upper arm. The little fellow was surprisingly strong for a walking corpse. In no time she was out of reach of her luggage. Ros resisted as he forcibly tugged her further away from the other passengers.

"No, I don't think so, Miss Talmadge. You'll be coming with me," the undertaker commanded.

"Hey! Let me go!" Ros protested.

The party gauleiter did not favor her with a reply. She was a self-important bitch, who had yet to grasp the gravity of her current situation. Soon he would have her safely into a more secluded section of the station where he had appropriated space for such *discussions* as he had planned for her.

"Am I under arrest?" Ros demanded.

He almost broke into laughter and wondered whether the woman was attempting humor. With Americans, one could never be sure. "Consider this protective custody, Miss Talmadge."

"I want to see a lawyer!" Ros insisted.

"Yes, of course you do," the gauleiter pulled the reporter harder.

Noticing the deserted tunnel she was being dragged toward, Ros pulled hard enough against his grip to stop his forward progress. That wasn't well received. When he turned to face her, Ros felt scared for the first time. His grip on her arm tightened then his free hand came up and slapped her face so hard she would have fallen had he not been gripping her arm so tightly.

The lighting where they stood wasn't good, and her focus was on her tormentor, so Ros barely noticed the blur that rushed in behind the angry wart. But she did know what the butt of a Colt pistol looked like and Ros was pretty sure it was one of those that slammed down upon the base of the little man's skull. It took what seemed like a very long time before the grip on her arm released and the undertaker collapsed to the floor. Ros looked down at the crumpled form. She didn't trust the little bastard to be unconscious and kicked him in the balls with the business end of her shoe. Ros smiled because if he wasn't limp down there already, he sure would be now. Looking up, Ros saw a familiar face.

"Hey, I know you," Ros realized. "Yeah, the wise guy in uniform from Prague. Thanks mister."

"Just helping out a fellow American, lady," Bulloch looked past her, anxious to make sure they had not been seen.

"I never dreamed of seeing you down here--" Ros wondered how he had turned up to save her.

"--No time for that," Bulloch interrupted her. "You need to be on that train before this gunsel wakes up."

"No need to be rude," Ros didn't appreciate the brush off. "Anyway, I need my suitcase first."

"Then find it while I get this guy out of sight," Bulloch sent her off.

Ros retrieved her passport from the fascist's coat. In case anyone asked she had been checked out and was told could go on her way. No one would think a woman would be out of the clutches of that Nazi weasel without permission. While she retraced her way back to her bag, Bulloch dragged the body to a nearby door. He cursed when he tried the latch and it was locked. Close by was another door that he figured led to an electrical room given the hum coming from inside. It was locked too but he was able to jimmy it with his knife. Bulloch dragged the body as far back and out of sight as he could. Looking around, he saw a roll of spare electrical wire. There was plenty to tie the unconscious goon up. Also handy was a crate half full of folded oil rags. Bulloch used one of these to gag the Nazi. With all the equipment noise, no one would hear him when he woke up. Done, Bulloch went to the door and carefully peered out. No threats awaited him so he exited the electrical room and was securing the door as Ros returned.

"No uniform, huh? I knew you were up to something shady that morning I saw you talking with that Czech cop," Ros wanted to needle him for being a jerk.

"Oh lady, why don't you just shut up and get on your train," Bulloch pleaded as he finished securing the door. "You know, I can always go back in there, untie that goon and let you fend for yourself."

"You don't have to get nasty," Ros snapped at him. "I get it, you want me to go."

"No offense, doll, but that would be best," Bulloch heard a train whistle blow its final boarding warning. "If this was a movie that would be your train about to leave without you."

"Yeah, that's my train. Ah hell, how am I going to reward you? I owe you for saving my skin," Ros felt guilty despite his surly manner.

"You can pay me back later. Right now, get on your train and don't look back. With any luck, no one will find your friend in there until you're over the border and out of reach," Bulloch shoved her in the right direction. "See 'ya when I see 'ya."

"Unless I see 'ya first," Ros got in the last word. He wasn't off the hook, she swore to herself. Not by a long shot.

PART III
15. GRUDGES

Sudeten German Party leader Konrad Henlein

JULY 31, 1938
PERSONAL JOURNAL
FRANTIŠEK MORAVEC, PRAHA

Czechoslovakia was next on the German list.

After the easy conquest of Austria our sources reported Hitler summoned Field Marshal Keitel for a final polishing up of Plan Green. In the summary of the discussion that came into our possession, Hitler is quoted as saying that there were three possible ways to carry out the aggression. The simplest – a straightforward unprovoked attack – was undesirable because: *this might create hostile world opinion, which might lead to a critical situation.* The second possibility – *action after a period of diplomatic discussions that would gradually lead up to a world crisis and ultimately to a war* – Hitler did not like because this would take too long. Therefore, the Führer preferred the third alternative, described in the summary with undiplomatic frankness as: *a lightning action based on an incident such as the murder of the German envoy in the course of an anti-German demonstration.*
 Inside Czechoslovakia, Konrad Henlein's Sudeten Deutsche Party, started in 1933 with Henlein's professions of loyalty to the Czechoslovak republic, was culminating its own preparations against us. We learned this from official documents describing Hitler's instructions to Henlein. Shortly after the Austrian anschluss, Hitler summoned Henlein and

explained to him the plan that was to be followed. First, negotiations in Czechoslovakia between the Sudeten German Party and the government during which Henlein's was instructed to ask for ever-wider concessions but never to be satisfied when concessions were made. Second, Henlein was instructed to make propaganda outside Czechoslovakia, mainly in France and Britain, presenting himself as a fighter for the national self-determination of the Germans and promoting the fiction that the Czechoslovak state was disintegrating and unworthy of salvation. This last argument would be given substance by increased Nazi pressure on Poland and Hungary to formulate their own demands for ethnic Poles and Hungarians in Czechoslovakia.

Early in May reports came flooding in via our intelligence network indicating unusual concentrations of German military units near the frontier in Saxony and Silesia. Units from distant garrisons were identified including motorized divisions from Bremen and Hamburg. Although training was normal in May much larger scale German military exercises than usual were now being held close to our territory with unit strength substantially increased beyond normal peacetime levels. These reports were confirmed by information forwarded to us from British Intelligence.

Finally, the intentions of the Germans were signaled by the fact that SS transmitters, using the same codes that we possessed, began to order SS regiments to our frontier much the same as had been done before the march into Austria. The Germans were concentrating units in the strategic areas of Leipzig, Chemnitz and Zwickau – nine to twelve divisions in all.

As troop-movement reports from our agent-observers came in, A-54 requested an emergency meeting in the Sudetenland. It took place on May twelfth. He reported the Germans were preparing a campaign of sabotage and agitation against Czechoslovakia designed to culminate in an anti-Czechoslovak coup in the German territories on the eve of municipal elections set for the twenty-second, only ten days away. He also reported that weapons, ammunition and explosives were being clandestinely transported across the frontier and provided us the places where this ordinance was being stored. Karl further provided evidence where units of the Sudeten German Legion newly formed in the Reich and under the command of senior officers of the SS, were being concentrated along the border in preparation for an uprising.

According to A-54, officials of Henlein's party in the Sudetenland were under instructions to listen for the watchword, *Altvater*, on the German radio broadcasts. On receipt of this code word the sabotage was to start with destruction of railroads communications and bridges and attacks on Czechoslovak customs posts and police stations. The uprising would climax when the *martyred* Sudeten Germans were to call for help from their brothers in the Reich. That, in turn, would be the signal for the Sudeten German Legion to invade Czechoslovakia with support of SS units.

I went straight to the chief of staff with what we had discovered and he swiftly informed the president and the necessary individuals within the government. We were ready. On May 20, the password Altvater was broadcast over German radio. The cabinet met in emergency session and President Beneš ordered a partial mobilization. In all, we mustered about one hundred and seventy-six thousand soldiers who were sent into the threatened areas to maintain order and to prepare for any eventuality. All the bridges and crossroads were placed under guard, roadblocks were set up and fortifications manned.

The international press called it the *Czechoslovak Crisis*. The president's firm response to the facts on the ground was supported by Britain and France, whose ambassadors in Berlin acting on information supplied by British Intelligence, made official protests against the army concentrations on our frontiers and declared that their countries took a serious view of the situation. We learned later that Premier Daladier had summoned the German ambassador to his office in Paris on May twenty-first and pointed to a mobilization order lying on his desk: *It depends on you Excellency whether I sign this document or not.* In Berlin, the British ambassador visited the German Foreign Ministry four times that day to make clear Britain's support for France. To place further pressure on Hitler, the British and French governments made their press aware of the warnings they had issued to Germany.

Demonstrations in the Sudetenland ceased with the arrival of our military units. The sieg-heiling and goose-stepping demonstrators who had been spitting and hurling insults at the police disappeared from the streets of the border towns. The British ambassador in Praha informed British foreign secretary, Lord Halifax in London, that the radical Sudeten German elements had apparently been taken by surprise by the government's swift action.

Obviously we could not publicly reveal the secret intelligence information in our possession that lead to President Beneš' mobilization orders. The Nazi propagandists soon characterized our response as a Czechoslovak *over-reaction*, a Prag *trial balloon*, or even as a *blunder*. Without knowing what we knew some commentators in friendly quarters wrote that our government could have misinterpreted German intentions. The truth will come out in time. The fact remains, our analysis of the situation was not only highly justifiable – as was the government's reaction to that analysis – it stopped Hitler. The May attempt by the Nazis to make an Austria out of Czechoslovakia had failed.

Hitler's reaction to this frustration was typical. A strong protest was sent to Praha, in which the Czechoslovak defense measures were classified as an unfriendly act. To emphasize his position, the Führer sent a wreath to be laid on the grave of two Sudeten Germans killed by Czechoslovak gendarmes during the mobilization period. The truth about the German *martyrs*, like that about the German troop movements, was different from the story put out by Nazi propaganda. In a village near

Eger in western Bohemia, during the state of alert on May twenty-first at three-thirty in the morning, two couriers from Henlein's party rode a motorcycle in the direction of the German border. When ordered to stop by Czech guards the men instead turned the motorcycle directly at the officers to run them down. Henlein's men were shot during the attempt. Their subsequent funeral was turned into a great Sudeten German political demonstration. I sent Burda and Furst to observe as the Sudeten newspapers were treating the matter as a front-page sensation. The estimate reported back to me was a crowd of twenty thousand attended the funeral service to watch Hitler's wreath – with the dedication, *To Fallen Heroes* – placed on the graves. Since the procession was orderly it accordingly was permitted to take place without intervention by Czechoslovak police.

In Berlin Goebbels made much of these Sudeten German *martyrs*. Hitler invited the French and British military attachés in Berlin to visit the Czechoslovak-German frontier areas to see for themselves that no aggressive action was being prepared by Germany. Needless to say the attachés saw nothing as intended. But their reports did cause the governments in London and Paris to question their resolve at the worst of times. Having forced Hitler to back down, they now fretted about how close Europe may have come to war and sought not to come so close to the precipice again.

Reports from our agents during the summer were growing ominous. A new Sudeten revolt was being prepared. We had evidence of a new epidemic of weapons smuggling from the Reich, plus further German troop movements and concentrations on our frontiers were reported.

At a meeting in Komotau in July, Karl confirmed these reports and brought us documents revealing a plan for a new deployment of German forces. The preface was a quote from Hitler:

> *It is my unalterable decision to smash Czechoslovakia by military action in the near future. It is the job of the political leaders to await, or bring about, the politically and militarily suitable moment.*

In a letter accompanying this directive to his military commanders, General Keitel mandated the execution of this revised Plan Green be assured by Oct. 31, 1938 at the latest. Major changes to the plan involved massing units on the Southern Moravian frontier from the Austrian side against our unfinished fortifications. This was in addition to the divisions that were massing along the Moravian frontier in the north. Three other German armies were dedicated to bursting through our lines in the west. Five German armies, composed of 36 divisions, three of them armored, were to take part in all. The directive ordered that the offensive take no more than four days to complete so that France and Britain would have no time to react to the invasion. Karl provided further documents describing how Hitler had made his closest advisors sit through a two-hour tirade that began: *It is my unshakeable will that Czechoslovakia be wiped off the face of the map.*

Naturally we shared this intelligence windfall with our allies. Yet unlike their stout reaction in May, now they vacillated. Premier Daladier, buffeted by contentious parties in France, wavered between a resolve that France should fulfill her obligations to Czechoslovakia and an ever-growing inclination for France to step back and have her ally, Britain act as the principal protagonist of democracy vis-à-vis Hitler. The latter inclination won out. That's how it came to pass in late July, despite President Beneš' protests that the Sudeten German question was purely an internal matter, we found ourselves saddled with an unwanted British *mediator*.

AUGUST 1, 1938
ROAD TO KARLSBAD

The Czech capital had been tense for weeks as negotiations between the government and the Henleinists fitfully started and stopped with no compromise of a settlement in sight. The last round of talks had seen the Czechoslovaks propose a new formula for greater ethnic autonomy based on proportion of population. But the Sudeten Deutsche team rejected the Nationalities Statute proposal as falling short of Henlein's Karlsbad Program unveiled during the spring. The Czechs were unlikely to cozy up to what amounted to making the Sudeten border areas a province of Germany so the parties respectfully called it a day. The dance had gone on like this all summer. Beneš' government would make a new concession and the Henleinists would reject the offer as not enough. All the while the German press over the border would stir up ethnic resentment with claims of continued Czechoslovak oppression.

Under the circumstances Minister Carr felt duty-bound to stay close to Prague should the crisis everyone felt was around the corner flared up. Then during the last week of July the embassy got word from Washington that the Brits were sending a retired shipbuilder, Lord Walter Runciman, to mediate between the Henleinists and Prague. The development was a complete surprise. We had learned that members of the British embassy had been dispatched throughout Czechoslovakia on fact-finding forays, but no one had expected British government taking a position of leadership in Central European diplomacy when they had always been content with France in that role. In that week until the Runciman mission arrived in Prague all the opposing parties paused. Minister Carr seized on the suddenly quiet conditions to schedule an impromptu half-vacation, half-official tour of the Sudeten German districts. He wanted to see for himself how the people lived and what the conditions were. That's why Carr chose Karlsbad as their first destination. It was the symbolic home of the Sudeten Deutsche movement and Carr felt he would understand them better having visited the people there. If time and circumstances permitted, after they had toured the ethnic German areas, then the disputed Polish districts would be visited as well.

That's how Bulloch found himself sitting in the front passenger seat of the embassy Škoda on the road to Karlsbad. That Carr had declined to bring either Chapin or Elbrick along on the trip gave Bulloch tremendous satisfaction. They would see it as a snub but the minister wanted to keep his tour looking as unofficial as possible. Knowing Bulloch had already been guided through the Sudeten territories by the Czech military Carr thought his attaché would do nicely as a trustworthy guide through the area when the minister's own social connections were not available. Either Chapin and Elbrick could have done the same – they both were well acquainted with the area. But with the possibility of violence weighing on Carr's mind, and with Mrs. Carr along for the trip, the minister appreciated Bulloch riding shotgun. While the minister had not inquired too far into the details of Bulloch's activities in Austria during the spring he had read-between-the-lines of the official report and understood there were some dangerous spots Bulloch had to navigate. Carr would never have asked yet if the need arose Bulloch's Colt pistol was nestled underneath the comfortable tweed jacket.

PRAHA-KBELY AIRFIELD

The flight was late. To avoid actually setting foot in Germany, Endicott and Sylvie had booked a plane out of the Netherlands direct to Prague. Endicott was still holding a grudge where the Nazis were concerned. All of these months later and his ribs were still sore. He also remembered how much of a chore they had getting out of Austria. The party hacks never missed a chance to make their exit to Hungary as miserable as possible. Thank God he'd had Sanderson and Sylvie to lean on. With his broken bones, Endicott had been a magnet for fascist slime – poking, prodding, and forcing him to stand at every checkpoint. He envied Roland who could slink back into a dark corner of a crowded train and not be noticed. So Endicott could do without dancing with German border goons for a while. That obviously was a popular sentiment. The Amsterdam to Prague run they were on was fully booked with passengers. That hadn't stopped Sylvie from finagling a window seat though. He hoped Sanderson and Ros had waited for the late flight to arrive in Prague.

The months since Austria had left him more irritable than normal. Even he had to admit that. Caged up in the London bureau while his bones mended was bad enough. Then when the Czechs and the Germans nearly came to blows in May his bureau chief wouldn't let him out of the cage to make the trip. If Endicott went anyway, he was off the payroll... forever. That damn Jenkins had to get himself killed in Shanghai, which had spooked the bosses. It was one of the few times Endicott envied Ros working for Lasky. That son of a bitch didn't care who died as long as a story came attached. Since Harry and his ilk didn't pay much, Endicott had stayed put. He had expenses and Hearst was paying the bills. At least Hitler and Beneš had been compassionate enough to postpone the fireworks long enough for him to get back in the game. That shill Runciman getting sent to Prague to *mediate* was just the screwball stunt Endicott had been waiting for. Who could object to Endicott covering a damn peace mission? It was a perfect opportunity. Shots were going to get fired and sending Runciman only delayed the inevitable. And when war broke out Endicott would already be on the front lines. Who were the Brits kidding? The Czechs weren't going to cave and give the family silver to Hitler without a shot no matter how much Chamberlain wanted them to. Endicott sensed the engines being throttled back as the Douglas banked to the left.

"Hey buster," Sylvie looked away from the window in his direction. "Looks like they're bringing this bird in."

2ND DEPT.
MINISTRY OF NATIONAL DEFENCE, DEJVICE

The British had been very busy indeed. Not only was there disturbing news from London, Minister Krofta's senior aide had turned over a fat dossier on recent British activities within Czechoslovakia. With Viscount Runciman about to arrive these developments could not be coincidences. Although they had suspicions about the fairness of Runciman's mission, Tichy and Burda now had to take evidence to Moravec that the English were attempting to stack the deck against them.

"Sir, we have serious problems with the British," Tichy took the lead as Burda closed the door.

"More than usual? What are our friends up to now?" Moravec put down the case file he was reading and leaned forward in his chair like a predator preparing to pounce.

"Our people in London just discovered that Prime Minister Chamberlain recently received Hitler's personal adjutant, Captain Fritz Wiedemann, with a private message from the chancellor," Tichy placed the file on the desk before the boss.

"Do we know what was said?" Moravec tapped the file.

"We have a good description from a reliable source that Wiedemann delivered an assurance of Hitler's good will toward England and his strong desire for a peaceful solution to the Sudeten problem. Hitler promised that he could restrain himself for six months, perhaps even a year, from any military action against Czechoslovakia. The condition is that there are no further grievances added to the *sad lot* of his fellow Germans. But let but one Sudetendeutsche be murdered and Hitler would take immediate action," Tichy paraphrased what had been relayed to Praha.

"Ah, Herr Hitler is making things clear for the British," Moravec picked up the file. "When he is ready he will sacrifice several of Henlein's minions as a pretext and put the blame entirely on us. Wiedemann... he was Hitler's company commander during the war, correct?"

"Yes sir, exactly right," Tichy was always impressed with the boss' command of details. "Our files show that Wiedemann was attached to Hitler's personal staff sometime within the last few years and our London sources tell us that he has carried out a number of these confidential courier missions for Hitler to Britain, and perhaps elsewhere."

"And now we have good Lord Runciman foisted upon us so soon afterwards. Hardly seems like a coincidence, does it? As if President Beneš did not have enough doubts about the good faith of this *mediation* mission. Gentlemen, we're going to have our work cut out for us to affect a positive outcome from this travesty," Moravec doubted they could sway Runciman from the agenda he had been assigned.

"It gets worse, sir," Burda stepped forward to make his report.

"I was wondering what had you looking so irritated, kapitán." Moravec noticed the foreign ministry dossier Burda was holding was rather large. "Tell me."

"Minister Krofta is close to filing a formal complaint with the British Foreign Office. The British assistant military attaché, Major Sutton-Pratt, and consul Henderson are continuing their fact-finding tour of German-speaking regions. Only now they are filing official missives on that blue paper of theirs regarding the most inconsequential of Sudeten grievances. A German is consistently late to work and has a deduction from his wages and they call it discrimination of SdP party members. Further, for every one of these cases the British are now petitioning our Foreign Ministry regarding what is do be done about such discrimination. Krofta is being flooded with these blue notes and finds such meddling intolerable," Burda let the dossier fall to the desktop with a thud.

"Very busy bees indeed our British friends," Moravec saw an opportunity, however. "I'll talk to Minister Krofta. No need to cause a diplomatic stir when we can potentially benefit. Obviously they are building a portfolio for Runciman to operate from. Our job will be to turn these facts to our advantage in questioning the veracity of their commitment to objectivity. It will put Lord Runciman on the defensive and allow us to dump a fuller set of grievances perpetrated by the Henleinists for the British to digest in the coming weeks."

"I fear it will all be a waste of time. It seems to me the British have drawn a conclusion and merely are in the process of procuring data to support that conclusion." Tichy had seen the same reports that Moravec had. A pattern was emerging that would end with Britain giving Hitler what he wanted at Czechoslovakia's expense.

"That very well may be the case. We still have to play the hand we have been dealt. Remember, every week's delay allows more tanks and aircraft to roll out of the factories and more troops trained in the use of their equipment. Like you, I have no illusions of what is going on. Our job is to make the process as laborious as possible for our adversaries and friends alike," Moravec needed his men to retain their composure.

"But what happens when these games come to a finish and we find ourselves alone facing the wolf?" Burda was having difficulty envisaging how to turn that to their advantage?"

"So good of you to ask. I have assignments for both of you that addresses this very point," Moravec smiled. He hadn't planned to set his lieutenants upon these tasks just yet, but now he saw no reason to wait.

U PINKASU – NOVE MESTO, PRAHA

They were far away from home and no one would look out for them like one of their own. Whether it was Shanghai, Madrid, Addis Ababa or Vienna, you'd always find foreign correspondents huddled together. No one remembers who picked the bar or the restaurant because often times that happened by chance. At least that's what Ros had been told countless times by old hands stateside. Back then she would latch onto anyone who had been anywhere, reporting on anything. She wanted to soak up every anecdote and metaphor... every bit of grizzled observation or opinion there was to be had. When she got her shot – and in her mind that had always been when not if – Ros was going to be ready for action. As a woman in a man's biz she didn't have the luxury of learning the ropes on the job. True, she hadn't banked on that foul rodent accosting her at the Vienna train station but someone was looking over her shoulder and put her army friend in the right place to get her out of that jam.

Now that she was in Prague again tracking him down was on top of Ros' list. Ever since she had first met him during the Masaryk funeral something about that guy was fishy. Bulloch had odd friends and something to hide. His being in Austria right in the middle of an invasion didn't seem like coincidence either. The other thing was that most army or navy guys, sadly, had little interesting to hide except their girlfriends from their wives. Ros wasn't a beauty queen but she knew she wasn't hard to look at either. Yet this guy Bulloch wanted nothing to do with her. That wasn't the word on him in Prague when she had dug a little with the society ladies around town. Seems like the good captain had held the attention of plenty of lovelies during his short period stationed in Prague.

Back in May when she had been in town for a bit to cover the little war that wasn't, the boy had made himself positively scarce. The man had done her a huge favor so Ros had no interest in ratting him out. But she at least wanted to thank him properly and possibly satisfy some of her curiosity about him. He also might turn out to be a great source if she could finagle him into the arrangement. This time she was going to nail Captain Bulloch if it took lashing him to one those old statues on the St. Charles Bridge. First things first, though... right now she wanted to get the gang acquainted with their new home base in Prague.

"Welcome to our new haunt folks," Ros announced as she waved her arm in a circle around the pub's main room – oblivious to the many curious stares from the other patrons.

"It's a little dark in here isn't it?" Endicott was always the first to complain.

"I like to think of the place as comfortable and cozy," Ros wasn't going to let Charles ruin the mood.

"All I want to know is whether the beer is any good," Sylvie had her own priorities.

"This place has some of the best Pilsner in the city," Ros lifted a glass as proof.

"So you are familiar with this joint, are 'ya kid?" Endicott played a hunch.

"Yes indeed. Found it last year when they planted Masaryk. This establishment came highly recommended by the locals," Ros put full glasses in front of the other four.

Sylvie ran her hand along the weathered bench. "Cushions might be a pleasant addition though."

"We won't have time to worry about the creature comforts, sister. Not with a war on our hands," Ros reckoned it would take a month for the bullets to fly.

"Really now. Aren't you rushing matters a tad," Sanderson found her gusto for covering the big events entertaining. He had come to terms with her keeping him at arms length months ago. After Vienna, with her in Paris and him in London, getting Ros off his mind had been easier to accomplish. Career was all or nothing for the yank. He knew this and putting his personal feelings aside was something he had to live with. The situation didn't prevent him from enjoying Ros' company, however, and he wouldn't abstain from his casual flirtations when he so chose. There was always hope for compromising circumstances to take their course but he wasn't going to place a wager on it. He was a big boy. One had to accept women for the enigma they were. For now he was pleased to see the old group back together again. Along with Roland, Ros and Sanderson had gotten to Prague the week before. How such an unassuming fellow as Roland was so good at getting around always intrigued him.

"I am in total agreement," Roland threw in his support. "An establishment like this, a bit under ground, will be very good for when the bombs start dropping."

"Is that the voice of experience talking? Where have you experienced bombs dropping?" Endicott hadn't seen Roland around when bombs were falling on his head.

"Along the Rio Verde in the Gran Chaco, my dear friend," Roland was not to be underestimated.

"You covered that dust up down there between Paraguay and Bolivia?" Sylvie whistled approval.

"Damn nasty place. If you yanks had not found oil in the Andean foothills in twenty-eight it would have stayed an obscure, dusty backwater and yours truly would not have had to dodge Bolivian bombs," Roland had won his spurs fair and square.

"Unbelievable," Endicott was forced to retreat. "I never took you for the type."

Sanderson knew a bit more of his fellow countryman's credentials. Roland simply wasn't the buttoned down little business reporter he appeared to be. His non-threatening, unassuming demeanor had worked in his favor on more occasions than Sanderson could count. He felt it proper to burnish Roland's reputation a bit. "If you check the library archives you'll also find Roland's byline on a number of excellent reports from Abyssinia in thirty-six."

Everyone looked at Endicott for the usual unkind remark, but he had none. "I'm speechless... honestly."

"Bravo!" Sylvie applauded. "So you had to dodge Italian bombs too, Roland?"

"Oh, I can't claim such accolades, my dear," Roland reveled in the moment. "If the damn Italians could not find it within themselves to hit a camel in the Cyrenacian desert, their dandy tri-motors were not going to come within a full mile of me in Abyssinia."

After a good laugh Endicott thought it was time for another round. "Drinks are on me. I'm buying."

"How delightful. That's a change" Ros couldn't help needling him when the opportunity presented itself.

"Look who's talking... not like you pick up the tab much," Endicott returned the favor. "We all know how much that cheapskate boss Lasky of yours doesn't pay.

"Point taken," Ros found herself forced to admit as she slumped down onto the wood bench.

"Now, now... don't feel poorly," Roland patted her on the shoulder. "No one pinches pence as well as some of the British publishers I've had the questionable fortune to be employed by."

"Thank you, Roland. You're a champ," Ros leaned closer to him.

"Cheer up kid. It could always be worse," Sylvie chimed in. "Hey, when does that Brit mission get here again?"

"Wednesday afternoon," Sanderson had seen the latest announcement.

"The day after tomorrow. Great. I can't wait to nail Lord Runciman's ass to the wall of the train station," Endicott vowed.

HEADQUARTERS
SERVICE DE RENSEIGNEMENT, PARIS

The large envelope rested uneasily in Colonel Thollon's hands. Under-secretary of the air La Chambre had delivered it to him personally. The contents were a report from La Chambre's boss, Armee de la Air commander-in-chief Vuillemin. The latter had just returned from a lavish inspection tour of Luftwaffe airfields sponsored by Göring himself. Such meddling in intelligence matters by career military officers rather annoyed Thollon. They couldn't report what they saw without coloring the data to fit the needs of their service budgets. Thollon was forced to sift through each such report to gleam what was accurate and what was hyperbole. The process consumed too much of his already scarce time. Worse, he never got such reports prior to everyone else on the distribution list, which meant he usually had to clean up affairs afterward.

Thollon looked inside the envelope and retrieved the report. Naturally there were the wasted pages on needless exposition. He flipped past them. To his surprise he read that Vuillemin had been toured through design bureaus and aircraft factories. The Germans were putting on quite the show for their French guest. A few cigarettes later, Thollon leafed through to the général's conclusions. Vuillemin's conclusion that the Luftwaffe was vastly more modern than the Armee de la Air was not such a surprise. But the général went on to presume that his air force wouldn't last a week against the Luftwaffe. That would get the politician's attention, as was intended. Vuillemin was fishing for higher budget allocations, Thollon was sure. Of the général's seven-hundred planes he presumed none of them to be modern and all of them obsolete in comparison to what Göring was fielding. Next Vuillemin used Thollon's own intelligence report estimating aircraft production in the Reich at between five hundred to seven hundred planes a month, whereas France was turning out fifty planes a month, and Britain seventy planes per month: *Germany had such a lead that France could not catch up for years.*

Thollon rolled his eyes while lighting another cigarette. Vuillemin had just complicated his life tremendously. He understood what the air force général was after... authorization to buy more warplanes from the Americans. Perhaps he was also encouraging the government to crack down on the trade unions to make home production more efficient. Unfortunately, that myopic agenda would help feed other agendas within the government with enormous repercussions. Half the cabinet sought to stand firm beside the Czechoslovaks in the fight to come. The other half was seeking a way to postpone the fight or keep France out of the hostilities. The prime minister wavered between both camps depending on what happened on a particular day. Thollon was sure Foreign Minister Bonnet would seize on Vuillemin's conclusions to sway official policy against supporting the Czechs. The battle between cabinet members would be brutal and eventually, Thollon would be called on to lend credence to one position or the other.

Thollon was in a vise. Very soon the cabinet would squeeze him for an answer and he would have to choose sides. How Thollon chose would have a vital impact on thousands of lives and probably on the future state of international borders. The problem Thollon thought, pausing to exhale, was that he wasn't yet sure which side to choose.

44TH FIGHTER FLIGHT, POLERADY – BOHEMIA

He contemplated putting the fighter down on the rough grass field with a three-point landing. That would be a challenge of sorts to the newly minted pilots under his command. Competition worked wonders but sometimes he had to remind himself that the duties of a squadron leader were different than those of a perfectionist. The pilots were improving. They weren't where he wanted them to be yet, but progress was progress and now wasn't the moment to push them unnecessarily. Bozik had welcomed the order to disperse the squadrons to their operational airfields. Getting the men to concentrate on their skills was easier without the distractions of their home base near Praha.

If war came, they would be squaring off against a faster, more modern foe. Each of his pilots would have to be at their wily best to down the Messerschmitts the Germans were flying. Their Avia B-534 bi-planes could be outrun and out-dived. Survival meant drawing the Germans in close where the Avia's superior maneuverability and rate of climb would let the Czechoslovak pilots loop, turn and roll into firing positions. The smart thing for the Germans to do would be to dive away from a dogfight, gain altitude and re-engage. The good news from Spain was that German pilots thought their fighters were maneuverable enough, and their skills superior enough, to dogfight with their shiny new monoplanes. That hubris would cost them dearly.

Today Bozik had been putting his men through in-flight firing drills to better their aim. He wanted them to improve at accurately gauging the speed and direction of their targets so that they could swiftly aim at a spot in the air ahead of where the opposing fighter was going and hit the target with a full burst. This was important since Avia pilots couldn't depend on the standard impulse of getting on the other pilot's tail and staying there long enough for a straight arc of fire to take the enemy down. True, the Avia was very close in performance to the Messerschmitts the German pilots were flying today, but take too long chasing one of them and soon one of the German's comrades put himself on your tail.

What Bozik had in mind was a more *athletic* strategy. At first his pilots thought he was crazy. But now they were beginning to see what their squadron leader was after. Bozik was training them to descend on the Luftwaffe squadrons like angry wasps where they would cross over the enemy pilot's field of fire at odd angles and be gone from view in seconds. Bozik was betting that most of the Germans pilots would be unable to calculate speed and position within such short windows of opportunity to aim accurately at such wildly moving targets. But if a Messerschmitt crossed in front of Bozik's men at an oblique angle, even for a moment, his pilots *would* be ready to fire short, quick bursts from their machine guns. Thankfully all four of the Avia's weapons were on the fuselage. With four guns pumping bullets into the same concentrated target area their short bursts would do significant damage.

An experienced enemy pilot would adjust to the tactic. Bozik was wagering, however, that his pilots could gain enough of an advantage to rule the early dogfights. Germans aces blooded in Spain were known to dictate that their wingmen follow them into the attack like guards. These wingmen were not permitted to hunt themselves just protect their commander's flanks. These wingmen would not have the target acquisition skills to shoot down his wildly moving Avias and neither could their Messerschmitts match the highly maneuverable bi-planes in aerobatics. If the Czechs could shoot down enough of the enemy aces in the early encounters his squadron would have the advantage against the leaderless wingmen.

Bozik brought his B-534 around in a banked turn for the easier two-point landing after all. Both of the front wheels touched the grass solidly with no bounce as he had planned. Throttling back the engine further, he felt a minor thud through the structure as the tail came down firmly. Looking over his shoulder Bozik saw his two wingmen bring their fighters in behind him. One of them found a rut under the grass that forced his main wheels to bounce the plane off the ground. The pilot would be red-faced about that but Bozik wouldn't tease him too much. The wingmen followed Bozik as he taxied his Avia off the airstrip to where they parked the fighters after a flight. Before he had come to a complete stop a ground crewman was already latching back the cockpit canopy of Bozik's fighter. He climbed out of the Avia and jumped to the ground. Pulling off his leather flight cap, Bozik stood gazing at his returning pilots gunning their engines and making their landings. Flying was always a dangerous business and he never relaxed until the last of his men were down on the ground. Leading a squadron turned a man into a den mother.

After all of the Avias had landed, Bozik went looking for the two Letov S.328s that had been pulling the target banners. He'd had instructed the Letov pilots to engage in erratic maneuvers. Just enough changing of direction so that his fighter pilots would have a harder time aiming at the banners but not enough hard flying for the targets to get their towing lines tangled. The long white banners had large black dots painted on them. Ground crewmen were unfurling the banners as Bozik approached. The pilots would have their look after the targets had been staked to the ground. Bozik examined the circular dots carefully. The number of bullet holes in each would be counted. But from what he could tell it seemed like more shots were landing in the circles than the last time they practiced... he was pleased. Bozik was forcing his men to approach the banners at high speed and oblique angles that would leave the pilots precious little time or opportunity to fire their guns. Hitting the targets under those conditions was not easy.

The idea for the tactics his pilots were learning had come up months ago in an animated discussion amongst the squadron leaders in the air regiment. Several had been part of the flight team during the Zurich International Aviation Meeting in May of the previous year. They had seen first-hand the latest prototype of the German 109: the E model. The Czech team had done well with the latest model B-534, not only besting the Fiats of the Italians, but also the Dewoitines of their French allies. That had caused some consternation and worry with the strategic planners within the general staff. If little Czechoslovakia could field superior fighters to their protector, France, then how viable would France's support be in the air?

The new Messerschmitt was envy of all the pilots present in Zurich. With the latest Daimler-Benz engine the form of the plane was significantly enhanced – sleeker, deadlier and swifter – compared to the D model now in service. Equipped with a variable-pitch airscrew, the E model could disengage from any fighter then in the air, either in a straight line or a dive. Not even the Soviet Polikarpovs could keep up with it. Bozik hoped the American Hawk 75s the French were buying would at least be able to stay close to the 109. The B-534 had the advantage in tight turns and rate of climb. Within those advantages is where they were forced to craft their strategy. The longer it took for war to come the more E models they would have to face. Bozik hoped war came soon while the current model one-o-nines still predominated. The difference in performance between the older Messerschmitt and the Avia was not so great.

Bozik spied the base commander, Luža, walking stiffly in his direction. He had flown for the Austro-Hungarians during the Great War. Luža was the kind of man who never talked or bragged about his number of kills. At their first meeting, Bozik had been so curious that soon after he did some digging and learned his new superior had a significant number of Italian aircraft shot down to his credit. While Luža would not discuss his accomplishments in the air his eyes lit with fire when the topic turned to fighter tactics. Luža's mind was as acrobatic as his instincts in the air must have been. Such a shame his left leg had been cut open by metal shrapnel from an explosion in the air. The wounds had left the leg as stiff as wood and ended Luža's flight career. To his credit, when the squadron leaders had come to propose training their pilots to combat the more modern Messerschmitts, Luža had been enthusiastic. He immediately dedicated whatever fuel, ammunition, aircraft maintenance or other resources necessary to support the effort. He also made a point of sitting in on every squadron's post-flight debriefing to keep track of progress.

"How well did they do today?" Luža looked over the target banners.

Bozik gestured at the bullet-ridden circles. "See for yourself. Steady improvement, there are more holes inside the targets than when we went up yesterday."

"Then why do you not look happier?" Luža was puzzled. "Your boys are doing a fine job."

"Yes they are," Bozik admitted, rubbing his chin. "What bothers me is that our entire strategy is predicated on having an altitude advantage. I've been thinking though. It's only twenty to thirty minutes from the border to Prague and we're between the border and the capital. If we wait for the alert to come in from the border, no matter how fast we get our guys off the ground, and they're pretty quick, we'll have a hard time climbing high enough to intercept the enemy from an altitude advantage... if we can intercept them at all. Hell, if the German fighters weren't enough to worry about, their Dornier and Heinkel bombers are damned fast too."

"That has been bothering me as well. If you and the other squadron leaders think the pilots are ready I've been pondering some tactical thievery," Luža had worked out a possible solution a few nights before.

"Stealing from whom?" Bozik was intrigued.

"The U.S. Navy. A few years ago I was part of an officer exchange program. The Americans love those aircraft carriers of theirs. Amazing ships. It's an exhilarating feeling to stand on the officer's deck of the Lexington, wind at your back, watching a squadron launch. The American navy has a doctrine that keeps their fighter patrols up in the air to intercept incoming enemy aircraft and give the carrier time to launch additional fighters. I think we should do the same," Luža knew there might not be any other way to catch the Luftwaffe planes in time.

"That makes a lot of sense," Bozik latched onto the strategy. "Putting up regular air patrols would give us a chance to slow down the enemy while the rest of the squadrons scrambled to get into position to do some damage. I cannot wait to start training my boys. We would have to set up specific grids to patrol, I would imagine. Do we have the fuel for continuous flight operations?"

"Leave that to me, we will call it advanced formation training for now. Praha loves it when they think we're accomplishing more training. If we need more fuel, we'll get it," Luža already had a requisition order prepared and waiting at his desk.

AUGUST 2, 1938
SCHLOSS REITEMEYER, KARLSBAD

Bulloch assumed the minister had found his collection of non-radical ethnic Germans via the discreet dinner parties Carr was fond of hosting and attending in Prague. Mostly business or civic leaders with a lot at stake and more to lose if war came, Carr felt they would be the best filter through which to get at the facts of the region. He also had wanted to see the area with his own eyes, and experience the people and their problems for himself. For his hosts there was also the prestige that came with being visited by a United States envoy. The accommodations weren't bad either, Bulloch had noticed. If the rest of the estates on the itinerary were anything like this castle-like mansion in the hills, Bulloch wouldn't complain. The bed in his room was huge. Too bad Petra wasn't along to share it with him. Luckily for Bulloch, her budding interest in politics had grown so that she hadn't complained a bit when he told her he'd be away from her for most of the month. There were articles to write, rallies to plan and. she was quite consumed by it all. Truth be told, he was starting to miss her more than she missed him.

A persistent tugging on his sport jacket sleeve interrupted Bulloch's thoughts of Petra. It was one of the estate staff, a kindly middle-aged lady who was in charge of the upper floors. She probably found guests staring aimlessly out of the oversized hall windows all of the time. Bulloch was still embarrassed though. He realized he had just been told in German that there was an important message for the minister. He smiled and took the envelope from her.

"Thank you very much," Bulloch told her with sufficient charm to make her cheeks blush. He was shameless. It was an impression he was much happier leaving the woman with.

Opening the envelope, Bulloch found the note was from Bess Flynn back at the embassy. Short, sweet and to the point as usual. The U.S. ambassador in Berlin, Hugh Wilson, was on his way to Prague to discuss the Runciman mission. Minister Carr would have to return to the capital and so much for the road trip. This wasn't all bad though if Wilson was bringing Truman Smith along. The two attachés had a lot to catch up on. Oh well, maybe it all was for the best Bulloch told himself while heading down the hall to the Carr's suite with the message. Call him selfish, but his little reverie just before had planted a strong desire in him to throw Petra between the sheets.

ŠKODA WORKS, PLZEN

His notations filled the form on the clipboard and if anyone else could make sense of them he would be surprised. Srom used his own shorthand when making inspections to keep prying eyes from looking over his shoulder. The factory managers would have little to worry about from his visit today, however. Not only had they remedied the reliability problems with the LT vz. 35 tank, they also had gotten quite speedy at returning broken down vehicles sent back to the factory for service. The proof was in the delivery ledger. There were fifty percent fewer tanks in the repair yard than when he had dropped in on them three months ago. Srom was pleased that his mobile divisions would have their tanks in the field and not in repair when war came. The next step was getting Praga into full production with the LT vz. 38. That was the tank he envisioned leading a counterattack into Germany. But that vision was still held hostage by the bureaucrats and the procurement process, Srom sighed.

After closely examining the tread wear on a particular Škoda, Srom noticed Tichy, the spy, approaching. Srom knew Moravec. Espionage was something the man had been assigned to so he brought a level of efficiency and effectiveness to the work one rarely saw from the fops usually found in the job. Starting from scratch Moravec had surrounded himself with men like himself. Srom could respect the spymaster and his right hand, Tichy.

"Striking fear into the factory managers?" Tichy was aware of Srom's reputation.

"Fear is relative. They know me now. Few of them run when I growl these days," Srom jested. "What brings the cockroaches out into the sunlight today?"

Tichy took the insult in good humor. Srom remained suspicious of the intelligence service liked most career officers. The difference was Srom would accept anything that gave his tanks an edge in battle. "This cockroach has brought you a present. Walk with me."

"What stolen morsels are you carrying today?" Srom followed the Second Department man out into the open factory yard.

"We are not supposed to know that General Krejčí has issued a secret directive to prepare for an aggressive defense should the politicians waver. Nor are we supposed to know he has tasked you with creating the template for that aggressive combat strategy should the contingency arise," Tichy cut right to the chase.

"My God, it is high time you people sniffed that out. I like to think your bunch are earning their pay every month," Srom was actually quite pleased. He would rather have the Second Department on board to assist them. "The question is how does your boss intend to use this knowledge to his advantage?"

"He appreciates the point-of-view behind the directive and stands ready to be supportive when required," much more Tichy did not want to elaborate upon.

"Very well, cockroach, please relay my regards to Mister Moravec. Now then, you mentioned a present?" Srom expected some useful information.

"First, advice," Tichy was obliged to scold the tactician. "Your working group is drawing attention. When the same little club of officers gets together without drinking, gambling, women or sports involved it gets noticed. We have rooted out many of the Hungarian and German sympathizers from the ranks but we have to assume there are more of them who are ready to report such comings and goings."

"But we have been very careful," Srom had personally taken reasonable measures to be discrete.

"Yes, you have. But better precautions must be taken from now on. Watching your back is one of the ways we can support your endeavor," Tichy hoped that would be enough to assuage Srom.

"Duly noted. Changes will be made immediately." Srom casually checked around them to make sure there was no one that could overhear them. "Now tell me something I do not know."

"You may have noticed the German's new 150mm howitzers have not entered Wehrmacht service. The reason is they have no shells for them. There is a severe shortfall in artillery ammunition production in general. I'm sure you see the advantage in possessing that knowledge," Tichy knew that morsel would be of extreme interest to Srom.

"Indeed," Srom's mind raced through the implications. "This is verified, you say?"

"Completely," Tichy knew the data had triple confirmation. "I can present you the supporting documents if necessary."

"No, not necessary. The Second Department's track record is impeccable." And if the information proved false, Srom could guarantee the body of the cockroach would occupy a shallow grave without its head.

AUGUST 3, 1938
WILSONOVO STATION – PRAHA

Getting through the crowded rotunda was challenging. The station was packed with gawkers of all kinds from the politically well connected to the patriotically fervent. None of these people would give an inch as Ros waved her press pass in their faces while attempting to squeeze by. As polite was not cutting it, Ros delivered a couple of well-placed New York subway shoves that did wonders for clearing some wiggle room. When Ros finally reached the platforms she understood the complete disregard of her press credentials. The place was crawling with news hounds. Ros figured there was probably a couple of hundred correspondents waiting for Runciman's train to arrive.

It took a few minutes but she finally spotted where Sanderson and Sylvie had staked out some prime territory near where Runciman would likely walk by after getting off the train. In navigating through this pack of wolves to get to them, Ros saw no sign of Roland or Endicott. At least she recognized enough of the huddled press corps that a chirpy hello and a big smile got her closer to where she was trying to go. After inching her way halfway, Sylvie spotted Ros and waved but Sanderson was oblivious as usual. Ros waved back and continued on. Reaching them, she finally caught sight of Endicott standing a few paces off chatting with his CBS pal.

"Glad you could make it," Sanderson was no longer ruffled by her tardiness.

"Oh be quiet, you," Ros dismissed teasing entirely.

"Where you been, sister?" Sylvie was curious what had delayed Ros.

"I swung by the embassy looking for that fellow American who helped me out in Vienna," Ros swooned a bit on purpose to get Sanderson a little worried.

Sylvie clued right in and elbowed Sanderson on the arm. "See that Robbie, you have competition."

"I realize it is not in your nature but please, at least make a shallow attempt not to be cruel," Sanderson retorted without looking at his tormenter.

"It doesn't matter anyway the guy wasn't there. The bastard is out of town again," Ros went easy on her Brit companion.

"He isn't off your hook yet. I think its love," Sylvie saw no reason to end the fun prematurely.

"Oh hush! The man got me out of a jam, I just want to do the right thing," Ros didn't need Sylvie prying on this subject.

"How romantic. I can picture it now when you finally corner your hero in uniform," Sylvie was merciless.

"Assuming with a high degree of probability that you pulled the wings off of insects as a child, why don't you run off and find some unsuspecting Czech bureaucrat to dismember," Sanderson got in a broadside of his own.

"Looks like I touched a nerve," Sylvie declared with complete satisfaction.

"Has anyone seen Roland?" Ros slyly looked around the platform.

"Not a sign of him all day," Sylvie was done needling the two lovebirds for now.

"Knowing Roland he probably left early to meet the train at the border. I can picture him casually approaching Lord Runciman to strike up some polite conversation with an offer to share some hot tea," Sanderson gathered Roland probably had an exclusive interview ahead of all of them.

A steam whistle blew in the distance causing a hush to fall over the platform. The human mass turned as one in the direction of the approaching locomotive. As the train came into view several more short bursts of the whistle were accompanied by the hiss of steam purged from the engine's lines.

Three groups waited for the train to arrive. The larger group was the domestic and foreign reporters who were rifling through pockets to prepare notebooks and pencils. Then there were the newsreel crews who were rolling film to capture the train pulling up to the platform. The smallest group was composed of official dignitaries: Dr. Smutny, Beneš cabinet chief; the lord mayor of Prague; the British minister, Sir Basil Newton; and all the associated aides. A stern and humorless bunch they were too, Endicott observed. While waiting for the action to start Endicott got curious about the rest of the congregation and took a look around. With so much attention focused on Runciman's approaching train, Endicott doubted many were looking in the other direction to witness a fourth entourage making their way forward. Endicott was pleased with himself that he had checked the archived newspapers at the library the day before. He recognized the man clearing the way. It was one of the British Foreign Office goons who had been giving the Czechoslovaks fits lately, Frank Aston-Gwatkin. In tow were the primary Sudeten German negotiators: Ernst Kundt and Wilhelm Sebekowsky. The Czechs would be furious with the Brits now. Sure enough, the Czech delegation had noticed and they were none too pleased with the uninvited SdP men.

"If looks could kill," Endicott muttered while scribbling down notes.

Shirer leaned closer to Endicott while watching the first passengers get off the train. "What was that?"

Endicott tapped his friend on the shoulder to turn him around, then pointed at the SdP representatives.

"That can't be a coincidence," Shirer could not believe the British were being so blatantly biased. "Runciman's whole mission smells."

That's when Endicott noticed that Roland was following closely behind Aston-Gwatkin and the Sudeten Germans. Before he could ruminate further on another of Roland's triumphs, the sound of rustling feet announced that the man of the hour was stepping off his train. With barely a nod Runciman waved his top hat at the crowd, returned it to his head, and then shuffled down the platform with his delegation following close behind. Correspondents called out questions but Runciman blithely ignored them. By the time the British mediator came close enough to Endicott the reporter could not see why he should bother.

"The hangman with his little bag came creeping through the gloom," Endicott hoped he had spoken loudly enough for the old fart to hear.

Shirer chuckled at the description. "Actually, the quote is: *The hangman, with his little bag, went shuffling through the gloom.*"

"Oh please, I have my Brit friend over there who can correct me on Oscar Wilde quotes," Endicott pointed at Sanderson. "I don't need it from you, pal. Creeping works better anyway."

Endicott watched Runciman continue on to warmly shake hands with Czechs. Then the viscount proceeded to just as warmly to do the same with the Henleinists after Aston-Gwatkin made the introductions.

"I come as a friend of all and an enemy of none," Runciman announced to the crowd. With that, shipping magnate bid his farewells and made to leave.

"If that don't beat all," Endicott put his notebook away.

"If I were President Beneš, I would be very worried right now," Shirer had seen enough British missions at work to be wary of their true intentions.

Roland appeared out of the thinning throng. "Glad I found you chaps."

"Come over to rub it in, did you?" Endicott groused. "How much did you get out of those Sudeten Nazis and their chaperone?"

"Plenty, my friend... and out of friendship I've come to tell you that Lord Runciman is setting up over at the Alcron Hotel. This evening he's holding a reception for selected correspondents there. You should attend," Roland suggested with a tip of his bowler.

PRESIDENTIAL CHAMBERS
PRAŽSKÝ HRAD, PRAHA

Moravec didn't relish flirting with insubordination with the president. That Moravec believed he must persist in pressing his point came from necessity, not disrespect. Moravec needed to know the president's mind. While gracious and tolerant, Moravec sensed Beneš' growing irritation at being pressed, which had led the president to pace silently between the wide windows overlooking the courtyard.

"Mister President," Moravec moved in closer to intercept Beneš' path. "Forgive my impertinence but I must know. Are you playing for time with the arrival of the British mission or do you actually believe a political solution to the crisis can be mediated?"

"There is always a political solution, František, we only have to find it," Beneš replied wearily. As often was the case with politicians, Beneš' sincere reply had not been an answer to Moravec's question.

"Your optimism has always been a source of strength to me, sir. Yet I am a pragmatic man by nature and pragmatism demands that I advise you that the only thing of value we can gain from this British mission is the opportunity to stall Hitler. No other good can come of this." Moravec imagined Beneš would either throw him out of the castle or entertain the spymaster's point.

"Go on, my friend?" Beneš finally spoke. "I know you have more to say."

"Mister President, it is imperative that you stall for time," Moravec would take his best shot at persuading Beneš. "There are several incontrovertible facts we know from verifiable sources. Last week Herr Henlein was summoned to meet Hitler at Bayreuth. He pleaded that Germany not use force to attain the Sudeten districts. Hitler refused the request. *The Wehrmacht needs blooding*, Henlein was told. If you accepted Henlein's Karlsbad Program on Sudeten autonomy in full tomorrow it would not change a thing, we would still face a military crisis. Anything short of ceding these territories to Germany outright means nothing. Hitler means to make war upon Czechoslovakia. Therefore, there is no hope in mediating a settlement with the Sudeten Deutsche Party. However, we can string out this mediation process to our advantage."

"Do you expect me to negotiate in bad faith?" Beneš was not at all pleased with that implication.

"Yes, quite right, sir." Moravec pressed ahead. "You are a student of history. I've taken it upon myself to undertake some study of my own recently. The British have a very defined sense of their own interests, as well as their own outward image. They have no qualms about taking an uncomfortable or prejudicial course of action if doing so is in their interests. Remember 1919? The British tacitly encouraged Venizelos to occupy Western Anatolia to help pacify the defeated Ottomans. It was in British interests to do so. Two years later the British looked the other way when the Greeks overreached and Ataturk pushed them into the Aegean... because it was in British interests to realign policy toward the resurgent Turks. The British are very conscious of their image, however. They never officially promised the Greeks support so they could properly, if sadly, deny support to their wartime ally later. The key to the British sense of image is propriety. If they must renege on a promise then their image must be shielded by some legal stipulation that absolves them of guilt. They made their promise of wartime aid to the French yet can be released from that promise if the French promise to Czechoslovakia becomes moot. Lord Runciman's mission of mediation is the process by which the British hope to absolve themselves of their promise to France. It is the conclusion of my staff, and myself, that the fuse to Hitler's territorial ambitions runs much shorter than the fuse to Britain's fondness for process. Feed Runciman's plodding mediation efforts long enough and Hitler will short-circuit the negotiation process before the British can properly abandon it themselves. Denied their face-saving process the British will be forced to honor their promises when war comes. You need to keep Runciman trundling along for a month, maybe six weeks. We have confirmation from multiple reliable sources within Germany that Hitler will not wait longer than October first to *blood* his forces."

Beneš had listened intently. No doubt Moravec had chosen the Venizelos example with care. Beneš and the Greek prime minister had been principal participants during the peace negotiations that ended the Great War and Beneš held the man in warm esteem. Punctuated thusly, Moravec's pragmatism was compelling. Czechoslovakia could not benefit from this mediation charade her allies had foisted upon them. Was it dishonorable then to approach the charade in bad faith?

"You are uncomfortably persuasive as usual, František," Beneš found himself appreciative to Moravec for adding sharp clarity to his thoughts. "Let us entertain your perspective for a moment. Do you suggest I employ the normal legislative procedures to retard whatever findings and proposals Lord Runciman makes to us?"

Moravec smiled... the president had been swayed. "Yes, those are exactly the measures I suggest you eventually employ. But for now I seek permission to retard the progress of Runciman's mission in concluding their findings and proposals. Leave that to my department, sir. We have a deep understanding of how Henlein's people operate against the nation, as well as the direct tether to their masters in Berlin. The British are a very thorough people. By the time we're done briefing Lord Runciman on these finer details his team will be forced to take weeks to substantiate and verify the volume of facts we are planning to deluge upon them."

ALEXANDERPLATZ, BERLIN

The chancellor was full of surprises of late. His opening of a private channel to the British prime minister had come as a surprise within the Abwehr. Personal diplomacy was out of character for Hitler. Oh he was good for a show one-on-one – embodying the blunt instrument to bludgeon unsuspecting politicians, as Schuschnigg had learned earlier that year. But sending Wiedemann with a message of good will to Chamberlain was an overture more in keeping with von Ribbentrop, Ottke thought. Yet the accounts Ottke was receiving pointed to Hitler by-passing the Foreign Ministry entirely. Did Hitler no longer trust his foreign minister, as well as distrusting General Beck? After confronting Hitler and naively demanding the chancellor not embark on a military misadventure in Czechoslovakia, Hitler lost his temper with the general, unleashing a torrent of angry invective starting with: *The military's role is obedience!* With no other option but retreat, Beck promptly resigned as army chief-of-staff. Hitler's will may be unshakeable but rank insubordination rattled him. If this row with Beck had led Hitler to irrational suspicion of all of his army subordinates the road ahead would be complicated immeasurably.

Now the British were sending their Lord Runciman to mediate between the Sudetens and the Czechs. Were Hitler's personal overture and this British mission connected? Ottke was intrigued. A great deal depended on concluding correctly how the British would react in the coming crisis. Falling in line behind the French and Czechs during the previous May had been the predictable response. Yet having shown backbone then why now was Chamberlain going out of his way to accommodate Hitler? That wasn't predictable. Ottke would have to discuss the contingencies with Admiral Canaris as soon as possible.

For now, Ottke was curious how the Foreign Ministry would choose to frame the Runciman mission. He approached a well-stocked newsstand on the crowded Alexanerplatz that carried most of the more obscure papers he was fond of regularly tracking. Scanning the racks Ottke found what he was looking for, the latest edition of *Deutsch Diplomatische-politische Korrespondenz*. The publication was the Foreign Ministry's official voice. The article on Runciman was enlightening. It concluded: *The task of the Runciman Mission is to expose Czech subterfuges and to establish the facts and conditions in their true character, in order, perhaps, to draw appropriate conclusions.* Was Chamberlain's accommodation a sign that the British had already drawn the *appropriate conclusions*? Ottke needed to find out.

UNIVERZITA KARLOVA, PRAHA

He owed Otto. They had made amazing time getting back to Prague. Of course Otto's primary concern was that Minister Carr had pressing business to attend to in Prague. Bulloch benefited all the same, however. He had pressing business of a different sort and hoped that he had positioned himself in front of the right university hall to intercept Petra after her last class. Petra told him the university dated to the 14th century one time he had walked her to class. Bulloch took notice of another gaggle of students exiting the hall. None of them was Petra. She had gotten so distracted by politics lately that the girl could be off at some meeting somewhere instead of heading home from class. That thought made Bulloch irritable for he wanted to see her with a power he was not accustomed to.

Bulloch had chosen the right spot after all. There she was chatting with two other women and heading in his direction. At about twenty feet away, Petra noticed him, stopped, and smiled in that mischievous way that drove Bulloch to distraction. Sending her girlfriends along, Petra closed the distance to park herself up close enough that he could smell the fragrant soap she bathed with.

"You are home early," Petra sounded pleased at the surprise visit.

"I couldn't stand being away from you any longer," Bulloch fed the moment.

"Honey lips," Petra drew the words out in a sly way that suggested he was insincere, yet she appreciated the facade nonetheless. "I do not believe you."

"Let me prove it to you, madam," Bulloch proposed in the cultured drawl of his Virginia forbearers.

Petra saw how his eyes danced and she fixed her gaze upon them so strongly that Bulloch never noticed her right hand reach up to grab his jacket lapel... until she pulled him down so his lips were within inches of hers. "You are not getting any sleep tonight."

HOTEL ALCRON, PRAHA

Lord Runciman was to hold court in the hotel lobby where close to two hundred eager reporters were arrayed to greet him and his team. And what a lobby... the joint was swank. Everything from the wide stairs up from the lobby, the Italian marble floors and the fancy chandeliers exuded the luxury treatment. The doorman said the Alcron had been built only six years prior to match the best hotels in Paris or London. At least the old British coot had good taste in accommodations.

After being snubbed at the train station the assembled press were still rather cranky and worried that Runciman was going to waste their time by reading a prepared statement before retiring to his suite. The old man had taken his good sweet time settling in at the hotel after arriving from Wilsonovo, keeping the reporters waiting for several hours. Except for the surprise appearance of the SdP negotiators at Wilsonovo Station there was no news to report and most of the reporters had editors chomping at the bit for something more substantial from the British mediator. Ros was growing impatient like all of the rest. When Endicott, Sylvie and Roland had suggested going off in search of something to drink, Sanderson had suggested going along but she wasn't in the mood. Instead Ros did what she always did when bored to tears – she started people watching. The reporters were their usually scruffy lot. What surprised Ros was how many of them she recognized. Maybe she was part of this little club after all.

Ros' eyes caught some movement along the edges of the group where the light wasn't very good. Curious, she watched the man wearing the dark suit as he circled casually around the lobby. She could not make out much until he stepped into better light. He was sly about it but the guy was watching everyone there. Ever since Vienna she had grown much more aware of whom was around her and what they were up to. One near miss did that to a person. Ros admired the man's suit. It was well tailored without being flashy or drawing attention to itself. He wasn't very tall but she also had to admire the cut of the upper body filling out the suit jacket. That's when it hit her… she'd seen this guy before.

"What has you so stumped?" Sanderson was curious what she on about now.

Ros didn't answer him. She kept on running mug shots in her head. Then it clicked. Ros matched the face with the place. "I've got it."

"Got what?" Sanderson could use a diversion himself.

"I'll fill you in later, wait for me," Ros commanded as she ran off.

His daft American charge was hurrying off to some new escapade. Sanderson had learned it was safer to allow her a long leash. Who knows, maybe Ros would come up with something tangible he could leverage. Although he wanted to watch where she was going his attention was captured by a wave of commotion coming from the area of the main stairwell. Runciman was finally making an appearance.

So intent on intercepting her target, Ros was ignoring Runciman's arrival. Ros had plotted her angle so that she'd reach a spot in the lobby a few seconds before the guy reached it himself. Ros had realized that the watcher was the same fellow sitting outside that Prague café last year with her pal Bulloch. Now he was here watching the show. The guy had, *spy,* written all over him. Blocking his way with her arms crossed over her chest, Ros forced Burda to stop.

Burda looked at the determined woman and smiled. His first inclination was to offer an evasive apology and move on but he recognized the woman as the reporter who had been chasing after Bulloch since the Masaryk funeral. She was quite persistent. Burda's curiosity got the better of him so he stopped for her. "Hello again, Miss Talmadge."

"What was your name again?" Ros jumped right in.

"Jan Burda," he answered amiably while raising his hand to shake hers.

The gesture forced Ros to soften her stance so she could shake his hand in return. "Ros Talmadge, Consolidated News. Our mutual friend, Captain Bulloch, never got around to introducing us when we met before."

"Yes, he was quite negligent. But very good to make your acquaintance now," Burda charmed her.

Making a mental note of the name, Ros was surprised the guy was being so sociable. "You aren't really a driver for hire, are you?"

Suppressing laughter, Burda answered honestly. "No not all."

Leaning closer to him, Ros whispered, "Are you a spy?"

"Would you like me to be?" Burda encouraged her.

Annoyed, Ros backed off and placed her hands on her hips. "Please be serious. I really want to know."

"I am sure you do," Burda consoled her. "Please do not be disappointed. I am merely a captain in the Czech army attached to the general staff."

"So you are not a spy?" Ros pressed again.

"Our mutual acquaintance is a military attaché. His job is to investigate into our military equipment and strategic doctrines. One of my jobs is to assist him in his needs," Burda explained matter-of-factly without directly answering her question.

"Then what are you doing here and out of uniform?" Ros was still skeptical and challenged him.

"My superiors are curious what Lord Runciman will say and do not wish to wait until tomorrow's newspapers to know," Burda whispered back like a long-time confidant. "The outcome of this mediation mission will have huge implications for my country. I am a fly on the wall."

"That is much less exciting than I had hoped," Ros felt like she had been robbed.

"There it is… I *have* disappointed you. My sincere apologies," Burda felt reasonably sure he had derailed her curiosity for now.

"I'll get over it. Getting disappointed happens all the time in my line of work," Ros admitted.

"I feel bad, perhaps I can make this up to you," Burda thought keeping a connection to her might be a useful tool in annoying Bulloch later.

"How so?" Ros pepped up.

"In a few weeks our army and air force will be staging joint training maneuvers. I am very sure I can arrange for you to be included in the official list of press observers. And if we are lucky, you may have an opportunity to interview our chief of staff, Generál Krejčí. I can't promise the latter but it is very possible," Burda laid out his bait.

"You're a real champ, mister," Ros thanked him. "I'm sorry I put the screws to you earlier."

"Think nothing of it. I enjoyed our conversation," Burda reached inside his jacket pocket to take out a small metal case. Opening it, he handed her a card with his telephone number on it. "Call me in the next few days, we'll make the arrangements."

"Deal," Ros put the card in a safe place within her purse.

Burda noticed that Lord Runciman was about to speak and pointed in that direction. "For now, it looks like we should direct our attention over there."

"Ah hell, you're right!" Ros hurried off to rejoin Sanderson. "I'll call you."

The encounter had gone well, Burda thought. He had been dismayed that her initial observation had been to place him as a spy. Reporters were generally perceptive, women reporters more so. He would have to review his wardrobe choices and mannerisms nonetheless. Burda didn't like being spotted. The best way to diffuse her interest was to feed her ambition with something she coveted. Burda was pleased with himself. He would have to consider in what way the woman might prove useful in addition to unnerving Captain Bulloch. For the moment he decided to slip back out of sight. Burda's primary reason for attending was to keep track of any SdP or German operatives that may turn up.

Runciman had placed himself in an over-sized chair in the center of the lobby. Not one who enjoyed oratorical endeavors, he felt more at home in a club-like atmosphere where he could relax as much as anyone could relax surrounded by these vile newsmen. The half-filled brandy glass in his right hand was mostly a prop in case he needed to pause to reflect on an answer.

"Well lads and ladies, thank you for joining me this fine evening," Runciman finally got started. "I want you to always feel free to present questions to myself and members of my mission. There is no hidden agenda to our work, although, I dare say, we have much work to do. Let me introduce my primary subordinates."

Runciman stood to better command attention as he pointed out his people nearby. "Frank Ashton-Gwatkin of the Foreign Office; R.J. Stopford, who has participated on several international committees; consul Henderson over there, who many of you may already be familiar with; and my secretary, Geoffrey Peto, formerly a member of Parliament."

Before Runciman had a chance to get himself halfway seated and comfortable in his chair a British reporter close to him launched into a question. "Trewett, Daily Mail, sir. Is it true that neither you, or any of the men you have just introduced, have any experience in Central European politics or ethnic minority problems?"

"Wish I had asked that," Ros nudged her way back alongside Sanderson.

Perhaps vile was too kind a description Runciman thought while taking his time responding to what he felt was an unwarranted attack. "Your question betrays a very narrow appreciation of competency, young man. Let me assure you that this mission is rich in individuals with long, distinguished service to the Crown. That experience is invaluable and counts for far more than you give it credit for. What counts is how we approach the problems here. I guarantee you that this mission will operate under the highest standards of integrity. What we do not know, we will learn. Our charter permits us to take whatever time necessary to investigate the conditions underlying local disagreements."

"Simons, Times of London," Roland edged in next with the obvious follow-up question. "Lord Runciman, even the most charitable predictions describe the window for avoiding conflict is mere weeks. How much time do you really have?"

"The principal parties in this dispute have pledged their good faith support of this impartial mission, and have assured me that our efforts will not be hindered. I may stay a month, or it may be three months," Runciman corrected Roland like a naive schoolboy.

"Lord Runciman," the Daily Mail man grabbed the floor again. "Given that Mister Aston-Gwatkin from your team personally secreted members of the Sudeten Deutsche Party into the official welcoming delegation today, there are already suspicions here in Prague that your mission is far from impartial. How can you avoid the perception of favoritism?"

Runciman took a sip from his brandy glass – earlier than he thought he would have needed to. If this was indicative of the treatment he had to look forward to in the weeks ahead he would have to navigate very carefully if he was to fulfill the promise he made to the prime minister.

"Please do not look for suspense where there is none," Runciman snorted with authority. "How can I mediate between the parties if I do not meet them? Are you suggesting that the Sudeten Germans are not legitimate parties in this mediation? Were these not duly appointed negotiators for their people? Doesn't a sense of fairness demand that I be introduced to them, as well? I sincerely believe so and you should too. My solemn duty, and yours, is to uncover the truth."

The old duffer was dancing much more sprightly than Endicott had expected. That didn't keep the performance from smelling any the less. Endicott thought he heard something extra insinuated at the end of the old Brit's last comment and decided to pounce.

"Endicott, Hearst International News. Are you suggesting the Czechs are keeping things from you, Mister Runciman? Is that why your sense of fairness seems tilted toward accommodating Nazis?" Endicott unloaded.

"That question is simply callous sir," Runciman sounded sincerely wounded. It was a cruel world indeed that forced him to suffer American as well as British scoundrels of the press. "What you are suggesting is preposterous. President Beneš has a well-earned reputation for integrity. Yet the Czechoslovak government also has a strong point of view. While I must respect the Czech position, my mandate calls on me to fully examine all relevant points of view if we are to reach a resolution to the crisis here in Central Europe."

Perhaps Endicott had infected him but Sanderson was also having a hard time swallowing what Runciman was proffering. Not after having lived through Vienna.

"Sanderson, Daily Telegraph, sir. There is a widely voiced perspective that there is no possible outcome from mediation between the Czechs and the Germans. Whatever concessions may be wrung from the Czechoslovak government are pointless given the Sudeten Germans have been instructed by Berlin not to accept any concessions. Therefore, since any mediation efforts are bound to fail, the real agenda underlying your mission is to provide the political basis to solve the German-Czechoslovak crisis via a four-power conference sometime later between Great Britain, France, Germany and the Soviet Union. How do you respond to such allegations?" Sanderson pushed Runciman into a tight corner.

The question was dynamite and left the room in silence. Sanderson had intentionally neglected to mention that he had pinched the analysis from an article in Pravda from the previous week. He doubted that Runciman or any of his team dutifully read the Soviet journal and felt his chances were good that they would not recognize the source of his question. While he waited for a response, Sanderson was oblivious to the admiring gaze he was receiving from Ros.

"That was a good one, hon," she whispered appreciatively to pump him up.

"Let's see him wiggle out of that," Sanderson whispered back not wanting to take his focus off of Runciman.

"I am not familiar with anyone who holds that spurious perspective," Runciman huffed. "Next question please."

With Sanderson momentary in shock at being summarily dismissed, Trewett took the lead again. "So you are denying that *prudent* minds back home have come to the conclusion that there is so much bad blood between the Czechoslovaks and their ethnic Germans that the only solution is for the unification of the Sudeten territories with Germany?"

"Of course I have heard that proposal, most prominently in the editorial pages of your competitor, the Times of London," Runciman was able to rouse some laughter from the reporters. "That is one possible solution to the crisis. Now suppose for a moment that the parties here, through mediation, agreed to a plebiscite in the German territories on the question of autonomy or unification with Germany. Would that not be progress?"

One of the reporters from the major Czech daily Národní Listy jumped up. "But sir, during the last election, Henlein's Sudeten Deutsche Partei polled eighty-five percent of the ethnic German vote. The outcome of such a plebiscite would be disaster for Czechoslovakia as a nation."

"Mister Runciman," Endicott interrupted to punctuate the Czech writer's point. "Do you think Prime Minister Chamberlain would endorse a similar plebiscite for the Scots to see whether they want to stay unified with England?"

Endicott's barb was good for sustained laughter at Runciman's expense. The mediator waited for the commotion to die down before replying.

"That's a question for the prime minister, is it not? I dare say, however, the two examples are not distinctly similar. The people of Great Britain share a fraternal heritage that the Slavic and Germanic peoples simply to do not possess," Runciman backpedaled.

"Lord Runciman," Sanderson had recovered sufficiently to push his point. "Six months ago I was in Vienna. I can tell you quite honestly that if I were in your position, I would worry about my role in making His Majesty's government complicit with another territorial land grab by Herr Hitler."

"Don't be so dramatic, son," Runciman advised in a grandfatherly fashion. "I understand the parameters of my mission well and I have no such worries."

16. INDIGNITIES

British envoy Lord Runciman (L) visits Czech president Beneš

AUGUST 4, 1938
KOPECKY'S FLAT
VINOHRADY DISTRICT, PRAHA

The arrival of the Runciman mission had left the generáls at headquarters in a foul mood. They did not appreciate the appearance of groveling to the retired British industrialist and Kopecky could not blame them. The whole facade was an insult to a sovereign nation. The generáls believed the country would not be in such a position were Masaryk still alive. They say Masaryk could look you in the eye with his piercing gaze and there were no questions here was a man not to be toyed with. So Krejčí and the rest worried how President Beneš would respond to the stream of lies funneled to Runciman that would be regurgitated as facts. Already there was a long list of Nazis stooges Runciman was scheduled to meet, and there would be no end to the cheap theatrics the Henleinists would stage in the Sudeten districts for the Englishman's benefit. Every Henleinist provocation would require another action memo to keep the generáls up to date. That is all Kopecky needed... more reports to write.

As Kopecky's weary hand rested on the brass knob leading to the sanctuary of his flat, a new worry presented itself. Why was his apartment door unlocked? Kopecky doubted that he had forgot to secure the door properly in the morning. Such was a possibility but Kopecky did not believe so. Looking inside the apartment he found the lights were on. Was Capka playing with him again? But turning on the lights was not Capka's style. Kopecky stepped slowly through the entryway to looking around thoroughly before closing the door. If his modest home was going to be violated with such frequency, Kopecky was beginning to think he should start carrying his service pistol more often. Moving into the front room there was a fellow sitting in his leather chair, someone much smaller than Capka. Kopecky recognized the Second Department man from headquarters.

"You shouldn't leave your door unlocked," Burda advised from the comfort of the Kopecky's favorite chair. "All manner of undesirable types could let themselves in."

"I suspect you have abundant experience in letting yourself inside other people's homes, kapitán," Kopecky was not going to waste time arguing about the door lock.

"Unsubstantiated fiction, major, I assure you," Burda denied the accusation because such denials were expected.

Burda thought Kopecky an interesting character. He was bright and well trained in the Czech academies and the French school as well. This was uncontested. Yet Burda had nonetheless come to consider Kopecky as soft. He appeared too enamored with the safety of headquarters work to be involved with a faction of senior field officers. Burda desired to clear of this mystery face-to-face.

"Do you know why I have come to visit you?" Burda asked like a gymnasium administrator about to paddle a troublesome student.

That was a very leading question and Kopecky pondered silently whether he wished to answer it. A surreptitious visit from one of Moravec's lieutenants was a bad sign. Srom's mandate from General Krejčí did not include disclosures to the Second Department. They had been careful, but perhaps they had been naive to believe the group's activities would not be noticed.

"Oh, I am sure you will tell me when you are ready," Kopecky chose not to fall into the trap. "Until then, allow me to be a good host."

Kopecky knelt in front of a small cabinet in the front room. He had moved his selection of good wines after Capka's recent incursion. Choosing a decent vintage from inside, he put the bottle plus two small glasses on top of the cabinet. Kopecky uncorked the bottle, poured the wine into the glasses, and offered a glass to Burda.

"Thank you," Burda happily accepted. "Very fine. You used your time in France well, I see."

Kopecky seated himself on a nearby chair and appraised his guest carefully before tasting the wine he had poured. Burda was toying with him and obviously enjoyed doing so. This Second Department officer had a reputation for diligence and loyalty. There was little else to know. The truth was that no one else who worked at the general staff wanted to get very close to Burda and his colleagues. They were always watching, taking mental notes and making judgments as their peculiar profession dictated. But now Kopecky had one of Moravec's men sitting in his front room uninvited playing with him like a cat about to swallow a mouse.

"So nice to find a staff officer with a taste in anything other than pivo. Obviously the Service de Renseignment treated you well on all of those trips to Paris to coordinate intelligence gathering between the services," Kopecky demonstrated that Burda was not the only person in the room who could be overly familiar with someone else's life.

"Touché," Burda conceded, resting his glass on the side table. Kopecky was keeping a level head. That warranted respect. "You are full of surprises, major."

"I have my moments, kapitán," Kopecky made sure to emphasize he outranked Burda.

"Which is why I paid you this unannounced visit. You do not have a reputation for skullduggery. And yet, here you are involved in a very secret undertaking. That intrigues me greatly," Burda would let him dangle a while longer before getting to the point.

"To be honest, I am not in a position to affirm, or deny, anything you may or may not know, Mister Burda," Kopecky chose his words carefully.

"No need. We became aware of Colonel Srom's working group some months ago. Inquiries were made, an investigation was completed, and the findings were conveniently misplaced," Burda remembered how Moravec was not keen on Krejčí keeping them in the dark. It led one to wonder what other secrets did the generál have, and why?

"Well then, if you already know everything what brings you to my front room, Kapitán Burda?" Kopecky chose a formal and demanding tone.

"As much as I hate to admit it my section is at a disadvantage. I cannot very well discuss this matter with you at the Ministry of Defence if we are not supposed to know of what you are working on. So here I am bearing gifts," Burda threw up his hands and smiled.

"Gifts?" Kopecky was still too wary of this fellow to believe him yet.

"As long as we are going to be complicit in your scheming, the best choice was to amplify your chances of success. When the dust settles, everyone loves a winner," Burda ventured as he reached underneath his jacket and retrieved several large, unmarked envelopes, which he handed to Kopecky. It was material that unavailable when Tichy had visited Srom. "You are receiving this documentation under the strictest confidence. If you are careless we will deny having any contact with you. Our position will be that you used your position within the general staff to steal these sensitive documents and evidence will be planted that will support that accusation." Burda warned.

"That sounds rather harsh, but I get your point," Kopecky inspected the envelopes. "Am I going to like the contents?"

"Without a doubt. Inside is the same information Colonel Moravec has presented to both General Krejčí and President Beneš. Fewer than a dozen people outside my department have read what you now hold in your hands. This material is classified as secret. It has come from trusted sources inside Germany… verified sources.

"What has changed?" Kopecky sensed something important had happened over the border.

"Hitler is pushing his generals for a different approach in attacking us. He has come up with his own plan: one big push into Central Bohemia from the west with everything they've got. Hitler's idea is to send fifty divisions in one huge wedge toward Prague. That is what is inside those envelopes."

BULLOCH'S FLAT – MALA STRANA DISTRICT, PRAHA

Different telephones had different personalities. The one in his flat had that peculiar ring common in Europe – rather like the small bell that dings when a merchant's door is opened. Somewhere in his muddled head the ringing registered and Bulloch lunged naked for the other room where the phone sat in a small alcove in the hallway wall. Mid-lunge Bulloch tripped over one of his discarded shoes from the night before. The giggling from the bedroom confirmed he had a future in slapstick should Howard Hawks ever call. As it turned out it was Truman Smith on the line. Ambassador Wilson was staying at the Carr's official residence but Smith had been lodged close to Vinohrady. He wanted to get together with Bulloch before Wilson and Carr were set to meet at the embassy that afternoon. Bulloch suggested getting breakfast at the Slezska.

Running back into the bedroom one of Bulloch's feet landed square on his keys that had somehow come to rest on the floor. Petra thought that was amusing enough to jump him when Bulloch fell back onto the bed to examine his throbbing foot for punctures. She wasn't done with him and soon Bulloch forgot about his foot. While his mind registered that bed boards under such stress resulted in a chorus of creaking that probably could be heard several buildings away, there was something she wanted and finally he gave it to her. Her final long, low moan was part contentment, part exhaustion and signaled his chance to make a getaway.

There hadn't been time for anything but a quick shower. Since there wasn't the luxury of waiting on the hot water to make it up from the basement to his showerhead, the cold water barrage he received encouraged Bulloch to get out of the tub in record time. By prior agreement with Smith, both officers had decided to leave their uniforms behind so at least Bulloch didn't have to fuss much getting dressed. Luck delivered a train at the neighborhood trolley stop right when he turned the corner so Bulloch reached Smith's lodgings almost when he had said he would – finding the senior attaché leaning against the low retaining wall outside the entrance.

"Good to see you, Bulloch," Smith met him half way. "Thanks for coming over so early this morning."

"My pleasure, major," Bulloch hoped Smith had not been waiting long. "Welcome to Prague."

"Thank you. Now, which way do we go? I have no idea where's what in this town," Smith regretted never getting to Czechoslovakia much.

"Not far... in that direction," Bulloch pointed down the street. "A nice spot the locals are fond of. I think you'll like it."

"I'll take your word for it. Let's go. We have a big day ahead of us," Smith followed his colleague.

"Yeah, big enough to pull minister Carr off his vacation," Bulloch hassled Smith.

"Sorry about that. Ambassador Wilson felt it was imperative that Carr gets a full briefing on what he intends to tell Beneš on Saturday. The State Department brass back in Washington feels this whole Runciman circus is going to put a ton of pressure on Beneš and they want us to give him the straight dope as we see it."

"And what is the straight dope? As we see it, of course," Bulloch followed along.

"Germany is not in a position to wage a large war. Look past the propaganda and the newsreels of all the new aircraft and tank factories. The current condition of the German economy won't stand for it. That's what we're seeing. Oh, Hitler may want the Sudeten Germans, and their territory, but there's plenty of old guard generals who aren't fond of going to war for them and are pushing back against Hitler."

"I thought all the malcontents had been purged earlier this year," Bulloch recalled the briefing reports he had read. "Who's left to push back? Didn't von Beck just resign?"

"Glad to see you're keeping up on the dispatches. I thought you might have been too busy. Nice work down in Austria a while back," Smith slapped the young attaché proudly on the shoulder.

"Thanks. There were some close spots but I got around them," Bulloch had chosen not to disclose the bit about waylaying Nazi secret police.

"With von Beck out of the way we now think von Brauchitsch is leading the opposition against war backed by a good number of other senior officers," Smith continued. "I don't want to go into names at this time. Hitler may jump up and down threatening to unleash his panzers but our bet is that he wants to wear down the English and French sufficiently that they'll give Hitler a blank check to take what he wants gratis."

"So State is advising Beneš to stand firm and not give in to the pressure?" Bulloch was surprised if that was the case.

"Nothing that forceful, only that our view from Berlin is we don't see war as Hitler's primary option," Smith knew that did not square with the documents the Czechs were sharing with Bulloch.

Wilson will have an interesting conversation with Beneš since that is not how they read the Germans in these parts... and I tend to agree," Bulloch made a rare detour into conviction.

"You're sounding like a hawk, captain," Smith was a little baffled. "Do your intelligence contacts, or the pretty young thing you've been courting, have anything to do with it?"

Bulloch was uncomfortable at how far gossip was traveling. He would have to have a little talk with Bess, it seemed. Smith had a point, however. Was Petra's fervor rubbing off on him? "Good question. Maybe the Nazis are just getting on my bad side. As for my lady friend, you've been talking with Bess again haven't you?"

"Guilty as charged. There's no one better informed on what's going with our people in this part of the world," Smith was having a good time at his colleague's expense. "And that old girl has her eye on you, bud. Lucky for you you're in Bess' good graces... mind if we take that table out front?"

"Sounds good," Bulloch agreed. "Outside is better." Bulloch waited until they had got comfortable at their table before continuing. "Let me assure you, Petra is a hard woman to ignore when she's set her mind to something but politics doesn't much enter into it when her and I get together."

Bulloch had a reputation within embassy circles for playing the field – one short, intense rendezvous after another. That wasn't abnormal for young, recently assigned attachés. Yet Bess had said Bulloch was sufficiently stuck on this girl that he hadn't moved onto fresher pastures in months. That knowledge had left Smith wondering if the attraction was more than carnal. It would have to wait because Smith noticed a tall woman marching up the sidewalk from behind Bulloch. The way her eyes were focused on the back of his head, Smith got the impression the boy was about to get a talking to. This one didn't fit Bess' description though. Her outfit looked more durable than fashionable yet the way the fabric draped her body, her curves were accentuated in all of the right places. This was a woman who knew her clothes well in a way that didn't look remotely Czech. And while there was passion in her eyes, he didn't see much affection as she reached spitting distance of them.

"You're cornered now, bub," Ros pounced on the unsuspecting captain. "I've been trying to track you down for months now and you know it. Lucky for me you are a creature of habit. I figured I would find you here eventually if I kept checking."

Bulloch lowered his forehead into the palm of his right hand, obviously embarrassed and annoyed. A server chose that moment to approach the table.

"Dobrý den," the kindly looking older man greeted them with cheer.

"Not now!" Ros waved the server off and closed the distance to Bulloch.

The waiter rolled his eyes and retreated to friendlier tables as Bulloch leaned back in his chair.

"Strange, I thought I put you on a train to Budapest," Bulloch recalled scornfully.

"You did," Ros was not at all pleased with the reception she was getting. "I didn't stay there."

"They could have at least have detained you until next year as a threat to state security," Bulloch wondered when he was going to catch a break with this pain in the rear.

The exchange drew a chuckle from Smith, which annoyed Ros all the more.

"Hey, you don't sound very happy to see me," Ros was going to teach this lug a lesson.

"To be honest--" Bulloch couldn't finish the thought as Ros threw her purse down on the table with a loud thud.

"--Didn't your mother teach you any manners?" Ros declared more than asked.

"She didn't have much time. My mother ran off when I was five," Bulloch explained in a low, slow drawl for maximum dramatic effect.

The admission caught Ros off guard. With her mind scrambling for the right response she dragged a nearby chair over to the table and sat down with the two officers. "Oh, that's rotten... who's your friend here?"

"Truman Smith," he was happy to interject some civility into the odd encounter.

"Nice to meet another American around this town, Mister Smith. Ros Talmadge. Sorry to interrupt your conversation but I've been trying to catch up with our friend here for months," she gave Bulloch the evil eye. "He's been avoiding me."

Curious why Bulloch would be giving the woman the slip, Smith decided to play along. "Back alimony?"

Bulloch rolled his eyes and sighed. "Oh please... don't encourage her."

"No he did me a big favor a while back," Ros tried to set the record straight.

"Just helping out a fellow American," Bulloch discounted his contribution.

"Don't be so modest. What you did meant a lot to me. You saved my neck," Ros wasn't one to let a good deed go unrewarded.

"You're very welcome. Now why don't you run along and infuriate someone else," Bulloch desperately wanted to share her questionable charms with some other victim.

Smith was finding it difficult to suppress more laughter watching these two go at each other. "Miss Talmadge doesn't seem all that bad. Why not let her have her say?"

"Thank you," Ros tossed extra sweetness toward Smith. "All I want to do is tell him thank you."

"For what exactly?" Smith was still curious.

"Mister Bulloch got me out of a serious jam when the Nazis rolled into Vienna last March," Ros still got a chill thinking about that day.

"I jammed the side of Nazi's head, that's all," Bulloch corrected her.

"Oh... that item wasn't in your report if I recall," Smith teased him. Naturally, accosting Nazis would not make it into official dispatches if they could be gotten away with. "Either way, there doesn't seem much harm in allowing the lady to say thank you."

"That woman is a reporter, Truman," Bulloch gestured in Ros' direction. "She wants something else. They always want something else."

"Why does there *have* to be another reason?" Ros tried to sound as reasonable as possible.

"Oh stop. You're trouble. I knew it the first time I laid eyes on you. You're working another angle. What is it?" Bulloch wasn't going to let her off easy.

"You know, you think way too much of yourself, buster. It's not like a girl can't get along fine on her own. I ran into that nice Mister Burda the other day and he's going to help me out. I don't need you for anything," Ros tossed in the name of the captain's Czech accomplice to needle him.

"Who? What?" Bulloch sat up. "How did you sink your claws into him?"

She had hit a sensitive spot, especially in front of Smith. Of all people Bulloch didn't want Talmadge to get close to, his contact in Czech Intelligence was on top of the list.

"You really don't have a very good opinion of me, do you? Don't worry I'm not working behind your back. I happened to run into Mister Burda last night at the Alcron right before Lord Runciman sat down with the press," Ros shifted her attention toward Smith. "We're talking about another one of Captain Bulloch's *friends*. I bumped into the two of them here last year, and remembered the guy, a very nice officer in the Czech army. He's going to get me an invite to their troop maneuvers later this month."

Smith's raised his eyebrows. Burda was the name of the Czechoslovak agent who had provided the German war plans Bulloch had come into possession of the previous year. "Oh really. How hospitable of him."

"He was a straight up guy. Turns out he has to work with all of the military attachés like this bum over here," Ros explained.

"I'm one of those bums, as well," Smith thought it best to divert her attention.

"The government is paying for two of you in this place?" Ros was surprised.

"Oh no, I'm based in Berlin. Like you I'm in Czechoslovakia to observe this Runciman mission up close," Smith gave her a solid explanation.

"Hey, did you have anything to do with that dog-and-pony show with Lindbergh last year?" Ros grew excited.

"Sure did," Smith was too modest to admit that he had set up the whole event.

"Ahhh, I wish I could have tagged along on that one... my luck for being based in Paris. It would have been great to get my byline on some of the copy that came out of that tour," Ros looked back at Bulloch to continue her assault. "How come everyone else is nice to me but you?"

"They don't know you like I do, sweetheart," Bulloch kicked the comment back to her. After listening to Ros he realized Burda was a smart guy. He obviously hadn't given her anything to be suspicious about. "Anyway, what does it matter, your new buddy Mister Burda is going to be helping you out, right? Like you said, you don't need me. So scram!"

"Maybe I was hasty," Ros acted coy.

"See. Here it comes," Bulloch looked to Smith for vindication.

"You are an exasperating louse," Ros growled at him.

"Is that right. Funny... I'm not the one putting on the false pretenses. C'mon sister, spit it out. What else do you want?" Bulloch scolded her.

"It wouldn't hurt you to help a girl out in getting another interview with Minister Carr," Ros sounded a little hurt at his appraisal of her. "That Chapin fellow at the embassy won't return my calls."

Bulloch smugly folded his arms over his chest, "Looks like Chapin is smarter than I gave him credit for. The answer is no."

Ros bolted up out from her chair wagging an index finger dangerously close to Bulloch's nose. "Aren't you forgetting something, buster?"

Bulloch pushed her finger away from his nose. Such as?"

Undeterred, her finger went right back to work, "Just what were you doing in Vienna right in the middle of an invasion, captain? Listen fella, I know your name and I know where you work. How would you like if your name started getting into the papers? I get paid regardless, so it doesn't matter to me whether its an interview with your boss, or an exposé on the valiant rescue of one woman reporter by one of America's finest."

"You don't play fair," Bulloch grumbled.

"No I don't," Ros' hands came to rest confidently on her hips.

"I should have let the Nazi run off with her," Bulloch lamented to Smith.

"That's the only reason I never wrote you up before. Do you think I'm heartless?" Ros tried to get touch something in that dense noggin.

Before Bulloch could answer, Smith leaned forward and extended an arm to push him back in his chair. Smith's expression sent a clear message: *Don't answer that question.* Next Smith gestured for Ros to sit back down. "I don't think it would be too much trouble to help the lady out in her request."

"C'mon, play nice like the man said," Ros latched onto Smith's advice.

"I'm going to regret this," Bulloch complained to no one in particular.

"No you won't. I'm just new in the neighborhood. All I need is a leg up with the minister. After that I'll be out of your hair for good," Ros promised... for now.

Bulloch cocked his head unbelievingly at her. "Can you put that in writing?"

In response Ros lurched forward in his direction and slugged Bulloch hard on the upper arm.

"Ouch. Cut it out already," Bulloch conceded while massaging the spot where she hit him.

"That's better," Ros gloated.

"It's going to take a few days to set up," Bulloch warned her honestly. "You have a hotel where I can reach you?"

Ros reached for her purse and pulled out a hotel card to give to Bulloch, "You can get a hold of me there."

"Nice joint," Bulloch commented after looking at the card. He had spent a few nights there with Jirina.

"Hey, I think that's the first time I have ever seen a smile land on that mug of yours," Ros teased him.

Brought back to reality, Bulloch pocketed the card and genially leaned closer to Ros across the table, "I do this for you, and you're going to behave, right?"

"Deal!" Ros happily agreed... for the moment.

FARMHOUSE, CENTRAL MORAVIA

The choice had been specific. The property was large with the house secluded from the road by distance and a stand of old trees. The owner was a decorated veteran who had lost his left arm below the elbow on the long march home through Russia twenty years before. Srom counted him as a personal friend. Someone who would not be inclined to chatter about hosting a curious meeting of army officers and didn't desire to learn who owned the vehicles stashed safely out of sight in his barn. Since Srom had formed their group they had met regularly every six weeks. For each occasion Srom had chosen a different location. He thought he had been sufficiently discreet in those selections but after Tichy had approached him it was obvious to Srom that he had failed. Srom was determined they would not to be noticed again.

During the previous seven months they had worked to identify which tank and motorized regiments could best make the leap from their normal defensive posture into assault formations of various sizes. Trusted brigade commanders had made sure these regiments got extra training in coordinated maneuvers between tanks, armored cars and motorized lorries. This had been done under each commander's personal authority. Now Srom had a new challenge for Vrana, Kucera, Janouch, Hanus, and Plzak had been in that endeavor.

The owner had cleared the huge family table in the kitchen and had been hospitable beyond expectation in placing, rye bread, snacks and several jugs of water out for the army men to take advantage of. And take advantage they did while settling in. Kopecky staked out territory at the table and made a point of patting his dossier case in a reverential way.

Srom had made him guardian of the secret package from the Second Department. Srom lifted his left leg high enough so his boot rested comfortably on an available chair and got the discussion started.

"Gentlemen, now that you are comfortable, thank you for making the long journey deep into Moravia. We have done excellent work together and I appreciate that this was to be the final meeting before completing the task at hand. Yet in the last few days I have become privy to critical information that must be evaluated before we can call our work complete," Srom commanded their full attention. "Mister Kopecky..."

"Change of plans, gentlemen," Kopecky stood up. "We have new intelligence from the Second Department that comes straight out of Germany. Hitler is unconvinced in the value of committing large numbers of units against our heaviest fortifications in Northern Moravia."

"Sounds like a reasonable deduction. What took him so long?" Janouch scoffed.

"I would rather know what the loud one wishes to do instead," Kucera had been expecting just such a change.

"Hitler wants a campaign of less than one week," Kopecky reached inside his dossier case to throw a thick file on the table. "To that timetable OKW has been instructed to commit practically every available Wehrmacht motorized division for one huge thrust into Central Bohemia. Hitler wants to be in Prague within four days before the French can mobilize."

"His senior generáls are balking at this strategy, disregarding directives from Keitel, and hoping to wear Hitler down. We do not have the luxury to depend on their succeeding, however. We now must re-evaluate most of our own tactical assumptions to be prepared for a completely re-written Fall Grün," Srom pointed at the file.

"Four days... that is beyond wishful thinking. Absurd really. Is the man so ignorant of geography in that area?" Plzak was incredulous.

"Mad is more like it," Hanus joined in. "Can Hitler really believe that the Czechoslovak army will fold like a house of cards? Duty be damned... if I were von Brauchitsch I would shoot the bastard myself before allowing him to bleed my army dry."

"This ridiculous story sounds like a ruse to me. The Second Department is being led around by the balls," Vrana never placed too much trust in what the spies told them.

"Given their track record, especially back in May when Moravec provided detailed warnings of when and where Henlein's people would sabotage government installations, if the Second Department says multiple sources have confirmed the intelligence, I am inclined to believe them," Srom reminded them how good their intelligence had been to date.

"I wouldn't put it past the Germans to leak something preposterous like this on purpose to fool our spies," Janouch had seen such ruses before.

Srom appreciated the spirited back-and-forth discussion, as it made them sharper. But there was one voice yet to be heard who was fidgeting in his chair.

"And what is your opinion, Štábní Kapitán Capka," Srom called out the usually outspoken tanker who had been invited into their working group. Based on what Srom had observed of the man so far he was destined for a promotion.

"Hitler is bold. Detached from the realities of the battlefield, perhaps, but bold," Capka stood to refill his water glass from the jug on the table. "It's all there to read in the newspapers. Someone tells him no and he furiously fights back all the more to get what he wants. He took back the Rhineland and snatched Austria that way. This new battle plan is bold. I believe the intelligence and I believe Hitler will get his way."

"It says here that the Germans are giving Henlein's irregulars two days to secure a bridgehead into the Sudetenland," Plzak noted rummaging through the dossier Kopecky had provided. "That's odd. The whole plan assumes a extreme level of surprise and ignores that we will have moved our new ready units into the area during the crisis that is bound to occur before the invasion."

"That's what I was thinking as well," Kopecky agreed. "Were they not paying attention last May at how swiftly we secured these areas after the alert?"

"Our fast-reaction units will grind Henlein's insurgents into the dirt. There will be no bridgehead when the Wehrmacht moves in. That will be a rude surprise. The ready units will just fall back in support of our fixed fortifications while our tank divisions move up. The Germans may end up controlling a sliver of territory on our side of the border, but there will be no bridgehead for them to pour in through. The whole invasion will bog down while our heavy guns pummel them from the hills," Hanus predicted to a chorus of assent.

"Which leads me to another morsel of critical information," Srom grabbed their attention again. "The Second Department has also verified that the Germans have no shells for their new 150mm howitzers. If the battle comes in the next month those new cannons will not be deployed with the enemy's artillery regiments."

"Thank God we don't serve in that army," Kucera could hardly believe such good fortune.

"Don't get smug," Capka would not let them forget the facts. "We are still short of everything that runs on tracks or wheels at the brigade level. They have problems and so do we. The deficiencies are just different."

"No, I feel quite good about our chances. Look, the Germans could not even ride into Austria unopposed without more than a third of their vehicles breaking down. And that was with no one shooting at them. The Germans will bog down in the west. What worries me is that the president will embrace our stopping them at the border as a means to further a political settlement," Vrana had been contemplating this particular factor for some time. "I do not believe Beneš will see the necessity of our crossing the border in strength to take the battle to Hitler's doorstep."

"Srom, has the president been briefed on this intelligence? If so, then he will likely anticipate the Germans stalling on the battlefield and certainly push for diplomacy," Plzak agreed with Vrana.

Srom and Kopecky looked at each other and nodded solemnly in unison.

"Yes, this same intelligence was presented to the president before reaching our hands," Srom had hoped not to be drawn into this topic.

"Well then gentlemen, we are screwed," Janouch blurted out to the general agreement of the others.

"Perhaps not," Srom countered in a steady and firm voice. "I trust in your professional discretion, gentlemen. Take what I am about to tell you as a guarantee. Generál Krejčí, despite his respect for, and loyalty to President Beneš, will not sacrifice the security of the nation to diplomacy."

"What does that mean exactly?" Janouch insisted on clarification.

Kopecky knew full well what Srom meant. Not only was the republic rushing toward a military crisis, Kopecky was sure they were all lurching toward a constitutional crisis, as well.

"What this means is that Generál Krejčí will make the necessary decisions, and take the necessary steps, to ensure the welfare of the republic without compromising the office of the president," Srom dared not say more.

"Although the *authority* of the president may come away somewhat mangled," Vrana contently tore off a large piece of baked bread to chew on.

AUGUST 6, 1938
PRESIDENTIAL CHAMBERS
PRAŽSKÝ HRAD, PRAHA

If most of Prague was storybook beautiful, the castle was a step above, literally. Bulloch had never been inside the presidential offices before. The city was full of ornate buildings with dazzling interiors but nothing he had seen on this scale before. For a boy from humble circumstances, getting a taste of Old World opulence was one of the better perks of the job. And this visit to President Beneš' offices had been a surprise. Given Truman Smith's frequent visits to German military installations and armaments factories, Ambassador Wilson had wanted him handy in case there was need for verifying a particular question Beneš or Krofta may have. As long as Smith was coming along for the meeting, minister Carr decided he would prefer to have Bulloch tag along to balance out the party.

That's how Bulloch and Smith had ended up cooling their heels in an adjacent chamber appreciating the expensive oil paintings on the walls while the diplomats were in with the Czech leader. Bulloch stashed his service cap under one arm while trying to appear stoic to Beneš' staff as they passed by. Considering how Czechoslovakia had come into being an American in full uniform still carried considerable weight with the locals. It was one of the few ways he had found to not feel small during official functions in rooms such as this.

"Hey, what are you doing Monday morning?" Smith broke the silence.

"Unless the minister has plans for me that I don't know about yet, nothing too important," Bulloch had nothing but status reports to work on. "What do you have in mind?"

"The Czechs have invited me to watch their new light tank put through its paces. Want to come along?" Smith would appreciate the company.

"You don't waste any time, do you pal? Damn. They haven't even shown me that model yet. You're putting me to shame," Bulloch felt a little left out.

"Don't act so offended. You coming?" Smith didn't know Bulloch had not seen the new Praga model yet.

"Hell yes. I have to protect my territory," Bulloch agreed.

"That's better. The opportunity fell into my lap. I couldn't say no," Smith added to reassure his colleague.

"You watch, one day I'll be a attaché to the stars myself and they'll all be inviting me to the swankiest events," Bulloch teased him.

"Insulting a superior officer will land you in the stockade, mister," Smith switched to his army voice.

"Around here that might not be so bad," Bulloch laughed.

"True enough," Smith looked at the oil paintings around them.

"So in your ambassador's learned opinion, Hitler is all bark and no bite," Bulloch changed the subject. "You haven't said yet whether you agree with him?"

"Off the record... frankly no," Smith answered.

"That's a relief," Bulloch turned his attention to the next painting.

"Diplomats," Bulloch sighed.

"Diplomats," Smith concurred.

Beyond the closed door between the rooms the meeting in Beneš' office had grown tense. Foreign minister Krofta stood protectively beside the president, growing increasingly perturbed with the American diplomats. The appointment had started off pleasantly enough off to one side of the room with Beneš, Wilson and Carr seated in a less formal fashion around a table just large enough to hold refreshments – perfect for private receptions. Carr had been received this way numerous times over the last year and had deeply appreciated the deference and access Beneš had shown him. Protocol demanded that he attend this visit by Wilson, or else Carr would have considered declining the invitation.

Carr believed there was a reliable probability that Wilson's assessment on the German posture in the crisis would ring hollow to Czech ears. But

Carr could not tell a colleague that his personal observations were inaccurate when Carr wasn't an eyewitness to the events that shaped those observations. So Carr found himself sitting quietly, sipping his tea, and watching the Czechs bristle at Wilson's presentation.

"Forgive me, ambassador, but you cannot be serious," Krofta finally chastised Wilson.

"No sir. I am convinced Hitler does not contemplate military action against Czechoslovakia," Wilson responded, sincerely taken aback at the Czechs disbelief in his advice.

"Unfortunately, sir, that view is little more than fantasy and not supported by the facts," Krofta's voice edged higher.

"Foreign minister, when viewed objectively, Hitler is a man who knows what war means. Beneath the bluster and threats he is not a person disposed to throw his people into another war that will shed German blood. His whole course since coming to power has been to avoid bloodshed with his neighbors," Wilson reasserted his point.

Removing his spectacles for a moment to rub his eyes was a sign Beneš had heard enough. It was time to table the argument in the furtherance of peaceful relations with a friendly government.

"Ambassador Wilson," Beneš began. "We appreciate your initiative and consideration in sharing with us the fruits of your experience in Berlin. However, we do not share the same confidence in your belief that the Germans do not contemplate an attack on Czechoslovakia."

"I am sorry you feel that way sir. What I have said here today was spoken in sincere good faith," Wilson decided it was time to retreat.

"We understand that fully," Beneš was generous despite the envoy's dreadfully faulty conclusions. "There is factual information privy to my government that would never cross your desk. Some of this data I have shared verbally with Minister Carr over the months. I would be happy to provide you with useful portions so that you can better understand our positions vis-à-vis the Germans."

Wilson shot a wounded look at Carr before continuing. "In the interest of our ongoing relations I would be pleased to peruse any information you thought was useful and necessary Mister President."

"Excellent, I will see to it," Beneš took a handkerchief out of his jacket pocket and cleaned his spectacles while shifting his focus to Carr.

"Minister Carr, I am curious to hear your evaluation on this matter," Beneš forced Carr out of his respectful silence knowing the American minister disagreed with his counterpart in Berlin.

Carr had expected to be put on the hot seat eventually. While he had tried to be as gracious as possible toward Wilson, Prague was his mission, and Carr was duty-bound to answer the Czech president honestly.

"Mister Hitler wants much," Carr commenced more scholarly than diplomatically. "And from where I sit, Mister Hitler has every intention of getting everything he wants. Men of sound reason can disagree in good faith regarding how far Mister Hitler will go to obtain his objectives. I am convinced that if German objectives can be had without resort to war, then that will be completely preferable to him. Yet the longer Mister Hitler is denied what he seeks the more fixated he will become in the pursuit of Czechoslovak territory. Timing is everything. Today, Mister Hitler is averse to shedding German blood, as Ambassador Wilson has aptly conveyed. Three months from now, his mind may favor violence instead.

AUGUST 7, 1938
SUMAVA MOUNTAINS

How does the chief of a military intelligence service whisk the special representative of a foreign government off to a remote location without causing a diplomatic row, Burda wondered? The whole affair was akin to the plot of an American gangster movie. He believed the English term was *bagged*. They had bagged the British mediator and spirited him to a musky hunting lodge up here in the mountains – away from the press and away from the Sudeten separatists. Although the latter task was easier than he would have anticipated. Burda's informants had reported that Runciman had wanted to meet with Henlein straight away but Henlein was playing hard to get. On the drive up to the lodge, which he learned belonged to a long-time comrade of Moravec's, Strankmueller also confided to Burda that Berlin had instructed that there be no discussions between Henlein and Runciman until *other* events played out. That was a euphemistic way of saying until a planned series of incidents that would be labeled Czech provocations for Runciman's edification.

Moravec had seized on the opportunity to monopolize Runciman's attention for his first weekend in Czechoslovakia – concocting this trout fishing expedition with less than a day's notice. Both the president and foreign minister Krofta had supported the plan – believing Moravec had hatched a fine idea. There were no illusions that the Second Department men could talk Runciman or his staff out of their existing biases yet Moravec felt there was a good chance of undercutting Henlein's credibility.

Shrewdly, Moravec had played upon the Englishman's love of sport and sense of aristocratic entitlement to suggest the weekend get-away to an exclusive mountain venue. And that's how Runciman now found himself standing knee-deep in the shallow water of a run-off stream amiably chatting with Moravec while both extended their fishing rods for another cast. It was up to Tichy, Strankmueller and Burda to keep Runciman's staff equally occupied. That way the boss could keep Runciman to himself. Geoffrey Peto, staff secretary to Runciman, was Burda's charge. For the moment he had left Peto agreeably in Furst's hands for a joint foray into the lodge's wine storage while Burda lit a cigarette and observed the boss in action.

Moravec had been dancing around the topic of Henlein's duplicitous intentions for most of the afternoon. As he had suspected, Runciman, knowing he was in the company of a respected intelligence officer, had politely inquired about a range of factual topics. The Englishman was keen to know more about the conditions of the Sudeten German minority and how that minority interacted with their Czechoslovak civil administrators. He wanted to know how and why those interactions had turned violent in the past. Throughout the afternoon Moravec had played the socially tactful host who chose not to speak ill of his enemies out of respect to his guest. The British were an odd lot regarding social protocol. Getting Runciman's ear was not sufficient but earning his respect was essential. That's why when Moravec finally turned to Runciman as one society chum to another might do he knew the Englishman would listen carefully.

"I feel it is my obligation to forewarn you of what sort of public spectacle you are about to endure," Moravec let slip.

"Oh, how so?" Runciman adjusted his rod.

"How much did your Foreign Office tell you about my portfolio and the operations of my department?" Moravec had to establish his bona fides.

"They hold you and your section in very high regard. Both for the quality and quantity of intelligence you're able to ferret out of Germany," Runciman knew he was in the company of a top-notch operator.

"I am honored my department is held in such esteem. This is why I can caution you that very soon Herr Henlein's people will stage a series of dreadful civil disturbances in the hope this unrest will elicit a violent response from Czechoslovak authorities. It is the reason he has declined to meet with you so far. If successful, Herr Heinlein will seek to exploit the results as legitimate grievances for your benefit when he does finally meet with you," Moravec carefully laid out the ruse being played on the Englishman.

"How do you know this?" If what the Czech had just explained were true, Runciman would not be pleased with such theatrics.

"Because the various government ministries in Berlin with direct responsibility over the matter made no effort to conceal their instructions to Herr Henlein. If British Intelligence cannot confirm this I would be happy to provide you, discreetly of course, recorded telephone conversations to support these facts," Moravec once again wanted the viscount to feel like he was being befriended.

"Indeed?" Runciman was impressed.

"Oh yes, my counter-intelligence personnel routinely record such conversations between Berlin and Karlsbad, and relay them to our Interior and Foreign Ministries. Since our relations with the United Kingdom are friendly there are many times we share this information with your government so I would be very happy to provide you with the same courtesy if it would assist your mission," Moravec proposed graciously.

"Gentlemen do not listen to the conversations of other gentlemen," Runciman would not let himself slip into such impropriety.

"That is understandable. But if I were the mediator between two sides during a crisis – say the Irish Catholics and the Irish Protestants – knowing whom was negotiating in good faith, and whom were not, would be of great import to my mission," Moravec had decided to draw out his guest.

Runciman visibly bristled at using the Irish example. It was the first time his host had strayed from congeniality the whole day. For months now newspapers in the United States and the Continent had dragged out the Irish as a blunt instrument to suggest that Britain was hypocritical in entertaining the imposition of a German anschluss on the Czechoslovaks when it denied union of Northern Ireland with the Irish Republic. Runciman knew full well the underlying point Moravec had intended and wasn't pleased at all by the ruse. "The two examples are not remotely similar, sir."

"On the contrary, Lord Runciman, the example is quite apropos," Moravec was satisfied that he was getting exactly the reaction he had intended from the aristocrat. "If I were to tell you exactly where and when the Irish Republicans would foment civil unrest in Belfast with malice aforethought and the full intent of initiating a violent response from the local constabulary, a response that later would be twisted to seek sympathy in the press, that information would directly speak to the lack of good faith of the Irish Republicans, would it not?"

Moravec had just swung a heavy steel trap down upon Runciman and the viscount saw few satisfactory options to extricate himself. The Czech had wily played the Irish card in sympathy to the British position. This Moravec was a sly one indeed. Instead of arguing a supposed contradiction in British policy in relation to Germany and Czechoslovakia he was pointing out a similarity between His Majesty's government in Northern Ireland and Czechoslovak administration in the Sudetenland. If Runciman were to deny that similarity, however, he would empirically prove the contradiction of British policy in Central Europe – very neat indeed.

"I suppose that scenario, if validated by the evidence, would carry some weight," Runciman felt forced to admit. "Are you are saying you have evidence of this sort implicating the Sudeten Germans?"

Moravec allowed himself a small smile before going on. "Lord Runciman, I can share with you the day, time and location of every riot or attack on government property that Henlein's people will carry out during the next three weeks. I can further detail which Berlin newspaper will have a reporter on hand to witness each so-called *provocation*."

Out of his vest pocket Moravec pulled a folded sheet of paper containing a typed list and handed it to Runciman. "This is an inventory of what invitations you will receive next week from the Sudeten German side and from whom. There are details on what the planned topics of discussion are to be and what propositions will be made to you."

"That is quite astounding intelligence work," Runciman was conciliatory. "However, such information is not the sort of evidence you were referring to a moment ago."

"Sadly, for your benefit, this week riots will be staged in Reichenberg and Ostrau. Czechoslovak policemen and administrators will be injured and possibly killed. When you peruse that inventory carefully you will see invitations that directly reference these premeditated disturbances and who will contact you regarding them. I believe the evidence will speak for itself.

Peto had admired so many different vintages that Furst had encouraged him to uncork a few bottles in order to make an informed selection for dinner that night. His British guest much appreciated such hospitality and had taken a liking to his easy-going host. Furst could think of far less agreeable ploys than letting his target sample a selection of fine wines. He had been instructed to sideline Peto, but if Furst could get the man's tongue to wag in the process what was the harm? Peto obviously enjoyed his wine so why not indulge that little vice and see what happened. Furst set a new bottle down next to the others crowding the top of the little wood table inside the cellar. "Here then, you were looking at this one, as well. Let's give it a try."

"Perhaps we shouldn't. I feel bad enough as it is. The owner will surely be cross with us," Peto did not wish to precipitate a row.

"We are here on official state business. The owner will strut around for weeks puffing his chest out in pride at the honor of hosting such an important retreat. Trust me, the more we drink the more honored he will feel," Furst sounded plausible even to himself.

"When you put matters that way, how can I refuse?" Peto reached for the bottle.

Furst could tell the bureaucrat was no stranger to liquor. Yet it was just as obvious that the more he drank the more amenable he became. Bottle for bottle there was no chance he was a match for Furst in this regard.

Peto poured a small amount of the red wine into his glass then held it under his nose for a moment to savor. "This is a good bottle, my friend."

"Then by all means let us share it," Furst encouraged him further.

Peto poured ample portions into each glass, which both men sampled liberally. Soon a sad expression came upon Peto's face. "You're a right chap, captain. I feel I will be quite remiss if I am not brutally honest about something important."

"What is troubling you now?" Furst egged him on like a good beer hall chum.

"I respect what your superiors are attempting to do during this retreat. You and your colleagues are obviously very professional and the information you have presented our team so far is admirable in its depth.

No matter what conspiracies by Henlein's people your side substantiates, nor how well you substantiate them, Prime Minister Chamberlain sees the only way of keeping the Sudeten German problem from evolving into an armed conflict is to deliver the Sudetenland to Germany," Peto thought this right fellow should know the truth.

U PINKASU – NOVE MESTO, PRAHA

So ravenously fixated on the approaching pork and cabbage was Sanderson that he hadn't noticed Ros approaching from the other direction. The waitress was placing the deliciously aromatic plate under Sanderson's nose at the same moment as Ros sat next to him. Ros looked at the dinner, contemplated for a moment, and swiftly snatched the plate away from him with both hands.

"Thanks pally. I haven't had a bite to eat all day," Ros sliced off a generous portion of pork to wolf down to Sanderson's consternation.

"You cheeky tart! Give that back," Sanderson demanded in disbelief.

"Too late for that, hon," Ros mumbled while hastily placing a second slice of meat in her mouth. "I don't think you'd like it now. Why don't you order another, I'll pay."

"Have you no shame, let alone manners? You can't just abscond with a man's meal in that cavalier fashion," Sanderson was of a mind to grab back the remaining meat.

"I think she just did, bub," Endicott pointed out upon arriving with Sylvie and Roland.

Ros cocked her head in Sanderson's direction and batted her eyes to telegraph the message: *I'm bad, but what are you going to do about it.* He was this short of throwing Ros over his knee so that she may witness him eating *his* food while spanking *her* bottom.

"Put the plate back where you found it," Sanderson's voice deepened.

"I say, our Robin is starting to sound a bit like Clark Gable," Roland observed.

"You're not acting very much like a gentleman, you know," Ros waved a fork at Sanderson.

"Ha! *Gentleman* is what they say every time they want something from a man," Endicott threw Sanderson some support. "What a racket."

Sanderson's raised a fist in a threatening fashion... something no one could ever remember seeing him do previously. "You are this close from getting a--"

"--Here, dig in," Sylvie clanged a fresh plate of pork and cabbage onto the table in front of Sanderson. "This one is on me."

Sanderson looked over his shoulder at Sylvie not sure he was altogether pleased she was defusing the disagreement. "I do not know where you conjured that meal from but thank you for being a good sport, my dear."

"Hey, we're all friends here," Sylvie reminded the group. But before sitting down she looked upon Ros disapprovingly. "Sister, didn't your grandma tell you never try taking a bone from a dog?"

The comment got a laugh and broke the tension at the table. Even Sanderson chuckled before turning his attention to devouring his dinner.

"She did actually... but I never listened," Ros was still a little surprised at the smoldering determination in Sanderson's eyes. Brit boy had his limits after all.

"Why am I not surprised," Endicott threw in. "Well, if you're done causing trouble, did any of you get leads on where the hell that old fart Runciman has run off to?"

"No luck at all," Ros confessed in-between bites of cabbage. That Czech army officer I chatted up the other night is nowhere to be found.

"That may not be a coincidence," Roland speculated while the rest of their meals were delivered – Sylvie's handiwork once again.

"What? You think the Czechs snatched Runciman?" Endicott was intrigued with the idea.

"Nothing so dramatic. Just that if Lord Runciman is not in evidence, and a Czech officer we know was tasked to follow his whereabouts is also not to be found, then maybe they are in the same spot... wherever that might be," Roland explained his logic.

"That still leaves us with a whole lot of nothing," Sylvie hated dead ends.

"Maybe I can charm the details out of the Czech later when I can find him," Ros sliced off some more pork.

"Charm... that's brilliant," Sanderson nearly choked on his food. "If he has any sense the poor fellow has probably run for his life after your last encounter."

"Hey! Did I miss the wedding or did you two just not invite me, because you both are acting like an old married couple," Sylvie blasted them.

"Married to him?" Ros pointed the knife at Sanderson in disbelief. "Ha!"

"Only if I want to be disinherited by my family and thrown into a facility for the insane," Sanderson glared back at Ros.

These two were starting to annoy Sylvie. She had a mind to tell Ros right there to plain give it up to Sanderson or leave the poor man alone. This keeping him on the hook was getting old fast. Sanderson had been stuck on Ros for months and they all knew it. Ros knew it too but she couldn't make up her mind what to do about it. Sylvie rose up from her bench, grabbed the back of Roland's collar, and firmly pulled him up next to her. "We're leaving. You too, Chuck."

"I'm not done with my dinner," Endicott protested.

"You are now, brother," Sylvie commanded in a tone not to be refused.

Endicott thought better of arguing with her. Instead, he shoveled in one last helping of food, grabbed his hat and got up.

"Listen," Sylvie wagged a stern finger between Ros and Sanderson. "The both of you need to talk a few things out. When the bullets start to fly around here, I don't want to worry about being distracted by this nonsense. You both need to grow up. Either take it to a cheap hotel, or not... just decide."

Having said what she needed to say, Sylvie stormed off with Roland and Endicott in tow. Her outburst had left Ros and Sanderson somewhat stunned. Their eyes separately canvassed the room looking for a safe spot to focus – only to find the uncomfortable stares of other patrons. Embarrassed, and with nowhere else to direct their attention, Ros and Sanderson slowly turned to stare sheepishly at each other.

A Czech LT vz. 38 on the Milovice proving grounds

AUGUST 8, 1938
PROVING GROUNDS
1ST ARMORED REGIMENT, MILOVICE

Some poor četař would have to pry him loose from the commander's cupola with a crowbar. That's how good this new model LT vz. 38 light tank performed and Capka wanted them for his regiment. He had been yearning for weeks to get at one of the prototypes to test whether the design was as good as it was reported to be. None of his entreaties through the chain of command had been successful. Capka knew all of the excuses by heart: limited number of prototypes, an accelerated test and evaluation program, priority assigned to purchasing commissions from foreign governments to amortize design and production costs, etc., etc., etc. Back at the farm house in Moravia the previous week, Capka was so frustrated that he had pulled Srom aside and asked if he knew which arms could be twisted to get Capka and his personal crew into one of the new Pragas. The invitation miraculously came through a few days later.

This particular prototype had only recently been reassembled after being taken apart for study after extensive trials. Despite close to eight thousand kilometers of testing the manager from the factory had told him that there was amazingly little wear, unexpected structural damage, or mechanical design failures. There were plenty of refinements that had been suggested by the trials but few if any serious problems to fix. Compared to the troublesome gestation of the Škodas now in service no one had expected to be so fortunate the next time around with the nation under the threat of war. After months of tinkering at the factory and in the field, the Škoda's complicated mechanical drive and pneumatic steering could now be labeled reliable. With more than a year of familiarity with the LT-35, Capka was confident that the tank was the equal or better than anything the Germans could field. The Škoda was solid yet he never would describe the vehicle as an agile mount. The Praga was both solid *and* agile – aptly demonstrated by the series of ruts his driver had just taken at speeds that would have annoyed the suspension of their trusty Škoda. Despite its solid virtues the Škoda was not the mount that Capka wanted. This new LT-38, however, was everything he wanted. The Praga was faster, more maneuverable, less complicated and mounted a better 37mm cannon. Sadly, they'd probably be at war before the factories began delivering the tank in volume early next year.

Back where they had started their run, Capka noticed someone was waving the flag that signaled his time was up. Luckily, there was no wireless set installed so he could feign ignorance for a bit longer before returning this prized new toy. Capka lowered himself down into the turret and barked orders for his two crewmen to take one last circuit on the far end of the grounds before delivering the Praga back to its handlers.

Bulloch and Smith gazed through their binoculars as the new Czech tank pivoted on a dime and then sped off away from them again.

"Look at that baby go," Bulloch watched through his field glasses and whistled.

"Yeah, I don't think they want to bring it back to mommy and daddy," Smith cranked his thumb over his shoulder at the Czech army team behind them.

"I wouldn't." Not with the way the Germans were knocking at the door, Bulloch understood the Czech tank crew perfectly.

"When are these things entering service?" Smith wondered.

Bulloch lowered his binoculars to look at Smith. He had a general idea of the answer but a young Czechoslovak lieutenant had heard the question.

"Poručík Bohuslav Kolar, sir," the Czech stepped forward confidently.

Smith lowered his binoculars and glanced over his shoulder at Kolar. "Glad to meet you, son."

"The army expects to receive the first batch of version 38 light tanks at the end of December with the bulk of the production order due by the first-quarter of next year," Kolar explained.

Bulloch double-checked the man's rank badges. So authoritative a response seemed odd coming from a second lieutenant. "No disrespect, but in my army poručíks rarely know such details, let alone speak of them."

"That would normally be the case in my army as well, sir. But I've been the official shepherd of this prototype most of the year so I get to know such things," Kolar handled the question affably. "What do you gentlemen think of her?"

"From a distance, that may be the best light tank in the world out there on those grounds," Smith was calm and precise in his evaluation. "I am well familiar with the new designs reaching production in Germany, France, and Great Britain – plus our own – so I do not make such a statement lightly. It's always possible the Soviets have a surprise up their sleeves, though. Unknowns aside, and while a riveted hull is a liability in combat compared to the welded hulls the Germans are using, in all other respects that is one honey of a tank you have there, lieutenant."

"Thank you for the positive evaluation, Major Smith. "But am I correct that all American tanks also use riveted hulls?" Kolar cheerfully teased the prominent U.S. military attaché.

"Don't torment an old man with the truth, son," Smith feigned injury to elicit a laugh all around. "Our factory owners are like your factory owners – rivets are a common and cost-effective way to join steel plates. That doesn't make rivets the best choice. Welds are better. They don't come exploding off when a cannon shell hits the tank. But welds take longer to apply than riveting and are more expensive. Until we start needlessly losing boys in battle and Congress sees the light on this, I'll just keep repeating myself to my superiors."

"Ah, bureaucrats," Kolar sighed sympathetically.

"Don't get him started on that subject," Bulloch stuck his nose in. "Not unless you want the conversation to last into dinner or beyond."

"Tell me I am not that bad," Smith pleaded.

"Okay, I won't tell you," Bulloch caught engine noise approaching on the wind. "Looks like they're coming in. Mister Kolar, what was the final decision on the main cannon? Will the production models mount the Škoda A7 or A8?"

The very informed inquiry caught Kolar by surprise. "The A7, kapitán. Both models share the same improvements on the 37mm cannon already in service but the A8 was proven to fire fewer rounds per second and costs more to produce."

Czechoslovakia was Bulloch's responsibility and once in a while he needed to remind people that he was on top of the job. While Bulloch could have continued with another question he became aware that the tank was hurtling toward them at full speed. The safe thing would be diving into a nearby ditch but pride kept his feet planted where they were. Bulloch locked his focus on the tank commander's square-jawed face. What was it with these guys? If it was game of chicken this Czech wanted Bulloch wouldn't be the man to blink first. Kolar flinched, however, trying to yank the American major to safer ground but Smith shrugged off the attempt. The Praga's brakes were finally applied at the last minute – locking up the treads and kicking up dirt, rocks and a dust cloud before the tank slid to a noisy stop a few feet in front of Bulloch's boots.

Satisfied, the tank commander wasted no time in extricating himself from the top of the turret cupola and leapt down from the turret to the ground with a grace Bulloch did not expect from a stocky man. Removing the leather glove from his right hand, Capka thrust the latter in Bulloch's direction.

"Štábní Kapitán Capka, Československá Armáda," the slow, heavily accented greeting boomed out with authority.

Bulloch showed no hesitation in shaking Capka's hand firmly while staring straight into the guy's eyes... just as his daddy had taught him to do when sizing up a potential friend or enemy. "Nathan Bulloch, captain, U.S. Army."

Not sure if Bulloch was intent on shaking the man's hand or slugging the Czech in the face, Smith stepped forward to introduce himself as genially as possible. "Major Truman Smith, U.S. Army."

"Major," Capka shifted to his left to shake Smith's hand. "Did you enjoy?"

"Yes, very much. But not as much as you did I am sure," Smith wagered.

Capka chuckled while removing his leather helmet. Looking back at the Praga he signaled his crew to exit the vehicle. "Fine design. I wish my regiment had them now, not next year."

Kolar dusted himself off as he approached the other men. Perturbed, he looked ready to challenge Capka's handling of the prototype but chose not to embarrass a fellow officer in front of the Americans.

As long as the rest were busy with the social pleasantries, Bulloch took the opportunity to poke around the suspension system, drawing a territorial stare from Capka.

"So you believe the new Praga here will give you an advantage in battle?" Smith continued.

"Hmmmmmm, yes," a distracted Capka replied. "Like horse is better than mule. Easier for me to explain in Czech... you speak Czech?"

"Sorry no," Smith conceded. "My German is very good."

"German. I prefer not," Capka grunted while trying to keep track of what Bulloch was up to. "Francais?" Capka suggested next in perfectly accented French.

"Looks like I strike out again, kapitán. My French is horrible," Smith admitted.

Capka looked at Kolar for an explanation. "Strike out?"

Bulloch smiled at Capka's driver then peered down into the turret through the commander's hatch as Kolar explained the term to Capka in Czech. Not as cramped in there as he had anticipated, Bulloch observed. On the way up he had noticed that the driver's hatch was open. As long as the rest were distracted he moved forward and nonchalantly lowered himself into the driver's seat – snug, but comfortable. Controls where you would expect them, Bulloch noticed.

"Mind if I ride your horse?" Bulloch shouted in Czech at Kolar through the driver's hatch. Before he got an answer, Bulloch pushed the starter button and let the warm engine roar to life.

Stunned, Capka whirled around ready to rip the smiling American's head out of the tank. But Kolar was already on the move and swiftly climbed onto the deck plating close to Bulloch.

"Not today captain. That is not authorized," Kolar explained.

"A shame... maybe next time," Bulloch yelled above the noise as he reached down to switch off the engine. Climbing out of the hatch and then down to the ground, Bulloch walked over to stand next to Capka. "She looks like a fast ride. I guess we'll just have to take your word for it, Štábní Kapitán Capka."

This American had balls. Capka could appreciate an insolent bastard like himself, especially one who took the time to learn how to speak Czech. He found he suddenly liked this military attaché. Dropping a heavy paw on Bulloch's shoulder, Capka pointed him toward the Praga. "Why wait? Get in turret, Americké. You replace my loader this run."

Kolar was unsure if he was more incredulous about Capka's change of heart toward Bulloch or Capka's impetuous decision to give the American a ride in Kolar's precious prototype. "Wait a minute kapitán."

Capka waved Kolar off then pointed at his driver. "Mount up!"

Shaking his head, Kolar backed up to stand next to Smith as Capka, Bulloch and the driver climbed back into the tank. All of this amused Smith no end as he watched the Praga roar back onto the field. "We're going to regret letting those two meet each other."

AUGUST 10, 1938
CNS HEADQUARTERS, NEW YORK

Lasky prowled the aisle like a lion looking to pounce upon some stray creature caught away from its herd. He had been in the business so long that he had a sense when something was about to go wrong. Times like this when it felt like a lump of coal was sitting inside his stomach slowly poisoning him. Or when his head started to throb as if it was in a vise being twisted tight by the stout arms of his pugnacious feral pig of a mother-in-law. Something bad was about to happen. Maybe every other wire service had a big story that Consolidated had missed. Or maybe one of Lasky's reporters was about to do something supremely stupid. The problem was he had reporters all over the globe and not a clue which one was about to stand on a land mine. Lasky wasn't happy.

Des heard the distinctive slap of Lasky's expensive shoe leather against the floor getting closer. "What's worrying you this morning, coal or the ex-mother-in-law?"

"The former, you insufferable smart ass," Lasky never got any respect from this crowd. "Have you heard anything from the kid yet?"

"Nothing yet, Boss. Last I heard she finally caught up with that Lord Runciman fellow far away from the capital. But all he did was cozy up to some wealthy industrialist kraut in the mountains behind high walls and a locked gate. The Brit isn't budging from behind those gates to give interviews either. Too busy taking tea and listening to wails of woe from his host from what I understand," Des spilled all he knew.

"That's your upper crust Brit for you. If it ain't important to the upper class in the world, it ain't important," Lasky opined.

"The strange angle is that old Runciman isn't talking to the Sudeten German leader, Henlein. Seems like the young gymnastics teacher made good won't grant Runciman an audience yet," Des filled in the final details.

"Oh, playing hard to get, is he? That won't sit well with the old fart – very bad form. Runciman may have been sent to give the Germans everything they want on a silver platter but he'll at least want the Sudetens to go through all the motions of assisting in his dutiful investigation," Lasky could write this one himself.

Des caught sight of an agile form sprinting in his direction. It looked like the new copy boy – Jenkins – dodging carts and reporters by mere inches. "Slow down kid. You're going to hurt somebody. What's the hurry?"

"Sorry sir," young Jenkins paused to catch he breath before handing a folded piece of paper to Des. "Important wire from Mister Hauth in Berlin, sir."

Lasky snatched the note. After a quick read he wheeled around to face Des. "Ah crap! The German papers are all reporting Czech police beating ethnic Germans in some border backwater called Reichenberg. Get a message off to Ros and tell her to get on it!"

SUDETEN DEUTSCHE PARTEI HQ
KARLSBAD, SUDETENLAND

His body was tense like piano wire wound tight at both ends. Pulling him one way was very specific instructions from Herr Hitler that left little room for deviation. Wrenching him in the other direction were realities that cared not a wit about his instructions. Konrad Henlein was not sure anymore whether he was a leader of a political movement or a prisoner of cruel circumstance. In his heart he was sure he could wrest near total autonomy for the Sudeten territory from Prag. Perhaps economic and cultural anschluss with Germany, as well, without violence. The British would see to it and the French would *reluctantly* go along. Wasn't that the whole point of the Runciman mission? Creating a justification for a decision that had already been made. The war had already been won so why was he compelled to wage these unnecessary battles? He feared Hitler craved the fight more than the rewards.

In peering from his window at the lovely spa town below, Henlein usually found a welcome distraction when he felt tense but not today. The last eight months had aptly demonstrated that the Czechs were disinterested in taking the bait the SdP had been ordered to lay for them. Their discipline was admirable. When attacked, Czech police reacted with restraint not violence. Vandalize a customs office and the damages were quickly repaired with injured officers supplanted with dutiful replacements. Henlein was tasked with delivering an international incident and the Czechoslovaks were simply not cooperating. Now his people were launching widespread riots and he feared the official response to those would be just as muted. At this rate Berlin would need to take the initiative to get the job done. If past examples were any guide that would likely mean Henlein would find himself assassinated on the steps below with accusations of blame immediately leveled at the Beneš administration. One more sacrifice for *One Reich, One Führer*.

Henlein grew aware of the rustling of footsteps behind him. He turned away from the window to find Karl-Hermann Frank ready to report on the day's progress. Frank was Henlein's deputy and an able deputy at that – both intelligent and ambitious without being a threat. Henlein hoped the news was good for all their sakes.

"Konrad, the riots in Reichenberg went off as planned. Plenty of local Germans joined in with fervor once our people got started," which was Frank's good news.

"And the Czechs?" Henlein dove straight into the critical question.

"Nowhere to be found. It was like all of the policemen and government employees had melted away from each target before our paramilitaries got there. I fear they knew we were coming," a suspicion Frank had held for a long time.

While Henlein had no doubt that there were informers within his party, he suspected the government's intelligence service received ample and reliable information from traitors within Germany. Such foreknowledge would explain why the Czechs always reacted so calmly to each provocation.

"What was the last status report from Reichenberg?" Henlein felt he already knew the answer.

"The army is poised to enter the city in force to restore order," Frank relayed the same old result.

"The arrival of armored cars will send the good people back to their homes," Henlein lamented. "Yes, I would say our adversaries knew what to expect... and when."

"Shall we call off our people in Ostrau? Why waste the effort?" Frank was as pragmatic as ever.

"No, we have our instructions. Repeated civil unrest will have a positive effect on world opinion regardless of government restraint. Who knows, maybe we will finally get lucky and discover a Czech hothead who will fire his weapon indiscriminately," Henlein glanced with frustration at the portrait of the Führer gracing his wall.

LOBBY – AMBASSADOR HOTEL, PRAHA

Why the Ambassador Hotel had become the recognized lodge for the international community in Prague had never been adequately explained. The best reason suggested so far was that over the years the establishment had been favored by diplomats, so when it came time for the newspaper reporters to swoop in during the May crisis they followed the diplomats. Whatever the reason, Sanderson was pleased for the distractions provided by so many raucous newspapermen in one location. This was especially true after the recent awkwardness between him and Ros. In her own brash fashion, Sylvie had been correct in her assessment. The problem, as Sanderson saw it, was there was precious little he could do about the situation short of bashing Ros on the head and carrying her off to some cave. He had made his feelings known the rest was up to Ros to reciprocate or demur. Only she knew why she chose this discomfiting point in-between yes and no. A part of him still hoped Ros would land in the yes camp. She was a fresh and exciting personality and he was fond of her beyond words at times. At other moments Ros frustrated him no end.

Now was not the moment for his mind to be ruminating on this topic, however. Not when Sanderson was in a mad rush to secure a car and driver to take the lot of them to Reichenberg. Transport was decidedly scarce but Sanderson had been lucky in finding a German-speaking driver. The word of riots in the town far north close and close to Germany had reached the members of the press colony at the Ambassador at about the same time via telegrams and phone calls from frantic bureau chiefs who had seen reports in the Berlin papers. Now all of them were in a hurry to get to Reichenberg yet few of them could converse in Czech or German. Sprinting into the lobby from the entrance to share his success, Sanderson only found Endicott.

"Where are the rest of our charges? I have a vehicle and driver waiting" Sanderson's exasperation was showing.

"The girls? You're too late, they're gone already," Endicott filled Sanderson in. "Some Frenchie Ros knows had room for two more so they took off."

"Disloyal trollops," Sanderson could smack them both. "Well then, are you ready to leave then?"

"All set buddy," Endicott from got up from the lobby chair and grabbed his bag.

"Did anyone locate Roland?" Sanderson inquired while retrieving his own gear.

"No luck there. No one knows where he got off to." Just liked always it seemed to Endicott.

"His loss then. Let's be off," Sanderson headed for the door.

Outside the hotel a very loud commotion came crashing up the street in their direction. Sanderson and Endicott joined a group of other reporters gawking out the main window as a demonstration of hundreds marched past them.

"My boy, there is a God," Endicott beamed. "The girls may beat us to the border but they missed this little gift here. Looks like students."

"And more..." Sanderson pointed to the pedestrians cheering on the procession with some deciding to join with it.

"C'mon, this is a story we need to get now before the cops break everything up," Endicott tugged on Sanderson's jacket sleeve.

Marching by the Ambassador had been no coincidence. It was no secret that the hotel had become the favorite of foreign nationals staying in Prague, especially the newspaper reporters. Even the foreign ministry and the SdP had taken notice – both of which sent daily couriers with official pronouncements to the lobby for the benefit of the foreigners. Their rhetoric professor had not revealed how he had learned of these facts but everyone knew he was very well connected in political circles. Their instructor was adamant that they had to show the foreign nationals that Czechoslovaks would stand up for their rights and would not be bullied. Petra ardently shook her fist in the air in unison with her comrades. She couldn't describe the pride she felt seeing so many normal people join them to shout – *Protect the Republic!* and *Stand Up to Aggression!* All of this was happening in front of the foreigners who were filing out of the hotel to watch. And did Petra notice some of the reporters cheering them on, as well? Her classmate, Sofia, saw them too. The two women shared the moment with wide grins and the knowledge this was a memory they would prize for the rest of their lives.

Sanderson and Endicott pushed and shoved their way through to where he had left his driver on the adjoining side street. The man with the graying temples and square shoulders was leaning on his front fender calmly smoking a cigarette and watching the students march by. The reporters dropped their light travel bags on the pavement.

"Thank you for waiting," Sanderson began to relax.

"No way to get out anyhow," the driver gestured at the marchers.

"I suppose not," Sanderson agreed. "What exactly are they shouting?"

"Very patriotic. They want the government to stand up to the Nazis. And I think they very much want people like you to notice," the driver editorialized.

"Looks like students," Sanderson suggested looking back at the main street.

"Yes from the university but other people now to," the driver added.

"Reds?" Endicott grunted.

"The driver didn't know much English but he understood that word and knew perfectly well what the chubby, boar-like American was driving at. "No doubt. But patriot first, unionist second."

U.S. EMBASSY
MALA STRANA DISTRICT, PRAHA

Bulloch rounded the corner of the hallway en route to Minister Carr's office with a copy of his latest report. Carr never asked for a revision or quibbled with anything that Bulloch submitted to the Military Intelligence Division. From time to time the minister would ask Bulloch to tea or coffee and congenially request a clarification here, or ask for more data there. Bulloch was fond of the old man and respected him immensely. So when Carr remarked on how useful such information was to him in formulating his own reports back to the State Department, Bulloch felt a special sense of pride.

Billings exited from Carr's door and hurried toward Bulloch. "Captain Bulloch. Good timing. The minister is looking for you."

"What's up, Geoff?" Bulloch sensed some unease in his diplomatic colleague.

"Haven't you heard? Another riot in the Sudetenland... Reichenberg this time," Billings filled him in.

"Ah hell, that's all we need. I'll go right in. Thanks for the head's up." Bulloch passed Billings in the hall and reflected on how their relationship had mellowed over the months. He wouldn't call them chummy but the hostility that was once there had dissipated. Bulloch could work with the man now. Carr was up from his desk standing by the window deep in thought when Bulloch reached him.

"Ah Nathaniel. So good of you to come so swiftly," Carr pulled himself away to greet his attaché.

"Actually sir, I was coming to see you," Bulloch presented the envelope he was carrying. "This is my latest report on the new Czechoslovak light tank they're bringing into service at the end of this year. This armored vehicle is quite an improvement on their existing models and better than anything the Germans will have in service anytime soon."

"Thank you for keeping me up to date on these matters, captain," Carr accepted the report. "I will read this later today. Right now we have a crisis brewing. Have you heard about Reichenberg?"

"Mister Billings just told me about riots there. I've been finishing up that report since this morning and had not heard a thing. Do we know what's going on?" Bulloch suddenly felt out of touch.

"Not much really, just what's been reported on the radio. Most of that is originating in Berlin so I suspect we cannot place much trust in those reports. I am attempting to get an appointment with foreign minister Krofta but nothing is set as of yet." That was all the details Carr had so far.

"What do you need me to do, sir?" Bulloch asked, knowing the minister's moods well.

"You're very well connected with many of these Czech military people, son," Carr continued. "It would be a great help to me if you could inquire with some of them to find out what the real facts are. I need to know what the situation is with a minimum of the tinting Mister Krofta's people will no doubt provide."

"I'll get working on that for you immediately, Minister Carr," Bulloch was glad for a little professional adventure.

"You are a great help to me, captain," Carr would have to do something nice for the boy when time permitted. "Thank you."

"I'll let you know as soon as I know more sir," Bulloch assured the diplomat as he made to leave. Closing the door behind him, Bulloch wondered what his old friend Burda was up to. Now seemed the perfect time to drop in on him for a visit.

WEHRMACHT MANEUVERS
SACHSEN, DEUTSCHLAND

His pretty boys were finally shaping up. Austria had been a holiday ride in the country. To his annoyance what little resistance that had been put up by the unionists had gotten snuffed out by some other company. Since then Morgen had kept his boot down hard on these party men. He trained them relentlessly until they could do simple things like dismount from a half-track silently in total darkness and instinctively stalk their prey like old wolves. The SS divisions were getting some of the best of the new equipment pouring out of the factories and Morgen was adamant that his bunch would put it to good use. How many bastards were lucky enough to get delivered into battle in a new half-track instead of the back of an old Opel beer truck? This SdKfz 10 could handle terrain that would bog down the wheels of a commercial truck. The time for admiration was over, however, as their armored personnel carrier braked sideways to a sudden stop. They were at their assigned position for the war games.

"Time to get out! Let's go!" Morgen waved them over the side. His squad moved with precision to take up crouching positions on either side of the vehicle. Morgen jumped down then spied the terrain from both sides of the half-track. "Where are those damn tanks? I'll have those sissy tankers for lunch."

Seconds later an army light tank roared up on the right. His men on that side wasted no time in falling in close behind the armored vehicle. Morgen joined his first group moving out because that was where the first tank arrived. In earlier days he would have needed to use a hand gesture to tell his remaining soldiers to pick up the next tank but they knew what to do as expected without being told anymore. It was as close to being a proud papa as Morgen thought he would ever get. Any children he may have fathered were growing up bastards and he would never know them. The tank they were hugging lurched right suddenly, coming close to sliding into two of his men.

"Don't get your sorry examples of soldiering run over by this Mark One!" Morgen shouted over the exhaust while bashing the butt of his rifle hard against the rear armor plate of the tank in anger. "Who taught these idiots how to drive?"

Morgen looked back over his shoulder pleased to see his other men had fallen in behind another tank. This army of theirs was coming together after all. A real *mailed fist* as the tacticians were fond of calling their new instrument of destruction. Morgen wasn't much for the fancy names colonels and generals were always coming up with but he had to admit he liked this term. It brought back memories of all of the alley brawls he'd ever been in – bashing faces and bones with nothing more than his God-given fists.

CZECH BORDER WITH SACHSEN

If the field glasses he was using had been a bit longer, Kopecky would have felt like a Caribbean pirate. They were so huge a tripod was needed to hold them steady. The Germans were sending them a message. Never before had they maneuvered so close to the border in such strength. He would have to thank the knowledgeable cetař who found the general staff delegation their excellent perch on the hill. They had a perfect view of the show.

"Not like Austria, eh?" Kopecky peered into the glasses again.

"Much better coordinated," Mayer answered. He and Kopecky worked on the same team at the general staff. "The Germans have been busy."

"Did you spot the Mark Fours in with the rest?" Kopecky remarked backing away from the field glasses.

"No, I'd like to see that," Mayer was eager to peer through the binoculars.

"Try over by that stand of trees at two-o'clock. I saw one, maybe two prowling around over there," Kopecky extended his arm toward the position.

"That's bad news. Their Mark Fours are probably the only tank they have that can give our Škodas a hard time," Mayer had read the intelligence reports on the new German tank.

"The good news is that if there are two Mark IVs for us to see they may be the only two yet taken into service. How much you want to bet that after the Germans give us a good look they truck both of them over to Schlesien for our people to get a good look at over there," Kopecky was not very trusting of their adversary.

Mayer laughed loudly as he pulled away from the glasses. "You may be right. I can't spot them at all. The bastards are probably backing those two new tanks up on a trailer as we speak. A shame we won't be able to return the favor and let them get a good look at our war games next week."

"You obviously have not seen the invite list," Kopecky teased him.

"Have you been reading Krejčí's mail again, major?" Mayer often wondered where his colleague acquired so much unpublished information. "What have you heard?"

"The army is bringing in a train load of reporters. Lots of foreign press types who arrived along with Runciman: newsreel crews, photographers... the whole carnival. Our boys will be seen in newspapers and cinemas everywhere in the world," Kopecky was feeling some pride for a change.

"That is a good thing," Mayer said returning his attention to the nearby German troops. "Having our neighbors operating so close to the border makes me nervous with all of the trouble they are causing in Reichenberg. We need to send them something stronger than a pretty post card."

SOKOL STADIUM – PRAHA

They were only completing their first circle around the track. Bulloch had been there before during the Sokol national sports event when the place was stuffed wall-to-wall with patriotic Czechs cheering on their favorite local athletes. Which was quite a contrast with the empty stands today – empty except for Bulloch, Burda, and Burda's perpetually surly partner. The latter was leaning against the wall of a ground-level tunnel they were nearing reading some magazine. The magazine was likely a prop since Bulloch suspected the man was always watching carefully anywhere he was.

"Your partner doesn't like me very much, does he?" Bulloch reckoned as much but though he would toss the question out to Burda anyway.

"Furst doesn't like anyone much. He just likes you less than most," Burda was only being truthful. "That judgmental nature of his is why Furst will be the first to spot something that would otherwise get both of us killed. I have come to realize my partner's general philosophy of life is that he expects everyone is a potential threat until proven otherwise. A cynical approach but useful."

"Where do I fit into that philosophy?" Bulloch wondered.

"If you must know, he believes you are a general waste of our time, captain. By itself that would not be so terrible but your enviable success with bedding Czech women really annoys him," Burda managed to keep a straight face.

"Now that's a reason I can understand," Bulloch looked back over his shoulder. "Your friend going through a dry spell?"

"Not that I have noticed. No, it is more like he has a problem with sharing in general, and especially sharing with foreigners," Burda never pried too far on the topic.

"Fair is fair. How about I give him our reporter friend Ros to play with. She probably bites but I'm sure he can take care of himself," Bulloch thought he had hit on a great idea.

Burda looked at Bulloch as if he didn't understand what the American was getting at.

"C'mon, drop the act. You know exactly whom I am talking about, my personal millstone, Talmadge. She told me about finding you at that Runciman reception and how you were so swell to invite her to the Czech army maneuvers next week," Bulloch reminded him.

"Ah yes, Miss Talmadge. Charming woman," Burda feigned ignorance.

"It's all right, I understand. You're talking with her to annoy me. Just remember I was the one who told you that skirt is trouble," Bulloch wanted no recriminations later.

"Captain, I do believe you have my best interests at heart," Burda acted surprised.

"Okay, I realize my motives tend to be fairly self-centered but I think about others... sometimes," Bulloch argued his case.

"Is today one of those days? Why did you ask for a meeting, Mister Bulloch?" Burda decided to steer the discussion back to business.

"Maybe I can help you, maybe you can help me. This border trouble up in Reichenberg, for example. The German papers are out in front screaming murder. That usually means they're the ones causing the trouble. But none of your people seem all that concerned. There's the usual righteous indignation coming from your foreign ministry guys but no one seems all that *worried*. And that's with the bulk of the Wehrmacht on maneuvers not far away. Hell, I call you up in the middle of a crisis and you suggest we meet all the way out here like you have the day off," Bulloch laid out the facts.

"Perhaps you are reacting only to our professionalism and training at work?" Burda suggested.

"I'll give you that," Bulloch admitted. "Especially the way your troops swooped in there and shut the Henleinists down. The reason we're here is that Minister Carr has a crisis report to file back to Washington. I want to know what's going on between you and the Germans. The real story no one is talking about. Maybe if Carr passes the truth along now it will make a difference for Czechoslovakia later."

"The real story? The real story is that my government is under intense pressure from our *allies* in Paris and London to reach a negotiated settlement giving the Sudeten territories total autonomy. The truth is Henlein has been given orders from his masters in Berlin to stage a series of attacks on Czech officials and state property in the Sudeten districts. Today it was Reichenberg tomorrow it will be Ostrau. The intent is to bait a violent response from our side that can be used as evidence of Czech oppression. They want to give Runciman every reason to propose Sudeten autonomy as the only viable solution to *Czechoslovak aggression*. It is a deadly game, captain. All staged for Runciman's benefit. That's the *real* story," Burda had probably said too much.

"You guys are good," Bulloch's admiration was genuine. "For the record, Minister Carr can share this knowledge with Washington?"

"What I just told you is nothing that has not already been shared with the French and British governments. If the U.S. administration knows something of what our allies have been told I doubt that will cause problems for us," Burda knew Moravec still wanted information funneled to the Americans.

That moment Bulloch made up his mind he would be renting a motorcycle from one of the local garages the embassy did business with and would kick up some dust getting to Ostrau. It would be tight. The city was on the other side of the map, northeast of Prague in Moravia near the Polish border. The travel books said it was an industrial town, the third-largest urban center in Czechoslovakia. Bulloch had never been there. Racing down unknown roads would make for a fun trip. He couldn't leave Prague without seeing Carr first. The minister needed to briefed, and know why Ostrau was important before anything happened there. Carr had to send a flash signal to Washington tonight to get their attention, and Bulloch needed to be in Ostrau on Thursday as a witness to validate the tip Burda had given him.

REICHENBERG – SUDETENLAND

On the road north from Prague, Sylvie was sure there was a good shot at getting to Reichenberg with the embers still hot since the city was a manageable distance from the capital by car if the driver was heavy on the accelerator. But when they reached the city the show was over... long over, as in curtains drawn and the janitors already sweeping up the joint. Whatever excitement there may have been they had missed it. Sylvie hated being behind the story. Lately all she had been was behind the story. Now that they were on the scene the local Czech officials were all holed up for their own protection and not talking. The police and army boys on the street didn't have much to say either. The folks causing all of the trouble had run for the picturesque hills around town as soon as the Czech armored cars had come rumbling from all directions into the center of the city.

All there was left for Sylvie and Ros to do was run after townspeople and ask whether they had seen what had happened. But none of the people they had cajoled into talking would trust them enough to say much about the riot that busted into a consular office and bloodied several of the Czechs who had worked there. Oh sure, there were plenty of people who decried living under Czechoslovak occupation, the daily indignities of having to submit to condescending Czech authorities or the shame of a proud people discriminated against at every turn. Sylvie could find plenty of Henlein sympathizers but no openly rank-and-file SdP members. There were rumors of an SdP spokesman in the area but the man couldn't be found if he really existed.

What stuck with Sylvie was the insanity of setting a beautiful city like Reichenberg on fire. The books said it was originally a big textile center but most of the modern city was built up in the 19th Century. The place was lovely much like newer districts of Paris and Prague and was the second largest metropolis in Bohemia. At least Ros enjoyed chatting up the soldiers standing guard around the pretty Baroque buildings. It was obvious the girl had a weakness for handsome men in uniform. At least she had gotten some good material on the Czech army's instructions in dealing with the Sudetens: respond immediately, respond in force, subdue without firing weapons.

But it was time to call the effort for what it was, a bust. They weren't going to get anything else that day and the Frenchies they had hitched a ride with were more anxious to get what they had back to the editors than find some nook to occupy for the night.

"Hey girl." Sylvie waved in Ros' direction. "It's getting late, we need to get going. Somewhere in this little backwater is a working phone line, and we have to find it."

CNS BUREAU
QUARTIER DE L'OPERA DISTRICT, PARIS

Ambassador Bullitt had been loquacious as usual. There was a very good chance he hadn't a clue what actually was going on in the Sudetenland but that would never stop him from commenting on the latest crisis. One thing about Bullitt was that his aides kept him well appraised of what the Berlin papers were saying. The Ambassador wasn't a German sympathizer... he'd call it political realism. Yet Bullitt could be damn deferential to Nazi interests when sizing up a crisis. Today had been no different when Clarence had rung him up looking for a few quotes. There was the usual official and personal regret that the two great powers in Central Europe were once again close to blows. With so many German units on maneuvers near the border and the Czech army undertaking its exercises the very next week, matters could get out of hand.

What Bullitt could not say openly, and what Clarence alluded to in the report he had just filed, was that the Roosevelt administration had no policy regarding Central Europe beyond urging restraint and offering a vague promise to assist efforts at peaceful negotiation. The ambassador to France was all for urging the parties involved to allow Runciman's mission complete its job before either committed any rash actions.

At least he had gotten Bullitt on record. Clarence's attempt's to reach premier Daladier had been politely rebuffed. The feeling Clarence got was the French were spooked. While never genuinely optimistic about Runciman's prospects, Clarence could sense the relief from Daladier's staff that for a few weeks at least there would be a lull in tension between the Czechoslovaks and the Germans. The May crisis had come too close to war and the French were scared of getting that close again.

That was a story for another day. For now, he had filed his dispatch, Lasky would be appeased for another twenty-four hours and Clarence could focus on which local bistro to treat his wife to. He rose from his chair, straightened his tie and grabbed his satchel from the desktop. There were only a few steps to the hat stand to retrieve his straw fedora.

"Clarence, I'm glad I caught you. Something has come up," Tucker hurried to intercept him.

"No worries, that's William Bullitt with two Ts at the end," Clarence baited his bureau chief.

"Stop kidding around... and good story by the way," Tucker let the reporter's slight drop. "There's another angle I want to ask you about though. The Hungarians and the Italians are cozy aren't they?"

"Pretty much," Clarence confirmed. "Musso sells them airplanes."

"I thought so," Tucker was pleased with himself. "If war in Central Europe is coming, we're going to need the Hungarian angle. Will they join in with Hitler or sit out the whole show? We should be on top of that."

If Tucker kept having such worthwhile inclinations, Clarence would have to change his impression of the man. "The spirit would be willing, sure enough. There are plenty of ethnic Hungarians on the Czechoslovak side of the border that Budapest would be more than happy to *liberate* if they don't have to pay too much for the reunion. Hard to say which way they'd decide to go right now though."

"That's it, you're going to Budapest to find out. The Italians are your beat, which makes the Hungarians part of the same package as far as I'm concerned. Besides, no one I know speaks Hungarian and there has to be a few big wigs in Budapest that can speak Italian or French. So you're my guy," Tucker's mind was made up.

"On it, boss," Clarence was pleased to take the assignment. Budapest would be lovely this time of year and the cuisine was always delightful. "I can check on booking train tickets on the way home tonight."

"Scratch that. Book an airline if you can. Who knows what's going to happen in the next forty-eight hours. Don't worry about the expense I'll pay it directly from the bureau accounts. Just get there and get me the story. Harry won't bite as long as he gets copy," Tucker liked to keep that tiger fed.

MECHANIC'S GARAGE – NEAR SVITAVY

Chances are Bulloch could have pushed his luck to reach Ostrau without too many stops to tank up with gas. The big BMW was well tuned, no problem there, but he wasn't intimately associated with this particular motorcycle. The smart thing was to re-fuel at safe junctures along the way.

Bulloch had no clue concerning the name of the village he was passing through – the place wasn't on his road map. But he knew he was over half way to his destination and seeing the lone pump outside the old repair garage sealed the deal.

No sooner had Bulloch leaned the big bike on its kickstand than he had the suspicion they didn't get many motorcycle riders stopping by in these parts or simply never liked the ones who did. Then again, he must have been a sight all decked out in that leather trench coat, plus the leather cap and aviation goggles. The latter two were Army Air Corps issue from the Great War and still in great shape. They were gifts from an old drinking pal of his father's, a local crop duster who had flown over France. Since the old pilot had come home in one piece the items had to be good luck and Bulloch always needed more of that. Bulloch guessed he probably looked a bit like Frank Luke after flying his Spad through the smoke and debris of another destroyed observation balloon. Only in this case, Bulloch was patting off road dust from the coat.

Since these people might just have easily taken Bulloch for a Czech courier he put on his best manners making it very clear to the owner of the garage that he was an American who wanted to see the land of his fathers. Bulloch had German blood on his mother's side but that went all the way back to Pennsylvania and the Revolutionary War. The patched-together German he was speaking was learned at the knee of the barbershop owner back home who let Bulloch hang out after school. The old guy had grown up in Prussia in one of the big families. Big enough that the only career choices open to young men of age was either medical school or officer candidate school in the army. Rejecting his father's will, the barber left the aristocracy behind for the Bering Sea coast where he signed onto the crew of a merchant steamer. Several years later he liked what he saw of California and jumped ship to build a new life from scratch and never looked back.

The dutiful German descendent cover story seemed to break the ice with the natives. Bulloch had no problem refueling the bike. When his stomach growled a bit too loudly the mechanic suggested visiting the local version of a general store. There he found some snacks for the road: bread loafs, cheese and sliced meats. News got around town fast for the elderly owner with the lined hands and face already knew that the stranger before him was on a pilgrimage and asked about where Bulloch's family was from. Luckily, Bulloch didn't have to apologize too much for several generations of separation obscuring the family history since Henlein was on the radio so the owner cut the conversation short to listen.

Bulloch had heard Henlein speak before and had found his speeches to be far more measured emotionally than the usual inflammatory bombast Nazi leaders were known for. But not in this broadcast tonight. Hearing the urgency in voice and the angry tone, Henlein sounded like a different man. The proprietor was completely captivated, however, yelling *Ya!* at the appropriate points when Henlein paused for effect. Not since Graz had Bulloch felt the same sense of revulsion for how people worked themselves into frenzies over this Nazi spiel. Rather than wait for the inevitable grilling on his politics that would surely follow, Bulloch paid his bill and bid farewell.

REICHENBERG, SUDETENLAND

What was it about this city that made people such a pill, Ros pondered while trying to settle into their tiny room? Two girls in need of a place to stay overnight and none of the innkeepers wanted to answer the damn door. A matronly woman eventually took pity on them and offered her and Sylvie a room in her boarding house. The furnishings were sparse but would do.

At least they had found a live phone line to the outside world. One of the Czechoslovak army officers Ros had chatted up had come through there. Ros got her call into Paris and read what she had. It wasn't much but none of the other syndicates would have better unless they lied. What counted is the dateline read Reichenberg, CNS was reporting from the scene: *Ethnic German Agitators Run From Calm and Professional Czech Troops.*

"This just hit me," Sylvie thought out loud. "I am beginning to feel like we're in the middle of a cheap Hammett novel considering some of the characters we're running into. There's a whole tit-for-tat back-story going back years between these people. My God this place is starting to feel like Dublin or Belfast with so many old scores to settle."

"You've reported from Ireland, too?" Ros hoped one day she could claim as many dots on the map as her well-travelled compatriot.

"Yeah, I'm that old, sister," Sylvie was feeling her years.

"You know that's not what I meant," Ros was quick to backpedal. "There just are so few women that have made it around the world in this business the way you have."

"And here I thought it was all because I was such a pain in the ass that my editors were happier sending me as far away from the newsroom as they could manage," Sylvie got the laugh she was looking for.

"You know, maybe you're onto something there with that bit about settling old scores. Remember that doctor we ran down on the street today for a quote? Something he said won't get out of my head: *Next time...* The way he said it was dark, mean and scary like some of the mob guys back in New York would talk about other gangs after taking a hit. You think he was Sudeten Party material?" Ros paused brushing her hair.

"Oh yeah. That one knew much more than he would talk about..." Sylvie stopped on hearing a rustling outside their door.

"You think someone is listening," Ros whispered.

Sylvie grabbed the wood hairbrush in her purse for protection and moved to the door. "One way to find out."

Before Ros could stop her, Sylvie swung open the door ready to bash any interloper with the blunt end of the brush. All there was an empty beer bottle with a small note rolled up inside the throat. Sylvie vigilantly peered down both ends of the hall. Seeing nothing, she picked up the bottle and closed the door.

"No one there," Sylvie was kind of hoping she could bang someone on the noggin.

"What have you there?" Ros' curiosity perked up.

"Lucky for us, not a bomb," Sylvie removed the note. Placing the bottle down on the room's small table she unfurled the note, "Don't that beat all."

"What does it say?" Ros was anxious.

"*Tomorrow, Ostrau...* that's all it says," Sylvie scratched her head.

Sanderson and Endicott walked out of Reichenberg's main Post Office. It was being used as a temporary command center by the army. Sanderson had just finished a conversation with a sergeant they had been directed to by the soldiers milling about outside. The sergeant was keenly aware of everyone who had come and gone that afternoon just as the young conscripts had suggested. Sanderson was amazed that so many young Czechs understood his poor excuse for German.

"My German isn't so good so fill me in," Endicott tipped his straw hat back with a forefinger.

"Your German is non-existent," Sanderson corrected him.

"Okay, now that we have that all cleared up mister know-it-all, what did the sergeant-major have to say? Has he seen the girls?" Endicott prodded.

"Despite your paltry foreign language skills you have Sylvie sized up well enough: *Find the phone and Sylvie won't be far away.* The good sergeant told me that two women reporters perfectly fitting the description of Ros and Sylvie were here no more than two hours ago," Sanderson confirmed.

"Damn, Everything here is over and done with. The whole city is locked down tight. I'd kill to know what those two were able to get into their notebooks," Endicott chewed on a pencil. "We sure haven't pulled in anything juicy since arriving."

"That's open to argument," Sanderson was irked that Ros had slipped from his reach again. "There's a larger subtext going on around us if you are familiar enough with the people here to discern it. This city for instance, Reichenberg is rather a grand name don't you think?"

"Reich in the same way Hitler uses it?" Endicott caught on.

"Quite right. The local Gerries were none too pleased about the carving up of their empire and much less cheery about their little portion of imperial territory being lumped in with those *upstart* Czechs. As Czechoslovakia was being cobbled together the people around here discovered a newfound appreciation of your Mister Wilson's fourteen points and declared an independent Sudeten Deutsche state. Reichenberg was the capital of that short-lived experiment in self-determination," Sanderson explained.

"Oh wow... you mean the Germans around here have had been nursing that kind of grudge for twenty years?" Endicott understood immediately.

"Exactly. The Czechs were a subject people for centuries and the Sudetens can only see insult and indignity at being governed by those they once ruled." Sanderson wrapped up the history lesson.

"Thanks, I get your point," Endicott appreciated the tip. "You ever cover the Ku Klux Klan back in the States?"

"No, but I understand that dreadful organization has made a comeback in recent years," Sanderson knew that much.

"You got that right. I was sent South ten years ago to report on that bunch. The more I think about it there is a lot in common between these ethnic Germans and unrepentant confederates," Endicott remembered those people still hated Yankees with a passion.

"That's a marvelous connection I would never have made myself. Charles, on occasion, you sincerely surprise me," Sanderson complimented his colleague.

"Oh stuff it," Endicott shrugged off the praise. "We should find the girls if we can. Did the sergeant know where they went off to after using the phone?"

" Only that they went in search of lodging," Sanderson wasn't able to get more info.

"Broke off from the French contingent, did they? What next then?" Endicott was more than willing to let Sanderson take the lead. He knew more about the area by far.

"Get our headlines into our respective editors, procure some dinner and head back to Prague," was Sanderson's best suggestion. "That's what the girls will do."

18. TRESSPASS

Czech Škoda PA-III armored cars in the Sudetenland

AUGUST 11, 1938
OSTRAU, MORAVIA

Stashing the BMW had been easier than he had thought. A few extra crown coins and the kid at the garage downtown was happy to keep an eye on the BMW and the saddle bag, which was where he had left the long coat and goggles. Ostrau was an industrial town in a part of the country rich in minerals. Which meant the place was always busy. Lots of foot and vehicle traffic made it easy for an outsider to blend in and there was enough soot in the air to explain away the road dust he had acquired since Prague.

Bulloch was unsure of what he was supposed to do next. He had ridden all night to be standing on this street corner yet he had no clue when the fun was supposed to begin, what direction it would come from or what the targets were. This was a big city by Czech standards. The feel of the place was a lot like Pittsburgh. There would be plenty of potential government and trade targets for Henlein's people to attack if only Bulloch had an idea where to find them.

The best course of action was to move along and look purposeful. His impromptu plan was to stroll about the city and wait for the excitement to come to him. Food somewhere along the way would be welcome though. A full stomach would take some of the edge off the lack of sleep. The thought of steak and eggs from a good old diner nearly brought Bulloch to tears. He'd settle for some stout coffee, dark bread and fruit.

ORLY AIRFIELD, PARIS

The early flight to Geneva, followed by a connecting flight on the Hungarian state airline, was the best Clarence could do on short notice. The wife had been testy that there wasn't time for her to make arrangements to join him, as she quite liked Budapest. The blow was softened somewhat when he reminded her that getting to Budapest was one thing, getting back might not be so easy if bullets started flying next door. Ever the practical woman, she accepted the situation stoically and reminded him not to get his rear-end shot off.

There had been just enough time for Clarence to get a hold of an old Hungarian pal of his. The man came from old money. Finding Budapest much too dreary as the Magyar Empire was chopped up into little pieces, he had arrived in Paris shortly after the cessation of the Great War. No one much cared that he had been a serving officer on the Alpine front. His French was excellent and few took him for anything else but a Frenchman. The little limp he earned in battle was treated with great respect on the boulevards. When the family patriarch died in 1929 the Hungarian had returned to Budapest to manage family affairs.

Clarence knew his friend was as patriotic as they came but the man was also too civilized to care much for the politics of the day. There was no question when Clarence requested lodging under a false name. His friend owned the hotel after all, no one would question arrangements made for an *Italian* comrade of the boss and no one would ask to see his passport. They would just hand him the key as soon as he gave the name at the front desk. Clarence expected the Hungarian police would check hotel registers to locate foreign journalists as a matter of routine. If something went wrong, and that could very well happen given his recent experience in Rome, Clarence didn't want to be easily found.

As always, Clarence packed light. When his flight was called he picked up his bag and joined the other passengers waiting to board.

SCHLOSS HARTMANN, EGER

The garden patio of his current host was a most agreeable location for taking breakfast tea and perusing the morning editions of the regional English-language dailies. And there was much to read this day. The coverage on the *troubles* in Reichenberg the day before was voluminous. Lord Runciman suspected, rightly he thought, that much of what he read existed in that realm between exaggeration and outright fabrication. He would have to wait until the local foreign office chaps could sort matters out and brief him more intelligently.

"Quite the show yesterday," Geoffrey Peto joined him for tea.

"Yes, it seems Moravec's people have well earned their esteemed reputation," Runciman noted holding up one of the Berlin dailies. "The name on this report is Ernst Kruger, just as the Czechs told us days ago. Amazing. I wish our military intelligence people were half as reliable."

"Does that reliability change anything for you?" Peto was curious. "There are some back home in Parliament who will not appreciate extending the prestige of the Empire to assist rank provocateurs... either here or in Berlin."

Runciman sipped his tea and thought about his aide's question. As someone who had served in Parliament, Peto's observation was quite pertinent. "No change. Berlin and these Sudeten subordinates of theirs can complicate matters by continuing on with such incompetent provocations. And Beneš has every right to point to each incident with contempt given the evidence. But the problem remains. There are only two possible solutions to this crisis. Shipping the Germans out of the Sudetenland simply won't do. Herr Hitler would surely choose war in response. That leaves separating the Sudeten Germans from Czechs by negotiation as the only viable solution. I've taken my measure of Beneš, he won't go to war for the Sudetenland."

"Perhaps not, but neither can we promote negotiations while one of the parties is actively fomenting aggression against the other. It's unseemly," Peto cautioned.

"Quite so. We will do what we can. But if the Germans make it impossible for us to act in good faith then we will wash our hands of both sides. Herr Henlein must be accommodating to reality and see me immediately. Have we received any acceptance of our meeting requests?" Runciman was losing patience at being ignored.

"No sir. Just more polite regrets through intermediaries," Peto had even delivered the last request personally.

"That will not do. These amateurs are wasting our time... who was it from the SdP that Moravec told us would show up today to chat about events in Reichenberg?" Runciman directed his attention at Peto's notes.

Peto checked his book. "A Herr Roether, sir."

"Very well," Runciman pushed his teacup aside. I have no intention of allowing Mister Roether to follow whatever script he may be working from. It is time these people started listening for a change.

OSTRAU, MORAVIA

The small convoy of Czech army Škoda trucks rounded the traffic circle then exited onto the main boulevard. A safe distance from the circle the lead vehicle slowed to an unscheduled and illegal stop beside the curb followed by the drivers of the other Škodas who pulled in behind. As the convoy idled a soldier jumped down from the passenger side of the lead truck and ran to the back to lower the rear cargo gate. That done he cupped his hands and waited. Soon a woman's shoe took advantage of the impromptu footfall and Ros stepped down sprightly to the pavement.

Sylvie soon followed. The corporal retrieved the reporter's light luggage, closed the cargo gate and smiled ear-to-ear as Ros thanked him by planting a sweet kiss on his cheek. Seeing the reward the driver of the next truck whistled approval and then blasted his horn in short bursts. Waving goodbye, the soldier ran forward to take his seat and the convoy soon rumbled forward on its way out of the city. As the convoy moved off the reporters were cheered by the soldiers standing in the rear of the departing trucks.

"You'd think we had dated the whole regiment," Sylvie was kind of fond of the idea.

"Oh, they're just kids. We made their day," Ros was delighted army boys were the same the world over.

"That's all good for them," Sylvie noticed the harsh stares they were getting from all directions. "But did you ever consider that some folks around here may not take kindly to our arriving in the loving embrace of the Czechoslovak army?"

"We got here didn't we?" Ros figured now wasn't the time for second thoughts.

"Yeah, something good did come from all of that flirting you managed back there in Reichenberg," Sylvie ate her words.

The reporters picked up their bags, looked around, then looked at each other... and laughed.

"We're a mess after all night in the back of that truck," Ros pointed out.

"My bones are frozen, sister. Let's find a room where we can pull ourselves together," Sylvie had not gotten a chance to enjoy their last accommodations.

"Which way?" Ros hadn't a clue what direction they should choose.

"You crack me up. How the hell should I know?" Seeing a church steeple not far away, Sylvie pointed toward it. "Let's head over there. If we can't find a room along the way maybe the good Father will give us sanctuary."

PRESIDENTIAL CHAMBERS
PRAŽSKÝ HRAD, PRAHA

Was that an extra bounce in the president's step? He didn't expect such high spirits at such a tense moment, but no, Moravec was not mistaken. Beneš was very pleased with something upon ushering Moravec and Generál Krejčí into the room. Since Moravec was not aware of any recent good news the spymaster was rather curious what was pleasing his president so. Krejčí, however, was his usual embodiment of professional restraint.

Beneš had called the meeting as a precursor to the events expected to unfold in Ostrau later in the day. So far, Henlein had not deviated an inch from his itinerary. The Sudeten Deutsche leader was not stupid, just constrained. Changing the schedule of when and where his people would cause a tumult would mean the reporters from the Berlin newspapers would be in the wrong place at the wrong time. What Berlin wanted was assured propaganda value and misplaced reporters would not do. Henlein's could only hope for a mistake on the Czech side that would give Berlin what it wanted.

"Generál Krejčí, I am very pleased with the performance of the army in recent days," Beneš began. "Our troops have shown remarkable restraint. Their swiftness in calming the situation in Reichenberg yesterday was impressive."

"Thank you, Mister President. It helps when we already know what the enemy intends to do," Krejčí nodded at Moravec.

"That may be so but I relish illustrating to the British how theatrical and manufactured are the grievances being heaped at their feet," Beneš was still insulted by Runciman's presence in the country.

"Proving such may not make a difference in their position, sir," Moravec cautioned.

"I respectfully disagree. The British are a practical people and practicality dictates that they will not endorse a process driven by proven falsehoods. That is why it is imperative that discipline within our ranks be maintained at all costs," Beneš could not afford a breakdown in discipline.

"Understood, sir. The army will do its duty," Krejčí had very capable commanders on the scene to insure nothing got out of hand.

"Plukovník, any last minute discoveries? Will Henlein keep to his script today in Ostrau?" Beneš did not want any surprises.

"For now, Henlein has no choice but to obey his directives. That may change in the weeks ahead given the lack of success in securing their objectives so far, but for now, we anticipate no deviations from the script, sir. We would have heard about changes in SdP strategy if there were any," Moravec reassured the president.

"Very well. I am counting on the both of you at this critical time," Beneš commended them.

"Mister President, I realize that there is a tremendous diplomatic burden on your shoulders," Krejčí thought now was the time to broach an important issue. "You must be aware that the patience of the people is not infinite, however. British or no British, there will come a time when the people demand that Henlein's agitators be dealt with severely. Love of the republic is strong with the people. They rally stronger every day behind the flag. That is a strength you can count on... the people will fight. More than that, one day the people may demand that you choose to fight, as well."

It was not like the chief of staff to speak such thoughts so forcefully, Moravec noted. Krejčí was tiring of the game being played. Nevertheless, the general's advice was sound.

"I appreciate your position, Generál Krejčí. Now appreciate mine. War will cost us everything and I will do all in my power to avoid war without sacrificing the republic," Beneš was adamant. "If the people decide to toss me out because of this conviction, so be it."

AMBASSADOR HOTEL, PRAHA

The razor was drawing smoothly across the longer than usual stubble until his wrist shifted a few degrees further than intended and Sanderson winced – bleeding about the neck by his own hand. The underlying distraction was both Ros and Sylvie were not in their rooms. The staff at the front desk was sure no one had asked for their room keys in forty-eight hours. Sanderson was fixated on what those two could possibly be up to. More likely what angle had that industrious duo latched onto that he had missed out on? Then again, there was always the possibility both of the tarts had gotten themselves into an irreconcilable bind. Sylvie was the more sensible one of the lot and he would have to depend on her to dampen Ros' penchant for attracting pandemonium.

The rap at the door caught Sanderson unawares as he was soiling a towel in an attempt to stem the flow of blood from the razor cut. Perhaps it was Ros or Sylvie arriving from Reichenberg, or Endicott with some news of them. Not wanting to relieve pressure on the cut, Sanderson sacrificed modesty and went to answer the door shirtless.

"Oh dear," Roland was startled at seeing the bloody towel. "That looks nasty. There's a very capable clinic nearby I am told. Let me shepherd you over there safely."

"Thank you, Roland. No need though. A minor cut, really," Sanderson tried to hide his embarrassment.

"Self-inflicted?" Roland was still concerned.

"Completely. Too much on my mind, I imagine," Sanderson ushered Roland into the messy hotel room before anyone else saw his bloodied state. "I should not have access to sharp instruments."

"No word from our intrepid femmes, I take it," Roland zeroed in on target.

"Despite your unassuming manner you are remarkably astute, my friend," Sanderson noted, and not for the first time.

Satisfied his wound was done showering blood, Sanderson tossed the towel into the bathroom sink and made to throw on a clean shirt – khaki though instead of his usual preference for white. A much more practical tint should the cut reopen. "They are big girls. Well, at least Sylvie can be counted on for acting with maturity. We shouldn't worry about them too much, especially since they probably are likely scooping the lot of us and not suffering a bit of regret."

"Quite right," Roland had already set upon counter measures. "As the frontier towns are exhibiting the kind of civil strife that makes solitary travel unsavory, I have a spontaneous proposition for you. Why don't you join me, I'm off to Eger to catch up with Runciman to hear what the old man has to say about these border troubles."

"Is this a wager or do you have an appointment?" Sanderson had grown to learn that Roland rarely set off on an expedition without prior arrangement with his subject.

"All nicely wrapped together with Peto this morning by phone," Roland proved true to his reputation.

"Think they'll mind my coming along?" Such a kind offer required politeness of Sanderson.

"Most certainly," Roland laughed. "I am counting on it. We don't want the Lord Mediator to be too comfortable now, do we?"

"I suppose not," Sanderson agreed cheerfully. "Count me in and my thanks."

"My pleasure, old friend. I can't fathom Runciman being too cross at entertaining a representative of the Daily Telegraph," Roland relished the inside joke.

"You realize we'll never hear the end of it leaving Endicott behind," Sanderson was altogether pleased he would be out of earshot of the loud fellow.

"No doubt. But we could never take that impudent colonial along. Runciman would clam up and refuse to speak to any of us. Where is the impudent colonial at the moment?" Roland was curious.

"Mister Endicott is dosing peacefully in his room... sleeping off a recent visit to the hotel bar," Sanderson found the circumstances quite fortuitous.

"All the better to ensure our making a clean getaway," Roland mischievously nudged Sanderson with his elbow.

OSTRAU, MORAVIA

This neighborhood was rougher and less picturesque than the districts most foreigners saw in Prague. There were plenty of neighborhoods of the same character in New York City, Shanghai or Hamburg where you knew immediately that you did not belong. Weathered avenues where the stares from every window and doorway told you in no uncertain terms that you were in the wrong area. Sylvie certainly wasn't partial to the neighborhood Ros was marching them into. The old hands that had guided her through her early years in the reporting biz had drilled the same set of cardinal rules into Sylvie's head. One of the major injunctions was never wade into dicey neighborhoods unawares without finding the local street bosses first. That way if you got into trouble and had some smarts you might have a chance to talk your way out of a jam.

Yet here they were breaking all those rules. Ros had argued persuasively that there wasn't time to go asking around. The bad guys were going to show soon and if the reporters weren't on the street they would miss everything again like Reichenberg. And if that happened they would have wasted all the effort the previous night to get to Ostrau. But Sylvie hated going into a situation blind. "Can you at least tell me what it is we're looking for? After spending all night in the back of that truck, and trudging us through Hell's Kitchen here, you at least owe me that much."

"Have some faith, will 'ya sister," Ros kept pushing further into the risky district.

"Faith comes with a long bath and a change of clothes. As you are well aware, I have had neither," Sylvie reminded her compatriot.

"Trust then," Ros shot back while spying down a side street they were passing.

"For a bath I could trust you," Sylvie had only been allowed a quick wash up when they had finally gotten a room.

"You're almost as much trouble as Robin," Ros waved her off.

"I'm sure he would prefer you would choose sensible over trouble," Sylvie joked.

Ros had to laugh at that one and paused a bit to get her bearings. Truthfully, all Ros was working from was a hunch and didn't want Sylvie to find out.

"If I knew more about where we were heading I might be able to help instead of nag," Sylvie thought that was a decent bartering chip.

"Okay, it's something I learned in Vienna. Remember that tourist office front for the Nazis back there?" Ros finally opened up.

"Sure do, but the Germans surely wouldn't pull the exact same con here," Sylvie didn't believe the cretins were that dense.

"Not another tourist office, that's for sure. How about the same idea using a different front? There's supposed to be a local German trade federation located somewhere around here, and I am willing to bet if we find the joint, we'll find some goons to lead us to the party," Ros laid out her hunch.

"You might be onto something there. Sorry to doubt you, kid," Sylvie had to give the kid credit as she had come up with another promising angle.

A Daimler screeched to a halt outside the building a block ahead. Men dressed in black got out and ran around the side of the building.

"That's exactly what we're looking for!" Ros pointed ahead.

OSTRAU OUTSKIRTS, MORAVIA

The ready unit of PA-III armored cars was parked single-file beside the road leading into the city. What they were doing there the staff sergeant responsible for No. 23 car had no idea. No one in the unit expected the incidents in Reichenberg to spread so far east, although the generáls in Praha had a penchant for covering their bets. As he had a lieutenant colonel attached to his car the staff sergeant wagered the order of the day was a training exercise. For now, there wasn't much else to do but keeping the hatches on the Škoda open so the vehicle stayed ventilated, and killing time by sitting on the old wood fence between the private property and the road. The staff sergeant said a prayer for whoever had planted the trees near the fence line long before he had been born. At least they had shade while they waited.

The officer had not said much outside the courtesies of checking on the state of their vehicles, shipment of supplies and availability of maintenance for their unit. The četař of No. 9 car had told him this Srom fellow had a reputation for putting his boot to the backsides of anyone who didn't take their jobs seriously. That story made sense to the staff sergeant. Their young kapitán was studiously avoiding the colonel. For the whelp to be so intimidated the colonel must have a reputation. The staff sergeant had no such insecurities so he made eye contact with the colonel sitting nearby and waved.

For his part, Srom was having fun. He enjoyed the breakneck mobility of these ready units and was pleased to see them becoming more cohesive in the weeks since they had been formed. There had been much debate about pulling men and vehicles from the mobile divisions and throwing them together into these glorified scout units. Yet Srom felt pride in these men and the strength of their prior training. Each unit was coming together in its own unique fashion but they *were* coming together.

Srom checked his watch. It was time by his reckoning. Say what you will about Henlein's lot, Srom had come to appreciate they were always punctual. Jumping off his perch, Srom grabbed his leather helmet from the fence post and approached the waiting Škoda. This caught the attention of the rotný who had just waved at him. When the radio in the armored car crackled to life the man was off the fence and running.

"You know something I don't, sir?" the enlisted man called out to Srom.

"We're going to have a busy day, rotný," was all he was going to get from Srom.

The staff sergeant understood immediately. There would be no training exercises today. "Mount up!" the rotný ordered his crew without waiting for his radioman to decode the action orders.

UNIVERZITA KARLOVA, PRAHA

The study they were using for their meeting was little known outside the community of music students. To find it one would have to enter a music hall then navigate through a cramped instrument closet to a small door leading to the study. Some enterprising music student had acquired the key to the closet years ago and that key was solemnly passed to a trusted new keeper when the last key holder graduated. Many of the old buildings in the city like those here at the university possessed out-of-the-way chambers such as this. Not hidden, not obvious either. Such rooms were most valuable during the long years of Austrian rule when some conversations were best left private. The same could be said of the students arguing their points today. Many in Dr. Beneš Interior Ministry would not take kindly to the majority of the proposals passionately bantered back and forth by the student activists.

Petra had seen her fill of debate. The Sudetens were in open insurrection. The time was long past for the central government to take off the silk gloves they were applying to Henleinists. That rabble needed to feel a hard slap in the face. If Dr. Beneš would not apply the back of his hand then the people should do it themselves. "We need to go into their cities, march in their town squares, occupy their government houses and demonstrate for the republic. Thousands would come to join us. Let Hitler eat that!"

Neither did it help that Bulloch was again mysteriously away from Praha. Every time he disappeared without explanation something crazy happened. His leaving left her more anxious than she cared to admit and also removed the main target for venting her frustrations.

"It is not that simple, Petra," the normally placid Karel tried to reason with her again. "We don't want to delegitimize the government. If we waltz into Asch or Eger that way it will be an open rebuke of Beneš. He'll resign. The government will be paralyzed."

"Forget about Beneš," Paulina jumped in from the other side of the circle. "You have to ask: *What would Masaryk have done?* Masaryk would not have coddled Henlein the way Beneš has. Masaryk would have kicked his ass into Sachsen. These rejectionist Sudetens will never accept the republic. They all have to go."

"That's exactly right," Petra nodded in agreement.

"Fine, fine, fine... quiet down everyone, please," Ernst fought to get a word in. "There is what we would like to see done, and what we can do. Let's stick to the latter. Since we cannot come to a consensus, I propose we take a vote. Show of hands, how many say we begin organizing public demonstrations in the border towns with the other groups?"

Nine of the fifteen committee members lifted their hands in support of the proposal, including Ernst.

"That's it then. Argument over. Now comes the hard part – making it happen," Ernst put the onus back onto the rabble-rousers.

Petra didn't appreciate Ernst's suggesting they were all talk. She was serious. She had never been more serious about anything. Petra wished she could share this moment with Bulloch. When she got her hands on him Petra would make him pay.

POLICE STATION – OSTRAU, MORAVIA

As soon as they had set the charges the men in black jackets pulled their Mauser pistols and ran for the safety of the nearby bank building's solid stone foundation. They were unafraid of being seen since the Czechs had taken to keeping themselves out-of-sight within the safety of the station until needed. There were police at the front and back entrances, but the two-man patrol that circled station was now on the opposite side of the building. The SdP men had surreptitiously timed these patrols often in the previous weeks to be sure how fast each patrol made the circuit. The Czechs were very punctual. It would be at least three minutes before the current patrol returned.

The shock wave slapped the four SdP men onto the pavement despite the protection of the bank building. The explosion had not only caved the police station wall inward, as intended, but had collapsed a large section of the second floor above the blast point.

"You madman, you could have brought the entire building down!" the cell leader slapped his second who had placed the explosives. "Every time you have to set off a bigger blast than the time before. We are not here for your enjoyment we are here to get a job done."

"No harm done," countered the explosives man. The zellenwart was his part-time commander but full-time brother-in-law. There was little to fear. "How else am I going to learn? The SS trainers only show you so much. It was a pretty explosion though, was it not?"

"Pah!" the cell leader dismissed the question. "If you make your sister a premature widow, and survive, she will surely castrate you with a stick of your own dynamite."

While the brother-in-law contemplated that sobering warning, the echo of boots clacking on cobblestones announced a squad of party shock troops moving forward to take position at the recently opened breach in the side of the police station.

SIGNALS ROOM – 2ND DEPT.
MINISTRY OF NATIONAL DEFENCE, DEJVICE

The corporal on duty put down his headphones after getting the last of the message on paper. A river of tactical reports from the recent action in Reichenberg was still coming in and had to be deciphered into something intelligible. Now the radio sets were overheating with incoming reports from Ostrau. The Henleinists were causing trouble there too now. The group of Sudeten irregulars that were being watched was on the move, followed by confirmation the army was sending more units into the city. Now there were new reports flooding in that a huge explosion had gone off near one of the larger police stations in the city. The corporal, swiveled his chair to the left to better address Kapitán Burda who had been waiting patiently beside of the radio sets.

"Whatever those SdP bastards are up to, it's started, sir. Lots of talk coming in about a powerful explosion and a big cloud of dust. No confirmation yet... but the only target known to be in the vicinity of the blast is a district police station. Phone lines are down in the area so our people can't get a call into the police on duty," the corporal finished.

"Good job, desátník. I'll take this straight up to the boss. If anything else of consequence comes in you'll find me there," Burda broke into a run.

POLICE STATION – OSTRAU, MORAVIA

Fortunately for the reporters the men they were trailing never checked over their shoulders. Chasing after the SdP irregulars who were on the run with their guns drawn was either brilliant or foolhardy. The outcome would depend on whether the women ended up with an exclusive, or dead. Piled on top of that knowledge, Sylvie was keenly aware that their zigzag chase had left them more utterly lost than they had been before. There was also the explosion somewhere close that was strong enough to shake the pavement stones beneath their feet. None of that mattered to Ros who was too hungry for a story to focus on anything else but keeping up with the Henleinists until the men suddenly stopped and crouched for cover.

"Not so fast, sister," Sylvie had to grab Ros by the collar and pull her back close to the foundation of the nearest building.

"Got 'ya, thanks," Ros replied out of breath.

Satisfied with whatever they saw, the SdP irregulars hurried off again past the corner they briefly had occupied. A spat of gunshots rang out soon after from that direction.

"C'mon, that's our cue." As the two reporters inched carefully along the foundation to the corner, Ros was aware of an odd scent – a mixture of old dust and spent explosives. "Smell that?"

"Yeah, the last time I caught a smell like that was when a bunch of wise guys decided to make an overnight withdrawal from a bank," Sylvie recalled.

Arriving at the corner, Ros carefully peered around the edge, took a quick look and then yanked herself back out of sight.

"Wow, good nose, hon," Ros had to admit.

"What did you see?" Sylvie pumped for information.

"There's a really big hole where there should be a wall in the building around the corner," Ros did not think it was a bank though.

"Let me see," Sylvie anxiously stepped around Ros for her own view.

After a good look, Sylvie whistled then slinked back to kneel beside Ros. "Must be a police station. I saw dead cops inside the breach."

"Yep, I think we crashed the right party," Ros ducked as a gunshot punctuated the moment. "I'm really glad you're here with me, Sylvie."

"The feeling is mutual kid," Sylvie grabbed her hand and squeezed tight.

"No turning back now, huh?" Ros tensed up like she was ready to bolt.

"Ah hell, you're thinking crazy," Sylvie sensed what Ros had in mind. "It's too soon. We'll end up with bullet holes between the eyes."

"I wish I could say you're wrong but we have only one shot at this. If we don't grab them now we'll lose them for sure just like Reichenberg," Ros breathed deeply.

"Stop making sense, will you," Sylvie thought it was funny how the news business turned something crazy into something sensible.

"Time to get your press pass out," Ros retrieved her credential from her purse and pinned it to her hat.

"Now they'll shoot us for sure," Sylvie was half-serious as she followed Ros' lead. With their hats securely on their heads, the reporters rose to their feet.

"My idea... I'll go in first." Without waiting for confirmation she sprinted for the gaping hole in the police station. "Follow me."

"Too bad I'm not Catholic," Sylvie digressed as she ran after Ros.

"Why is that?" Ros wondered where that comment had come from.

"I would cross myself for both of us," Sylvie held onto her hat.

OSTRAU, MORAVIA

The second radio communication from command had contained more details including the location of the police station under attack and an estimate of the number of attackers. There were an unknown number of dead and no word on whether hostages had been taken. The explosion was reported to be huge, which suggested the Henleinists had plenty of explosives in hand. There was a risk the station might be booby-trapped by the time they arrived. The Sudetens would love to bring the rest of the building down on Czechoslovak soldiers responding to the attack.

His rotný had urged Srom not to ride exposed in the commander's hatch not wanting the VIP in his charge felled by sniper fire. But Srom was conceited enough to doubt the SdP had a sniper sufficiently skilled to successfully adjust for wind and the speed of the accelerating armored car. Besides, Ostrau was not a solidly Sudeten city. The SdP could draw support from the countryside to the west but this place the Czechs called Ostrava was not unfriendly territory. No, he would ride atop this Škoda proudly. The local Czechoslovaks would appreciate a show of valor and the local Sudetens would detest the show of bravado. One more audience were the Poles. Těšín was close to the east and the Poles openly coveted that city for themselves. A show of strength against the Sudetens was an equally useful message to Warsaw not to meddle.

A quick check of his watch told Srom that they would be arriving at their target within minutes. Swiveling around he was pleased to see the tankettes and trucks carrying their mobile infantry were both keeping pace with the lead armored cars in the column. Srom eased a shell into the chamber of his pistol then switched on the safety. Srom hoped the SdP were brazen enough to stick around to accept the lesson he had planned for them.

AMBASSADOR HOTEL, PRAHA

The banging he was perpetrating upon Sanderson's door was starting to harmonize with the steady throbbing between his ears. A maid passed by and looked at him cross enough that he gave up. If the rat hadn't answered by now he was probably off running down a lead. Endicott vowed to lay off the bourbon... again. Old chums turning up was not *that* special an occasion. The truth was Endicott was annoyed enough at missing the Reichenberg story to hit the bourbon and the old chums had provided the excuse.

Endicott's next step was checking out what was going on down in the hotel lobby. Maybe Sanderson was down there. But a quick look around the room produced no familiar Brits. He did recognize the portly backside of the Czech Foreign Ministry guy they always sent over with the latest list of nasty deeds associated with the local Germans. The hope of something substantial to gnaw on drew Endicott in that direction but his progress was interrupted by one of the hotel bellhops.

"Excuse me sir, a message was left for you," the boy prefaced prior to offering up the neatly creased envelope he had in his jacket pocket.

Endicott grunted and tipped the kid a few coins for his trouble. The banging in his head got worse as Endicott read the note from Sanderson. It was short. Endicott had been ditched. Roland and Sanderson were off to Eger to cultivate Runciman. Everyone was working an angle but him. Endicott contemplated the standard lecture he'd soon be receiving from his bureau chief if he didn't latch onto a story soon. Sanderson's note was soon a crumpled mound of pulp in his pocket when Endicott looked up to see the Foreign Ministry guy walking out the front entrance. Before Endicott could lurch into pursuit one of his drinking buddies approached.

"Holy crap! The party has moved on," the reporter called out across the room.

"What?" all the shouting made Endicott's headache worse.

"A police station just blew up someplace I never heard of in Moravia," was the news.

POLICE STATION – OSTRAU, MORAVIA

Bulloch had been close enough to hear and feel the explosion. The rest was following his nose once he had the general direction the blast had come from thanks to fleeing locals. The bad news was Bulloch had no idea what he was converging upon or what he might find when he got there. Slowing his pace the attaché slipped the safety off the Colt and slinked low in approaching the next intersection. Nothing was amiss, however.

Further down the street Bulloch heard something fall hard to the ground. The kind of sound bricks made when they were knocked over at a construction site.

Moving toward the noise, Bulloch used alcoves and doorways to mask his approach. A small cloud of dust drifted across the side street ahead. When he got to the corner, Bulloch paused to take a look. He saw a solid-looking building common to local police stations in Central Europe. There was a gaping cavity blown into the side of the structure with a number of Daimler sedans parked alongside guarded by a squad of jittery militiamen. SdP probably, Bulloch thought by the look of the Mausers. The guards were covering some of their comrades who were busy helping several injured pals past the debris and out of the station to the cars. Bulloch could hear some kind of a commotion and yelling from inside the building. First one, then a second woman were pushed out into the daylight toward the Daimlers. Bulloch rubbed the smoke from his eyes and realized he recognized one of the women. It was that damn Talmadge. She had gotten herself kidnapped by Nazis again but there was nothing he could do. Ros and her companion were too far away and there were too many SdP goons in-between. All he could do was watch the women shoved into the back of one of the waiting cars, which soon sped off in the opposite direction.

The embassy of the United States in Prague

AUGUST 13, 1938
AMBASSADOR'S APARTMENT
U.S. EMBASSY, PRAHA

Louise arrived with another tray of coffee, biscuits and jam from the kitchen. Minister Carr was entertaining a small delegation of important German industrialists from the Sudetenland again. Mister Carr called the musty, gray-haired men *moderates* when he let Mrs. Carr know they were having guests. The minister enjoyed chatting with all kinds of influential people and had invited many of them over for dinner parties or teas since arriving in Czechoslovakia. Carr was not the gregarious type, yet he possessed a very easy manner well suited to slipping through a room – hearing all, and revealing little. Louise always thought of her employer as the sly old fox in with the hens.

From the small bits that she picked up from the conversation while serving the guests today the minister was trying to get help releasing the two American women in the custody of Henlein's paramilitaries. Until now Dr. Henlein never impressed her as thuggish although many of his devotees fit that description. Whatever they were, they were not stupid. Louise felt sure the reporters would be released in short order as soon as these ethnic Germans had twisted whatever political advantage they could out of the Americans. Not a violent person by nature, Louise did not understand these dreadful people. Blowing up police stations and post offices, and killing honest civil servants, should earn Henlein and his followers a noose not diplomacy.

"Herr Seigenthaler, I understand that you have no active association with Dr. Henlein, yet you are a man of considerable standing in the German community. None of my overtures to him have been answered. Can any influence be brought to bear to encourage an honest dialogue between us," Carr beseeched one of his three guests as Louise served a second round of refreshments.

"Given that the SdP has yet to acknowledge that your two reporters are in its custody, I would expect Dr. Henlein would not wish to discuss them yet," Seigenthaler had seen this routine play out before.

"But I have it on very good authority that these women are the *guests* of the SdP," Carr added, Bulloch's full report still fresh in his mind.

"Of that I have no doubt," Seigenthaler wondered what sources Carr's information came from. "Regardless, the opportunity these newspaper women present is a political not a humanitarian question. Henlein will not be at leisure to hold them, or release them, without consultation with Berlin. That takes time so I advise patience. Germany has nothing to gain in needlessly angering the American people."

"That is very reassuring, sir," Carr accepted the industrialist's logic. "The United States does not wish to place blame on anyone. Yet these are perilous times and we are justifiably concerned for the safety of our citizens. If you have the opportunity to communicate with Herr Henlein, please pass along my sincere appreciation for any help he can offer in locating these young women and returning them to us."

"I believe we can convey that message to the right people," Vorbeck leaned forward to pour some cream into his tea. Of the three sitting with Carr, he was the only one with a direct line to Henlein. Seigenthaler liked to talk, however, and Vorbeck saw no reason to let more attention focus upon him than was necessary. Especially since there would be no overture made to Henlein regarding the meddlesome reporters. There was no need. Inviting unwanted attention from the Americans in what was transpiring in the Sudetenland would be stupid of Berlin. The women would be set free shortly. It would be assumed the quiet diplomacy of Vorbeck and his colleagues played a part in the release and they happily would bask in the good will generated with Carr's legation without lifting a finger. Quiet diplomacy being what it was, neither Vorbeck nor the others would ever be called upon to discuss the matter again.

ROSE GARDEN – BUDAPEST

Paris was nothing to sneer at yet Clarence truly loved Central Europe in a way that would make his French wife supremely jealous. The cities of the old Austro-Hungarian Empire were lovely in a meticulous way that was simultaneously more charming and sentimental to him than the flagrantly buoyant French capital. The small rose garden Clarence was strolling through was an apt example. Who tended it was unknown to him but the love and care that had been lavished on the flowers and the grounds was breathtaking. Every hue and vantage point had been placed with great care… like a note in a classical concerto.

The location for the rendezvous had been chosen by the man Clarence was awaiting, a Romanian introduced years before simply as Nicolas by an Armee de la Air general in Paris. Clarence had suspected the man was career air force, although the fellow was never seen in uniform during his many visits to Paris. The Romanians had a strong military trade relationship with the French going back many years – most recently in the area of aircraft engines. Clarence reminded himself that he should work in a question whether Nicolas had been to Warsaw lately. The Romanians were also licensing airframe designs from the Poles. Visits to Warsaw by the Romanian would suggest Nicolas' portfolio might include more than Gnome Rhone radial engines.

The note from Nicolas that Clarence had received at his hotel had been a welcome yet unsettling surprise. Welcome in that Clarence appreciated when a knowledgeable source appeared voluntarily, and unsettling in that Clarence was taking pains not to be conspicuous in Budapest. The Romanian was friendly but not a friend, and there was the question why the man was in Budapest at all since Romania and Hungary were often at odds. Clarence hoped his Hungarian compatriot had played matchmaker. There had not been time to check.

"Welcome to Budapest," a familiar voice boomed in French behind Clarence.

Clarence turned to face the source of the greeting and was pleased to see Nicolas, alone and relaxed, closing the distance between them. "And to you, as well. What business brings you to this fair metropolis?"

Nicolas smiled as he firmly shook the reporter's hand. "Honestly, a little competitive investigation on how our neighbors are fairing with their Italian Fiats. One can't be too careful in these matters."

"That makes perfect sense," Clarence thought it was a good cover story. "What have you learned?"

"A very smooth introduction into service as I see it." Thankfully, the Hungarians had far too few of the fighters to prove much of a bother Nicolas observed.

"I must admit I was pleasantly surprised to receive a message from you here in Budapest," Clarence circled closer to the circumstances behind their meeting.

"Our mutual benefactor here in Hungary mentioned you were visiting Budapest and I decided straight away you might appreciate hearing some interesting news I have learned recently," Nicolas put the American's mind at ease.

"Well then, let's hear what you have to say," Clarence felt comfortable to proceed. "That tip on the Yugoslavs you slipped me last year worked out to be a great story."

"Excellent. Shall we stroll then," Nicolas gestured to the path ahead.

"A pleasure. And might I add you chose a delightful location for a rendezvous. This is a beautiful garden," Clarence remarked as they walked.

"Yes, I am most fond of it myself," Nicolas appreciated beauty as a counterbalance to martial topics. "Are you inquiring into the posture of countries neighboring the Czechoslovaks should hostilities arise between them and the Germans?"

"Indeed," Clarence found Nicolas well informed as usual. "My take is there isn't much stomach around here for getting involved should the two come to blows. I can't say yet about the Poles. Have you been to Warsaw lately and what are they saying?"

"No, I haven't been there recently, although I suspect the Poles would welcome any opportunity to snatch Cieszyn for themselves. What I can tell you is we have word that the Soviets are preparing more than bluster should a Czech/German war break out," Nicolas presented his meaty morsel.

"What does that mean exactly?" Clarence could get vague statements from Moscow on his own initiative.

Nicolas saw a young couple ahead and stopped to the side of the path so they would not be overhead. "That the Red Air Force has assembled as many as three hundred and fifty bombers, complete with crews, ready to assist the Czechs against German aggression. Naturally those bombers would require an air corridor to reach Czechoslovakia, and quite unsurprisingly Moscow desires to fly them over Romania."

"That's huge." Harry would swallow his cigar when Clarence sent this one in. "Will Bucharest allow the over flight?"

"Let us say that is a sensitive topic within my government. The Soviets have not been told yes and they have not been told no. We will have to wait and see. What is important is that Stalin is serious and ready to commit his own military in Czechoslovakia," Nicolas expected the decision would be yes.

"Why me? Why are you giving this delicious scoop to me?" Clarence had to guard against getting played with false information.

"You have always struck me as more intelligent than most newspapermen I have had dealings with. In addition, you understand Europeans very well," Nicolas found the reporter much better than most foreigners in this regard. "I wanted you to have the benefit of this knowledge in guiding your other inquiries."

"And perhaps also because Romania is in a very delicate spot, my friend?" Catching onto a source's motives was one of Clarence's strong suits. "I imagine if news gets into the international press that Stalin is serious about going to war, Uncle Adolf might blink before sending in his tanks into the Sudetenland. Maybe then Bucharest might not have to say yes or no to Moscow."

Nicolas appreciated the American had not lost his edge. "Perhaps, perhaps... regardless, the tip I provided you is accurate. With a bit of digging you should be able to corroborate what I have told you."

"Thank you. Where can I reach you should I need to follow up?" Clarence didn't want to let this fish completely off the hook.

"Come to Bucharest, I will find you," Nicolas would only speak again from the safety of home. "For now, adieu."

With that Nicolas disappeared down the boulevard. Looking around to get his bearings, Clarence noticed a newsstand a few paces to his right stocked well with foreign dailies.

"Crap!" Clarence cursed after picking up the latest edition of the Herald Tribune. *American Women Reporters Held in Sudetenland*, the headline read.

CNS HEADQUARTERS, NEW YORK

Most times a reporter went missing the body could be dredged up in a dive bar somewhere. Not this week. First Marlowe went missing in Wuhan then Ros disappeared in some blue-collar backwater in Czechoslovakia. And no one could give Harry Lasky a straight answer, which probably annoyed him worst of all. China was such a mess all he could do was hope Marlowe was holed up with some local hottie like when he disappeared in Barcelona the previous year. If Marlowe was dead in some ditch they might never know what the hell happened to him. At least Harry knew the Sudeten Nazis had nabbed Ros and the other broad because that was actually making news. Thank God no one else had the goods yet to scoop Harry on his own reporter, but it was going to happen

"Walter!" Harry paced behind his desk with the phone. "You're the best I've got. Can't you get something out of the damn krauts? No one takes a piss in those German towns in Czechoslovakia without Berlin telling them how, when and where in triplicate."

Lasky listened to a few more explanations before cutting off his Berlin correspondent mid-sentence. "Bullshit. Someone there knows what the hell is going on you just have to find them. What do I pay you for anyway? You're supposed to have more sources on the hook than anyone else in Berlin. Break out the damn cognac and loosen some lips. We need to at least look like we're ahead of the pack on this one. Hell, it's our own reporter who's been bagged. Get the inside track and get it now. And while you're at it tell those bureaucrats in jackboots I want my reporter back unmolested. If I get back damaged goods they'll never hear the end of it on the wires."

"I'm not happy," Lasky slammed the phone receiver down on its cradle. The question was where to lash out next. He'd already complained to the State Department in Washington for what little that was worth. The Czech ambassador, on the other hand, had actually seemed competent. He at least knew what was going on. The same couldn't be said for the dolts at Lasky's own State Department. Which gave him an idea. Lasky stomped out of his office into the newsroom.

"Des! Get me the number of our embassy in Prague. I gotta make another call," Lasky called across the floor. "And what have we heard from Wuhan? I don't care if it's a war zone."

GENERAL STAFF
MINISTRY OF NATIONAL DEFENCE, DEJVICE

Srom had reported the majority of his observations to the generals. He was sure by their contented expressions that nothing Srom had conveyed had been unexpected. This was intended. The ready units had performed extremely well. Advance knowledge of the impending attack made a huge difference he had noted. Still, the units had held formation and closed swiftly on their targets. Srom felt sure that in the middle of a crisis they would prove a decisive counter to the kinds of paramilitary disruption applied against the Austrians. The tactical concept behind the ready units was sound.

As Srom had fulfilled the goals of his assignment to Ostrava the general staff would not expect his final conclusion, although Krejčí had endured Srom long enough to enjoy it when the colonel pivoted into a flanking argument.

"One more finding to report." What Srom was about to suggest was strategically advisable yet would leave the generáls with a political conundrum. "Our adversary is adapting his strategy. These attacks are no longer being perpetrated exclusively by local Sudetens at the target. There is a shift to ad-hoc paramilitary units drawing men from different districts. This trend will create complications for us in the future."

"So it becomes slightly more difficult to apprehend the scum," Generál Bohuslav Fiala did not see the problem.

"Initially yes, sir. The trend, however, is to larger and larger operations with more ambitious goals. As the Henleinist units get bigger they get harder to hide. We are already seeing a number of them slipping into Germany after disengaging. It is my conclusion that this trend will swiftly accelerate so that soon virtually all of the SdP's operations will be incursions over the border from Germany. That eventuality will create complications, especially as German regulars will undoubtedly be mixed in with their Sudeten allies in larger numbers."

"Are you suggesting the ready units will be unable to deal with this threat," Krejčí was still operating from the original briefing agenda.

"No, the major complication, as I see it, is that at some point in the coming weeks these incursions will cease to resemble internal civil unrest completely and could rightfully be labeled attacks by a foreign power. That is a military *and* political complication," Srom's next point would drop like an aerial bomb. "If you haven't already, I recommend the prudent course is to be prepared to mobilize the army by September first. The army must be at sufficient strength and prepared to react at a moment's notice."

"The president will have a cow at the very suggestion," Fiala warned.

"Yes, you are correct. Mobilization will be imperative regardless," Srom held his ground.

FOREIGN MINISTRY, HRADČANY – PRAHA

Diplomats had the good fortune of promoting civility as part of their portfolio, Moravec reminded himself as he sipped his tea: a fine mint variety. Which was why Moravec looked forward to his irregular visits to the Foreign Ministry. Having remarked once that he savored the mint tea they served, Minister Krofta made sure there was always some on hand when Moravec was in the building. Regardless of the tense topics of discussion, private meetings with Krofta always reminded Moravec of better times.

The agenda today was politics. Specifically, throwing a diplomatic wedge in front of Henlein so huge that he would have no choice but to take precious time away from his own timetable to deal with the impediment. Disallowed from operating independently, any change in the political landscape would force consultations with Berlin. Perhaps even necessitating Henlein's recall to the German capital for those consultations. Cleaving a week or two out of the SdP's order of battle was a tactical victory that diplomats and spymasters could relish equally.

The execution of that wedge is what had brought Moravec to see Krofta. Back in April Henlein had rejected as insufficient the government's proposal for a new Charter of Liberties to provide ethnic minorities more rights under the constitution. His eight-point counter-plan bordered on authorized secession and intentionally went too far. With his *just* aspirations rebuffed, Henlein had harangued during the summer how the rights of Sudetens continued to be trounced under Czech tyranny. Whispers out of the Runciman mission showed the British were taking such rhetoric seriously, which called for a political counterpoint that would cause friction between Henlein and the unwanted mediator sent by London.

The diplomatic side of the initiative would come in two days. Prague would propose a second plan on minorities that went much further than the first attempt the previous spring. Beneš would propose a decentralization of central government control between the capital and the provinces. Provincial assemblies would be transformed into parliaments with some restricted legislative power over local affairs including managing issues of nationality. This Second Plan would give provinces made up of a majority of ethnic minorities a legislative framework to peacefully further their interests and set up a system where any grievances would fall under the jurisdiction of distinct councils in each province to adjudicate. It was a bold proposal considering few sovereign governments would stomach ceding power to antagonists intent on dismembering the state. It was all show but Czechoslovakia needed to wrest the political high ground from Henlein.

"Then we are agreed on the timing," Krofta double-checked.

"Fully. Everything is in place. Tomorrow, as your ministers are briefing their opposites in Paris, London and Moscow on the details of the Second Plan, my *liaisons* with the intelligence establishments in each country will undertake our side of the bargain. They will provide a thick file of evidence detailing every act of unprovoked violence undertaken since last March by the SdP. This file includes the names of every Sudeten known to have participated, the identities of those who commanded the raids, the SdP officials connected with each attack plus the German ministries responsible for planning and ordering every operation. There is also an addendum listing money transferred by Berlin to Karlsbad: how much, when and to whom. Also listed are the specific dates, lists of arms and ammunition delivered to Henlein from Germany, as well as a complete breakdown of German military *advisors* known to be operating within Czechoslovak territory," Moravec slid a copy of the data over to Krofta.

"Impressive, my friend," Krofta was once again astonished at the breadth of detail Moravec's network continued to cultivate. "Now if you could only share with me what passes in private communications between Daladier and Chamberlain."

"Foreign minister... gentlemen do not spy on the mail of their trusted friends," Moravec made light of the diplomatic niceties.

"But of course," Krofta politely dropped the inquiry.

"Then again," Moravec's mood turned from jovial to serious, "there are no gentlemen in my line of work."

LIBRARY, UNIVERZITA KARLOVA – PRAHA

What an odd choice for a meeting, Burda had thought to himself as he hung up the phone earlier in the day. His first inclination was that the both of them would stand out blatantly amongst the students. That had turned out not to be the case. Burda made a note to himself that he could pass as an associate professor the next time an undercover persona was required. Perhaps Bulloch was onto something.

The intelligence captain spotted the American browsing a stack of recently returned tomes on a cart. At least he looked like he was fluent in the language while turning pages. Burda picked up a stray volume on rhetoric from a nearby table, stashed it under his arm to appear more studious, and redirected himself toward Bulloch. Arriving at the reading desk to Bulloch's side, Burda perched himself on the corner, opened the rhetoric book to a random page and feigned referencing a particular section for Bulloch's benefit.

"Ah, very enlightening," Burda commented studiously.

"What may that be?" Bulloch responded quietly without looking away from his own volume.

"Your girlfriend is obviously leading you to a firmer appreciation for culture," Burda tossed out a barbed compliment.

"We all can use a change of pace from our usual back alley surroundings, don't you agree?" Bulloch reminded him they both spent too much time in the gutter.

"I can appreciate the sentiment. Especially since I understand you have been very well traveled lately. The motorcycle was a nice touch, I might add." Burda liked to remind the American he was always watched. Not that he had any intention of admitting they had lost the attaché soon after he had sped off on the motorcycle.

"You're just jealous." The constant trailing by Burda's men no longer got under Bulloch's skin the way it once did. He could make fun of it now since he was much better at losing them than he once was.

"Hardly, I have a much nicer BMW available that once was attached to a German courier. Sadly for him he no longer has need for it," Burda boasted.

"Waste not want not, my aunt used to say," Bulloch completely agreed.

"A wise woman. So what did you wish to share with me today?" Burda cheerfully got to the point.

"Come upstairs with me, and we can discuss it," Bulloch tried to sound as professorial as possible. "Minister Carr is very concerned for the safety of the two American newspaper women who are the guests of the Mister Henlein."

"Yes, Mister Carr has been making all the correct inquiries. But you surprise me in taking up this task. I would have thought you would be pleased Miss Talmadge was *indisposed*," Burda teased him.

"Personally, I'd rather leave that nosey female on ice. But my boss is duty-bound to get her back and that makes it my duty, as well," Bulloch hated the way the world worked sometimes.

"You have my sympathy," Burda understood completely. "You may discreetly assuage Minister Carr's worry. As far as we can discern both women are in fine shape and are in no danger."

"Thanks. That should lift his spirits considerably. What's your best guess how long Henlein will hold onto them?" Bulloch imposed a bit further.

"That is much harder to estimate. Until they become too much of a burden to keep or until there is no further value in keeping them. I suspect the good Dr. Henlein will play their rescuer after a time. He will be full of apologies about how it is not the policy of the party to abscond with foreign nationals and how he only just discovered they were in custody. Our local Nazis are very good at wringing decent propaganda from such opportunities," Burda described as they reached the second floor.

"Do you know where the SdP has them?" Bulloch would have been negligent not to ask.

"I really can't say," Burda chose to evade rather than to lie. The American was impetuous enough to attempt a rescue on his own for the sake of Miss Talmadge's compatriot. "Honestly, the less we get involved the better for all."

"Message received," Bulloch acknowledged the discussion was closed.

COUNTER-INTELLIGENCE OFFICE
REICH MINISTRY OF WAR – 72-76 TIRPITZUFER, BERLIN

Something stank and there would be hell to pay until he found out why. They were dealing with incompetence of such magnitude someone was ripe for losing their head. That was Göring's frame of mind when he burst into Canaris' private sanctuary unannounced. Göring had tired of the back and forth of useless memoranda that explained nothing. He wanted answers from the source. With the good admiral cornered with his second in command Ottke, there would be no opportunity for evasions. It was one of the prerogatives feldmarschalls held over admirals and their obertsleutnants. "Has anyone noticed that the Czechs are very well informed about our business?"

Standing protectively next to Canaris, Ottke's inclination was to throw the fat bastard into one of the nearby chairs before proceeding to garrote the air from his lungs but the admiral would never permit it. Instead he would wait for Canaris to take the lead.

Canaris had a reputation for cool detachment yet that had not stopped his gun hand from caressing the grip of the Luger strapped out of sight to the underside of his desk. He had put the weapon there as a precaution. Now that it was obvious the commotion outside his door was Göring, the intelligence chief methodically rose from his chair – his hand still gripping the Lugar. Göring eyed the pistol carefully as Canaris carefully laid the pistol to rest on the desktop.

"Don't be alarmed, feldmarschall," Canaris coolly referenced the pistol. "I am sure you understand my line of work has its own peculiar hazards. One never knows what distemper might burst through the door at any time these days. Thankfully, I restrained myself from firing first and averted a tragedy. Please sit down."

Canaris' greeting had taken some of the air out of Göring's sails but there was plenty of fire left in him. He had no intention of relaxing. "No thank you I would rather stand."

"Suit yourself, pace as you wish," Canaris folded his arms to his chest to watch the show.

Göring didn't like the man's tone, yet mindful of the business end of the Lugar's barrel still pointed in his direction, he returned to his original inquiry. "How do these damn Czechs always know exactly what our plans are before they are put into operation? Who is responsible for this failure?"

"I will remind you, feldmarschall, that despite my official protests coordination of Sudeten Party operations does not fall under my jurisdiction. That is the responsibility of the political wing at the chancellery, as you well know," Canaris reminded him. "While we may participate in what's going on down there, many things are simply outside of our control. Besides, your Forschungsamt unit already has our phones tapped. If we were responsible you would already know it."

"Don't equivocate! Surely you have an idea what's going on," Göring had nowhere else to complain. He had already come to a dead end with Himmler.

"Let us review the facts, shall we?" Canaris raised a forefinger for effect. "Do not forget that we are faced with a very capable adversary in František Moravec. He has spent years building his network of paid informants here in Germany and in the Sudeten regions. No matter how many we root out the Czechs have more agents listening and watching. Many of them good party members, perhaps even in your own chambers or mine. It is impossible to say when we will get them all – there are so many. Another problem is that Henlein's organization is as porous as a colander. I have some of my own people watching them and I can no longer count the number of these SdP amateurs who cannot keep their mouths shut. This too is well known to you."

"Fine. Tell me something I don't know. I feel like I have been sleeping with some Slav bitch they know so much about my business," Göring was starting to perspire.

"Very well put, sir. What you may not know is that our operatives in Paris and London report that complete copies of many of our most sensitive war plans are circulating within the British and French intelligence services." Ottke joined in to throw Göring something to chew on. "We have verified that these documents were provided by the Czechs. I can only assume Moravec is being fed by individuals well connected in Berlin. We have reported this possibility personally to Himmler and are coordinating our efforts. The guilty bastards will be caught, but until then, if there is something you know expect Moravec knows it too."

"Why was I not notified immediately about the compromising of our war plans?" Göring's cheeks grew red as he blustered.

"Do not take offense," Canaris remained steady and reasonable. "You know very well how this works. We have an enemy agent very high up but we don't know who that person is. Procedure is clear. The fewer people who know of the investigation the better odds of us catching the fox."

Göring swallowed the argument well enough, but that didn't mean it was sitting well. "Access to sensitive documents is coded. You should be able to narrow down the possibilities."

"That would be correct if we had access to the documents in possession of the French and British. But we don't have anyone in place with such access. At least not yet," Canaris was tiring of Göring's tirade.

"I like your attitude. For once I'd like to know more about them than they know about us. Then maybe we could trap the fucker selling us out." That was one execution Göring wanted a hand in.

"Get in line, general," Canaris sat down and caressed the barrel of the Luger.

U.S. EMBASSY
MALA STRANA DISTRICT, PRAHA

The damned thing about broken ribs... they still felt broken long after the fool doctors pronounced you healed. Endicott reached inside his jacket and gently rubbed the area where the fascist bastard had kicked in the side of his chest back in Vienna. Now with the girls getting kidnapped, Czechoslovakia was starting to feel a lot like Austria and his ribs were aching like crazy. Endicott was so preoccupied he probably would have walked right by Shirer had both men not bumped into each other as Endicott meandered out of the embassy building.

"Those ribs are still bothering you, Charles?" Shirer observed keenly.

"Yeah, just my rotten luck," Endicott paused to shake his competitor's hand.

"No good news on Sylvie and the other one then?" Shirer looked past Endicott to the embassy.

"The last few days Carr has been chatting up every moderate ethnic German in the country. At least that's what the old duffer just told me. They're doing their best but no one seems to know anything. It's like those skirts completely fell off the map. I even went to the address that Henlein's negotiators call home. A whole bunch of nothing," Endicott reported sourly.

"Really, I was going to head over there later myself," Shirer was happy not to pursue a dead end.

"Don't waste your time friend. That bunch is useless," Endicott carped.

"That's discouraging. I spoke with Ed last night. The people back home are starting to take interest in our lost lambs. The story is getting traction and folks want to know what's going on," Shirer shared the feedback.

"Maybe it will do some good and Henlein will get the message he's pissing off the American public, big time," Endicott's blood pressure was starting to rise.

"While we wait on the release of our colleagues, what's up next for you?" Shirer could see Charles needed something to take his mind off the situation.

"The Czechoslovaks have their war games tomorrow. Should be great fun," Endicott was looking forward to seeing the show. "You going to be there?"

"Wouldn't miss it. The Czechs have their new radio transmitter up and this will be the first time I'll get a chance to broadcast over it." This was a big deal for Shirer's career. "No more telephone calls routed through Germany."

"Radio. One day you're going to regret giving up real reporting, friend," Endicott continued many months of taunting on the subject.

"Perhaps... but it's the future, Charles. CBS pays me well and we have a baby to feed," Shirer had responsibilities to consider.

"You're hopeless," Endicott led him away from the embassy by the arm. "Let's get a drink. We both need one?"

LUFTWAFFE AIR STRIP
ALTENBURG, THÜRINGEN

One by one the Heinkel bombers banked in low and fast over the trees at the end of the field as their landing gear tires plunged the last few feet to the ground in a burst of dust and gravel. The staffel had been sent up on another test run with live ordinance for the third day in a row. Many of the crews had cut their teeth in Spain and had only recently returned to Germany while others were fresh out of flight school. Stahl's new bombardier was on his mind as he eased the main gear onto the airstrip with a few bounces and let the tail wheel drift down. They were training on camouflaged targets but Stahl didn't think the kid could hit a gymnasium at noon.

"The bird will be parked in forty-five seconds," Stahl announced into his microphone. "No hiding this time. Lock everything down and everyone get off. Then we are going to review today's sorry performance."

The truth was that Spain hadn't presented much of a challenge. There rarely were targets where precision bombing was necessary. What they faced now were hardened installations that were well protected by anti-aircraft and easily blended in with the hillsides they were tunneled into. The job ahead was going to be hard and they were not ready. Bringing the Heinkel to a stop where the ground crewman directed, Stahl shut down the engines. He got out of the pilot's chair and worked his way down to the forward exit hatch. As soon as Stahl's boots hit the dirt he noticed Pilz jogging toward him. Pilz was one of what Stahl euphemistically called the *fresh* pilots in command of No. 8. As soon as he heard that Stahl had flown with the Legion Kondor, Pilz followed him around like a loyal puppy.

"Stahl! I have a question," Pilz wanted to prove himself to the seasoned veteran.

"What comes to mind today?" Stahl sounded like an old professor. He didn't wait to hear the query before starting an inspection of his bird.

"Aren't we supposed to get fighter escort training?" If so, Pilz never saw it listed on their mission agendas.

Stahl fought back laughter. "They tell you that in flight school?"

"Of course. Our Heinkels are fast enough to outrun most of the fighters the Czechs will put up but I would feel better knowing what we can expect of our escorts," Pilz was only being prudent.

"You can expect never to see fighter escorts," Stahl gave him the unfortunate truth.

"What?" Pilz paused to chew on the unexpected answer while Stahl continued on with his inspection.

"You heard me. It will be just like Spain. Fighter pilots don't give a damn about us. All they care about are kills. They have no time or inclination to shepherd our slow asses. As soon as they see something they can chase they'll disappear," Stahl wasn't going to sugarcoat the matter.

"You are not serious," Pilz quickened his pace to catch up.

"Face up to it, kid. The only way you'll ever see an escort is if by some chance the Italians are with us again. At least they stick with their bombers," Stahl was unappreciated in Spain for speaking that sentiment.

Having circled his aircraft and finding nothing wrong, Stahl noticed the staffelkapitän approaching. He removed his cap and leather flight gear and gestured to his crew to follow him.

"Gentlemen, let's not keep the headmaster waiting," Stahl hoped they were ready to take their medicine for missing the target. "You too Pilz."

SCHLOSS HARTMANN, EGER

His host had been so gracious these last few weeks that Runciman often felt as much at home as at one of his own manors. The food was wholesome and abundant, there was always house staff to attend to one's every need, and when visitors arrived they were shown the same decorum as if they were relations to the master himself. Runciman hoped one day he would be able to return the hospitality of Herr Hartmann. These were fine people, Runciman told himself. They deserved every consideration in their aspirations. But to the matter at hand, Runciman had guests of the most annoying variety – worse than politicians, certainly – newspapermen.

As by plan, Runciman would greet them in the foyer under Peto's escort. Runciman would no less have newspapermen running about unattended in his host's home than in his own. They could lodge themselves in the most private areas of the manor in no time like vermin.

At least they were English vermin. Men from the Times and Telegraph understood how to speak to a Lord and he already had the benefit of dealing with these two before. Having read their reporting from that encounter, Runciman found them to be as professional as could be expected of newspapermen.

"Gentlemen, welcome to Eger," Runciman extended his hand in greeting. "I trust your trip was a comfortable one?"

"Most agreeable, Lord Runciman. A fine time of year for travel in this part of the world," Roland answered in his cheerful, agreeable way.

"That's a weight off of my mind. There is so much anger and ugliness at work in this country, I fear for the safety of the rest of us who are attempting to help these people from themselves," Runciman lamented.

"Yes indeed, these are terrible times for Europe," Sanderson added. "That is why we are most curious to learn of what success your mission of mediation is having in averting such a tragedy."

"Straight to the point. I appreciate that... Mister Sanderson isn't it?" Runciman recalled.

"Yes sir. Spot on," Sanderson had not expected the viscount to study up on them.

"Well, you and your colleague Simmons here should follow me out to the patio and we can get going," Runciman beckoned. "Geoffrey, would you please let the staff know that they can serve refreshments in the garden now."

"At once, sir," Peto assured Runciman, who was well able to handle the reporters for a few minutes without his help.

"Oh this is lovely..." Roland admired as they approached the French doors leading out to the garden patio.

"Very true. It has been my good fortune to have an extremely gracious host here in Eger. If it is not too much to ask please be sure to mention Herr Hartmann kindly in your reporting. It is a small gesture but he has been of inestimable assistance to this mission," Runciman lobbied for his benefactor.

"Wouldn't hear otherwise," Sanderson agreed. There was no way Roland or he would leave out how cozy Runciman was with the Sudeten upper crust. "Are there any other ground rules we should know before we start, Lord Runciman?"

"Nothing more than my usual admonitions before speaking to those of your profession. I may not answer every question you ask but everything I tell you may be used for attribution," Runciman recited his well-worn guideline for interviews. While the reporters digested them, Runciman went around to the far end of the table to claim a chair that would put the sun comfortably at his back and directly in the eyes of his interviewers. "Gentlemen, please seat yourselves. No reason to wait for Geoffrey... we may proceed."

"Most kind of you sir," Roland accepted the invitation.

"Regrettable about all of this violence recently," Runciman expressed genuine sorrow as his guests made themselves comfortable. "Still, understandable when people are pushed too far."

"Is that an official finding, my Lord?" Sanderson again saw the level of sympathy for the ethnic Germans Runciman was volunteering so early in the discussion.

"Heavens no," Runciman fought off the inconvenient question. "No one will see my official findings before they are presented to the prime minister. No sir, I speak only of simple truisms that well-educated men cannot help but accept when witnessed."

"Quite right... so you have been monitoring this recent spat of ethnic German unrest in the region vigilantly," Roland tried a less direct approach.

"Too many hot heads if you ask me," Runciman adjudged. "While I can understand the motivation behind such outbursts they only end up making the resolution more complicated. Too many new loose ends to tie back together. Which reminds me, any word on your fellow reporters taken hostage the other day? Where was that now? Oh yes, in Ostrau?"

"Newspapermen were taken hostage?" Roland asked in total surprise. "We have been on the road and did not hear anything of that sort."

"Two women actually... Americans. Apparently scooped up by Herr Henlein's people in Ostrau," Runciman conveyed matter-of-factly.

"What women?" Sanderson leapt to his feet in alarm.

2ND DEPT. SAFE HOUSE, PRAHA

The cigarette hovered distressingly close to his ear. So close he could feel the heat on his skin yet the smoker said nothing. After each deep drag on the cigarette the Czech would flick hot embers next to his ear. The first time Nagel had reflexively turned his head to look at his tormentor. That had earned him a backhanded slap across the face. Nagel's hands were tied behind the back of his chair just as his ankles were lashed to the legs of the same piece of furniture. His body ached. He had been sitting there tied for hours before the smoker had arrived. At least the smoker had removed the sack covering Nagel's head since he had been accosted leaving his home in Karlsbad and thrown into the back of a black Praga. Nagel cursed himself for getting careless. Karlsbad felt like a part of Germany, after all. Though the Czechs stepped lightly there they obviously had not left. Those who had taken him had not worn uniforms and neither did the smoker. Regular police or army would not have resorted to such dishonesty. He had demanded to know who was holding him, and where, when the smoker had pulled the sack from his head. That had earned Nagel a powerful fist to the face. By the way his skin felt there must be a nasty bruise under the eye nearest the blow. After that Nagel had kept his mouth shut... waiting. Sensing movement from behind, Nagel tensed as the smoker circled in front of him.

"I want to know one thing and one thing only. Tell me what I want to know and this encounter can go very easily for you" Furst proposed with icy calm.

"What do I know? I am a nothing. I am not worth your time let alone all the effort behind this illegal abduction," Nagel protested.

"Strictly legal, young man," Furst countered, flicking his cigarette ashes in the bound man's direction. "You are a deserter from your unit. How you are dragged back to duty will not be questioned. Add to that there is ample evidence that you are a traitor to your oath of service. Maybe you'll end up lucky in Germany – exchanged for a Czechoslovak patriot in their custody. Or perhaps you will be the unlucky victim of a street accident. Ever see how a man looks after being run over by a heavy lorry? I have. Not a pretty sight at all."

The Czech casually drew on his cigarette while waiting for Nagel to think it over. Any hope Nagel had been caught up in a random sweep was now dashed. If his abduction had been random he could play dumb in the hopes of throwing his captors off. No chance of that now. They had wanted him specifically. Nagel had no reason to doubt the gravity of the Czech's sincerity. The choice was easy.

"What do you want to know?" Nagel submitted.

Furst knelt down like a big cat sizing up its prey before striking. He removed the cigarette from his lips and blew smoke contemptuously at Nagel. "Someone in the SdP ranks likes to play with explosives. Tell me who that person is."

MALA STRANA DISTRICT, PRAHA

Walking Petra home from her late classes was growing on Bulloch. His home actually... it was closer to the university than her tiny flat. Petra had pretty much taken possession of his place weeks ago anyway, and never headed back to her own apartment unless she needed to haul in more clothes, or she was mad at him. Somehow he hadn't given her much reason to be mad at him, which Bulloch had to admit was a switch. Usually he always found a way to disappoint whatever woman he happened to be with in the past. With the way Petra ensnared her arm tightly around his as they walked through another warm, lovely Prague evening, the girl obviously had not tired of him yet. The other surprise was the usual itch to try out another woman's bed was completely absent. Bulloch wouldn't bet on how long it would last, but for now strolling home in one of the world's most romantic cities with Petra on his arm made a lot of sense.

An orchestra was somewhere near. Bulloch thought he heard Smetana on the air. That wasn't unusual for Prague nights during summer. These people enjoyed their symphonies in a commonplace way that folks back home enjoyed baseball. Any night there might be a dozen places in the city where you could find an orchestra at work with normal folks filling the audience. Which gave him that an idea.

"Do you hear that?" Bulloch had caught a little whimsy.

Petra's eyes connected with his and she smiled. "The music? Yes... it is lovely."

"Why don't we go to a symphony this week?" Bulloch proposed.

"Does that mean I am not losing you to some international emergency for once?" Petra teased him.

As much as he trusted Petra, Bulloch was careful never to reveal too much of what he did or where he went. It was safer for her and for him that way. But the girl was bright as hell and connected dots pretty well. "I'm sorry," seemed like the safest response.

"Don't be," Petra squeezed his arm tighter. "We understand what is coming. Whatever you are up to is going to help us beat them. I know that."

PARK KOLIŠTĚ, BRNO

The shove out the back door was kind of sudden. The squeal of brakes bringing the old Daimler to an abrupt stop should have been a warning but the crazy driver had been making abrupt stops regularly for hours. Without so much as a good bye, car doors slammed shut and sedan sped off into the distance. Ros felt dirt under palms as she pushed herself up off the ground onto her knees. Pulling the blindfold from her eyes the late afternoon sun was still bright enough to be uncomfortable. When they adjusted, Ros realized there was a little girl in pigtails watching her with extreme curiosity.

"Hello," Ros managed fairly sweetly given the circumstances.

The greeting startled the youngster and she ran off calling for her mother.

"Great. We get cut loose and the first thing you do is start scaring the local small fry," Sylvie was just getting started. Once on her feet she dusted herself off as best she could with her blindfold. "Just look at us, we're a complete mess. The poor kid will probably be traumatized for life."

They were in a lovely downtown park with lots of trees and grass. But the people walking by were gawking at them, which started to make Ros self-conscious. Sylvie was right they really were a mess to behold. The passers by were definitely commenting on them in Czech. That meant there was a good chance they were in a safer neighborhood. Ros noticed their purses had been thrown to the ground with them. Ros picked them up and passed Sylvie her bag. Peering inside her own, Ros saw nothing missing. Documents, even the money was still there. A jumbled mess but everything was accounted for.

"At least they weren't total scoundrels," Ros snapped the purse shut. "Any idea where we are, sister?"

"No clue. Definitely not Prague," Sylvie could not recognize a thing.

"Great... lost again," Ros looked around for someplace promising to strike out for.

Sylvie pivoted around for a better view until she found what she was looking for and pointed in that direction. "Wherever we are that's a hotel over there. *Hotel Passage* the sign says. Looks rather up-to-date too. I'm dying for a bath."

"There you go again with the creature comforts," Ros protested. "What we need is a telegraph office. I have everything laid out in my head. Harry is going to drool all over it. No one else has this but us."

"Exactly," Sylvie growled as she seized Ros by the blouse and tugged her close. "That means the telegraph office can wait."

CNS HEADQUARTERS, NEW YORK

How he had missed the coffee cart lady escaped him. She was pretty good about stopping by to check to see if Des needed anything on her last run of the afternoon, and sure enough, people said she had shown up. Now Des would have to make his own tea in the side kitchen. Neither could he blame Harry since Des couldn't find Harry. The boss was getting crankier every hour. Somewhere he was annoying someone, Des was sure of that. The question was where. There was copy from their guy in Barcelona that was pretty juicy. As he cleaned the fairly persistent stains out of a pot to boil some water, Des decided to send his edited version of the Spanish story on through without Harry. That would piss the boss off and maybe teach him a lesson about disappearing. While relishing the thought, Des sensed Trevor the copy boy was hovering behind him. Des took it kindly that he was the only person on the floor the boy treated so politely.

"What do you have for me there, son?" Des asked without turning away from cleaning the pot.

"Telegram, Des... international too. I thought you'd like to see it right away," Trevor held out the page.

Des put the pot down in the sink, shut off the water and wiped his hands with a nearby towel. He noticed the telegram the boy was holding was rather lengthy. "Correct you are. Let me see what you have there."

Des let out a howl as he read and felt like dancing a jig.

"It's from the pretty lady in Europe, right?" Trevor had taken a quick look before bringing the telegram up from downstairs.

"Yep, our girl is all right! Aw, this is great news. Come with me kid," Des hurried back to his desk with Trevor in close pursuit. Des had long ago put up large maps of Europe and East Asia behind his desk. Checking the telegram again he looked closely at Czechoslovakia on the European map and poked a spot with his finger. "There... Brno, Ros is in Brno."

"Where's that Des?" Trevor was always curious of foreign countries and what their people were like. Des often thought the boy might make a fine correspondent some day.

"Moravia. That's a province in the middle of Czechoslovakia," Des added some details.

"What's she doing there?" Trevor fed on Des' excitement.

"Her job. *48 Hours with the SdP* – great headline. You have to love that girl. Held hostage for two days and she comes out swinging," the editor felt like a proud uncle. Des pulled a silver dollar from his vest pocket and slapped it into Trevor's hand. "I don't care how far, or under what barstool you have to look, kid. Track down Harry. This is something he must read, pronto."

20. BRAVADO

A prototype Czechoslovak Avia B-35 fighter

AUGUST 14, 1938
PRAHA-KBELY AIRFIELD

Usually Czechs were not about pounding their chests like angry gorillas. A cutting sense of humor was a much more common form of expression for most Czechoslovaks. But if the Germans were going to march the Wehrmacht up and down the border for weeks, Bozik couldn't blame old Krejčí for responding in kind. He just wished he had something a bit more modern to flaunt in front of the camera than his trusted biplane. Kopecky had let it slip that the single-winged successor to his Avia was in early testing and Bozik desperately wanted to fly it. If that damned prototype could fly level he prayed someone would take it over the reviewing stand. The new Avia monoplane would not be ready for the coming fight but his pilots would fly all the harder with the knowledge they had a Messerschmitt killer on the way.

The weeks of constant target training had turned his pilots into dangerously accurate shooters and his chief mechanic into a cranky pest. The old veteran was not happy with all of the flight hours the pilots were putting on *his* Hispano-Suiza engines. Then the planes had to be tuned again for what the chief considered a useless air show. But everyone needed to make sacrifices including the maintenance crews. For now they were back at their home field and Bozik was going to make the best of it. The ground crews had the engines of the Avia's warming up in the cool morning air as the pilots approached their parked planes so Bozik slapped his wingman on the shoulder to get his attention over the noise.

"Are you ready to put on a show for the people today?" Bozik yelled over the engine roar.

"I fully expect my top wing to shear off as I chase you around," Nedoma joked. "That should give the crowd a thrill."

The wingman's jest caught the attention of the chief who was closing up the engine hatch of the Avia they were passing. "Hey, Nedoma! Don't joke about such things."

"Oh shit. How did that old fart hear me over the engines?" Nedoma expected the chief should be deaf after working on planes all these years.

"Chief Soucek claims his hearing can pick out a bad piston at one-hundred meters," and Bozik had no reason to doubt the boast.

"Now you tell me," Nedoma sighed.

"Looks like he will tell you himself," Bozik noticed the chief chasing after them.

Nedoma felt his arm being grabbed by what seemed like a vise and his body yanked around to face the annoyed chief mechanic.

"Listen, never make fun of such things. Up there luck is all you young pups have. Never cut short what little supply you have," Soucek brandished a wrench under Nedoma's nose.

"Ah chief, don't take things so seriously," Nedoma pleaded.

"I am the one who has to sit here and wait for you young fools to come back, not you. During the Great War most pilots wouldn't last a month. I lost count how many Bergs we patched up in those days and never saw again. So don't make idiot jokes," Soucek poked Nedoma in the chest with wrench for emphasis.

"Bergs... really," Bozik grew excited. That was the first fighter built completely in Austria-Hungary. "What were they like chief?"

"At first, a pile of crap, but they got better at building them after several months. You could tell which letky had the early ones by all the parts strewn about the field. Gear would just fall off in flight. The damn Austrians rushed the plane into service too soon," the mechanic grimaced at the memory. "Thank God we build them better today."

Nedoma felt comradeship for the first time with the salty little man who had seen much in the last twenty years. "Chief, I appreciate you."

The mechanic brought the wrench up again. "Oh shut up with that stuff. Get in your Avia and get going."

"Well said, chief," Bozik twirled his fist around in a wide circle above his head to get the attention of the other pilots following behind them. "Let's get these birds up, now!"

PROVING GROUNDS
1ST ARMORED REGIMENT, MILOVICE

The radio guys were getting all of the perks these days. In this case a specially constructed deck with tables just for the microphones. Part of that made sense since the ground crews had to string all the wires to one spot. But the radio reporters also got to sit higher than everyone else. Radio didn't make one reporter any better than any other and Endicott suspected the opposite would be true: that radio would make news hounds lazier than they already were. At least that's what Endicott took away from bumping elbows with the newsreel guys the last few years. At least his pal Shirer still went about the job the old-fashioned way and Shirer was the only reason Endicott was ever setting foot on a radio stand.

"How's it going, buddy?" Endicott announced as he plopped down into the empty wood chair next to Shirer.

"You're a welcome sight. I am jumpy as heck here," Shirer felt better having some company.

"What about? You have the best seat on the field with these other loud mouths," Endicott swept an arm in the direction of the other radiomen.

"You know very well that I, of all people, am no loud mouth. This is the first time I've done a live report outside a studio. How Murrow talked me into this business I'll never know," Shirer missed the safety of a comfy studio.

"Murrow knows talent, that's how," Endicott reassured his friend.

"Hey, I hear you got good news this morning," Shirer was happy to focus on something else than fidgeting with his notes and warily appraising his microphone.

Endicott pushed the brim of his hat higher up from it resting place. "Yep, the broads turned up safe in Brno."

"Lucky, very lucky. It is hard to know what the Henleinists are capable of," Shirer had given the abduction of Ros and Sylvie a great deal of on-air coverage.

"Trust me, those two alley cats are a magnet for trouble but they have plenty of lives left. Especially where Henlein's half-assed outfit is concerned. That bunch wouldn't last a week on The Bowery," Endicott had noticed these Nazis always seemed to run from a real fight.

Endicott's rough assessment amused Shirer. "When you put it that way you make it very difficult to disagree with you. But in the context of Czechoslovakia I fear we're about to see worse than the odd customs house bombing."

"Nothing the Czechs can't handle. This won't be Austria. That's why we're here, isn't it?" Endicott gestured at the field. "Their General Krejčí wants to send a message to Uncle Adolph: *Stay out, fool.* "

Shirer pointed out a group of uniformed officers milling about nearby. "Look, the military attachés."

"There is no doubt in my mind that the evidence Moravec's people have put together is convincing. The SS is colluding with Konrad Henlein in this Sudeten uprising," Général Faucher argued. "You both have seen pictures of the weapons, yes? The Germans are so brazen they did not even file off the production stampings from the barrels."

"Listen, Louis... quit bragging about how many secret dossiers you read, I'm not the one you need to convince," Bulloch did not want to admit how much material the Czechs were sharing with him and turned to British attaché Lieutenant-Colonel Stronge to divert attention. "The real question is has Lord Runciman seen the same stuff?"

"Who funds and advises Henlein's little party is somewhat outside our portfolios, is it not gentlemen," Stronge felt annoyed at being put upon by the very junior yank. "We are here to appraise how well the Czech army will stand up to the German army."

"They go hand-in-hand, my friend. Herr Henlein is to be considered a weapon just as surely as any Krupp cannon in a Wehrmacht artillery unit," Faucher took a fuller view of the situation.

"Dreadfully less accurate, however," Bulloch laughed at his own joke.

"Is that actually what you intend to report to Paris?" Stronge ignored the annoying American.

"Without a doubt. It is my duty to report all," Faucher declared proudly.

"The Sudeten militia with their hand-me-down equipment is an annoyance not a realistic threat. If that is not obvious to you then perhaps you belong in a different, less martial ministry," Stronge was done with the self-important Frenchman.

"That is a low blow--" Faucher had choice words to offer about the Irish until Bulloch butted in.

"--Hold the artillery, boys... we have company," Bulloch spotted Major Moericke, the German attaché, approaching.

"I'm surprised he hasn't been kicked out of the country," Faucher groused after glancing in that direction.

"All the better for the Czechoslovaks to show their adversary what he will face if the border is crossed," Stronge found the strategy commendable.

"The time for publicity is long over... now is the time for action," Faucher fussed with the tilt of his kepi.

"What did you have for breakfast this morning?" Bulloch was surprised by Faucher's verve.

"Good afternoon, gentlemen," Moericke comfortably called out in English as he neared his three opposites. "I see you all are your regular contentious selves."

"Nice of you to come over and brighten our day, major," Bulloch tended to agree with Faucher regarding whether Moericke should be in the country at all.

"Aren't you a tad young to be an attaché, captain," Moericke goaded him. "I hope, for your sake the Czechoslovaks are not insulted in Washington's choice of appointments to a major Central European capital."

"Where I come from we don't keep a large army on hand to bully our neighbors so we don't always have senior officers for every posting," Bulloch never avoided a direct challenge.

"You are obviously going to be unsociable, captain," Moericke dismissed further banter with the American.

"I understand your previous assessments on the Czech army have been favorable," Faucher decided to play a card he had been given by the Service de Renseignment.

"General Faucher you are well informed," Moericke wasn't sure whether Faucher was guessing but decided not to deny the statement. Moericke had said much the same in social conversation many times in Prague. "Compared to much of the region the Czechs can be considered a formidable opponent."

"Admirable of you to be so honest. But this sparks my curiosity. Will your superiors in Berlin pay any attention to your assessment?" Faucher belittled the German.

"About as seriously as your assessments are received in Paris, I would imagine," Moericke played on the lament of every attaché.

The boom of nearby Škoda heavy artillery tabled all interest in the petty argument. All four attachés instinctively brought their field glasses up to their eyes and turned toward the area where the salvos came from.

"Sounds like 150mm field guns," Faucher observed.

"I hear a good number of them are drawn by motorized lorries instead of by horses these days," Stronge added.

"They still are well behind us in that regard," Moericke clarified.

"Perhaps," Bulloch decided to leverage a rumor that Smith had dug up in Berlin. "But at least the Czechs have shells for their big guns. Can you say the same, major?"

The stare Moericke leveled on Bulloch was all the proof the American needed to know he had landed a direct hit on German major.

The artillery salvos were dropping a little too close for Capka's liking. Some artilleryman behind the opposing team's lines was laughing it up at all of the mud and rocks showering down on Capka's head. He would track down the prankster later. For now Capka needed to disperse his forward tanks into a wider formation.

"Point! Fan out!" Capka ordered into the wireless microphone above the roar of Škoda's engine.

The front echelon of his tanks split evenly to the left and right as they had practiced. The maneuver would not be obvious from the vantage point of the reviewing stands as they were at ground level and their perspective was from the side. But the opposing team would see the first echelon from the front and be forced to react. Capka was with the second echelon of tanks that would then come together to wedge up the opening in the middle. The plan was to catch the opposing forces just as they were reacting to the flanking maneuver of his lead tanks. But before he gave the order for his group to close ranks, Capka looked skyward and hoped Bozik was on time for once. Capka needed a little distraction before forming his wedge.

Thousands of feet above the ground Bozik checked his watch. Capka had been adamant about the strafing run being a complete surprise. To carry that order off meant coming in from an insanely high altitude. Since progress on the ground couldn't be seen they were forced to time the dive. At least there were plenty of puffy white clouds beneath them to mask their approach. Bozik switched on his microphone and ordered his pilots to dive. Capka's tank wedge had better be were it was supposed to be when his birds got down there.

Not far above the field a wing of Letov S-328 attack bombers were completing their patrol arc when the flight leader craned his head to the left and saw the formation of tanks on the ground splitting apart. He cursed in the same low voice reserved for a losing hand in cards. The tactic reminded him of those used by some of the fighter squadrons his wing shared a base with in Moravia. The goal was to pull the lead defenders far enough away from supporting comrades to make them vulnerable – in this case to distract from the main attack. It was lucky he even noticed the maneuver at all as his Letov's had been caught on the wrong side of their patrol area. His old bi-planes could get back to where they needed to be in time but it would take a high-speed slanting angle of attack. At least as high a speed as these slow Letovs could manage. Lifting his arm out of the open cockpit he gestured to his pilots to follow his lead. Unfortunately, his was the only aircraft equipped with a radio. Sure that his signal had been seen the flight leader banked his bomber left into a dive.

Capka stole another glimpse skyward but instead of Avias screaming down in support of his attack all he saw was an attack wing of Letov light bombers approaching his position from the wrong direction. Opposing ground attack patrols had been considered but Bozik had been sure the ground attack pilots would be just as confused by the tactics Capka's tanks were using as the ground troops facing them. Conceited fighter pilots... they thought bomber pilots were stupid. Capka grabbed his radio microphone to instruct his tankers to increase speed. The opposing team's defense line was close. Perhaps they could break through before the bombers could mark them for bomb hits.

The Avias burst through the bottom of a huge cloud with Bozik's plane in the lead. Within seconds Bozik realized he had a problem. There was Capka's wedge of tanks about where it was supposed to be. But vectoring toward his friend was a wing of Letov's setting up a mock attack. The problem was the fighters and the bombers were heading for the same patch of sky at full-speed. All Bozik had time for was to order his pilots to evade and hope his men could successfully avoid the slower Letovs.

The attack wing flight leader was adjusting his bombing run when he felt his rear gunner insistently slapping the side of the plane. Usually a signal they had dangerous company incoming. Looking over his shoulder and above the veteran bomber pilot saw it was worse than that. He had a squadron of Avias in the opposing team's colors diving into his formation. He crossed himself and did the only thing he could do: break away into another direction and pray enough of his crews did the same to save themselves. The wood spars connecting the fabric wings of his plane groaned under the strain of the sudden maneuver but they held together. He heard the snarl of a Hispano-Suiza engine pass far too close for comfort but had no time to check to see how close the Avia had missed them by. His gunner would have to tell him later.

Leveling out frightfully close to the ground the flight leader risked a look behind him. Miraculously he saw no explosions and there was his wingman matching his every move. Their escape had brought them very close to the audience assembled to watch the mock battle. Joy turned to alarm, however, as his eyes spotted something amiss on his wingman's plane. The lower left wing of the other Letov was separating from the fuselage and soon tore away. The aircraft was suddenly thrown out of control – careening toward the field directly in front of the review stands.

The reporters had a perfect view of the near collision of aircraft. Shirer was broadcasting live and had stayed composed, describing every detail despite the shock he felt at watching a near disaster unfold before him. Then one of the slower bi-plane attack bombers that had just escaped collision fell wounded out of the sky mere feet in front of them – impacting the turf in a furiously loud crash. All Shirer could manage was a stunned, "My God."

Endicott saw it all happening and was out of his chair at about the same moment the Letov cratered yards away. Looking down at his friend he yelled, "Keep talking!" Turning to the rest of the reporters, Endicott gestured to the crumpled fuselage of the bomber. "C'mon guys, let's see if we can save those poor bastards."

A pair of Avias swooped so low the undercarriage of the lead fighter missed Capka's head by a few meters at most – forcing him to duck down into his turret at the last moment. Bozik's boys were badly out of formation, but whole. Despite the near collision he could see they were reforming and heading onto their targets ahead. Capka admired their very professional work. He would commend Bozik for their excellent training later. Capka did a calculation in his head and concluded that by the time the scattered group of light bombers formed up and came after him it would be too late for the opposing team's main defense line, which his attack wedge was swiftly closing on. Capka refused to be distracted by the aircraft accident. He had needed a diversion and had received one of huge proportions. Capka recognized this was a perverse sense of luck, yet on the battlefield, there was no other variety.

The first ambulance crew to reach the crash felt their hearts sink as they saw the crumbled wreck of the Letov up close. It appeared as if the biplane had hit the ground askew on the same side where the bottom wing had torn away. The fuel tanks had not exploded on impact but they had to be ruptured and loose fuel could ignite at any time. Many brave souls from the reviewing stands had already reached the aircraft and were working together to cut away parts of the plane to get at one of the limp crewmen. The četař brought the ambulance in as close to the wreckage as he could manage and ordered his medics to get moving. Looking the scene over quickly as his feet hit the ground the četař deftly retrieved a pair of heavy cutters from the side of the ambulance and ran to the plane. The rescuers saw the fabric covering and thought they would find wood underneath. Hacking away with pocketknives wouldn't help. The Letov had a metal frame under the fabric. Pushing some of the amateurs out of the way, the četař planted a boot for leverage and put his weight behind the cutters.

Bulloch had lunged for the crash site mostly on instinct. He had sprinted half of the way there before noticing that Moericke was keeping stride with him. Whatever surprise he felt got buried in the demands of the moment. The two attachés had reached the wrecked bi-plane right behind a gaggle of reporters who had been closer to the crash than anyone else. The aircrew appeared badly injured. The cockpit had been crushed in around the pilot and the rear gunner had been thrown from the aircraft. Some of the reporters were trying to make the man comfortable while the rest went to work attempting to pry open enough space to get the pilot out of the wreckage.

"Many doctors in my family, I'll check on that one," Moericke moved toward the unconscious gunner.

"Right, I'll see if I can help over there," Bulloch responded as both attachés split up.

Moericke got a few stares as the nationality of his uniform was recognized. There wasn't time to worry about that. The gunner was splattered with blood and oil making it hard to tell how extensive his injuries might be. Moericke checked the man's wrist for a pulse then laid his ear close to the gunner's chest to check for breathing. Moericke noted faint results on both counts. There was little that could be done for whatever internal injuries the man had and Moericke suspected there were plenty. But what he could do was stop the bleeding – most obviously the nasty gash on the forehead. Moericke threw off his jacket and then tore off a section of his white shirtsleeve. Fashioning a head bandage, Moericke applied it tightly to the forehead over the gash and gently lowered the gunner's head down to the grass when finished. Checking the fit closely, Moericke became aware of a Czech army medic hovering above him.

"Good job," the medic commended in accented German. "We'll take over now."

Moericke stood up and backed out of the way, very much surprised at the respect present in the medic's voice. Perhaps he was getting much too used to Faucher's constant volleys. Forgetting his jacket, Moericke hurried back to the wreckage to see if he could be of further use. Arriving after the ambulance sergeant, Moericke took in the situation. The assembled rescuers were trying to cut away the fuselage around the pilot and were making slow progress with the crumpled metal – much of it bent inward dangerously close to the injured man. The reporters had torn away nearly all of the fabric in the area so it was easy to see what needed to be done.

Moericke circled the military ambulance until he saw what he wanted mounted with other heavy tools on the vehicle side: a very long crowbar that would do nicely. Moericke grabbed the tool and rushed to Bulloch's side. The American was smartly attempting to pull metal in the fuselage away from the pilot with the clawed end of a hammer. Moericke would have to ask him later where Bulloch found the hammer.

"Let's try this instead," Moericke suggested as he grasped Bulloch firmly by the upper arm with his free hand. Bulloch eyed the crowbar and smiled.

"That's much better than this thing," Bulloch agreed as he dropped the hammer to the dirt. Bulloch took the crowbar in his hands and guided it in-between strips of fuselage metal until the rounded end of the tool was evenly centered. The German attaché was on the same page. Without a word, both men pulled backward with all of their strength. The metal gave under pressure. Choosing other adjacent sections the two attachés repeated the operation several times.

"That will do it!" the četař yelled – moving in deftly with the cutters.

Minutes later enough of the frame had been cut away. The četař and some of the closest men eased the pilot out of the wreckage and back to the ambulance. Examining the wounded man as the sergeant tore away portions of flight suit, Moericke noticed numerous punctures... some of them substantial. If the pilot survived it would be a miracle.

"Quick thinking back there, major," Bulloch praised his rival. "If you ever need someone to put in a good word for you let me know."

"I appreciate that greatly, captain," Moericke was caught off guard by the American's change of heart. "One never knows what will happen tomorrow."

A fire truck pulled up next to the crash site. The well-trained crew hit the ground and was unraveling the hose in seconds. As a precaution they began wetting down the Letov and the surrounding area to keep any fires from igniting as the medic crew finished securing the two airman on gurneys and gently pushed the men into the back of the ambulance. In a few moments they were on their way to a nearby Czech army medical facility.

Bulloch thought of Moericke and remembered stories his father had told him about life on the front during the Great War. Some days the carnage would suddenly stop and some small bit of humanity would take its place. It was a crazy world. Bulloch noticed the American reporter stepping into the space between the two attachés.

"Very nice work, gents," Endicott was uncharacteristically praiseworthy.

"Not bad yourself. I noticed you were the first person to reach the crash," Bulloch wasn't used to being outrun.

"Professional instinct. We can chase ambulances almost as well as lawyers," Endicott's joke was not far from the truth.

Bulloch was happy for the levity. He didn't always get along with reporters but thought he could throw back a few beers with this one. "So what's your headline going to be?"

"That depends on whether those two poor fellas pull through or not. But I have to tell you I am intrigued with the subplot here," Endicott eyed both attachés.

"Subplot?" Moericke was curious what the American newsman was getting at.

"I'll be straight with you, major," Endicott had been studying up on German rank badges. "How does it feel helping to save that Czech aircrew today knowing your countrymen might have to shoot them down some day soon?"

"That irony is not lost on me. Despite what may happen between our nations I am not at war with these men today. My duty was clear," Moericke tabled any further discussion.

KARLOVY LÁZNĚ – STAROMESTSKE, PRAHA

The bathhouse was already old but the Roman-style spa pools added a bunch of additional centuries onto the feel of the place. All of which suited Ros fine. The marble and stonework felt very safe after a week of uncertainty. The massage treatment followed by soaking in pools of hot water was delicious she had to admit. Ros regretted missing the Czechoslovak Army maneuvers but Sylvie had been adamant about the hot soak since they had been dumped in Brno. Now Ros didn't mind so much. After getting back on safe ground in Prague there had been no shutting Sylvie up, especially since Roland had already told her of this bathhouse in the Old Town district. It was amazing the details that that little Brit dug up on a town.

"Hey sister, how does a little worm like Roland know about fun places like this?" Ros wondered aloud while swishing water with her toes. "I can't picture him in a posh joint like this."

"You need to pay better attention," Sylvie managed tiredly like a mother asked one too many questions by a young child. "How do you think Roland gets all of those exclusives? You never see him chasing politicians down the sidewalk like the rest of us. That's because he'll be the unobtrusive little fellow hanging out at the garden tea, smoking a cigar in the club lounge or who just happens to be sharing the same steam room with the high and mighty. Roland is probably more clever than all of the rest of us put together."

"Why am I hanging out with Sanderson all of the time then?" Ros joked.

"Because he puts up with you," Sylvie chose the honest answer.

Ros giggled knowingly before continuing. "What's your excuse then?"

"If you had not already noticed you happen to be one of the luckiest brats I have ever known. Every day is like Christmas with you. I'm just hoping Santa throws a couple of extra presents my way since I'm in the vicinity," Sylvie explained her theory.

"Hey! I work hard," Ros took offense.

"Hon, I never said you didn't. You're good *and* you're lucky. That's the honest truth," Sylvie clarified the theory.

Ros sloshed around a bit in the warm water while contemplating what Sylvie had just mentioned. "Does everyone else feel the same way?"

"None of us are stupid, sweetheart. Well, Endicott is pretty dense but when it comes to the news business he's right on the money. Don't fret about it," Sylvie advised.

"Oh, I'm not worried about you guys, it's just I never think of myself as being that lucky. Especially working for a little prick like Harry," Ros wasn't quite sold yet.

Sylvie stretched her legs then sat up a bit straighter. "I'll grant you working for Harry Lasky isn't the height of good fortune but think about it from a different angle. We're women in a man's business, foreign correspondents at that. No matter how hard we work at it we wouldn't be where we are without a lucky charm in our pockets. And that's all the business I want to discuss for the rest of the afternoon. I want the last week to soak out of my pores before going back to work."

"Amen to that," Ros agreed as both women slipped lower in the hot water.

SCHLOSS HARTMANN, EGER

Lord Runciman descended the stairs to the waiting Daimler LQ20 limousine he had grown to appreciate far too much during his stay with Herr Hartmann. The delightful vehicle had been put at his sole disposal and was just one more example of the civility the German people here had continually shown him. Runciman's eye caught another vehicle approaching up the lane to the mansion and paused on the steps. Upon closer examination he recognized the automobile as one of the ubiquitous Škoda cabriolets that middle-level Czechoslovak officials employed to get around. Whatever the reason for the visit, Runciman was sure the usual dour demeanor of most Czech functionaries would certainly cast a pall on an otherwise lovely day. The Škoda pulled in behind the Daimler and sure enough a Czech bureaucrat emerged from the passenger door with satchel in hand.

"Lord Runciman," the Czech greeted the British mediator in well-enunciated English. "I am pleased we arrived to find you in residence. These are important documents from Foreign Minister Krofta."

The youngish diplomat presented the satchel in a respectful manner that pleased Runciman. He was well aware of the disdain many Czechoslovak's held for the British mission and was impressed with this fellow's sense of professionalism. "What have we here?"

Jicha knew full well what he was delivering but had been instructed to feign ignorance if questioned. If Lord Runciman had questions the foreign minister wanted the mediator directed back to Praha for answers.

"Such details have not been confided in me, Lord Runciman. I have been instructed to tell you that you have been presented with a complete document preceded by a detailed summary," Jicha explained.

"Fine, fine. Anything else young man?" Runciman would be pleased to send the fellow on his way.

"Only that I am to wait at your pleasure should you have any immediate requests that I can pass along to the foreign minister, sir," Jicha added.

As he considered the diplomat's offer Runciman became annoyingly aware that Peto was nowhere in sight – most unbecoming of a senior aide. Peto may have had something to add that had escaped him. No reason to keep the man waiting though. Very bad form, that. "You are most accommodating but I have no reason to detain you further here. Please convey my compliments to Minister Krofta."

"As you wish, sir. Good day," Jicha concluded very happy to leave. His personal sentiment would have led him to immediately deport the British interloper but that was not his decision or authority. The sooner he was away from the stale old shipping magnate the better he would feel. Jicha returned to the waiting car and took his seat. Closing the door he gestured for his driver to take the Škoda 420 back to the road.

Curious, Runciman released the lock on the satchel. Inside the case was a large envelope containing a very substantial document. The Czechs were nothing if not thorough. As promised there was an ample summary on top. He had just been delivered as a courtesy a new negotiating platform from Beneš intended for the Henleinists. Scanning the summary Runciman realized the proposal he held was shocking. This new minorities plan was a near capitulation from Beneš' earlier positions. It proposed decentralization of the government between the Prague and the provinces with provincial assemblies transformed into parliaments with some restricted legislative power. These parliaments would even possess control over some nationality affairs. If there were ethnic grievances they would fall under the jurisdiction of distinct councils in each province. Runciman's hands shook as he read further. This was exactly what he needed to close the matter.

"Lord Runciman, I was told there was a delivery," Geoffrey Peto emerged from the mansion.

"There you are at last! We have work to do," Runciman waved the document in Peto's direction. "No more excuses. What I have in my possession is critical and I must see Herr Henlein immediately. If he declines to meet with us once again inform him we are done here and leaving for England immediately."

PROVING GROUNDS
1ST ARMORED REGIMENT, MILOVICE

The crash of the Letov had been tragic yet most of the army units engaged in the mock combat had continued on their assignments unawares of their stricken air force comrades. As the medics sped the injured men to the hospital, Capka's tank assault created a huge gap in the defensive lines that the other motorized units swarmed through. Bulloch had missed it all. When the maneuvers were done he found himself drawn back to the crash site to contemplate what he had experienced. Bulloch had never been in actual combat and probably never would since attachés rarely got close to the actual blood and guts.

If Bulloch was expecting solitude he didn't find it. There were plenty of curious Czech soldiers milling about observing the air force investigators examining the wreckage. When yet another army lorry pulled up behind him Bulloch completely ignored the distraction. What he could not ignore moments later was the huge paw of a hand that fell commandingly on his shoulder from behind. Expecting to be told to leave the scene, Bulloch swung around to discover the paw belonged to the outspoken Czech tanker he had met a few weeks previously, accompanied by another officer Bulloch did not recognize.

"Capka, isn't it?" Bulloch recalled the face.

"Your memory is good, kapitán," Capka tone was melancholy.

"Who is your friend there?" Bulloch felt like being direct that evening.

"Him, he is my keeper. All of this is my fault," Capka outstretched his arms in the direction of the stricken Letov. "The generáls want to have a word with me and he works for them."

"Major Kopecky. I work for the general staff," Kopecky was curious how Capka had befriended the American.

"Captain Nathaniel Bulloch, U.S. Army." He could not grasp what possible connection the tanker had with the crash.

"Ah yes, I am glad to finally make your acquaintance. Your reputation precedes you," Kopecky knew the attaché mostly for the casual inquires about him from military representatives of other foreign powers in Praha. Kopecky often wondered why this attaché was so interesting. So far there was not a satisfactory answer.

"Would you be referring to a brunette, about five-foot, six? That one, she's trouble," Bulloch made light of his notoriety.

"I see you two have similar tastes in women. Both of you stay away from my sisters or I will break your necks," some lightheartedness returned to Capka.

"Warning noted, stábní kapitán. But I am curious. Why would your generals want to talk with you about a plane crash? You are a tanker. I was standing right over there and watched with my own eyes. This crash was caused by a near miss in the air," Bulloch didn't think the man could pilot a plane as well as a tank.

"Yes, that's my fault. My brigade led the ground attack today. I wanted to decisively show what we could do. So I arranged for a little air support, which ended up funneling too many pilots into the same damn little space and *that* was the result," Capka turned to the wreckage.

Kopecky felt Capka had volunteered about as much as the American needed to know. "Trust me. He's in much less trouble than you are with that brunette. Accidents happen. It is regrettable. Senior officers still need to know why accidents happen."

"That's Kopecky's way of saying I talk too much... the bastard never talks straight," Capka chided his companion.

"You both have been friends a long time then?" Bulloch could see the bickering between them was much too comfortable to not be of long standing.

"Very perceptive of you, kapitán. I have found it is much safer to be a friend of Capka than the alternative," Kopecky was only half joking.

"I'm thirsty," Capka shifted topics. "I know a place on the way into Praha that serves a good Řizek. Let's go. Join us Bulloch."

Bulloch hesitated a moment before answering – suspecting a long night ahead, and a fearsome hangover tomorrow if he accepted.

"In case you didn't notice, that was a command not an invitation, kapitán," Kopecky advised Bulloch. "Please join us."

A squadron of Soviet Polikarpov I-16 fighters

AUGUST 17, 1938
U.S. EMBASSY, MOSCOW
MOKHOVAYA BUILDING

A last final review of the cable turned up nothing amiss. Any further second-guessing was confined to whether the contents of the memo were to be believed. He saw very clearly where Europe was heading even if many of his peers back home did not. Czechoslovakia was not an end but only the beginning. That's why chargé d'affaires Alexander Kirk dearly wanted the Soviet statement he was forwarding back to Secretary Hull to read like the genuine article. It had come from Litvinov's office and Kirk didn't see such a correspondence being generated without Stalin's approval or knowledge. But was the pledge therein bankable? It would not have been the first time the Soviets had played them. It was common knowledge with the embassy staff that their temporary offices were well laced with surreptitious microphones. The building overlooked Red Square for heaven's sake. The NKVD probably knew more about what went on inside these walls on a daily basis than Kirk did and could ably determine what the Americans wanted to hear.

Kirk decided he was too old to question his instincts. Whatever Litvinov's ultimate agenda Kirk always came away feeling the man was serious about drawing a line at the Czechoslovak border with Germany. Serious in a way the Soviet people's commissar for foreign affairs had never been about Spain. Aiding the Spanish Republic was more theater and a test of what could be accomplished when the fascists were challenged. Litvinov had looked Kirk in the eye and stated firmly that the Soviet Union would honorably and effectively fulfill its obligations to Czechoslovakia even if it were compelled simultaneously to wage war in the Far East with Japan. Kirk had taken the encounter to heart.

There had been rumors circulating for weeks between informed personages in Moscow about hundreds of Voyenno-Vozdushnye Sily light bombers and crews being readied for deployment to Czechoslovakia at the first word of hostilities breaking out. Unfortunately, Kirk could find no evidence to support those rumors and that bothered him, but not sufficiently to change his mind about the cable in his hands. Kirk decided not to waver. He wouldn't change his recommendation that Litvinov was playing straight with him. With the argument in his head settled, Kirk rose from his desk and headed toward the cable room to send the memo.

SLEZSKA CAFE
VINOHRADY DISTRICT, PRAHA

Prague was proving different than Vienna. Back then the crisis marched relentlessly on Vienna. But in Czechoslovakia the action was everywhere but Prague. The city was geographically well placed to get to the many different Sudeten cities, and the Czech government was here, yet Prague itself was still pretty much the calm and beautiful metropolis any traveler would read in last year's tourist brochure. The reporters were always splitting up to track down some story lead in some small village on the map no one had heard of. When they realized the Ros and Sylvie were safe and everyone was back in Prague at the same time, Ros suggested the little neighborhood café she had caught Bulloch at all of those months ago for lunch.

"Nice choice, Kid," Endicott looked around as he got comfortable in his chair.

"Especially for this time of year too," Sylvie liked a spot where you could enjoy the coming of fall. "When did you have time to find it?"

"Just someplace I stumbled upon when I was in town for the Masaryk funeral. It really is a lovely spot," Ros wondered if Bulloch would ever turn up again.

"What a nice change to have you providing the venues instead of pinching them from the rest of us," Sanderson tossed in. "Bravo!"

"Leave you to yourself for a while and you turn nasty. Wait until I tell your mother on you," Ros swatted the back of his head.

"Better watch out!" Sylvie whistled while concentrating on filing her nails.

"Feel free to make a reservation. My mother's social calendar is set for the next thirty-six months and there is rarely a cancellation," he raised both hands in submission.

"Didn't we tell you, hon? Robin here comes from one of those hoi polloi families," Sylvie threw in. "You'd have to elope with the boy before getting dear old mum's attention."

"Marvelous chance of that," Sanderson scoffed at the hilarious notion. "On both counts."

Ros pursed her lips in dissatisfaction while a waiter brought them the wheat beers they had ordered. Endicott appreciatively beheld the golden liquid placed before him and rose to his feet in a toast.

"Here's to great pals, worthy competitors and crazy bastards," Endicott raised his pint glass.

"Didn't I hear that same toast in Madrid... from somebody else?" Sylvie eyed Endicott suspiciously.

"Shut up and drink you crazy broad," Endicott hated it when Sylvie was right.

"And to Endicott here," Ros felt honors were in order. "I here you were quite the brave one the other day – jumping in to help rescue those crashed pilots."

"Someone had to help those poor suckers. I wasn't alone either, turns out your army attaché buddy was there too with a Kraut alongside helping out. Can you imagine that?" Endicott was setting up for further embellishment.

"Perfectly well, old friend. I read your dispatch the next morning," Sanderson threw cold water on Endicott's storytelling.

"Really... Captain Bulloch was getting his hands dirty?" Ros thought he wasn't the type.

"That was sure harsh, sister. Especially about someone who pulled your rear out of the fire," Sylvie didn't see the use in ripping up good boys the way Ros did.

"Hush!" Ros didn't need reminding on that count.

"Well here you all are," Roland appeared with a short balding Czech festooned in a cheap suit tagging along.

"Roland! Glad you finally got here," Endicott was pleased for another excuse to order more of the tasty summer beer. "Who is your new friend there?"

"This good fellow is a bona fide representative of the Czech Communist Party. He came by the hotel looking for our dear ladies," Roland was going to enjoy this.

"What can we do for you, comrade Pudgy?" Ros just had to accept that she was a magnet for totalitarians.

"Pudgy?" The party man recited back, confused. "No, Petrov is name. Miss Anderson and Miss Talmadge report honestly in Vienna. The chairman of the Czechoslovak party extends his regards. He would be pleased to speak with you both regarding the international crisis with Germany."

Sylvie leaned forward to take the business card the communist was offering. "That's very sweet, Mister Petrov. I'm sure we can arrange something.

SUDETEN DEUTSCHE PARTEI – HEADQUARTERS, KARLSBAD

Everyone who had been summoned was present. Lord Runciman had been insistent on speaking personally, *and in detail*, with Henlein. The party leader had been demurring for weeks not wanting the mediation process to make progress and to prevent the old Englishman from pinning Henlein down to any concessions. That's the way Hitler wanted it and Henlein knew better than to veer from the path selected for him. Still, Henlein felt strongly that war would cost the Sudeten Germans significantly in lives and property – a sacrifice that could be avoided. Looking at the population maps a good argument could be made that self-determination alone would bring the Sudetenland into the Reich in short order. It was an argument Henlein was sending Frank to make in person before Hitler with little hope of success. It was obvious war was what the Führer wanted. The Czechs had insulted Hitler in May when they mobilized and Hitler had been keen ever since to deliver them a severe comeuppance.

Frank's appointment with Hitler was a week hence, however. For now he had a more immediate chore to complete. As Henlein could avoid Runciman no longer, Frank was tasked with preparing the rest of the senior SdP delegation on how to deal with Runciman's team. When the Englishman went to his colleagues for counsel it was imperative that the same message Runciman had received from Henlein was echoed back from mediator's own people.

"It is our duty to convince His Lordship that the nationality problem in Czechoslovakia cannot be solved within the state and that the Czechs are in no way prepared to make concessions of a kind that could lead to a real justice for ethnic Germans," Frank understood this had been Sudeten negotiating position for months yet no deviation could be allowed. "His Lordship must take away with him the impression that the situation in this country is so confused and difficult that it cannot be cleared up by negotiations or diplomatic action. Lastly, Runciman must accept that the blame for this crisis exclusively lies with the Czechoslovak government and thus Prag is the real disturber of peace in Europe."

BRITISH EMBASSY, BERLIN

The change in tone was rather noticeable... and disquieting. Hermann Göring was a boastful provocateur and a known agent of opportunity. What he had never been before was openly belligerent to a representative of His Majesty's government... at a social encounter no less. Sir Neville Henderson was left with the strong impression there had been a policy shift within the German government. The British ambassador had always viewed the Sudeten question as an issue of great import to Hitler yet Henderson also well understood many of the institutional barriers within Germany to an overly aggressive stance toward Czechoslovakia. The country had lost too much in the Great War to view a return to hostilities with anything but aversion. Austria was a different scenario of a mostly Germanic populace very willing to join with their Germanic brothers. Czechoslovakia would take a fight and a bloody one at that.

In the past Göring was always good for a bellicose denunciation of Prague or Moscow but on their last encounter the field marshal had included Britain. Henderson reread the quote in his cable to the Foreign Office in London one last time for accuracy.

IF ENGLAND MAKES WAR ON GERMANY, NO ONE KNOWS WHAT THE ULTIMATE END WILL BE. BUT ONE THING IS QUITE CERTAIN. BEFORE THE WAR IS OVER THERE WILL BE VERY FEW CZECHS LEFT ALIVE AND LITTLE OF LONDON LEFT STANDING.

Following the boast Göring had added for emphasis that the Luftwaffe was numerically superior to the air arms of Britain, France, Belgium and Czechoslovakia combined. If Göring was casually tossing such threats about, to Henderson that meant a line had been crossed at the highest levels in Berlin. It was no longer about *if* the Wehrmacht would roll against the Czechs but was now a matter of when. The message was abundantly clear to Henderson. Göring obviously did not want to see a repeat of the crisis of May when Prague ordered mobilization, followed soon thereafter by Paris and London delivering a diktat to the Germans: *back down or we mobilize as well.* So now the field marshal was issuing threats to deter British interference.

COMMUNIST PARTY SAFE HOUSE, PRAHA

Stalin's man had been droning on for two hours and wasn't winded yet. Not even the delegates from the French and British communist parties could get a word in. She figured that was expected. This seemed more like a relaying of orders than a back-and-forth discussion. The meeting and its location were strictly secret. That Petra was there at all was a fluke. Her professor was on the invitation list not her. But he needed someone who could understand what the Soviet was saying because his Russian was abysmal. At first they did not want to admit her but the professor demanded and here she was. Petra was excited at the opportunity, and she was honored, but this Andrei Zhdanov fellow was a conceited bore.

And she definitely didn't care for the way he looked at her. Zhdanov made her skin crawl. Neither did Petra appreciate fellow Czechs being dictated to by outsiders. But she'd leave that for later when she could talk to her instructor alone.

What she was translating in a low voice was annoyingly self-serving. The final strategy of the Communist International was that fascism was a threat *and* an opportunity. If war between Czechoslovakia and Germany broke out it was the duty of all party members to fight the fascist aggressor. At the same time party members would have to utilize the economic and political crisis to accelerate the downfall of capitalism in Československo.

To Petra it seemed like Zhdanov's priorities were all wrong. What kind of ally was Stalin if he was more concerned about who ran Československo than the Germans marching into Praha? The way Zhdanov was talking it seemed the Soviets saw fighting the Nazis as their last priority after overthrowing the republic. Then maybe the party would have a better chance of doing the same in Hungary and other places – all of this at Czechoslovakia's expense. She had heard enough of this drivel.

"Forget all of your worthless words," Petra stood up in the middle of the room to interrupt a stunned Zhdanov. "Get to the point. How many soldiers would comrade Stalin send to help defend Československo from the Nazis?"

VACANT BAKERY, HRADČANY

The long flights of steps up the narrow streets close to the palace never got any easier to surmount. Naturally Srom had chosen an address that automobiles could not get close to so there was no choice but the stairs. Capka seemed unaffected by the climb but Kopecky was panting more than he wanted to admit.

"You're out of shape," Capka rubbed it in. "That desk job is making you soft."

"Stop gloating," Kopecky shrugged off the comment. "I still swim twice a week. I just wasn't born a mountain goat like you."

"I'm serious, you need more exercise. When was the last time you were on a track or a football field?" Capka pressed his friend further.

"No time for either. Despite your misconceptions I actually have substantial responsibilities," Kopecky not only was overworked he was getting grief for the results.

"What about women? You used to have them fawning all over you. Women are excellent exercise. When was the last time you had one in your bed on a regular basis?" Capka was delighted that roles had reversed so he could pester Kopecky on this subject.

"Not since Lola and I got un-engaged," Kopecky tensed at the memory. "I just haven't been in the mood to deal with women for a while."

"Before I head back to my division you and I are going to visit a place I know with pretty women that is not too expensive," Capka had decided on the proper exercise regime.

"Thank you my friend but that's really not necessary. I promise to add more exercise to my schedule," Kopecky saw Srom approaching in the company of Hanus and Plzak, which would divert Capka from his fitness lecture. "Looks like we have arrived at our rendezvous."

Srom gestured for them to follow him to the door of a shuttered bakery. Producing an antique key from his coat pocket Srom opened the door and the five officers went inside. By the amount of dust Kopecky estimated the shop had been closed for months.

"When did they stop baking bread here?" Hanus asked as Srom shut the door.

"Last fall," Srom peered out the window to see if anyone had followed them. "The owner was a friend. He died suddenly and his wife did not have the heart to run the place by herself. She asked me to sell the shop for her but I have yet to find a buyer."

"I see," Kopecky realized old acquaintances meant a great deal to Srom. Kopecky found an old table and chairs that would suit their needs well while Capka strolled to the back kitchen.

"These are beauties… top of the line back in their day," Capka admired the ovens. "The bread must have tasted marvelous."

"The aroma was the best part. The smell caressed your senses in the most tantalizing fashion," Srom shared the fond memory.

"A baker... that is a profession I would enjoy," Capka closed the oven he had been inspecting and returned to the outer shop. "Good honest work feeding people is an art when done well. With ovens like these that would not be difficult."

"Maybe you should buy the shop. I am sure I could negotiate a fair price for all concerned," Srom encouraged the tanker.

"What do you know about baking? Your father runs a mill." His friend often strayed into odd undertakings that left Kopecky incredulous.

"My uncle on my mother's side is a baker, and a damn good one too. If a German bullet doesn't finish me, you watch, I'll buy this shop." Capka had some money saved.

"I have no intention of allowing you to resign your commission, mister," Hanus flung the words at Capka like cold water. "Your job is riding point at the front of a division and will be so until I say differently."

The door opened and Vrana slipped inside. "Damn, I had high hopes to feast on a fresh loaf. But this place hasn't baked a morsel in ages."

"Sorry about that. I did not realize I was in the company of so many bread lovers," Srom found all of the bakery talk was making him hungry.

"No pumpernickel for you," Vrana looked over his shoulder to deliver the bad news as Kucera shoved himself past Vrana into the shop.

Vrana closed the door and came inside. "Rather dark in here with all the shades down. Is there still electricity?"

Of course," Srom walked to the nearest hanging light bulb and pulled the cord to light the filament. "Capka, come help me with a few items." Capka followed Srom to the back of the shop as Vrana busied himself with turning on more lights.

"Shall we begin," Kopecky grabbed a large section of rolled up cloth that Srom had placed on a nearby chair. Unrolling it on the tabletop unveiled a finely hand drawn strategic map of the western half of Czechoslovakia with symbols for Czech and German military units. "This is the big show, gentlemen."

Srom returned with Capka from the Kitchen lugging simple refreshments and snacks that they placed on the far side of table. Plzak and Kucera volunteered to set out the food while Srom positioned himself back at the map.

"My friends, this is the current order of battle as accurately as I can pull together," Srom took a long wooden spoon he had found in the kitchen to indicate specific details. "Our First Army in Bohemia can field eleven divisions plus two rapid divisions. The Second and Fourth Armies in Moravia bring another twenty divisions plus one rapid division. That leaves the Third Army in Slovakia with six divisions and one rapid division to deter Hungary and Poland. Facing us in Bohemia and Moravia will be fifty-six German divisions. We can expect another thirty-five or so incomplete reserve divisions in their rear areas. It is estimated that our adversary will keep five divisions in the west to deter the French and send almost everything they have against us in the initial attack."

"They have been busy bees indeed. In June they only fielded thirty-six regular divisions," Hanus leaned closer to the map to better see the enemy deployments. "I cannot foresee these twenty new divisions of theirs having developed much unit cohesion and probably aren't much good beyond occupying captured territory. Where it counts, in trained combat-ready units, I'd say we're pretty much even with the Nazis. They will come after us with eleven motorized divisions, which I expect our border forts can bleed down to something very manageable. This is a fight we can win."

"That's how I see it," Kucera looked over Hanus' shoulder.

"How recent is this intelligence," Vrana was concerned with how long the Germans had been training these new divisions.

Our sources within the Second Department assure us the information was assembled within the last month and has been independently verified," Kopecky felt comfortable that these division totals were what they would face in battle.

"If we can impale their best armored divisions on the fortifications while keeping our own mobile tank divisions intact I'm sure we could breakout without problems and cut through any of those soft reserve units that get in our way. The opportunity will be ours if we choose to seize it," which was Capka's code for questioning the political will to take the initiative.

**Sudeten Freikorps paramilitaries
ambush a Czechoslovak unit**

SEPTEMBER 10, 1938
PERSONAL LOG
OBERTSLEUTNANT BALDRIK OTTKE, BERLIN

We were hurtling toward war... the real thing. The Führer had long ago ordained October first for the attack on Czechoslovakia. Yet with barely twenty days left Hitler and the general staff were still arguing on how to prosecute the battle. Since April Herr Hitler had been advocating a massed attack of armor and aircraft in the west of Czechoslovakia. Everything the Wehrmacht and the Luftwaffe could spare funneled into one huge wedge to break through the Czech border defenses, overload their secondary siege lines, smash the enemy's main tank divisions, and then race east to seize Prag within a week. All during the summer the stalemate simmered. The Führer fumed and the general staff simply ignored his strategic input.

On August twenty-second General Halder went to Kiel to brief Hitler on the current status of Case Grün for the first time as the new chief of general staff. Lucky for the general, Hitler was in a good mood relaxing on the state yacht, Grille. None of the Führer's tactical instructions had been entertained, let alone incorporated. Halder dutifully explained updates to the original plan in detail: attack at both north and south Moravian choke points, split the Czech Republic in two, consume Bohemia, then push the remnants of the Czech army into Slovakia. Seeing the Führer's face during this recitation would have been priceless. I do know that before Halder was dismissed he received a spirited lecture on his ineptitude, and the ineptitude of his fellow generals. Could they not discern the facts for themselves? The Czechs were far too well entrenched to risk the stale offensive the general staff continued to advocate – one that would bog down for weeks or months on the border.

Hitler summoned the generals to the Berghof ten days later for a tongue-lashing and a lengthy harangue on the necessity for the strategy he had instructed for months. My sources reported that the Führer was especially hard on commander-in-chief Brauchitsch – insisting that attacking in north of Moravia with Second Armee would bleed them dry like Verdun in the Great War. Could they not see that a massed force of tanks from the west as Hitler instructed was unexpected by the Czechs? Amazingly, the generals continued to brush off the chancellor after their visit to the Berghof.

Through it all General Keitel was Hitler's man. No rabid national socialist just a realistic officer attempting to fulfill his duty to the man in charge. By September eighth Herr Hitler was seething. No progress on realigning divisions according to his directives had been undertaken. Here he was at the Reichsparteitag in Nürnberg with every ear in Europe waiting to hear what he would say and his own generals were defying him. That would not do.

Keitel was flown back to Berlin from Nürnberg to investigate. He begged Brauchitsch and Halder to comply with the chancellor's commands. They refused. The next morning Keitel flew back to Nürnberg and reported the facts. Hitler was livid. He ordered the generals to present themselves in person that night at the Deutcher Hof, the Führer's hotel. The row went on for five hours. By all accounts Hitler wore them down into submission. By early in the morning the chancellor informed Brauchitsch and Halder that there would be no more argument. They would comply or be sacked. They had their orders... redeploy their tanks as instructed and do so by the end of the month.

There would be no more stalling by the Army now. The old guard generals did not favor a wider European war in 1938, as their accelerated rearmament programs would not be complete until 1945. If forced into a battle that committed the Wehrmacht's best divisions in Czechoslovakia, the French advantage in divisions would overrun Germany in the west while the Red Army flanked them in the east. Brauchitsch, Halder and the rest sensed their own weakness and had stalled Hitler for months to give the French and British ample opportunity to come to the same conclusion. The problem was the Führer was correct. Their old adversaries were consumed with fear of war. That fear in Paris and London was the much greater inertia. So the German general staff had waited in vain for a show of backbone in the major powers that was not forthcoming.

I have to admit some sympathy for Czech president Beneš. The dithering of Daladier and Chamberlain was humiliating. His own allies were forcing Beneš to bend over for a troublesome minority. Most leaders would have imposed order or expelled the troublemakers but not the Czechs. They were civil to a fault and had been most reasonable in dealing with Henlein's Sudeten party. Their reward was to have that old codger Runciman shoved down their throats with a mandate to force further concessions. Beneš' failing was two-fold: first his belief in the doctrine of collective security, second that he was a diplomat to his core. The Czechoslovak president could not conceive of operating out of concert with his alliance partners, and by nature, was inclined to work toward consensus. So every time Paris and London pushed, Beneš accommodated.

In late August, our microphones recorded French Ambassador Francois-Poncet in Berlin telling Czech minister Mastny that it was vitally important for Prag to accept whatever Lord Runciman recommended. If Beneš accepted these terms before the Reichsparteitag in September, then Great Britain would stand by France and Czechoslovakia, after which Hitler would suffer a defeat. If Prag rejected Runciman's recommendations, Britain would abandon Central Europe to Hitler, and France would not be militarily capable of preventing the complete destruction of Czechoslovakia even if the Third Reich was eventually defeated. So Beneš' response was to accommodate these demands, as well as employ a sly attempt to preempt what he wagered would be a far worse conclusion penned by Runciman. The tool employed was an expanded Sudeten proposal – Beneš' third – drawn up hot on the heels of its predecessor. This very generous offer went far beyond his previous proposals to divide up the country into new administrative cantons, each with a state appointed representative and an elected president. Every such district would be ethnically homogenous with at least three of the total guaranteed to be wholly German. These new administrations would also significantly increase the number of German public servants, an important gift to areas of chronic unemployment. Any sensible negotiator would have happily accepted the proposal. Beneš had no illusion that Henlein was in a position to be sensible. That's why the document was given to the British directly. Beneš still harbored hope that Daladier and Chamberlain would come to their senses. So this third plan was not intended for the Sudetens it was really directed at convincing his alliance partners enough was enough.

Beneš' read on the British was excellent. They were impressed enough in these new concessions for Runciman to summon Henlein to a meeting at which the mediator presented this third plan directly and advised Henlein to get Hitler's opinion in person. Henlein's deputy was already in Germany to argue for moderation by Hitler when this was all going on. The Führer's response to Henlein's suggestion that a popular vote in the Sudetenland could decide matters had been to send Frank home with the firm instructions that SdP militias were to start staging incidents against Czech authorities as of September fourth. Whether or not Moravec's annoying network of informants had learned the outcome of Frank's visit, Beneš well understood the chancellor's overall strategy and that Hitler would just as assuredly reject Beneš' third plan when he became aware of it. In fact, Beneš astutely saw no reason to wait for an answer before playing his next card in motivating Chamberlain, and by extension, Daladier.

So while Henlein was en route to present the third plan to Hitler, Beneš called in the SdP negotiators, Kundt and Sebekowsky, to deliver a more sweetened offer. For months Henlein had argued nothing less than his eight-point plan for the Sudetenland would be acceptable. It was the standard negotiation line that had been directed at the Czechs and Runciman. This Karlsbad Programme was well thought out and supported by the Führer. Henlein's eight points were designed to be so odious to the Czechs that they could never be accepted, and in return, Henlein would never have to sign an agreement that would settle the crisis. I wish I could have been there when Beneš in his cordial manner sat Kundt and Sebekowsky down to tell them that he was ready to accept Henlein's eight points. All I have is the report from Kundt and Sebekowsky, which indicates they were stunned silent. As Beneš prattled on about how he would not object to the program being gradually implemented, the SdP men could say nothing. They were never prepared for a negotiating victory. After Beneš requested a clear yes or no answer to the proposal be returned within three days all Kundt and Sebekowsky could do was scurry off without a word.

To fully submit in the complete knowledge unconditional surrender could not be accepted was a brilliant diplomatic move. Beneš made this offer on August thirtieth, two days before Henlein would visit Hitler. Kundt and Sebekowsky were not even able to get word to Henlein prior to his meeting with the chancellor. The result would have been no different, however. Hitler saw all concessions on autonomy as a sign of weakness to be exploited to further his war goals. It cannot be denied Hitler has a penchant for political brilliance. Henlein was sent home and told not to reject Czech proposals outright. Instead, the chancellor gave instructions to continue negotiations in supposed good faith. At the same time, Henlein was to see to it that the situation in the Sudetenland deteriorate in the coming weeks with as many street disturbances as the SdP could muster. Our propaganda machine would lay the blame on the government in Prag for these *outrages*. Hitler understood the British and French mindsets very well. As long as there was a chance for a negotiated settlement Chamberlain and Daladier would stay on the hook and continue to pressure the Czechs to avoid a conflict. I am sure Beneš acceptance of Henlein's eight points would have made no difference in the Führer's instructions.

Comically, word of Beneš' acceptance of the eight points program did not catch up to Henlein until he returned to Asch on September second. That allowed the Kundt and Sebekowsky farce to continue in Prag. Beneš' deadline for an answer was also the second and all Frank could do was tell them to stall Beneš lacking further direction from Henlein. The two SdP negotiators walked into Beneš' office and proceeded to deliver a lengthy exposé on whether the Czechoslovak state had a legal right to administer the Sudeten territories. This exposition neither accepted nor rejected Beneš' offer. When finished they bid the bemused Czech president farewell.

Whatever sense of victory Beneš may have felt at the success of his strategy was quickly dashed, however. Not long after the SdP negotiators fled, Lord Runciman paid a visit. Instead of receiving the most minor display of support from a supposed ally, according to a knowledgeable source on Runciman's staff, the British mediator duly noted Beneš' many concessions to the Sudetens yet went on to lecture the Czech to have no illusions that Great Britain would go to war on behalf of Czechoslovakia. To punctuate the point the next day, the British minister in Prag, Basil Newton, visited Beneš to instruct him that in the event of war Czechoslovakia would surely be overrun and devastated. Therefore it was vital for Czechoslovakia to accept great sacrifices and if necessary considerable risks in order to avoid a much greater disaster.

Sometimes I suspect Beneš is a betting man. Faced with such British intransigence he doubled his bets. Kundt and Sebekowsky were recalled on September fourth for the most amazing display of deception. Beneš sat them down, and by their accounts, lacked his usual energy and dispensed with the usual diplomatic chitchat. Sliding a sheet of paper and a fountain pen across the top of the desk, Beneš invited the negotiators to compose a complete list of demands, and implored, *I promise you in advance to grant them immediately.* What could Kundt and Sebekowsky say to this offer? They were dumbfounded, which both noted later in their report. Beneš saw the game for what it was and had bet correctly – the SdP was in no position to accept its own diktat. With Kundt and Sebekowsky silent in their seats Beneš finally reached across the desk like a slow moving tortoise and reclaimed his pen and paper. *Very well. If you won't write it down, I will. You tell me what to say,* Beneš instructed them. The SdP men dictated every demand Henlein had ever mouthed and the Czech president captured each word in exacting detail. When Kundt and Sebekowsky could think of nothing else to add, Beneš signed the list. His one stipulation was that Czechoslovakia's international commitments be honored. Outside of that one provision, Beneš had just accepted creation of an ethnic system of cantonal government with complete local control except in matters affecting unity and security of the state, complete equality of minority languages with Czech in official affairs, a guarantee of a set percentage of positions in government offices reserved for Sudetens plus loans to assist economically depressed Sudeten districts. There could be no more concessions without the dismantling of the Czechoslovak state. Beneš could never have gotten such a proposal passed in his own legislature but he didn't have to.

Kundt and Sebekowsky called an SdP conclave the next day to deliver the terms Beneš had signed his name to, during which Frank is said to have exclaimed, *My God, they have given us everything.* Frank immediately telephoned Henlein in Asch with the details. Henlein had been hard at work preparing a lengthy justification for rejecting parts of Beneš earlier compromises. After the call from Frank he dropped everything and crossed the border back into Germany accompanied by the SdP leadership available in Asch. The Führer received Henlein promptly. It is said the chancellor reacted irritably to learning of this latest capitulation from Beneš. Whether the Führer doubted the sincerity of the concessions, or was annoyed at the prospect losing the opportunity to punish the Czechs militarily as he desired, no one can say. Either way, Henlein was ordered to cut off negotiations without explanation and carry out the schedule of incidents already planned throughout Czechoslovakia.

As for Beneš he dutifully reported all of his negotiations with the SdP in complete detail to London and Paris. It did not take long for a response. Unfortunately for the Czechoslovak president, it was not the response he had labored so masterfully to bring about. Instead of receiving acknowledgment of the impossibility of a negotiated settlement with the Sudetens, Beneš' answer came in a slew of newspaper editorials.

The first appeared four days ago in *La Republique,* penned by Emile Roche. Roche is a close associate of foreign minister Bonnet and is known for floating sensitive policy the latter does not yet wish to own publicly – such as a direct threat to Czech sovereignty:

> *Can Prague still persist in counting three million, two hundred thousand Germans among its loyal subjects? If so, all will be well. But if not, the two races which cannot agree to live together within the framework of the centralized Czech state must be separated. In any case, a peaceful solution must be found.*

Two days ago, Lord Halifax's close friend Geoffrey Dawson, editor of The Times, published essentially the same recommendation:

> *It might be worthwhile for the Czechoslovak Government to consider whether they should exclude altogether the project, which has found favor in some quarters, of making Czechoslovakia a more homogenous state by the cession of that fringe of alien population who are contiguous to the nation with which they are united by race.*

Faced with the verified intransigence of the Sudeten negotiators, Daladier and Chamberlain had now established their new negotiating position: break Czechoslovakia apart and cede the Sudetenland to Germany. It bears noting that neither Henlein, Hitler, or Runciman ever made such a proposal but here were the guarantors of Czech independence selling out their charge. This was a very realistic approach given the Führer's ambitions but the message had to be devastating to Krofta and Beneš in Prag. Her allies would dismantle the Czechoslovak state rather than help defend her integrity. And if it was good enough to give the Germans back to Germany, what about the Poles to Poland and the Hungarians to Hungary? All would come calling for their piece of flesh. Czechoslovakia would cease to exist in very little time. It was a new development well recognized by Herr Hitler to his great satisfaction.

The French and British editorials coincided perfectly with the onset of civil disruptions that Henlein had set in motion on the chancellor's command. To the rest of Europe it must have seemed like there could be no peaceful living side-by-side between Germans and Czechoslovaks. As planned, Sudeten militia members provoked confrontations with Czech authorities throughout the border areas. Early reports show that dozens of Czech police and custom officers were slain outright on the streets or ambushed at their posts. These raids were carried out during the night to protect the identity of the militiamen who usually slipped into Germany to elude any Czech investigations. The idea was to incite a harsh response by the Czechs that could be used as a pretext for further conflict. During an attack on Czech policemen in Ostrau a mounted policeman used his riding whip to strike an SdP deputy. Henlein astutely publicized the event as a brutal attack on ethnic Germans, and under the circumstances, officially broke off negotiations with Prag.

With riots breaking out throughout the Sudetenland, and the crisis escalating, Henlein waited for the Czech response... the bloodier the better for the chancellor's strategy. He would speak in Nürnberg on September twelfth and the world would hang on every word. No one doubts that he will call on Germans to save Germans. Even now two hundred thousand troops are massing on our side of the Czech border. Under these circumstances it will be impossible for our generals to disobey the order to protect the Sudetens when the directive comes.

SEPTEMBER 12, 1938
ROAD TO GRASLITZ – SUDETENLAND

They were racing through a raging fire to dive into a hornet's nest. Everyone in the Daimler was tense. The Second Department's garage had a number of the German sedans that had been confiscated in recent months that came in handy when motoring through ethnic German villages as the four men were doing tonight. Burda appreciated the thick metal panels of the sedan's body, which had an excellent chance to stop a bullet. After the last two weeks he would have preferred a Tatra armored car. Henlein's people were setting fire to every symbol of Czechoslovak authority and administration within easy reach of their strongholds – another reason not to be seen in a Praga or Škoda tonight. Dozens of Czech policemen and civil administrators had been injured or killed. It was a bloody mess on the border and Burda found it hard to accept that Praha had yet to clamp down on the provocations. He knew the pressure coming from Paris and London not to respond was intense but enough was enough.

Thankfully the general staff felt the same way. Yesterday, the boss had shared with them something extraordinary. Generál Krejčí had broken all of the rules by sending the president a respectfully worded demand to carry out a partial mobilization. That wasn't supposed to happen. The protocol was the military did not set policy. That was the prerogative of the politician yet Krejčí was undeterred. Burda had filled with pride when Moravec had shared the contents of Krejčí's memo stating there was a limit to compromise, how the army was well armed and eager to fight, and the Wehrmacht should not be over-estimated:

> *This is a decisive moment in our nation's history and it calls for resolute decisions... If we do not defend ourselves there will be no mercy for us. We would be annihilated in the most barbaric manner. If we must die let us do so honorably.*

Those had not been hollow words. With no reply from President Beneš, early this morning Krejčí put all units on full alert and ordered the mobilization process ramped up without a presidential signature. All leaves were cancelled and all regular troops were restricted to barracks. As these orders were being issued there was a telephone call from A-54. Karl had requested an emergency rendezvous in Praha before Hitler gave his speech at Nürnberg tonight. That had been unusual because Karl had a preference for staying close to the German border. We always supposed it was so he could return to wherever he was posted quickly without being missed. That the agent had come all the way to Praha in the middle of a crisis suggested either the man possessed much more latitude in his affairs than we had suspected or that he already was in Praha on other *business*.

Karl was their most valuable source so there was no hesitation. Moravec gave the German an address and a time then ordered one of the department's private villas in the suburbs readied immediately as soon as he put down the telephone. When they met the German a few hours later he dropped a bomb on his hosts: the complete order of civil disruption set to unfold during the next seventy-two hours. The dates, places, and objectives Henlein's militias would strike following Hitler's speech. There was no reason to doubt any of what Karl presented. Everything he had presented in the past had been completely accurate. There was a chance that the volumes of data received from this agent previously had set them up for this moment and that was suggested to the boss, yet Moravec trusted his intuition and his gut told him that what Karl had to share was entirely valid. When he had finished what he had come to Praha to accomplish, A-54 made it clear that he had to make it back to Germany before Hitler's speech and asked for transport to the border town of Graslitz. That's how Burda ended up seated next to Karl in the back seat of the Daimler with Furst up front driving like a mad man through the mountain roads.

Luckily the Henleinists were glued to their radios waiting for Hitler to speak instead of making mischief so good progress was made. Not progress enough, however. They were not going to get Karl across the border before the speech. When a stop was made for petrol in one town they heard that shrill voice blasting from a radio speaker near an open window. Herr Hitler had worked himself into a full lather and was sparing no fury in the lies he was spreading. He went on about how the Czech government was systematically attempting to annihilate the Sudeten Germans. How the Czechs were hunting them *like helpless wildfowl for every expression of their national sentiment.* It took every ounce of personal restraint not to react to these diatribes amongst the local Germans who were excitedly devouring every word.

> *If these tortured creatures cannot obtain rights and assistance by themselves, they can obtain both from us. We will not allow another Palestine in Central Europe. The poor Arabs are defenseless and perhaps deserted but the Sudeten Germans were not.*

Burda dared a glance at Furst who had tilted his head in the direction of the dinner house where the radio blared – asking for permission. Burda discretely shook his head in the negative and Furst contained the urge to rush into the dinner house and bust up the radio. Not soon enough for Burda the Daimler was fully fueled and they returned to the road as the German leader droned on,

Down the road a ways Burda turned to Karl to ask a question that he was not supposed to ask. "Why? Why not you? What keeps you from joining in with this chorus of madness? What leads you to work against it?"

"Call me pragmatic," A-54 answered in his cool, professional manner. "I have seen enough ruin since the end of the Great War and this adventure against your nation has the potential to force Germany so far into the gutter I could not stomach going along. Given that Daladier and Chamberlain have no spines the Führer may yet secure his ambitions regardless. I won't be a party to it, however."

No one said much for a long while until they rounded a curve in the highway and were surprised by a roadblock fifty meters ahead manned by a dozen rifle-toting paramilitaries with swastika bands around their arms. One of the men fired his Mauser in the air as a warning. Furst cursed under his breath and applied the brakes to slow the heavy Daimler. As they rolled up to the makeshift barrier barring further passage Burda and the young četař in the front with Furst discretely slipped off the safety catches on their concealed service pistols. Furst gently removed his weapon from under his arm and slipped it out of sight under his right leg. One of the Henleinists directed a torch at Furst as he brought his gun hand back up to rest calmly on the wheel. Despite the glare in his eyes Furst figured there were at least ten rifle barrels pointed at his nose. Although Furst considered accelerating through the roadblock with the tank-like Daimler, the mission was to return A-54 to the border without incident, and he reluctantly brought the vehicle to a stop a few meters from the recently cut spruce tree that had been used for the makeshift barrier.

One of the SdP paramilitaries approached the open driver's window and gestured for the headlights to be switched off. Furst complied because the drill was to talk their way through the situation. Furst had a wide selection of forged documents patterned after those confiscated from SdP members who had been arrested by Czech authorities. Then there was another set of very authentic-looking Abwehr documents to choose from. As Furst was fluent in German he was usually convincing. If he met with an argument then Furst was to pass the conversation back to Burda, his *superior* officer. While this was rarely necessary Burda was quite capable of browbeating one of these subordinate militiamen in the German fashion. But this night neither Furst nor Burda got the chance.

Karl impulsively opened his door and jumped out of the car to engage the Sudeten. In more of an order than a request the agent said he wanted to be taken to the commander of the roadblock. The three Czechs watched intently as Karl was led to a tall fellow who was hard to see well in the low light of the lanterns the militia squad had set up. How they would rescue the man if his ploy went wrong was a worry. The three watched as Karl handed over some documents and chatted amicably with the Henleinists. In short order the commander saluted sharply then commanded four of the other of the paramilitaries to raise the spruce tree to allow passage. A-54 returned to the Daimler. Upon getting in he instructed Furst to drive on.

All three of the Second Department men were impressed with the speed at which Karl had gotten them clearance through the roadblock but Furst was the first to put it to words as soon as they were well in the clear. "What did you tell them to make the leader snap to attention like that?"

"I produced my credentials as an officer of counter intelligence," the German explained.

"That doesn't explain why they did not check out our papers, as well," Burda pointed out as he secured his pistol.

"That was fairly simple," Karl went on. "I informed them that the men in my company were Czechoslovak officers in my pay as spies. The best lie possesses a kernel of truth. I think I could have passed you three off as Czechoslovaks."

The Second Department officers appreciated the joke, which broke the tension of the previous moments back at the roadblock.

"German, I like you," Furst returned his pistol to its shoulder holster.

"That's a high honor. Furst doesn't much like anyone," Burda could remember an occasion when his partner had made such an endorsement.

"I am flattered," Karl doubly felt the need to ensure their safety. "One more thing though. The Sudeten back there told me there are several more road stops before we reach Graslitz. Accepting the importance of my mission he gave me the code to speed our journey. When we approach them tonight's password is *March 15*. That should get us all the way to Graslitz and get you three back to Praha unmolested."

MARKET SQUARE – EGER SUDETENLAND

A quarter hour had passed since Hitler had ended his speech in an emotional fusillade against the Czechs. If these border Germans were any barometer the whole western third of Czechoslovakia must be celebrating like New Year's Eve in Times Square. That's what it seemed like to Ros. Eger wasn't very big as towns went but it seemed like the entire population was out of their quaint homes and dancing through the streets cheering, shaking hands, and singing Deutschland uber Alles in the rain. There wasn't a Czech policeman in sight. For the most part it was a spontaneous outpouring of joy at Mister Hitler standing up for them. No shenanigans at all from what Sanderson and her could tell.

"Rather seems like poor orphans who have finally been claimed by a rich uncle," Sanderson ventured as another group of locals waltzed happily by.

"Oooooh, good description. Can I use that?" Ros might ignore him if he said no.

"Certainly not. I'm surrounded by thieving magpies," Sanderson felt like checking the contents of his pockets.

"You're lucky I even let you tag along after selling me that bill of goods about there being too much danger for Sylvie and I to come out here alone," Ros smelled a con. "Do these folks look dangerous to you? I think you have ulterior motives."

"More like a hole in the head my dear," Sanderson was already questioning his own motives. "Despite this island of joviality surrounding us tonight you know full well the chicanery that your friends the Henleinists have been up to."

"There you go again. You are just jealous that Sylvie and I got all of the attention," Ros could not believe he still was smoldering over that.

Sanderson pulled the collar of his jacket up, lowered the brim of his hat against the rain then turned to Ros. "I have half a mind to kiss you full on the lips and then leave you flat, madam."

A nearby window shattered loudly before Ros could respond to Sanderson's flippant threat. Before the smashed pieces of glass could finish falling to the ground another window succumbed to a brick in a sharp discharge of sudden demolition.

"You were saying something about lack of danger," Sanderson reminded her.

"Quiet, you! Let's find out what's going on," Ros darted off through the crowd toward where the sound of breaking glass had come from.

No one could accuse the girl of wiggling out of harm's way, Sanderson thought while sprinting to close the distance between them before Ros rounded the next corner. It was difficult since Ros was smaller and could more easily slip between people out on the street. Sanderson had just pulled even with his errant compatriot when they turned onto the side street and saw a mob of hundred Henleinists with clubs and bricks approaching from the opposite direction. Both reporters moved off to the side and instinctively took out their notebooks to note shop addresses and other details. The lead Henleinist pointed out a specific establishment and the rest promptly went about breaking in the window and door.

"Why that one?" Ros could not tell what the business was.

"It's a jewelry shop," Sanderson determined after squinting in the low light. "I would wager the owner must be Jewish."

"Oh, that's nasty," Ros grimaced while recalling Vienna.

Their larceny finished, the Henleinists continued forward again without a care that they were being observed by the reporters and others on the street. Suddenly, a dozen of the men broke ranks to pursue a very well dressed young man nearby.

"Not so fast, Jew," one of the Henleinists raised a club. Catching up to the man the group beat him so mercilessly that he quickly crumbled to the ground where they proceeded to kick him repeatedly. Satisfied, the same Henleinist spat on the man. "Now maybe you will think twice before profiting on the blood of honest German people."

Eager to continue their work the mob swiftly moved past the reporters and the other bystanders leaving their victim to his own devices. With great effort, the injured fellow managed to rise on wobbly legs to rock dazedly in place while blood streamed down his face.

"Follow me, let's get that guy to a doctor," Ros lunged forward.

"During which we can get his story for the early editions... blood suckers that we are," Sanderson filled in the second part of the proposal.

"Of course! Don't go soft on me now, bub. If ambulance chasing were so distasteful we wouldn't be in this business. C'mon, I can use those strong arms of yours right now," Ros reached out to steady the injured man.

"Very well, we should get on with it then," Sanderson realized that was the first compliment she had volunteered to him in many weeks.

DAS POSTAMT – KARLSBAD, SUDETENLAND

The BMW had been stashed behind a convenient spruce not far from where the spa houses started up the road from the center of town. Then again any tree would have been convenient since there were so many of them in this village. Bulloch had grown so attached to the big motorcycle on his forays through the countryside that he had purchased it from the garage owner. Today was his first time in Karlsbad. This guy Henlein knew how to live: clean air to breathe, therapeutic hot springs to dip into and strolls through relaxing gardens. It would be like orchestrating a revolution from The Hamptons or Palm Beach

And just like everywhere else there were Germans in Czechoslovakia these town folk had been enthralled with Hitler. Minister Carr had explained how these border towns had voted to be included with Germany back in 1919 and had been ignored by the Allied leaders divvying up the Austro-Hungarian Imperial spoils. A formula had been agreed upon and there wasn't motivation to open up the discussion now that they had a deal in place. And what was the harm? As rulers went the Czech were pretty easy. Everywhere you looked you could see evidence of public works and civil investment that Masaryk had shepherded into place for the whole country. Yet that didn't matter much to these Germans who had been stewing for nineteen years. Their kind had been on top for centuries and they didn't much take to the reversal of fortune that put the Czechs in control. They had been riveted to their radios tonight while their hearts hung on Hitler's every word. He was their savior. Bulloch was just hard-pressed to discover what they needed saving from.

A beer hall had been Bulloch's choice to listen to the speech. He had found playing an American on vacation touring the land of his German grandparents had been as well received here as in other towns. The facade also gave him plenty of opportunities to ask questions when he couldn't make the meaning of something out. Buying a few rounds didn't hurt the cause either. When word arrived that Henlein himself was leading a march through town after the speech, Bulloch's new found *cousins* hauled him along with them. That's how he had ended up in the pouring rain outside the local post office – a rather impressive building at that for such a small community. The rain wasn't bothering him much because Bulloch had a bottle of Becherovka stashed in his jacket pocket. At least that's what they called the spicy distilled bitter in Prague. It didn't take long to figure out they called it Becherbitter in these parts. The stuff kept you warm and was only produced in Karlsbad. Amazing that they could take the not-so-great tasting mineral water here in town and turn it into such a delightful liqueur. Bulloch was sure he tasted gingerbread and cinnamon.

A roar of cheers exploded nearby and then several more rounds after that. A heavy hand thudded against Bulloch's back as his little group saw their man approach and hands clapped in wild applause. Bulloch got his first direct view of Konrad Henlein. The Sudeten leader was marching down the main drag accompanied by his lieutenants and other Sudeten Deutsche Party members. All of them were wearing swastika armbands. There had to be thousands marching behind Henlein in that procession despite the weather. But what set Bulloch aback was when those around him spontaneously burst into a rousing yell for the passing Henlein: *Down with the Czechs and Jews,* which was returned in deep baritone by the passing SdP men.

SEPTEMBER 13, 1938
CHURCH OF ST. NICHOLAS
ASCH, SUDETENLAND

Amazing what a generous donation to the clergy could produce. Endicott was hoping the good German father would put in a good word with a parishioner in the possession of a working telephone. As it turns out the old fellow was in such good graces with the Almighty he had a phone in his office. Wonders of wonders Endicott was even able to connect to Shirer in Prague. Endicott had made a deal with the CBS man so that Endicott's copy got sent to the bureau in exchange for Shirer using some of the broader details for his nightly radio broadcast. Such arrangements were frowned upon by the big dogs at Hearst but it would give him a lead over most of the other hacks out here on the border trying to file their stories. Since Sylvie would have blackmailed him silly if she knew, he had ditched her when she cozied up to a squad of goons outside party headquarters. They enjoyed the attention so she seemed safe enough... that was one broad who could take care of herself.

"Buddy, you have to get out here," Endicott spoke loudly over the line. "Everything is going to hell. This is big. All of these local Germans are sure the tanks will roll into Czechoslovakia today or tomorrow... yeah, I'm ready to read you what I've got. Thanks for the courtesy. I'll be out in front for a change. Okay, here goes:

> *Dateline Asch, Czechoslovakia. On the day after German chancellor Adolph Hitler gave a rousing address in support of their right to self-determination, the people across the border in the Sudeten territories of the Czechoslovakia rose up against the central government in Prague. New graph.*

> *Thousands of ethnic Germans are rioting throughout the Sudetenland demanding unification with their big brothers a few steps to the west. Police stations, rail stations, post offices and customs houses – anything flying the Czech flag – has been attacked or occupied by members of the Sudeten Deutsche Party. Many Czech civil servants and policemen have been injured and those unlucky enough to be caught have been arrested with many of them spirited off into Germany to be held until Sudeten demands are met. New graph.*

> *Here in Asch, all is quiet. As this town is surrounded on three sides by German territory, the Czech authorities pulled out overnight*

leaving Sudeten leader Konrad Henlein in complete control of the enclave. The plundering of Czech-owned and Jewish-owned businesses – a common occurrence since these ethnic Germans rushed out into the streets in joyful delirium last night following Herr Hitler's speech – has subsided but not ceased. In Habersbirk this reporter has learned four Czech policemen were shot dead at their station and now lie under sheets in the street. As a result of the widespread civil unrest we have received word that Czech president Edvard Beneš has declared martial law in the Sudeten districts of Eger, Elbogen, Falkenau and Habersbirk. In response, Dr. Henlein has sent President Beneš an ultimatum to lift martial law, withdrawal police and barrack the Czech army by midnight. New graph.

Not all Sudetens on the streets support the violence and worry about the consequences. Radio stations in the Czech capital, Prague, have announced a partial mobilization of reservists to back up Czechoslovak army reinforcements reported heading west to bolster regiments already on the Czech-German border. With a showdown between Prague and the Sudetens looming many here expect German tanks and troops will cross the frontier at any moment to support their aspirations. Spirits are high that the vaunted panzer divisions can wrap up the Czech army and be in Prague within a week. But after months in Czechoslovakia this reporter can attest that the Czech army is a well-prepared fighting force with defensive fortifications rivaling France's Maginot Line. If war comes, the Czechoslovaks will not go quietly and Europe may find itself embroiled in a new World War if the contest over these Sudetens drags on. France and the Soviet Union have mutual defense treaties with Prague and could be pulled in on the Czech side. New graph.

What transpires in these picturesque villages during the next seventy-two hours will affect the fate of millions of people in Europe.

"That's it. Do you have it all?" Endicott double-checked "Thanks pal. Pull some of that material in for your broadcast like we talked about. Now catch a ride on one of those Czech Škoda tanks heading west."

OTTKE RESIDENCE
WILMERSDORF DISTRICT, BERLIN

Many times Heiden would have preferred a rendezvous at a random location. A very remote corner of the Berlin zoo immediately came to mind. Ottke had nevertheless overruled such locations when the meeting was reserved for Abwehr staff. There was no perceived impropriety in staff members associating at any location, especially in espionage work. Meeting out in the open would only open them to additional scrutiny by the Sicherheitsdienst or Geheime Staatspolezei. And as Ottke pointed out, his apartments were screened for microphones on a regular basis and directly before any discussions were held within.

Ottke had yanked Heiden in from the field due to a change in plans. As it would be late before Heiden could arrive it was decided he should go to Ottke's home. After parking the Horch 830 he checked to make sure the boot was well secured. The majority of his weapons and tools were stashed inside. One knock on the door was all that was required for one of Ottke's assistants to answer – leaving just enough distance between them to respond as needed. Heiden knew the man to be in fine physical condition, well trained in martial arts, and most definitely carrying a pistol under his left armpit. They nodded at each other and Heiden proceeded past him on the way up the stairs... he knew the way. The door to Ottke's study opened smoothly to his touch. Heiden stepped in, quietly closed the door behind him then threw his well worn but *lucky* leather jacket over a nearby guest chair. Heiden's shoulder holstered pistol drew no attention at all.

Ottke was seated beside Gisevius discussing something critical. The latter was another of Ottke's direct subordinates who Heiden had worked closely with in recent years. Gisevius had been Gestapo who had later spent some time in the Interior Ministry before Canaris had recruited him into the Abwehr. Gisevius was very well connected and had proven a reliable conduit of confidential Gestapo information.

"What's the bad news? I doubt you would have pulled me in at this late hour if something was not amiss," Heiden took a seat next to Ottke.

"Your mission is aborted." It was a directive that Ottke needed to deliver in person for Heiden was of a kind to pick and choose which dispatches he acknowledged while in the field. "Hitler will not order the army to move tomorrow in support of the Sudetens as we expected. He has decided to hold to the October first timetable since the general staff was so tardy in acceding to his deployment strategy."

"Damn, my boys were all ready to go," Heiden did not like postponements.

"Regrettable, but necessary. We cannot move unless the Führer orders the invasion. Halder will not condone it," Ottke reminded his subordinate.

"We can do this without Halder, obertsleutnant." Heiden was done waiting on the general and his list of conditions.

"No, if we act on our own there will be consequences," Ottke was growing tired of repeating the point.

"Only if the target is not terminated," Heiden was positive his team would complete the mission.

"Not everyone supports that solution," Gisevius had seen Heiden take a mission contingency and turn it into a mission priority before.

"Enough!" Ottke ended the debate with a raised hand. "Stand down, gentlemen. Major, take your unit off alert and vacate your staging area. Keep them close, however. We may get another chance at any time between now and the first."

"Yes sir," Heiden acquiesced. "So what is happening on the ground? I feel somewhat out of touch holding position with my men with nothing to do but listen to the propaganda on the radio."

"Henlein's people are panicking," Gisevius volunteered. "They had been promised the Wehrmacht would enter Czechoslovakia in support of the SdP today. Frank has been on the phone to Hitler directly asking where are the tanks? Beneš is mobilizing reservists and Czechoslovak regular units are rolling toward Eger, Karlsbad and Asch. Frank expects his people will face Czech shock units no later than tomorrow and he's not happy with Hitler's assurances that, now is not the right time. There are reports that Henlein will flee for Germany tonight if he has not already done so."

"Such a brave lot they are," Heiden mocked their *associates* across the border. "No matter. Why did the chancellor back down?"

"Hitler believes he has a tacit agreement with the Western Powers giving him a free hand in Central Europe," Ottke described the latest development. "The chancellor has the luxury of allowing Henlein and the rest to dangle in the wind. It matters not in the grand scheme, Czechoslovakia will be crushed in *His* way on *His* schedule."

KARLSBAD, SUDETENLAND

A feeling told him to stick around a while... and there was the rain of course. Wet and muddy mountain roads didn't appeal to Bulloch despite how comfortable he felt on the BMW. Yet what was really nagging at him was where were the Germans? The local Deutsche had been quite certain that Wehrmacht regiments would be taking up positions in town today. That hadn't happened. Bulloch could sense the unease in every conversation and furtive glance toward Germany. It was well known that Prague had declared martial law and had begun mobilization. Vandalizing a police station was one thing but staring down an armored car was a much more dicey proposition. Most of these town folk didn't have the stomach for digging trenches and shouldering a carbine.

He had spent most of the day hanging around the fanciful colonnades dotted throughout the old town quarter. Each address seemed to have its own mineral water fountain that squirted up an ample stream of the warm liquid. Bulloch tried hard to better appreciate why the bitter water made this particular village famous in Central Europe but found familiarity did not make him fonder of the recuperative beverage. If he must drink the stuff he would happily stick with the Becherbitter he had purchased in town. Luckily there were plenty of places to buy the thin wafer cookies that he had discovered were also a hallmark of Karlsbad. These sweet treats were supposed to be eaten after drinking the foul mineral water. After a while Bulloch forgot the mineral water entirely and munched wafer cookies while watching events in town from different vantage points.

There was a summit behind the town that had an observation tower. With nothing better to do Bulloch hiked up thinking he could get spy the surrounding territory for arriving Czech or German troops. A squad of Henleinist paramilitaries was already in residence when Bulloch arrived at the top. Although they scrutinized him severely Bulloch brushed the hostility aside and joined them on the tower. The SdP men had already pegged him for the German from America they had heard about. Karlsbad was a small town indeed. Volunteering the last of his cookies and Becherbitter broke the ice, after which Bulloch got an earful about what they thought would happen if no military support from Germany arrived soon. Like every private in any army the guys on the front line always got stiffed and they weren't happy about it.

With the better part of the afternoon gone, no armies in sight, and whatever information possible had been gotten from the Sudetens, Bulloch bade them farewell and headed back down to town. He was really hungry now and the beer hall from the previous night presented itself as a decent candidate to wait out the hours until something happened. Inside Bulloch found plenty of nervous locals who needed to drown out their fears in good lager and semi-digestible food. Most of them had some rumor or another they felt compelled to share. The telephone lines to Germany were still active and anyone with a nearby relative across the border had tried to get some word of any movement of regular troops on the German side. Then someone had spotted a flight of Dornier bombers overhead and the place emptied as people's hopes got up and they thought it was a sign of Hitler's promise fulfilled. An hour later the establishment was fuller than before with sad Sudetens.

The sun had mostly set when Bulloch heard an angry voice shout, *Du Hurensohn,* out front. There had been a lot of swearing that day yet this time the source possessed the kind of immediacy and potency that screamed something juicy was actually happening outside. Once again everyone in the room dropped their steins on the wood tables with a communal clank and ran out the door to see what was going on. Bulloch edged his way to the front of the pack and saw a line of black sedans speeding down the main cobblestone drag heading west. Most of the grumbling and curses muttered around him featured Henlein's name in one form or another and Bulloch gathered the party leader had decided to get while the getting was good. By the looks of it the rest of the party leadership in Karlsbad had made their getaway with their boss.

Bulloch found himself feeling some pity for these people who were abandoned by their Führer and their party all in the same day. In less than twenty-four hours emotions had gone from sky high to straight into the gutter. When the Czech ready units got here Bulloch doubted they would be greeted with much resistance.

SEPTEMBER 14, 1938
MARKET SQUARE – EGER, SUDETENLAND

The driver kept the Tatra coupe positioned between two Škoda armored cars for protection as the convoy sped into the center of town. The army was setting up administration at the government house, which was where the driver veered away from the safety of the convoy at the last moment and braked the staff car to a dramatic stop in front of the building. Kopecky thanked the desátník, grabbed his service cap and opened the passenger door to jump out. He was feeling quite a deal of pride at how well the operation was going and it showed in the way Kopecky assertively snapped the cap onto his head at a roguish angle. He saluted two passing enlisted men and found he liked the way the lower half of his new leather long coat flapped in the morning breeze. It was air force issue. Bozik had just procured the coat for him as a good luck charm shortly before the current crisis had flared up.

They had entered the Sudeten districts without opposition. The president had rejected Henlein's ultimatum and the SdP response was to evacuate their leadership to Germany. Whatever fight there was in the people those cowards left behind had completely evaporated with their leaders gone. When passing through Marianbad Kopecky had learned those Sudeten party members still around had openly presented themselves to the commanders of the Czechoslovak army and police entering the town and publicly welcomed the restoration of order by the government with a pledge to work peaceably with officials.

As for Henlein's militiamen left behind, they had either laid down their arms or melted back into their communities as troops and police took up positions throughout the ethnic German areas. The only locality excepted in the general order to recapture territory was Schwaderbach on the border. Generál Krejčí expected some resistance there and the town was so situated that any Czech fire would have spilled into German territory. No one wanted to give Hitler a direct provocation to use as a pretext to declare war. The official tallies Kopecky had received that morning by wireless had registered twenty-seven confirmed dead so far since Hitler's Nürnberg address: sixteen Czechs and eleven Sudeten Germans, which was much fewer than Kopecky had feared.

Disregarding some mischief none of the border fortifications had reported problems, and the German side of the border had remained quiet as a mouse. Hitler had given Krejčí a pretext to mobilize, as well as lock down Western Bohemia with zero opposition. Czechoslovakia would never be as secure as it would be in the coming weeks. Kopecky intercepted an adjutant as he strode up the government house steps. "Major Kopecky, attached to the general staff."

"Welcome to Eger, sir," the lieutenant saluted. "Plukovník Stefanik is expecting you upstairs."

"Excellent. Thank you, nadporučík," Kopecky examined the route he needed to take to the next floor. "From what I've seen on my journey regaining control has gone smoothly. Has that been the case here?"

"Mostly, major, except for the SdP headquarters over at the Hotel Victoria," the adjutant raised an arm in that direction. "A bunch of hard heads would not come out when ordered so our boys had to storm the place. Six dead. It could have been much worse."

TOWN HALL – LEITMERITZ, SUDETENLAND

The four of them had headed north from Prague that morning to take a look at the fighting first hand. The problem was there was no fighting. Shirer was flabbergasted. The night before everyone had thought German bombers would strike the capital at midnight when Beneš, as expected, had rejected Henlein's ultimatum. But no bombers came. The next day dawned with thousands of enthusiastic reservists reporting for duty and normal citizens remarkably holding their composure. The other three journalists on the foray were Cox, Hindus and Morrell. Shirer's first inclination was to have journeyed alone but there were not four cars to be hired in the city. The Czech army had already taken the best vehicles available as part of the partial mobilization. The rolling junk pile they had procured was the best that could be had and was not cheap either. So it made sense for the four of them to chip in together. On the plus side the company would be welcome if the sedan broke down along the way.

Their intention was to cover two hundred miles and it would be miraculous if the car continued to hold together that long. Hindus had conjectured that they were going easy on the old horse since their progress had been so slowed by roads clogged with Czechoslovak troops moving to the border. The further north they ventured into the Sudeten areas it became obvious the Czechoslovaks were in firm control. If there had been fighting it was all over. Czech police and military could be seen taking up positions and dismantling Henleinist roadblocks and emplacements. When members of the SdP were seen under guard it was blatant that the Czechs were operating under the utmost restraint. Several times the four stopped in different villages to speak with the locals themselves. The people Shirer spoke with were very puzzled. They expected the German army to march in on Monday night after Hitler's speech and when the Czechoslovak army arrived instead their spirits sank.

By the time the correspondents had arrived in Leitmeritz steam had begun to escape from the radiator and the group decided this was as good a place to stop as any other. Shirer was familiar with the area, which was well known for growing fruits. The town itself was old and built in the gothic style. Leaving the sedan to rest the four newsmen fanned out to discover what had happened there during the last seventy-two hours. Although the Czech presence was substantial it did not feel oppressive in the slightest. Shirer was keen to discover why these ethnic Germans hated the Czechs so much. What had Prague done to them that was so horrible that they needed to revolt?

Shirer was directed to the town burgomeister to answer his many questions. The man seemed most willing to sit down and discuss his grievances. So Shirer put it plainly to him, "What is the worst thing the Czechs did to you, Herr Burgomeister?"

"That is a very easy question to answer, sir," the magistrate grew animated. "Only today they have perpetrated their latest horror upon me. It was frightful, unbelievable, that the Czechs have taken away my radio so I can no longer hear the Führer's words. Could any crime be more terrible?"

CZECHOSLOVAK EMBASSY
GROSVENOR PLACE, LONDON

The alarms were going off in his head once again. He had spent all day at the Foreign Office as reports came in from Bohemia. Czech troops and police had been so disciplined in the use of force that more Czechoslovaks had been killed than Sudeten trash. Henlein had fled and Praha was in total control. Given the explosion of terror that had been unleashed the day before the conservative estimate was that the republic would be at war with Hitler this day. They were not, which made it a good day diplomatically. Jan Masaryk, however, would have preferred the two adversaries would be at blows by now. By forcing the issue their erstwhile allies would be compelled to either support the Czechoslovaks as they were obligated to or desert the republic in the full view of daylight. Win or lose it would be cleaner all around.

But something was up with these damn British. Masaryk could feel he was being avoided. He was used to hearing all manner of convoluted policy justifications from Halifax's people. These Foreign Office snakes may have been shoveling manure but they had never shied away from the assignment. Yet today the same snakes would not look at him, the official envoy of Czechoslovakia, directly in eye. What were they guilty of? What had they done or were about to do? Masaryk hoped it would not be too late before he found out the truth.

And now he had Krofta on the phone line. This worried Masaryk for there was a rumor the Germans had tapped the telephone cables to Britain. Moravec's people had yet to get proof of this breach of confidentiality, leaving Masaryk no excuse to refuse Krofta's urgent calls.

Today the foreign minister had learned of a cable from Daladier to Chamberlain. The gist was that the deterioration in relations between Czechoslovakia and Germany since Hitler's address at Nürnberg would force the French to fulfill their treaty obligations. Now Krofta wanted to know what the British reaction was.

"Kamil, I honestly wish I could tell you," a frustrated Masaryk explained again into the phone. "This is the first I've heard of Daladier's cable. If you asked me yesterday if everybody else should march, I would tell you that after a while the British would march too. You have to understand though that today these stupid people would say little and they would not look me in the eye."

Masaryk listened to Krofta's worries for a while before continuing. "Of course, yes, I can see where signs of French resolve would send the British into a dither but this is different. Something is afoot I tell you. Lord Halifax's worms won't talk to me and they are behaving like guilty school children that have just stolen sweets from the bakery. That my father ever placed faith in these people astonishes me. Mark my words. If they have not done so already, Halifax and his master are selling us out. I am only sorry that the two-thousand pounds a year I've paid all of these senior British politicians to bring down Neville Chamberlain and his government will not bear fruit in time to save us. My gut tells me I am wasting my time here."

REICH FOREIGN MINISTRY, BERLIN

The buzzer wired to a button on von Ribbentrop's desk quivered into life once again. There had been substantial tasks to attend to as a result of the Sudeten crisis. The last three days had been exhausting yet today the foreign minister had obviously been pre-occupied with something else – an unfamiliar project. All of the senior personal staff members were running errands and the only one left for von Ribbentrop to buzz for was Platen. The sensitive file he had been working on would have to wait. After returning the contents to the folder he carefully placed the dossier into the middle drawer of his desk, which he locked immediately. Picking up the notebook and pencil he reserved for when the foreign minister beckoned, Platen straightened his rumpled suit and entered the inner office.

"Oskar, come in," von Ribbentrop called out as Platen closed the door. "I'm sorry to have been so pre-occupied today. You have done an outstanding job since joining my office staff and I am very thankful. No rest for us though, as we have much work ahead. I suggest you take an hour to go home so that you may clean up and change into some fresh clothes. Our advance group is flying to Munich tonight. We will be there for one day for sure, perhaps two."

None of what the foreign minister had just mentioned corresponded with anything on the official assignment record von Ribbentrop's staff had been working on. Platen considered how best to inquire about further details.

"Sir, I cannot think of anything that we have been working on that is consistent with an abbreviated trip to Bavaria. So that I can bring the correct materials what exactly will be our mission? I would like to be as prepared as possible," Platen hoped that explanation would pry loose a few details.

"Good man," von Ribbentrop saw progress in the little fellow. "As Herr Goebbels has released this information for distribution to editors of the evening newspapers I can tell you what is up. The British legation in Berlin hand delivered a telegram from Prime Minister Chamberlain to the Führer late yesterday. The communiqué was a proposal by Herr Chamberlain to come to the chancellor to discuss a peaceful solution to the Sudeten problem. The meeting will take place tomorrow at Berchtesgaden and all of us have to be there to assist the Führer."

"Do I understand correctly that the British prime minister initiated this conference entirely of his own volition, sir? That would be nothing short of astounding," Platen was suspicious of why Chamberlain was being so accommodating.

"Astounding indeed... and true. Here, see for yourself when you have a moment before locking it away," von Ribbentrop handed him a slim folder that Platen secured under his notebook for the moment. "Yes, Herr Goebbels is most pleased with the opportunity that has been presented to us. Imagine the newsreels... millions around the world will watch and see the Führer ascendant. That will make our job all the easier... but only after the next forty-eight hours are done. Go now and get ready. Tomorrow we make history."

"Yes sir," Platen nodded in dutiful agreement. Upon returning to his desk he took a moment to open the file the foreign minister had presented him. Inside was a copy of Chamberlain's cable. Platen's hands trembled faintly at possessing such a document.

IN VIEW OF INCREASINGLY CRITICAL SITUATION I PROPOSE TO COME OVER AT ONCE TO SEE YOU WITH A VIEW OF TRYING TO FIND A PEACEFUL SOLUTION. I PROPOSE TO COME ACROSS BY AIR AND AM READY TO START TOMORROW.

"PLEASE INDICATE EARLIEST TIME AT WHICH YOU CAN SEE ME AND SUGGEST A PLACE OF MEETING. SHOULD BE GRATEFUL FOR VERY EARLY REPLY. – NEVILLE CHAMBERLAIN

KAFKOVA STREET
VÍTĚZNÉ NÁMĚSTÍ, DEJVICE

He needed a long stroll to clear his mind and the lateness of the hour appealed to Moravec. There were fewer distractions, and he had dealt with more distractions since Sunday than he cared to number. Through it all, his department had performed brilliantly. Forty-eight hours ago he thought sure the nation would be tested in the most severe fashion. A-54's narrative of the terror that the Henleinists would unleash had proven deadly accurate. Yet tonight the government was in complete control of the situation and the nation was better positioned to meet the challenges ahead.

A glance upward pleased him. Citizens were supporting the blackout decree yet the midnight sky held no Luftwaffe bombers menacing the capital. Why? The glaring inaccuracy in Karl's account was Hitler did not declare war this day as scheduled. Not knowing the why nagged at the Czech intelligence chief.

Had this erroneous detail been intentional? What was to be gained had the flaw been deliberate. There was one potential benefit as far as Moravec could deduce: to encourage a mobilization by the Czech army that could be viewed as a provocation by Hitler. Yet their partial mobilization to counter Henleinist violence could only be seen as a reasonable response. Therefore, this raison d'être was weak in Moravec's estimation despite Hitler's easily bruised ego. A-54's record of accuracy to date had been extraordinary. To take years building up such confidence only to expend it upon such a weak ploy did not make sense. Another viable theory came upon the Czech spymaster. Perhaps A-54 was one of Heydrich's men planted at Abwehr. In this scenario, a premature Czech mobilization, and the timely revelation of a conduit between Abwehr and Moravec's department, would be a set up to implicate Canaris and remove him. But Heydrich's SD recruits were typically too blunt in their methods for such finesse. Ruling this theory out, Moravec was forced to conclude that A-54 was certain Hitler planned to order the invasion or he would not have divulged that information. If he were to wager, Moravec ventured that Canaris and his staff had fully expected Hitler to order the invasion. Which returned Moravec to the same question he had started with: why had the invasion not been ordered? What had changed?

Hustle and bustle closer to the ground caught Moravec's attention. One of the local newsboys was scurrying up the street in Moravec's direction. "Extra! Extra! Head of the British Empire goes begging to Hitler!" the boy ran by.

Curious, Moravec beckoned the child over and purchased several copies of the late edition. A quick scan of the front page revealed the worst of news and Moravec cursed the fates. He had wanted an answer and his request had been granted. That swine Chamberlain was flying to Germany in the morning to supplicate before Hitler at Berchtesgaden.

**Prime Minister Chamberlain is greeted by
Chancellor Hitler on the steps of the Berghof**

SEPTEMBER 15, 1938
CNS HEADQUARTERS, NEW YORK CITY

Chamberlain's surprise trip to Berchtesgaden had caught them all napping and Harry was throwing a fit. Not a whiff of warning got out before the official announcement at nine o'clock London time the previous night, although the Nazi rags had *miraculously* gotten the news early enough to make the evening editions – lucky bastards. The only consolation was that every other American news organization seemed to be in the same predicament. The only bureau chiefs they knew that had reporters on the ground in Berchtesgaden were the Germans but it was likely that Chamberlain would be bringing along some approved British hacks to get the message out the way he wanted.

The problem vexing Lasky was CNS didn't have anyone near Munich. Walter had been following Hitler up and down the country during the Nürnberg Nazi Party brouhaha the last week but had just arrived back in Berlin when it looked like there would not be a war after all. Hauth volunteered to make a mad dash for Munich via train but Des had told him to stay put. With all of the delays going on thanks to the troop movements Hauth could not guarantee when he would arrive and Chamberlain might already be gone by then. Better for Walter to stick in Berlin and hit his contacts at the various Reich ministries for details. He also would have first look at the German editions since they were obviously being fed details before everyone else. No reason not to take advantage of the opportunity to steal from them.

Ros was turning in great work from the area around Eger. Once the Czech police got a hold on matters they were letting the reporters use station phones to file stories as long as the conversation was in a language they understood. Thank God enough of them spoke some French. But train service between Czechoslovakia and Germany had been suspended, as was passage through the border crossings. Right now he didn't know where Ros was. And everyone in Paris was needed to cover the French angle.

None of that sat well with Harry, however. Something big was breaking and he had no one on the scene. He was having a bloody cow and nothing Des could say would shut Harry up for more than twenty minutes. Now he was back jabbing his forefinger at Des' big map of Europe tacked to the wall.

"C'mon boss, you're going to poke holes in the damn thing pretty soon," Des couldn't get any work done on account of the constant thumping.

"There's supposed to be a war going on in Czechoslovakia. All the smart money said so," Lasky's arms flew over his head. "One day I'm on top of the world with Talmadge turning in great eyewitness copy and the next day I've got nothing! I'm *not* happy! Not happy at all I tell you!"

"Yeah, we have a clue about that," Des wagged a pair of scissors at the boss. "At least the nothing you have is the same nothing everyone else in this business has."

"That martinet Chamberlain... it's all his rotten fault. I'll admit I never expected the old duffer could pull off a publicity stunt this big. Wait a minute, what time is it at Berchtesgaden right now?" Lasky jabbed at Bavaria on the map.

Des checked the wall clocks. "Should be after five o'clock, I guess."

"Hitler and Chamberlain should be talking by now, right? Chamberlain landed at noon their time then took the special train. It can't take that long to get up to that mountain whorehouse of Hitler's. I sure wish I had one fly... just one fly on the wall to know how much that mealy-mouthed Chamberlain is giving up to old Adolph. I'm not happy!" Lasky pounded the map with his fist.

PRAŽSKÝ HRAD, PRAHA

Beneš had not slept since nine-thirty the night before when he had taken Masaryk's call from London with the news of Chamberlain's sudden diplomatic gambit. The British prime minister had no authority to negotiate terms for Czechoslovakia, especially without prior consultation. Beneš had already offered to give away all that a sovereign nation could reasonably part with without being able to sate Hitler's appetite. What more could Chamberlain parlay with at Berchtesgaden except for the dissolution of the Czechoslovak republic? What had Europe become that Beneš' best hope lay in the madman miscalculating his advantage and wasting the opportunity presented him. Beneš had two hands left to play: pray and wait, or order full mobilization and take his chances leading the nation to war. The opportunity for the latter course was available. The people were ready. He saw them on the streets: their conduct calm, disciplined and showing no fear. Czechoslovakia could fight but could she win? Beneš had precious little time left before he had to choose. For now he needed to discuss what to do in the meantime with Krofta.

"What happened, Kamil? When Hitler undercut Henlein the Sudeten will to revolt collapsed. We were steady and firm when tested. Why was that not enough? Why is Chamberlain sitting in Berchtesgaden?" Beneš was looking for something he may have missed.

"Jan and I have discussed it several times since last night. Masaryk believes Daladier's note of the thirteenth to Chamberlain is what triggered the overture to Hitler. Faced with French resolve to fight on our side if German troops crossed the border, Chamberlain engaged Hitler directly to pre-empt that eventuality from taking place," Krofta had no other explanation for the British prime minister's actions.

"That tells us all we need to know," Beneš made up his mind. "Mister Chamberlain would do anything to escape being forced to fight. Checking German ambition matters not at all to him. Whatever Hitler demands at Berchtesgaden will get a sympathetic response from the prime minister. You and I know what that will mean: severing most of Western Bohemia from the Republic. There is no time to waste. Chamberlain will infect Premier Daladier as soon as he returns to London from Berchtesgaden with whatever accord has been reached. We must get to Daladier first and impress upon him the consequences if France loses Czechoslovakia as a curb against Hitler. Keep pressing that point and do not let up. We must stall for time. Hitler has no patience. If we can keep Paris from signing onto Chamberlain's concessions long enough then Hitler's nature will overtake him with such a rage that he will order the attack upon us. The French and British will finally fall in line in the end."

"You realize Bonnet will block our envoy, Osušky," Krofta already had such problems with the French foreign minister. "I am sure it was Bonnet who was responsible for that defeatist tripe in *La Republique* earlier this month. Don't be surprised if that bastard attempts to keep himself between Osušky and Daladier so that the premier has no chance to be swayed by us."

"The attempt still has to be made. You may have to fly to Paris yourself," Beneš would not let Bonnet get in the way without applying the upmost pressure.

"Very true. Regardless, I would advise we open up a secondary channel to Daladier," Krofta understood they had scarce hours to act only to waste them on Bonnet alone.

"Good idea, I will bring in Moravec," Beneš hurried to the phone. "I know the Second Department has strong contacts with the French general staff. Perhaps he can help us find a way to prevail upon Generál Gamelin to entreaty with Premier Daladier."

EGERER BURG – EGER, SUDETENLAND

They needed to plan their next move. There was no way Ros and Sanderson were getting to Munich. It was possible to get across the border. There were places and a few of the local Henleinists were willing to see the reporters safely to the other side for a small fee. From there it was thirteen miles to Marktredwitz where they were told the train to Munich stopped. Who knew whether they could hitch a ride despite Sanderson's enthusiasm for Ros hiking the hemline of her skirt to better their chances? Since Chamberlain's journey had been so sudden, and would likely last no longer than a day, it made little sense to make the effort unless they were planning on staying in Germany. That would prove difficult without a valid entry stamp in their passports. Ros had her fill of creepy Nazis in Vienna. There was no way she was giving them any ammunition to put their greasy paws on her again.

Since there were too many ears around town they had walked up to the old ruined castle in the woods to the northwest. It was on top of a rock and offered a good view of the countryside, which was the same reason a Czech reconnaissance unit had set up residence on top of a nearby tower. The old Romanesque chapel was empty, however, and they found it a good place to map out their options. Despite evidence of recent reconstruction the interior was hollow. A couple of intact pews would have been nice although Sanderson had found himself a large stone to perch himself on.

"This chapel is lovely. How old do you think this place is," Ros asked, since Sanderson always seemed to have an encyclopedic memory of odd details.

"Hard to say really... not much of it left," Sanderson looked over the structure. "Thirteenth Century, perhaps Twelfth Century. One of the townspeople told me the grounds had been used for an armory for a couple of hundred years towards the end."

"That makes sense. Looks like a powder magazine blew the joint sky high," Ros thought it was a real shame to use such a special place for a powder magazine.

"Back to matters at hand, my dear. What is your vote? We must make a decision," Sanderson reminded her.

"Fine. I vote we get back to Prague. The war seems to be on hold for now with the Czechs in control here," Ros watched the lookouts in the tower. "With that wily prime minister of yours flying the olive branch to

Adolph the ball is going to be in Beneš' corner and Prague will be where the action is."

"Agreed. There is not much for us left to do out here. We've gotten as many personal testimonies as we'll ever need for future use. Barring a rebuff from Hitler, Chamberlain and Daladier will be making life most uncomfortable for the Czech president... and swiftly I'll wager. Prague it is then and we had better be fast about it," Sanderson jumped off the stone.

CZECH/GERMAN BORDER
WESTERN BOHEMIA

The weather was turning foul with too many clouds building up between them and the ground. In theory this would be a proper test of his navigator-bombardier to keep the flight on the right side of the border but Wunsch had yet to earn such confidence in his flight leader. The boy had made steady progress during the previous weeks of training but this area of the frontier was difficult for the most experienced navigators, of which he had none at the moment. The way the border jutted one direction and then the next at changing elevations made charting a straight line to stay on the German side a chore, especially without visual checks of landmarks on the ground. All Stahl needed was to stray far enough onto the Czech side to draw the attention of one of their forward fighter patrols. There was a good chance Stahl's Heinkels could outrun the Czech Avias in level flight but he didn't want to risk getting shot down or interned before the war even started. The prudent action was to verify their location. "Attention all birds. "Hold formation and follow me. We're descending under the cloud cover."

Stahl should have waited for the other pilots to confirm his order but they were an observant flock and would follow him down regardless. In combat they would not have the luxury of waiting for confirmations so this was a good test as well. It took four hundred and fifty-seven meters to break through the clouds. Thankfully the descent had left them a comfortable distance from the ground and nowhere near a mountain peak. A quick check over each shoulder found the other bombers were where they were supposed to be. Satisfied, Stahl felt enough at ease to look for something recognizable on the ground to confirm where they were supposed to be. As a child his parents had vacationed to the spa towns now on the Czechoslovak side so Stahl was familiar many of these villages in the border area. Looking to his left he recognized a church spire and main square to the west. Several seconds later was when Stahl remembered what town the spire belonged to.

"Wunsch! You idiot," Stahl scolded the navigator over the intercom. "We are east of Weipert on the Czech side. Figure out what you did wrong because you and I have an appointment after we get back to the field to discuss it."

Stahl swiftly scanned the airspace around the flight. No bad guys were around but that wouldn't last. It was time to get back home... fast. "Attention flight. Our position is east of Weipert over enemy territory. Change direction to due west. I repeat, due west. Full throttle, maximum speed… let's get our asses out of here."

THE BERGHOF
BERCHTESGADEN, BAVARIAN ALPS

To be here, at this high place, took his breath away. Yet the circumstances made it difficult to keep his limbs from trembling. Here was Oskar Platen, a lowly functionary in the Foreign Ministry, standing in the chancellor's mountain chalet. The same Oskar Platen who also happened to be in the pay of Czechoslovak Intelligence. Not a comfortable condition when surrounded by the highest levels of the Gestapo, SS and military officers. Never in his worst nightmares did Platen ever imagine himself being in such a vise. Damn the weakness that put him in this position.

It had started all those years ago with that loan he had taken out with the newly chartered bank in Aussig. Platen wasn't political but he needed more deutschmarks than he could earn honestly. There were no rich family members with means to help him provide for his wife and children. It was those wily Czechs who had been behind the Sudeten bank in Aussig. They knew who he was and they knew his finances. One night on the way home from work a man of upstanding appearance approached and called him by name. The proposal was simple. For a generous monthly retainer all Platen had to do was share any important details that concerned Czechoslovakia. Platen could not refuse such a proposal. Little of any importance passed under his nose so where was the harm? That was until Minister von Neurath had promoted him somewhat and now von Ribbentrop was allowing Platen to see copies of cables from British prime ministers.

The volume of information he secretly deposited as instructed by the Czechoslovak agent had steadily increased over the last year. The information must have been valuable, as his retainer had been generously increased without a word. His debts were paid but now Platen had to worry about where to hide this surplus in the Swiss account. He couldn't spend it or deposit it in Berlin... that would draw attention. If Platen should be discovered one whisper from any of these men at the Berghof could end his life in short order.

There had been much to do between leaving Berlin the previous night and getting everything prepared by this afternoon. But after the British arrived there had been little to occupy Platen but pass the time in the main entrance hall attempting to appear inconspicuous amidst the peculiar cactus vegetation sprouting forth from the colorful Italian pottery. The whole residence was decidedly odd in its decoration. But as the person responsible for the decor was the chancellor himself, best to leave such impressions unspoken.

The chancellor had met Mister Chamberlain on the steps just before five o'clock and brought his guests to the Great Hall for tea. It was a huge room with a fireplace and a magnificent view through an enormous picture window. Platen could have remained in the room with them and the rest of the foreign minister's staff yet was happy to stay nearby in the hallway during this social experiment. The insincere discourse annoyed him. Every few minutes Platen would enter following an unobtrusive circuit through the room before exiting again – just enough time to give von Ribbentrop an opportunity to make eye contact should he require anything.

After twenty minutes of polite discussion it was decided that the two leaders should get to the business at hand. The British were wary of the foreign minister so they had suggested a private chat between the chancellor and the prime minister. This maneuver had infuriated von Ribbentrop and Platen was sure his superior would retaliate in some fashion. The two leaders had retired to Herr Hitler's study on the floor above accompanied only by the chancellor's interpreter. Platen had seen this study earlier in the day while assisting the foreign minister. It was a large room with comfortable furnishings... a good choice for two powerful leaders to negotiate in. What he learned from von Ribbentrop was this was the very same room the chancellor had used to corner Premier Schuschnigg seven months previous. The foreign minister strongly believed the study was very good luck for the Führer.

During their long wait Platen could tell his boss was most eager to know the outcome of the meeting up the stairs. Platen could plainly hear the chancellor giving Herr Chamberlain a passionate scolding, as was the Führer's nature. Platen never once heard the Englishman speak though as the chancellor's strong voice had never paused. Then Platen heard nothing more from the study and gathered the two had settled into actual conversation. Later, after the British had returned to their lodgings in the village, von Ribbentrop summoned Platen to join him in the study to take notes as the chancellor described to the foreign minister and his other senior advisors what had been agreed upon that day. He could barely keep up with Herr Hitler's recitation, which was fortunate. Platen had to concentrate so deeply on the chore at hand that he had no chance to faint standing in such close proximity to Hitler.

What Platen found himself privy to was simply extraordinary. The chancellor had been most firm with Herr Chamberlain. There should be no doubts about his absolute determination not to tolerate further that a small, second-rate country should treat the mighty thousand-year-old German nation as something inferior. One way or another the three million Germans in Czechoslovakia *must* return to the Reich. The Führer was forty-nine years old, and if the Czechoslovak question led to a world war, then he wanted to lead his country through the crisis in the full strength of manhood. The rest of the world might do what it liked he would not yield one single step.

The Führer then went on describe the back and forth that had ensued between the two men and Platen imagined this part had taken place after he could no longer overhear Herr Hitler's voice from the staircase. Apparently the prime minister had the impertinence to interrupt the chancellor to ask why he had been allowed to come to Berchtesgaden if Herr Hitler was already set on applying force to settle the matter. Of course there was still an opportunity for a peaceful settlement Hitler had argued. What the chancellor must know was whether Herr Chamberlain was agreeable to a secession of the Sudeten region enforced on the basis of the right of self-determination? To no surprise to the Führer, Chamberlain expressed little shock at this proposal – accepting it most calmly as a basis of negotiation. What spell did the chancellor have over the Englishman, Platen wondered as he continued to take notes.

The two leaders then went on to haggle over the details. Chamberlain suggested that all Sudeten areas with eighty percent or more ethnic Germans be taken away from Czechoslovakia and turned over to Germany. The chancellor would have no talk about percentages. He was only concerned with those areas with a simple majority of Germans. Any Czechs who lived in those areas could leave without incident and without compensation. The prime minister did want some assurances, however. He reminded the chancellor of his words... that the three million Sudetenland Germans must be included in the Reich. If this were accomplished would Hitler be satisfied with that? Could Chamberlain have his assurance that there was nothing more that Herr Hitler wanted? The question had to be asked because there were many people who thought these Sudeten Germans were not all Herr Hitler desired. The Führer's response was brutally honest. When the German lands in Czechoslovakia were returned to Germany the Poles and Hungarians would successfully press their claims. What would be left of Czechoslovakia would be so small that the chancellor would not bother his head about it.

Herr Chamberlain confessed that he personally recognized the principle of the detachment of the Sudeten areas yet could not authorize this agreement at that moment, however. First he was obligated to return home to report to the rest of his government and secure their approval of his personal attitude. He would also need to consult with the French at the earliest opportunity. These consultations Chamberlain would pursue immediately with dispatch. But while he was doing so would Herr Hitler agree to refrain from taking military action against Czechoslovakia? The Führer said he was sincerely moved by Herr Chamberlain's initiative and pledged he would not order an invasion while the prime minister carried out his promise. The Führer did advise that the Englishman not take too long in his deliberations for who knew what provocations the Czechs might engineer.

Platen recalled the many troop transports he had seen that morning motoring toward the Czechoslovak frontier and wondered whether there was anything that would prevent that blunt force from being applied. Chamberlain would have seen the same display as well and Platen questioned how the Englishman could draw any different conclusion. Chamberlain told the chancellor he would return to Great Britain the next morning and departed the Berghof soon after. The prime minister had said he would return to Germany in several days to discuss his progress. With these final details noted, von Ribbentrop hurried Platen out of the study. With another Chamberlain visit looming they all had a mad week ahead of them.

As he descended the stairs behind his foreign minister to the first floor, Platen felt deathly faint. He had a decision to make: provide the Czechs with knowledge of what had been said at the Berghof this day or share none of what he knew. Platen would not sleep that night or for many nights thereafter.

RATHAUS DER STADT
ASCH, SUDETENLAND

All of the influential Henleinists had cleared out. Not much of a last stand either. Henlein had left that morning having retreated here from Karlsbad a few nights before. The Czechoslovak authorities had issued an arrest warrant on the guy for treason. His parting shot was a general proclamation that the crisis could only be averted by the achievement of a union with the Reich. Sylvie didn't see how that had pumped up the locals much with Henlein skipping out of town like a moonshiner just ahead of federal revenue agents.

For now the Czechoslovaks were firmly in control. Everyone in German or mixed German-Czech districts in Bohemia had been ordered to give up their arms and ammunition. Here in Asch the local SdP administrators at the town hall had been sent home. The government in Prague had dissolved the Sudeten Deutsche Partei and seized all of its property. To fill the local leadership gap a Bohemian German Party had been established by four moderate leaders of the SdP. This group appeared to have some encouragement from Prague but until they got up and running the Czech army was the only show in town. Sylvie's opinion of Henlein might have been more positive if he had given her the interview she had been nagging his people about since the guy had arrived from Karlsbad. Oh well, if a heel is how his own people viewed Henlein, a heel is how she would describe him.

Endicott had been lobbying for a return to Prague since they learned Chamberlain had flown to Germany but Sylvie had disagreed. He was right about how much diplomatic back and forth would go on in the next week between the respective capitals yet Sylvie also felt strongly that the story here on the border wasn't done. The next challenge to Czech authority from Henlein or the Germans was going to roll right through Asch. Sylvie had talked Endicott into staying put for twenty-four hours. Her ace in the hole was that German newspapers were still slipping into town in large numbers. Since the German editors were getting tips early, the Americans had a pretty good window on what was going on as long as you stripped out the bull. The headlines on these broadsheets were plenty entertaining if you actually knew the truth:

Prag Unleashes Bloody Terror
German Population Without Self-Defence
Czech Terror Overreaches Itself
Mob Rule In Bohemia
Sufferings of Sudeten Germans Worsen
Germany's Patience Almost Exhausted
All Warnings Fall On Deaf Ears

There was another reason Sylvie wanted to stick around Asch. Endicott had found that church telephone the other day and the rat didn't tell her, so this was her revenge. One of the mid-level Henleinists who had stuck around had confided to Sylvie that the thousands of party men who had fled to the German side would be back soon… and armed to the teeth. He also hinted that the Germans had their own guerrilla and sabotage units ready to slip into the Sudetenland to cause mischief. It could all be bluster but that was not how the man struck Sylvie. No way she was going to miss out on a scoop like that.

24. SCURRILOUS

Czech pilots relax by their Avia B-534s

SEPTEMBER 18, 1938
CZECHOSLOVAK EMBASSY
GROSVENOR PLACE, LONDON

Chamberlain had returned to London Friday evening. As soon as he had stepped off his plane he walked up a radio microphone and told his countrymen: *I had a frank talk with Herr Hitler and I feel satisfied now that each of us understands what is in the mind of the other.* Masaryk had advised Krofta that the bastard was selling them out and he saw no reason to change that advice. Especially since Runciman had conveniently turned up in London a day after Chamberlain himself to deliver his *report,* a document that Henlein himself had already boasted recommended the prompt transfer of the Sudetenland over to Germany.

The British Foreign Office was still keeping Masaryk at arms length. Their line was the prime minister was obligated to consult with his cabinet first, which had taken most of Saturday. Neither would they grant him an audience today as the French had arrived and Mister Chamberlain naturally must consult with his partner Daladier next. Regardless, Masaryk believed he had a fairly accurate notion of what was being negotiated behind their backs. The newspapers said it all. The News Chronicle reported from Berchtesgaden: *That optimism among German officials is immense.* Then there was the Daily Mail also from Berchtesgaden: *The Germans are entirely satisfied with the conversations.* The Daily Mail seemed very well connected indeed:

It is believed that Mister Chamberlain will discuss with his Ministers a plan for a four-Power conference between Britain, France, Italy, and Germany to discuss the Czech issue. Chamberlain is reported to be fresh, vigorous, and calmly optimistic after his twelve hundred mile round air trip. He went to Germany with the determination to preserve the peace of Europe by drastic measures to reorganize the Czechoslovak state. It is further stated that there was not much difference of opinion between Mister Chamberlain and Herr Hitler.

Masaryk hurled the newspaper into the nearest wastebasket and cursed. On the plus side his campaign to encourage British legislative opposition to tie Chamberlain's hands was showing some progress. The Labour party contingent in parliament was making noise by demanding that the prime minister brief them on exactly what was agreed to with Hitler. And among the conservatives Churchill was on record describing the Berghof meeting as the stupidest thing that has ever been done. These were useful developments yet Masaryk calculated that they would not be sufficient to prevent Chamberlain from delivering up as much Czech territory as Hitler demanded. The whole concept of a four-power conference was to put a civilized seal on the betrayal as well as divvy up the responsibility.

The phone rang. The operator said President Beneš was on the line from Praha. Masaryk told her to put him through. "Hello Mister President... Oh yes, they are still talking. I have that on very good authority."

Beneš was desperate to know what the British and French had in store for them. He was reading the same newspaper reports as Masaryk and had little illusion what was going on. All that they lacked was the extent of the betrayal. "No sir, I cannot tell you what Chamberlain and Daladier are offering. The uncles are only speaking to themselves. I have already sent Halifax a démarche that we took it for granted that no decision regarding us will be taken without our being consulted, and in the absence of such consultation, we would take no responsibility for decisions made without us. Naturally I have received no response. It doesn't really matter anymore. They are *obviously* discussing the ceding of Czechoslovak territory... No, I won't go over to Ten Downing Street. They have not sent for me... What do I recommend? What I say is fuck them, Mister President."

44TH FIGHTER FLIGHT, POLERADY – BOHEMIA

Many chief mechanics would have viewed Bozik's daily rituals as a lack of confidence in their maintenance routines. Soucek, however, took pride in pilots taking an interest in the health of their aircraft and was happy to toss them a wrench when needed. Bozik always took time to examine the four machine guns on his Avia as part of the normal visual inspection pilots were prone to. As they were mounted on the fuselage behind the engine all manner of carbon and sludge could work its way to the weapons. The last thing Bozik needed was a jam during a dogfight. So he removed access panels to check the guns on a daily basis. When checking this regularly the process went swiftly if cleaning and oiling were needed. A necessity since a Luftwaffe raid could happen at any hour. The combat air patrols gave them a time cushion but not much. The fruit of their months of drilling was Bozik's pilots could get their birds in the air in less than five minutes on the sounding of an alarm.

Luža snuck up on Bozik while the pilot was concentrating on the ammunition feed to one of the starboard guns. He always appreciated how Bozik was constantly searching for an edge in the air. The base commander could not expect all of the squadron leaders to be so driven but the natural competition between the men meant many of Bozik's strategies were filtering throughout the wing. "I am fairly certain those guns shine more brightly than my wife's crystal."

"Please do not tell her that, sir," Bozik saluted casually with an oily hand. "She is a nice woman and I would not want her to hate me."

"Hardly! But I would be forced to loan you out to her for cleaning duty if she knew of your good work," Luža enjoyed bantering with Bozik.

"What brings you to my office? You have that spark in your eyes, sir," Bozik knew his commander's ways well.

"Walk with me and I will tell you," Luža pulled him along by the arm.

Bozik wiped his greasy hands with a rag and followed. These walks usually meant something entertaining was brewing. Luža's heart was really in the sky. Administrative shacks were confining to him. So he looked for any viable excuse to be out among the crews and aircraft.

"I have good news," Luža continued. "Odd given British diplomacy of recent days, yet encouraging."

Bozik had no idea where his commander was going but played along. "Don't tell me they are sending a squadron of Gladiators to help out."

"You are not far off," Luža thought such a laughable token commitment would be typical of the British. "No, apparently we recently exchanged some staff with the Armee de l' Air and they are telling us some of what the French air service is planning. Vuillemin is putting his squadrons on a war footing at last. If the French fight they intend to send us four bomber groups at the outbreak of hostilities to operate from Bohemian airfields. Their mission will be to disrupt German troop movements toward Austria, Bohemia and Moravia by attacking the rail network in Bavaria. They will also be tasked with raids against Luftwaffe bomber bases in Eastern Bavaria, and Western Saxony to take away some of the German advantage."

"What are they sending? I hope it's not those old lumbering Bloch's," Bozik assumed the worst.

"What aircraft the French plan on sending is unknown at the moment. But since they are intent that most of the French sorties should take place at night you might be entirely correct." There was little that got past Bozik, Luža admitted.

"Night missions, eh?" Bozik did not like the sound of that as the two officers were reaching the outer edge of the airstrip. "That won't be very effective. They won't do much damage."

"My thoughts exactly," Luža was onto an idea. "Who knows whether the French will actually come through but the possibility brought to mind the matter of protecting bombers."

"As in those slow buzzards are going to need some lions to keep them alive," Bozik would hate to see their French allies die early deaths.

"That is why I am adding some new drills for your boys to master," Luža had come to the same conclusion but not only for the benefit of the French. "Starting tomorrow I want your squadron to practice fighter sweeps and bomber escort protocols. I will find you some B-71 crews to practice with by Tuesday. What do you say?"

"That is a marvelous plan," Bozik was already working out how to set up the drills. "Having new skills to master will give my men something to keep their minds focused on. They really want to get at the Germans for all of this shit on the border. At least the army has some action on the ground. All we can do is patrol and wait."

"They will get their opportunity soon enough," and sadly some of them would not survive, as Luža knew well from personal experience.

U.S. EMBASSY
MALA STRANA DISTRICT, PRAHA

Minister Carr had something on his mind but he had yet to get to the point. Sometimes on these strolls around the grounds Carr would ask advice on a particular question while at other times he would assign Bulloch a task of importance. Bulloch had returned to Prague at about the same time Chamberlain had landed at Munich. The attaché had shared a copy of his report to Carr the next day yet that was several days ago and Carr rarely took this long to comment on something he had read.

"That was a most excellent report, captain," Carr raised his hand to his chin as he moved on from casual conversation. "Despite the calm conditions with the Czech authorities in control of the situation I fear conditions remain volatile. I regret putting you into this position but I require you to make a prediction for me given your recent observations and your *special* knowledge of German intentions. Will these Sudeten Germans stay cowed and will the Czechoslovaks be able to keep them controlled?"

"My best estimate is that more violence is coming soon, sir. Tens of thousands of ethnic German men are slipping over the border to join up with Henlein in Germany. Even the newspapers are onto that," Bulloch wasn't going too far out on a limb.

"Oh, where has Herr Henlein taken up residence since the Czechoslovaks issued their arrest warrant for him?" Carr had been told the location was unknown.

"Selb is the village I heard whispered the most but there is no way to be sure," It was impossible for Bulloch to know how connected the Sudetens he spoke with were.

"I see... so you are expecting some mischief then," Carr circled the conversation back.

"Without a doubt. The Germans still need a few more days to get the rest of their regular divisions in position. Don't ask me why but it took Berlin until the beginning of this month before the order went out to get their tanks, artillery and infantry moving into their attack positions. What I have been told is Hitler intends to attack before October first and the Wehrmacht redeployment will be finished by then. I expect you'll see Henlein's people hopping over the border to generate confusion and keep the Czechs busy between now and then," Bulloch gave the minister the short version.

"I had a long chat with foreign minister Krofta today," and Carr had required the attaché's counsel to confirm what he had been told. "We're all in the dark as to what terms Prime Minister Chamberlain agreed to with Chancellor Hitler. This state of affairs is very vexing for the Czechs as you might well imagine. Krofta is of the opinion, and we can expect president Beneš shares this opinion, that Mister Chamberlain has endorsed separation of the Sudetens from Czechoslovakia. By treaty, arbitration is the stipulated method of deciding territorial disputes between both nations. Believing that whatever Anglo-French plan that emerges from Chamberlain's and Daladier's consultations today will focus on stripping away the Sudeten territory, the Czechs are hoping to press for arbitration with Germany."

"That's a very optimistic strategy," Bulloch suspected there was an ulterior motive.

"There is the presumption that Chancellor Hitler may engage in such arbitration while his armed forces finish gathering on the frontier knowing full well he will terminate that arbitration when the army is ready to invade. Krofta believes such bad behavior would be sufficient to force Chamberlain and Daladier to exhibit some real firmness with the dictator. With only two weeks before Germany invades that is a timeline that would support Krofta's theory," Carr had his answer.

"I see." Such a diplomatic maneuver never occurred to Bulloch. "From my vantage point, Hitler is a man who has wanted something for a very long time and he means to have it soon. Too much talk will only make him more inclined to try taking what he wants."

"I tend to agree with you, son," Carr had taken a call from Ambassador Wilson in Berlin during which he learned British minister Henderson had much the same analysis as Mister Bulloch. Hitler would not wait if the democracies did not accept Sudeten annexation immediately without conditions. The wild card was whether Beneš would accept those terms and that is what Wilson wanted Carr's advice on. In Carr's estimation, Beneš might submit to such a humiliation yet he thought it unlikely given the growing public sentiment to resist the Germans on display every day in Prague. "My mind is made up. With war around the corner I have decided on two courses of action. The first is the building of an air raid shelter here on the embassy grounds. With all of those shiny new bombers you tell me the Germans have available Prague is sure to be hit very hard. I want our staff to have a place of refuge in that eventuality. Which leads me to my second decision. It is my intention to withdraw our embassy women and non-essential staff from Prague as soon as possible. Locomotive and river transport between Germany and Czechoslovakia has already been suspended. It is also near impossible to hire enough vehicles to drive our people to safety. Air service may be the next transport to become unavailable. I won't risk any more of our staff as necessary. I am putting Secretary Chapin and yourself in charge of shelter construction and arranging the evacuation of our people."

"Of course sir, I will coordinate with Vinton immediately," Bulloch took a deep breath thinking of how many people were now depending on him.

"Thank you, son," Carr rested a hand on the attaché's shoulder. "There are already several bids in my office so let's go evaluate the plans. You'll know best how strong the shelter will have to be to withstand the latest weaponry. Pick the best option and I will issue the construction contract today. I'll leave it to you and Vinton to make the most expeditious arrangements for our people."

Bulloch saw there was one matter Carr had neglected to consider, however. "You realize Bess will never leave."

"That is true. She's absolutely necessary to running this legation. Ask her anyway. It will give Miss Flynn a reason to remind us how indispensable she is and I imagine she will quite enjoy that," Carr's eyes twinkled as he made the suggestion.

COUNCIL CHAMBERS
PRAŽSKÝ HRAD, PRAHA

The president had been in non-stop discussions with his cabinet for most of the last two days. There was no word whatsoever from London and the delay was infuriating. Beneš and his ministers had nothing concrete to formulate policy around. The educated rumors being bandied around in the British and French press portrayed an intolerable scenario made all the worse for how consistent these dispatches were from newspaper to newspaper. As these reports were all out in the open the public mood was growing uglier with every hour. There was also the increasing initiative

Generál Krejčí was showing. He had not waited for presidential approval to start partial mobilization. The generál was a loyal patriot, and Beneš did not fear an army coup, but if the will of the people demanded it Krejčí would be encouraged to show still further independence in the name of protecting the republic. Beneš' government would have to issue some proclamation soon or they risked losing the people's trust and matters might spiral out of his control. All of this made young Masaryk's recommendation to tell the French and British to fuck themselves a very tempting choice.

Since Chamberlain had flown back to London, Moravec had his department hard at work hunting for a verifiable account of what Hitler had brokered with the prime minister. The problem was the flurry of governmental activity stirred within Germany in the aftermath of Chamberlain's Berghof gambit was making it nearly impossible for Moravec's German sources to share what they knew. Nor did the border closures between Germany and Czechoslovakia help matters. All Moravec could say is that when he had possession of anything useful he would bring it to Beneš and that moment had come. Moravec slipped into the chambers, circled in behind the president and whispered into his ear. "I have something."

"Tell us," Beneš' spirits lifted.

"This is better for you to hear alone, sir," Moravec advised softly.

"No, please tell us all," Beneš ordered for all to hear.

Moravec straightened himself and nodded at Burda who had waited at the door. The Second Department chief had expected this. Burda would wait outside to make sure no one else entered, or listened from the outside, until Moravec approved.

"Very well, Mister President," Moravec shifted his position to better address the cabinet ministers. "Gentlemen. I implore you. What I tell you now must not be shared outside the participants in this room. The cost would be grave. I have the account of a reliable individual who was at the Berghof on the fifteenth. This is one source and we have not received corroborating evidence, as I would prefer. Yet given the individual, and the urgency of the matter, I cannot wait for verification as I do not know when conditions will permit it."

"Understood. Go on Plukovník," Beneš urged.

"The understanding between chancellor Hitler and Prime Minister Chamberlain is compact and of few points. Those points, however, are explosive. One, the prime minister entered these discussions fully prepared to transfer much of Western Bohemia to Germany. He did not need to be persuaded nor did he argue against such a transfer at the earliest opportunity," Moravec paused a moment for his restless audience to compose itself. "Two, Chamberlain proposed that areas populated by eighty percent or more ethnic Germans be transferred to Germany. Hitler countered that a simple majority would suffice but that he would compromise to the outcome of a plebiscite in these areas. The prime minister did not argue the point any further. But he did pledge to take the matter up with his cabinet and expected to return to Germany within a week carrying a proposal that would meet with the chancellor's satisfaction. Three, Hitler anticipates that the Poles and Hungarians will press for transfer of Czech territories that contain significant populations of these ethnicities. More importantly, it is Hitler's expectation that these Polish and Hungarian demands will be successful. The implication being that Hitler will not be satisfied with the acquisition of the Sudetenland alone and the peace will be predicated on the satisfaction of Warsaw and Budapest. Once again, the prime minister did not argue against this demand and promised that he would pursue this issue with equal dispatch. That is all, sir. Whatever plan Chamberlain and Daladier agree upon today it will be based on this understanding with Hitler."

The intelligence chief nodded to Beneš and backed away to pass control of the floor to the president. "Thank you, Mister Moravec. That report was extremely valuable and thoroughly distressing. We will take it from here."

QUARTIER DE L'OPERA DISTRICT, PARIS

Le Soir was a good read as French broadsheets went. That newsroom had a voice of its own unlike many of the paper's competitors that printed whatever message their powerful patrons wished promulgated. If Clarence had time to kill he always procured a copy of Le Soir first. He shouldn't have had time to kill yet the entire country was in a state of suspense waiting on Daladier and Bonnet to wrap up their negotiations with Chamberlain in London. Daladier had been talking tough in the days prior so there was hope the premier might have developed a backbone where selling the Czechoslovaks down the river was concerned. But the line on Daladier around Paris was he always talked bigger than he acted. It didn't help having that evil little gnome Bonnet sitting on Daladier's shoulder whispering foul defeatist advice into the premier's ear.

Clarence had spent all day attempting to get something substantial out of his usual sources. He had gone from one ministerial office to another looking for a lead but there were none to be had. Clarence was about ready to give up. His last shot was charming one of the lesser secretaries who worked for one of the lesser parliamentarians. They had met on several occasions socially and Clarence was getting desperate. Surprisingly, the aide did not shoo Clarence away like all the rest. Instead the address of a humble cafe near the CNS bureau was written on a note. Clarence knew the place well. The proprietress was a saucy lady with a great little menu. The secretary told Clarence to go to the cafe and wait.

That had been a couple of hours previous and Clarence was starting to get nervous. The sun was ready to go down, things were getting rolling back in New York, and Harry was stirring up a tornado looking for copy. Clarence took a sip from his fourth glass of Bordeaux when an undistinguished businessman of small frame left the cafe and placed his rump onto the extra seat at Clarence's sidewalk table without asking.

"Would you be Mister Clarence?" the man inquired with an overly friendly manner.

"That would be correct," Clarence put the copy of Le Soir down on the tabletop. "Who is asking?"

"I am Didier," the man in the frumpy suit answered as if the name meant something.

"Yes, but who *are* you?" Clarence wanted a better idea who Mister Didier represented.

"That is totally unimportant, my friend. You made an inquiry earlier today and now you have the good luck to have your enterprise rewarded," Didier did not have time to play with this reporter.

This fellow was friendly enough, yet Clarence didn't like the eyes. Those eyes were very serious and the message they were sending was: *Don't trifle with me.*

"This is my lucky day after all," Clarence changed tack. "Can I buy you a drink?"

"You are most generous but no thank you. Today has been very busy and there is much left to do," Didier reached into his jacket and pulled out a folded envelope for Clarence. "In this you will find the text of a joint French-British statement that will be issued by tomorrow. Some words may change but what you now have in your hands is close to a final version."

"Don't take this in the wrong way," Clarence turned the creased envelope over in his hand. "But I have never worked with you before. I appreciate the gift enormously but I don't like going out on a limb without a level of trust between me and my sources."

"Totally understandable. That is a quandary I cannot assist you with. There is risk in every endeavor. Look at the contents and decide for yourself," Didier had been told to deliver the document... not babysit the man. "Good evening Mister Clarence."

With that the Frenchman rose from the chair and swiftly disappeared into the procession of Parisians passing by on the sidewalk. Clarence had either just been delivered a gold mine or he was being taken for a ride. It was time to look inside the envelope.

BRITISH & FRENCH PROPOSALS PRESENTED
TO THE CZECHOSLOVAK GOVERNMENT

The representatives of the French and British Governments have been in consultation today on the general situation and have considered the British Prime Minister's report of his conversation with Herr Hitler. British Ministers also placed before their French colleagues their conclusions derived from the account furnished to them of the work of his mission by Lord Runciman. We are both convinced that,

after recent events, the point has now been reached where the further maintenance within the boundaries of the Czechoslovak State of the districts mainly inhabited by Sudeten Deutsche cannot, in fact, continue any longer without imperiling the interests of Czechoslovakia herself and of European peace. In the light of these considerations, both Governments have been compelled to the conclusion that the maintenance of peace and the safety of Czechoslovakia's vital interests cannot effectively be assured unless these areas are now transferred to the Reich.

Clarence whistled loudly. In his hands was the real deal: an eight-point plan to strip the Czechs of their border regions. It was a carbon from an original typed on a lousy typewriter – the government-issue variety – that appeared authentic. But he had seen elaborate hoaxes before. The major details did correspond remarkably well with speculation that had been published during the past two days. This document could either be an elaboration of those reports or a confirmation of them. What won Clarence over was the formal diplomatic language. It reeked of the seemingly sincerely yet insincere niceties politicians employed while picking someone else's pockets. Yep, Chamberlain and Daladier had their paws all over this baby.

The courier had been right. There was a huge risk but you only die once and he hadn't landed something this big in ages. Clarence couldn't quote the document exactly, that would get him arrested, but he could describe the major points in detail and that would be plenty good enough. If he were lucky, Clarence's story would run in papers at about the same time the French and British got around to giving Beneš his copy.

The only matter nagging at Clarence was the not knowing which patron he was serving by acting on this gift. The obvious suspect was Reynaud who might benefit from breaking the details early in an attempt to build opposition sufficient to derail the plan. And as minister of justice he might have been able to get his hands on an early copy. CNS seemed like an odd choice in this little scheme at first but giving the documents to a French outlet risked having some mole on the inside snitch on the windfall. Bonnet would have a hard time stifling an American wire service in the same way he worked the French papers. Clarence's mind was made up. He was going to make Papa a happy man back in New York.

SEPTEMBER 19, 1938
ASCH, SUDETENLAND

Wow, did she make the right decision. All hell was breaking loose. Yesterday Henlein issued an angry proclamation. It was datelined from Asch but Sylvie knew for a fact that the stooge hadn't been in town for almost a week. Besides, the proclamation Sylvie held in her hand was issued through the official German news agency in Berlin. She did give the Henleinists credit for getting copies into Asch so quickly. But wow, such tough talk from such a mousy guy.

> *The Sudeten Germans for years have sought the collaboration of the Czech people. The Czechs have continued to intensify their hatred of everything German. The Prag Government has carried on a ruthless war of destruction. The Czech authorities in the last few weeks have let fall their mask. The Prag Government is no longer master of the situation in face of Bolshevik and Hussite elements. President Beneš is still cheating and deceiving his people about the real state of affairs. He is too cowardly to admit the collapse of his policy, and sees a last hope in a European catastrophe. He is letting loose Bolshevik and Hussite hordes in the uniforms of malignant Czech soldiery on defenceless Sudeten Germans. Ten thousand racial comrades are forced to fly across the frontier in order to avoid destruction or are being taken off as defenceless hostages. We therefore take the right which peoples have always exercised in times of extreme need to take up arms and form a Sudeten Freikorps TO FIGHT CZECHS IN SUDETENLAND.*

Another big surprise was that the Henleinists actually meant business. Since she had been in Czechoslovakia this bunch had been big on talk. But to her surprise this new Freikorps didn't waste any time getting into action. Henlein issued his proclamation in the afternoon and that night the Freikorps started hitting Czech targets. Asch was total chaos and all night Sylvie had been running after Czech officials and troops. Her bureau chief was going to love the story if Sylvie could only find a way to deliver it to him. The Czechs were way too busy to let her use any of their phones. Now that dawn had arrived things were quieting down. Sylvie elected to be a pest and wait at the police station until someone took mercy on her or a hand grenade sailed through the window. As long as she was stuck waiting Sylvie decided to review her notes. If they let her on the phone she wouldn't have time to dawdle.

> *Overnight Henleinists had kidnapped eighteen uniformed Czech frontier guards in the area, while another squad of ten Freikorps men had approached and machine-gunned the customs house at Asch. Asch was the most defenseless town in the Sudetenland because it is almost surrounded by German territory. During the attack Czech officials were forced to retreat until daybreak when they returned with reinforcements. By that time there was no trace of the aggressors. The customs officers, two of whom were wounded in the course of the attack, refrained from shooting and fired rockets as a call for*

assistance. Czechoslovak troops have moved up and now occupy trenches at some points on the German frontier.

Elsewhere in the region, Henleinists attacked the Custom House at Neusorge, near Braun, and the defenders replied with hand-grenades. When reinforcements arrived, the attackers withdrew. An hour later they returned, resumed the assault, and were again expelled by Czech defenders. Six Czechoslovak customs officials were carried off as casualties. Two soldiers were also wounded. Another Freikorps unit armed with hand-grenades and machine-guns twice attacked and set fire to the custom house at Ober Kleinaupa near Marchendorf and were repulsed. Two Czechs were wounded. Nine Sudeten deserters from the Czechoslovak Army attacked and set fire to still another custom house at Trautenau, throwing hand-grenades at the occupants, killing one Czech and taking another a prisoner.

In response, the government in Prague has taken additional measures to maintain order in the Sudeten areas on top of the state of martial law previously established. Three more districts, including Pressburg, have been added to the proclamation demanding the surrender of arms. New emergency decrees have suspended immunity from arrest without warrant, the inviolability of private houses, secrecy of the mails and the freedom of the press. Those caught in the act of violence, or suspected of participating in violence, are now subject to confinement in fixed areas. The government will also impose censorship as required to maintain order.

In an interesting turn of events, many ethnic German men who fled in days past are returning from Germany to escape conscription. They say all male refugees in Germany between the ages of eighteen and fifty are being drafted into the Freikorps. Henleinists who returned from Germany gave themselves up to Czech police declaring that the alternatives to taking up arms was either forced labor on the German fortifications or being sent to a concentration camp.

The only item Sylvie had left out was only a hunch that could not be confirmed. The Czech soldiers she had spoken with in the area were getting very edgy about being surrounded on three sides by German territory. It was a bear to defend this sliver of land under the circumstances. The feeling Sylvie was getting from some of the conversations she overheard was that they wanted to pull back, perhaps to a more defensible position as far as Eger. But since the Czechoslovaks she was talking also detested giving ground to the Henleinists, Sylvie was hedging at mentioning the possibility when she already had plenty of other good material to report.

As soon as she got her copy in Sylvie would have to figure out what happened to Endicott. He had disappeared Sunday. At first she had not minded since the lug had been nagging her for days about sticking around Asch. The respite had been kind of nice. Now Sylvie was starting to worry about him. It wasn't like Endicott to go off and leave Sylvie flat without hollering at her first.

RADIO-TELETYPE ROOM
CZECHOSLOVAK EMBASSY
GROSVENOR PLACE, LONDON

Daladier and Bonnet had spent eight hours sequestered with Chamberlain and the three ministers that made up his inner cabinet. The cabal had not concluded their discussions until after midnight. With the British blocking his every entreaty, Masaryk had next set his sights on the French contingent. He learned that Daladier and Bonnet were not flying back to Paris until the morning. There was a chance he might personally prevail upon them for an audience before they left London but the attempt failed. Masaryk doubted his messages ever got past Daladier's guards and by now the pair was already in the air. It would be up to Osuský in Paris to corner them. All Masaryk could do was update Beneš on what little he knew. The ambassador swooped into the teletype room like a tempest. "Get this out immediately to the castle in Praha," Masaryk threw the first half of a handwritten cable down in front of the machine operator.

> *MISTER PRESIDENT. CHAMBERLAIN AND HALIFAX STILL IGNORING ME. THEY HAVE NOT SENT FOR ME OR FORWARDED TEXT OF JOINT BRITISH-FRENCH POLICY CONCLUDED LAST NIGHT. OFFICIAL DOWNING STREET PUBLIC ANNOUNCEMENT AS FOLLOWS.*

Masaryk presented a second document typed on the letterhead the operator recognized as the kind used by the British prime minister's staff.

> *After full discussion of the present international situation the representatives of the British and French Governments are in complete agreement as to the policy to be adopted with the view to promoting a peaceful solution to the Czechoslovak question.*
>
> *The two Governments hope that thereafter it will be possible to consider a more general settlement in the interests of European peace.*

Masaryk placed the second half of the cable to Beneš before the operator.

WILL CONTINUE TO PRESS ON TIRELESSLY FOR CLARIFICATION ON NEW POLICY. FEAR WORST SINCE I HAVE NOT BEEN SUMMONED. ADVISE YOU DELAY AS LONG AS POSSIBLE WHEN BRITISH AND FRENCH DICTATE TERMS. PUBLIC OPINION HERE TURNING. LAST NIGHT THOUSANDS MARCHED FROM TRAFALGAR SQUARE DOWN WHITEHALL SHOUTING, "STAND BY THE CZECHS." LABOUR MP WILKINSON LED MARCH CRYING OUT: "WE SAY TO NEVILLE CHAMBERLAIN, WE DON'T TRUST YOU." POLICE HAD TO BLOCK ACCESS TO DOWNING STREET. ARRESTS MADE. POLICE FORCED TO CLEAR DEMONSTRATORS FROM WHITEHALL. STAND FIRM. OUR EFFORTS WITH CHAMBERLAIN OPPOSITION MAKING PROGRESS. NEED A LITTLE MORE TIME. SEND MORE FUNDS.

There sadly was nothing more for Masaryk to add. "That's all, send it."

COUNTER-INTELLIGENCE OFFICE
REICH MINISTRY OF WAR – 72-76 TIRPITZUFER, BERLIN

The arrangements had been formalized. The chancellor would host Prime minister Chamberlain at Bad Godesberg in three days. Ottke preferred the Führer being close to a large city such as Cologne. Berchtesgaden was far too isolated considering how fast events were progressing. The diplomacy was a sideshow, Ottke thought as he calmly sipped a cup of tea while peering out his office window. One only had to look to nearby rooftops to know where the country was heading. Each day he saw preparations against potential air raids were proceeding in and around Berlin with new antiaircraft gun emplacements being manned day and night. Travel anywhere and the picture was the same. The new autobahn segments already built between Berlin and Dresden were packed with troop divisions moving south. All the roads around Breslau were jammed with military traffic and transport. Trains loaded with guns and material were moving to the Czech border. Hitler could not stay so far away for much longer with war near and Ottke expected him to return to Berlin after his second meeting with Chamberlain.

Ottke doubted the Englishman could conceive of the trap being laid for him. The embarrassing circus would be so well documented that Chamberlain would never be allowed to forget his role. The Propaganda Ministry had commandeered every last room at the Godesberger Hof. Space for one hundred foreign correspondents was being made ready there. The chancellor himself had taken possession of all one hundred and seventy rooms at the nearby Hotel Dreesen. The proprietor was one of the Führer's oldest compatriots. Hitler already had a permanent suite there with a huge balcony with one of the best views of the Rhine. Chamberlain was walking into a finely prepared web indeed.

The poor prime minister thought too highly of his negotiating skills. What he lacked was the knowledge that he had few secrets from Hitler and hence little leverage. Every hour Göring's Forschungsamt delivered a new set of Brown Pages to the chancellor. These were the transcripts of telephone wiretaps of foreign diplomats in Berlin and telephone calls to and from Central European capitals that transited through Germany. Thanks to these Brown Pages, Hitler undoubtedly already knew what Chamberlain's last, best offer would be and he could bludgeon the seventy year-old politician silly until the old man delivered. Even Admiral Canaris admired the wealth of intelligence that the Forschungsamt produced. It was a highly efficient operation with tentacles stretching everywhere, which had to be respected. That Göring also spied on Himmler and Heydrich was a given. It kept them loyal to the Führer and provided Göring a certain level of personal security.

Ottke finished his tea and returned the cup to its saucer. The trap would close on Chamberlain and they would see what resulted. He sensed the fate of millions would be sealed during the next five days.

RATHAUS – PLAUEN, DEUTSCHLAND

Another new town and another stay in the hoosegow... Endicott wasn't even fully sure where the hell he was. This was all Sylvie's fault. She couldn't leave Asch when the getting was good. No, that wouldn't do. By the time he had decided to drop the broad flat there wasn't transportation available. It took an hour before Endicott had talked that Czech sergeant into letting him hitch a ride to Eger. Two miles out of Asch the Czechs heard gunfire whizzing nearby and they put him off right there and drove off on a side road. No way he was giving up and retreating back to Asch so Endicott had grabbed his suitcase and hoofed it in the direction of Eger.

About forty-five minutes later Endicott noted the landscape was getting more wooded, and he could see some rural buildings looming in the distance. That was a welcome sight since no one had passed him on the road going in either direction. The hike wasn't bothering him but he wanted to get some water to quench his thirst. Perhaps he could buy some from whoever lived up ahead. Concentrating too much on that goal, Endicott didn't notice the two goons in vintage German helmets until they made themselves plain from their cover behind some large tree trunks. The pair honestly looked like they had stepped out of a cartoon. Who dressed these guys? They looked like ridiculous Swiss yodelers. But the business end of their rifles was serious enough and the swastika armbands made it pretty plain he had walked into a Henleinist scout patrol.

All of that was three days ago. Endicott had since learned his new friends were Sudeten Freikorps. They didn't shoot him or rough him up but Endicott soon found himself walking into Germany under escort. Having successfully gotten across that he was an American had developed into something of a problem, which led to Endicott getting passed to one senior Henleinist after another. They didn't know what to do with him. Along with Endicott on the cross-border hike were some Czechs and conservative Germans who also were under escort. It was obvious that the Freikorps knew exactly where to take those guys – poor chumps. Endicott had finally ended up in an archaic jail cell in what looked like some provincial capital where he was passed off to civil authorities.

Eventually Endicott was informed he was in Plauen, which he made out to be around sixteen miles from the border based on what the cop on the last shift had explained. On his way into town Endicott noted the place was packed tight with regular German army troops. Plauen was so full of soldiers that they were billeted in every one of the quaint shops near the town hall where the police headquarters was. There was a great story in this misadventure if Endicott could ever find a way to file it with a bureau. Endicott had hoped there was an American consulate not too far away. Maybe in Munich, he was told. They had his passport and he wouldn't get it back until everything was sorted out. Endicott was not being charged yet neither was he being released. It was an odd situation and guidance from superiors was required. He had been told that on Sunday and they were now way into Monday.

A tall guy wearing a tschako on his head walked down the hall in Endicott's direction with one of the local cops in tow. By the stiffly pressed uniform he looked like Grenzpolizei, the German border police. The cop unlocked the cell for the border guard to enter. Endicott politely stood as attentively as his rumpled suit would permit.

"Herr En-di-cott," the Grenzpolizei made out from what the reporter recognized as his passport and press pass. It was more of a statement than a question.

"That would be me," Endicott confirmed, stifling the urge to salute.

"Please accept my apologies for your confinement. These are unusual times. You are not in Germany by your own will yet neither are you in the country with permission. Returning you to the Asch crossing would be the normal solution, but as you know, passage into Czechoslovakia has been suspended. So we had to determine what was to be done with you," the Grenzpolizei explained in labored English.

"What *are* you going to do with me?" Endicott asked hopefully.

The border guard handed Endicott his credentials and wallet. "You have been issued a temporary entry visa. You must leave Germany within two weeks or arrange a proper visa for a longer duration. The American consulate general in Leipzig has been notified of your presence in

Germany and of your visa status. I recommend you see your countrymen there."

"Does that mean I'm free to go?" Endicott wanted to be sure that was where the conversation was going since the Grenzpolizei had clammed up.

"Ya," the Grenzpolizei was just as happy to be rid of the troublesome situation.

"But you may not stay in Plauen. This is now a restricted area," the local cop spoke up. "You will follow me to my desk and I will help you make arrangements for passage to Leipzig. From there you can call on your consulate and make arrangements to leave the country."

QUAI D'ORSAY, PARIS

So this was how it was to be. Abandoned like a faithful spouse to the vagaries of a cheating scoundrel. Despite all of the warning signs and the advice of good friends, the fleeting hope that the one who you had invested so much history with would not betray that which had taken so long to build, was dashed. What Masaryk had said on the phone was right: *screw them!*

Štefan Osušky could not remember when he had felt so embittered. The Franco-Czechoslovak Pact was dead. It had been dying for months through the long summer. For the last hour Bonnet had hammered the death certificate onto a public wall. Osušky had been summoned to the Quai d'Orsay to meet with the French foreign minister. Daladier and his cabinet ministers had been meeting since ten-thirty in the morning at the Élysée Palace to approve or reject the Anglo-French plan that Daladier had crawled back to Paris with from London. When they had finished, Osušky was to be waiting at Bonnet's office to hear the results. No audience with the premier was available.

Osušky held no illusions as to what Chamberlain had proposed to Daladier. The newspapers had been shockingly detailed in their presentation of the expected major points. So many leaks to such a plethora of reporters usually suggested a raison d'être behind the disclosures. Osušky calculated there was a chance those ministers in Daladier's cabinet that opposed ceding Czech territory to Hitler might be setting the stage for an uprising against Chamberlain's cravenly acquiescence to the dictator... but a very small chance.

When Bonnet arrived back from Élysée Palace he got right to the point. Daladier's cabinet had unanimously approved the Anglo-French plan. As Bonnet read off the terms it was just as the press reports had purported. The only difference was that Bonnet had the full list while most of the newspapers lacked one component or another. The next hour was a blistering back and forth between the two diplomats. Osušky reminded Bonnet of the last two years of French assurances, to which the Frenchman countered the break-up of Czechoslovakia was, *the least unpleasant solution.* Osušky went on to reiterate the fullness of France's treaty obligations only to be instructed they were mere words on paper. The British had said in no uncertain terms that if Prague refused the Anglo-French plan then Britain would disassociate itself from the dispute. Without British solidarity the assistance that France could offer Czechoslovakia was of no effectiveness. The Czechs would not be allowed to drag France into a war over three-and-a-half million Sudeten Germans. Osušky's further protests only fed Bonnet's burgeoning hostility. France demanded that Czechoslovakia accept the plan. That was the message Osušky was to take to President Beneš without further argument.

There was nothing more to say to such intransigence so Osušky made his leave. Heading down the hall to the main entrance, Osušky felt his own emotions exploding as he replayed Bonnet's words in his head. The ostiary opened the tall, narrow door Osušky had been through so many times in better days and the Czechoslovak envoy stepped out to overlook a courtyard full of anxious correspondents. He couldn't restrain himself.

"Do you want to see a man condemned without a hearing?" Osušky played to the crowd while descending the stairs. "Here I stand!"

WENCESLAS SQUARE, PRAHA

Securing transport back from Eger had been arduous. The whole trip to Prague had been in a succession of small doses and had taken several days. They finally arrived tired, grimy and ready for a break from each other. He was sure they had made the right decision to return. Whatever the terms the British and French governments had settled upon had yet to be delivered to President Beneš. They had gotten back to Prague just in time. Ros had told him in no uncertain terms that she would find him when she was ready, not the other way around. The *Do Not Disturb* sign on her hotel room doorknob was merely punctuation.

After cleaning himself up Sanderson found it impossible to fall asleep. So he decided to lurk around the hotel for a while. There was no evidence that Roland, Sylvie or Endicott had been seen in days. Heading downstairs to see who was about, Sanderson found some chums in the Ambassador Hotel lounge who filled Sanderson in on the latest news about the joint Anglo-French statement, how Daladier had returned to Paris Monday morning, the latest Sudeten Freikorps attacks and the various rumors circulating through the city. The banter mixed with the fine whiskey from the bar did the trick and Sanderson was able to return to his room for the sleep he so sorely needed.

Since there was no word from his erstwhile compatriot, Sanderson set out to check on what was happening about the city. The mood in the capital had taken on a dark and bitter patina in the days Sanderson and Ros had been away. Chamberlain's jaunt to Berchtesgaden had been received as a low blow. After conversing with several of his man-in-the-street sources Sanderson learned that the French papers had been well stocked for days with leaked accounts of the wretched territorial sacrifices the Czechoslovaks were expected to make. The Czech broadsheets were quick to turn these reports around so nearly everyone in the capital was well informed of the ghastly news. Not even the strong radio address by premier Milan Hodža had done much good. His declaration that the country would not submit to a plebiscite if Hitler and Chamberlain had made such an agreement, and that Czechoslovakia was willing to go it alone with Germany, should have been good morale boosters but they were not sufficient to lift the spirits of his countrymen in the face of a never-ending stream of bad newsprint.

After more than four hours of taking notes Sanderson felt he was fairly well up to speed again. And for the first time he was sensing hostility toward his British nationality. Throughout the summer, and during the farcical Runciman mission, Sanderson had never felt any ill will directed toward him. To be sure there was more animosity being directed at the French since it was they who were the Czech's official allies yet Sanderson distinctly perceived the harsh feelings toward him during the day. Many of the other British correspondents he had chatted with since returning had experienced the same hostility.

Sanderson's meandering had brought him to Wenceslas Square, the traditional focal point where the citizens of Prague gathered during a crisis. The government even had loudspeakers set up for delivering important announcements. Sanderson immediately felt something was odd, however. People were not traversing the square in their normal Point A to Point B fashion. Everyone was gravitating to separate fixed locations in the Square. It finally hit Sanderson what was happening. Everyone was gravitating toward the nearest newsstand.

"Daladier and Chamberlain tell Czechs to surrender!" the nearest newsboy barked.

Sanderson nudged his way closer to a newsstand and paid for the latest edition of Lidové noviny, the nation's largest daily. Printed there was the full list of terms to be imposed on President Beneš. The curt headline mirrored the seething public sentiment completely: *UNACCEPTABLE.*

PRESIDENTIAL CHAMBERS – PRAŽSKÝ HRAD, PRAHA

The undertakers in top hats had been in with the president for more than thirty minutes. They had turned up together, unannounced and without an appointment. Diplomatic protocol demanded that such an audience go through Foreign Minister Krofta. Yet here they were nonetheless: British Minister Newton and French Minister de Lacroix. Beneš should have kept the envoys waiting, as was his habit. But he had admitted them immediately. Drtina phoned Krofta's office as soon as the door to the president's suite had shut. There was no question Beneš could handle the situation himself but it would be better to have support. The castle staff had already brought in the afternoon newspapers so Drtina saw the arrival of the undertakers as confirmation that the cruel rumors of what Chamberlain had promised to Hitler were obviously true.

After the travesty of the Runciman mission there was no reason to rely on the British. But here was the envoy of the republic's closest ally following behind the English diplomat like a frightened mouse. Drtina had been a lawyer long before agreeing to assist his long-time compatriot as a personal secretary. Drtina could read opposing counsel well and sensed that de Lacroix had no confidence in the brief he was to present this day. No surprise that the undertaker Drtina overheard the most from the other room was Newton. The conversation was not a pleasant one. Beneš was clearly agitated, his voice taking on a hard edge Drtina rarely experienced. At one point he plainly heard Newton argue that the Czechoslovak government accept the transfer of an unspecified amount of territory to Germany. Newton also had the gall to demand an immediate acceptance of these vile terms as Mister Chamberlain had an appointment to keep with Hitler later in the week. At that further insult Drtina was pleased to hear Beneš' snarl at Newton to be silent. Beneš was a democratically elected president of a constitutional government. There would be no reply without further consultation with his government and parliament. There was a long break with no discussion then the door opened.

"Make your choice then," Newton directed back at the president. "Reject our proposal and you will be at war with Germany. A large percentage of your population will be butchered and your ancient capital will lie in ruins. Your actions will precipitate a general European war and the international community will rightly label you, President Beneš, as the warmonger. Accept our proposal and His Majesty's government, and the French government, will guarantee Czechoslovak national security against any further demands by the Third Reich."

"Forgive me if I am doubtful of the value of such a guarantee," Beneš shook a document clutched in his hand at the envoys. "What of the treaty guarantees already in my possession. They have proven to be worthless. Furthermore, what your governments propose is woefully naive if you believe it will solve the crisis. Far from it! This so-called solution of yours will ultimately prove to be no more than a stage towards the eventual domination of Czechoslovakia by Germany. The truth of the matter is, that after all of my efforts and the efforts of my government to reasonably resolve this crisis, we are being abandoned."

"Good day," was all the undertakers could manage following such a summation and they swiftly made their escape.

Without further comment, Beneš walked over to Drtina and handed him the document typed on the blue stationary of the British legation.

"Please have this translated as soon as possible for the cabinet ministers who do not read English" Disgusted, and lacking desire to say anything more, the president returned to his suite.

Drtina's heart sank as he read the blue pages. Not long thereafter as he dictated his version in Czech to a staff typist, Drtina noticed tears were welling up under her eyes. With fingers busy tapping on keys the young woman could not wipe away the teardrops before they fell on the paper below. They were tears for the nation.

25. COERCION

Czech broadsheet decries the Anglo/French ultimatum

SEPTEMBER 20, 1938
HOSPODA – DEJVICE DISTRICT, PRAHA

It was as if every Czechoslovak in the capital was holding their breath. On the street it was common knowledge what ultimatum the French and British governments had delivered the previous afternoon. Bulloch had it on good authority that President Beneš had been in consultation with his cabinet ministers continuously since then with no break. That had to be twenty-five hours ago at least. Thanks to the newspaper reports there was no mystery about what Beneš and his government were debating. If they accepted those terms those men would have a revolution on their hands, Petra was quite definite on that point and Bulloch had no reason to doubt her.

After Bulloch's last little fact-finding jaunt west Petra had spent hours debriefing him. There was no hiding from her since she had long ago claimed his apartment as her own. As there was little in what he had observed on his journeys that could be considered sensitive, Bulloch gave Petra what she wanted until the girl was satisfied.

While the country waited to hear how Beneš' government replied to the Anglo-French plan, Bulloch had a chance to escape out of town with Petra. She loved riding out of the city on the back of the BMW and Bulloch was rather fond of the way her arms wrapped tightly around him. Heavy work on the embassy shelter would not start until tomorrow and arrangements with Chapin to ship the embassy's women staff out of the country were proceeding well. Bulloch didn't know when he would get another opportunity to spirit Petra away before all hell broke loose so he told her to be ready for him to pick her up at work.

With so many private cars requisitioned for army use there was plenty of parking for the motorcycle close to the hospoda. No sooner had Bulloch set the kickstand than a military policeman approached pointing at the BMW. It wasn't the first time someone had attempted to confiscate the motorcycle. Bulloch had the drill down by heart now and had his embassy credentials ready by the time the officer reached him. "United States Embassy property, this vehicle is not to be touched."

The officer snatched the embassy documents to examine each page thoroughly. "Very well, your papers are in order. Don't leave the motorcycle unattended for very long. The way things are going it might disappear."

"Thanks for the advice," Bulloch took back his documents. When they were safely stashed in his jacket pocket he dashed inside.

Petra was wiping down a table when the door opened and Bulloch stepped inside. She ran up and kissed him sweetly on the lips. "I won't be long, my kapitán. Have a beer while I finish up with my customers."

The place wasn't especially busy that evening but Bulloch was sure the joint never had been louder. A dozen animated discussions were going on and all of them were political. Bulloch found a sliver of space at the bar and leaned his torso against the edge. One fellow at a nearby table was attracting quite a crowd. Then again he was louder than the rest. Bulloch sensed there was someone uncomfortably close on his blind side.

"Welcome back to Prague, Captain Bulloch," Furst addressed the attaché in that politely sinister fashion of his.

"Hello yourself," Bulloch shot glanced at the owner of the voice.

"I was hoping our paths would cross last week in the west," Furst was curious what exactly the American did on his forays.

"So you got to see the dust-up first-hand." It was too early in the conversation for Bulloch to give away much.

"You could call it that," Furst was equally obscure.

"Not where I was. The party kind of fizzled early," Bulloch wondered what the intelligence officer had been up to.

"That seems to be a common complaint," Furst was proud at how they had locked down the Sudeten unrest yet he felt unfulfilled. "Personally, I would have preferred to put my service pistol to much further use."

"That is a sentiment I can appreciate," Bulloch had found a least one thing both men shared in common. "Any word yet on how your government will respond to London and Paris... or when?"

"The president likes to leave no stone unturned before making a decision. The when is difficult to predict. The answer is not. He will reject their proposal," Furst sounded very confident in his assessment.

"You are sure of that?" Bulloch still had his doubts. "They have been talking an awfully long time."

"The British and French deserve to wait to receive their rejection," Furst could imagine far worse sorrows to mete out to those supposed allies.

"I doubt they will take a rejection lying down with Chamberlain going off to meet Hitler this week," Bulloch decided to draw the intelligence man out. "What do you think Beneš will do then?"

Furst pointed to the loudest man in the room Bulloch had noticed before. "I believe that one has it about right."

Bulloch turned his attention to the fellow who had just pounded his fist on the table.

"There is no question that we will fight!" the loud one implored. "The first German soldier to cross our frontier will be shot. It is impossible for the Czechs to agree to these proposals. The loss of this territory would mean the end of our country. Hitler will not be satisfied with the Sudetenland. He will demand the whole of Bohemia. We should fight now rather than being wiped out piece by piece."

"Who is that guy," Bulloch was curious about the rabble-rouser.

"Him... that is President Beneš' nephew," Furst nonchalantly turned back to his beer.

HAUPTBAHNHOF, LEIPZIG

The looks he was getting made him feel like a dustbowl Okie, lone suitcase in hand, looking for a job in Central California. Four days without a shower will do that to a fella. The police sergeant back in Plauen was too much in a hurry to get rid of Endicott to arrange for such a courtesy. The hell with him anyway... Endicott had seen plenty and had written the whole piece in his head dozens of times on the train ride up to Leipzig. Now all he needed was to find a phone out of earshot of any nosy cops. The question was where? The train station was so cavernous you could fit a damn Zeppelin in the place. Endicott could probably walk the length of what looked to be the largest train station in Europe and not find an out-of-the-way phone.

He did spot a nearby newsstand, however. With the money he had changed back in Plauen, Endicott could afford to pick up a few papers. There was no escaping the German rags and their sensational headlines:

> *Women and Children Mowed Down*
> *Poison Gas Attack on Aussig?*
> *Extortion, Plundering, Shooting*
> *New Czech Murders of Germans*
> *Czech Terror in Sudeten German Land!*

Soon enough Endicott found some English language dailies – mostly British papers. Endicott scanned the headlines and bit his tongue in frustration. He had missed plenty since Friday. Chamberlain was about to scurry back to report to Hitler. This time near Cologne. And it was going to happen tomorrow or the next day. Then there were the Czechs who were still chewing on the rubbish the limey prime minister had brought home from Berchtesgaden. Endicott whistled, annoying the Germans standing beside him. The real Anglo-French plan was worse than the rumors he had read in print. This called for a change of plan. Endicott decided right there on the spot that he was going to this Bad Godesberg resort town. Why not, he was half way there already. Okay, the whole trudging across the border with a rifle barrel pointed at the back of his head and getting locked up for days all really stunk, but maybe providence was shining on him after all. The rest of the bunch back in Prague wouldn't be able to get to Cologne in time but Endicott damn well could.

Endicott paid for the papers then whirled around to locate a sign showing the way to the ticketing windows. When he spotted what he was looking for he set off in that direction. The new plan was to buy a ticket for the night train to Cologne. He needed only enough time here in Leipzig to file his stories to the Berlin bureau. The first was his exclusive on being kidnapped by the Sudeten Freikorps. The second was a report on the German army build-up at the border. That second piece could land him in some hot water with the Nazis but by the time the story ran the show in Godesberg would be in full swing. Maybe the party goons would be too busy to care. That would allow Endicott to report from Bad Godesberg then beat it out of the country before his temporary visa ran out. He was running a risk but a slew of big stories would be a huge feather in his cap.

Endicott decided cut out his visit to the U.S. consulate. There was no time to waste and he had no desire to endure the kinds of complications that came with visiting bureaucrats. Scrutinizing the departure board, Endicott figured he could fit in the phone call to the bureau in Berlin plus checking into a cheap hotel near the station to clean up and change clothes. He was starving but could keep his growling stomach in check until he could eat on the train to Cologne. If his luck held Chamberlain wouldn't arrive until Thursday, which would give Endicott a day to get acquainted with his new surroundings.

Yeah, he was top of the world now. Maybe someone would offer him one of those cushy radio jobs like Shirer had with CBS. Wouldn't that be a turn of fortune? Endicott even felt like giving Sylvie a smack on the lips for setting him up. That broad was going to hate herself silly for giving him the leg up like this. Read it and weep, kid.

CZECHOSLOVAK MOTORIZED BRIGADE, NEAR EGER

It could have been worse, at least their brigade had been kept whole. Capka's company alone could have very easily been reformed into several ready units without motorized infantry or artillery. He suspected Srom was largely responsible for the brigade remaining intact when so many others had been subdivided. The ready units were useful and even Capka would now admit to their being necessary. The rapid response in quelling the civil disorder by the Sudetens directly after Hitler's Nürnberg address proved the strategy was sound. But in the last few days his company was encountering much more organized and much better equipped irregulars. Hardened positions with multiple machine gun posts were becoming commonplace with this Sudeten Freikorps. A platoon of his had even captured one of their officers and Capka was sure the man was a Wehrmacht regular.

The heavier fighting was good for his men. Against a foe almost as dangerous as a regular army, Capka's tankers were granted an opportunity to build needed communication and joint tactical skills with the rest of the brigade. Every ounce of operational experience between his tanks, their motorized ground troops and the big guns was essential. That would be a distinct advantage in the battles to come. The Germans had theory up the ass but it would be Capka's men who would rule the moment of decision. How had de Gaulle put it so long ago: *A tool of ruthlessness and suddenness that will take whatever is required, wherever it is needed and with all speed.* Capka had thought about the French officer a great deal in recent weeks. He wished they could speak together again and wondered whether the man would even remember the young Czech who had challenged him in class.

The last Capka had heard, de Gaulle was still a colonel and he liked to think that man would be leading a brigade as the French broke through Hitler's puny West Wall and lunged for the factories on the Ruhr. The French officer had published a new book earlier that year on the history of the French army. In those pages Capka could tell de Gaulle was still the same firebrand: *France was fashioned by the sword* is how the volume began. *From the day which marked the union of a strong government and a powerful army, France became a nation.* De Gaulle saw the world for what it was and would never stop goading those who saw otherwise. Capka was sure it had cost the man gravely with the politicians in Paris, the same politicians who were toying with the future of Capka's nation. A shame there were not more like de Gaulle to spar with them.

Capka's attention was torn away by more pressing issues such as keeping his tanks out of sight. What worried Capka were German dive bombers. His brigade was operating so close to the border there would be no warning of an aerial attack. Capka also had to wager that the local Henleinists who hadn't fled over to the German side were reporting the location of his tanks on a regular basis. So Capka kept moving the company around and made use of as much natural camouflage as possible. His men were getting quite good at covering up their Škodas. These efforts would be good for a day, maybe two at most. Much depended on the Freikorps. The Sudetens liked to make mischief at night. If they had action after dark the company would redeploy tomorrow.

At least the gloves were off with the Freikorps. The general staff had made it clear these irregulars were a serious threat and there were no directives to play nice with them. Capka's company already had two engagements with Freikorps units and he had much enjoyed the bloodying his platoons had delivered upon them. Hitler was not a patient man. The more of these Freikorps bastards they killed the more frustrated Hitler would become and the sooner he would send in his panzers. That suited Capka fine.

ASCH, SUDETENLAND

The army major was being annoyingly uncooperative in that completely civil way the Czechs had about them. In her case, the officer intended to put Sylvie on the back of the nearest truck and nothing she had to say about it counted for much. The army was pulling out and the decision was made: Sylvie was pulling out with them. She couldn't blame them for leaving since Asch was situated on this sliver of territory stuck up Germany's rear. That meant the Czechs had one small open corridor behind them that could easily be cut off. The Freikorps attacks had grown fierce and more frequent, too. The army had been able to handle the Henleinists but it made no sense digging in to hold an indefensible little town with no real military value. She got that. Sylvie just wanted to stick around to write up what happened after the Freikorps rolled in.

Her decision to stay put had been the right one. Sylvie had filed some great material in the last couple of days. Every night the Freikorps would turn up somewhere nearby and lob a bunch of grenades at one Czech post or another. The idea was to draw a Czechoslovak counter-attack and lead them into an ambush of machine gun nests. The Czechs were savvy to that trick though and usually turned up with armored cars or the tiny little machine gun tanks they often used. But all of that was prologue. Sylvie was sure the whole German army would be coming right through this little village and she wanted to watch that in person.

There was also the matter of Endicott. She had no idea what had happened to him. There was no sign of the goon. None of the soldiers or townspeople seemed to know what had happened to Endicott either. It had been days and Sylvie was sincerely beginning to worry about the guy. He was a big boy and could take care of himself. That didn't stop her from feeling guilty though. It didn't feel right leaving Asch without finding out if the dumb lug was okay.

"Listen, I am not a Czech national and you have no responsibility for my safety," Sylvie pleaded to the major.

"That is true. It is my safety that I am concerned about," the major was weary of the reporter's unwillingness to submit.

"What exactly do you mean?" Sylvie was confused.

"Mesdame, my orders are clear. This district is under martial law. Foreign correspondents are not allowed to publish reports from Czech territory under martial law without first submitting those reports for review by Czech authorities," the major explained patiently.

"But the army is leaving! How can you review my stories if you are all gone?" Sylvie figured she had found a loophole.

"Exactly. Whether there are Czech administrators here or not this remains Czech territory. You are not permitted to stay and submit reports if there are none of us here to check those reports. Therefore, you will leave," the major closed the issue.

"Oh what kind of wacky logic is that?" Sylvie was getting knocked silly boxing with this guy.

"The logic of inevitability," the major smugly folded his arms over his chest.

Right then Sylvie noticed a corporal march by, his rifle slung over a shoulder and both hands holding her travel case. By the looks of it the case had been hastily packed. Portions of a blouse were hanging out the side.

"Hey! Those are my things," Sylvie pointed at the enlisted man.

The corporal ignored her and tossed the travel case onto the back of the waiting Tatra. Distracted, Sylvie didn't pay attention to the officer as he stepped behind the reporter, then very surely reached down and swooped her off her feet.

"Yes they are and you are leaving with them," the major announced.

"I don't want to go!" Sylvie flailed her legs and arms to no avail.

"We can't have you becoming separated with your belongings, can we?" the major dropped Sylvie's rump a bit roughly onto the bed of the troop transport. "Have a safe trip, mesdame."

The corporal shut the gate with a firm clank and latched it securely. Sylvie found herself sitting at the feet of a half dozen or so Czech civil servants staring at her like she was some rude child. Undaunted, she leapt to her feet with the intention of getting out... just as the driver put the truck into gear and accelerated. Sylvie's feet slipped out from under her and she found herself thrown right back down on her rear. "Ow! That hurt."

The road was bumpy, uneven and not good for getting one's footing. Sylvie looked behind her and saw one open place on the bench. Reaching back for support, she grabbed a hold of the closest wood stake and pulled herself up onto the bench next to a pudgy, middle-aged Czech woman.

"It's for the best," the plump neighbor consoled the reporter.

"Oh please... I've been in worse scrapes than this, sister," she stood up and raised her fist in the air. "That guy hasn't seen the last of Sylvie Anderson!"

Sylvie glanced ahead and behind the truck. They were moving fast down the rutted road, which made the ride extremely uncomfortable. She could also see they had an armored car and motorcycle escort at point and at the rear. There was no way Sylvie was getting away even if she managed to jump off the back. That would only get her injured in the process. Wherever they were destined she was stuck for the duration. In looking around Sylvie noticed that the landscape was changing. It had been fairly open near Asch but the foliage and tree lines were getting denser the further along they went. As long as she was stuck, Sylvie sat back down on the bench and let her mind wander a bit. She observed the sky was actually rather pretty this late in the day.

Somewhere not far off Sylvie half recognized the crack-crack-crack of heavy machine gun fire that sounded like one of the older Czech models. Just as her brain processed the command to turn her head in the direction of the gunfire, Sylvie felt the blast of an explosion without really hearing it. The truck lurched violently to the left and Sylvie had the odd sensation of being catapulted upside down into the air. Soon the reporter perceived she wasn't flying anymore. Her vision focused long enough to make out a very pretty wildflower swaying in the breeze close to her, right before everything wiped to black just like in a Hollywood picture.

FOREIGN MINISTRY – HRADČANY, PRAHA

The French and British ministers were ushered into his office like two misbehaving children. Unlike the president, Krofta had made them cool their heels for a time. The two were decidedly anxious as it was close to eight o'clock at night and their governments were displeased at having no reply to the plan that had been presented to Beneš yesterday afternoon. When Newton and de Lacroix had pestered him earlier in the day for an answer, Krofta had sent them away then and he cared little now if Chamberlain was forced to postpone his travel to Godesberg. On top of his desk were two envelopes, each containing the official response of the Czechoslovak government. As a slight to the arrogant one, Newton, the diplomatic notes were both written in French. Neither did he invite the two envoys to sit as both of them were undeserving of such niceties. They would stand and take what he was about to deliver as men.

"Gentlemen," Krofta let his disfavor with the envoys show openly as an aide handed the envelopes to the diplomats. "The government of the Republic of Czechoslovakia has rejected the Anglo-French plan. The acceptance of this proposal would result in the complete mutilation of the Czechoslovak State in every respect and would not lead to peace. The international guarantee of revised frontiers that you propose is no deterrent. Czechoslovakia already possesses international guarantees. Despite these guarantees you propose Germany will acquire the Sudeten territories at no cost. The outcome is that you will have given Hitler every encouragement to demand more territory wherever he pleases. You would put Czechoslovakia, sooner or later, under the complete domination of Germany."

"You cannot seriously be taking this position, sir," Newton interrupted.

"This is not a conversation, minister," Krofta cut off Newton coldly. "Even if my government was inclined to accede to your ultimatum, to do so is impossible. May I remind you this is a democratic republic. Only parliament may decide questions pertaining to national borders. There is one legal option for a speedy resolution of Germany's territorial demands. By our 1925 treaty with Germany territorial disputes can be submitted to arbitration. My government would be bound by any judgment that might be pronounced. Arbitration would forestall conflict and it would make possible an honorable solution worthy of all interested parties."

"My government will not accept this rejection of its efforts to secure European peace," Newton shook his envelope at Krofta.

"And what have you to say?" Krofta ignored the Englishman to focus on the visibly uncomfortable de Lacroix.

"I... I am in a terrible position," de Lacroix stammered. "On behalf of France, my government has associated itself with our British allies."

"Then tell your government," Krofta stepped within inches of the Frenchman, "Czechoslovakia has been bound to France by devoted friendship and an alliance no Czechoslovak government and no Czechoslovak will ever violate. We still believe in the great French nation. For reasons already stated we appeal to France again and for the last time that she reconsider her opinion. It is our conviction that we are not only defending Czechoslovak interests but also the interests of our friends. The truth of the matter is that at this decisive moment, not only is the fate of Czechoslovakia in question, but also the fate of France."

The embarrassment Krofta's words provoked in de Lacroix left him no words to voice in disagreement. Newton, however, was about to offer a retort when the Czech foreign minister preempted him.

"That is all, gentlemen," Krofta made it obvious the audience was over.

ASCH, SUDETENLAND

They approached the town on foot as quietly as possible. At least the deserters from the Czech army possessed the discipline of military training. He kept them close behind. The rest were little better than an armed mob. The hauptsturmführer had ordered them to hang back a far as possible. When they protested he told them they were guarding the rear. That was a lie but the captain did not need one of these fools to start a firefight with a dog or a tree to alert the whole district of their approach. That was the consequence of throwing together the Sudeten Freikorps in one week's time. Fourteen days ago he was happily attached to his SS platoon. Tonight he was slipping into Czechoslovakia with this rabble armed with ancient Austrian weapons and orders to seize Asch. The last report they had received promised that the Czechs had pulled out. The hauptsturmführer did not quite believe it. Often times these reports were more optimistic than accurate. The night before his unit had gotten its nose bloodied by a Czech shock unit that was not supposed to be where it was.

Hauptsturmführer Horst silently motioned for his men to stop. As the order made its way back through the line he kneeled long enough to bring his field glasses up for a look around. There was no movement ahead and a few lights could be seen from buildings in Asch. With no sign of Czech military about perhaps tonight they had gotten lucky. At least there was a tree line handy to mask their approach. The hauptsturmführer gestured for the rest to follow him. As they weaved through the trees the hauptsturmführer spotted someone ahead and signaled for an immediate halt. Looking through the long-range lens' he made out a guard with a rifle. The hauptsturmführer whispered to his two best Sudetens to go check the guard out. Before long they had returned with the man. It was a local SdP member wearing a Swastika armband and bearing an antique hunting rifle.

"It's all I had left after the Czechs took everything," the local man lamented.

"Understood," the hauptsturmführer was concerned with more important matters. "Is it true? Have the Czechs abandoned Asch?"

"Yes, they left yesterday… maybe they are as far back as Eger now. We have not heard for sure yet," the Henleinist told all he knew.

"Good enough. Listen carefully. I require a defensible location to set up my headquarters. Preferably not the same location the Czech commander used. That would be too obvious. Can you direct me to such a place?" the hauptsturmführer hoped the fellow had some military sense.

"There is a good position near here that's close to everything. Very old with a heavy stone foundation that will suit your needs well," the local party leader promised.

"Excellent, take us there immediately," the SS commander was pleased. "We have much to do. First we must set up radio contact then my men will to take up positions securing the town. You will be pleased to know Herr Henlein will be setting up a provisional government in Asch. And this time he means to stay. In addition to additional Freikorps units that will be arriving, two SS battalions have been ordered to lend their support. And they are bringing anti-tank cannons and artillery with them.

CZECHOSLOVAK EMBASSY
AVENUE CHARLES FLOQUET, PARIS

When the message came he was still up reading a book in the study. There would be no sleep for Osušky as long as this direct channel connecting Chamberlain and Hitler was operating. Between the efforts of the prime minister and that no good Bonnet, Osušky had to remain vigilant. Oddly, the French foreign minister could easily been mistaken for a member of Chamberlain's cabinet given the vigor that devil devoted to supporting the English leader's venal agenda. Osušky was still livid at Bonnet's conduct earlier in the week at the Quai d'Orsay. Later that very same day a French parliamentarian had revealed that Bonnet was under strict instructions not to exert pressure on Praha to accept the Anglo-French plan, an instruction Bonnet had repeatedly violated to Osušky's face and thereafter through Bonnet's minions operating in Praha. This knowledge only infuriated Osušky the more. Czechoslovakia had friends in the French government. From them Osušky had learned the extent of Bonnet's orchestration of lies and deceit – seizing on military reports critical of the Czech Army and misrepresenting positive analysis from none other than Generál Gamelin. At every turn, if there was an opportunity to work against the interests of the Czechoslovak Republic, Bonnet embraced that opportunity with verve.

Krofta had alerted Osušky Tuesday night that the government back home had justly rejected the Anglo-French Plan. But in the last few minutes a courier had delivered a note, the content of which was a warning from another friendly source describing how that rejection had not gone down well with the British, who had set up a late night telephone conference between Chamberlain and Daladier. The short of it was the Czech rejection was itself being summarily rejected. Minister Newton was being sent back to the castle before dawn to threaten President Beneš. He could either accept the Anglo-French plan or Britain and France would wash their hands of Czechoslovakia. If Germany invaded, France would not honor her treaty obligations. The Czechoslovaks would suffer the consequences alone. All the more galling, the note informed Osušky that Bonnet had ordered de Lacroix to accompany Newton and confirm France endorsed the latest ultimatum.

The note was not signed but it did not need to be. Osušky recognized the hand as Mandel's. The last tantalizing item was that Mandel, Renaud and possibly more of Daladier's cabinet intended to resign over such treatment of France's most loyal ally, especially after the cabinet had instructed Bonnet that there was to be no such pressure tactics. Osušky knew for a fact that these ministers had interrogated Daladier point-blank during the afternoon:

> If the Czechs said no to the Anglo-French Plan would the premier cow to a German attack on her ally? Was it true the premier had informed Prague that neither Britain nor France would stand by Czechoslovakia if their proposals were refused?

To each probing Daladier had replied, *non,* and all the while Bonnet was carrying out every atrocity the premier denied. The burning question for the ministers was did Daladier know and approve of his foreign minister's actions. Resignations had been tendered for far less. If they did resign this was good news. The Daladier government might fall and all of Bonnet's dastardly efforts might yet be derailed. President Beneš had to be wakened and informed of these developments before Newton and de Lacroix arrived at the Castle. Osušky picked up the telephone receiver and instructed the night operator to place a call to Beneš immediately.

MALA STRANA DISTRICT, PRAHA

Before they had gotten the news of President Beneš' rejection of the Anglo-French proposal, the foreign correspondents had been milling about the lobby of the Ambassador for the next shoe to drop. The Foreign Ministry runner to the hotel had felt sure that an announcement would come by noon. When noon had come and gone Sanderson had cooked up a strategy. Far better to work their way up to the Foreign Ministry building at the Castle to catch officials and ordinary people along the way. Perhaps an interview with Mister Krofta could be had after the announcement had been made. Ros had endorsed the scheme immediately. Although Sanderson suspected it had less to do with the merits of his proposal and more the fact that the lovely Miss Talmadge had no patience for remaining stationary for longer than five minutes.

The night had been quiet and warm, which was welcome medicine for a dramatic and frenzied day. The entire capital had been on a knife's edge waiting in suspense for the government to make its decision. People had left their jobs and homes, unable to work or play or study while the fate of their nation hung in the balance between two simple words: yes or no. The average Czech on the street desperately longed for his president to step onto Wenceslas Square, strike a defiant pose, and declare in the most forceful oratory that the British and French proposals were rejected outright. In their hearts they knew Edvard Beneš' was a true patriot, but not the fierce protector of the Republic they yearned for. When the news spread on the streets that the government had, in fact, rejected the Anglo-French plan after more than twenty-four hours of deliberations, the people were satisfied the president and his ministers had stood firm. Yet that satisfaction was tempered with a deep wariness. Why should it take so long to refuse such onerous demands when one minute should be sufficient? They feared their president was sitting on a fence and could still manage to fall on the wrong side.

While Sanderson and Ros were some of the first reporters to learn of Beneš' formal rejection that night, they did not get their interview with Minister Krofta, however. That setback did not deter Ros. The enterprising woman managed to pull together an audience on the spot with Dr. Gottwald, president of Czechoslovak Communist Party, whom she had been introduced to with Sylvie. Gottwald should have been a thespian. The man could dominate a stage with the best of them, and was never in a pinch for dialogue. Tonight he was understandably harsh on Beneš... for hours. Yet the message Gottwald pounded on again and again during their visit was defiance: *We shall not stand by and let our Republic be destroyed. We shall defend ourselves in the sure knowledge that the Soviet Union will be loyal to her treaty obligations.* That last part Sanderson had quizzed him on repeatedly. Yet Gottwald had never wavered. Stalin would help even if France did not. Ros reminded him that the USSR was not treaty bound to assist Czechoslovakia if France did not act first but the doctor was sure it did not matter. When cornered he would pour another round of delicious cognac and then change the subject.

When they left it was very late and Dr. Gottwald's cognac had left them in grand spirits. A lovely night to be walking arm-in-arm in the company of a lovely woman down the gas lit Thunovská. Before long they were passing the entrance to the British embassy, a narrow side street off Thunovská that led to the walled compound of what once was an old palace. Some say Mozart had even stayed there. At this early hour there strangely was a sedan waiting with its engine running.

"Well then... look at that," Sanderson stopped to observe the automobile.

"Oh forget that bunch," Ros tugged on his jacket sleeve. "You have no business there anymore."

"What are you going on about?" Sanderson stood firm.

"You're one of us now," Ros happily poked at his American press credential. "Remember, it ain't safe to be British in this city anymore. You can thank me later."

"Right," Sanderson caught on. "No, I meant the automobile. Rather late for one to be on standby."

The compound door swung open. Not long after Minister Newton emerged in a dark suit that was hard to see. The driver got out of the vehicle and opened the rear door for him. Once Newton seated himself the driver closed the door, got back behind the wheel, then drove past the reporters and turned right to go up toward the Castle.

"No kidding, something *is* up," Ros realized Sanderson was right for a change.

"You suppose he is heading up to pester President Beneš?" Sanderson feared the worst of his nation's envoys at the moment.

"C'mon, let's find out," Ros pulled Sanderson by the arm back up Thunovská.

PRAŽSKÝ HRAD, PRAHA

It was going to be a busy night. First the two foreign envoys had turned up unannounced at two o'clock in the morning and now there appeared to be a government issue Praga Super-Piccolo approaching the gate at high speed. The two palace guards at the main gate were already a suspicious lot. Many were legionnaires who served in the Great War where fighting your way home in the middle of a Russian civil war tended to reward the eternally vigilant over the careless... and a speeding Praga meant trouble. As they were considering whether it was time to un-sling rifles from over their shoulders, the vehicle skidded to a stop before the gate. The guards recognized the driver as a man from the Palace staff, and the president's personal secretary as the passenger who exploded from the rear seat like a shell from a barrel.

"The French and British ministers... are they still here?" Drtina rushed up to the legionnaires.

"Yes sir," the senior guard grew concerned for the president's safety.

"God help us," Drtina pushed in through the main gate.

It was near three o'clock and Drtina feared he was too late. The president had told him to go home after the government's rejection had been delivered by Krofta around eight o'clock. The last two days had been a complete blur of ministerial deliberations and everyone was physically drained, especially Beneš. Yet Drtina could not rest. All evening long his instincts nagged at him that something was amiss. When he had rung up the castle operator to check that all was still quiet that is when he was informed that the undertakers had roused the president from his bed. This meant Beneš had been at their mercy for almost an hour. Drtina would apologize later to the driver for having prodded him to such reckless speeds through the vacant streets of the city.

Throwing open the staff door leading to the office wing, Drtina hurried inside in the direction of the president's office. He was furious that there was no one to support Beneš against whatever coercion the envoys were wielding. It was the old legal advocate in him... his friend required a defender. Drtina felt no hesitation as he knocked solidly on Beneš' office door. It was a breach of protocol yet necessary under the circumstances. The voices from inside paused as footsteps approached. A weary looking Beneš slowly opened the door.

"Mister President, would you please step outside for a moment," Drtina commanded more than requested.

"Of course," Beneš complied, shutting the door behind him.

Moving them a short distance away from the envoys on the other side of the wall, Drtina drew close to the president. "I am sorry for the intrusion, Edvard. This is not an hour for protocol, however. What are those two demanding of us?"

"Complete submission. Nothing less," Beneš admitted. Chamberlain and Daladier refuse to accept our rejection of their proposals in the face of an imminent German invasion. I am instructed to withdrawal our formal rejection and urgently consider an alternative that takes account of the realities. If I refuse to do so immediately and unconditionally Britain and France will wash their hands of us. Czechoslovakia will stand alone and France will break her legal obligations."

"No, they must be bluffing," Drtina knew such tactics well.

"Quite the opposite. I demanded this in writing from de Lacroix, and after a telephone call to Bonnet, de Lacroix provided me this ultimatum in writing," Beneš confirmed by pulling a piece of paper out of his pocket and giving it to Drtina to read.

"Edvard, send them away. You have seen the streets and you have heard the people. If we accept this garbage the British and French are peddling there will be a revolution in the country. The people will not stand for it. What then?" Drtina was convinced the war would happen with or without Beneš leading the fight.

"If there is a revolution then we will have to deal with it," Beneš was sadly resigned to his fate. "We will speak more of that later."

With that, Beneš tiredly patted Drtina on the shoulder signaling the interruption was concluded. He then walked back toward his office and the waiting envoys.

26. INSURRECTION

The Hotel Dreesen on the banks of the Rhine River

SEPTEMBER 21, 1938
HEADQUARTERS
SERVICE DE RENSEIGNEMENT, PARIS

Well then, what surprises were in store today? The players to watch were the Poles and Hungarians. Mister Chamberlain's finely wrought concessions to Hitler might not survive the chicanery of Warsaw and Budapest. That is if Bonnet's strong-arming of Prague proved successful, of which there was yet no guarantee. His man at the embassy in Prague had reported that de Lacroix and Newton had debated with Beneš until the four o'clock hour, leaving thereafter without an answer still. Beneš would take hours to argue options with his ministers so Thollon had taken the opportunity to break away. Time enough for a needed shower and a change of clothes after a very long day. On his return Thollon had also taken time to peruse the morning papers and procure a small snack to maintain his stamina. By eight-thirty he had arrived back refreshed and ready for another tedious day. Thollon diverted his course to visit the new lieutenant in the operations department, a very promising young fellow.

"Is Warsaw up to anything this morning?" Thollon inquired with as much gravity as asking about a new cafe down the boulevard.

"Yes colonel, Foreign Minister Beck is sending this out to all of the legations," the lieutenant handed a file to Thollon. "We intercepted that about an hour ago."

"Excellent, that will do fine. Continue on lieutenant." Thollon removed the document and read the main points on the way to his office. He had suspected this. Beck was informing his ministers that Poland would make a formal demand for the return of Teschen from Czechoslovakia and that this demand would be made of Beneš this very afternoon. There was blood in the water and the sharks were circling the wounded prey. Thollon suspected that Beneš and Krofta would not be surprised by the demand. The previous day Hitler had summoned the Polish and Hungarian representatives to speak with him, separately of course. Thollon had no doubts about the reason behind Hitler's timing. The German chancellor was surely going to blindside poor Chamberlain. The prime minister expected to deliver the Sudetenland on a platter and Hitler would inform him in the clearest terms that Polish and Hungarian demands must be satisfied promptly as well.

Such confidence in this scenario was justified since Thollon had seen an intercept of the report Polish ambassador Lipski in Berlin had submitted to Beck following his audience with Hitler. Hitler wanted Czechoslovakia assimilated and done away with. He had been most frank with Lipski on this count. All at once with military force was the chancellor's preference. Yet he was not opposed to the goal being accomplished in stages as long as Chamberlain was openly acceding to his wishes without need for a fight. The remaining Czechoslovak territory would come later and Hitler was happy to see Warsaw and Budapest regain their countrymen and join in the dismemberment. These added demands were sure to upend Chamberlain's apple cart when the two met in Godesberg. That rendezvous would most likely be tomorrow unless Prague's obstinacy continued.

Thollon could immediately forward these Polish memoranda to the premier, who would likely sit on them for a while. Thollon could similarly forward them to Reynard, Mandel, Champetier de Ribes and Campinchi. These ministers would use the intelligence as a tool to bring down Daladier and Bonnet. They were already livid at Bonnet's subterfuge in his dealings with Prague. They would seize on the Polish documents as evidence that Chamberlain was promising concessions in France's name that the full French government had never endorsed yet the premier had obviously conceded. Thollon was not convinced now was the time for the government to fall, however. Better to wait until Chamberlain was about to start his conference with Hitler then forward the documents to all concerned. The delay would only be twenty-four to forty-eight hours at most. Timing was everything.

Then there was Général Gamelin. Thollon wanted to give the old warhorse the opportunity to exact his own demands of the government. Gamelin was most displeased with Foreign Minister Bonnet. The latter had taken the général's report on French and Czechoslovak preparedness and seriously misrepresented Gamelin's words during the conference in London after Berchtesgaden. Bonnet had over-emphasized the weak points of the French forces reviewed in the report and had suppressed Gamelin's favorable conclusions. Thollon had learned from an associate attached to the War Ministry that Gamelin had chosen today to press

Daladier on a change of policy. The general rightly argued that France's diplomacy throughout the summer and into the current crisis had been weak in reacting to Hitler's bellicosity. As if the republic was itself weak and possessing of little leverage to deter Germany. That was an absurdity to Gamelin. Such weak diplomacy was completely out of proportion to France's military strength. So today the good général would insist of the premier that at least a partial mobilization of the army was in order to add teeth to Chamberlain's negotiating position. Gamelin was naively under the illusion that Chamberlain had intentions of negotiating firmly with Hitler. That did not detract, however, from the soundness of the strategy Gamelin intended to leverage upon Premier Daladier.

Godesberg would be a mess Thollon was sure of that. Therefore, dropping the Polish memorandum into his desk drawer for a day was the prudent measure for now. The government must remain intact, focused and operational as Chamberlain's initiative fell to pieces. But that was for tomorrow. Today, Thollon expected some more surprises to surface. Comrade Stalin would not appreciate being left out of such momentous European diplomacy. The Soviets would surely play a wildcard today to remind Berlin, Paris and London that Moscow demanded respect.

HOTEL PETERSBERG
KOENIGSWINTER, DEUTCHLAND

The hotel was huge, swank establishment sitting on top of a hill with a commanding view overlooking the Rhine and the charming little hamlet of Bad Godesberg that was about to make history. At least that's how Endicott thought he would set up the story he would file later. The train to Cologne had gotten him in the area with loads of time to spare. Lots of other hacks were making the journey so it wasn't much trouble to tag along on a ride the rest of the way into Godesberg. So far he had yet to run into other Hearst correspondents though. First order of business had been getting registered with the German propaganda goons. On the plus side they were putting everyone up for free at a place on the river aptly called the Godesberger. Much less tony accommodations than at the Petersberg here, but free was free, and Endicott was nursing his small cash reserve for as far as it would go. The pricey Petersberg was where Chamberlain and his people were staying.

After setting up at the Godesberger, Endicott had checked out his options for filing copy back to the bureau. The Germans were making lots of phones and teletype machines available under the watchful eyes and ears of their propaganda people. But get this many reporters all clamoring for a connection out at the same time and it would be hard to interfere much. They probably would not have much incentive to make much of a stink either given the worldwide attention on the conference. Walking through town was a laugh. The Germans had the whole place plastered with swastikas and Union Jacks. Thousands of the emblems decorated walls and light poles, plus many more that were hung from lines strung across streets between buildings. The analogy in his head was of all the hoopla before an old-fashioned state wedding between monarchies. This was one honeymoon Endicott would rather not visualize in his head.

As long as he had hotels on the mind Endicott had gone to check out the Dreesen where Hitler was going to stay. Like the Godesberger, the Dreesen was a nondescript joint built of white brick and stucco right on the Rhine. Despite the chancellor reserving the whole place it was easy enough to walk in and check out the lobby. There was a crew setting up an area for radio broadcasts and Endicott wondered if Shirer would make it in from Prague. The set up crew was German and didn't seem to know. Endicott asked around and couldn't find anyone who could say for sure. A very friendly desk clerk did mention, however, that the restaurant and bar remained open to all if he wanted to come back later and wait. That struck him as rather strange. No one seemed to care much who was hanging around the big man's hotel. Such a relaxed atmosphere was not what Endicott had expected in a filthy dictatorship. It was the doorman who pointed out the Petersburg high up on the other side of the river when Endicott had asked where he could find Chamberlain's hotel. It had taken a ferry ride and bus but he had made it up here in less time than he had figured.

The decoration on display was much the same as everywhere else: Union Jacks and swastikas inside and outside. Going out the back entrance the hotel grounds were nestled amid the handsome green trees that lined the hillside. Endicott whistled as he spied down and spotted the Dreesen where he had just been. It had to be a thousand feet or more down below. Back inside the lobby and dining hall were lined with more flowers than Endicott had seen in a long while. Lots of pine tree branches too, although he didn't have a clue what the significance of those were. Endicott would have to ask since it might make for good color in his story. Meandering around the dining hall, Endicott was impressed with the gloss shine on the marble floors.

"Hey Charles!" a familiar voice called out from behind him.

Endicott tried to locate the direction of the voice. A few tables away he spotted Shirer. "Good to see you, Bill. I was hoping I'd find you around these parts. You staying here, Murrow must have deep pockets?"

"Oh no. I wish otherwise, but no. The truth is the Germans want to show off Chamberlain's suite upstairs and there was time for quick bite. Why don't you join me?"

"Don't mind if I do," Endicott found no reason to argue.

"The last time we talked you were in Asch but the border is closed. How did you get here, good man? Murrow had to fly me out to through a half-dozen neutral airports to get me here in time," Shirer embellished a bit.

"You can read it all in some paper today," Endicott boasted. "I was kidnapped by the Sudeten Freikorps and ended up on the German side. Once they let me go a couple of days ago I made a beeline for Cologne. You got to love the rail service in this country. "

"Glad to have you with us. That sounds like an adventure. Did they rough you up?" Shirer had bad memories of Vienna.

"You and me both," Endicott felt his ribs ache at the mention. "Nah, after I got passed off to some local police cooling my heels in a cell for several days was the worst of it. The authorities let me go and told me I had a couple of weeks to get out of the country so I headed here and arrived early this morning."

"Did you see any of the military build up?" Shirer leaned forward hoping for an eyewitness account.

"Plenty friend. I've never seen so many troops... tanks too. Thousands moving south and you could see them from the train to Leipzig. The Czechs will have their hands full," Endicott reckoned this was going to be a doozy of a war.

"All the reporters based here in Germany are saying the same thing. Hitler is betting everything he's got on the invasion. I don't think he's bluffing for Chamberlain either," Shirer wondered where he would broadcast from once the war started.

A German in a propaganda ministry uniform approached the table. "Mister Shirer, the tour of the prime minister's suite will take place in twenty minutes. Please meet us in the lobby at the time."

"Of course, thank you," Shirer checked his wristwatch.

"Notice how all of the Nazis are on their best behavior for this little show," Endicott had spotted a trend.

"Yes, they all are very sure of themselves. I don't like it one bit," Shirer did not trust friendly Nazis any more than the bellicose variety. "Say, want to tag along for the tour? I'm told the view is magnificent."

"Wouldn't miss it, buddy," Endicott was hoping he would get that invitation.

TRAFALGAR SQUARE, LONDON

The crowds were getting larger every day. The more these Britons thought about their prime minister subordinating himself to Hitler like a vanquished enemy the more they disliked the idea. No war had been fought, no battles lost, yet here was an overly anxious Mister Chamberlain publicly impatient to hurry off to the Rhine to deliver desperate and horrible concessions. None of these people on the street today yearned for war but they did see the essential error in yielding to a thug. Britain had not yielded to King Phillip, nor to Napoleon, why should she yield to the likes of an upstart dictator? Masaryk saw the change in the crowds and slowly he saw the change in the newspaper editorials. Support for peace at any price was waning.

In his hands Masaryk held the results of national polling that would be released tomorrow to coincide with Chamberlain's departure for Germany. These findings had been shared with him early as a courtesy and they filled Masaryk with vigor. Forty percent of the British public firmly opposed Chamberlain's policy. Nearly double the twenty-two percent who were in support. That left thirty-eight percent who were unsure of what the prime minister was about. This was amazing news. Masaryk's efforts to prod public opinion in favor of the Czechoslovak cause had helped but what this poll proved was that ordinary people in Great Britain were seeing the truth for what it was.

As much as Masaryk yearned for the freedom to speak freely to the thousands of good people assembling for the day's march down Whitehall he could not deliver the fiery oratory they would have appreciated. Masaryk was an envoy to the British government and it would be unseemly to bash those he was solemnly entrusted to serve. For that reason he had stayed away from these protestations at first as not to add fuel to those who opposed standing by his nation. But as it was strongly suggested to Masaryk that his presence alone would have a substantial impact upon the crowds, he had begun to attend to listen to the fiery speeches of these members of parliament and other well-intentioned souls. The most that Masaryk would permit himself to say was that all of Czechoslovakia appreciated this outpouring of support for a small nation in Central Europe and may God bless them all.

Some of the best oratory against Chamberlain was coming from Winston Churchill. That pugnacious fellow was a fount of winning slogans like: *The government is choosing between war and shame. They are choosing shame and they will get war too.* Masaryk held no illusions... Churchill was positioning himself for a run at the prime minister's job. Yet the man's potent oratory was genuine and greatly influenced the public mood. Masaryk had stayed in close contact with Churchill and his allies in the opposition within Chamberlain's own party: men such as Anthony Eden. The latter was a behind-the-scenes operator with strong connections within the Foreign Office and other ministries. The picture that Masaryk was getting from Eden and Churchill was that many in Chamberlain's own inner cabinet were wavering in their support of the prime minister's German policy. That was the message Masaryk had wired to President Beneš. After Krofta had informed Masaryk of the British and French counter ultimatum of early that morning, Masaryk had wasted no time in imploring Beneš to stand firm. If the president could hold out until at least the twenty-sixth, Chamberlain would come under severe fire at home. That is what Churchill and Eden wanted Beneš to know. Public support here for Czechoslovakia was growing like wildfire. The tables would turn if Beneš could just hold off making a formal decision on the Berchtesgaden plan for a few more days.

POLISH CONSULATE – KIEV, USSR

There were many ethnic Poles living in the Western Soviet Union. It had been an article of faith that one day Poland would reclaim them. Had they not beaten back the Bolsheviks and the Germans after the Great War? The communists would misstep... it was only a question of how long before that rotten edifice consumed itself in vile avarice and bloodshed. The executions continued with dozens of innocent lives extinguished each day. Some not so innocent it was true but life was cheap in the USSR. As ethnic Poles made up a large portion of the population in Kiev many sought out members of the Polish legation at great danger to themselves – even minor and insignificant staff such as him – with information damaging to the communists.

That's how Urbanowicz ended up with bruised knees and aching back muscles. He had left the consulate to buy some food for lunch. While minding his own business a passerby unexpectedly struck him with such force that Urbanowicz was thrown forward to the ground. The apologetic peasant was horrified at the accident. While helping Urbanowicz to his feet the man whispered a warning in Polish. As Urbanowicz was preoccupied with getting his footing the peasant disappeared. Smart man that one. Like every Pole at the consulate, Urbanowicz was shadowed by an NKVD officer every time he left the building. To maintain the facade Urbanowicz calmly purchased his lunch from the closest vendor before heading back to the consulate. He didn't break into a run until safely inside the walls and away from scrutiny.

Urbanowicz's scraped knees protested under his trousers as he hurried to the room the Dwójka had made its own many years ago. The military intelligence branch of the army had been operating in the Soviet Union from the moment diplomatic relations had normalized during the 1920s. Mostly concealed within consulates like this one in Kiev. The disheveled Urbanowicz burst through the doorway, caught his breath, and then slammed the door behind him.

The duty officer of the intelligence station appraised Urbanowicz severely for the interruption. "Why are you in such a state, young man?"

"A local Pole just knocked me down outside the consulate. He has seen with his own eyes... the majority of the Red Army garrison is preparing to depart Kiev. The first units are already moving out. Toward the west... toward home," Urbanowicz blurted out.

CABINET CHAMBERS
PRAŽSKÝ HRAD, PRAHA

The ministers had been debating what to do about the French ultimatum since the president had summoned them at close to five in the morning. All were showing signs of strain. General irritability, short tempers, and progressively foul moods were on display. The written demarche that de Lacroix had presented to President Beneš lay at the center of the table. Every possible course of action proposed during the long hours had failed to overcome the severe weight of the words on those still sheets of paper. Many of the men in this room had loved the French like a beloved patriarch and now their parent was casting them aside. So on top of the weighty issues of state they carried on their shoulders these men also carried a heavy burden in their hearts.

Although the British had crafted their current predicament it was the French who were the center of these deliberations. The French were the ones who bore the burden of obligations with Czechoslovakia. What did those harsh terms in writing really mean? What would the French really do if events escalated? Beneš had been focused on two possible strategies. Reject the ultimatum and risk the outcome, or accept the Anglo-French terms as a stalling tactic while hoping for a fortuitous change in circumstances as young Masaryk was predicting from London. Either of those two strategies shared one essential component: fending off a German invasion. The reports that Moravec was receiving from within Germany were uniform on that count. Hitler intended to occupy the Sudeten districts without need of further negotiation and to do so prior to October first. As London and Paris needed the shield of a formal negotiated settlement to protect them from political repercussions at home, an outcome Hitler was unlikely to wait for, there was every chance a Czech acceptance of the French ultimatum would be nullified by Hitler's impatience.

That was one of the topics that Moravec had been invited that afternoon to flesh out for the cabinet ministers plus the leaders of the senate and legislature. Beneš had invited the legislators since accepting the ultimatum without a vote in parliament would be unconstitutional and the president would need these leaders on board in that eventuality. Moravec laid out the facts for them succinctly. In many ways, there was little material difference between the Second Department's intelligence work and what the German newspapers were printing. What Moravec could give them was more substantial detail. He had definite information about the latest Wehrmacht unit concentration. For example, seven divisions were taking up new positions east of Dresden in the area of Zwickau and around Passau.

The wild card was Poland. The intentions of the Poles were a major question since they had been moving troops in along their side of the border for weeks. The cabinet session was even forced to pause that afternoon so that Beneš could confer with Krofta after the Polish envoy had delivered a formal demand that Teschen be handed over to Warsaw as part of any agreement with Germany on the Sudetenland.

When the meeting resumed Moravec was invited to discuss the second topic on his agenda. The USSR was bound by treaty to assist Czechoslovakia if Germany invaded. The difficulty was that the Soviets were not bound to act unless France acted first. The president had been seeking clarity with the Soviet envoy in Prague, and via staff in Moscow, if the USSR could be counted on to provide assistance in the absence of French action. Diplomatically, the Soviets were remaining coy in answering that vital question. It was up to Moravec to provide a more revealing assessment of Soviet intentions. "Gentlemen, to the question of whether Stalin will come to our aid without prior French action I cannot foretell. What I can impart with extreme clarity is that the Soviets are prepared and able to do so."

"How do you know that?" the senate leader questioned.

"Because in recent days General Jaroslav Fajfr has been in Moscow negotiating with the commanders of the Voyenno-Vozdushnye Sily at the behest of the Soviet government. Fajfr has secured an agreement whereby the Red Air Force will immediately dispatch seven hundred modern aircraft of various classes to airfields in Czechoslovakia. This is contingent on suitable airfield facilities with adequate anti-aircraft defenses being made available for these aircraft. To this end we will soon receive Soviet officers who will assist us in properly preparing these airfields near Košice, as well as other locations in Slovakia, for their planes. Once these squadrons are in the country and operational they will be available for defence of the republic."

The silence in the room was profound. The general consensus had always been that Soviet promises were many and determined actions would be few. As much as Moravec detested the communists, this time, their actions were bankable. But would President Beneš come to the same conclusion?

WENCESLAS SQUARE, PRAHA

The citizens of Prague were in a grim and bitter mood. People were so anxious that merchants were closing up early, schools were emptying out and factory workers were abandoning their machines. Rich and poor all seemed to feel milling about together to share their worries was the best course while waiting to hear how their government would respond to the pressure from Paris and London. The people expected their government to stand resolute against pressure and fight alone. The rumor that Dr. Beneš intended to resign rather than accept such onerous surrender terms, after which he would turn the country over to the army, was well worn. For those who fretted that the president would succumb to British and French pressure, talk of the army taking control and completely sacking the government from top to bottom was nearly as popular. Many Czechs felt revolution was the only answer and they wanted the armories opened up to take matters into their own hands.

But none of them had seen what Ros and Sanderson had seen... the British envoy calling upon President Beneš so early in the morning. As the afternoon dragged on the two reporters impatiently waited like everyone else to learn what Beneš would do in the end. Weaving through the huge crowd, joining conversations and listening to these people's hopes and fears at least gave the journalists something to do. The government was clamping down on the press. Many foreign newspapers were being confiscated and Czech papers were being censored. Ros and Sanderson had also found out that their international phone calls were being tapped. Each measure made it harder for them to do their jobs. Whatever was coming they hoped it would come soon.

Ros had other worries on her mind though. The border with Germany was enormous and the Henleinists had done a spiffy job at stirring up trouble up and down every mile. No one knew what had happened to Sylvie and Endicott. They had been in Asch but there had been no word on either of them in close to a week. Now reports were coming in that the army had evacuated Asch to the Sudeten Freikorps goons. Both reporters were big kids yet Ros would feel much better knowing they were okay.

Sanderson had gotten ahead of her again. He kept looking for the arrival of late editions at the newsstands. So every time they got close to a newsboy he darted through the crowd to have a look while she tried to catch up to him. Up ahead she saw Sanderson had his gotten his paws on some broadsheet and he was gesturing for her to hurry up.

"Look what I found," Sanderson thumped the newsprint with the back of his hand. "At least Endicott is alive and kicking."

"What does it say," Ros asked when she got close enough to be heard."

"Our dear compatriot managed to get kidnapped by the Freikorps and lived to tell about it," Sanderson was reading the story as fast as he could.

"Makes sense. Endicott will leave a bad taste in anyone's mouth. As soon as they realized what they had gotten they probably wasted no time in coughing him back up," Ros could take shots at Charles knowing he was okay. "Where did he file from?"

"Leipzig... a couple of days ago. Seems like the Henleinists took him over the border and released him to some local authorities on the other side," Sanderson read aloud.

"Oh great!" Ros snatched the paper away. "That louse got lucky. He's in Germany. How much you want to bet that little rat is making tracks for Godesberg right now?"

"Don't be jealous dear. Endicott won't be privy to anything that several hundred other reporters won't be sticking their noses into. You and I are in much better shape," Sanderson tried to argue the bright side.

"He doesn't say anything about Sylvie here," Ros scanned the account. "Can you believe it, Endicott cut out on Sylvie?"

"He was abducted by the bad guys, remember," Sanderson reminded her.

"C'mon, this is Endicott we're talking about. He probably paid those guys to take him across the border and lied about the whole thing," Ros could make money on that bet.

"That would be in character," Sanderson had to admit.

Suddenly there were angry shouts ahead. The reporters could see a crowd had just encircled a delivery truck on a nearby side street that had pulled up to drop off the latest Czech editions.

"Tell us what is happening!" a woman who looked like a schoolteacher pleaded.

"Everybody knows but us!" a businessman yelled in agreement.

Ros briefly caught sight of huge headline in black: *UTTERLY ALONE.*

"Wait, did you hear that?" Sanderson drew close to her.

"Hear what?" Ros could hear nothing else but the angry crowd.

But others had caught the strange sound as well and the square went eerily quiet in seconds. The government loudspeakers had crackled into life.

> *Citizens... Citizens of the republic. After twenty years of peace and order a grave European crisis has broken out. Our Western European friends, France and Britain, are not prepared to help, and the Government was placed in the dilemma either of accepting the Western Powers' suggestions or fighting alone without hope of success. Therefore, the government has been forced to accept all the conditions proposed, even the greatest sacrifices, to preserve the state's independence. Do not let your courage sink. Remain firm in loyalty to the republic. In a case unparalleled in history our allies impose conditions which are usually dictated to vanquished enemies. It was not lack of courage that induced the government to take this decision. God knows that it is more courageous to live than to commit suicide. We stand alone, but we shall rise again. Nothing can be solved by acts of violence.*

A bottle crashed against the closest loudspeaker. As broken glass showered down upon everyone in the vicinity more bottles launched into the air with the same result.

"Throw Beneš from the palace walls," a woman shouted from the open window above the reporters.

"Down with the capitulators," a university student ahead of them protested with a raised fist.

"I believe the revolution has started," Sanderson pulled Ros close to protect her from falling shards of glass.

U.S. EMBASSY
MALA STRANA DISTRICT, PRAHA

Work on the air raid shelter was progressing well. The plan was for the property's ample wine cellar to be remade via the application of sandbags and cement. The crew had already made good progress putting up the necessary reinforced wood framing. Mister Carr did not seem overly concerned with the cost, which was pretty steep. The minister wanted the job done fast before a full mobilization was called and construction workers got scarce. By the looks of the workmanship the final product would more than get the job done. The workers Chapin and Bulloch had hired were top notch. Petra had been a huge help there in providing a few key recommendations. Those guys, in turn, had come up with a bunch more skilled hands. But these men were human too and Bulloch could tell their concentration was distracted. Chapin had picked up on their mood as well. This morning he had reminded the workers that this was an embassy, and the legation staff would be some of the first in Prague to know if there were any important developments. Chapin's overture to the crew did the trick and they had been hard at work the entire day.

Given the circumstances, Bulloch had stayed at the dig to keep an eye on progress. When an extra hand or shoulder was required to move something heavy into or out of place he jumped right in. Bulloch had long ago sworn off of the hard labor he had known and hated in his youth yet he could still swing an axe with the best of them when required. Bulloch still preferred dishonest work but chipping in today was the right thing to do. As long as Bulloch was there side-by-side with the Czechs, pride would keep them from scurrying off the job. There was no guarantee how many of them would show up tomorrow so the more work that got done today the better. But they would be losing daylight soon and Bulloch would have to turn the crew loose.

A stray dog from the neighborhood had adopted them when the embassy grounds had to be opened to bring in equipment and materials. The little guy had a very expressive face. Bulloch could tell exactly what the dog wanted based on the way he cocked his head and stared. For now Bulloch was calling the mutt Leon. The dog was trying to talk Bulloch into playing fetch by running up close with a purloined workman's glove in his mouth and pressing his nose against Bulloch's leg. Suddenly, Leon's face got very serious and he dropped the glove. Then his ears went straight up. That's when Bulloch heard the bells from a nearby church as their ringing rode the breeze like a big wave toward shore. It wasn't a happy ring.

The Czechs heard the alarm and stopped whatever they were working on. Each of them turned to Bulloch, their expressions a silent request for permission to hightail it out of there. He was about to tell them to scat when Chapin trotted toward them from the main building. A trot was fast for him so something was up.

"There is news... not good, I am afraid," Chapin addressed the Czechs. "Your government has reversed itself and accepted the Anglo-French ultimatum."

The Czechs froze for a moment in stoic poses. Then came the muttered curses –colorful ones at that. Bulloch felt deeply for the men. "Go Take care of what needs taken care of. Come back when you can and we'll finish the job then.

Instead of dropping their tools where they stood, each man stowed his gear properly on the makeshift racks they had nailed together for the purpose. They may be going but these guys were pros. "How bad is it out there?" Bulloch asked Chapin.

"Bad. Krofta presented the surrender to Newton and de Lacroix at the foreign ministry around five o'clock. Word has been spreading like fire through the city. Thousands of people are dropping everything and joining together on the streets. They're angry and many are marching up toward Hradčany," Chapin pointed toward the castle.

"Crap! I have got to go," Bulloch took off his work gloves.

"Captain, that doesn't sound very wise," Chapin needed the attaché close at hand if the riots got out of hand.

"No choice. I have to find Petra," Bulloch snatched his leather jacket from where it had been resting atop a wood pole.

"How do you intend to find her? There are tens of thousands of people flooding those streets." Now was not the time to strike out impulsively, Chapin reasoned.

"Easier than you think. All I need to do is find the loudest group of rowdy Czechs, and she'll be right in there with them," Bulloch ran off to secure the compound and then run down Petra.

HOTEL DREESEN, GODESBERG

Nazis of every description had flooded into the establishment since earlier in the day. There were plenty of the high muckety-muck types milling around as expected yet what intrigued Endicott was the large contingent of kitchen table Nazis chewing the fat with each other over beers. This was an odd combination. It was like all of the bankers in Boston getting together with the city's gritty union hall crowd... and all of them were getting on famously with each other. Oil and water just didn't mix like that. Not even at a Red Sox game. Endicott couldn't get over it. The whole scene was dodgy, as Sanderson would say. Endicott wondered what the Brit was up to. Given what old Neville the prime minister was up to, Endicott wouldn't want to be a Brit in Prague right now.

"Hey Shirer, when did you leave Prague?" Endicott decided to follow this line of thought.

"Early Monday. Why?" Shirer shifted his attention away from the conversation at a nearby table in the lounge.

"My curiosity is peaked. How were the Czechs treating British nationals with everything going on? I was thinking of a buddy of mine back there," Endicott would hate to see Sanderson get his neck stretched.

"Growing impatience," Shirer paused to reflect on recent days. "The Czechs I know understand the British are not their fast allies but the feeling is sinking in that the British are turning out to be a meddlesome enemy. There is great anger brewing and I am afraid those emotions will spill over before too long. Many of the British correspondents have acquired American press passes in the last few days as a precaution."

"Oh that must stick in their craw," Endicott would have to needle Sanderson about that later. "The world is a crazy place, and you realize you have the best seat in the house for the show tomorrow."

"The Germans are very keen to have news of the conference broadcast live across the world. They are very confident of the outcome. Godesberg is a great victory for them," Shirer felt a tad uncomfortable at helping them promote their success.

"Yeah, that's what I have been reading in the local rags," Endicott found the towing of the government's pitch lines to be remarkably uniform.

"Don't be too hard on us, my friend," an overly cheery German broke into the conversation to sit down at the table without waiting for an invitation. "Godesberg is one of those rare occasions where everything we print is actually true."

Shirer laughed and slapped the tabletop. "Eavesdropping again, Manfred?"

"Of course! And so do you. I am just better at snooping than you are," the German boasted, although he ranked Shirer's attention to detail as amazingly high.

"Charles," Shirer turned to Endicott. "Meet Herr Culemann, one of Germany's leading editors."

"Pleased to meet you. Charles Endicott, Hearst International News Service," Endicott reached over the table to offer his hand.

"I just read your story. Great work there: *Kidnapped By the Sudeten Freikorps*. I am glad you survived unscathed. Many of their number are severely undisciplined," Culemann was sincerely pleased no harm had come to the American.

"Thanks on both counts. Sometimes I get lucky," Endicott hoped the roll lasted for a while longer. "Say, you look like a man in the know. When does Herr Hitler arrive?"

"Oh, the chancellor is already in Godesberg... upstairs as we speak," Culemann informed them.

"Now you're talking," Endicott perked up. "When do you think we will get a chance to see him?"

"Any time really. One never knows. He could stroll through the lobby in five minutes on the way to his river yacht. The vessel is tied up at the water's edge," Culemann located the vessel through the window and showed them.

"Somehow I expected something more formal," Endicott sounded let down.

"Do not despair, the Teppichfresser will not disappoint," Culemann lowered his voice as he teased the Americans.

"The what?" Endicott did not understand the term.

"Carpet eater?" Shirer's translation did little to ease his own confusion.

"You two have obviously not been paying attention to the discussion at the next table," Culemann nodded in the direction of two party hacks nearby.

"I imagine not," Shirer had been ignoring their boorish neighbors on purpose.

"Perhaps you have heard... the chancellor often has *strong* reactions to bad news," Culemann continued in a whisper. "Chamberlain promised him that he could deliver the Sudetenland on a platter and all of the news from Prague says Beneš is obstinately refusing to go along. Those two over there were just mentioning how this continued stubbornness by the Czech president has brought on one of Hitler's rages causing the leader of the great German Empire to fling himself on the floor where he chews on the edge of the carpet."

"You have to be kidding," Endicott found such a tale difficult to believe.

"Trust me, on such matters, I never *kid*," Culemann wagged his forefinger at the Americans.

MALA STRANA DISTRICT, PRAHA

The long dark line of people stretched back as far back as they could see. Back over the Charles Bridge they had just crossed and far into the Old Town district across the river. This is the way it had been since the angry crowd had poured out of Wenceslas Square in the direction of the seat of government across the Vltava. At every intersection hundreds more people funneled into the mob. Sixty to one hundred thousand people would be a fair estimate from Sanderson's vantage point. Where they were the procession swelled twelve across taking up the entire narrow street. Sanderson could see no end to the supply of Czechs joining the protest – shouting slogans and grimly focused on the castle looming ahead of them. That usually romantic Baroque architecture was taking on a more baleful silhouette as the last bits of daylight waned.

Somewhere after leaving Wenceslas Square several large red, white and blue tri-color flags – the national symbol of Czechoslovakia – had been commandeered and were proudly being carried at the front of the growing throng. The march had spontaneously set off from where Ros and Sanderson had been listening to the government broadcast. They had been swept into the march with all the rest and been near the head of the procession the entire time. To the front were some factory workers in leather jackets, their hands still blackened from the shop floor. To the right was a businessman carrying a briefcase who had been on his way home when the bad news had been announced. Mothers led their children by the hand and students still carried their schoolbooks. Well-heeled patrons left street-side cafes to join the march.

Sanderson would describe the mood of the Czechs as more resolutely determined than fanatical. At the beginning there certainly was the occasional endorsement of comrade Stalin but as more people joined the protest the tone became less political and it was obvious the majority of them were simply patriots demanding the right to defend their nation. Sanderson recalled a soldier who had been watching the burgeoning march wide-eyed from an adjacent street. The passing crowd surged out and enveloped the young man, hoisted him on their shoulders, and cheered him wildly. As the soldier was carried along, women started to chant: *Our army, our army is our only home now.* Soon every Czech in the vicinity rousingly joined in.

Sanderson now saw a particular pattern develop. The further they moved inward on this side of the river more stern-faced policemen lined the narrow streets. The poor fellows were obviously in a bad spot as it was obvious these constables were wholly sympathetic to the marchers. Several times a large group of police had begun to get into position to block progress of the protest. As soon as the policemen started moving in, the leaders at the front of the procession would start singing the national anthem and instantaneously thousands of people were singing those patriotic words with undeniable fervor and emotion. Each time the police stood at attention and added their voices to their fellow citizens while the march continued up the hill toward the castle unimpeded. Ros and Sanderson had never seen anything like it before. They did not know the words but the correspondents were inspired so thoroughly they tried to hum along with the melody. Some of the Czechs nearby in the crowd glared at them for not singing until Ros pulled a small American flag out of her purse.

"Comrade Americké," Ros announced in her cheery fashion.

With the question of nationality settled the reporters were soon coached in the lyrics. Despite Ros' handy flag, Sanderson realized their route would take the protesters perilously close to the British embassy. From the beginning the mob's greatest wrath had been reserved for London and Paris. When they weren't singing the national anthem, or praising the army, the marchers angrily denounced their supposed allies: *Down with England, down with France!* Sanderson glanced down at his American press credentials with relief. If there were to be a violent scuffle the British embassy would be the place it would start. The street they were on began to narrow sharply as it curved around a building. Ros rose up on her toes and pointed toward a squad of mounted police, perhaps sixty strong, blocking the way ahead. The lead protesters broke out into the national anthem again as they approached the imposing horses. There was no change, no quickening of pace. Just continued forward momentum from people who had no quarrel with their police. But the mounted officers did not yield as their brethren had done before. Surprisingly, the procession stopped. Then without a display of anger or force, the leaders in front attempted to push their way non-violently past the horses. Every time the police line held off the incursion in that narrow corridor without resorting to threats or violence. After several attempts the march simply stopped where it was. If they could not go forward, they stubbornly would not go back.

What happened next was totally unexpected. Both Ros and Sanderson were used to mounted police who after stopping a protest such as this would then attempt to stampede protesters in the opposite direction with raised batons. But with thousands of angry citizens approaching this obviously was not an option. Having momentarily stopped the march from going any further, the policemen casually began to dismount and mingle with the demonstrators.

"Long live the republic," the lead officer's deep voice boomed.

"Long live the republic!" those before him in the crowd joined in.

And so the cheer flowed back through the ranks and was taken up by thousands. In four simple words one Czech policeman had assured his countrymen and countrywomen that the defenders of public order shared their emotion. While everyone else was focused on cheering the republic with the police, a wiry middle-aged man who had glared menacingly at the reporters several times before wheeled around and pointed at Sanderson. He pushed people aside until he came right up to them and repeatedly poked his forefinger forcefully into Sanderson's chest. While he did not recognize the man, the reverse was obviously not the case for the testy little fellow.

"I know you. I remember now," the man poked harder. "You are not Americké, you are a damned Anglická. Everyone! This one is a filthy Anglická!"

For his troubles the unruly herald was forcefully dropped hard onto the cobblestones in a single blow executed so swiftly it was intimidating. The unknown perpetrator hovered over their accuser long enough to apply several deft punches that left the man limp and unconscious. Most of the Czechs around them had been too caught up with their patriotic cheering to notice what had transpired. That was how quickly the whole altercation was over. Sanderson's savior gently picked up the comatose Czech and securely held him upright next to the reporters in a friendly fashion.

"Sorry about that fella," Bulloch apologized to the unconscious Czech. "No hard feelings, I hope."

"I know you. You are her private yank," Sanderson blurted out.

"Bulloch, where did you come from?" Ros couldn't believe where the captain had been that she would not have noticed him.

"Keep it down you two," Bulloch commanded while struggling to hold the unconscious Czech steady.

A little girl was staring at Bulloch with suspicion while tugging insistently on her mother's dress. When the woman stopped to see what her daughter wanted the girl was pointing accusingly at Bulloch.

"He slipped and had a bad fall and I have to find a doctor for him," Bulloch tried to sound concerned and authoritative at the same time.

The explanation seemed satisfactory enough for the mother who much preferred returning her attention to what was happening up front with the police. The little girl was no so well convinced yet complied when her mother pulled her along through the crowd to getter a better look at the front of the march.

"What are you doing here, Bulloch?" Ros leaned in close to him.

"Saving your boyfriend's rear end if you care to pay attention," Bulloch never pretended to expect thanks from the woman.

"He's not my boyfriend!" Ros protested the assumption.

"Well you certainly don't have to put that so declaratively," Sanderson raised his own objection.

"What do you take me for, a chump? You two go everyplace together," Bulloch was growing weary of the pair.

"And how would you know that? You spying on me, pal?" Ros wagged her little flag under his nose.

"Don't flatter yourself, sister. The world doesn't revolve around you despite what you may think," Bulloch was regretting his decision to help out.

"Forget the song and dance. I think you *are* a spy. You sure do act like one--" was all Ros got out before Bulloch had reached over and cupped his free hand firmly over her mouth.

"--Shut up," Bulloch spoke slowly and decisively.

Ros' eyes darted back and forth toward Sanderson telegraphing the message: *Aren't you going to do something about this?*

Sanderson ignored her and turned toward Bulloch instead. "There has been many an occasion I have contemplated taking the very same course of action."

Furious, Ros bit down on one of Bulloch's fingers.

"Ow!" Bulloch tried his best to muffle discomfort as he yanked his hand back.

Satisfied, Ros gritted her teeth and then hit Sanderson in the stomach hard with the business end of her purse.

"Ow!" Sanderson nearly bent over while Bulloch examined the teeth marks on his finger.

"You both need to practice your manners," Ros admonished the men. "Now what are we going to do with this guy you're propping up, Bulloch? People are watching us."

"Help me get him over to the alley there behind us. There is a hip flask in my back pocket. We'll give him a little sip then I'll deposit him close by one of the cops down the road. Cops love locking up drunks. When pally here wakes up and starts singing, they'll just figure it's the liquor talking," Bulloch proposed.

"Sounds plausible," Sanderson endorsed the scheme.

"Then what?" Ros prodded wanting to know what the captain was really up to.

"Then I lose you two and get back to what I came up here to do," Bulloch adjusted his hold on the unconscious Czech. "Man, this little guy is getting heavy."

"We'll come with you," Ros invited her and Sanderson along.

"Fat chance, hon. I'll do just fine on my own," Bulloch did not want her company.

"You have a nose for action, fella and I am not letting you out of my sight. If you give me any guff I'll start screaming at the top of my lungs until one of those cops over there comes riding over," Ros threatened him.

"You'd do that, wouldn't you?" Bulloch fumed.

"Bet on it," Ros stared him down.

"Arguing with her is quite useless when she gets into one of these moods," Sanderson advised the American.

"Fine. Have it your way," Bulloch gave in. "You both might come in handy if I need a distraction. There's another way around up to the Castle and we're going to take it right after I ditch this dead weight."

FRENCH MILITARY MISSION, PRAHA

Non, he could no longer wear the uniform proudly. Faucher loved these people far too much to scurry away in the night like a thief who had gotten what he came for and now made his escape. The scene on the street below his balcony broke Faucher's heart. Had a mob arrived to burn the mission to the ground he would have understood completely and perhaps joined them in their rage. But what could he say to the grown men, so many of them, who paused under the tri-color of France and wept. Weeping for the betrayal of France, whom they loved. What could he possibly say that would make up for what his government was perpetrating upon these fine people. These Czechoslovaks had been a part of his life for nearly twenty years. Louis-Eugene Faucher would not abandon them now. He would not see his years of his efforts thrown away. If only in a small fashion, French honor must be preserved.

Faucher left the balcony and returned to his study. Slowly and deliberately he removed the valorous decorations of many years and many battles from his tunic, placing each one into a small box. The box would be mailed to Premier Daladier along with a letter he had yet to pen. Effective immediately Faucher was resigning his commission in the Army of France and was surrendering command of this post. Tomorrow Faucher would seek out Général Krejčí and place himself at the service of the Czechoslovak Army if they would have him. Should he be so fortunate then Faucher would devote himself fully to defending this land. It was a small gesture insignificant to the damage that had been done this day by his countrymen yet Faucher saw no other avenue to cleanse the stain on the reputation of his homeland.

Taking a seat at his desk, Faucher drew a sheet of paper, and retrieved the pen from its well. He thought of the Institut Francais in Prague, where once proud graduates were returning their diplomas, and the parents of current students were withdrawing their children. Then there were the Czechoslovak officers who had sought Faucher out to ask why France was assuming the duty of Hitler's executioner. Finally there was the pain of reading the Czech newspaper headlines that shouted out the harsh truth of betrayal. Having gathered his thoughts, Faucher set his pen to work as surely as a saber unsheathed in battle.

MINISTRY OF NATIONAL DEFENCE, DEJVICE

The sun had already retreated below the staff buildings to the west. The architects had done their best to bestow ornamentation to the army facilities that was in keeping with the rest of the city when the district was built up during the last decade. Faux facades and doorways, along with their sheltered nooks, were plentiful and useful for those looking for a quick repose to nurse a cigarette and contemplate. Wherever they had gone today the news was terrible. The mood of the people was rightfully combustible. Burda and Furst expected the coming night would provide their wounded capital with still further anguish as they returned to their headquarters from another hectic undertaking on a day overflowing with hectic undertakings. Neither did tomorrow look to be any better.

"Does the boss know the communists are stirring up trouble?" Furst raised the subject in-between drags on his cigarette.

"He knows," Burda leaned back against the side of the stone alcove.

"Are we going to do anything about it?" Furst pursued the thought further, anxious to put some of the fury inside him to good use.

"That would be difficult to explain to Stalin at the same time we are asking for Soviet assistance against Germany. Besides, I am not sure it is altogether wrong to be leading the people up to the castle to demand weapons instead of capitulation," Burda was melancholy enough to join them.

"You know Gottwald's instructions from Moscow as well as I do. Inciting a communist revolution that deposes President Beneš is what they are after," Furst was not as charitable as his partner.

"That too might be an opportunity," Burda was tired of feeling like a hog being led to a butcher's shop.

Furst had never heard such conspiratorial notions from his partner before. "As a pretext for the army to assume control?"

"As I said, an opportunity," Burda had been running through the options in his head all afternoon. "All of our sources inside Germany are telling us that Hitler will invade regardless of our official concessions. You heard them out on the streets this afternoon. The people would embrace the army coming to the salvation of the republic. They are so distressed they would approve of Generál Krejčí taking power to save the nation from anarchy. Beneš could be forgiven the predicament forced on him by our *allies* that saw him deposed, and Krejčí forgiven for the necessity to restore order. We could say the enemy had been chaos not the communists. That would keep Soviet military support in play," Burda wrote one possible script.

Furst saw the steel point of his friend's reasoning. "Do you think it will come to that?"

"Who knows? Tomorrow is a lifetime away," Burda flicked the stub of his cigarette to the concrete. "Let's go back up. There will be no sleep for any of us tonight."

PRIEGER FARM, NEAR ASCH

He should have sent the unterscharführer on such a task. The man was certainly competent enough to appraise the situation. The area was quiet, however, and it was useful for Horst to get a direct view of as much of the surrounding terrain and structures as possible. The Czechs had very conveniently pulled out but they could just as quickly return to occupy any of these isolated properties on the periphery of Asch. The bastards had definitely made his life complicated by commandeering every vehicle to be had in the area before evacuating. At least they had left some farm horses, one of which a local landowner had generously volunteered for the hauptsturmführer's use. It was good to see the hope in these people's faces that expressed they had not been forsaken by their brothers. He was German, an officer, and that counted for a lot for these good men and women. That was the other reason he had decided to ride out here for himself. These people living outside of the village needed to see who was leading their liberation – negligible a force as it was until the arrival of reinforcements.

The wife was already hurrying out the front door of the house to greet him as the horse was trotting up the dirt and gravel lane from the road. There was so much excitement bubbling out of the middle-aged woman you would think her own son was coming home after a long time away. She rubbed her hands on her apron then placed them on her hips in that way women did when they wanted to size up the measure of a man. He swung his leg around and jumped down from the saddle to walk the last few steps to her.

"Hauptsturmführer Horst," he introduced himself. "My apologies for the lateness of the hour."

"Oh thank you for coming all the way out here. I hope it was not dangerous. I am Frau Prieger," she gushed.

"No danger at all. And if something went amiss I came prepared," Horst gestured cavalierly back to the carbine stowed on the saddle and then the holstered pistol on his belt. "Is Herr Prieger here?"

"No, I told him not to go out to mend equipment today but he never strays from that routine of his. I'm sorry," she apologized.

"That is fine, I was only being polite as my mother taught me," Horst tried to make her feel better.

"I am sure she is very proud of a good son like you. I wish my daughters were still single," she blushed.

"You flatter me madam," Horst felt like blushing as well. "Where is the injured woman?"

"Come inside. We are caring for her in there," Frau Prieger turned and beckoned for Horst to follow.

Whomever the woman was she amounted to one more complication. All he had been told was that she was a foreigner, as if Horst needed an international complication on top of his other worries. He needed to find out how badly she was injured and who she was. The home was tidy and modest, as he had come to expect in the region. Frau Prieger led him down a hallway to a back bedroom where a young woman was tending her unconscious patient.

"That is my daughter, Konstanze," Frau Prieger introduced them. "She is very good with the medicine."

"Thank you both," Horst moved close enough to the bed to check the woman's pulse. It was steady. Noticing the wet towel the daughter had resting on her patient's forehead, Horst felt underneath. There was a nasty bump there. "She's very warm."

"And there is another large bruise on the back of her head, poor thing," Konstanze reported.

Horst looked the patient over once again. She was a handsome woman. He rolled up a shirtsleeve and saw the female had a few deep gashes on her arms. There were scratches and dark bruises everywhere he could see. But the clothes she was wearing appeared locally procured.

"What happened to her clothes?" Horst doubted the woman had been found naked.

"They were torn up terribly. I have been mending them. They will never take a good washing in the state they are in," Frau Prieger's concerns were practical.

"Amerikaner," Konstanze knew what was behind his question. She reached into a basket on top of side table and pulled out a badge and a wallet to hand over to the officer.

Horst checked the identification and inside the wallet. His English wasn't good but he could make out that the woman was a correspondent and her home was in the United States... Dallas. Horst remembered the Hollywood westerns he had seen and thought about that barren place called Texas. "What exactly happened to this woman?"

"Our men attacked a Czech convoy a few days ago. There were lots of explosions. We heard later that those Czechs who had not been killed had been taken across to Germany. She had been left for dead. My husband found her not far from an overturned truck. We think she had been on the truck when a grenade blew it up," Frau Prieger felt sorry for the unlucky girl.

"The Czechs had probably ordered her to leave with them," Horst guessed. "Does anyone remember her?"

"I spoke with the burgermeister myself. He remembers a woman of her description poking around and asking many questions ever since Herr Hitler's speech," Konstanze had already checked.

"There was no passport buy by her documents she appears to work for a news wire company," Horst saw the clues fit together. "Unfortunately, I do not have a physician assigned to my unit. Do you think she can be moved? I would like to get her to a place where her countrymen can be notified and take responsibility for her."

"No, I would not move her until she is awake and lucid. There are no broken bones that I can find just those terrible bruises and gashes. That's the good news. The worst of it is she has a concussion... I am sure of it," Konstanze made her diagnosis with authority. "Moving her could be dangerous. I will care for her until she is conscious and able to move on her own two feet."

"Very well then," Horst saw no benefit in arguing with the daughter. "That seems very wise. Thank you both very much for giving this foreigner such excellent care. Is there anything you need?"

"Please check with the doctor in Asch. I could use some real cold compress ice bags instead of these towels. If he has aspirin that would helpful when she wakes up. Those superficial injuries are going hurt terribly," Konstanze finished her checklist.

"For your safety and hers I will be sending out one my rottenführers. He is a good boy and no trouble. I will have him bring out the items you asked for. He is very self-sufficient so don't worry about putting him up. When the Amerikaner wakes up I don't want her running off. He will be instructed to help you if she proves troublesome," Horst felt a lost American national could be a huge headache.

"I am not worried. She is nothing I cannot handle," Konstanze vowed confidently.

"Perhaps, but I would feel better all the same by taking every precaution," Horst held his ground.

"Have it your way," Konstanze waved the matter off with a sigh.

"Oh, our own soldier. I feel so honored. I will have to prepare a special meal tonight," Frau Prieger anticipated happily.

"Madam, please do not pamper my man too much. I might need him to fight when I get him back," Horst pleaded with the woman.

PRAŽSKÝ HRAD, PRAHA

Drtina could not relax. The city had been close to anarchy for almost five hours. He had warned Edvard that the people would not swallow such a humiliation and Drtina had been proven correct. No sooner had the capitulation announcement been broadcast over the radio than citizens had begun milling about around the castle perimeter around six o'clock. Then came the reports of tens of thousands of protesters marching across the river to protest. The municipal police had somehow worked wonders. Those throngs never made it up to the compound as a unit. But Drtina had been keeping a careful watch outside the gates. Even in the flickering light of the gas lamps he could tell there were many more people out there now at nearly ten o'clock.

Naturally the president was unconcerned with the potential danger. In fact, he was in an unusually good mood that Drtina could not account for. Perhaps it was the Soviet Minister, Aleksandrovsky. Somehow the envoy had managed to sneak past the demonstrators and the police to pay a visit to Beneš. When Aleksandrovsky had stopped to speak with Drtina after bidding adieu to the president nothing about the Russian's demeanor suggested good news. If the minister had brought positive news it was his nature to say something encouraging on his way out. But Aleksandrovsky was his usual coy self when Drtina asked him of Soviet preparations to aid Czechoslovakia. At least the president finally had a few moments to relax in his study. The day had been grueling for all, especially for him. As there were still documents to file and distribute, Drtina picked up a stack of paperwork from his desk and made down the hall where he could delegate the work to the staff. They were a good lot who had refused to leave during the crisis.

Drtina was startled by a shout outside the window that seemed much closer than it should be. He hoped it was the palace guard rooting out an interloper. But the rapidly mounting commotion outside suggested numbers far greater than the guard could muster. Peering out the nearest window confirmed Drtina's suspicions. A very large crowd had materialized under the windows of the presidential suite. His mind raced almost as fast as his breathing. The president was in grave danger. This mob was at the right spot to break in and seize Beneš. If they were so inclined they could easily toss the president from the ramparts long before help could arrive. To his great relief Drtina saw the palace guard move in to disperse the mob from the area. The legionnaires were seriously outnumbered yet firm in their efforts and had gotten the demonstrators to start yielding. Then Drtina's ears made out singing. It was the small group organizers at the lead of the disturbance. They were singing the national anthem at the top of their lungs. Their followers lost not a moment in taking up the patriotic verses with equal vigor. *That old trick*, Drtina fumed. He fumbled with the latch but failed to get the window open in time to yell a caution to the guards below. Each of them stopped what they were doing, stood rigidly at attention, and saluted in honor of the republic.

It was too late. In those few moments of shared patriotism a second wave of demonstrators flooded into the area – far too many now for the guards to fend off. The swarm of protestors peacefully weaved in between the legionnaires, separating the guardsmen from each other. The protectors of the president were isolated in a sea of fellow citizens without any physical leverage to control the crowd. Drtina threw the documents in his possession to the floor and ran down the hall. He needed to rouse the staff. They had to organize quickly to bolt every door and window possible. Once he set his people to that purpose, Drtina would attempt to call in the state police. The mob leaders were disciplined. They knew exactly where the president's suite was and it was plausible they also knew where to cut the telephone lines to the castle. If Drtina could not raise the alarm he feared the worst for all of them.

All that she wanted, all that any of her friends wanted, was a chance to fight the Germans. Most of the people who had marched beside her today would answer the same way if asked. But there were some whose motivations were not so pure. While Petra had waited with her fellow students in Wenceslas Square for a positive sign from the government she had noticed many of the Czech communists who had attended the lecture by comrade Zhdanov. They were prepared for Beneš' capitulation. When the loudspeakers blared the shameful bulletin it had been these communists who stepped forward immediately within seconds imploring the people to advance on Hradčany. Petra knew what was going on. She well remembered the details of Zhdanov's agenda. But rage was surging in her blood. What did it matter if there were communists in the lead? The government needed to hear the voices of the people regardless who were leading the throng. So they raised their voices, shook their fists and marched. Soon they were tens of thousands. This was truly the most important day of Petra's life.

Along the way what the communists had started was transformed into something much nobler. The Bolsheviks were still out in front since they had many tricks at their command that were most useful. But her fellow citizens were dictating the message. They shouted down the self-serving slogans of the reds, replacing them with a roar that buoyed every soul on the street that day: *The republic deserved to be protected; set the army free to do its job; give the people the weapons to protect their homes from the fascists; and let no other nation guarantee or threaten our freedom, it is for us to decide and no one else.* Even the communists could not argue with such pure motives. When the police had stiffened to block their way there was no violence. Again the communists were clever. There were too few police to secure every route. The word passed amongst the people to break into smaller groups and split off onto smaller streets and alleys that would lead up to the castle gates.

Hours after streaming out of the Old Town they arrived at the gates – a score here, a dozen there. As there was no threatening activity the palace guards were watchful but they were not alarmed. Slowly, steadily, the number of citizens grew into the thousands once more. The legionnaires decided it was wise to secure the gate but the people pushed their way past the guards. Once again the communists were useful. They knew exactly where the president's quarters were located. Petra found it miraculous how quickly so many people reached the third courtyard unmolested before more legionnaires arrived. Those men were so few and so brave as they attempted to carry out their duty. As they had done many times during the evening the demonstrators sang the national anthem with devotion. The legionnaires shared that love deeply and the emotion in their voices brought tears to Petra's eyes.

In the pause after the singing ended the guards pulled back and everyone looked to each other. What were they to do next? No one had come to meet with them. No window opened to reveal President Beneš or Prime Minister Hodza. Were their leaders cowering and afraid? These men needed to hear the people. At that moment, Petra decided that they *would* hear her.

"Give us weapons! Give us weapons!" Petra passionately beseeched her government. "Give us weapons! Give us weapons! Give us weapons!"

The hundreds of citizens streaming in through the gate after the legionnaires fell back took up Petra's call. Still no one from the government possessed the courage to appear. That's when several of the communists took advantage of the moment. They began pounding on the door to the apartments. But it was a very solid door with metal plating that would not yield. Someone she didn't recognize produced a crowbar and attempted to force the door's locking mechanism.

Drtina had sent a young typist to bolt the main entry door to the wing while he had hurried to make his call to the state police. They were aware of the situation but it would take them time to assemble enough men to clear the area. As he lowered the phone receiver on its cradle Drtina heard new shouts building from outside on the compound. Cursing, he rushed back down the hall to the entry door. The typist was still there and Drtina could tell being so near to the protest was unnerving her.

"Get to safety, I'll stand watch here." It was Drtina's obligation, not hers. "I'll be fine."

"Are you sure? Someone should stay with you," the typist objected.

Heavy boots approached down the hall. Drtina and the typist were relieved to see the guard commander and a lieutenant heading in their direction.

"Go," Drtina pushed her along. "Look. I have company."

As the typist departed the guard commander arrived just as they heard a heavy tool applied to metal on the other side. "Sir, I have redeployed inside the building. My men are securing every point of access. As you can tell an attempt is being made to force open that door. If that mob gains entry I will have no alternative than to start shooting."

The initial surge of people pushing past the main gates was a complete shock. There was no preparation or warning. One moment the Czechoslovak civilians were keeping watchful vigil on the palace while deep in their own individual conversations, the next moment they were like salmon heading up river. Bulloch was attempting to catch up with Petra but she was nowhere to be found as he weaved through the mass of Czechs. Bulloch acutely wanted to ditch his two shadows but that Talmadge woman was sticking to him like glue.

"Who are we looking for?" Ros demanded for the umpteenth time.

"We are not looking for anybody. I am looking for somebody," Bulloch corrected her.

"It would be easier if we knew what to look for," Ros wouldn't take the hint.

Bulloch wasn't pleased at having to stop to explain matters to her. "Listen, why can't you both trot along and do what your bosses pay hacks to do."

"I think I take offence at that description," Sanderson thought the captain was getting a bit menacing toward Ros.

"Tell it to the crowd, pal. I think they have far worse descriptions for Limey's these days," Bulloch piled on a further insult.

"Point taken but you needn't be rude," Sanderson's feathers were ruffled.

"Okay, let me lay it out for you straight. There is a young brat who is probably inside those gates right now. You know the type… she's going to get herself in trouble. There's no stopping it. But I am going to pull her rear out of the fire before it gets singed," Bulloch felt his hands clenching into fists.

"What's this skirt to you?" Ros tapped her shoe on a cobblestone.

"She shares my bed. That good enough for you?" Bulloch was done with the endless questions.

"You! You have a girlfriend. How is that was possible? You're a first class jerk," Ros stepped closer to Bulloch.

"Yeah right. Remind me to let the damn Nazis cart you away when they get their paws on you," Bulloch was sure she would get herself snatched a third time.

"That old spiel again. You're like a broken record," Ros belittled him.

"I am beginning to think that down deep you both really like each other," Sanderson hit on that disturbing realization while watching them go after each other.

"Shut up!" Ros and Bulloch shouted in unison at Sanderson.

In the short cease fire that followed, a chant from the inside courtyards grew louder: *Give us weapons... Give us weapons... We want to fight!*

"You hear that?" Ros turned in the direction of the shouting.

"Sounds like the natives are restless," Sanderson was near setting off in that direction.

Bulloch had heard the defiant calls but he was more interested in the uniformed army officer approaching the gate in the company of several junior adjutants. Which gave him an idea on how to ditch the reporters.

"Don't look now but here comes General Syrový," Bulloch tipped the reporters off.

"The inspector general of the Czech Army?" Sanderson looked over his shoulder.

"The very same," Bulloch confirmed. "All four stars of him: hero of the Great War, lost an eye fighting the Austrians, led the Czech Legion home through Bolshevik hordes and lived."

"I have been trying to get at him for weeks. Here goes!" Sanderson pulled a notebook and pencil from his jacket and ran to intercept Syrový.

"I can't let him get that interview all to himself," Ros pulled herself away. "You wait right here. Don't go anywhere, you understand?"

"Yeah sure, run along," Bulloch lied.

Ros sprinted off after Sanderson. When she looked around Bulloch was where she had left him, arms folded against his chest. Catching a second glance back she saw the captain hadn't budged so Ros introduced herself to the general.

"Sharks," Bulloch critiqued the reporters. Now that they were preoccupied, Bulloch was inside the gates within seconds running alongside the latecomers to the party. Seeing Syrový had given him an idea. Bulloch had seen enough angry crowds in the past few weeks to know what was coming next. Someone was going to get cocky and a rock or a gasoline cocktail was going to get thrown. He had seen the palace guard before. They were badly outnumbered yet still disciplined veterans. Push them too far and they would defend themselves. Bulloch had no reason to doubt they were all excellent marksmen. Past the second courtyard, Bulloch knew what he needed to do to keep the situation from boiling over. He had to stall this bunch before they got out of hand. Forcing his body into the final courtyard, Bulloch scanned as far as he could see but he couldn't spot Petra amongst the raucous Czechoslovaks shouting themselves hoarse. It was now or never he figured. Giving himself a few seconds to catch their beat, Bulloch joined the Czechs in shouting their demands.

"Give us weapons or give us Syrový!" Bulloch added in a twist to the slogan as loud as his lungs could force the words into the night air. "Give us weapons or give us Syrový! Give us weapons or give us Syrový!"

The people around him picked up on the chant as he had hoped. Bulloch got what he wanted... he had just hijacked the mob. The general was a popular war hero and beloved by many Czechoslovaks. The people surrounding him approved of the new demand. It fit their mood completely. They weren't revolutionaries by nature but they prayed for their army to save them. Within a minute the entire courtyard was making the same demand: *"Give us weapons or give us Syrový!*

There was no way the general could not hear that demand back at the gate. Bulloch counted on what he knew of the man, especially with two foreign correspondents as witnesses. Syrový would come and that would create the diversion that would keep Petra out of more trouble than she already was in.

The prying at the main door had ceased. Drtina worried that the mob had found something more destructive to break their way in with. The guard commander pointed down the hall for the benefit of his lieutenant.

"Quick, check the rest of this wing to see if they are trying to enter someplace else," the commander instructed.

Drtina canted his head so he could listen better with his good ear. "Syrový? They want Syrový now? Why, to replace the president?"

"The eye patch," the guard commander chuckled. "That damn eye patch reminds people of the great Žižka... leading the common folk to victory."

"We should be so lucky," Drtina scoffed.

Four legionnaires jogged toward the president's secretary and the commander. Drtina hoped they had come with good news.

"We are here to reinforce your position, sir," the četař announced upon arriving with his small squad. "No telling when they will start in again."

"What do you mean, soldier?" Drtina butted in

"The lead agitators on the other side of the door have broken off their attempt to break in. We checked the courtyard when we heard the crowd start calling for Generál Syrový. The leaders seem quite annoyed by this and are vigorously conferring with each other," the sergeant reported.

The commander holstered his pistol and laughed heartily. "That will teach them."

The četař and the other legionnaires were unsure what was so funny, each looking at the other in puzzlement.

"No demand for comrade Gottwald, no pleas to comrade Stalin. The rabble wants Syrový to lead them. That is not what the Bolshevik instigators want to hear. Be proud of your fellow citizens this day. They may be ready to hang President Beneš but they are not communist stooges.

Syrový's adjutant heard the voices rise from inside the gate. At first he did not believe his ears, but the general could hear them too, as did the two foreign pests. The reporters were impeding their progress and the adjutant had been contemplating which lamp pole to lash them to... the annoying man especially. No matter what the identification clipped to his jacket pocket professed, the accent betrayed the Englishman and the adjutant had little patience for Englishmen at the moment. But the generál was showing the two opportunists polite regard, which left the adjutant little recourse than to glare sinisterly at the reporters.

Syrový had been at Hradčany all day shuttling between the palace and different ministries while the president's cabinet explored every option. When news arrived that thousands of protesters were making their way to the castle the generál had decided to remain close by. The police had reported delaying the main throngs on the streets below but small groups of citizens managed to find their way to the top. Even at this late hour more people continued to turn up outside the palace gate. This assemblage concerned Syrový sufficiently that he decided it would be best to return to the castle to lend whatever aid he could. They unfortunately had arrived just as the crowd had pushed their way past the legionnaires. Despite the unwanted attentions of the reporters the general proceeded forward in the wake of the protestors while curtly responding to the torrent of meddling queries. But when he heard the mob call his name Syrový stopped abruptly to gather his thoughts.

"That's you they are calling for... isn't that true, General Syrový?" Ros was quick on the draw.

"Do you have designs on deposing President Beneš, general? Is this a military coup d'état?" Sanderson thought the theory plausible.

"If this were a military coup, Anglická... there would be a bullet with your name on it," the adjutant meticulously unsnapped the pistol holster on his belt.

"Please be serious the both of you," Syrový admonished the correspondents. "There has been quite enough drama today. Please do not manufacture fairy tales."

"What are you going to do, general? That is your name they are calling," Ros reminded him.

"I will speak with them, of course." Without a further word, Syrový threw his shoulders back and marched deeper into the castle compound in the direction of the boisterous demonstrators.

2ND DEPT.
MINISTRY OF NATIONAL DEFENCE, DEJVICE

The Germans were not making trouble while they played at being magnanimous hosts to Prime Minister Chamberlain. The same couldn't be said for the Freikorps along the border but that was to be expected with the army pulling out of indefensible zones. The best news, however, had been the uneasy quiet in the streets of the capital after nightfall. Despite earlier in the evening when a small group of protestors had forced their way into the Radio Praha studios to broadcast arguments against capitulation the radio had proven to be a reliable source of tactical information on what was happening in the different districts of the city. That calm ended when Colonel Tichy burst through the operations room door.

"Listen up people," Tichy had taken the call from the state police. "Gottwald and his people have managed to force their way into the castle compound with a considerable quantity of hooligans - far too many people for the guard to repel. The communists have surrounded the presidential wing and are making trouble. The state police have been roused and are preparing to sweep Hradčany in force. Given the Soviet connection there will be complications. The state police do not have our counter intelligence background to know which suspects are *sensitive* and those individuals who are of no consequence. So we need to be there to help sort things out. Get your gear together... live rounds too, gentlemen. We have no idea how bad this hornet's nest is going to be. We leave in ten minutes."

Furst leaned over from his desk and backhanded Burda's arm. "See! I told you."

PRAŽSKÝ HRAD, PRAHA

Whoever had spoken the name of Generál Syrový was a genius. The government that had agreed to capitulation without a fight must be sacked. The nation must defend itself and the government needed new blood like Syrový who would not capitulate. Petra was sure that was why everyone got so much louder shouting *Give us weapons or give us Syrový* than the other demands they had made that night. She spun around to witness the heady passion and energy on display from everyone except from the poor communists who were upset they had lost control of the crowd. Petra thought that was a good thing. These were good people here. They were deeply angry with President Beneš but they did not want any harm to come to him. If he would come to a window to hear them out that would be enough.

While Petra observed the bickering communists she noticed it was getting quiet behind her. When Petra swung around she saw the mass of her fellow citizens part like the Red Sea. Through the opening marched a portly army officer in full uniform. As the man approached some of the gaslight got past the brim of his service cap and Petra saw the black eye patch. It was Syrový! Not only had he come the generál stepped past her by only centimeters. Even the communists stepped aside for the generál. When Syrový got to the very front of the crowd he found a pedestal to stand on.

"I know your hearts," Syrový took in the sea of people before him. "Do not condemn the president and his ministers too harshly. Our *allies* had dictated to them two unconscionable choices: death by suicide or death by murder. Our defence was predicated on the concept of the Czechoslovaks being a bulwark in Germany's side, holding the enemy in place while our allies throttled him from without. But without allies how much can we accomplish? That is what the president has agonized over these many hours. His love of the people is extraordinary and he does not want to see his countrymen slaughtered."

The explanation was politely received but not what the ireful citizens wanted to hear from a potential savior. Syrový recognized the mood of the crowd and adjusted. "I have known duty my entire life. If commanded to sacrifice myself for the defense of our republic, I have no reservations in making that sacrifice. But what of you fine people? You had taken no oath to serve. Does the president have the right to sacrifice your lives? That is the question that has tormented him. That is the question that guided the government in making its fateful decision. Yet look at you here. Look at the tens of thousands who rose up today. You made your choice clear to all. You have taken your oath! This will not go unnoticed. Nothing is written in stone. The army and the people are ready to defend their republic. That is what counts. That is what has substance. Words on a sheet of paper can be ripped apart and replaced tomorrow."

The mob roared its approval... and kept roaring. A student took up a new call – *Lead us Syrový! Lead us Syrový!* – that spread swiftly through the courtyard.

"No, no, no," Syrový held up his hands in protest. "I am not a politician. I am not a leader. I am a servant of the people. But I will speak with President Beneš. I will speak of your devotion and I will speak of your loyalty. You have lifted the burden from the president's shoulders."

"Why does the president not speak with us himself? Where is the president?" Petra had not intended to interrogate the generál. Her excitement had gotten the better of her, the query had blurted out and now the crowd had gone suddenly quiet. Syrový stared at her for a long moment, sizing Petra up. But she held his eyes with hers. She was not ashamed of speaking her mind. Syrový's expression turned fatherly and he stepped down from the pedestal to approach Petra through the crowd.

"I do not know child," Syrový answered sincerely. "The president may not be here at the moment. There are many little known exits and passages away from the castle. His protectors could very well have spirited him away hours ago for his own safety. That is their responsibility. Trust me though. All of your voices have been heard. Tomorrow there will be changes."

Further back in the thick of the mob, Bulloch had recognized Petra's voice. She was where the action was, as he knew she would be. Now that he had a direction to move toward Bulloch started squeezing past the tightly packed Czechs as quickly as he could.

Whatever Syrový had told the angry demonstrators had an effect. They were not leaving yet the attempt to break down the door had ceased. The generál was not known as a dynamic speaker but his words had defused the immediate danger. Now Syrový was walking between the demonstrators engaging them in conversation. From his vantage point it looked like Syrový was answering questions from whoever wanted to speak up. That could go on for hours. Drtina let the drape fall back over the window. Syrový had purchased enough time for Drtina to escape the entryway for a few minutes. He had sent a staffer to check on the president but the man had not returned and neither had Drtina seen Beneš. It was Edvard's curious nature to investigate a situation such as this. That there was no sign of him worried Drtina.

"Commander. I believe we can safely steal a few moments for an important matter. Please accompany me to the presidential apartments. I want to confirm that the president and Mesdames Beneš are secure and would appreciate your company," Drtina courteously ordered the legionnaire.

"You read my mind, Mister Drtina. If the mob stays quiet we may be able to get the president away through a different wing of the palace," the commander advised.

"If he will leave. President Beneš is stubborn that way," of which Drtina was well acquainted.

"You four," the commander addressed his men. "Stay alert. If those outside start their mischief again, attempt to keep them out without injuring them. But if they enter by force use live ammunition to prevent this position from being overrun."

"Yes sir," the four legionnaires confirmed their instructions.

Drtina and the commander hurried up to the portion of the wing that was reserved as living quarters for the Beneš family. Drtina hoped to find the president in the drawing room. The entrance to that room was closed as they approached. Drtina stopped to lean his ear in to the painted wood door. He heard nothing, however. Rather than knock, Drtina grabbed the door handle. After catching the commander's eye to verify the soldier was ready, Drtina pushed open the door for them to enter. Inside he saw his clerk pacing around a small decorative table – alone – no Beneš.

"Where is the president?" Drtina was distressed at why his man was loitering about.

There was a small dose of panic in the clerk's eyes. Before the youngster could answer, Mesdame Beneš slipped through the interior door to the bedroom.

"Gentlemen, please lower your voices," the president's wife scolded them like a school librarian to a child. "My husband is resting."

"The president must be roused, mesdame," the commander's voice lost no authority at close to a whisper.

"That is impossible. The poor dear is exhausted. I will not allow it," Mesdame Beneš held her ground.

"Are you aware of what is going on out there in the courtyard, good woman," Drtina challenged her.

"Oh yes, I saw for myself even before this kind young man came to warn us," Mesdame Beneš lavished a sweet smile in the direction of the clerk.

"You must understand, the president and you must be seen to safety. It is our duty," the commander reasoned with her.

"Your devotion to us is very much appreciated, and I am sure my husband would agree wholeheartedly with you, but I will not have it. Forgive me, gentlemen but I really cannot wake my husband. That is that," Mesdame Beneš gestured for them to leave. "Now Shoo."

Drtina looked toward the clerk. "You did the right thing. Stay here until the president wakes of his own volition. Until then see that he is not molested in any fashion."

"Thank you, Prokop," the president's wife savored her victory.

Drtina let the clearing of his throat suffice as his answer. They had known each other many years and he knew she would not take any offense.

"Call for us if there are any emergencies," Drtina urged her firmly.

"We will be fine. Go attend to more important matters," Mesdame Beneš bid them farewell.

Shutting the door to the Drawing Room behind them as they left, Drtina looked up at the commander with resignation. "What will the history books say? While Praha burned, President Beneš slept?"

MAIN ROAD, NEAR EGER

There was no radio in the staff car, which was an annoying deficiency. Kopecky had been recalled to Praha and he had no idea why. The order had been relayed out to him in the field where he was inspecting the most recent forward positions that army units were settling into. The last Kopecky had heard was that Beneš and his cabinet were still deliberating on a second response to the French and British. The communiqué had interrupted a spirited discussion after dinner with the colonel in command of the battalion that Kopecky had come to inspect. No reason given, just return immediately. The not knowing why was a major irritant. Especially since local Germans he had come in contact with during the day seemed especially smug – as if they knew something important that Kopecky did not. Orders were orders, however.

Neither did Kopecky relish traveling at night. The Freikorps were very active in the area and were causing a great deal of mischief. The colonel and Kopecky discussed their options and decided faster was preferable to more protection. So the plukovník dispatched a motorcycle escort to accompany Kopecky's car until they were well east of the frontier: one motorcycle on point and one motorcycle at the rear. Despite the escort his driver Hruska had produced a personal pheasant-hunting shotgun, which he was keeping close by on the passenger seat. It was not a standard issue weapon but Kopecky had no reason to argue with the choice. For himself, Kopecky had the vz.33 carbine from his own collection beside him. It was lightweight and easy to handle in delicate situations. Kopecky had broken the weapon down and oiled it before leaving for the frontier so the rifle felt almost new as he gently caressed the barrel.

The road was generally in good condition and they were making a high-speed run with little or no opposing traffic to slow them down. Kopecky checked his wristwatch. They had been on their journey for almost a half hour. Before he had a chance to look up, Kopecky felt the concussion from a grenade exploding ahead. The lead motorcyclist disappeared from view – obscured by a blur of dust and dirt. Neither would Kopecky get a chance to determine what had happened to the man. A machine gun opened fire from the left forcing Hruska to respond by lurching the Tatra to the right off the road and into a field. The rear motorcyclist zoomed past on the road when his front tire was hit by bullet fire and the machine crumbled underneath him before careening off the road into a tree. The way the staff car was bouncing up and down on the uneven dirt was making the vehicle hard to hit. Whether this had been intentional was another story as Kopecky attempted to ride out the harsh conditions. "Try to get us back on the road as soon as possible."

"That's what I am working on, sir." In the darkness Hruska was unaware of a deep irrigation ditch to their right. With a pile of cut lumber suddenly looming ahead he swerved further to the right and ran the Tatra into the unseen ditch. The car flipped on its side and skated wildly along on the rock and dirt surface until natural obstructions slowed the injured vehicle to a stop. Hruska pushed the collapsible windshield down and slipped out with the pheasant gun out using the engine hood for cover. Before he could assist Kopecky out of the back of the Tatra the major's carbine was tossed out a window and his officer was already climbing out of the skyward facing rear passenger door. Since that was the most elevated part of the stricken staff vehicle, Kopecky immediately drew machine gun fire.

"Bastards," Kopecky cursed when he landed roughly at the bottom of the ditch. "Stay down, we have company!" Kopecky rolled over several times until he could reach his rifle. He chambered a round, jumped up high enough to nestle against the top lip of the ditch and acquired a target in the dark. Easing off a round, Kopecky chambered another bullet, aimed then fired a second time. He hadn't noticed Hruska had taken up station next to him.

"Nice shooting for an officer," the corporal whispered. "Right between the eyes both of them."

The machine gun nest sprayed the dirt in front of their eyes forcing the Czechs back down in the ditch.

"I think I just made them angry," Kopecky chambered another rifle round.

"No, I am sure you made them angry, sir," Hruska pressed back against the ditch wall. "Sorry about the car."

"Couldn't be helped," Kopecky patted him on the shoulder. "Who knew someone had put a ditch here." Kopecky looked at the Tatra with a mind to pulling the vehicle back down on all four tires and making a run for it. But he noticed straight away that one of the front wheels was badly bent – too much so to roll true.

"Looks like we're not driving out of here," Kopecky pointed out the damage. "What else is in the Tatra that we can use?"

"Extra ammunition, an infantry Mauser, three or four grenades, some flares and rations," Hruska itemized from memory.

"Those will have to do," Kopecky started going over their options. The machine gun fire had dropped off so Kopecky snuck up high enough to spy the field and saw the outlines of an old Austrian helmet rising up between the Czechs and the machine gun emplacement. Kopecky brought his carbine to bear and hit the helmet square with a loud clang.

"You got him sir?" Hruska heard the bullet strike metal.

"Just gave him a headache I am afraid," Kopecky reported as he slid back down into the ditch. A second later, bullets impacted the dirt close to where his head had been. "Those Freikorps are going to figure out they shouldn't charge us from the same line as their machine gun is firing from. We can expect they will try and flank us from the sides and the rear. Let's get ready to give them a warm welcome."

44TH FIGHTER FLIGHT, POLERADY – BOHEMIA

The news on the radio had been bad all day. His men had been training tirelessly for months and were ready to fight yet now the government was openly capitulating. Such news was disastrous for the morale of Bozik's pilots. Morose airmen would be easy pickings should the Luftwaffe appear overhead. They needed something to occupy their minds for a while. After dinner, Bozik rounded up his pilots and forced them to follow him to the shed they used for flight briefings. It wasn't much, with only two electric light bulbs hanging from the rafters over twenty beat up chairs, but they would be away from the damned radio.

"Gather around and have a look at this," Bozik unrolled a large map onto the table using a few rocks he had picked up from the field to hold down the edges. "This is the central portion of the frontier we are responsible for. Notice these arrows I have drawn here, here and here. These are all recent incursions by Luftwaffe bombers over the border."

"Verified how, sir?" Franek knew of no squadrons that had caught the Germans.

"Verified by ground spotters," Bozik moved on. "Note the angle that takes them from their territory over ours before they veer off back to their side of the border."

"Could be pilot or navigator error, sir. Nedoma saw nothing importance in those areas worth violating the border.

"I considered that. But these incursions are happening with greater frequency and they are cutting deeper into our territory. They could be testing us to determine how far they can cheat over onto our side before we challenge them. If we do not challenge them it would be a simple thing for them to veer east toward our industrial zones with a head start. Their bombers are too quick so we cannot let that happen," Bozik was about to put the hunt back into his pilots.

"But our orders are not engage unless fired upon," Hasek had his own view of what challenge meant.

"That is correct. Starting tomorrow we are putting up an extra patrol over this area. Any of those Luftwaffe birds that stray over the border are to be escorted back in the other direction... short of firing on them but turn them back," Bozik laid out the strategy.

"Is this even necessary anymore," Cervena stepped away from the table. "Why challenge the German bombers if all we're going to do is surrender?"

"Do not believe everything you hear on the radio, poručík," Bozik pursued the young pilot and turned him about. "Politicians always speak from both sides of their mouths. What is said for the benefit of the French and British politicians does not dictate our reality in the air or on the ground. At this moment Hitler sends those Sudeten Freikorps traitors further and further inland to provoke us. Hitler does not want us to surrender he wants to pummel us in battle. He yearns for this. Nothing Chamberlain offers Hitler will change that fact. We have a fight ahead of us, and mark my words, we will cost Hitler dearly."

PRAŽSKÝ HRAD, PRAHA

The state police had been securing the perimeter around the castle for almost an hour. Their strategy was to flush the citizens from the inner courtyard into a natural funnel between buildings to a side gate where they would be forced down the hill away from the compound. It was close to midnight and the state police kapitán in charge hoped the these people where just tired enough to call it a night in favor of going home to a warm bed. There would be no more compatriots arriving to bolster the number of demonstrators. Every street and alley leading to the castle was under guard. The policemen had made no effort to hide their preparations for the benefit of the demonstrators so everyone understood the situation clearly.

Burda and Furst approached the kapitán accompanied by a half dozen Second Department cohorts wearing their army uniforms. They were here to assist the police and the uniforms would lead to less confusion once the operation got going. Burda stopped beside the police kapitán at the small guardhouse adjacent to the main gate.

"Kapitán Burda, Second Department General Staff, reporting," Burda saluted crisply.

"Kapitán Grof here. Good to have you with us," Grof returned the salute.

"Those are the individuals to watch for," Burda produced a dossier, which he handed over. "All have direct connections to foreign governments. There are two groups, however. The members of the first are relatively benign and arresting them would prove troublesome diplomatically. The second group is known provocateurs. Participating in this disturbance is a good pretext to hold them for swift deportation."

Grof quickly perused the contents of the dossiers before tendering it to a nearby sergeant. "Excellent. This information will prove most useful. My thanks."

"These men are available to assist with identification," Burda gestured to Furst and the other Second Department men.

"I can put them to good use," Grof was pleased for the aid. "Gentlemen, follow my četař here. He will show you where your services can best be applied."

When the others had left, Burda peered inside the gates at the citizens milling about inside the courtyard.

"Seems fairly peaceful. What is the current status near the presidential wing?" Burda thought the scene felt too quiet.

"We have direct telephone communication with the president's personal secretary. No attempt has been made to break inside the building for nearly two hours," Grof considered it lucky the situation on the grounds was not urgent. "Did you know that Generál Syrový marched in there alone earlier tonight?"

"I had no idea," Burda wondered what other improbabilities the night held for them. "What was he trying to accomplish?"

"Turns out the rabble was calling for him by name. Very loudly too I am told: *Weapons or Syrový*. Give them weapons to fight or give them a new leader who will fight for them," Grof described what he had been told by a legionnaire.

"Sorry I missed that," Burda felt a chill that he had foretold the circumstances so closely. "What was the result?"

"I don't know the words he used but they listened to him. Whatever Syrový said the attempts to force entry into the presidential quarters ceased and the angry mood of the crowd dissipated. The situation is still tense but no longer volatile. The problem is these people still won't leave," Grof summed up their position.

"What is your plan of action?" Burda shifted to the more pressing issue.

"Sadly, I do not have specific instructions for this state of affairs. Therefore, my goal is to clear the castle compound with a minimum of violence with as few arrests as possible. We just want the people out of here and Hradčany secure," Grof pulled out a pocket watch to confirm that it was almost midnight. "We might as well get started then. Follow me, kapitán."

It would have helped if Petra didn't move around so much. While General Syrový had been mingling amidst the crowd she had followed him everywhere to ask more questions. More annoyingly, the general kept moving away from Bulloch's position. And since Petra never left his side, Bulloch couldn't rush in and scoop her up as he wished. Now that the Syrový had finally left, Bulloch was inconspicuously getting close to her. Petra was going back and forth between her student friends. He could tell none of them quite knew what to do next. Syrový had calmed the crowd and gave them hope yet no one trusted the government enough to take the pressure off by leaving. So they sat, and talked... and talked some more.

At least Talmadge and her boyfriend had trotted off after Syrový. That ungrateful harpy got under his skin in the worst way. With the Federal police arriving Bulloch reckoned the reporters would have plenty of new victims to keep them occupied for the rest of the night. The protesters had been nervously eying the police build-up and a little bit of apprehension and fear was seeping in.

Suddenly, sharp whistles started blowing from behind them. Bulloch stepped up on a bench and saw men on horseback in the lead followed by a solid line of police advancing behind them. The crowd hesitated not knowing exactly how to respond. Now was Bulloch's opportunity. He launched swiftly through the crowd and planted himself in front of Petra.

"Nathan, you found me! I am so glad," Petra wrapped her arms around him.

"Me too darling... time to go." Bulloch bent down and roguishly threw her over his shoulder so swiftly and securely that Petra had no chance to object. With the crowd focused on the approaching police Bulloch made off with his prize in the opposite direction.

27. REVERSAL

A Tatra sedan shot up by the Sudeten Freikorps

SEPTEMBER 22, 1938
MAIN ROAD, NEAR EGER

All through the night the pesky Czech soldiers had held them off. One of them was a damn good shot with eyes like an owl's. After the unterscharführer lost one man, and had another seriously wounded, he would not leave the area without taking possession of two dead Czechs to show for their efforts. At least they thought it was only two. That was all the members of his squad had seen escaping from the overturned Tatra. His own relic of an Austrian helmet had stopped a round directly in front of his forehead. God bless whoever had manufactured that old bucket. It had saved his life but the squad leader's head still ached like someone was pounding his skull with a hammer. Several times during the night he had attempted to flank their prey with no success. The irrigation ditch the staff car had rolled over into was deep enough to provide the Czechs a natural defensive trench. Another problem was the night was clear and there was a good deal of moon and starlight that betrayed their approach. And that damned shooter never slept. The Freikorps squad leader hoped this devil wasn't the officer. One of the men escaping the staff car was wearing the kind of fashionable long coat only officers got to wear. To be thwarted by an officer would be embarrassing.

The sun would be rising soon and the unterscharführer figured he would have one last chance to overcome the Czechoslovak position before the area got hot with enemy transport. For this attempt he had sent two of his men far to the right, and the unterscharführer was flanking with a fourth corpsman far to the left. Both approaches were well covered by thick brush and trees. The two teams would hug the ground until they had worked themselves over to the opposite side of the Czech position and approach their targets with the benefit of the rising sun behind them. The shooter wouldn't be much good with the sun in his eyes. The remainder of the squad leader's men would launch a distracting attack from the direction of the road to draw the attention of the Czechs.

The unterscharführer and his corpsman had worked themselves into position while it was still dark. It had taken less time than he had anticipated. Using the extra minutes to relax, he cranked his head to listen carefully but could hear nothing from the direction of the Czechs. That was not to his liking. Much better for the targets to be making some noise for that would betray their exact locations. The squad leader didn't much like approaching a marksman who was waiting for a trophy goose to present itself. After about twenty minutes the sun was above the tree line, and unterscharführer felt more confident. He gestured to his companion to follow and they crawled slowly on their stomachs toward the Czech position – each pushing their Mauser rifles in front of their noses. A breeze was picking up, which would help mask their movement. By the time they closed within twenty meters of their targets his comrades by the road open fired right on schedule. There was no return fire or movement from the Czechs, however. This lack of activity bothered the unterscharführer for he did not trust that devil marksman. They would just have to push forward, regardless. The squad leader saw the second team on the other side was slightly closer to the ditch and in position to pounce. He signaled them to get ready.

Now the unterscharführer picked up his pace the last few meters to the ditch. His attention was focused intently on the lip above the depression in the dirt. If the shooter's head popped up there would only be one quick chance to get a rifle shot off first. But still there was nothing to see or hear that would betray what the Czechs were up to. The unterscharführer had gauged the distance of the other team correctly... they reached their edge of the ditch first. Rather than wait to attack jointly, as they had been told, both of the morons leapt in with their rifles drawn. The squad leader cursed under his breath at their lack of discipline. Now he would have to further expose himself. But there was nothing else to be done. The unterscharführer rose to a crouch and sprinted the final distance to the ditch and jumped in with his trooper right behind him. But there was nothing. Nothing at all between him and their two compatriots slowly approaching from the far side of the stricken Tatra. Had the two Czechs snuck away to safety in the dark? The unterscharführer was growing frustrated at the prospect of losing his quarry. All he could see was empty shell casings and debris strewn around the vehicle. And since his men at the road had ceased shooting when they saw their comrades jumping into the ditch, all that could be heard was his boots crushing dirt and rock as he slowly stepped closer to the Tatra.

Something did not feel right. But the squad leader could not tell exactly what was out of place. Then he sensed something – a small disturbance in the earth along the side of the ditch behind his two approaching corpsmen. Loose gravel and pebbles were sliding to the floor of the dugout alongside the wall. Before he could call out an alarm one of the Czechs burst out of the ground where he had buried himself. The unterscharführer saw the double barrel of a huge shotgun come level with his other team. One chamber fired – blowing the first of his men back into the air from the force of the shotgun blast at close range. Before the squad leader could aim his own rifle to return fire the Czech unloaded the contents of his other barrel into a second victim. Two more of his comrades lost, their torsos ripped open and replaced with gaping holes. This Czech was going to die. As the trigger of the unterscharführer's Mauser squeezed tight he sensed another disturbance from behind… and cursed. A rifle shot rang out.

Pivoting around the squad leader found himself face to face with the second unaccounted for Czech. The officer. The ends of that unbuttoned long coat flapping on the wind sweeping through the ditch. That devil marksman was out of his hiding place and had already downed the squad leader's last trooper with a bullet through the back of the skull. The youngster's body fell limp to the earth with a hard thud. Now three of his men had died this morning. The squad leader was going to die as well but perhaps he would not die alone. Off balance, the unterscharführer got off a single round from his rifle. The shot missed to the right as his target shifted to the side to discard his carbine. There was no time to chamber another round before the Czech devil's gun hand deftly reached for the vz.24 pistol nestled under the officer's trouser belt. There was such precision and economy of movement in the way the devil leveled the barrel of the pistol at a spot slightly above the bridge of the squad leader's nose. There was no delay in taking aim. The pistol simply rose up and fired instantaneously. The unterscharführer thought he glimpsed the 9mm bullet on its trajectory. Then his headache was gone.

GODESBERGER HOF, GODESBERG

The line to the Berlin Bureau was clear with none of the rotten static he had gotten used to for months. Endicott had to hand it to the Germans they really wanted to make a big impression. Just like the Olympics in 1936 there was no expense spared and every minor detail accounted for. Say what you will about the Nazis, they knew how to throw a party when they wanted to. These were the kinds of things a person making do on reporter's pay tended to notice. The voice from Berlin spoke up on the line. They were ready to take down Endicott's copy. "All right, here we go:"

Dateline Godesberg. After days of uncertainty, British Prime Minister Neville Chamberlain and German Chancellor Adolph Hitler are set for a diplomatic rendezvous today here in this picturesque little town nestled beside the Rhine River. Local residents awoke at sunrise to catch a glimpse of their beloved chancellor. A thousand of Herr Hitler's elite SS guards uniformed in black has cordoned off the streets of Godesberg to protect the German leader during his stay at the riverside lodgings of the Hotel Dreesen. Authorities here tell us that the chancellor's staff reserved the entire establishment for the occasion and Mister Chamberlain will conduct his negotiations with Herr Hitler there, as well. New graph.

The streets of Godesberg are lined with storm troopers in uniform and school children waving flags. From every building and every lamppost the German flag and the British Union Jack hang side-by-side. Groups of lovely young women sing patriotic songs on nearly every corner. Herr Hitler was accompanied to Godesberg by Foreign Minister, von Ribbentrop; Propaganda Minister, Doctor Goebbels; and the head of the State Police, Herr Himmler. New graph.

The British prime minister is set to arrive later this afternoon by air in Cologne, the major metropolis in this area of Germany. Mister Chamberlain is making a direct flight from Heston airport near London on a brand new and very fast airliner built by the Lockheed Company in America. The three hundred mile flight usually takes close to three hours to complete but British officials here in Godesberg expect Mister Chamberlain's trip will not take near as long. They want to give the British leader plenty of time to refresh before he starts discussions with Herr Hitler, scheduled to begin around four o'clock this evening. New graph.

Although there has been no official confirmation from British or German authorities, informed sources say Mister Chamberlain is set to negotiate based on the following agenda. One: The setting up of an international commission for the Sudetenland region to arrange for the withdrawal of the Czechs and the transfer of the German and Czechoslovak populations. Two: An appeal by the Western Powers for a period of peace and tranquility during which the present crisis in Europe can be calmed. And three: Putting an international guaranty in place for what remains of Czechoslovakia. End.

Endicott paused while the editor in Paris finished scribbling the story down. "Okay, you got all of that? Read it back to me. Yeah, all of it."

While he listened another reporter was standing too close, glaring at Endicott and tapping his foot while waiting for his chance to use the phone. Endicott cupped his hand over the microphone and stared back at the fellow. "Listen buddy... I waited my turn you wait yours. Next time hurry it up if you want to be in the front of the line."

The warning had its desired effect. The impatient newspaperman backed away a few steps. When Endicott returned his attention to the editor the read through was ending. He had not heard any errors.

"Yeah, what I heard sounds good. You're perfect... send that copy through. I'll file again after Chamberlain lands and probably tonight too... No, nobody has a clue what Hitler and Chamberlain will announce tonight. Whatever happens I'll let you know, bye," Endicott ended the call.

Quickly gathering his notes, Endicott rose to his feet and then planted himself nose-to-nose with the impatient reporter.

"That wasn't so bad now, was it?" Endicott taunted him. Not waiting for an answer, he headed for the exit as his foil hurried to grab the phone. Exiting the hotel Endicott ran to a waiting sedan. Getting in the back he sat down next to Shirer.

"Okay, let's go," Endicott commanded the driver before turning to face Shirer. "Thanks for waiting."

"My pleasure. We have plenty of time to get to the airfield," Shirer saw no reason to rush. "Our driver is courtesy of Doctor Goebbels. I doubt he'll let us miss the prime minister's arrival."

"If these Nazis didn't constantly give you the creeps a fella could get used to this kind of treatment," Endicott let his body relax back into the bench seat.

BULLOCH'S FLAT
MALA STRANA DISTRICT, PRAHA

The girl had been perched atop his groin teasing him mercilessly. Bulloch needed to check in at the embassy but Petra was pulling every little trick in her bountiful repertoire to persuade him to pal around with her for the day. She had the top sheet loosely draped around her legs and waist but the rest of her was completely bare in the morning sunlight streaming through the bedroom window. Carrying her off to safety the previous night had touched Petra deeply. The girl could take care of herself yet she really was touched that Bulloch had spent the whole evening locating her. His reward was a wonderfully sleepless night. That is how a very weary Bulloch found himself at eight o'clock in the morning with a young tigress straddling his waist irresistibly encouraging his manhood back to life.

"Do you surrender, my kapitán?" Petra demanded in a low purr.

"You are merciless, angel." Bulloch's protest was unconvincing.

"I know... and I get what I want," her legs applied more pressure. "Surrender, and I will let you out to do something useful. Resist, and I will keep you prisoner the entire day."

"I should be building a bomb shelter right now. We might have need of one you know," Bulloch appealed to her practicality.

"Wrong answer, prisoner," Petra passed judgment on him by reaching down and grabbing him firmly.

Part of Bulloch knew he should be sensible with all hell breaking loose around them yet he was enjoying this moment far too much as she had her way with him. Bulloch seized her securely at the hips with both hands and Petra gasped. "What are your terms?"

"Unconditional surrender." Without interrupting their rhythm she leaned down and kissed him full on the lips.

ASCH, SUDETENLAND

Communications with Asch had been established for more than a day. The Freikorps in the village had reported the town was secure and the Czechs were not contesting ownership. The situation around Eger was less clear. Berlin had been crowing on the radio that the Sudeten Freikorps had taken control of Eger but that wasn't what was described in the last action reports Morgen had read. The reports said there were plenty of heavy Czechoslovak army units operating further east and they were making themselves known. He would have to discuss the matter with the ranking Freikorps commander for more up to date information. For now, Morgen was tasked with adding some teeth to the Freikorps units already in Asch. Since the Sudetens controlled the border crossing it was a simple matter of driving the half-tracks straight up the road and into the town. Morgen was adamant that his company would be the first SS unit to cross the border. His spotters had noted Czech aircraft in the vicinity but they were not threatening the company's movement. All the better the Czechs got an idea of what they were facing, Morgen reckoned.

Morgen jumped down from his transport as soon as they reached the main square. Some of the Freikorps men were coming out of their positions to greet them. Morgen was not the social type and ignored them. He had little patience for deserters, regardless of their nationality. Morgen would just as soon hand them back over to the Czechoslovaks than depend on a deserter to cover his back.

"You there!" Morgen beckoned to a nearby Freikorps rottenf"uhrer. "Are there forward positions suitable for my guns?"

Morgen's demeanor was intimidating but the corporal focused on the anti-tank guns towed by the half-tracks and knew what the SS company leader wanted.

"Yes, there are some good positions with natural ground cover for concealment and protection," the rottenf"uhrer gestured head.

"That will do nicely. Get up here and show my men where to get set up," Morgen pointed a stubby finger at the front seat of the half-track.

As the Freikorps man enthusiastically climbed onto the vehicle, Morgen turned his attention back to his own men. "This man will show you where are the best spots. Get the guns unhitched and dug in within a half-hour unless your rear ends want a date with my boot."

His men were well drilled and equally well used to Morgen's bluster. The threat was more for the benefit of the Sudetens who needed to know who was the rabid dog to be feared as they witnessed the deadly efficiency of an SS-Verfügungstruppe up close. As the half-tracks left for the outer perimeter of Asch the officer in charge of the Sudetens strutted up to present himself. Morgen had not intended to salute a Freikorps fop regardless of rank but he recognized the man as SS.

"Sturmscharführer Morgen," he presented himself with a sharp salute.

"Hauptsturmführer Horst. I believe we have met before," Horst recognized Morgen, as well.

"Weren't you attached to Germania? We shared the road to Vienna with your regiment," Morgen recalled the unconscionable traffic caused by broken down vehicles.

"That was it. Good to see you again and very glad to have SS men on station," Horst was sincerely relieved to have the reinforcements that had been promised.

"The rest of battalion is not far behind. No worries now," Morgen reported proudly.

"Excellent. This area has been very quiet but that could change quickly if the diplomats fail," Horst confided.

"What is the situation in Eger? The picture I am getting is muddy," Morgen was eager for a fight if one could be had.

"The local population has seized some of the civil offices and other Freikorps units are very active in the city but my scouts tell me that the surrounding area is thick with Czechoslovak regular units," Horst knew those facts were not getting into the papers.

"Too bad we are so far away," Morgen would have no excuse to check things out personally.

"Looking for a fight, are you?" Horst could read the emotions of this old brawler well enough. The SS was full of such men. Tranquility unnerved them. "I doubt you will have to wait very long the way things are going."

"That is an attitude I can appreciate. Patience is not one of my strong suits," Morgen liked this man already.

P5RAŽSKÝ HRAD, PRAHA

He had awoken to find his wife sitting calmly in the chair next to the door leading to the study. Hana was reading the morning newspaper, something she never did in this room. This was odd in and of itself as his wife was very particular about such things. Beneš squinted to see what the headline was but his vision was too blurry to make it out. She told him soon enough what he had missed, which explained why his wife was standing guard at the door. Beneš' first reaction was to scold her for allowing him to slumber. He was the president and should have spoken to the people in the courtyard personally. Beneš soon reconsidered protesting further when he noticed the weariness around her eyes. His wife had been up all night doing what she thought best. He could not rebuke her. Perhaps it was for the best. These momentous events that he had slept through had provided Beneš with a solution to the problem he had faced since acceptance of the Anglo-French plan had been announced. Had Hana roused him, and Beneš had dealt with the crowd in person, his options would be fewer today.

Once he had made himself presentable, Beneš entered his study to find Drtina patiently waiting to fill him in on every detail of the previous night. His friend had been right. Giving in to Chamberlain's coercion had brought the country close to revolution. What no one had predicted was that the people would demand Syrový to save them. The generál was popular as a symbol but was not a man possessed with political inclinations. Syrový's public anointment was nothing short of brilliance, however. The people were angry and they wanted a blood sacrifice. As soon as the sun had risen thousands had flooded the streets once again to demand weapons and mobilization. For now they were not calling for the president's head but the people were demanding that the government that had accepted the British and French ultimatum must go. Each time the phone on Drtina's desk rang there was a new report from the heart of the city. Factories were closing, businesses were shuttered and a huge demonstration was forming outside the chamber of deputies. The crisis had brought normally warring political factions together in common cause. There was the communist Gottwald standing tall side-by-side with the Lord Mayor of Praha and conservative leader Ladislav Rašín. Beneš had to defuse the powder keg without resorting to the army and Syrový was the answer.

Beneš immediately sent Drtina out to find Prime Minister Hodza, and after that was accomplished, locate Generál Syrový. When the three sat down together Beneš was direct and honest. The crisis demanded that Hodza resign as prime minister. This was no reflection on Hodza but the people were demanding change in the administration of the country. The prime minister understood completely. Having a strong political base of his own, Hodza could have resisted yet he saw the emergency for what it was and agreed to resign as Beneš asked. Syrový was the harder sell of the two. Forthright and sincere, Syrový considered himself ill-equipped for political service, especially the job of prime minister. Beneš met the generál with equal earnestness. The people trusted the army veteran. Syrový's greatest asset was his humility and many years of service. Obtaining Syrový's acceptance took coaxing yet Beneš knew that his appeal to the generál's sense of duty would not allow him to refuse. Syrový agreed to become the next prime minister and form a new government of national defence. They decided former and current military officers would also take on portfolios in the new cabinet that would be formed. Men like Generál Husarek, who recently had been the director of fortifications could be counted on. Syrový himself agreed to take on the cabinet position of defence minister.

There was a risk for Beneš, however. The change he was orchestrating was a calculated political response to the public unrest sweeping the country. The truth was little in the actual governance of the country, or his polices, would change. His new cabinet would be weak politically with little leverage over the president. Beneš needed to assure the people that he had heard them. He needed to quell these protests without resorting to force. If the masses came to the conclusion that their president was insincere, however, Beneš *would* have a revolution on his hands and would be forced to resign. A further complication was that by installing this new government of national defence, with ministers possessing strong ties to the army hierarchy, Beneš would be increasing the likelihood of a coup d'état. Generál Krejčí was already exhibiting worrisome independence in his recent decisions. Forcing the partial mobilization on an elected government without approval was a message. Krejčí would take those measures he thought prudent for the defence of the nation regardless of the political implications. Would it also prove prudent to remove the president from office? Beneš thought not, yet the possibility was very real indeed.

The cold reality was Beneš was playing for time. Time to cajole the Soviets into a commitment to march regardless of whether the French did so, and time for Hitler to overreach in his demands, thereby forcing Chamberlain to terminate negotiations. If this change in government reassured the people and the military that the president would fight rather than surrender then the risk he was taking was perfectly sound. The next seventy-two hours would tell one way or another.

LUFTWAFFE AERODROME, KÖLN

As promised, the driver from the propaganda ministry had delivered Endicott and Shirer to the airfield with time to spare. It was closing in on twelve-thirty and Chamberlain's plane was due any moment. Just as Godesberg had been spruced up with every inch decorated with German and British flags, the same was true of this new military aerodrome, which was still under construction. Not that this was easy to notice with all the decorations. Once again the Nazis had gone all out for the five thousand or more people packed in front of the main hangar. At least that was the number Endicott and Shirer estimated. There was also an SS honor guard assembled and waiting for the prime minister's arrival – dress uniforms and all. The same ones they used for the Olympics and the Nürnberg party rallies: shiny black steel helmets and white gloves. There was even an SS band in the same outfits. Despite all of the pomp there was no Hitler. The press was told the chancellor was fatigued after his trip to Godesberg and needed a nap back at the Dreesen. Foreign Minister von Ribbentrop was on hand with his entourage, however, and Shirer recognized the German Secretary of State von Weizaecker.

"Did you notice? Dirksen, the German ambassador in London is standing next to von Ribbentrop. He must have come out early," a familiar voice commented from behind Endicott.

"Thanks pal. I was wondering if that guy was important," Endicott turned around to discover Roland looking rested in a fresh suit. "Roland! Aren't you a sight for sore eyes? When did you get here?"

"Oh, I have been in Germany for quite some time. I received a note right before the prime minister left for Berchtesgaden and I departed Prague post haste." Roland was not in a position to say whom the note was from.

"You little devil. I forget how well connected you are. Sounds like you had a much easier time getting to Godesberg than I did," Endicott needed to watch Roland's moves more carefully.

"Having read your recent article of the other day, I dare say so. I am so pleased you were not hurt," although Roland was a tad envious of the published outcome.

"Everything came up roses for Charles regardless," Shirer jumped into the conversation.

"Hey you two know each other don't you? From Vienna?" Endicott wanted to be sure introductions were not required.

"Oh yes, William and I are well acquainted," Roland knew Shirer from his old Berlin posting.

Shirer had a suspicion about Roland but nothing that could be proven… at least not yet. The next time he was in London Shirer would make some discreet inquiries. Maybe there was a connection through a gentleman's club or an old regiment in Roland's background that would account for his relationship with Lady Luck. Until then Shirer would keep his curiosity to himself.

"Glad to have you with us, Roland. Any idea whether Mister Chamberlain will have anything to say on arrival?" Endicott figured if anyone would know it would be Roland.

"Nothing prepared from what I am told," Roland had already inquired. "The prime minister is not a gifted orator. I suspect public speaking makes him a touch nervous."

The airbase public address system crackled to life with a quick announcement in German. Upon completion of the message the German dignitaries waiting for Chamberlain adjusted their suit jackets and hats.

"They just announced that Chamberlain's plane is on final approach," Shirer translated.

"Outstanding," Endicott checked his wristwatch. "That means they made the trip in under two hours with that new Lockheed. That will read well in the States."

The chancellor had slept little the night before and was in a foul of temper. The original plan was for him to meet the English prime minister in person but the Führer was wracked with headaches and in no condition to appear socially. Hitler was convinced he was wasting his time with the Englishman. There was no question the prime minister was arriving with the promised concessions but the chancellor was fixated on the vicissitudes of the Czechoslovak president and he had worked himself up into a punitive fury. Mister Chamberlain was in for a rude reception. Platen would not be surprised if Hitler demanded of Chamberlain that Beneš' head be presented on a pike.

For years Platen had heard rumors of Hitler's short temper and regular tirades. Leaders of great nations were expected to have their eccentricities but what Platen had seen for himself had gone far beyond his expectations. The last few weeks alongside the foreign minister in close proximity to the chancellor had been like something from the horrorfilms. Hitler could transform into a fire-spewing monster at the smallest provocation. Those high in the party said the Führer's manner was a symptom of true genius. Genius, or madness... Platen felt like a parakeet in cage hanging inside the main tent of a foul carnival. The atmosphere would surely kill him one day.

The foreign minister pointed skyward and Platen saw sunlight reflecting on unpainted metal. It was a twin-engined plane – very sleek and modern with a low wing – approaching very swiftly. Platen gripped his notebook tightly and breathed deeply. At least his mental control had improved. His hands almost never shook like they once did. Walking this tightrope between his duties to von Ribbentrop and his financial relationship with Czech spies was a condition Platen knew he could not maintain for much longer before he was discovered. There were eyes and ears everywhere reporting to the party. Maybe Platen could get his brother-in-law the doctor to help concoct a believable justification for a transfer to a less stressful ministry – someplace like agriculture where he could be a church mouse of no value to the Czechs or anyone else.

For now, Platen steeled himself. The agenda before them was grueling and that was before the chancellor and the prime minister were to meet late in the afternoon. He told himself if he could get through this day everything would get better. Platen turned his head to follow Chamberlain's aircraft roaring low overhead. The pilot probably was taking in the airfield before attempting a landing. Soon the show would be starting. Platen pulled a folder from inside his notebook and offered it to von Ribbentrop. "Mister Foreign Minister, the revised schedule."

PARLIAMENT BUILDING, PRAHA

The second day of mass demonstrations got rolling as the sun came up over the city. Ros and Sanderson had roused themselves early in the hopes of locating an open telex office. They had given up on finding an international phone line after returning to the Ambassador early that morning and being told international lines were no longer available. Both journalists had great quotes from General Syrový and needed to file their reports but they had no way of contacting their bureaus. The civil authorities had succeeded in gaining control of the seat of power up in Hradčany but the same could not be said for the rest of Prague. No one had to call a general strike since people on their own chose not to go to their jobs or their schools or their shops. Ros did notice a difference, however. The Czechs again went about their protests to surrender in an orderly manner but they weren't as positive as the previous day. The euphoria of tens of thousands coming together spontaneously had given way to a grimmer determination. Sanderson suggested that the dour mood might also be a response to the complete lack of knowledge of what was really happening at the border. Many people were sure Hitler's armies were already on their way to Prague.

When the reporters learned of the rally outside parliament via a post on a light pole they decided this was their best bet to find a focal point for the day's protests. Unfortunately, no trolleys were running and even foot traffic was a near standstill on some streets in the capital. It was like pushing past people to get close the Thanksgiving Day parade in New York. Along the way they discovered the long-winded Gottwald had organized the rally, which was supposed to be a demonstration of unity between political parties that usually hated each other's guts. As Ros and Sanderson closed in on the Czechoslovak parliament they were handed leaflets bearing the names the reporters recognized as some of the most influential legislators in the country. If as many of these flyers were being handed out along the other main thoroughfares leading to Parliament, there might be hundreds of thousands of copies circulating by now. The leaflets urged citizens to exhort President Beneš to rely on the full support a united nation to turn away from surrender.

What Ros and Sanderson finally shoved there way close to the parliament building they saw Gottwald in mid-harangue, flanked by many of the same men who had signed the leaflets, working the crowd into a patriotic lather. "Look around you! Who can argue that all Czechoslovaks stand as one? If Hitler wants to take our lands... let him come. Our people will fight the Germans from every cottage and every factory. Let them pay a price for their arrogance. Nothing should be given away for free. That is our message to the president. Fight for your nation and you will fight side-by-side with the people!"

"Wow, he's singing a different tune today," Ros was skeptical of this newfound solidarity. "If I didn't know he was a communist it would be hard to tell.

"Yes quite," Sanderson leaned his head closer to hers to be better heard. "Last night up at the castle he was going on about how Beneš and his ministers had brought the revolution upon themselves. A rather keen tactical adjustment."

"New day, new horseshit, as my grandmother used to say," Ros' position on politics was a simple one.

"I think I would like your gran," Sanderson saw where the girl got her cheek.

Ros thought about the possibility long enough to be amused. "Oh hush with your sweet talk... look at that!"

A young government staffer ran up to the makeshift stage to deliver a note to the mayor of Prague. After reading the message the mayor became very excited and motioned for Gottwald and the other dignitaries to come closer. The men discussed the matter together for several minutes until the mayor broke from the group to step to the microphone stand.

"Fellow citizens!" the mayor pulled the microphone closer. "I have amazing news. President Beneš has asked Generál Jan Syrový to lead a new government of national defence following the immediate resignation of Prime Minister Hodza and the president's cabinet. And what I have just learned is that Syrový has accepted and will become prime minister!"

The huge crowd deliriously burst into a cheer of approval. As the Czechs launched into singing their national anthem, Sanderson grabbed Ros by the shoulders. "We have to find an open telex office!"

FORWARD COMMAND POST, NEAR EGER

The brigade commander was examining a large map of the area around Eger spread out on the collapsible metal table that had been set up in the middle of the tent. As he consulted the message slips that were coming in regularly from the radio operator the commander made notations in pencil on the map. The Sudetens had moved into the Eger zone in force the day before. Cocky bastards thought they could waltz in and take what they wanted. Today they had learned differently. Generál Krejčí had approved his request to repulse the incursion so the commander ordered his entire motorized brigade into action that morning. The reports coming in were all positive. There was heavy fighting all over the area but his tanks and infantry had routed the insurgents. It was a good day. His concentration was so focused he paid no attention when one of his officers entered the tent.

"Štábní Kapitán Capka reporting as ordered, plukovník," Capka saluted, his face and uniform streaked with dust.

"Excellent," the brigade commander finished off the notation he was working on before he rose to return the salute. "Tell me, how was it out there?"

"Like angry bees, sir. Lots of them to swat but their equipment was light, mostly heavy machine guns and few anti-tank cannon. They were well dug in, however. Took a while to root them out of their nests. Their cannon are completely ineffectual against our tanks, however. If we had sent ready units in there the armored cars and tankettes would have had problems with those guns but not a problem for a first-line battalion," Capka indicated areas on the map that had enemy positions.

"Noted. So no mechanized vehicles are in use by the Freikorps?" the brigade commander wanted first-hand confirmation of what he had been told.

"No sir. Not yet. Those we did not kill we sent running back to Germany on foot. If they had something in reserve to ride or fight with we would have seen that," Capka had been keen to destroy any motorized transport if they had found any.

"Very well--" the brigade commander was interrupted by the arrival of another junior officer on his staff. "--What is it porucík?"

"Sir, I have news of that stranded staff car in Zone R that the Letov aircrew reported this morning," the second lieutenant had finally pulled together what had happened. "A platoon was diverted to investigate. When they got to the location they chased off the remnants of a Freikorps unit and recovered an Army major and his driver. It turns out the two held off the Sudetens the entire night – killing a half dozen or more as I understand it."

"Now that is soldiering," the brigade commander was impressed. "Where are these two now?"

"They are being delivered right outside, sir," the second lieutenant gestured out the tent's entrance.

"Follow me. I want to meet these men." The three walked outside as a Tatra sped down the dirt road leading to the command post. The staff car slid to a stop on the loose earth as the doors opened. Kopecky and Hruska stepped out of the Tatra. Their uniforms were filthy from mud and dirt but the men wearing them were whole. Seeing the senior officer approaching both crisply saluted.

"Major Kopecky, attached to the general staff, sir," Kopecky acknowledged Capka with a quick sideways glance. "And this is my driver, Desátník Hruska.

"Glad to have you both with us major," the brigade commander saluted the two rescued men. "They tell me you had a full night."

"Fuller than I would care to repeat for a while," Kopecky's aching muscles were testament to that observation.

"And what about you, desátník, what have you to say?" the commander shifted his attention to Kopecky's driver.

"I am glad to say my major is a very good shot, sir," the corporal would happily tell the tale of their adventure for years to come.

"Good to see your aim is good on something other than clay pigeons, Tomáš," Capka could no longer joke that his friend was soft.

"Oh you know each other then?" the brigade commander looked back and forth between them.

"Mister Capka is like the demanding older brother I never had as a child, sir," Kopecky nestled a bit of sarcasm into his response.

"I know exactly what you mean. My own brother was a cruel bastard," the commander remembered how much he relished proving his sibling wrong.

"Someone had to toughen up this fop. It was a challenge but I never accept defeat," Capka played along.

"Let's see, you both met at officer's school," the brigade commander guessed.

"Yes sir, I had little choice but dedicate myself to tutoring Mister Capka to assure his passing our classes at the Cole Special Militaries de Saint-Cyr. The honor of our nation depended on my efforts. There were so few Czechs there I was duty bound to undertake this Herculean task," Kopecky embellished the tale.

"Saint-Cyr... the both of you? No wonder you two are cool under fire. I want to hear more about your deeds in the field this day. Get cleaned up and return then we will share a drink. It's one of the few luxuries I can offer out here," the brigade commander was feeling gracious. "You too desátník."

"Thank you, sir!" Hruska was thrilled at prospect of being treated to some liquor – fine or otherwise.

"Most appreciated, plukovník," Kopecky elbowed Hruska. "But we may not be in a position to accept. I was recalled to Praha and have already been terribly delayed. I should secure transit as soon as possible."

"Very laudable. But securing transit is at my discretion and I simply have no vehicles to spare until tomorrow. You are stuck with us until the morning," the commander would have his way. "Mister Capka, direct your friend here to the radio operator so that he can report to his superiors. I expect you three back here in ninety minutes."

"As you wish, sir," Capka accepted the task.

The three men covered in dust saluted and waited for the brigade commander to return to his tent.

"This way, Tomáš," Capka grabbed Kopecky's arm to point him in the right direction. "So why were you recalled?"

"I wish I knew. I was out checking units in the field when the order caught up with me. It was a relay, no details unfortunately," Kopecky was impatient to know more.

"Don't worry about the delay. Given the circumstances I don't think the general staff will punish you too severely. Besides, I want to hear how you put down that Sudeten trash," Capka's voice was full of pride.

HOTEL DREESEN, GODESBERG

No one was talking but the way Endicott read the winds the day hadn't gone well for the Brits. He had gotten a good look at both Chamberlain and his personal advisor, Wilson, when they had come through the lobby after three hours up in Hitler's hotel suite. Those sourpuss expressions they wore on their smackers was all Endicott needed to see. The Germans weren't too cheery either. No one was patting each other on the back and heading to the bar for a drink. The Nazi party muckety mucks who made it downstairs after the Brits left all shook their heads *no* when their pals in the lobby walked up looking for good news. The way Endicott described the mood in that night's dispatch was tense and uncertain. One of the reasons he was hanging around was the hope that Culemann fella would turn up. He seemed very well connected and a good snoop on top of that. Someone like that could confirm what Endicott had dredged up on his own.

Chamberlain had come to Godesberg bearing gifts. If Hitler hadn't accepted them with a Cheshire cat grin, Endicott reckoned it could only mean one of two things had happened. Either Hitler had raised the stakes on the British or the Czechs had done something nasty to piss off *der Führer*. Yet no one had heard of anything to disadvantage the Germans in the Sudetenland. In fact, all of the German rags were crowing about getting their reporters over the border into some of the towns on the Czechoslovak side to witness the liberation. If things weren't going the German's way Endicott was sure those same newspapers would be crying foul loud and clear. Add all of these details up and Endicott would bet a month's salary that Hitler had given Chamberlain a major case of heartburn.

Educated hunches would have to do for now. It would take a day or so before word of what was said filtered down to the busy bees working for the big men – the drones where all good leaks started. The details would come later but Endicott was sure his report had delivered the big picture correctly. As Herr Culemann was not to be found, the other thing keeping Endicott planted was Shirer's final broadcast of the day. Actually the first broadcast of Friday since it was after one a.m. already. Endicott wanted to hear how his friend wrapped it all up for the folks back home where it was nudging up to suppertime. This radio stuff was something else and Shirer had a knack for it. After the broadcast there still was time for a couple of rounds of drinks. Endicott figured tomorrow was only going to get worse for the British and this show was going to shut down pretty quickly so better to enjoy a little libation now while they could.

Endicott wandered out of the bar area back to the lobby where Shirer's makeshift radio stage was. The German engineer was almost done fiddling with his settings making sure everything was just right. Endicott leaned against a column and shot Shirer a thumbs-up.

"Hello America. This is Godesberg, Germany, calling," Shirer began the broadcast in his usual fashion. "For the second time today I'm talking to you from the Hotel Dreesen in Godesberg where for more than three hours this afternoon Chancellor Hitler and Prime Minister Chamberlain were in conference together. What was decided or even what was discussed in the little room just above us here has not been made known. All we know is that the talks did not come to an end after the first meeting, as they did at Berchtesgaden last week. An official communiqué said they would be continued tomorrow. And then we have the appeal of the British prime minister issued from his mountain hotel above the Rhine tonight. Shortly after Mister Chamberlain left Chancellor Hitler's hotel at seven-fifteen this evening his private secretary convoked the correspondents to his hotel, the Petersberg. The ferry wasn't working so we drove five miles down the river to Bonn to find a bridge and arrived all breathless on the mountaintop a half hour later. I'll read to you the statement from Prime Minister Chamberlain, which we were given:

> The Prime Minister had a conversation with the German Führer which, beginning at four o'clock, was continued until shortly after seven p.m. It is intended to resume the conversations tomorrow morning. In the meantime, the first essential, in the opinion of the Prime Minister, is that there should be a determination on the part of all parties and on the part of all concerned to ensure that the local conditions in Czechoslovakia are such as not in any way to interfere with the progress of the conversations. The Prime Minister appeals most earnestly therefore to everybody to assist in maintaining a state of orderliness and to refrain from action of any kind that would be likely to lead to incidents.

That was Mister Chamberlain's appeal."

It all sounded like a stall to Endicott. Hitler wasn't signing onto the deal and Chamberlain couldn't afford an incident in the Sudetenland that would cause Hitler to call off the negotiations completely. The Brit still thought he could get Hitler to the table to sign. The way Endicott read the tea leaves that train had already left the station.

Es' tut mir furchtbar leid, aber das geht nicht mehr. Platen reread the words from his notes another time as he sat in front of the portable typewriter on the writing desk in his room at the Dreesen. Those three hours of Platen's life were excruciatingly vivid in his memory. The Englishman had sat there on the sofa in the Führer's suite, all proud of himself like a hunting dog that had retrieved the fox. Chamberlain explained how he had succeeded, after grueling negotiations in persuading not only the British and French cabinets but also the Czechoslovak government to agree in principle to what the Führer had demanded when last they met at Berchtesgaden. It was obvious the British had come to Godesberg with the necessary capitulations so all that remained in their estimation was to work out the formal details of transferring the Sudetenland to Germany in a civil and orderly fashion. Was that not the way great empires carved up territory between themselves? Then the chancellor spoke those words: *I'm frightfully sorry but that won't do any longer.* The shock on their faces was so complete Platen felt some sympathy for the British. The chancellor would have no talk of their commissions or plebiscites or census tallies. How could they imagine Hitler would reject a settlement that returned more than three million people, and their lands, to Germany at no cost to the Fatherland?

As the Führer began to lecture his guest, Platen recalled how the room grew thick with tension. It was no longer just about ethnic Germans. What about the one million Slovaks that had been tethered to the Czechs? There were also more than a million Hungarians living in Czechoslovakia against their will. What about them? There also were hundreds of thousands of Poles living in Teschen, the city the Czechs had stolen in 1920 when Poland was busy valiantly fighting the Bolsheviks. The Germans were the Führer's primary concern but it was his duty to remind the prime minister that there could be no peace in Central Europe while the claims of these other nationalities went unsettled.

And now Mister Chamberlain came to Godesberg with talk of international committees to decide who owned which bricks in every wall within the Sudetenland.   No, there was no time to delay in such dalliances. Was the prime minister not aware of the mass protests in Prague that showed the Bolsheviks could take the rudder? No more delays when over one-hundred thousand additional Sudeten German refugees had just fled Czech oppression and crossed into Germany after their villages had been depopulated, their men arrested and their wives and children had been parted from each other. Tempers were rising and action must be taken with all speed. The chancellor was adamant that within three or four days this state of affairs would develop into a full-fledged war. Not an hour should be wasted. In the interests of peace, Hitler demanded that definite and clear-cut facts be established now, not talk.

After this wretched day all Platen wished was to be somewhere else. To forget what he had heard, forget what he knew and move his family to some other country away from what was coming. The Führer was marching them to another World War. Platen calmed himself... the foreign minister was waiting on him. It was difficult but he measured his breathing and focused his mind. He had been tasked with creating one transcript that joined together his own notes with those of Doctor Schmidt, Hitler's translator. The assignment forced him to double check both accounts as he merged them. There was no escape from the words or his memories. How would he describe the festering tension in that room? Platen recalled Chamberlain's eyes and how those eyes had narrowed and the fire that grew behind them. The Englishman's calm talk of puzzlement at the Führer's new conditions didn't match what Platen saw in those angry eyes. Yet some of the agitation in the Englishman's expression made it into his words. Did Herr Hitler not appreciate how Chamberlain had risked his political life to secure the chancellor's demands? Could Hitler not urge moderation on the Hungarians and Poles while the proper methods be applied to the agreed upon principle of cessation of territory by the Czechoslovaks? Could the chancellor show some small cooperation?

Knowing whom would be reading this transcript Platen continued typing with an eye to make the Führer sound as reasonable as possible. How Hitler had responded that the only possibility of avoiding violence was to draw a frontier at once based on nationality, beyond which the Czechoslovaks would have to withdraw their troops and government. How troops and civil organizations of the Reich would then enter the zone thus created. As spokesman for the Germans it was the only peaceful solution he could see. The alternative was a military solution in which the new frontier would be established by the military authorities on a strategic basis.

In retrospect, Platen marveled that Chamberlain had continued to reason with the chancellor for so long. Had he not gotten exactly what the Herr Hitler wanted and without the expenditure of a drop of German blood? Why should the chancellor resort to war when he could get everything in a peaceful manner? In the event of German troops moving into the areas as proposed, there is no doubt that the Czechoslovak government would have no option but to order its forces to resist. This would mean the destruction of their agreement of the previous week, namely an orderly settlement of this question rather than a settlement by the use of force. Why, if Herr Hitler could establish this *strategic frontier* at any time, why was he wasting the prime minister's time? Furthermore, what was to be gained by conflict, which was an uncertain enterprise? Even if Germany were to win, precious lives, lands and resources would be destroyed in the process, nullifying the gain. If a few weeks gave Germany what she wanted without such a cost, was this not preferable?

The Führer did not back down in the face of such reason. He reminded Chamberlain in a shrill tone that the situation was almost intolerable. At any moment, while the negotiations were going on here in Godesberg there might be an explosion somewhere in the Sudeten German area that would make all efforts for a peaceful solution fruitless. To bolster his argument the Führer often reached for one of the little scraps of paper that were arriving for him throughout the meeting. Each slip held news of some new outrage the Czech army had committed against the Sudeten Germans. Hitler would read aloud from these notes and work himself back into a frightful lather. Finally he cut off Chamberlain mid-sentence. No, the territory within the so-called German language boundary must be ceded at once, without any delay and occupied by German troops no later than the twenty-eighth. That was the quickest and best solution. There would be no further discussion.

After sustaining himself for three hours against such tongue-lashings, Chamberlain reached his limit. Visibly drained, he reclined back on the sofa and gathered his thoughts. If this was the chancellor's final position the prime minister declared he had done what he could for peace and his conscience was clear. Before leaving, Chamberlain asked for a map showing those areas of Czechoslovakia Hitler had determined fell within this language boundary. The map would be useful in preparing for their second meeting the next day and for Chamberlain to report back to his cabinet. The Führer provided just such a map he had previously prepared and the British retreated to their hotel for the night.

There was nothing more to add. Platen typed the last few sentences of the transcript, collected and organized the pages then left to find von Ribbentrop so he could deliver his work.

SEPTEMBER 23, 1938
FOREIGN OFFICE
KING CHARLES STREET, LONDON

The call had come exceptionally early. There were the usual apologies for the frightful hour but his presence was required on a matter of the greatest urgency. The British prime minister was in Germany ready to separate large chunks of territory from his country for Germany to swallow... of course the situation was urgent! Masaryk calmed himself for he needed to hear what they had to say. Perhaps there was some advantage he could extract while Chamberlain was out of the country. The reports from Godesberg were positive that Germany and Great Britain had not come to any further agreements. While being driven on the quick journey across London Masaryk ran the possibilities through his head and how best to respond to each. The sun had barely started climbing above the rooftops overlooking Whitehall when the sedan carrying Masaryk stopped abruptly and the Czechoslovak minister was ushered through a nondescript side door into the Foreign Office structure by a pair of youngish staffers.

The path that had been chosen for him did not show off the best features of the grand old building. Masaryk had come to think of the structure, built in the Italianate style, as a metaphor for England – representative of better days and in sad disrepair. Parliament really should procure funds to fix the old place up. But that was their problem. Masaryk's task was finding a way to undercut what Chamberlain was up to. Soon enough he was deposited into a moderately sized reception room that included a settee and several leather chairs and asked to wait. Hot tea was already available on the table. Masaryk poured some of he beverage into one of the waiting china cups. Too tense to sit, he paced the room while sipping from the cup. After a few minutes the door opened and in walked an older man with weathered features and a prominent mustache. Masaryk recognized him as the man second only to Halifax at the Foreign Office.

"Cadogan, isn't it?" Masaryk inquired without offering his hand in greeting since he remembered Churchill stating this fellow was a supporter of appeasing Hitler.

"Exactly right. Alexander Cadogan, permanent undersecretary. Thank you for coming out at this un-Godly hour," Cadogan noted he was being met with suspicion.

"Things going poorly at Godesberg?" Masaryk probed before another sip of tea.

"Shall we say yesterday did not go as the prime minister expected," Cadogan intimated the difficulties that would become public soon enough.

"So the papers say," Masaryk paused while he set the cup and saucer down on the table. "As a critic of current British policy in Central Europe I find this admission encouraging. How can I assist you Mister Cadogan?"

"As a professional courtesy, I brought you here at the earliest opportunity to disclose that there has been a change of heart within the inner cabinet," Cadogan kept his annoyance with the Czech under wraps. Cadogan knew full well how Masaryk was seeding opposition politicians with large contributions but he had other imperatives to discuss with the man. "Herr Hitler has breached the terms of the agreement made with the prime minister a week ago at Berchtesgaden. The new German terms for a settlement require an immediate Czech withdrawal from disputed Sudeten territory and an occupation by Germany by September twenty-eighth. As there is all the difference in the world between an immediate but orderly settlement of the Sudeten question, and an immediate forcible annexation to be followed by the activities of the Gestapo, the British and French cabinets can no longer take the responsibility of advising the Czechoslovak government not to mobilize. British and French envoys in Prague will deliver this guidance, in writing, to your government this afternoon."

"Would this be some cruel jest?" Masaryk had gone through too much in recent weeks to believe his ears.

"No, my government is deadly earnest. The prevailing view is that Hitler has trampled British and French good will so completely with these new demands that there is no reason to provide him any more latitude than we already have," Cadogan was also speaking for himself.

"Please do not consider me ungracious… but thank you for finally coming to your senses." Reality had finally settled in with these people, Masaryk marveled.

"While we are not prepared for war there is only so far this government can allow itself to bend to petty tyrants," Cadogan summed up the inner cabinet's position.

"Very sensible given the most recent national public opinion polling," Masaryk could not help himself from throwing in a bit of sarcasm. "But does the prime minister share the same virtues as his cabinet? As I recall, he still is in Godesberg and plans further negotiation with the petty tyrant."

"The situation is fluid, as you can appreciate. The prime minister feels duty bound to finish what he started. Yet he left the United Kingdom with specific guidance from this government and Herr Hitler's latest claims go beyond that guidance. The change in advice your government will receive today is firm and will not be rescinded. If Germany is set on invading unilaterally, Czechoslovakia must have the freedom to act accordingly," Cadogan clarified the guarantee.

"You have the appreciation of my government and our people," Masaryk's praise was sincere. "As you can well appreciate, there is much for me to do now. I should take your leave immediately."

"We have a driver waiting. But before you go there is a warning I must give you. The prime minister's staff in Godesberg reported that Hitler boasted of having transcripts of telephone conversations between members of His Majesty's government, as well as wire taps capturing telephone conversations between you and your government. He even offered gramophone recordings to listen to as proof. We are investigating this assertion, but given some of the sensitive subjects the chancellor had knowledge of during yesterday's discussions with Mister Chamberlain we must assume his boast is accurate," Cadogan gathered from the Czech's expression that the possibility had come up before.

Masaryk recalled the content of his recent outbursts on the phone with Krofta and cringed. "If Hitler's boast proves accurate, then for certain German ciphers and future historians, I have now become a subject of some ribald amusement."

HOTEL PETERSBERG
KOENIGSWINTER, DEUTCHLAND

Something sure the hell was wrong. It was way past lunch and Hitler and Chamberlain weren't talking. The long black sedans were all lined up, their engines running for hours while the drivers waited to ferry the British delegation back down to the Dreesen. Not only had Uncle Adolph gotten the better of Chamberlain the previous night, it looked to Endicott that the British prime minister wasn't going to get another audience until he came around to Hitler's way of thinking. The particulars were still rather fuzzy, however. With Chamberlain and his aides endlessly pacing the terrace of the hotel, Endicott had cornered a few of the lesser members of the diplomatic corps who had nowhere to run. The most that he could wrangle out of them was that Chamberlain had sent a personal message directly to Hitler right after breakfast with some kind of overture. The response had been a cancellation of the scheduled eleven-thirty meeting.

The way Endicott saw the situation, with Chamberlain already willing to negotiate away Bohemia, Hitler must have demanded something grander. Shirer's opinion was that the British liked these affairs between empires nice and tidy. Negotiate a settlement, set up an orderly process to carry out the provisions, then stick to the agreed upon schedule. Hitler wasn't neat and tidy though. Hitler was hand it over now or I will beat you to a pulp. Shirer was usually right on target and that's what Endicott thought had happened too. Hitler must have told Chamberlain the Germans wanted the Sudetenland now and would send the tanks tomorrow to prove the point. Since Endicott had seen lots of those tanks swarming near the border it wasn't a far-fetched notion. He even put the theory as a straight question to one of the junior British diplomats. The poor fellow's face went ashen and he stammered for seconds before calling up a less than convincing denial.

For the moment Endicott was just another of the dozens of news hacks waiting impatiently for some action from either the German or British camps. Every one of them was probably thinking the same thing: *Do I take the time to file an update on the suspenseful pause in the negotiations and risk missing something big happening or sit put watching boats slowly pass by on the Rhine?* Just then Endicott spotted Roland walking through the lobby... just the man he needed to talk to.

"Roland! Hey Roland. Hold up there," Endicott hurried after him.

"Hello Charles, good to see you," Roland peered nervously over his shoulder before returning to his usual cheery self. "Where have you been?"

"Treading water with everyone else. Listen, I have a question since you're usually the person well connected with British civil servants," Endicott chased after him.

"Oh you give me far too much credit. I am just lucky to be in the right place at the right time," Roland kept trundling along.

"I like your kind of luck. So tell me, are you lucky enough to know what the prime minister wrote to Uncle Adolph this morning?" Endicott cut to the point.

Roland looked around to see if anyone close by had heard the query. Satisfied that there were no eavesdroppers, he beckoned Endicott closer.

"Well, I do know a small morsel," Roland teased softly. "Yesterday the chancellor was very firm in wanting to occupy the Sudetenland within the week."

"I knew it," Endicott was pleased with himself.

"Naturally, the prime minister cannot agree to such a thing," Roland continued. "So this morning he suggested, most reasonably, that Herr Hitler consider a compromise whereby the Czechoslovaks could pull out of the disputed territory in short order, after which the Sudetens could then self-rule until an international settlement could be worked out."

"Chamberlain doesn't have liberty to make such an offer," Endicott was incredulous.

"No, I rather think he does not," Roland whispered back.

HOTEL DREESEN, GODESBERG

The Führer was not in a mood to entertain the British in their frumpy business suits. It was the chancellor's strong opinion that the sloppy attire of Chamberlain and his aides was an insult. Had they not had time to dress themselves appropriately? Had their rooms not been provided with the finest bath salts, hair lotions, shaving creams and soaps produced by the Eau de Cologne conglomerate? More likely, Hitler railed, they had spent their free hours enjoying the fine cigars that had been placed in their suites. The Führer knew for a fact from Göring's wire taps that the British were inclined to make all of the necessary concessions yet Chamberlain still sent him notes complaining about what he could not do... nonsense. Better to make the British cool their heels. That was why the chancellor had cancelled the scheduled meeting. He could not bear to hear more of the prime minister's sorry protestations. At least not until the ciphers had broken the code used to protect Chamberlain's report to his cabinet. As soon as Hitler was in possession of Chamberlain's true positions, then they would talk.

The foreign minister had been strategizing with the Führer since early in the morning, which had left Platen running back and forth to the communications room to deliver the latest communiqués arriving from Berlin or completing the odd tasks von Ribbentrop needed tending to. With a few minutes to himself, Platen caught his breath in the hallway outside Hitler's suite. Platen's respite was fleeting, however. One of the corporals from the communications room was approaching him with a memo slip in his hand. There was no chance this message was intended for anyone else as the soldier's eyes were focused uncomfortably on Platen's.

"This just arrived from Berlin for foreign minister von Ribbentrop," the obergefreiter was intent to relieve himself of the memo slip as quickly as possible.

"I will deliver it, thank you," Platen took possession of the dispatch.

As the soldier left the way he came, Platen read the message and felt faint. Berlin had received a notification from the Polish government in Warsaw. The Polish chargé d'affaires in Moscow had been presented a formal warning early that morning. The Soviets were unhappy with Polish military concentrations on the Czechoslovak border opposite Teschen. Should Poland commit aggression against Czechoslovakia, the warning stipulated that the Soviet Union would consider itself released from the Soviet-Polish non-aggression agreement of 1932 and would respond accordingly. President Mościcki in Warsaw was of the opinion the Czechoslovak government was behind this Soviet threat, which had to be taken seriously since there was evidence the USSR was mobilizing more than three hundred thousand troops along Poland's borders.

Platen closed his eyes and gathered his strength. News such as this would cause Hitler to explode. He already was convinced that Beneš was stalling. With the Soviets making threats and deploying their army, Beneš will have more reason to hold his ground against the concessions Chamberlain was brokering. The Führer would be done with negotiations for good. Platen straightened his back, took a deep breath and opened the door to Hitler's suite. The chancellor and von Ribbentrop were sitting side by side on one of the sofas with a number of hand-written notes strewn about the table in front of them. Platen had learned that hovering was a sign of weakness so he wasted no time in placing himself by von Ribbentrop's side.

"Herr Foreign Minister," Platen broke in. "Apologies for the interruption but this communiqué has just arrived from Berlin. It is important."

"Let me see," von Ribbentrop rose from the sofa to snatch the message way.

"What! What does it say?" Hitler demanded without waiting for von Ribbentrop to finish reading the message.

Furious at what he had just read, von Ribbentrop folded the paper into smaller sections while he chose his words. "Mein Führer, Stalin is threatening Poland with war should they invade Czechoslovakia. As an illustration of Soviet veracity the Poles note more than three hundred thousand Red Army troops are mobilizing in the western Ukraine and Belorussia."

"There! You see! I told you the Bolsheviks were angling to take the rudder. While we play act with the British, Stalin takes advantage. I am done wasting time with this charade. The Wehrmacht occupies the Sudetenland by the twenty-eighth. That is that! Whether the Czechs stay or go makes no difference. That is what we tell Chamberlain!" Hitler thundered.

MINISTÈRE DE LA GUERRE
BOULEVARD SAINT-GERMAIN, PARIS

The sun was on its way out and Clarence was wondering whether he had spent too much time lurking about this part of Paris. Daladier and his cabinet had been mostly silent since Chamberlain winged off to Germany. Neither had any more fortuitous documents dropped in Clarence's lap. Now that all of the news out of Godesberg was cautionary, Clarence was keen to see if there was any reaction on the streets that the British mission was in rough water. Earlier in the afternoon Clarence had dropped by two locations that were good barometers of the public mood in Paris. The Café de la Paix was as full of people as ever. No war scares there. Next he checked around the Paris Bourse. Stock traders were easily spooked creatures. Yet here again no special urgency was evident. A Reuters staffer had tipped Clarence that the British envoy had delivered unsavory details from Godesberg to Daladier and the premier had responded by closeting himself with his generals. So Clarence headed to the Ministry of War next to see what was happening there.

Looking around Clarence recognized a number of French reporters already on station taking notes of who was coming and who was leaving the building. That seemed like a worthwhile enterprise so Clarence took out his notebook and pencil and started jotting down those officers and politicians he could identify. Sadly this wasn't as many as he would care to admit. After an hour of watching Clarence was convinced something more than government consultations was going on inside the building. The only question was how to confirm what he suspected. Looking about for a French journalist he knew well, Clarence spotted Rene Coiffard. Older than Clarence by a long shot, Coiffard was sill slim as a pencil and in great health. He had made his name during the Great War. With little left to prove Coiffard didn't mind talking to the competition if he liked you. Since Clarence had never been shy in sharing a bottle of wine with the old veteran over the years, he figured he was in Coiffard's good graces. "Coiffard! I have a question for you."

"What took you so long? I have been waiting more than an hour for you to come over and keep me company," Coiffard scolded the American.

"Sorry, my pride got in the way. I thought I could identify more of these youngsters on my own than was possible," Clarence pointed at another. "Like that fellow there."

"Him?" Coiffard's keen eyes tracked the army captain passing nearby. "He is attached to Gamelin's staff. Nothing special, just a runner."

"I've seen lots of them today," Clarence tried to draw the old fox out.

"Indeed," Coiffard made another notation.

"To me this has the feeling of mobilization," Clarence went for the money question. "You have been on this beat a lot longer than I have. Is mobilization the way you read all of this activity?"

"So it would seem. But mobilization is not war," Coiffard hedged. "But what do I know? Mobilization is not war is what they said in 1914 too."

PRAŽSKÝ HRAD, PRAHA

One of the palace secretaries dropped another stack of evening newspapers on his desk. All of the headlines read that the British were having a rough time with Hitler. The bastards deserved everything they got, Drtina gloated as he scanned the various international journals. Drtina had also received word through diplomatic channels of the USSR's warning to Poland and was anxious to learn what else the Soviets were up to. Their ambassador, Aleksandrovsky, was in with the president again, and as much as Drtina detested the communists, their pressure on the Poles was most useful. The colonels in Warsaw thought they could take advantage of the crisis, and now they knew differently.

Looking up from the newspapers Drtina noticed Counselor Tomes from the Foreign Affairs ministry approaching with an envelope in his hand. "What have you there, counselor?"

"Minister Krofta sent me to deliver this envelope to the president. My instructions are the envelope is to remain sealed until in the possession of President Beneš," Tomes met no disrespect but those were his instructions.

"Well then, that sounds important," Drtina dug for more details as he rose to his feet to receive the envelope.

"Yes, we just received another visit from French and British envoys," Tomes gave Drtina a morsel to chew on.

Before Drtina could ask anything further the door to the president's office swung open as Aleksandrovsky bed his goodbye. Tomes used the distraction to turn and leave. The Soviet minister was in one of his jovial moods. He usually had perfunctory good words to share with Drtina whenever he visited Beneš. This time he grabbed Drtina's hand firmly and shook it enthusiastically. "Stand firm! Now it is up to you."

Aleksandrovsky had yet to release Drtina from his grip when Beneš began pressing the buzzer indicating he wanted to see his next visitor. The summons was welcome because it gave Drtina ample reason to send the Soviet ambassador on his way. "Thank you, sir. As you can see, however, the president needs me."

"Of course, to your duties. We will talk again soon," Aleksandrovsky released Drtina from his grip and marched off down the hall.

Without delay, Drtina entered Beneš' office and closed the door behind him. "Edvard, there is an important message that has just arrived from Minister Krofta." Drtina unsealed the envelope and presented it to Beneš.

Beneš got up from his chair and started pacing back and forth through the office while reading the memorandum. "Yes, yes, yes!"

Drtina had not seen his colleague so excited in what seemed like a lifetime but the suspense of not knowing the contents of the message from Krofta was killing him.

"Do you know what this is?" Beneš shook the pages above his head. "Read it for yourself, my friend. The French and the British have withdrawn their objection to our defending ourselves. We can now order a full mobilization of the army.

PUBLIC TELEPHONE BUREAU
NOVÉ MESTO, PRAHA

They had finally found working international phone lines to dictate their latest stories back to their bureaus. Ros couldn't seem to get a line to Paris so Sanderson's went first while the manager hustled to get a connection to New York for Ros. This worked out fine since Sanderson's people were on European time and it was darn near ten o'clock already. Ros' luck was picking up again. She had literally bumped into the kid manager of the telephone bureau outside a cafe close to the Wenceslas Square. Thanks to his job he had picked up English pretty well and he was fascinated with the newspaper business. Young Otmar went out on a limb and asked her if she was having problems getting a phone line out of Prague during the crisis. Boy, was that an understatement. So he insisted on her and Sanderson using his bureau from then on.

Some details were finally getting through from Godesberg. Chamberlain would indeed finally see Hitler again. What they were hearing was that the Nazi demands were pretty harsh, which had caused all of the delays in the two leaders getting together. With that knowledge in hand, Ros and Sanderson had gone out to see how the populace was taking the news. When they returned they checked with the Information Ministry spokesman who hung around the Ambassador and were told there was no further government announcements scheduled for that night. So Ros and Sanderson grabbed their notes and went to visit Otmar.

Ros was just about done with New York when she noticed Otmar waving to her through the glass like something was important. While she was listening to Des read back her last paragraph, Ros silently mouthed, *Okay, I'm hanging up,* to the kid. In response, Otmar sternly rapped the glass and gestured that she should stay on the line.

"Hold the line Des. Something is happening," Ros opened the door to her booth. "What's up, hon?"

"I have scoop for you, miss," Otmar appeared rushed. "A friend at the Ministry of Defence just called me. He told me to go home and say goodbye to my family. In a few minutes the government will announce a general mobilization."

Ros grabbed the lapel of his jacket with her free hand and pulled him close. "You sure this is on the up and up, Otmar?"

"My friend would not joke about something so important," Otmar wondered why the woman doubted him. "It will happen. He said the French and British say Hitler wants too much so they gave their permission. All of us reservists will be called up tonight."

"You're an angel, kid. I owe you. Take care of yourself. I'll be out of here in a minute so you can get home," Ros kissed Otmar on the cheek then settled back onto her stool. "Des, listen... this is major. New headline: *Czechs Order Mobilization, British and French Give Go Ahead...* That's right! Now be quiet and hold onto your shorts. You need to keep up with me because I'll be losing this line soon. Here's the new lead."

28. DECLARATIONS

Czech newspapers announcing army mobilization

SEPTEMBER 25, 1938
PRIEGER FARM, NEAR ASCH

There was worse duty... latrines came to the rottenführer's mind. When the daughter was at the farm looking after the unconscious woman he busied himself with helping the parents with their daily chores. This made the mother so happy he was sure the old house frau was bragging to all of her contemporaries in the area. On the plus side, the home-cooked meals were very welcome. The rottenführer would miss them terribly whenever it came time to leave the farm. It was still early and the daughter had yet to arrive to look after the Amerikaner. For now he sat by the bed and read a book from the farmer's library. The old man's collection was surprisingly well stocked, especially with history and biography tomes. Otherwise the corporal would have nothing to do at times like these. Hauptsturmführer Horst had ordered that he not stray more than a few meters from the woman if she was unattended. If she rolled off the bed of her own accord and broke her neck an international incident would ensue and the Hauptsturmführer would have none of that.

Despite lacking any medical education whatsoever, the rottenführer believed the woman was resting more lightly than before. Her breathing was less labored plus she moved around in her sleep a great deal more than when he had first arrived at the farm. From what he could tell the daughter had mended the Amerikaner's bruises very efficiently. Perhaps that was the wrong term, yet he had watched closely and her techniques and medicines had resulted in swift recuperation of the patient's visible injuries. The woman simply neglected to wake up. So he continued to read. He had never picked up Homer previously but the farmer had highly recommended this translation of the Iliad. The rottenfuhrer found the whole drama about the assault on ancient Troy quite fascinating. So engrossed was he in the current passage that he completely missed the first signs that the Amerikaner was waking up. What finally captured his attention was the cloying, contented moan that floated in his direction from the bed. Lowering the book below eye level he watched as the woman stretched her arms away from her torso like a cat stretching after a relaxing nap. She was older than him by a number of years yet still was a very pretty female. The rottenfuhrer studied her intently as she placed her arms behind her for support and rose up to a sitting position.

"Guten morgen, fraulein," seemed like the appropriate thing for him to say.

"Hey, you're kinda cute," a very drowsy Sylvie purred sweetly.

CNS HEADQUARTERS, NEW YORK

The congratulatory phone calls had been coming in all day long. It was after midnight and Harry was still deliriously pleased. That kid Talmadge had come through big time with the scoop on the Czech mobilization. None of the other American wire services had it. As far as Des could find out only the Brits at the Daily Telegraph had the story early and Lasky could live with that. The competition Lasky hobnobbed with weren't in London. Spread out on his desktop was as many of the front pages headlining the story as his secretary could get her hands on. By the morning the glory would all be gone – that was the news biz – glory never lasted longer than twenty-four hours. But for a little while longer he was going to relish their victory. Pulling his personal bottle of scotch from the desk drawer he poured another tall shot. How many times he had circled the prized clippings didn't matter, Lasky slowly went around the desk another time while sipping his liquor.

Des had been witnessing this ritual for close to a day now and the appeal was wearing thin. It was good to see the boss in a rare good mood, which happened about as often as a solar eclipse. But he needed to get out of there to catch up on some rest and couldn't leave as long as Harry hung around ogling his trophies. A lot was going to happen in the next few hours and Des may not get another chance for decent sleep for days. Checking the wall clock, Des grunted disapprovingly and headed to

Lasky's office where he propped his shoulder against the doorframe and folded his arms over his chest.

"What?" Lasky challenged without taking his eyes off the clippings. One thing Harry Lasky wasn't was oblivious.

"Boss, it's time to call it a night. Tomorrow is going to be a roller coaster ride," Des was considering the purchase of a cattle prod.

"You're getting old Des," Lasky hoped the man wasn't going soft too.

"No, I am getting tired of hanging around while you gloat. Why don't you head back for another couple of rounds at the clubs and lord over the other syndicate moguls while you still can," Des decided to exploit Lasky's weaknesses.

"That's not a bad call," Lasky took a stiffer sip from his glass. "I love rubbing it in with those swine. What's happening out there?"

"It's morning in Europe. The Royal Navy has recalled sailors to base and has started ordering ships to sea in the Atlantic and the Med. The French are mobilizing one million reservists. Chamberlain is back in London and set to face his cabinet by ten o'clock, the Frenchies are flying over from Paris in the afternoon to discuss what they're going to do next and the Czechs are supposed to respond to Hitler's Godesberg memo," Des rattled off the main items from memory.

"What's the final word on that little document?" Lasky wanted to get up to speed.

"About the same. Chamberlain was bidding adieu to Hitler in a last minute audience that looks like it was a pretty rocky affair. Hitler had been playing hard to get all day and the Brits' last move was requesting the Germans put everything they wanted down in writing. That's what Chamberlain went back over to the Dreesen to get... that and a chance to talk Hitler down from launching an invasion. But when the good chancellor got the news the Czechs had ordered full mobilization he blew a head gasket. All Chamberlain walked away with was the memo. From what Walter just sent in that little document reads like a broadside from your ex-wife's lawyer," Des whistled for punctuation.

"That bastard tried to cut off my left testicle along with everything else I own," Lasky winced at the memory. "Never mind that. Tell me what Walter dredged up."

"The Germans who were at Godesberg have a chip on their shoulders and aren't averse to talking. What's in the memo is what Hitler hit Chamberlain with during their first meet and greet on Friday. Not one iota of difference. Hitler hasn't given an inch. He wanted the Czechs to clear out of the Sudetenland starting on the 26th with only two days to get that done," Walter's copy was still fresh in Des' head."

"That does sound like her rat lawyer," Lasky agreed. "Go on."

"On top of the short deadlines to get the army and civil servants out, Hitler made a point of explaining that the Czechs had to leave everything behind unmolested. And I do mean everything: military and government facilities, factories, raw materials, farms, merchant inventories and anything else of value," Des ran down the list.

"And Hitler would send the panzers in on the twenty-eighth," Lasky added.

"Nah, that's the one minor change Chamberlain got. Word is the prime minister balked hard at Hitler's demands to the point of getting out of his chair to leave. An orderly transfer down the road, with prior sign off by all parties, is one thing. Opening the front door on the 28th for the Visigoths to run through to rape and pillage is something else. No way Chamberlain could sell that to anyone in his own government or anywhere else. So Hitler tells him, okay, I'll give you until October first," Des finished.

"What a ball buster," Lasky was impressed. "That Adolph could set himself up on top of Capone's old organization in a second."

"No lie there," Des had to laugh, Hitler running the rackets in Chicago fit like a glove.

"So what was Chamberlain's final word before skulking off in the wee hours of the morning?" Lasky wondered.

"I think it went something like: *Thanks for wasting my time, I'll pass your memo along*," Des embellished somewhat from Hauth's wire.

Lasky rubbed his hands together gleefully. "We're going to have a war, I tell you! We're going to have a war and I'm going to make a mint."

WILSONOVO STATION – PRAHA

Carr had rung up Bulloch late Friday night when he had heard the broadcast announcing mobilization. The minister had been intently interested in observing how the mobilization was going and what was the state of the capital following the call-up of reservists. Carr thought it vital that they get a first-hand look at how the Czechoslovaks responded to the order so they roused Otto and took to Prague's avenues in the Škoda to witness what was happening first-hand. The passionate outbursts of patriotism that had rocked the city during the last week were no fluke. People who had heard the radio announcement were waking their neighbors and men subject to the call-up enthusiastically rushed to train stations in the city. Carr kept a notebook that Bulloch spied from time to time. He liked the Minister's description:

> *Railroad stations are full of cheering, laughing reservists packed solid into outgoing trains. No confusion evident just everyone falling into their places with the upmost promptitude. Air raid drill at three a.m. conducted calmly and in good order. Men on their way to report, and soldiers on duty, are cheered loudly by their fellow citizens.*

Next they decided to have Otto motor them out to the surrounding countryside to see if public reactions were as rousing outside Prague. Throughout the suburbs Bulloch noted for his own report that everywhere the mobilization was proceeding with haste but without disorder and showing fine organization. He estimated that many of the reservists had reported to their regiments within six hours, which was an amazing achievement. Bulloch's evaluation was that these Czechoslovaks were fine soldiers who were strong of character, dutiful and ready to fight.

By Sunday morning, the Americans found many changes were already taking place. Those automobiles and horses that had previously escaped requisition were now happily given up. Otto had been forced to show their diplomatic credentials several times when the Škoda drew too much attention from the boy scouts and civil guards who were replacing police to direct traffic. Notices were going up pointing out where people could find bombproof and gas proof shelters. Workmen had begun digging out shelters where there were none close by. A few quick checks showed that there were no more gas masks to be had in the street-side shops although the merchants the Americans spoke with felt sure most people they knew had them by now.

Bulloch had Otto swing by the main rail station for a last look. Instead of reservists, Wilsonovo was full of uniformed soldiers lugging full loads of gear and waiting for transport to their destinations.

"That's all we needed to see, Otto. Take us back to the embassy," Carr instructed the driver. "I am merrily shocked that the Czechs got their reservists called up and to their regiments without any interference from the Germans. This was supposed to be the German's great advantage: the complete superiority of their air force to disrupt just the orderly mobilization you and I have witnessed. But look to the skies... more than twenty-four hours later and those skies are completely devoid of German bombers."

"It does seem the Germans have been caught off guard again," Bulloch remembered the same thing happened in May. "Hitler wasn't prepared for the Czechs to actually call out the troops. I don't know what playbook he's working from but launching a major invasion without the benefit of surprise is a bad idea."

"Yet all of the military experts I speak with, yourself included, tell me a German attack is probable," Carr disliked such non sequiturs.

"Neither would I change that assessment, sir. It's like Hitler has no respect for the Czechoslovaks. Remember the Nürnberg speeches? All of the Nazi bigwigs talked down the Czechs as an inferior people. I think Hitler truly believes all he has to do is order his divisions to cross the border and they'll roll all the way through Bohemia and Moravia without much difficulty," Bulloch doubted force of will would be sufficient.

"Such bluster and hubris," Carr sighed. "What awaits the Germans is a bloody hornet's nest."

MINISTRY OF NATIONAL DEFENCE, DEJVICE

The trip back to Praha had taken the better part of two days. No one could spare a vehicle for the entire trip. Kopecky and Hruska were forced to sit idle waiting to find drivers who were heading in their direction. They would go some distance and get dumped at some out-of-the-way post until they could attach themselves to some other scheduled trip east. Many a time Kopecky considered requisitioning a car without permission yet restrained himself. With full mobilization declared the army was pumping men and machines in the opposite direction he wanted to go. All of the eastbound trains had been cancelled for the same reason. Even when they acquired a seat in a lorry they often were forced to wait until the road cleared of whatever convoy that was heading west. The delays would complicate his life enormously.

Kopecky knew the general staff was supposed to relocate to secure wartime headquarters in expectation of a German invasion but he did not know whether that had already happened or was going to happen soon. Therefore, he was unsure where to rejoin the general staff as was ordered. Neither was there anyone he could ask since these relocation plans were not discussed widely. Kopecky would have to take his chances and see who was on hand when he arrived back in Dejvice.

The last few blocks until the lorry driver dropped them off told Kopecky everything he needed to know. Men, files and equipment were flowing out of the ministry buildings into waiting trucks and cars. Kopecky made arrangements with Hruska to rendezvous later and headed inside with the carbine slung over his shoulder. Arriving on his own floor in the ministry, Kopecky checked in with the adjutant who confirmed that Generál Krejčí had already departed Praha. Instructions left for Kopecky instructed him to report to Srom. Since the colonel was in a different wing on a lower floor, Kopecky dashed there as fast as he could dodging past other soldiers hurrying through the hallways. Arriving a bit winded, Kopecky was very happy to see Srom's assistant in a corner of the room sealing up a box. Before he had a chance to ask if the colonel was still in Praha, Kopecky heard Srom's voice through the open door to his small office.

"Kopecky! Glad you made it back in one piece. Come in," Srom beckoned.

"Podplukovník, sorry I am so late reporting in," Kopecky felt like a tardy schoolboy.

"No apologies necessary. We got a report Friday morning from Eger about your run in with the Freikorps. Fine work there, son. I am sure there will be a commendation coming your way for heroism," Srom handed Kopecky a file box from his desk.

"Thank you sir," Kopecky was puzzled why he was holding a moving box. "I would be glad to help but I have been delayed for days and I must learn where can I catch up to the general staff?"

"After we announced the mobilization everyone worried we were open to Luftwaffe bombing attacks or even airborne units parachuting onto the army compounds here in Dejvice. Last night Generál Krejčí and the rest relocated to Klanovice outside the city. We don't want to move them during the day. Tonight they will be moving onto the wartime headquarters at Vyškov in Moravia as planned," Srom explained.

"I had better collect a few things and then be onto Klanovice before they depart for Brno," Kopecky felt sure he could secure an automobile in Praha.

"That is very diligent of you, major, but there has been a change in your orders. You have been assigned to me, indefinitely. You are where you need to be... attached to that box," Srom enjoyed having a little fun with his new aide-de-camp.

"Well then, how can I argue with that," Kopecky acquiesced. "After moving these boxes what is your first order of the day?"

"You and I have some strategizing to do based on the latest intelligence on Wehrmacht deployments then we are heading back west to our forward post at Saaz. Our job is to help coordinate the swift response to any advances by German armor. Cut off the head of the snake wherever he rises up, if you will," Srom was pleased Kopecky had already seen action as they were heading for a hot zone.

"We will need to pull many of the ready units back and reconstitute those crews back into something like regular divisions," Kopecky adjusted his hold on the file box.

"Almost, my young friend," Srom picked up another box and nodded for Kopecky to follow. "You and I are going to do a little mixing and matching first. Our assignment is to recommend what assets go where. When we are done the best tank and motorized infantry regiments will be brought together."

"I am going to like this assignment," Kopecky trailed Srom to the outer office.

"I thought you would," Srom and Kopecky stacked their boxes with on a hand truck. "After we review that intelligence you'll need to gather together any personal gear you think you might require in the field. I would think that carbine of yours, especially."

"That rifle goes where I go," Kopecky patted the carbine affectionately.

"Good. Any questions?" Srom had a timetable for them to meet.

"Yes sir. Is the president still in Praha?" Kopecky was concerned at how fast events were moving while he was out of touch.

"For the moment. Too bad you won't have time to see the palace before you go. The place looks like a military compound. Generál Bláha has troops everywhere for the president's protection and to secure communications. Cots for the enlisted men have filled up usually empty corridors and officers are shaving each morning in some of the finest rooms in the palace. Beneš even has a gas mask at the ready on his desktop. The president is a brave man and reluctant to leave his post but he'll have to go soon. We can't have him exposed where the Germans can find him," Srom was glad he didn't have Bláha's assignment.

"I am still shocked the French and British finally came around and advised us to mobilize?" Kopecky had given up hope Daladier and Chamberlain would see reason.

"More like they admitted it was impossible to continue advising us against mobilizing," Srom corrected him. "Even Paris and London could not swallow Hitler's Godesberg memorandum."

"What exactly was in that memo? I've only had old newspapers to read the last forty-eight hours," Kopecky felt too far out of touch.

Srom reached over to his desk and retrieved several typed pages. "Read for yourself. Even Napoleon never dared to demand everything down to the last house cat as tribute... so much the better for us. Today, Masaryk will deliver our rejection of that memorandum in London. While Hitler bellows we have mobilized 1.3 million men unmolested and they are ready in their assigned positions. Let the Germans come now."

OTTKE RESIDENCE
WILMERSDORF DISTRICT, BERLIN

The Turkish coffee poured slowly from the Cezve into the small porcelain cups. The engraved brass pot was one of the many curios his uncle had brought back from his assignment in Istanbul during the Great War. The oddness of the design had always fascinating the young Ottke. So much so that his aunt made a point of giving the vessel to him after the sudden death of his uncle by heart attack. The economic depression had been cruel to them. The stress of losing their modest savings when the bank the funds were deposited at collapsed was too much for him. Ottke always suspected his uncle was a naval intelligence agent, and although the truth was never divulged during his childhood, the admiration Ottke held for the man was strong enough to prompt him into the service. Years later after he had risen in rank, Ottke gained access to the old files for himself and discovered his suspicions were correct. His uncle had meandered through much of the Eastern Mediterranean keeping logs on British naval deployments. Every time he used the Cezve, Ottke thought warmly of the man. Following his uncle's death, Ottke had made sure his aunt lived a comfortable life without money worries. There were no children to care for her so Ottke happily did so.

"You seem somewhere else today," Heiden inquired delicately. Usually Ottke's focus was uncomfortably piercing.

"Indeed, that would be your fault for requesting the Türkischer Kaffee," Ottke put his personal thoughts away. "The cezve belonged to my uncle. I think of him every time I make use of it."

"Fondly it would appear," Heiden picked up the cup and sipped the coffee. "The taste is strong and smooth without sharpness. That is a most excellent pot indeed."

"Thank you," Ottke put the cezve to rest on the serving tray and leaned back on the sofa. "This is the least I could do before sending you back out into the cold again."

"With the negative outcome at Godesberg your summons was not unexpected. I have already alerted my men to be ready," Heiden often took such liberties.

"Very good. The momentum toward war is now too strong. With the Czechoslovak army at full strength and in the field there will be no lightning victory. What lies ahead is a very bloody affair," Ottke savored the coffee.

"Is there a date? I am not aware of one yet." It would be difficult for Heiden to fulfill the mission without firm timing.

"Not officially. Thursday night Keitel phoned OKW from Godesberg with news that the British were not submitting to the Führer's will. With more negotiations expected, the general could not ascertain the exact date for the invasion. Therefore, Fall Grün would not be launched prior to September thirtieth and no later than originally planned on October first. Keitel did note the chancellor's growing impatience, however. Hitler could order an invasion prior to September thirtieth but the circumstances would be improvised not deliberative," Ottke could be no more specific. "There has been no changes in Keitel's instructions during the last forty-eight hours."

"Then sometime in the next six days. Excellent, we will be ready. Our targets are now accessible. There is only one matter left to confirm," Heiden circled back to the same argument they had grappled with previously.

"What is your trigger to strike?" Ottke inserted the critical missing subject.

"Precisely," Heiden was happier pressing the issue without Gisevius present to argue an opposing view. "I would prefer to take action as soon as the invasion is ordered without waiting for Halder's directive – a directive I fear will never come."

Ottke had been reconsidering the issue intently himself with some sympathy as his own appraisal mirrored Heiden's. There were risks in acting too brashly, however. Ottke weighed the options and made his decision.

"Major, initiate action alone, without support and odds are you will not accomplish your mission objective. Therefore you will wait until we can guarantee that sufficient units necessary to ensure success are actually taking part in the mission... Halder or no Halder," Ottke gave Heiden half of what he wanted.

"I can live with that," Heiden acceded to his superior's wishes because he was certain the men under his command were sufficient to complete the mission.

DOWNING STREET, LONDON

His driver maneuvered the embassy's Škoda slowly onto the lane past the watchful eyes of uniformed police and the concealed watchers assigned to ensure the prime minister's safety. In his satchel was Czechoslovakia's official reply to Hitler's Godesberg memorandum. Masaryk patted the leather side of the case contently and smiled. Krofta had dictated the major points from Prague yet had left the finer points of the composition up to Masaryk, which pleased him. There was much he had wanted to say for weeks and now he would have Chamberlain and his entire inner cabinet as an audience. Since Masaryk had been invited to deliver his government's decision, protocol demanded that the Czech envoy not be interrupted. After what Chamberlain and his dog Runciman had wrought upon Czechoslovakia during the previous months, Masaryk had no compulsion against appropriating the tidy rules of these British to his own ends.

His driver rolled the Škoda to a stop before the most famous door in English politics. Masaryk let himself out, as was his custom, and strutted purposefully inside when a staffer swung open the entrance into the residence. Masaryk had never before been in the room where he would speak. After the words he planned to deliver were spoken he may never be allowed back in again. Masaryk's hand tightly gripped the handle of the satchel while he waited in the lobby to be announced. He used the time to gather his thoughts. The words he was about to deliver would come from memory. Only when he was done would Masaryk provide the written statement bearing his signature. The wait was not long. A more senior assistant to the prime minister approached to beckon Masaryk to his destination. Going in, he passed Cadogan, whose stoic face betrayed nothing. The foreign office undersecretary's eyes, however, burned with mischief.

"Mister Prime Minister, and gentlemen... let me offer the appreciation of my government, and myself, for this opportunity to address you directly," Masaryk prefaced as the door closed behind him.

"We are pleased to offer you this audience," Lord Halifax spoke for the group. "And we are most eager to know the decision of President Beneš and his government to Herr Hitler's demands."

The way Halifax characterized the memorandum was not in the diplomatically polite words of the appeasement camp the foreign secretary was a member of. The sonorous drone was the same yet Masaryk sensed a change by the careful choice of words. Emboldened,

Masaryk placed his satchel upright on the tabletop and launched into his denunciation without further delay.

"After careful review, the Czechoslovak government rejects Herr Hitler's Godesberg terms in full. They were a de facto ultimatum of the sort usually presented to a vanquished nation and not a proposition to a sovereign state, which has shown the greatest possible readiness to make sacrifices for the appeasement of Europe. My government is in amazement at the contents of the memorandum. The proposals go far beyond what we agreed to in the so-called Anglo-French plan. They deprive us of every safeguard for our national existence. We are to yield up large proportions of our carefully prepared defenses and admit the German armies deep into our country before we have been able to organize it on the new basis or make any preparations for its defense. Our national and economic independence would automatically disappear with the acceptance of Herr Hitler's plan. The whole process of moving the population is to be reduced to panic flight on the part of those who will not accept the German Nazi regime. They have to leave their homes without even the right to take their personal belongings, or in the case of peasants, their cow," Masaryk paused briefly on that extreme absurdity.

"My government wishes me to declare in all solemnity that Herr Hitler's demands in their present form are absolutely and unconditionally unacceptable to my government. We rely upon the two great Western democracies, whose wishes we have followed much against our own judgment, to stand by us in our hour of trial. Against these new and cruel demands my government feels bound to make their utmost resistance and we shall do so, God helping. The nation of Saint Wenceslas, John Hus, and Tomáš Masaryk will not be a nation of slaves," Masaryk was confident his words would not be misconstrued.

The power of those words had left Chamberlain's cabinet members momentarily without a response. Since he believed no response was required, Masaryk threw open the cover to his satchel, removed the typed pages therein, and slapped them against the top of the table before him. "Good day, gentlemen," Masaryk closed up the case, and made his exit.

LAKE SCHLACHTENSEE, BERLIN

If war were coming you would never know it from the good citizens of Berlin. From what these keen eyes could see the people of the leading metropolis in Central Europe had everything but war fever on their minds. That's pretty much how Endicott planned to sum up this Sunday in the German capital in his next dispatch. Shirer had talked Endicott into joining him on the train trip to Berlin. There was still time on Endicott's temporary visa, plus being on the German side of the battle might be a winning ticket. That is if he could hitch a ride with some division crossing the border into Czechoslovakia. Back in Godesberg, Endicott had chatted up one of the fellows with the Propaganda Ministry about getting a press visa and the response had been positive. The advice was to apply with a certain someone at ministry headquarters in Berlin. So tagging along to the capital suddenly made a lot of sense.

After getting set up in a cheap hotel for the night, Endicott made a point of getting out early to get a feeling for the city. He hadn't spent much time in Berlin and needed to find out what was where. Shirer had an interview to conduct at the American embassy but before he disappeared they met for coffee in the morning and he gave Endicott the low down. On warm Sundays like they had today the city emptied out. Even in bad weather the government ministries all shut down on Sundays. So pretty much nothing was supposed to be happening in Berlin. But that's not exactly how Endicott found things when he ventured out on his own. First stop was the Wilhelmstrasse where Hitler's Chancellery, the Foreign Ministry and most of the other government ministries were located. But instead of a lifeless street Endicott found a hell of a lot of coming and goings at each building he passed. The German government was sure working this Sunday. There were a lot of civilian and military traffic swarming the area, which told Endicott that Hitler's people were getting ready for a show down with the Czechs.

The next thing on his mind was what were the Berliners up to? That would make for good color for his story. The day was lovely... what folks called an Indian summer back home. Locating the nearest elevated trolley line he found the platform swarming with people waiting for the next train heading out of town. After asking around, Endicott got mostly the same answer: they were all heading to the woodland area called The Grünewald. What surprised the heck out of Endicott was how close this area was from the city center by trolley. Good thing too since it was standing room only. And when they got to their destination what Endicott found wasn't the large park he expected but a whole damn forest with multiple lakes. Central Park had nothing on this.

Seeing the lake seemed like a decent idea so he got directions and hiked through the trees to the larger body of water the locals called the Schlachtensee. Along the way he saw people sunning themselves in every direction. What seemed like every family in Berlin was there that day having a picnic or playing ball with the kids on the ample grass. When he had the opportunity to strike up conversations with the locals, Endicott would ask what was on their minds on such a fine day. It was well reported, even in the German papers, that Godesberg had not produced the peace so many normal people in Europe yearned for. Yet not one person he spoke with recommended beating up on Czechoslovakia as a solution. War was the last thing on these Berliner's minds.

Endicott thought this state of affairs was odd. On the train from Cologne Shirer had gone on about how Germans were a very patriotic people. Before the Great War started there had been huge public parades and protests outside foreign ministries. But Endicott had seen no such activity as he walked through the city. He was hard pressed even to spot a policeman. The government was working overtime but the people seemed like they were trying their best to avoid thinking about possible hostilities. The water looked so inviting and people were having such a good time splashing around, Endicott was jealous he didn't have swim trunks available. Checking his wristwatch, Endicott decided to head back into the city before the afternoon sun was gone. He didn't want to get himself lost on his first day in Berlin. Arriving back in the city Endicott noticed plenty of posters going up with the same announcement. The Propaganda Ministry had something big planned. For the first time in the country's history one solitary radio broadcast would be heard throughout all of Germany.

> *On Monday, the 26th of September at eight o'clock in the Sportpalast in Berlin, there will be a great Popular Mass Meeting. The Führer will speak. This mass meeting will be broadcast by all German radio stations. Those who do not possess a radio apparatus will listen to it through community loudspeakers in every town and village in Germany. All party leaders in each district must begin immediately to prepare for the reception of the community broadcasts. There must not be a single person in Germany who shall not be a witness, by means of the radio, of this historic mass meeting.*

Endicott scratched his brow. The good people of Berlin were not focused on the international crisis with the Czechs but starting at eight o'clock tomorrow night their government was going to coerce their attention.

CHURCH OF SAINT BARTHOLOMEW, PLZEN

The hand-delivered message has arrived early that morning. The code was the agreed upon simple shifting of letters several positions backward. Say using the letter M when the actual character intended was J. The content of the message was direct. A-54 was requesting an urgent rendezvous in Plzen for that evening. Although he was tempted to make the journey, Moravec was too pre-occupied with transferring critical operations of the Second Department to their various wartime locations. Since Karl was comfortable with Burda and Furst, especially following their previous escapades together, Moravec sent his junior officers to Plzen.

Given the congestion on the roads driving there was out of the question. A call to Kbely put an Aero bomber at the disposal of the intelligence men for the flight to Plzen. To be honest, Burda and Furst would have preferred driving themselves in the Baby. The metal benches they had to sit on during the flight were hard, and since the interior of the huge aircraft was drafty, those benches were uncomfortably cold. Lucky for them the weather was still warm. There had been no time to requisition proper flight suits, which were rather scarce at the moment. Their business suits had to suffice.

A car was waiting for them on the ground in Plzen so no time was lost heading to the rendezvous point A-54 had specified. Burda had come to the conclusion their most valuable agent had a flair for the dramatic. Saint Bartholomew was one of the principal landmarks in the city – a stunning church in the Gothic tradition. Definitely not the drab, concealed hideaway one in this profession would expect. Furst circled the car around the perimeter of the church yet nothing appeared out of place or suspicious. They parked the sedan close by to watch the church a bit further while they checked their weapons.

"Let's go," Burda holstered his pistol.

The short distance to the main doors of the church was unremarkable except for dodging the mostly older women intent on lighting prayer candles. To better fit in, both men paused to cross themselves upon entering. This also gave their eyes an opportunity to adjust to the low light inside. Luckily there was no service in session to interrupt. Separating, Burda moved up the center aisle toward the middle of the church where he found an open pew to sit on. Furst kept to the left side of the vestibule, hugging the wall while slowly moving deeper into the structure. Burda tensed at hearing quiet steps approaching from close behind. An old woman passed shuffling down the aisle and Burda allowed himself to relax. He caught Furst's eye long enough to worry his partner would draw a pistol on the aged parishioner but Furst continued his search pattern instead. Just as Furst was as far into the church as he would get before retracing his route, Burda heard someone slip into the pew behind him.

"Hello kapitán," a familiar voice whispered. "Please do not turnaround. I will be gone in thirty seconds but you will find an envelope. Put the contents to good use."

"Do you need transportation or other assistance?" Burda could do without another wild ride if possible.

"No thank you, I am well taken care of unlike last time," Karl's manner was un-rushed and confident. "Good luck kapitán, I do not know when we will meet again."

Burda did not waste the effort to peer over his shoulder. He knew the agent was already gone. Waiting thirty seconds, Burda stood up and turned around. The envelope was there on the next pew as promised. He bent down, picked up the envelope, then calmly walked up the aisle and left the church. Furst caught up with him halfway to the borrowed automobile.

"Did you see him?" Furst was uneasy having noticed the envelope and knowing he had missed whatever had happened inside the church.

"No, but Karl saw us," Burda confirmed while opening the passenger door of the car.

When both men had got into their seats and closed their doors, Burda signaled for Furst to start driving. After they had traveled several blocks he opened the envelope and browsed through the pages inside.

"What has he given us this time?" Furst was too curious to wait.

"The exact location of each Luftwaffe airfield assigned to the invasion," Burda flipped pages swiftly. "In here is where we can find every one of their bomber and fighter squadrons. Go faster, we have to get this information back to Praha immediately."

GARE DE L'EST, PARIS

Coiffard had been right on the money. It wasn't a general mobilization yet the Parisians were treating it that way. Clarence had risen early, to the consternation of his sleep-adoring wife, to check for any announcements. No sooner had he rounded the first corner from their apartment did Clarence see an *Affiche Blanche* pasted on a public building. Clarence suspected that old fox General Gamelin was sending the message because he didn't think Daladier had the balls. The government was announcing a partial mobilization but they were using a poster that symbolized a general mobilization to Parisians. As the city awoke from its slumber and people went about their business, the call up of Categories Two and Three reservists caused quite a stir. The message Clarence divined was *get ready* and that's just how the French he spoke with saw matters.

This call-up system was new. Clarence remembered how the French civil and military institutions found themselves with egg on their faces during the Rhineland crisis. While Hitler waltzed in, the French lost time struggling to get their reservists to their regiments under the old system. Now, instead of calling specific social classes of men, these new categories selected males of various ages and occupations. The six-hundred thousand men Clarence estimated were getting their orders today came from a much larger cross-section of society so a lot more families were feeling the anxiety of sending a loved one to service.

Clarence thought the best place to see all of these personal stories play out was the Eastern rail station facing the Boulevard de Strasbourg – one of the major avenues in Paris. The Gare de l'Est was where so many of the troops had passed through on their way to the front in 1914. It was a good hunch. Traffic was stopped all around the station. There were so many people heading in that direction on foot that autos simply could not maneuver. The crush of people was so bad the authorities had stopped allowing family members into the huge station. There were barricades out front with notices affixed to them stating the entrances were for reservists alone. And the military police didn't flinch at turning people away as Clarence found out when he tried to go inside to see the last train for Metz pull out at four-thirty. All people could do was wave their handkerchiefs at their boys as they disappeared into the foyer and out of sight. Clarence saw a fairly even mix of workers, bourgeoisie, and poor men swallowed up by the station as they left their tearful wives and girlfriends behind.

Journalists like Coiffard remembered how Parisians approached 1914 with a romantic notion of victory. Yet no one that Clarence could see seemed excited about fighting the good fight this time around. No singing of the Marseillaise and no desire for glory. Serious and dutiful was how Clarence would describe the mood of the reservists. For their women it was an outpouring of worry. When a young wife holding her baby began to sob nearby, Clarence approached her and offered his handkerchief. She gladly borrowed it and wiped away the moisture from her face.

"Who do you blame?" Clarence inquired in a fatherly tone.

"I blame Hitler," the woman accused without hesitation. "Push, push, push... all of the time pushing us. Haven't you heard him on the radio? That pig. What else are we to do but push back?"

Walking down the boulevard known for its shops and cafes, Clarence found many Parisians expressed the same sentiment. They were not happy about sending their boys off to danger and they were angry at Germany for creating the crisis that was forcing France to respond. In fact, Clarence found the mood of the families crowding the cafes to be much more realistic than the daily commentary in the French newspapers that promoted mollifying Hitler. These Parisians knew exactly what the score was and they were not keen on rolling over for *les Boches*. That's how Clarence would lead his story. The average Frenchman was ready even if his ruling class was quaking in its boots.

NEAR GORKAU, SUDETENLAND

The spotter tracked the flight of German bombers heading northeast. The aircraft were quite low under a blanket of clouds and moving fast in the direction of the fortifications defending Brux. The Germans had picked a section of territory between anti-aircraft nests to fly through. No doubt following a path mapped out by Sudeten traitors to avoid ground fire. Could the war have started already? The spotter did not know but those bombers were too far inside Czechoslovak territory to be tolerated.

"Someone get on the phone to the command center at Brux and report three enemy Heinkels heading northeast in their direction," the spotter followed the bombers with his field glasses. "Estimated time to their position... under ten minutes."

Stahl's gloved fingers kept thumping the control stick. Wunsch had been the paragon of accuracy since getting his ass kicked after taking the whole flight over Weipert in enemy territory ten days before. The flight leader had been determined to demote the boy to ventral gunner. That open-air pod was *the* most uncomfortable position on the plane – cold, lonely and buffeted non-stop by angry gusts of air forced back along the Heinkel's metal skin. Wunsch had pleaded for another chance. Along with fear, Stahl had seen enough determination in those eyes to relent. Since that day Wunsch had given Stahl every reason to believe he had made the right decision. But today they were late reaching their assigned training target, and more worrisome, Stahl could not identify where they were after he took the flight down under the clouds. So much for trust... Stahl switched on his intercom microphone.

"Wunsch, you have been a good boy lately. But if you cannot tell me where the hell we are in the next sixty seconds, I assure you I will take us back up to nine-thousand meters and personally shove you out the access hatch," Stahl sounded most convincing over the intercom.

"Understood, sir," Wunsch responded quickly. "We encountered more wind than was forecasted. I have been trying to compensate. There's a good chance we are over the border but not too much."

"I already know we are over the border, Wunsch!" Stahl looked out the cockpit window again. "Can you tell me where?"

"Maybe close to Komotau if my last calculations are accurate," Wunsch ventured an estimate.

"Komotau! That's far worse than the last time," Stahl saw they were coming up fast on one of the Czech defence lines. The damn things were set back into hillsides and so well camouflaged you wouldn't see one until you were right on top of it – as they were right now.

"Stahl to schwarm..." He could see the barrels of the AA guns rising up to take aim at his nose. "Boys, that's the Czech army down there and they don't look happy to see us. Set course due north... full throttle. Now!"

Stahl banked his Heinkel hard to the left as he opened up the engines. North was the shortest way, although the new course would leave them dangerously close to the enemy guns for a while if the Czechs started shooting. Stahl got a quick answer to that question as a heavy anti-aircraft shell exploded to the right and above the aircraft. Flak was one of his least fond memories from Spain as more detonations boomed around the escaping bombers.

"Everyone but Steinhausen... roll out your machine guns," Stahl ignored the bomber shuddering and rattling severely. "I expect we will have company soon. But do not shoot at any Czech planes unless they shoot at you first. I repeat... do *not* shoot first. If you see anything suspicious call it out first."

The Czechoslovaks were taking their accidental incursion seriously and Stahl could not blame them. The Führer was promising to invade within days, after all. With their military fully mobilized, Stahl had to expect the Czechs had fighters up in the air. The question was could his flight make a speedy retreat before those fighters could vector on his position.

"Stahl to schwarm. Stay low and check your sixes for enemy fighters." Following his own advice, Stahl looked over both shoulders, and through the canopy above. No bad guys... yet. "Position check..."

"Clear," the radioman Gutzman spoke up first from the dorsal gun.

"Nothing down here but scared sheep," Steinhausen joked. His ventral *dustbin* was retracted to prevent added drag on their top speed. He still had to stay at station though in case they were attacked from below later.

"All clear ahead," Wunsch added from the nose. "Time to border, fifteen minutes at this speed."

"You positive about that, Wunsch?" Stahl had no choice but to ride the youngster.

"Ya hauptmann... I fixed our position at Brux. Fifteen minutes should be correct," Wunsch did his best not to stutter under the pressure.

The flight was outrunning the flak. They had not lost anyone so Stahl could relax a little, but only a little. All he could do now was hope their luck held.

They were fortunate. The alert that came in from Brux over the wireless said the intruders were heading north fast at treetop level. That would bring them right into the zone Bozik's squadron was patrolling. They had been anticipating such an opportunity for weeks. The enemy had been straying into Czechoslovakia airspace on a regular basis yet they always got back to their side of the border before anyone could intercept them. This time, however, the intruders were deep into Czech territory. The Luftwaffe planes had not done anything belligerent according to the report. If the bombers *had* attacked something it would make his job much more simple. The ground spotters had identified the Germans as Heinkels. That was lucky. Heinkels were slower than the Dorniers and had a distinctive wing that was easy to spot from above. If they were fired upon Bozik had ordered the pilots to shoot the intruders down. Otherwise, they were to force the Heinkels to land on Czech soil so the aircraft could be interred and examined.

Their sixteen planes were broken up into four flights, each vectoring at high speed toward the area where Bozik reckoned his Avias could intercept the Heinkels on their last known course. One flight would remain at high altitude to protect against the rest being jumped by waiting Luftwaffe fighters if this were a trap. Bozik's and another flight were ready at medium altitude waiting to pounce as soon as the German bombers had been located. The final flight was at lower altitude scouring territory for the approaching Heinkels.

All of Bozik's pilots were itching to prove themselves. Part of their motivation was demonstrating their prowess after months of Bozik's grueling training. His men also had a little chip on the shoulders. The Germans had ruled over them for centuries. A people who were once subject to another were eager to prove they were every bit the match of those who had ruled them. With the Germans always boasting of their superiority, his pilots were eager to prove that Germans could die as well as other men.

Bozik's headphone buzzed over his ear. The scout flight below had spotted the three Heinkels in a *V* formation and had provided their direction and estimated air speed. Now the fun began.

"Team two," Bozik activated his microphone. "Anything to worry about above?"

"All clear." was the efficient response drilled into the pilots.

"Team one, we're coming down." While the Germans worried about the four fighters they could see, Bozik would lead his two flights on a diving vector that would surprise their prey from the front. It would be tricky to pull off since the Heinkels were so low to the ground but Bozik relished the surprise he was about to spring on his adversaries.

"Teams three and four, follow me down," Bozik pushed the control stick forward.

By his estimate, Stahl figured they had covered half the distance to the border with nothing but small villages below as expected. So far his planes had drawn sparse ground fire. In those moments between the routine of checking the skies above, Stahl had contemplated what to do with Wunsch. It was his own conceit that he could mold any crewman into a reliable asset given time. In Wunsch's case, Stahl was forced to admit he had failed. There was such a shortage of trained navigators that Stahl had kept working with the boy, hoping to turn him around. With war but days away it was obvious that Wunsch had to go. Experience told Stahl it was time to push such thoughts aside to check above for enemy aircraft when he was startled by four Czech biplane fighters crossing over his nose. Looking out his side window Stahl saw them banking back around to the rear of the flight.

"We have company back here," Gutzman announced with a bit of urgency. "Four biplanes taking up position on our tails."

"Damn!" Stahl's luck had run out. "What are the Avias up to?"

"Slowly closing distance, a little high and dipping their wings from time to time," Gutzman cocked his MG 15 machine gun.

Stahl thought that was good news. The Czech pilots were just having a look.

"Shit!" Wunsch yelled over the intercom.

An Avia dove past the Heinkel's nose with millimeters to spare at high speed. A quick glance around and Stahl saw four or five more of the Czech fighters were harassing the rest of his schwarm in the same way. They were being toyed with. "Do not fire! I repeat, do not fire," Stahl commanded the other crews over the wireless.

The Czechs were attempting to draw fire from the defensive machine guns to justify shooting his birds down. If the Czechs had wished them dead they would have fired on their first pass. Stahl was pleased at the discipline of his crews.

"The four in back are closing on us," Gutzman warned."

Stahl watched the two new flights of Avias aggressively harassing his three Heinkels. Soon an attempt would be made to force the schwarm to land. If he refused then they would shoot his planes down. It was what Stahl would do if the roles were reversed.

"Taking fire from the ground!" Wunsch warned from the nose.

Focused on the Czech fighters closing from behind, Gutzman only heard *taking fire,* and took the alert to mean the other biplanes had opened fire on the schwarm. Gutzman depressed the trigger on the MG 15 machine gun that was aimed at one of the Czech fighter biplanes to the rear. Seeing tracer fire reaching back toward them, the quick reflexes of the pursuing pilots took over and they hauled their aircraft out of the way of the incoming bullets. Without hesitation, the Czechoslovak pilots picked their targets and returned fire. The machine gunners on the other two Heinkels saw the exchange of gunfire and began shooting at the Avias to protect their comrades.

"What's going on? Who fired first? No, no, no!" Stahl called out over the radio.

The dorsal gunner on the closest Heinkel opened up on Bozik's Avia but was a poor shot. If that's the way the Germans wanted it, Bozik was happy to oblige. The Avias converged on the flight of Heinkels at full speed like angry wasps. The concentrated fire of the four fuselage-mounted Model 30 machine guns on each Czech fighter swiftly ripped gaping holes in the metal skins of the Heinkels. The German pilots valiantly attempted to hold formation to maximize the fire of their own guns but there were too many attackers. The right wing of one of the bombers sheared off and the Heinkel tumbled out of the sky into a hillside. The same fate befell a second H-111E when its tail was shot away. That left the flight leader. This pilot was obviously well skilled. He flew his Heinkel between tall trees and banked perilously close to rock formations to throw off the Czech pilots nipping at his heels. Bozik admired the man trying so hard to make it home alive but not enough to let him go. Lining his gun sight up on the left engine, Bozik eased down on the trigger. His wingman, Nedoma, was lined up on the right engine. With both engines on fire the Heinkel rapidly lost airspeed until it stalled and careened into a hillside – exploding on impact.

Bozik and Nedoma circled the crash several times but saw no survivors. "Leader to letka, let's go home," Bozik pulled back on the stick and pointed the Avia east.

29. HOSTILITIES

**Chancellor Hitler addresses the nation
from the Sportpalast in Berlin**

SEPTEMBER 26, 1938
WILHELMSTRASSE, BERLIN

Having gotten familiarized with Berlin over the weekend, Monday morning was reserved for getting his visa status fixed with the authorities. Forgoing breakfast to get an early jump on the day, Endicott blended in with the crowds of Germans on their way to work and headed back to the Wilhelmstrasse. If you ignored the over-the-top trappings of the Nazi party that were plastered throughout the city, there wasn't a whole lot of difference mingling with Berliners, versus Londoners or New Yorkers. But the party did seem to have its fingers into everything. Case in point, his visa. Endicott followed the instructions given to him once he got to the Propaganda Ministry. Sure, he got passed around a few times to different clerks but Endicott still walked out with a new visa. Regular consular officials never dispensed that kind of service.

The other item that Endicott managed to get his paws on was a pass to Hitler's speech that night at the Sportpalast. No sooner had Endicott gotten his credentials approved and pocketed the pass than all hell broke loose in the building. Something big was happening. A woman in such a hurry to get down the hall almost knocked him to the floor. At least she was polite about it and stopped to apologize, which gave Endicott a chance to roll out his sparse vocabulary in German.

"Fraulein, what happened?" Endicott raised his arms.

"I knocked you down," the woman already sounded exasperated with him.

"Nein, why all of the excitement here?" Endicott tried again.

"Oh... the Czechs. They shot down three of our bombers yesterday. We have proof from Sudetens in the vicinity," the copywriter explained.

"Photographs?" Endicott wasn't keen on many of the claims the Henleinists made.

"Ya," she confirmed. "The crews are all dead."

Endicott was surprised something like this hadn't happened sooner. With German planes straying over the border it was only a matter of time before the Czechs shot first and asked questions later.

"Are you a foreign correspondent?" the copywriter switched to a slightly accented English.

"Why yes," Endicott was happy to ditch his stilted version of the local lingo. "How could you tell?"

"It's my job. Follow me. You can get the latest information and statements from the government," the woman instructed him.

She was already making headway down the hall before Endicott could thank her properly. Hurrying after her he marveled at how well his luck was holding. He might even be first to get the story out on the U.S. wires. Now the big question was what would Hitler say tonight? After what Endicott witnessed in Godesberg, getting three of his prized airplanes shot down would probably send Hitler's blood pressure through the roof. Once Hitler got done tearing up the carpet at the Reich Chancellery, Endicott imagined the chancellor would respond by calling for Czech blood. Lucky for him, Shirer was scheduled to broadcast from the Sportpalast tonight. He told Endicott that the broadcast stage was being set up in a balcony right above where Hitler would speak and Endicott could tag along if he could get in.

DOWNING STREET, LONDON

The British were sufficiently backed into a corner to bear their teeth... not at Hitler but at their French ally Daladier. The premier was furious at his treatment on Sunday by Chamberlain and his henchmen like Sir John Simon. Daladier knew for a fact that the majority of Chamberlain's cabinet was against further concessions to Hitler yet those men remained uniformly silent while Daladier was rudely interrogated regarding what were France's battle plans should Germany take military measures. The premier's consistent response – that France would fulfill her obligations in the event of unprovoked aggression – was not sufficient for them. Was France prepared to declare war immediately? What was France's battle plan? Could the premier provide exacting details on those battle plans? Obviously, Daladier could not. The premier had never been briefed on such minutiae. So Gamelin had been summoned to fly to London early that morning to shut down Chamberlain's interrogation. Why the British prime minister was so intent on pushing this line of questioning eluded Gamelin until he arrived at 10 Downing Street where he was greeted by Daladier and Bonnet in the foyer.

"Général Gamelin," Daladier hurried over to his army chief of staff. "Finally someone who can silence these annoying questions. Chamberlain wants one more go at negotiating with Hitler and is trying every possible tactic to erode our resolve to permit him to pursue that course."

"Further attempts at negotiation are a wasted effort," Gamelin had a mind to tell the British prime minister the same to his face.

"That is exactly what I told him. Hitler has already gone too far and won't back down now. It is no longer a question of reaching a fair arrangement. Is it not apparent Hitler's sole objective is to destroy Czechoslovakia by force? My council of ministers unanimously rejected the Godesberg memorandum. To grovel to Hitler and accept his demands now would be political suicide for us all. But this morning we heard whispers that Chamberlain is close to resigning if he doesn't get his way. That explains the silence of the opposition within his inner cabinet – at least in front of us. Now we have learned that Chamberlain has already dispatched a personal emissary to Berlin on his own authority," Daladier was quite weary of these *surprises*.

"Another direct overture to Hitler without prior consultation," Gamelin quietly huffed. "When will this emissary depart?"

"We are told he is already in the air," Bonnet spoke for the first time.

Gamelin held a dim view of Bonnet. The foreign minister had repeatedly misrepresented the chief of staff's reports and findings to his own defeatist ends, so Gamelin had to weigh carefully everything that came out of the diplomat's rascally mouth.

"This emissary will fail. Do not place any hope in a negotiated settlement," Gamelin had to be careful about clearly phrasing his words lest Bonnet twist any ambiguities.

"That is a rather final assessment, général," Bonnet felt Gamelin was speaking outside of his portfolio.

"Perhaps, but I find the général's assessment refreshing," Daladier cut in, obviously anxious to push back against their treatment at the hands of their British allies the previous day. "I want to hear more. Let's go."

"Premier, it would be best if we discussed some matters privately first," Gamelin attempted to hold the premier back.

"No, the British need to hear our position as soon as possible. And they are waiting for us. Follow me," Daladier continued on.

Bonnet glared at Gamelin, yet held his tongue as they both followed after Daladier through the open door into the cabinet room.

"Gentlemen, have a seat," Chamberlain gestured at the three spaces at the table reserved for the French delegation. "And thank you for joining us on such short notice General Gamelin."

"I am ready to go wherever duty requires," Gamelin decided to set the tone of the discussion.

"Of course, as it should be," Chamberlain sat back in his chair. He had been led to believe the French general was an ambivalent fellow when it came to actually fighting a war. Ambivalent was not how this man seemed in the flesh.

"The Général is fully prepared to answer the technical questions you posed yesterday," Daladier courteously raised an arm toward Gamelin.

"Very good. General Gamelin, if Herr Hitler cannot be deterred from invading Czechoslovakia, England is bound to come to France's aid. My government has a responsibility to learn how exactly the French military will successfully prosecute war against Germany," Chamberlain would leave the probing questions for a bit later.

If Chamberlain was still thinking in terms of deterring Hitler, it was obvious to Gamelin that the British leader had not been appraised of the same news that Gamelin had received before leaving Paris.

"May I remind the prime minister that I have personally and repeatedly requested the exchange of liaisons between my staff and their English counterparts over many months, and if your government had approved these requests, you would have a much better understanding of our capabilities and strategy at this urgent hour," Gamelin purposefully slapped his host... for his own reasons and for the rude treatment of Daladier.

The room went dreadfully silent. No one expected Gamelin had any intention of reproaching the prime minister, let along rebuking him so bluntly. Bonnet was aghast, and while Daladier would not have approved of such impudence, he nonetheless enjoyed watching Chamberlain put on his guard.

"But now is not the time dwell on such matters," Gamelin continued before someone rose up to interrupt him. "This crisis has taken a fateful turn. It is my duty to inform you that yesterday evening three German Heinkel bombers penetrated deep into Czechoslovak territory, their crews fired upon Czech fighters sent to intercept them and these German aircraft were swiftly shot down over Czechoslovakia. I was informed of this encounter while boarding my plane this morning.

Daladier leaned in close to his army chief of staff while forcing a calm expression on his face, "This has been corroborated?"

"Yes sir, from both Prague and Berlin," Gamelin was pleased to see his premier remain composed.

Chamberlain's weary body deflated into his chair like a burst balloon. He had weathered Hitler's constant harangues at Godesberg and had witnessed how the man would erupt at each slip of paper with some supposed Czechoslovak provocation was passed to him. Most of those were wild tales and obvious fabrications. Chamberlain had watched as something as minuscule as a report of a dead cow would set Hitler off on another diatribe. But this... losing three bomber crews to Czech fighters would irrevocably send Hitler over the edge. There would be no finding a peaceful arrangement with him now. Germany would invade and the only question was what day later in the week the attack would come.

"That would settle the matter, I would think," Duff Cooper, First Lord of the Admiralty spoke first while rising from his chair to pace. "Is anyone at this table still willing to contend that Hitler can be deterred from aggression?"

Cooper did not wait for a response, as no protest was forthcoming. "Right, it doesn't really matter who fired first, does it? The Germans were caught where they shouldn't be. The Czechs have every right to protect their territory and Hitler will have a legitimate provocation to justify his invasion. I do not see a way to avoid the matter any longer. Whether we like it or not we are in it now, gentlemen. The discussion must now turn on how we intend to prosecute this war. For my part, I have already ordered all ships in the Royal Navy to full complement, recalled all men from leave, sent two-thousand men to support the fleet in the Med, as well as manning defenses on the Suez Canal. Before the day is out I would recommend ordering our ships to sea and putting the Royal Air Force on full alert. We might as well show Chancellor Hitler we are serious. General Gamelin, upon the onset of hostilities between Germany and Czechoslovakia what will be your strategy?"

Gamelin rose to his feet so that he could use a nearby map of Europe to demonstrate. "Within five days of Germany invading Czechoslovakia, twenty-three French divisions will attack weak points in the unfinished West Wall and then push into the Saarland toward Saarbrücken. Facing us the Germans have mustered but eight divisions and that force will not be sufficient to stop our advance. The worst of it on the ground will be clearing the minefields that have been sown in the area. Upon full mobilization, the French army will add an additional thirty-seven divisions to the offensive. Having dispatched opposition in the area, and secured our incursion, our next step will be to fan out further into the German industrial districts to disrupt Hitler's war effort. This will continue until we meet opposition, at which time we will evaluate our options. To deal with us, Hitler will be forced to draw divisions away from Bohemia, which can only bolster the fortunes of the Czech army."

"And what of the French Air Force?" Chamberlain roused himself. "Certainly you must admit that you are at a disadvantage in the air."

"Much depends on how many Luftwaffe squadrons will face us," Gamelin had to admit. "The Armee de l' Air will bomb German targets and our fighters will defend the airspace over the front. If Hitler dedicates the bulk of his aerial assets to the Czechoslovak front then we shall not do too badly. If this is not the case our inferior aircraft will suffer terribly, I am afraid. Our pilots are well trained, however, and they will do their best. Despite these discrepancies in aerial armament the outcome remains the same: the democratic nations would dictate the peace. It is the whole and not the parts that count. I hold a high opinion of Czechoslovakia's military capabilities. They will give a good account of themselves and France can hold her own in a war with Germany. But in order to win the war it is indispensable that the French government and the high command know without delay which important British forces your government is prepared to send?"

During the previous day it was the British that had fixated on how far France was willing to go in waging war on Germany. In fifteen minutes Gamelin had turned the spotlight around and all eyes burrowed in on Chamberlain. Daladier was particularly impressed with the général's performance. Gamelin had been unflappably confident in his briefing, which had obviously had the effect of fortifying the resolve of the British ministers.

"It has been my unwavering desire to avoid just this very state of affairs," Chamberlain let his growing annoyance show. "The United Kingdom is not prepared for another world war."

"The prime minister will have to admit that the state of affairs have unavoidably embraced us," Secretary of State for War Hore-Belisha stood up ready for a fight. "I know extremely well how woefully unprepared we are for this conflict yet the general's question is legitimate. With conscription, we can raise five hundred thousand men for the army. Unfortunately our modernization program was only initiated this summer and we do not have the mechanized equipment to supply all of those men. If war comes this week, His Majesty's Government could only commit a modest expeditionary force drawn from our peacetime complement. Mister Cooper is correct, however. Squadrons of the Royal Air Force would be available to support your offensive in the Saarland and the Royal Navy is more than capable of bottling up the Kriegsmarine."

"It would also be prudent for both nations to order full mobilization and introduce conscription simultaneously, as well as pooling of our resources where possible," Gamelin's proposal was both pragmatic and intended to further vex Chamberlain.

The discussion was proceeding far too swiftly for Chamberlain's comfort. Hore-Belisha was a loud proponent for meeting Hitler with force and the prime minister did not want to air their disagreements in front of the French delegation. Chamberlain accepted that he faced a rebellion in his cabinet but better to move for a temporary adjournment so that he could hash out matters with his ministers in private.

"I beg the premier's pardon," Chamberlain rose to his feet. "My ministers and I need some time to sort out General Gamelin's disclosures. I am sure there is much for your delegation to discuss as well before we continue. My staff will make you comfortable in the interim. I promise this interruption will be as brief as possible."

Daladier was actually thankful for the intermission. While Gamelin had proven to be stunningly good, the premier had a thousand questions of his chief of staff. It was also obvious that Bonnet was squirming in his seat at the direction of the discussion. Daladier collected his papers and pushed his chair back as Gamelin moved to stand supportively by his side.

"Let them have their chat," Daladier whispered in their own language. "I do not think the prime minister will be able to wiggle out of the vise you just put him in, général."

DERELICT CATHOLIC MONASTERY, VYŠKOV

Their new home was going to take some work. Emperor Joseph II had closed monasteries throughout Bohemia and Moravia during the late Eighteenth Century. Most of them had stood abandoned ever since. This one had attracted a substantial hive of dwellers over the decades. Unfortunately for them the Czechoslovak intelligence service could not afford to allow potentially unreliable persons under its nose. Tichy instructed the counter-intelligence branch to clear out the compound with as much restraint as possible. The larger problem was most of the twenty thousand people living in the area were German farm families that had been settled in Vyškov after the town had been decimated by plague long ago. When the general staff learned of how well the monastery had been cleared, counter-intelligence teams were assigned the same task throughout Vyškov. It was unpleasant work since the families ordered to leave their farmhouses quite naturally refused.

Why relocate the headquarters of the military to a German town? A central location within the country was convenient. Mischief by the Poles to the north plus the Hungarians to the south was a very real worry. The high command also had to be concerned with coordinating expected Soviet support from the east. As the army already had a presence in Vyškov via a training facility, the town proved to be an excellent geographic choice. There already were good communications links in place and more could be added thanks to the closeness of Brno about thirty minutes away. Eventually the local Germans would make the presence of the general staff known to Berlin. When the Luftwaffe bombers came they would endanger a far fewer number of civilians than if a large city like Brno had been selected.

There were drawbacks to the location, however. The existing anti-aircraft batteries were thoroughly inadequate. That was being tended to with dispatch but it would be days before the air defenses in Vyškov were up to the task. They would have to hope the fighter regiments further west would keep most of the German bombers from getting to Vyškov. For the moment there were a few fortified shelters that could be used to ride out air attacks. Constructing more would also take precious time to complete.

Everything considered, the Second Department had fared very well in drawing the old monastery as its headquarters. The site was situated at a higher altitude and was somewhat secluded from the rest of the town. Their monastery would be easier to defend as they could spot anyone approaching from a distance. But the monastery's greatest asset was her deep cellars. The thick walls of stone in the cellars were perfect natural bomb shelters. After appraising the existing structures for defensibility, state of repair and habitability, Moravec selected for their headquarters what must have originally been the House of Novices. Once it had been cleared of debris the old chapel was of such decent size that they could use it as a primary work area. Six rooms adjacent to chapel would be set up as section departments. The nearby Infirmary structure had possessed similar virtues and would be next on their list for occupation.

A platoon of regular army troops had been assigned to secure and protect the monastery compound in concert with Second Department personnel. They were good boys and didn't balk upon learning *securing* also meant cleaning out the results of several generations of decay and leftover rubbish. Moravec's main worry was the cloister. It was large and must have been beautiful in its day. But the cloister's generous open area was also a problem to defend since it was a perfect landing zone for paratroops with swift access to the rest of the compound. After talking it over with the platoon leader, Moravec agreed the best solution was to sew together large tents into a tarp of the proper size, paint the fabric to resemble roof tiles in the Roman fashion and then secure their deceptive creation over the cloister like a roof.

It was their good luck that several of the soldiers were professional house painters who managed a stunningly good job of visual subterfuge. Climbing up to the roof, the men took careful mental note of the rake of the original structure, the materials used and the discoloration after many years. From memory they went to work on the stitched-together fabric and worked a miracle. From up in the air their artful work of deceit looked like one more section of the existing roof. It would have to do, as there was no guarantee when Moravec's request for heavy machine-gun crews would materialize to protect them from German air attacks. Moravec was so impressed with the soldier's final work that he requested that they create camouflage for the petrol generators that had been set up to provide electricity for the department's operations.

As their headquarters was transforming into space that was actually useful, Moravec drew together his chief lieutenants. The necessary telephone and teletype lines had already been strung into the old chapel where the communications department had their machines up and running. Burda and Furst had also supervised setting up various wireless stations in several of the rooms off the chapel. Either for monitoring German radio traffic, or the department's own sensitive communications, the added seclusion was prudent. As they were now connected again with the outside world, Moravec desired an update on what was happening outside of Vyškov.

"Excellent job everyone, our new home is operational much sooner than I had anticipated," Moravec consulted his clipboard. "First order of business, what is the word coming out of Germany?"

"Our assets in Berlin are all reporting an enormous surge of activity at every government ministry since yesterday. There has also been an explosion of Wehrmacht wireless chatter since the downing of the Luftwaffe bombers – all operational in nature and much of it coded. We are still divining which intercepted messages require priority with the ciphers. There is much to sort through." Now that communications were up the backlog of intercepts was dropping on Strankmüller like an avalanche.

"What we are most concerned with are operational instructions that differ from what we were intercepting prior to yesterday," Fryc the code expert clarified his task.

"During the last twenty-four hours we have not discerned any evidence that Hitler has ordered a military response at sea or in the air," Strankmüller ran down the available facts. "No changes in the status of the Kriegsmarine. No orders for the pocket battleships to raise steam and no hurried orders to sea for other units of the surface fleet. The submarines are much harder to track but we're trying. Luftwaffe squadrons are already deployed to their forward airfields. We cannot yet confirm if their alert status has been raised. The Luftwaffe doesn't usually issue orders over the radio."

"Very good," Moravec made notes on his clipboard sheet. "While we are on the subject of the Luftwaffe, what is the status of that aerodrome data from A-54?"

"Furst and I hand delivered the material to General Janoušek before leaving Praha," Burda spoke up. "He said his pilots would put the information to good use."

"I would think so," Strankmüller had marveled at the completeness of the inventory. "The meteorologists are predicting westerly winds and heavy fog on the German side of the frontier in the coming days. If the Luftwaffe cannot get off the ground I can see where the chief of air operations would be pleased."

"Excellent. Now what about security in Sudeten districts where the army must operate? I want to keep their spying and sabotage to a minimum." Without a detailed agenda from Karl this time, Moravec's network had a much more difficult job ahead.

"All of our field centers remain operational," Tichy was still pulling together the latest action reports. "Customary Henleinist activity has actually decreased with the onset of Freikorps raids. Our people in the field will be sweeping German villages with regular army units to intern all known SdP agitators we can put our hands upon."

"Where are you going to put them?" Moravec had some concern for the political ramifications if those interned were treated harshly.

"We have arranged for several secluded villas tucked far away in Slovakia. The Sudetens will have quite a nice vacation at the expense of the government," Tichy was considering the sending of a photographer to document the comfortable conditions.

"I approve," Moravec was amused at Tichy's choice for internment.

"What about the evacuation of President Beneš, sir? Are we assisting in any way?" Furst had heard the president was still in Praha.

"Not directly. That job is already well supervised. The president will be moving out of Hradčany today. For now I have other plans for Jan and you," Moravec had a special assignment he had not told them about.

"Where are we needed?" Burda was curious about this latest surprise.

"For now, Plzen. A-54 might need to meet with us again. Regardless, with the war about to start I will need an extra set of eyes, ears and hands closer to the front lines. Plzen is perfectly located for that purpose. Now the both of you get moving before all hell breaks loose," Moravec sent them on their way and adjourned the meeting.

TIERGARTEN DISTRICT, BERLIN

No one had a moment of rest upon returning from Godesberg. Without a firm understanding reached with the British much energy was devoted toward monitoring Chamberlain's return to London. Sympathetic persons in Britain were enlisted to press for further accommodation with Germany in this fateful hour. Both the Führer and the foreign minister believed strongly that Chamberlain was desperate to meet the demands of the Godesberg memorandum if his ministers could be coerced into going along. Had the prime minister not acceded to convey the memorandum to Beneš? Chamberlain would not have agreed to associate His Majesty's Government to such a document had he been opposed to the contents. So von Ribbentrop had gone to work leveraging many of the personal associations he had made while ambassador there to add more pressure on Chamberlain to push for peace on Germany's terms. In the early hours of Sunday morning, the foreign minister acknowledged Platen's hard work and showed him a great favor. Having not spent time with his family in more than a week, Platen was told to go home to them and not to return until Monday.

Platen could easily have collapsed on his bed for several days. His wife, however, had many questions about whether peace or war was upon them, and Platen relished the time with their children so greatly that he relaxed the best he could in his favorite chair. His girls were wide-eyed that their father had been in the same room as the Führer many times. He only half-believed it himself, really. In the sanctity of their bedroom Sunday night, Platen described the tense negotiations at Godesberg and the unsettling outcome. Mercifully, she let him fall into a deep sleep and did not wake him until much later than usual the next morning.

Everyone had finished their breakfast and the children had been sent off to school when the knock came at the door. Platen was almost finished dressing so his wife went to check the door herself. It was about the right time for a delivery from the baker.

"Oskar," he heard her call from the first floor in the voice she reserved for summoning him to duty.

"Yes dear?" Platen descended the stairs still fidgeting with his tie. He saw two uniformed soldiers waiting just outside the front door. Pausing halfway down to the first floor, a thousand possibilities raced through Platen's mind – all of them bad.

"These men are here to see you, dear," his wife made the introduction in as pleasant a way possible, yet with worry in her eyes.

Platen took a breath and descended the rest of the way down into the entry lobby of their apartment. "Good morning, and how can I help you young fellows?"

"Sorry for the interruption, Herr Platen. General Keitel dispatched us to bring you to Oberkommando der Wehrmacht," the taller of the two soldiers announced. "The foreign minister is there now and requires your assistance."

"Thank you gentlemen, we should not keep them waiting," Platen turned to locate his jacket but noticed his wife had silently gone off and fetched it for him. Her eyes were full of questions as she handed him the garment. "Sounds important, does it not? I will be home as soon as I can, dearest."

"We have a car waiting," the tall soldier urged politely.

"Lead the way, son," Platen donned his coat and grabbed his satchel in the hallway.

Platen's wife watched them depart for the waiting staff car from the open doorway. After Platen sat in the back he waved to her and smiled. He had never been in a military vehicle before. The driver put the car in gear and they drove off. The tall soldier then handed Platen an envelope. Inside was a memo in the foreign minister's hand.

> *Platen. At eleven o'clock last night the Führer and Supreme Commander of the Armed Forces ordered all troops and divisions scheduled to participate in the attack on Czechoslovakia must be so ready for action that operations supporting Fall Grün are possible from 28 September. We have much to do. – Ribbentrop*

PRAŽSKÝ HRAD, PRAHA

Oblivious to the ongoing evacuation underway, Beneš stood by his desk focused totally on the correspondence grasped tightly in his hand. Had not Minister Carr promised in this very office the day before to forward Beneš' appeal to Roosevelt that the American president urge Britain and

France to stand by Czechoslovakia? And what was Roosevelt's response? This letter addressed equally to Hitler and Beneš, as well as Chamberlain and Daladier. The Czech president was livid. Roosevelt in a single stroke of the pen had elevated Germany to moral equivalence with Czechoslovakia. It was an insult. Neither did Roosevelt urge support of the Czech cause. Far from it!

> *I most earnestly appeal to you not to break off negotiations looking to a peaceful, fair and constructive settlement of the questions at issue.*

There was nothing fair or constructive in Hitler's Godesberg memorandum to negotiate. Roosevelt's letter was pure, naive folly. Beneš took a deep breath. Roosevelt's message would have been sent without knowledge of the incursion of German bombers deep into Czech territory and their subsequent demise. Now was the time for the democracies to stand firm. That is what Roosevelt had to understand. Beneš searched the desk for his stationary set but it was nowhere in sight. The drawers were empty, their contents no doubt packed for the journey to Zátiší. He stopped a soldier to check the box he was carrying, but there was nothing to write on, just more dossier files.

"Prokop! Where is my writing set?" About the only items remaining in the room were Beneš and his military uniform hanging on its rack.

"Already on a truck to Zátiší," Drtina answered calmly from the outer office. This was a lie but he chose not to encourage further delinquency by the president.

"Then find me something to write on. I must compose an answer to Roosevelt immediately," Beneš would not relent.

Drtina dodged several soldiers carrying additional boxes out of the presidential office. They probably would have the same conversation several more times before Beneš could finally be sat down in the back seat of his Tatra. "You can compose such correspondence very well on the way to Zátiší and I will be happy to take dictation."

"President Roosevelt's support is vital and no time can be wasted in my appeal to him. This is important, my friend." When it came to his beloved diplomacy, Beneš was a hard man to sway.

"So is your life," Drtina had no intention of yielding. "I have it on good authority that if Hitler sends more bombers it is only twenty-five minutes by air between the border and Praha. They may be on their way as we speak. It is just as vital that we get you out of the city as soon as possible."

"I agree completely, Mister President," Generál Bláha pushed his way into the room. You must leave immediately."

"And if I choose not to abandon my post?" Beneš was perfectly ready to ignore these demands.

"Then I will personally carry you to your vehicle and suffer the consequences. But you are leaving immediately, Mister President," Bláha removed his jacket and rolled up his shirtsleeves.

AMBASSADOR HOTEL, PRAHA

None of them were being allowed anywhere near Hradčany and its government ministries. Many had tried but you don't argue with soldiers who have rifles slung over their arms. The foreign correspondents had been told in firm language that they were to stay put at the Ambassador. The Ministry of Information would come to them. From the looks of things – the way army trucks were driving down the hill from the castle – large parts of the government were picking up and moving somewhere else. No confirmation on that observation from the Czechoslovaks was forthcoming, naturally. The dearth of facts was annoying. All they knew from the local papers was that the air force had downed a flight of Heinkels that were not where they were supposed to be. That left the gaggle of reporters chomping at the bit in the lobby. The information ministry had promised that a representative would arrive on the hour with announcements. They could only hope Czech punctuality held up in a crisis.

"One fifty-six," Sanderson spied his wristwatch again. "This does not look hopeful."

"Yeah, these hacks are about to riot," Ros was just as tired of waiting as the rest. From her perch sitting on one of the lobby tables Ros had a good view of the entire first floor up to the main entrance to the hotel and saw the doors thrown open to admit a small entourage of public servants. The youngster in front Ros recognized as one of the deputies from the Ministry of Information. Accompanying him were two assistants carrying boxes filled with printed sheets. Ros had seen this before when the Czechs had something important to say and couldn't wait for their own newspapers to print the news. "Now we're in business."

The government delegation navigated their way through the restless herd of reporters to the center of the room. Along the way the deputy claimed a chair, which he carried to the spot he intended to speak from.

"Hello again. I am Deputy Stachura from the Ministry of Information. We have a great deal of material to cover, after which I will take questions." Stachura paused to be sure he had the attention of the correspondents. Reporters were unruly creatures by nature, and when deprived of what they clamored for, devoid of discipline.

"Yesterday afternoon at approximately five o'clock in the evening, a flight of three Luftwaffe bombers of the Heinkel one-eleven class penetrated deep into Czechoslovak territory," Stachura got straight to the topic the reporters cared about. "Their mission was unknown. As these aircraft were approaching our defensive emplacements near Brux in Bohemia, fighters were dispatched to intercept the German aircraft. Our pilots were under orders to escort these intruders to where their crews could be compelled to land safely on Czechoslovak soil and interned. Our pilots were also under orders not to fire unless fired upon first. As our fighters approached these aircraft fleeing at high speed they were fired upon by machine gun positions on by all three bombers. Our interceptors returned fire and the German aircraft were shot down. The wreckage of all three downed aircraft has been located but no survivors have been found."

Stachura waited for the sound of pencils scribbling on paper to subside before picking up one of the printed sheets his assistants had brought. "Prime Minister Syrový has issued the following statement regarding this unfortunate incident:"

> We remind the world that the Czechoslovak Republic is under constant attack by armed forces under direct instruction by the German government. Even now paramilitary units are attacking our border districts from Germany, and in some cases, occupying Czechoslovak territory. Our military has exhibited great restraint in responding to these attacks but a nation under siege has a right to defend itself. Not one of our soldiers stands in foreign territory. On the other hand, attacks from the enemy side continue without pause. These German aircraft were deep into Bohemia and they open fired on our pilots over our territory. The Czechoslovak people and this government deeply regret the further loss of life but we will not shirk from our responsibility to defend our nation from those who seek to drive us from our homes.

It was a good statement, Stachura thought. Well in keeping with the general's public persona. As proof the statement had generated the desired effect, the foreign correspondents were reacting like hungry wolves hovering over fresh red meat.

"As news of this incident has spread, the Czechoslovak government is receiving numerous telegrams from all parts of the world sympathizing with our nation. The Czechoslovak legation in London has received many offers of enlistment in our armed forces. Many foreigners residing here in Praha have offered their services for the national defence and have been accepted as volunteers. What's more, the Slovak Autonomist Party, which at the beginning of the crisis was aligned with the Sudetens, now fully supports the government in the defence of the nation and has urged all of its members to join the colours." As more notes were jotted down, and before he lost the attention of the newsmen Stachura moved onto the final part of his announcement.

"Lastly, the government has decreed that all women between the ages of seventeen and sixty have been brought into the compulsory national service. In addition, the charges against Herr Kundt, the arrested Sudeten parliamentary leader, now include the operation of a secret wireless station from which Berlin was informed of sensitive decisions taken by the Czechoslovak government," Stachura readied himself for the barking dogs. "I am open for questions."

"Has your government received any direct communication from Chancellor Hitler," the correspondent for the Daily Mirror blurted out the first question.

"No. There has been no official message directly from the German government, nor via third-parties." If there had been a communiqué he would have mentioned it.

"Do you have proof that the Germans fired first," one of the Italian reporters challenged the official announcement.

"We have only the statements from our pilots. But I think it is obvious the well-deserved reputation for discipline that the Czechoslovak military has earned after the many weeks of provocations orchestrated on our soil. The larger issue is the un-deniability of the deep incursion into Czechoslovak territory made by these German bombers. We are distributing maps today showing how far east these planes had gotten and the exact locations of the three crash sites. Even if our pilots had shot first that action would have been justified under the circumstances. I doubt Signor Mussolini would believe differently faced with enemy bombers over the naval base at Taranto," Stachura shut the meddlesome Italian up.

"Do you think Herr Hitler will declare war during his speech tonight in Berlin?" Ros raised her arm high while outshouting everyone else.

"That is a question better put to the German embassy," Stachura paused a moment to compose the right answer. "The Czechoslovak government must consider such a declaration as a possibility, however. As I said earlier, we have not had direct talks with the chancellor despite repeated attempts to arrange direct negotiations. What has been conveyed to us by representatives of the British government is that Chancellor Hitler was most bellicose in his dealings with Prime Minister Chamberlain last week in Godesberg. We can only wait and see what he says tonight."

"How soon before we know what those Heinkels were up to?" the Prague correspondent for United Press called out.

"It is too early to say. The wreckage at each crash site is being thoroughly investigated by our best aeronautical experts. But I can tell you there is not much left of the aircraft as the aerial bombs they were carrying exploded on impact with the ground," Stachura personally believed it was a pretense to create a provocation for war.

"Robin Sanderson, Daily Telegraph," Sanderson grabbed the floor. "Does this incident complicate matters between your government and its allies in Paris and London? To the point, does the downing of these three aircraft create such a provocation that a German military response is seen as justifiable and Czechoslovakia is left to her own devices?"

Stachura intensely disapproved of the question and his annoyance was evident. "I believe Generál Syrový said it best. Not one of our soldiers stands in foreign territory. It was not Czech bombers discovered deep inside Germany. The Czechoslovak government has a right to defend its territory. You will remember not one week ago that my government accepted wide-ranging territorial concessions in the interest of peace. Those concessions were made predicated on a negotiated, orderly process. It was Herr Hitler who decided to jettison the agreed upon orderly process. If Germany decides to invade Czechoslovakia after having *perpetrated* this provocation upon us, it is my government's firm belief that France will still honor her treaty commitments."

"What a mean question. He hates you now," Ros whispered to Sanderson. "I'd better move."

"Stay put," Sanderson felt like spanking her.

"Will the bodies of the German airmen be repatriated and how soon?" was the question from a Japanese newsman.

"My Government's intention is to return all remains with dignity as soon as possible. But as you are aware, our western borders are under siege, and all direct commercial transportation by air and rail has been severed on the German side. When such a transfer can be made cannot be said. We are open to working with an intermediary if that will speed the process," Stachura managed quite politely. Personally, he just as soon would throw the bodies into a deep hole.

"Your general mobilization seemed to go off quite smoothly," the New York Times correspondent jumped in. "How prepared is the Czechoslovak army if the Germans attack tomorrow?"

"As President Beneš said the other night, we are prepared for all eventualities. Our armaments are second to none in Europe plus our troops are well trained and supplied. As you pointed out, the army was able to mobilize without interference or interruption. Today I am proud to report we have a million and a half men under arms and in their assigned positions. No one can say what the outcome will be in war but the Czechoslovaks promise that any invasion will not be cheap in blood and material for the invader. That is the lesson to be taken by the shooting down of these German bombers. We are alert and we are prepared to defend our homeland," Stachura again sought to put the onus on Germany for the incident.

"We have heard reports that the Soviets have mobilized their army near the Polish border," the well-connected United Press man went fishing. "Is this action in support of Czechoslovakia?"

"There definitely is a relationship," Stachura made a gut decision to use the question to his advantage. "My Government's position is to settle territory disputes by negotiation and that remains our policy with Poland. We have noted, however, the continued concentration of Polish divisions along our shared border during this crisis. As Moscow is pledged by treaty to aid in the defense of Czechoslovakia, a few days ago the USSR issued a formal warning to the Polish chargé d'affaires in Moscow for Warsaw not to commit aggression on the Czechoslovak Republic. I believe you can fill in the blanks from there."

"Is it true Soviet warplanes are now being sent to Czech air bases in Slovakia?" the correspondent for *La Republique* sought to illuminate the growing communist influence.

"I cannot confirm nor deny specific security matters of that nature," Stachura chose to evade the question.

"Can you confirm your government is evacuating the capital?" Ros bounced up a second time.

"Once again, I cannot confirm nor deny specific security matters of that nature," Stachura repeated himself. "And that concludes the questioning. Please come forward and my colleagues will distribute the supporting materials I promised earlier."

Stachura knew the clamor created by the reporters rushing forward to get their copy of the printed documents would drown out any of the correspondents with serious questions still to be asked. The cacophony would also serve to mask his exit.

"That weasel. He didn't answer my question and he's getting away," Ros thought about chasing after the spokesman. "And I didn't get a chance to ask about missing persons in the border districts. It's been forever since there was a report and I am worried silly about Sylvie."

"Me too. We will just have to try a different way," Sanderson suggested. "Everything sounds so serious. They are even drafting women. If hostilities break out it may be a long time before we will learn anything solid on her whereabouts."

"I *am not* giving up on Sylvie," Ros tugged on his jacket lapel.

ŽIŽKOV DISTRICT, PRAHA

Without too much arm-twisting she had coerced him into helping to convert into an air raid shelter what once was the storage cellar of a prominent merchant some centuries ago. After all, wasn't Bulloch an expert on air raid shelters now? Not the kind of girl to wait for a summons, Petra volunteered to help defend the capital and had been assigned as an air raid warden in the district. This was an admirable decision on her part and having a personal bunker was a plus in keeping her safe. This one started off looking rather like something out of the Roman Empire the way supporting arches and columns had been used throughout. The government had provided a generator but there was a shortage of able-bodied men to string and secure the lines down to the cellar, as well as set up the new incandescent lamps. That's how Bulloch had come to be sweating side-by-side with the three reservists who had been assigned to the task.

When his compatriots in manual labor decided it was time to break for cigarettes, Bulloch excused himself to go topside. Petra had raced up the stone stairs not long before on some errand. She was hard at work coordinating the deliveries of provisions and other supplies that would be needed if the folks in the neighborhood were forced to stay put in the shelter for any length of time. The stairs let him out into the hallway of the old building. The original wood door to the cellar was leaning against the opposite wall. It was huge, thick, solid and built to last. Rather than waste time fitting a new metal hatch like you would find on a battleship bulkhead they had made the decision to upgrade and fortify the hinges so that the old door would serve its new purpose safely. Walking through the hallway the glare from the sunlight coming in off the street was blinding his eyes so he had to follow the sound of Petra's voice on the sidewalk.

"How is it going down there, darling?" she looked over her shoulder while conducting an inventory on a recent delivery.

"Better than I had hoped. We'll have the lights all strung this afternoon before I have to get back to the embassy." Bulloch could only spare one day to devote to the job.

"I'm sorry to pull you away," she stopped counting to come over to kiss him on the cheek. "You won't get in trouble, will you?"

"No, I am calling it a fact-finding mission to report on how much protection the citizens of Prague will have if the bombers come. But I also have a selfish reason," Bulloch rested both hands around her waist.

"You love me madly," she teased him.

"No question there," he puller her a little closer. "I have a proposition for you, too."

"Do tell, my kapitán," Petra held the inventory clipboard close to her chest to keep a little distance.

"What you are doing here is amazing but I really want to talk you into working with us at the embassy," Bulloch squeezed her a little tighter around the waist.

"What?" Petra was surprised and a bit suspicious.

"You know Minister Carr sent most of our women staffers back home. We are terribly understaffed and someone like you who speaks English so well would be a great help. I'm sure we could talk your government into approving us borrowing you from national service. We really need the help. Orders just came in from Washington this morning. On top of everything else we now have to get more than five thousand American nationals out of Czechoslovakia as soon as possible. I want you to come work with us," Bulloch finished the pitch with a winsome smile.

Petra soft punched Bulloch in the stomach. "You! What do you call it? You are a frog oil salesman. What you really want is to have me where you can keep an eye on me."

"Ow, okay," Bulloch stifled a laugh at her mangling of the snake oil phrase. "You got me. But I really did mean it. You could help us a lot at the embassy."

"I love the way you think, my love, but I need to help my people. There are so many old ones and young ones we have to protect. I could not live with myself if--"

"--Stop," Bulloch held up a hand to quiet her as he listened. The streets were much less noisy since mobilization and he thought he heard something familiar droning off in the distance... familiar in a bad way. "Aircraft engines!"

Before he could say more, air raid sirens started wailing. In the distance Bulloch could hear heavy ack-ack guns booming.

"Oh God, we are not ready. The people don't know what to do yet," Petra started looking up and down the street for pedestrians. Bulloch could tell she was about to go building to building to corral people to safety.

"No time for that!" Bulloch grabbed her securely around the shoulders and shoved Petra back into the building and toward the cellar entrance. The sound of bombers overhead was growing much louder and the heavy machine gun installations nearby were firing toward the sky.

"No! We have to help." Petra struggled unsuccessfully in Bulloch grasp. "Nathan no!"

"Downstairs, now!" Bulloch felt like they were moving in slow motion. As he dragged Petra near the stairs leading down to the cellar, Bulloch heard a piercing shriek cutting through the noise outside – bombs. Then the explosions reverberated closer and closer. Two hundred and fifty kilograms by the sound of it he guessed as the concussion from the nearest explosion threw them down the stairs in a wave of dust and debris.

ASCH, SUDETENLAND

Horst had sent for him and the timing was inconvenient. Morgen had squads out reconnoitering close to Haslau where the Freikorps had a forward command post. He wanted to locate where the troublesome Czech regiment had gone to ground. That was the bunch that had been bloodying the Freikorps irregulars for days. The Czechoslovak commander was a wily one who was always shifting position on a random basis. They would need to know the whereabouts of that regiment, and soon. He could always feel extra adrenaline pumping through his veins when a brawl was imminent. The sensation had never failed him and he felt it strongly now. The Hauptsturmführer had been a good compatriot who had left Morgen alone to carry out his assignment without impediment so it was obvious that Horst had something important to discuss or he would not had bothered Morgen to begin with.

For his headquarters Horst was using the former office of a Czech insurance broker who had previously done business in Asch. It was a less obvious choice compared to one of the recently looted Czech administrative offices. No reason to be easy to find if that Czechoslovak regiment decided to make a sweep through the village.

"What has happened?" Morgen stepped into the back room Horst was using for his personal office.

"Herr Morgen. Thank you for coming in so swiftly," both men had found no use for perfunctory salutes or other military greetings in their own presence. "A courier arrived earlier today with new instructions that concern us both."

"They finally have set a day for the battle to begin," Morgen predicted anxiously.

"Quite right," Horst got up to hand Morgen a large envelope. "Wednesday morning for the ground invasion. The Luftwaffe has already been unleashed. Here is your copy."

"About time they put those expensive aerial toys to use," Morgen took possession of the envelope. "It is criminal that most of our SS units are without their own tanks. All so Göring has more shiny planes to awe foreign ambassadors with. This war won't be won in the air."

"Speaking of armor, between now and tomorrow we will be getting a strong dose of reinforcements," Horst decided to ignore discussion of party procurement policy for now. "An armored regiment to secure this zone for the rest of the army to push through the next day. Ours is one of the few frontier zones not protected by Czech barbed wire and other hindrances."

"Finally someone has grown a set of balls. Thank you for calling me in. This news was worth the interruption." Morgen brandished the closest thing to a smile Horst thought he would ever witness. "Anything on this paper about my boys in particular?"

"Yes, after the main line of enemy defences are broken through your unit has been ordered to take part in the race to Prag. It's all there," Horst was happy to give the old brawler what he wanted.

"Ha! These are good times," Morgen slapped the envelope against his leg. "And what of you? What have you to look forward to?"

"Command has not been so forthcoming in my case. Unlike your unit we are not motorized, if you except the horse out back one of the townspeople gave me. All I have been told is to select the best of my Freikorps men and be prepared to join a forward reconnaissance unit if needed. No guarantees though," Horst was buoyed by the thought of jettisoning the worst of his Freikorps underachievers.

"You are a good soldat, your time will come. They will not allow you to miss all of the fun," Morgen cheered him on.

Asch was a quiet place, even during the crisis. Any gunfire or grenade explosions were instantly noticeable. So there was no missing the powerful snarl of aircraft engines flying low over the village that drowned out Morgen's voice.

Horst's instincts told him to seek immediate shelter under his desk while his ears attempted to register the direction of the airplanes.

Morgen's reaction was to eschew safety to rush outside and peer skyward. "Those planes are coming from the west. They are ours!" Morgen clearly saw the Balkenkreuz painted on the wings of the biplanes.

Horst came out to join Morgen as the Henschel ground attack aircraft continued on eastward. "Off to soften up the Czech fortifications, I would imagine. That wasn't in the orders."

"What else is new? Just like artillery gunners who shoot their loads early like a schoolboy with his first whore." Where Morgen wanted to send those bombs was that Czech regiment... if he only knew where to find it.

DOWNING STREET, LONDON

The war had started. At last further diplomacy was a moot point. The genie was out of his bottle and there was no shoving him back inside. Yet the curtly worded telegram he had received an hour before in the relative safety of London had also left him burdened with the weight that his homeland was under attack. People he knew might now be injured or dead. Daladier had to be informed immediately. The premier's delegation had extended their stay to confer on the changed circumstances since Czechoslovak fighters shot down the German bomber flight. So it fell upon Masaryk to officially inform the French leader. If Chamberlain was present, all the better.

The one insider Masaryk had a chance of reaching swiftly and directly was Cadogan. The Foreign Service undersecretary had left that door ajar on their prior meeting. So Masaryk ignored proper protocol and dialed the private telephone number Cadogan had given him. The young voice on the other end of the line noted Masaryk's request without argument. The Czechoslovak envoy was told to stay by his phone to await a call from the undersecretary within five minutes. Four and a half minutes later Masaryk found himself on the line with Cadogan.

"I must speak with them. Prague is being bombed. But it must be myself who tells them," Masaryk had appealed to Cadogan.

"Come now," was all Cadogan needed to say.

So Masaryk found himself once again at No. 10 Downing Street. He took the moment afforded him while loitering in the lobby of the prime ministers residence to adjust the fit of his suit. There had been no time to change into fresh clothing. The door to the meeting room eased open enough to allow Cadogan to slip through.

"All Lord Halifax knows is that you bear critical news from Prague," Cadogan prepared Masaryk. "They are waiting for you."

"I am in your debt, Mister Cadogan," Masaryk now thought of the man as an ally.

"We have much ahead of us. Better to get started on it all now," Cadogan ushered the Czech ambassador inside.

Masaryk entered the cabinet room for a second time to find the table surrounded by a much wearier assemblage of politicians. Haggard in the way only hours of constant argument could leave a person. Gamelin caught Masaryk's attention. The general's face was more defiant than weary. Bonnet, on the other hand, appeared the broken man. Daladier's demeanor betrayed restlessness, while Chamberlain could best be described as resigned to whatever fate was under discussion. As there was very little room around the table, Masaryk stepped forward as far as he could while Cadogan entered behind him and the door closed.

"Thank you for receiving me on such short notice, gentlemen. I will dispense with the formalities," Masaryk paused to establish eye contact in the silent room. "An hour ago I received word from my government. This afternoon hundreds of German bombers and escorting fighters violated Czechoslovak airspace to bomb both Plzen and Prague. Our own pilots and ground defenses gave a good account of themselves. Many of the attackers were shot down and I am proud to report that the Luftwaffe squadrons heading toward Brno were turned away short of their objective."

The previously listless politicians sat alert in their chairs at hearing what Masaryk had divulged so far.

"Neither were the Germans able to catch our air force on the ground, as they intended," Masaryk let himself feed on the added energy in the room. "Not long after these air attacks commenced, German heavy artillery began shelling our border defences, bombardment which continues at this very moment. I do not know as of yet how badly our cities were damaged, nor the number of casualties sustained. What I can tell you is that these attacks are neither isolated, nor limited. My Government has instructed me to inform you, that as of this day, the Czechoslovak Republic is in a state of war with Germany."

SPORTPALAST
SCHÖNEBERG DISTRICT, BERLIN

The party faithful were rocking the house, which was saying something too as the auditorium was huge. The background on the place was that it was built as a hockey stadium and ice rink some thirty years before. Since then the Sportpalast had also become popular as a venue for the big political rallies the Germans like to throw. Set up for that purpose tonight, Endicott was told the building could hold more than fourteen thousand people. As far as he could see every seat was filled. Not a stunner given that not attending would be a mark of death within the party but impressive nonetheless. And what a sweet view of the auditorium Shirer had commandeered. From his radio perch they had a prime spot in the balcony about fifty feet above and to the side of the stage. This close up Endicott could see Hitler's blood vessels flex.

The good chancellor was in full vigor tonight. Reichsminister Doctor Joseph Goebbels did the introductions and Hitler wasted no time in getting right to the point. The capital had been on a knife's edge all day after news of the Czechs downing the Luftwaffe bombers had circulated. There were rumors of hostilities breaking out but no official confirmations or pronouncements of any kind from government sources during the afternoon. Dead silence was obviously the official policy. This Sportpalast address was already planned and the population was well aware they were supposed to listen whether they wanted to or not. Everyone Endicott spoke with during the day expected the response to the Czechs would come tonight directly from the chancellor, and Herr Hitler did not disappoint.

This was the first time Endicott had seen Uncle Adolph in front of a large crowd. He started slow then quickly worked himself into a lather. Endicott had never seen anything like it, save for some of the hellfire and damnation preachers down South. But even those fellas didn't come close to stepping into the shoes of the new Messiah the way Hitler could. This was a side of the man that wasn't on display back in Godesberg. A week ago, on the smaller stage, Hitler seemed the odd little fellow. Here, in front of thousands, he reached for the stature of modern Caesar – a very pissed-off modern Caesar.

Everyone was waiting to hear whether war had been declared. Yet Hitler didn't go there at first. Instead he kept the world dangling on his every word. Hitler thanked Neville Chamberlain for the prime minister's recent efforts and professed no quarrel with either Britain or France, yet the chancellor warned all of the governments in Europe that the patience of the German people was exhausted. Hitler then reflected on the burdens he set himself to early in his chancellorship to negotiate peace with other capitals and how the rejections he received steeled him to order the swiftest rearmament the world had ever seen. Make no mistake... the world would respect Germany now. It was a refrain he would return to time and time again during the night.

> I myself am a front-line soldier and know the hardships of war. I wished to spare the German people this experience. I approached each and every problem firmly determined to attempt anything to bring about its peaceful resolution. This was another burden upon me. At each turn I chose the more difficult route. What was my reward? At every opportunity those who dedicate their existence to plotting ill against the German nation have doubled their efforts. You know whom I speak of.

For weeks Hitler had railed about the plight of the Sudeten Germans. Endicott had spent plenty of time in that part of Bohemia and knew no such atrocities were taking place. So as the chancellor elaborated on those tired accusations at length in his speech, Endicott wasn't impressed with the cheap theatrics. But then Hitler shifted gears to lay out what he was going to do about the situation. Never before had Endicott or Shirer heard Hitler call out President Beneš directly as he did tonight. Thankfully Endicott could crib from the translation notes his colleague was taking during the broadcast as the dictator unloaded on his nemesis in Prague with both barrels.

> *Until the last, we told those who would do Germans harm to leave our lands peaceably, as they had promised to do, and we would leave them in peace. That was my final word last week to Prime Minister Chamberlain to convey to Herr Beneš. And what was Herr Beneš' answer? Yesterday, his reply was to brutally murder twelve of our brave young airmen. A cold-blooded act of violence carried out without mercy. This is the point at which his game is up!*

> *Today, Herr Beneš received the answer of the German people. Our Luftwaffe delivered that message today over Prag, and will do so again tomorrow, and the day after and all of the days following until the Czech is driven from the Sudetenland.*

There was the money line. Hitler had sent the bombers to bomb the Czechs and from the sound of it he was sending lots of them. If the tanks had not already been ordered into Bohemia they were going in soon. Next to him Shirer was as excited as Endicott had ever seen him. They were right in the middle of the biggest story on the planet and his buddy was broadcasting the news live. What the radio audience was actually hearing in their living rooms was another question. The Nazis in the auditorium raised such a raucous cheer at every jab Hitler took at Beneš, Endicott wondered if the microphone was still capable of picking up Shirer's calm voice above the roaring party faithful. Feeding off the crowd's wild adulation, Hitler continued to reward them with more oratorical home runs.

> *Until today, Beneš sat comfortably in Prag believing: "Nothing can happen to me. England and France will always back me." And after all he could still turn to the Soviet Union should all else fail. What could happen to him? My fellow Germans, the time has come to tell him what's what. While it may be a characteristic trait of us Germans to bear up under something for a long time and with great patience, once our patience has reached an end... that is the end!*

"Those are the Chancellor's words and they brought the house down with a burst of yelling and cheering the like of which I have never before heard at a Nazi meeting," Shirer spoke to his radio audience. "Fifteen-thousand people have leapt to their feet in a frenzy, raising their right hands in salute and yelling at the top of their voices in approval."

No exaggeration there, Endicott agreed. The chancellor could not continue for more than a minute without interruption. The average Berliner probably was not enthusiastic at the prospect of marching on Bohemia but those were not the people the world would be hearing from tonight. The delirium on display in this hall would be what the world remembered. The crowd was calling repeatedly for Czech blood and Hitler was feeding on every shout and every boot pounding on the floor.

> *Herr Beneš chose this war. We will finish it! There are two men facing each other down. Over there stands Herr Beneš... and here I stand! We are two entirely different men. While Herr Beneš danced on the world stage and hid himself there from his responsibilities during the War, I was fulfilling my duties as a decent German soldier. And as I face this man today, I am but a soldier of my nation. The world must avow that in my four and a half years in the War, and in the long years of my political life, no one could ever have accused me of one thing: I have never been a coward!*

> *Now I march before my people as the first of its soldiers. And behind me, let it be known to the world, marches a nation. At this hour, all Germany unites itself with me. Herr Beneš may have seven million Czechs, but here there is a nation of seventy-five million!*

> *We stand as strong as in the fighting times, a period in which I strode forth as a simple unknown soldier and set out to conquer a Reich. A time in which I did not doubt our certain success and the final victory, just as I do not doubt our victory against Herr Beneš. Nothing can prevent the united German people from putting a stop to this crazed man's crimes against three and a half million of our brothers and sisters. Once and for all!*

"Listen to that frantic cheering greeting Chancellor Hitler," Shirer had to wait for the ruckus to die down. "The crowd has started yelling in unison: *The Führer commands, we follow. The Führer commands, we follow.* Over and over again they keep shouting it until I think they'll take the roof off."

"No lie, brother," Endicott said aloud knowing no one else could possibly hear him over that racket. He watched Hitler acknowledge the crowd before sitting down. Suddenly Doctor Goebbels jumped up to the microphone looking very eager to say something.

"Mein Führer! In this historic hour I shall speak in the name of the German people as I solemnly declare: the German nation is solidly behind you to carry out your orders loyally, obediently, and enthusiastically. Never again will a November 1918 be repeated," Goebbels vowed.

Hitler looked up at Goebbels like no truer words had ever been spoken in the history of the world. True conviction and fire were blazing behind those eyes as Hitler leapt to his feet to stand side-by-side with his propaganda minister. In one fanatical movement, Hitler raised his right hand up in the Nazi salute, brought that arm around in a theatrical sweep to the right, then pounded his hand down on the lectern as he shouted: *Ya!*

The hall went nuts. Endicott knew there was a ton of pent up anger at having lost the last war. That's why you couldn't find socialists, communists or Jews on the streets. Those were the people who got blamed for Germany losing twenty years ago. But this was crazy and Endicott had never seen anything like it. This war wasn't about the Sudetens this war was about getting even for 1918.

30. SHOCKWAVE

A Tupolev SB (B-71) bomber in Czechoslovak colors

SEPTEMBER 27, 1938
PRIEGER FARM, NEAR ASCH

Yesterday the German aircraft flew back and forth over the farm the whole day without a let up until the sun went down. She longed for her favorite set of winter earmuffs but those were an ocean away. At least the Czech pilots were not making it worse by dogfighting with them over Asch... not yet anyway. The poor farm animals were spooked by all the noise so Sylvie decided to get up at five in the morning to help work with the livestock before the air races started up again. There were plenty of farm animals to feed and she owed these dear people a lot for looking out after her the last couple of weeks. Sylvie had grown up on a ranch so there was some nostalgia in taking up these chores again. And since the Freikorps corporal was under orders to stay close to her, he joined in too... at least when he was awake. How that boy could snooze through so much racket escaped her. After pulling on some work clothes, Sylvie went outside to help Frau Prieger with the cows.

Walking through the thick layer of ground fog, Sylvie thought a few things over. Up until yesterday she had been determined to get off the farm as soon as possible. But the family was adamant that it was not safe for a woman to be traveling with so much going on. And now with the Luftwaffe flying attack missions further east the Priegers were not taking no for an answer. But if the war was going to roll through the neighborhood, perhaps Sylvie was in the perfect spot to hitch a ride with whatever army rolled down the road.

In Sylvie's presence the family never talked politics. Given the circumstances, she had stifled the urge to ask them questions about the crisis and how they felt about it. Keeping her lip zipped didn't come easy to Sylvie but now she thought maybe there was an opportunity to nibble at the edges a bit. The reporter found her hostess milking a cow out in the pens. Without a word, Sylvie grabbed a pitchfork and started moving hay to where the cows could get at their breakfast.

"Danke," Frau Prieger was happy for the company.

"How are the animals doing after all of the noise yesterday?" Sylvie pitched hay closer to her benefactor's cow.

"Better now. This must be frightful for them. I haven't seen the dog since yesterday. The horses are settling down finally and these old cows seem to be doing fine. None of them are eating as much as they normally do but they are eating," Frau Prieger wished she recovered as easily.

"How are you doing?" Sylvie sensed the middle-aged woman was a little frazzled.

"Glad I don't have a son of military age here at home," was the answer any mother would appreciate. "My husband served in the Austrian army and that was worry enough for one life."

"What do you think will happen next?" Sylvie inched a bit closer to what she wanted to learn. These local people were less isolated than the picture postcard scenery would suggest and knew a lot more than they let on.

"The whole Deutsche armee is coming right though here. Nothing to be done except hope they do not take our animals with them," Frau Prieger was resigned to what happened during a war but still didn't like it.

"Sounds like you have been through this before," Sylvie hinted.

"I am so tired of wars for this and that. Wars are nothing but trouble for everyone. It is true... Deutsche should be with Deutsche. We have no business being tied to Tschechische. But if we have nothing left at the end, what will be the use?" A horse whinnied nearby and Frau Prieger stopped milking the cow to rise up from the stool she was sitting on to listen. One thing Sylvie had forgotten about farm life was a set of keener senses. When you were on your own you better be able to smell trouble coming.

"Do you hear that?" Frau Prieger slapped her thighs in exasperation. "More aeroplanes."

At first Sylvie could not hear anything but soon her ears picked up of the droning of gasoline engines – lots of them. "This is not like yesterday though. West, they are moving west. I am sure of it."

Frau Prieger moved out into the open between the shed and the house to peer upward. "Can't see through the fog though."

"Don't have to," Sylvie joined her. "I'll bet twenty dollars those are Czech planes."

REICH AIR MINISTRY
WILHELMSTRASSE, BERLIN

Hans-Jürgen Stumpff was making scant headway in his briefing. The Luftwaffe chief of staff essentially had an audience of one who demanded specifics that the general simply did not possess. A lack of specificity was a sure method of antagonizing a feldmarschall and Hermann Göring was fuming. The others in the briefing room were content to do nothing other than watch as Stumpff was poked like a game pig. This weight Stumpff had to bear on his shoulders alone. His steadfast loyalty to Göring did not deflect from the reality that the Reich air marshal himself had to answer to the Führer.

"How can you stand there and tell me there is no confirmation of damage to Czech targets. There are over three million Germans living in that wretched country and none of them are in a position to sneak around to report on what our bombers were able to accomplish? Unbelievable." Göring had expended his small reservoir of patience.

"I will remind the feldmarschall that the latter deficiency is best taken up with the Abwehr," Stumpff at last found a point he could defend. "We do know that the Hradčany area and the palace compound were hit but I have not yet received confirmation of how significantly."

"What about the Czech air fields? I already know their fighters were up in the air but did we at least catch their bombers on the ground?" Göring went onto the next action item from of the previous day's attack.

"The main bases at Pilsen, Prag, Budweis were all hit. We have visual confirmation from our own crews on this. But there was nothing on the ground when our crews got there. Every Czechoslovak aircraft had already dispersed," Stumpff gritted his teeth.

"Fine, just fine," Göring felt like bashing his baton against the table. "Damage? How much damage did we do to those damn fields?"

"Moderate, at best," Stumpff was embarrassed to confirm. "By the time our bombers reached their targets we had already suffered significant losses: approximately twenty-six percent of the mission complement."

"Those losses are unacceptable! Where were the bomber escorts?" Göring paced around the table in frustration.

"From the debriefings I have read so far it appears one force of Czechoslovak fighters would lure them away from the bombers not long after our squadrons had crossed the border. Soon after a second and larger number of Czech fighters then pounced on our unprotected bombers," Stumpff was furious at how easily their fighter pilots had been lured away from their assignments.

"How many Czech fighters did we shoot down?" Göring went looking for some saving grace to all of the bad news.

"Unconfirmed," Stumpff knew what he was about to say would only add kerosene to the fire. "But an insignificant number at best. The Czech pilots had altitude when they engaged. While slower, their Avias are more nimble, have tighter turning radiuses and can climb faster than our Messerschmitts. Our pilots were unable to use their speed advantage except to escape battle. But the Czech pilots never followed them. We didn't lose many fighters, but neither did we shoot many down."

"Two years of combat experience in Spain and you are telling me we were outsmarted by these Slavs? This sorry performance must change immediately. Order the fighter groups to stay with the bombers when they go back out today," Göring commanded. "When are they expected to take off?"

"Ground fog has most of our operational air fields shut down until eleven o'clock, the meteorologists estimate. Maybe longer," Stumpff sensed Göring was ready to strike him across the face with his baton.

"Get my planes in the air as soon as that damn fog lifts and do whatever is necessary to guaranteed better results today. We've spent the last four years building an aerial weapon of terror, not a puny church mouse." Göring stormed out of the room.

There was no use in chasing after Göring to explain that all of those measures had already been ordered. Saying so would not have softened Göring's temper. Even now the bomber crews were making their way to their planes where they would sit with engines running until the fog cleared sufficiently to get airborne. Directives had also been sent to each of the Jagdgeschwaders making it clear that the bombers were not to be left unattended. Today would be different, Stumpff was certain.

KAMPFGESCHWADER 153
ALTENBURG, SACHSEN

The previous day had been a fiasco and Rohrer had little reason to believe today would prove to be different. He had seen it all before over Madrid. Dogfight hungry fighter pilots always left the bombers to their own devices. At least by the end of 1937 they had attained air superiority in the skies over Spain and few Republican interceptors ever rose to molest his bombers. Neither did the leftists possess enough anti-aircraft artillery to worry about. By comparison, what they encountered yesterday was a nightmare. As soon as their formations had crossed into Czechoslovakia their bombers took a day long pounding. Once the Messerschmitts abandoned them to chase after the first Czech fighters that had shot their way through his formation, those agile and hard-hitting Avias harassed the Kampfgeschwader all the way to Prag and back. By the time his Dorniers made it to Prag they were so spread apart Rohrer could only watch as the bomb loads fell on different parts of the city with little or no concentrated damage. By the time they had gotten back over Germany his gruppen had lost four aircraft to the Avias and another to heavy flak over Prag.

Now they were going back over Bohemia for more. There was no surprise to exploit and it was obvious the Czech squadrons were prepared and waiting for them. That is what they got for allowing thousands of Sudeten irregulars to attack Czechoslovak government buildings for most of the month. All it accomplished was to give the enemy a reason to move into his wartime positions. The whole idea behind their tactical doctrine was to surprise the enemy and destroy his air force on the ground. With that strategy thrown out the window the best the Luftwaffe could hope for was to get its bombers off the ground early for a dawn attack and perhaps the Czechs could be caught off guard. But even that was out of the question today. The ground fog was as thick as his mother's lentil soup. By the time these birds got into the air the Czechoslovaks would again be ready and waiting for them. If their own fighter pilots stuck close maybe the losses would be less. But as Rohrer and his crewmates neared their Dorniers he saw another long day of hardship.

Stepping up to his Do 17E, Rohrer made his way to the open access hatch. The ground crews had already warmed up the engines. All that was left was for him and his two men to sit at the ready inside until the tower gave the go ahead to take off. As Rohrer was about to pull himself inside the fuselage he paused to listen carefully. He definitely heard aircraft engines above. Motors at high throttle made a much different sound than the idling BMWs of their Dorniers. What fool was up in this soup? With the bomb lorries and gas trucks still all over the place a bad landing would cause chaos. Whoever was up in the air was flying dangerously low and moving at high speed. Rohrer had a bad feeling as he scanned the near horizon. That's when he saw the twin-engined bomber break through the fog over the tree line. He had seen that slim airframe before in Spain. Soviet Tupolevs.

"Everybody into the plane" Rohrer shouted to his crew as the enemy bomber screamed low above their heads.

Glancing upward, Rohrer saw the Czech red, blue and white tricolor insignia on the underside of the wings. Rohrer didn't hear the Tupolev drop its bombs, or the explosion when those bombs hit a gas truck on the other side of the airstrip, just the blast of air and heat that knocked him flat against the damp ground. At least the bonfire had gotten the attention of whoever was asleep at the alarm crank. Unfortunately, the flames would also serve as a signal flare to the other enemy bombers overhead.

"Move your asses, we're getting out of here," Rohrer urged his dazed crew as they picked themselves off the dirt.

Rohrer pulled himself into the Dornier, rushed into the cockpit and strapped on his harness. While adjusting the fuel mixture he looked out the lower window to see his dorsal gunner diligently pulling the chocks away from the tires. Nearby crews were doing the same thing. They had to get in the air or their planes would be destroyed. This is what they should have been doing to the Czechs. Rohrer looked back and saw his gunner jump in after the bombardier. He pushed the throttle levers forward ordering power to the engines before the hatch had a chance to fully secured. The Dornier lurched forward toward the strip as more Tupolevs zoomed low ahead, dropping bombs that ignited ammunition and detonating nearby aircraft. Rohrer was pleased to hear the dorsal machine gun open up to spit bullets at their tormentors. A token fist shaken at the enemy yet the sound made him feel better. Rohrer would have one shot at getting his bird lined up on the airstrip. Not so easy given he had the bomber moving much faster than proscribed. Rohrer applied what he hoped was the proper braking maneuver and the plane came around more or less as intended. But as he was about to feed full power to the BMWs, a Czech bomb exploded to the left of the tail, pushing the back of the Dornier violently to the right. That was too much abuse for right landing gear, which collapsed under the strain. The propellers on the right engine soon dug themselves into the ground as the stricken aircraft staggered to a jarring stop in the dirt. Thank God, none of the bombs in the bay went off... at least not yet. Rohrer cut power to the engines and prayed the three of them could get away before the Dornier exploded of its own right.

"Everybody out!" Rohrer ordered the crew out as he unbuckled his harness and jumped down from his chair.

Listening to the radio chatter between the B-71 pilots the raid appeared successful in catching the Germans napping. The picture that Bozik got was of several enemy squadrons all loaded with ordinance and fuel waiting like game hens to be slaughtered. He could see the smoke and flames rising through the fog, which more than confirmed the damage being done on the ground. These raids today would take a good bite out of the German's advantage in bombers. Bozik only hoped his colleagues were tearing up the landing strip, too. Taking out the field so more bombers could not immediately replace those destroyed today would give them a short-term edge. Dipping low into the fog to raid the base at high speed took tremendous skill and guts from the bomber pilots and their navigators. When the opportunity presented itself, Bozik planned to buy those guys several rounds of whatever drinks they desired.

For now, Bozik's fighter squadron stayed high above the raid on the lookout for Messerschmitts. He was aching to take his planes down to strafe the field but the smart thing to do was protecting the bombers. They couldn't replace losses like the Germans could, so no risking the few modern bombers they had on indulgent whims of fighter pilots. They had been briefed that most of the Messerschmitt squadrons were stationed close to major cities in expectation of Czechoslovak or Soviet bomber attacks there. Bozik did not expect to encounter any bad guys before they escorted the B-71s back home. But since Altenburg was near Dresden there was always a chance a patrol of Messerschmitts was in the vicinity. That was why the B-71s were chosen to hit Luftwaffe bases further into Germany. The Soviet design was fast and had excellent range with every chance to get in and out before being overtaken by enemy fighters. The older, lumbering Aero MB.200s were assigned targets closer to the border so they could have the best chance to escape. After today, Bozik doubted command would risk losing valuable pilots on daylight missions with the Aeros. The Germans were unlikely to leave the skies over their airfields un-patrolled in the future.

Their first encounters with the Messerschmitt pilots the day before had gone very well for Bozik's boys. The weeks of drilling with the aerial targets had paid off. They had shot down two D model one-o-nines and had hit many more with no loss to their own. That had to have come as a shock to the Germans and Bozik knew they would be looking for every opportunity to even the score.

The headphone in his flight cap buzzed alive in Bozik's ear. The B-71 pilots were out of ordinance and pulling out. Time to go home.

"You heard the news," Bozik called out to his pilots. "Take up position on our charges as they rise up out of the fog."

LETIŠTĚ DOBŘANY, NEAR PLZEN

Long after departing Vyškov the radio operator on the Aero had come back to give them the news that they would be arriving in Plzen hours earlier than scheduled. The bomber was supposed to land at Saaz first to unload another set of passengers but a message had come in that the airfield there was out of commission. A reason was not provided. For all they knew, the German ground assault had already started. So the pilot was diverting directly to Plzen. One complication arising from an early arrival in Plzen was that it was doubtful transportation would have been procured yet for Burda and Furst. Naturally they preferred to get to the secluded property on the outskirts of the city with its waiting equipment and supplies as soon as possible.

Finding an automobile in normal times was not a problem but the general mobilization had requisitioned practically every working automobile available in the country. Burda was on good terms with the commanding officer of the army base at Strašice, who probably could be talked out of a civilian sedan once they landed and could contact him. Furst saw the visit to the base as an opportunity to requisition some heavier weapons ordinance not usually stocked at their safe houses. Burda thought the idea was overkill yet Furst would not be swayed. If the main component of the German invasion was pointed in their direction he wanted to be prepared.

Unless in a dire emergency, Burda and Furst would be carrying out their assignment without contacting the Second Department's operations post in the city. Moravec had wisely separated operational agents from headquarters agents. Personnel at the regional field offices and their outposts were well known to Burda and Furst but they rarely interacted with each other by design. Headquarters staff worked out in the open to a greater degree and could be more easily recognized. Operational agents, by nature, performed their duties in the shadows. To be seen with headquarters staff could easily compromise their operations. But Karl had cultivated Moravec directly so it had fallen to headquarters staff to run the agent. If Karl needed another face-to-face meeting close to the front lines Burda and his partner would be responsible for coordinating the rendezvous.

Furst backhanded Burda's arm to point out the pilot had turned on the flashing red light inside the fuselage, which meant they must be approaching the field at Dobřany. The large stork-like aircraft gently banked to the left and the view out the side windows showed the ground coming up quickly beneath them. The huge fixed undercarriage tires met the airstrip with a thud, bouncing the bomber back in the air for a moment before the pilot commanded the aircraft firmly to earth and the tail came down. Furst was already out of his harness to take up station by the fuselage door.

As soon as the pilot taxied the Aero to a full stop, Furst un-secured the new portable short wave radio set they had brought with them to make direct contact with the monastery in Vyškov. Furst and the radio were outside of the plane before Burda could unbuckle himself and reach the door. Burda was expecting they would have to walk themselves to the administrative building where they could easily arrange for a ride to the base at Strašice. All it would take was flashing their general staff credentials. But looking in that direction he saw a truck speeding in their direction.

"What? Are we getting lucky for a change?" Burda pointed at the incoming Tatra.

"I hope so, this wireless suitcase is heavy," Furst gently lowered the case to the ground. "But that bunch riding in back seems much too happy to be coming out here to move freight."

The Tatra skidded to a stop near the Aero with the engine running then the driver leaned out the window. "Hop in, we will take you back."

"Why is everyone so merry?" Burda asked while helping Furst with their gear.

"Of course we are happy!" one of the men in the back shouted. "Our boys just hit the German air bases hard. Caught the bastards fogged in. All those pretty new bombers lined up and ready to go and full of bombs and fuel. Boom! All gone now."

"We thought your plane was part of the attack and we wanted to congratulate you," the driver had put two and two together and realized he had got it wrong.

"Sorry, wish we had been there," the Aero pilot stepped down from the plane. "Maybe next time."

"Who cares, get in back and we'll take you where you need to go," the driver waved to the rear of the truck.

BULOVKA HOSPITAL – LIBEŇ DISTRICT, PRAHA

The evacuation of American citizens around Prague got a lot easier after the German air raid on Prague. Actual bombs falling had a way encouraging people to get the hell out. The problem now was so many U.S. nationals were clamoring to leave at once that it was a chore keeping them calm while everyone got processed. It wasn't easy to accomplish with a short staff but they were making progress. Then there was the twenty or so who had been injured during the air raid. All of them were in the major metropolitan hospital on the north side of the capital, and luckily, none of their injuries was life threatening. Regardless, Minister Carr decided he wanted to break away from the zoo at the embassy to visit each of his injured fellow Americans personally. Neither did the old gentleman advertise the visit. He wasn't looking for a publicity stunt. This was just another obligation he felt went along with the job.

While he was checking in on the injured, Carr also wanted to process their evacuation paperwork. Bulloch wasn't sure at first why Carr had asked him to tag along instead of an embassy staffer like Chapin or Elbrick. Maybe he felt those guys were better utilized where they were. Then Bulloch thought it might be his uniform. Perhaps Carr felt that seeing one of their own would help make these folks feel safer. Either way, it was Bulloch who went along. So as one of the nurses led them from one hospital room to another, Bulloch dutifully jotted down all the information about each person and their medical condition. After more than two hours they had spent time with every American in the hospital.

"I believe we have one more, do we not, captain?" Carr inquired in the hallway.

"Not that I have here," Bulloch checked his clipboard. "No, we hit everyone on the list, sir."

"There's another patient in Room 217 we must visit. I am sure of it," Carr insisted.

"If you say so, Mister Carr," Bulloch just figured the minister had information that he wasn't privy to.

The hospital was crammed full of people. By doubling and tripling up in the rooms it looked like the hospital staff had accommodated everyone. But count in the worried relatives and friends hovering about, and the facility was overcrowded. When they got to the room the door was open and Carr stepped right in. Bulloch was busy consulting his clipboard when he followed in behind. Looking up he was surprised to see the patient Carr was with was Petra. Her right leg was in a full cast held elevated in traction. There had not been a free moment since the bombs fell and the ambulance had taken her away. Bulloch knew she was in Bulovka but he had not found out which room yet. It was something he had planned on checking before they left.

"Hello dear," Carr picked up Petra's hand and gently caressed it. "My name is Wilbur Carr, and I believe you already know this young fellow behind me. We are here to check on you."

"Oh my," Petra was a bit puzzled. "Thank you very much."

She looked past Carr to Bulloch with a quizzical expression. Bulloch shrugged his shoulders and grinned in reply. Minister Carr was a sneaky and adorable old duffer, and Bulloch smelled Bess' handiwork.

"How is that leg of yours? I understand you are very brave... injured while overseeing the creation of an air raid shelter," Carr lightly patted her cast.

"They tell me the break is not too bad, but the leg would not be broken at all if someone had not fallen on me," Petra looked past Carr again at Bulloch.

"Now, now... I am sure that it could not be helped under the circumstances," Carr did not remember being informed of that detail.

Petra beckoned Carr to come closer so that she could whisper to him. "Don't let Nathaniel off so easy. A little guilt will go a long way."

"My wife would agree with you," Carr whispered back. After straightening up, he prepared to make his exit. "Is there anything we can do for you, dear?"

"Everyone here is taking very good care of me but all of the hospital staff has been working since the attack. How badly was the city damaged? These people do not know a thing," Petra was starving for details.

"Captain, why don't you describe what we have learned while I attend to another matter for a moment. I will return shortly to say goodbye, miss." Carr played the charade perfectly.

"Considering how bad we all thought an aerial attack was going to be, Prague wasn't hit so hard," Bulloch began as Carr slipped out silently. "The damage is haphazard with a little here and a little there all over the place. The Charles Bridge took a bomb near the west entrance but the explosion only blew off some of the stonework. Looks like the Germans really wanted to hit the castle but missed the presidential wings. At least the president and the government had already cleared out before the bombers reached the capital. I heard the cathedral up there has a hole in the wall where a bomb hit but I haven't seen any pictures. Did I really fall on you?"

"You most certainly did!" Petra admonished him. "Do you know how heavy you are?"

"I'm sorry," Bulloch moved up to sit close to her on the edge of the bed. "Will you forgive me for trying to keep the ceiling from falling on top of your pretty little head?"

"Don't tell stories now to make yourself look good. But after what that nice old man just did, I can't be too hard on you," Petra treated him to a small smile.

"Yeah, he is something special, isn't he," Bulloch owed the minister for getting him out of trouble. "Listen, the world is kind of crazy and I am going to be scarce a lot of the time, but I'll take care of you kid. That's a promise."

"You bet you will. I have plans for you, mister," Petra grabbed his tie and pulled Bulloch closer for a kiss.

CZECH FORTRESS
ELBLEITEN, SUDETENLAND

The German dive-bombers deserved credit for excellent aim on the medium fort, which was not an easy task given the elevated terrain. The bunker had been designed into the mountain in such a way to make both aerial bombing and artillery fire a difficult proposition. Most of the bombs had exploded on the mountainside. Kopecky verified that the worst result from all that expenditure of ordinance was some minor surface chipping. After seeing how the fortresses were standing up to bombing, Kopecky was not overly worried. When the German tanks moved through the Erzegebirge Mountain passes it looked like every Czech pillbox would be waiting for them.

Srom had insisted on seeing the status of the fortifications under fire with his own eyes. Not that he was a skeptic. Each bunker was uniquely designed and constructed to take advantage of its surrounding terrain with the strongest of materials available. Yet there was no substitute for live fire to determine whether the engineers had been successful in their work. Srom wanted an intimate understanding of how these fortifications were holding up for when the time came to decide how and where to commit the motorized divisions to counter German incursions.

Kopecky felt a tug on his trouser leg. Looking down from the armored bell used for spotting he saw Srom looking up at him.

"My turn," Srom urged from below the metal platform Kopecky was standing on.

Kopecky draped the field glasses back around his neck and climbed down. "You will be pleased, the bomb hits are ineffectual."

"I still want to see for myself from this vantage point," Srom scurried up the ladder, where he was quiet for a while. "Yes, I am confident these pillboxes will hold up."

"How do you think they will take a ground assault?" Kopecky wanted to confirm whether Srom agreed with him or not.

"Too high and narrow up here to mass much firepower," Srom climbed down. "With some anti-tank emplacements to support these small forts they should hold their own."

"Agreed," Kopecky needed to nudge Srom to their next task now that he had satisfied his curiosity. "Still we have the equivalent of two rapid divisions spread across the whole Sudeten uprising but nothing large enough to counter a divisional breakout."

"Exactly. I have a few ideas though so let's get moving," Srom started down the narrow corridor. "We have portions of the first and second rapid divisions in the field already plus a good measure of the third. They might be ad hoc units but our men have had two weeks of field operations under their belts side-by-side with platoons from other divisions. That's a tactical advantage I intend to leverage. Our next job is to go over the action reports and figure out what armored platoons have built up a relationship fighting together. You and I are going to create two new rapid divisions from the mix. That's not what we will call them, obviously, but when we are done that will be the result. We always planned that our armor and motorized regiments should be prepared to shift where needed on the battlefield, what I have in mind is slightly more ambitious."

"Won't the existing rapid division commanders object to losing their tanks?" Kopecky suspected he already knew the answer but was more interested to learn how Srom would deal with the politics.

"Those generáls have already lost that control and there is no time to put the rapid divisions back together," Srom was not going to waste any more time on the subject. "We already have experienced field commanders in the ready units operating on the border now. The ones who have shown the most affinity for large-scale formations will be the officers we will choose. For the sake of expediency we will be giving them field promotions on the border. That is what I intend to recommend to the general staff today. Do you see any gaping holes I have missed?"

"The smaller ready units have been ordered back behind the fortress line. How do we use the motorized regiments already engaging the Freikorps? We can't afford to throw those regiments against full divisions when the Wehrmacht crosses the border," Kopecky used the worst case.

"Good point. I believe we will see the invasion by tomorrow, Thursday at the latest," Srom stopped next to a pallet of stacked provisions, pulled a map out of his jacket pocket and unfolded it upon a wood crate. "We should pull those regiments out and let the Germans advance to the fortress line in the west. It is a risk but I have been thinking of recommending that these mobilized regiments feint the Germans a few kilometers onto our side of the border further to the southeast – here, here and here opposite the two German armies pointed at the Český les Mountains. They will be of a smaller number than their attackers, so when they turn tail and run, German pridefulness will see this as the obvious response to their superior numbers. What our boys will really be doing is leading the forward panzer regiments into an artillery kill zone that the enemy will not exit from. The meteorologists all predict bad ground fog in the mornings throughout Bavaria, Saxony and Austria during this time. As long as the Luftwaffe is not in the sky to harass us it should work."

"That old cavalry trick? Won't the Germans recognize the feint for what it is?" Kopecky appreciated the beauty of using geography to eliminate a large number of German tanks yet relying on intangibles such as weather and hubris was risky.

"Speed beats power. That is the dictum these newly minted German tank commanders are drilled in. Given the bait they will pursue. By the time their generáls back across the border spot what we are doing it will be too late," Srom folded up his map. "What would your friend Capka say about this strategy?"

"He would liken it to a provincial bandit luring a fat prize into a backwoods ambush," Kopecky laughed. "Beating the Germans is one thing. Humiliating them is something he would consider quite worth the risk."

"I suspected as much. That is why we will recommend that his regiment spearhead the feint maneuver against lead units of the German Tenth Army," Srom proposed. "I think he will appreciate the honor.

REICH AIR MINISTRY
WILHELMSTRASSE, BERLIN

Stumpff was back at the big table in the operations room hovering over a growing mountain of status reports from airfields stretching from Sachsen to Österreich. All told the same story of carnage. The ground war had not yet begun and Germany's best weapon had just suffered a horrendous loss. Had he been sole architect of the operational plans, Stumpff would have tendered his resignation. Given the challenges ahead, resignation might be a wise decision, regardless. Instead he had picked up the telephone and called Göring's secretary to request the feldmarschall's immediate presence. A few months previous the Führer had appointed Göring as his successor. Escaping to let Göring to fend for himself was not an option... not if Stumpff expected to be alive in a year. They would have to turn the situation around. The political consequences would need to be paid first. But after Hitler had exhausted his rage he would demand answers and they would have to be ready to provide them. There was simply no way to sugar coat the fact that in twenty-four hours the Luftwaffe had lost about half of the six-hundred bombers it had assigned to the war with Czechoslovakia.

"Are my bombers in the air?" Göring roared expectantly before completing his charge into the room. "Why do you all look like the farmer whose cow has just died?"

As the support staff receded into the safety of whatever crevices they could locate, Stumpff grabbed a set of reports he had been saving and straightened his back.

"No sir, as the fog began to clear, Czechoslovak bombers raided our bomber bases," Stumpff shook the paperwork in his hand. "Name the base – Altenburg, Ansbach, Erfurt, Jesau, Wels – every airfield with bombers participating in Fall Grün was hit. In most cases the ground crews had yet to move the fuel trucks and ordinance lorries away from the aircraft. Between the exploding bombs and petrol, the estimate is we have two hundred and fifty bombers destroyed or put out of action. We also lost most of the Junkers transports assigned to drop paratroops tomorrow."

"Impossible! Counting the aircraft lost yesterday, that's half of the bombers assigned to the invasion," Göring stared at the map markers showing the airfields hit. "The Czechs would have to have sent every single bomber they had."

"So it would seem. And they knew exactly where to send them," Stumpff was certain it was no coincidence that the enemy bombers appeared where they had.

"I will not take responsibility for this alone. Czech Intelligence has so many spies up our asses it is criminal. Canaris is supposed to root out these traitors. For his incompetence I have lost three-hundred aircraft," Göring pounded the table with his fist. "The Abwehr will pay for this."

Stumpff saw immediately how Göring would break the news to the Führer... with a politically astute attack on Admiral Canaris. With the feldmarschall directing his thoughts to career defense, Stumpff took the opportunity to steer the conversation back to more concrete matters.

"Herr feldmarschall, there are several measures that must be taken without delay. Most of our fighters are attached to bases near the major cities. The Führer must permit us to reassign as many as possible to defend the airspace above our operational fields. It would also be prudent to transfer Luftflotte Two from the north to the front. The losses we have sustained in the last twenty-four hours puts the Czechs at parity with us in bombers. We have to assume the Soviets will soon be sending their squadrons west within days. We do not want to be at a disadvantage. Both of us know keeping bombers and crews in the North that can't be much more than a nuisance to the British does not make much sense." Stumpff got the whole argument out without interruption.

"Good proposals," Göring weighed in after considering the options. "Draw up the orders. We have to pull ourselves up by the bootstraps but we will do so. In the meantime, I have something else for you to put into operation. Forget the Czech cities for now. Starting immediately we are shifting everything we have left into tactical support to the ground offensive. It is obvious that the Czechs do not intend to roll over for us in this war. Our troops will need all the help we can give them."

PETŘÍN HILL, PRAHA

The Interior Ministry wasn't disclosing how much damage Hradčany had taken from the German bombers the day before, nor were they allowing foreign correspondents up to the castle to see have a look for themselves. Sanderson thought a good view from the other hill in the area, Petřín, might be had. Hiking up through the parkland with Ros they met no obstructions on the way up. In addition to the fine view of the western half of the capital, they found the army had positioned an anti-aircraft company at the op. The soldiers waved and winked at them probably under the impression Ros and Sanderson were two lovers.

"Shall we put on a show for them? Besides, neither of us wants to fall out of practice in the romantic department," Sanderson's proposal bordered on cheeky.

"I'll smack you all right, pal," Ros elbowed him in the rib gage. "I swear, no more Clark Gable pictures for you."

"Ow! You are a vicious, angry woman," Sanderson tried to keep a relaxed demeanor.

"Stick to business, chump. You can hold my hand. But that's it! And only because I want to get the best view of Hradčany from over there near those machine guns," Ros set him straight.

The two journalists strolled by the gun crew holding hands and waved at the soldiers. "Dobrý den," Ros called out to the young men with a winning smile. Charmed, the soldiers returned her greeting enthusiastically.

"Pulling out the binoculars might not be wise under the circumstances," Sanderson patted the over-the-shoulder case at his side.

"Yes, a little obvious," Ros agreed. "I don't think mine will draw much attention though," Ros reached into her purse for the opera glasses she had brought along. "Oh, much better."

She was right, the soldiers did not care a wit about the compact magnifiers Ros was holding up to her eyes by the folding handle.

"Do not exaggerate. Those puny lens' are next to worthless," Sanderson scoffed. "Of course they are not going to care."

"Jealousy is so unbecoming in a man," Ros teased. "For your information, I have quite the good view. If there were major damage I would see it from here, but all of the buildings at the castle are still standing without any gaping holes."

"Let me have a look," Sanderson pinched the opera glasses from her hand. "You rapscallion... these are more than three-times magnification. No wonder you can see accurately that far in the distance. But true enough, no serious damage can be seen from our vantage point."

"When are you going to start trusting me?" Ros swiped her opera glasses back. "If I could find Sylvie I wouldn't waste my time with you at all."

"Quite. I wonder what has become of Sylvie, as well. I am beginning to fear the worst. It's as if the poor woman has fallen off the face of the Earth," Sanderson agreed. "Come on, let's see what the other views of the city have to offer from up here. From what we have seen so far from street level the damage has been fairly sparse. The Gerries were much more effective over Barcelona when I was there. That tells me our Czechoslovak friends really must have gotten to them in the air."

"Where are the Germans today? That's what I want to know. It's the afternoon already." Ros wondered if they had they just taken their ball and gone home after getting a bloody nose.

"Good question. It' does seem like the Czech lion has taken some of the fearsomeness out of the German eagle," Sanderson was sampling headlines again.

While strolling arm-in-arm around the perimeter, Ros and Sanderson saw an army motorcycle courier rumble up the road to pull close to a nearby gun position. Revving the engine several times before shutting off the motor and propping up the cycle, the courier gestured for the anti-aircraft crews to gather around. The reporters could see him explaining something in a very animated fashion but could not make out what he was saying. The courier used his arms to mimic an airplane in a dive. Whatever he was describing, the soldiers broke out in loud cheers upon hearing it.

"I wonder what that is all about?" Ros looked over her shoulder.

"Something we should investigate further," Sanderson steered them back toward the commotion.

MINISTÈRE DE LA GUERRE
BOULEVARD SAINT-GERMAIN, PARIS

Pity the poor spy who managed to gain entry to the War Ministry for the first time as one could go mad trying to navigate the frustrating maze of corridors, staircases and courtyards. Thollon suspected this feature had been intentional on the part of the architect since the stately structure near the Seine was under sixty years of age and purpose-built to the needs of the army. Even now, after many years searching out one bureau or another, he still made wrong turns and discovered new dead-ends. The first floor was mostly devoted to evaluation, generation and storage of documents. But there were also offices devoted to the standing commissions for each of the separate branches such as the infantry and cavalry. Thollon had been informed that Général Gamelin could be found with the Office of the Infantry, and without much architectural diversion, that was where he found the chief of staff closely examining new maps of the Saar region.

"Those look recent," Thollon commented over the général's shoulder as a way of introduction.

"Excellent eyesight, colonel. A virtue in your line of work, I am sure," Gamelin continued perusing the cartography. "You are correct. The Germans have been very busy since reoccupying the Rhineland."

"So then you *are* serious about launching an offensive. Most intriguing, what will be our first priority?" Thollon was skeptical the général truly intended to prosecute the war as vigorously as he procured exquisitely tailored uniforms.

"First priority..." Gamelin considered his answer while straightening his back. "I intend to put that pain in the ass de Gaulle and his regiment right in front to spearhead the attack."

"Very wise," Thollon stifled a chuckle. It was well known the lieutenant colonel and the chief of staff did not get along – so much so de Gaulle had been exiled from Paris to command a tank regiment at Metz. "But the last I heard those new Renault tanks you sent him last year are not the most reliable vehicles. A somewhat perilous condition if they run into any determined resistance."

"Such are the fortunes of war," Gamelin turned to face the intelligence officer. "But enough of such trifles. What bad news brings you to see me today, Thollon?"

"Some of my reputation is undeserved, général, for today I bring you excellent news," Thollon mildly objected.

"What an unexpected surprise. Please continue," Gamelin was now tepidly interested in what Thollon had to share.

"Moravec just communicated with us from Vyškov and forwarded the most amazing tidings. Taking advantage of heavy fog over the Luftwaffe's operational airfields, the Czechoslovak Army Air Force put every bomber it has in the air and they caught the Germans with their bombers waiting on the ground loaded with fuel and ordinance. The damage inflicted has yet to be verified but Moravec estimates conservatively that upwards of one-hundred and fifty German aircraft could have just been taken out of the battle if the enemy squadrons supposed to be at each airfield prove accurate," Thollon noted that the often fussy général was pleased with the report.

"That man has built an enviable network of agents in Germany. I do not doubt his claim," Gamelin praised Moravec knowing the French espionage service had been nowhere near as effective. "Such successes will make what comes next much simpler."

"Ah, Mobilisation Générale?" Thollon sought confirmation of what he had heard an hour earlier.

"Exactly correct. Daladier's cabinet approved the measure this morning. I have the signed orders on my desk. The announcements will be posted publicly tomorrow morning," Gamelin was ready to knock on Hitler's front door.

ANHALTER BAHNHOF, BERLIN

Next stop, Dresden... at least for Roland. After trailing British diplomats in Berlin for the better part of a week, and several lengthy interviews to his credit, the little guy was getting out of Dodge. At least that was how Endicott characterized it. Holding a British passport might soon be a liability whenever Britain got around to making it official to back up the French. The Wehrmacht would soon roll into Czechoslovakia, and whatever the outcome, Roland had it on good authority that Paris would be forced to declare war within days. By now when Roland said he had something on good authority, Endicott took it as gospel. So the little fellow was heading east toward the Polish border. Once there he had some cockamamie idea that he could make it back into Czechoslovakia. The Poles were on cordial terms with Hitler at the moment. The same could not said of Czech/Polish relations, however, as Shirer pointed out. Roland was undaunted by such arguments, and given his track record of slipping through dangerous situations unscathed, who could argue with him? That's how the three of them found themselves on the platform waiting for the conductor to announce boarding for the Roland's train.

"Did you know that sixty years ago this fine neo-classical structure was the largest terminal on the Continent?" Roland remarked to fill in his last moments in Berlin.

"Where do you get all of these snippets of information, Roland? You are like a walking encyclopedia," Endicott was going to miss the guy.

"I actually read the newspaper I work for," Roland cast an accusing eye at his colleague.

"Ha, ha, ha," Endicott pooh-poohed the slight. "Take care of yourself, Roland. I still think you are crazy heading east like this."

"No more crazy than yourself thinking you can pinch a ride with some German convoy crossing the border into the Sudetenland," Roland retorted.

"Fine, we're both nuts. Here's hoping we can meet up somewhere in Bohemia," Endicott had seen stranger rendezvous.

"That's the spirit. We will share a drink when the time comes," Roland agreed. "So you are set on remaining in Berlin, William?"

"Oh yes. Murrow wants me to stay put for now. We have solid access to radio facilities here and Germany is the center of the crisis." Thankfully Shirer felt safer in the German capital compared to Vienna.

The whistle blew to announce boarding was starting on the passenger cars.

"Well then, I'm off," Roland picked up his leather suitcase from the platform. "Wish me well. I understand the Pierogi is especially tasty on the Polish side."

"A good choice. Very tasty and they will fill you up for the long journey ahead," Shirer never got over the eccentricity of Roland's priorities.

"Take care of yourself, pal," Endicott added as Roland hurried off to board.

"You'll be next," Shirer told Endicott as they turned around and walked side by side toward the exit.

"Yeah, the propaganda people seem fairly confident about the whole affair. They won't give me any hard dates but looks like they don't mind allowing correspondents to follow in after the front line troops cross the border," Endicott's luck was holding.

"That strikes me as over-confident, honestly. Have you noticed no one is boasting about the Luftwaffe having pummeled Prague? That suggests to me yesterday's raid did not go well for them. From the people I have spoken to outside of the hierarchy, there is plenty of unease about the difficulties that lie ahead once on Czechoslovak soil. It might be like reporting on Verdun from a fox hole," Shirer hoped his compatriot knew what he was getting into.

"Hell, I made it through the Japanese attack on Shanghai in thirty-two and I'll make it through this fracas too," Endicott was actually looking forward to seeing things from the side doing the attacking for a change."

"Where are you heading," Shirer still felt his colleague was being much too cavalier about the matter but that was the nature of the profession.

"Back to the Wilhelmstrasse and the propagandists to see if there is any word..." Endicott pointed toward the weirdest site he had seen during his stay in Berlin. "Hey, look what is going on behind you."

Shirer turned around and saw what Endicott was talking about: a motorcycle brigade roaring by in escort of a troop convoy making its way down Saarlandstrasse. "I have never seen anything like the goggles those motorcycle riders are sporting. They look more like men from Mars than soldiers," Shirer observed.

"You're on to something there. Just like Flash Gordon's Trip to Mars. Of course, that would put Uncle Adolph in the role of Ming the Merciless," Endicott chuckled at his own joke.

KREUZBERG DISTRICT, BERLIN

His mission was a chancy affair. The head had to be cut off before the serpent became aware he was imperiled. Surprise was a crucial component of the procedure. Yet thanks to the improvised start of this war the serpent had his back to a corner, his body tensely coiled and ready to lunge while eyes searched for foes to strike. Whatever providence had caused those three Heinkels to be where they had no business to be had let loose an avalanche that had left Heiden's well orchestrated plans in shambles. He had two options: stay out in the cold and improvise to the new conditions facing them, or come in from the field and risk receiving a direct command to suspend the mission. Heiden chose the former course. The serpent still needed to be slain but getting to him was now many times more arduous.

Their original location had been closely guarded information known only to a handful of individuals. Despite this, after listening to the Führer's Sportpalast speech on the radio, Heiden had ordered the team to a secondary location known only to him. There were drop points around the city were messages could be left and retrieved but for the most part Heiden and his sixty hand picked men were now operating on their own until Heiden chose to contact Ottke. General Halder was no longer a factor. The quick start of the war would leave the useless career army officer unsure how to proceed. Therefore the general would do nothing while the units he had pledged to the mission were likely now racing toward the Czech border the same as the majority of Wehrmacht and SS divisions. Heiden saw this state of affairs as an opportunity. When he struck there would be other military assets in the vicinity that would not be committed to battle and would lend their support.

Heiden would wait for now. He and his men were quite comfortable inside the old factory tucked away within the district. Kreuzberg was the most populous section of the capital, which allowed his men to blend in with the thousands of people who lived in the dense tenement housing that had been built during the turn of the century. As the city planners had been hard at work de-industrializing Berlin during the years hence, there was plenty of unused commercial space in the area to choose from. All that remained was to lie in wait for the proper moment, which may come in hours, or after many long days. They were sixty coiled springs held tightly in place against their nature. The waiting would be their most difficult trial.

31. FOLLY

German motorized infantry enter Asch

SEPTEMBER 28, 1938
ASCH, SUDETENLAND

The local tree line was close to the road and did a fair job of muffling the racket made by most vehicles approaching from the direction of Selb until they got quite close to the former border crossing. The Czechoslovak guard shack had been torn down by the local Germans in a frenzy of joy following the arrival of the first Freikorps units. The same revelers had been excitedly clamoring all of the previous day to greet the first Wehrmacht companies to enter the Sudetenland. Everyone in the city knew the army was coming soon, they just did not know precisely when. As this was an invasion and not an occupation, Morgen and Horst agreed it was best not to tell the population that their saviors were arriving this morning. The incoming troops didn't need distractions to delay them from their appointment with the Czechoslovaks.

Waiting with his rifle slung over the shoulder near the demolished border guardhouse, Morgen enjoyed a cigarette while contemplating his growing respect for their adversary. The enemy regiment to the southeast was cagey. They never stayed in one place for very long yet were always nearby anytime a substantial force of Freikorps troops attempted to isolate Eger. When they were not moving these units obviously were well hidden. None of Morgen's scouts had been able to root out where the enemy was resting. They only could verify the carnage left behind by the

Czechs after the fact. These men were smart and no doubt worried about being caught out in the open by Luftwaffe ground attack aircraft. Morgen took a long drag on the cigarette before looking up at the overcast skies. If there were clouds here there would be dense fog over the airfields to the west so no air support this morning.

Morgen appreciated the crispness in the dawn air. Given a preference, he would rather accomplish his work when most soldiers were out of commission and vulnerable. The stillness heightened the senses. That's when he noticed the approaching column by the muffled din rolling closer. Soon he could discern the differences between the various gasoline engines approaching up the road but not yet visible. Morgen made out the angry growl of the BMW motorcycles the Kradschützen brigades favored. Flicking his smoke to the ground, Morgen raised his field glasses to his eyes in the direction of a dust cloud rising down the road. Moments later the full motorcycle rifle brigade was in full view and swiftly overtaking his location. Wisely, they zoomed past without breaking speed upon entering the city. Good... they were taking this invasion seriously. The resulting commotion did rouse the citizenry, however. Lights in buildings switched on and house fraus in their slippers and night robes hurried outside to see what was causing the racket so early in the morning.

Looking back at the road from Selb, Morgen saw a Mark IV tank leading the panzer column. Following behind were the puny Mark IIs and Mark Is of the brigade, then the Opel trucks transporting infantry. The more powerful Mark IV was likely the commander's tank given the way the officer riding the turret cupola was scanning the route ahead. The two men locked eyes and the brigade commander ordered his driver to pull the tank off the road near Morgen. The SS man straightened up to approach the idling vehicle.

"Greetings hauptscharführer," the brigade commander spotted Morgen's collar insignia. "Any enemy forces operating in the vicinity?"

"A full Czechoslovak regiment had been tearing up the Freikorps irregulars closer to Eger until the order came down for the Sudetens to pull back several days ago. The Czechs also have a number of mobile companies throughout the area further east. Very clever operators though – always on the move," Morgen reported what he knew.

"Berlin wants Pilsen taken within four days. Chasing after mice will delay our progress," the brigade commander considered the threat insignificant.

"Be warned, these mice have sharp teeth," Morgen advised as a professional courtesy.

ČESKÝ LES MOUNTAINS, NEAR PFRAUMBERG

The vz. 34 cannon recoiled backward as it launched a 37mm shell in the direction of the German Mark II tank Capka had targeted. The armor-piercing round caught the side of the enemy vehicle high at one of the return wheels – separating the latter from the hull and severing the track simultaneously. The stricken light tank would have pivoted in a circle had the driver not cut power to the suspension. Capka's loader already had a new shell in the chamber before the German crew had time to escape their motionless coffin. The hatches on the Mark II swung open too late as Capka depressed the trigger mechanism another time. The second round penetrated the enemy's hull, detonating the ammunition inside. A good kill, Capka thought as he glimpsed the ensuing fireball that sent metal plate careening skyward. This was fine sport but they were running short of armor-piercing shells. The Germans had put the few new Mark IV tanks in their possession on point. This model could almost match the range of their Škodas, so the companies in Capka's battalion concentrated their fire on the Mark IVs – immobilizing the lot of them while losing two LT vz. 35s in the process. Next the battalion's tanks pounced on the weaker Mark IIs. With armor unable to stand up to the Škoda's 37mm cannon and the Czechs having the advantage of firing from a further distance, the German crews were lambs to the slaughter. Looking at the ammo rack, Capka saw he had less than six shells left and grabbed the radio microphone.

"Break off," Capka ordered. After replacing the microphone to its hook, he yelled new orders down to his driver. "Stanislaus, turn us around and head toward the rendezvous point."

As he cranked the turret around to cover their retreat, Capka peered through the gun sight and saw the German tank regiment was taking the bait, regardless of their losses. This plan was working and Capka was pleased that someone back at command was on top of things for a change. No sooner had the Eger sector cooled down than the regiment was moved by train south into the Český les range where there were moderate elevations and plenty of forest to hide away from prying eyes in.

It was obvious there was a worry about a major German thrust toward Plzen. This was confirmed when new directives arrived late Tuesday. Their regiment would cover the approach to Pfraumberg by the German Tenth Army, while a different regiment was slated to cover the approach to Česká Kubice. Together both regiments amounted to one half of a full mobile division – enough to hold their own in the ruse they were orchestrating. Their job was to lure the lone panzer division spearheading this German army's attack into narrow valleys where massed Czechoslovak artillery would rain destruction down upon the enemy. Hopefully, few of the Germans would be left to run once the trap that had been sprung upon them. If Capka's tanks had to counter-attack later, it would not make much sense to chase the surviving Germans with only six anti-tank shells for the cannon. Spitting high-explosive shells was dandy when dispatching Freikorps but not for much else. Capka felt like kicking himself for not increasing each tank's allotment of armor piercing rounds above the standard twenty-four usually carried.   That would have to change for the next engagement.

The Czechoslovak armor was retreating. Odd since they held the advantage. The Czechs were known to carry fewer armor piercing rounds in their turrets than high-explosive shells as the company commander insisted yet Stürmann still had a bad feeling in his gut. After having just taken a nasty beating face-to-face with the Škodas, Stürmann thought it unwise to go chasing after them. He had been overruled, however. The Czechoslovak armor was retreating and this was the moment to press the attack, it had been explained to him. A sharp sound like a large bell being rung by a dozen iron mallets reverberated between the tank walls as the Mark II shuddered terribly.

"HE round!" his driver announced.

That settled the argument, Stürmann thought. The Czechs were shooting high explosives. There would be no justification now for *amending* a direct command, as he had been considering.

"Any damage?" Stürmann called out. "I wouldn't bet against our puny armor being breached by one of those."

"No damage," the loader confirmed after a quick check about the interior.

"Close range so that I can get off a response?" Stürmann repeated the same request he had made all morning long.

"They are staying just out of reach, sir," came the reply from the driver.

"Are you telling me we are no faster than they are?" Stürmann balked.

"Perhaps they are a little faster. Nothing I try does any good at closing the distance, and sometimes they pull ahead a little bit," the driver kept trying.

Nothing had gone right since they had engaged the Czechoslovak force a few kilometers inside the border. Several battalions of Škodas scurried out into the open from the dense tree line to converge on the precious few Mark IVs leading his formation. Stürmann's battalion only had six of them total to spread around. The tankers knew the Czech cannon had a range advantage on the 20mm auto-cannon on the Panzerkampfwagen II but few of them suspected the snub-nosed 75mm cannon mounted on the Mark IV would be so ineffective at longer ranges above three hundred meters. The low muzzle velocity of the 75mm made it difficult to hit and penetrate a moving target with the precious few armor-piercing rounds available for that caliber – once again giving the advantage to the Škodas. Once the Panzer IVs had been knocked out by concentrated fire, the Škodas turned about in the large canyon to target the Mark IIs. It was crazy, they had an advantage in numbers but could not get close enough to actually land hits on the Czech tanks. Stürmann's 20mm cannon could spit all ten shells in a magazine within five seconds. If he found a weak spot, unloading so many shots so quickly might be sufficient to disable one of heavier Škodas. But they never got close enough to test that theory.

The best that he could do was keep the platoon on the move to throw off the aim of their attackers.

"Leutnant, the road is opening up into a valley ahead," Stürmann's driver reported.

"Good, room to maneuver finally," Stürmann thought maybe they were coming into some luck. "Perhaps we can finally call in some artillery support now that that canyon is behind us."

Stürmann broke protocol to throw open the hatch on the top of his turret. He wanted a better view than the restricted angle through the slit in the forward turret armor they were forced to use in battle. Snatching his binoculars from the hook they were swinging on, Stürmann eased his head out into the air. Now would be an inopportune moment for another incoming HE round but none of the Czechs were firing in his direction. As the tanks behind him spread out into the more open area, Stürmann saw no defensive positions waiting ahead to heap more misery on their first day of war. Yet this was not the large valley shown on their maps that he was expecting, but a smaller one pot-marked by a few odd sheds that were probably used for grazing animals or farming. Double-checking the horizon, Thurman dipped back down inside the turret.

"Get on the radio," he addressed the loader. "Provide our position and see if you can call in some air support. I think we have outrun our artillery. At least now that we're out of that canyon we can maneuver but it would be smart to call in some ground attack planes if we get into more trouble than we can handle."

Stürmann froze on those words while the radio crackled to life. He fought off the sinking feeling that was distracting him. Taking a deep breath, Stürmann pushed himself back out into the air, risk be damned. The view through the glasses showed the retreating Škodas already on the far side of the vale. Now that the German light tanks were well into the basin it was more obvious the space was smaller than it had appeared upon entering. And like the Mediterranean, there were only two passages to freedom – the one ahead, and the one behind. If they wanted out the only sure route was reversing course back to the canyon, which was thoroughly plugged with friendly armor and infantry lorries. Pivoting around, Stürmann observed his compatriots dispersing wide just as they had been taught. They did not know the vale closed in further ahead. Stürmann's mind raced through the possibilities. His gut told him that not far into the next canyon the Czechoslovaks would be waiting to make a stand. Stürmann cursed... he had to make the company commander aware of potential ambush they were hurtling toward. But first...

"Give me that," Stürmann ducked back inside the turret and yanked the microphone out of his crewman's hands. "Stürmann to zug. Take up immediate position to the far left of the valley. Get your asses out of the middle of this valley!"

"Hearing the command loud and clear, his driver lurched the ten-ton vehicle to the left as Stürmann rushed to rotate the frequency dial.

"Why are we abandoning point, leutnant?" the loader was unsettled by the rash maneuver when there was no obvious threat.

"Because my friend, I fear that while our artillery is not trained on this valley, enemy guns most certainly are. We have a fifty percent chance those shells will come in from the left or the right. So I just gambled on which side is safer," Stürmann blurted out while fiddling with the radio set.

CZECHOSLOVAK ARTILLERY POSITION
NEAR LABUŤ

Troníček had fallen into a nervous routine of pacing, looking skyward, checking his wristwatch then repeating the sequence. The kapitán was anxious to commence with live firing of his 100mm guns. They were operating in an area of mountain ranges that an entire German army was desirous of breaking into. As the Czechoslovak pillbox line ran along the inner range of peaks, which was somewhat further from the German border in this area, the strategy was to draw the enemy armor division spearheading the attack into a few pre-determined depressions that came before breaking free of the mountains. It was the responsibility of the available mobile artillery regiments such as Troníček's to pummel the invading German units while they were still vulnerable. But that depended on his armored regiments not getting blown to hell before they could bottle up the enemy. The other thing worrying Troníček was German attack aircraft. The weather couldn't keep them on the ground forever. Despite the fine job of camouflage netting that blended his guns in with the green and brown countryside, Troníček still felt exposed. He was told friendly fighters were patrolling above, and there was an anti-aircraft company attached to their position, but Troníček was anxious for the order to open fire to arrive. So far, that order was tardy by about an hour.

Elevation and azimuth for the mix of Great War-era field guns, and the newer 1930 models, had already been computed. How close to correct those computations were would not be known until the first shells were sent hurtling into the valley. Dropping large rounds over a tall embankment was always tricky to pull off. Troníček expected the first salvo to be off. But with a spotter up over the target area in a Letov, and scouts watching at ground level, his cannoneers should receive ranging guidance almost immediately. An aircraft engine audible in the distance pulled Troníček's attention from plotting trajectory options in his head. The plane to which that engine was attached was too distant for him to see, however. Before he could trouble himself further about who was flying nearby, the field telephone buzzed into life. Troníček sprinted back to his makeshift command post before the third buzz.

"Troníček," he announced himself succinctly.

"Now," was the terse directive before the connection died.

"Fire!" Troníček shouted before letting the phone handle drop out of his hand.

The gun crews had gotten into alert position as soon as the phone rang. So there was no delay in pulling their trigger lanyards upon hearing Troníček's command. The near simultaneous sequence of booms sending shells screeching to their target was positively calming to the artillery kapitán.

ČESKÝ LES MOUNTAINS
NEAR PFRAUMBERG

The decision had been decided based on proximity. They were simply closer to the left wall of the valley so Stürmann had chosen the shortest distance over weighing the odds of what was the more likely direction of incoming artillery rounds. One of the two rock walls would provide cover from indirect fire. If shells came at them from the west, his decision would be fortuitous. But should the Czechoslovaks have placed their guns to the east then Stürmann had probably just killed his platoon.

"The company commander is responding, leutnant," the loader called up from the turret as he passed the microphone up.

"Sir, are you out of the canyon?" Stürmann had to make his superior understand. "I urge caution. This valley is small and there is another canyon ahead. If we get bottled up in here, the Czechs will slaughter us if they have artillery trained on this position."

The answer was much as he had expected. Push ahead and blast through into the next canyon before the pass could be blocked. Stürmann slunk back into the turret to hand the radio microphone back to the loader.

"We are moving through," Stürmann informed the driver. "Let's hope there are no anti-tank cannons waiting for us and those Škoda drivers are really out of AT ammunition."

The ground rumbled under their tank, causing the vehicle to tremble and making it difficult for the driver to maintain control. A second, closer concussion followed swift on the heels of the first. Raising his head out of the turret Stürmann witnessed a salvo of shells barely overshooting their position. He had gambled poorly. The next salvo would not be so off the mark. Stürmann's driver figured it out for himself and lurched their Panzer II to the right. Closing the hatch behind him, Stürmann reached again for the radio controls.

"Stürmann to zug. Looks like we have to take the canyon ahead away from the Czechs if we want to make it out of here alive. Prepare to re-engage the enemy," Stürmann ordered as the their tank shook terribly from a nearby shell hit.

The desátník returned the handset to the field telephone. From their position the reconnaissance team could view the entire valley. The Germans had rushed in as expected. As soon as he had noticed one of their platoons veer off, the spotter had called in the order to commence firing. There was no sign of smoke or disability to suggest mechanical error so it had to be assumed that someone down there had recognized the danger. The first fusillade was not as inaccurate as anticipated. There was a slight pause as the adjustments forwarded to the cannoneers were applied to the gun carriages. In the quiet the desátník could hear the engines on the German tanks revving higher. They had decided to rush the canyon. Brave, yet foolish. A nest of anti-tank guns awaited them. All it would take was killing a few of their number as the canyon narrowed and none would pass.

Checking his wristwatch, the corporal **instructed his men to lie prone.** He raised his field glasses and waited. Within thirty seconds the artillery barrage resumed. This time the range was perfect, covering the entire valley. Even at their camouflaged position above the floor the ground beneath the Czechs shook tremendously as the basin below took the full brunt of the explosive impacts. The concussion waves were deafening. Then again it was far worse for the Germans. Quite the demonstration of destruction as the light tanks employed by the enemy disintegrated in eruptions of earth and steel as the incoming rounds found their victims. The selection had enough randomness that a good number of the armored vehicles did cross the valley floor intact only to meet the dug in anti-tank crews inside the next canyon. He would learn later that these Germans had fought tenaciously to clear a passage into the canyon but were unsuccessful. As the extent of the carnage sunk in, the remnants attempted to retreat back to the canyon still clogged by their compatriots. When there was nothing left moving in the valley the desátník called in the order to ceasefire.

The debris clouds filled with dust and pulverized materials that once constituted fully whole armored vehicles cleared slowly. This was the first time the corporal had observed the receiving end of such a sustained barrage. Their training had not prepared them for the deadening of the senses that resulted. His mind understood that all about them should be silent but the signals his ears was sending to the brain were still relaying the deafening explosions of shells impacting on the valley floor. At least his eyes were still reliable. The desátník raised the binoculars up to search for survivors. Nothing moved. There was far more blood and intact human remains strewn about the ground than he had expected.

The field telephone rumbled to life, which the desátník felt more than he heard. Still lying prone, he reached over and collected the handset.

"Point Orange," was the proper code for their position. "No movement... no evident survivors in target area. Between forty and sixty armored vehicles killed. Unable to determine the number of infantry or artillery lorries destroyed. Remnants have retreated back into the pass."

The line went dead. Now they would wait to see how the Germans would respond to their mistake.

LES TERNES DISTRICT, PARIS

The French were lurching headlong into war, and what a sight. Everywhere on the street men went their ways clutching the same telegram announcing Mobilisation de Guerre. One fellow was good enough to show his telegram to Clarence. For those without an address to receive the notice, Paris was plastered thick with the same poster prominently bearing the flag of the republic and titled: *Ordre de Mobilisation Générale.* In case anyone missed either of those declarations, the headline gracing *Paris-soir* was typical of most French broadsheets: *Mobilisation Générale: The War Has Come.* Although some of the papers in Bonnet's pocket weaseled around the topic by editorializing that Gamelin was pushing the issue too swiftly. Regardless of what the fascist apologists wrote that old fox Coiffard had nailed it the week before. War *had* been around the corner just like 1914. The feeling Clarence got from people he spoke with on the boulevards was similar to what he had been told three days ago, only more magnified. Then he had described the public mood as simmering. Today Parisians were boiling over and very angry at being put through the ringer once again after twenty short years. No one he talked to, however, believed delivering the lesson Hitler deserved would keep their soldiers from home anywhere near as long as in the Great War. So there was great optimism mixed in with their determination.

Within days the cities and towns would be completely drained of their fathers, brothers, husbands and sons. All men in good health between the ages of twenty and forty-eight were called up. Getting all of those men to their regiments was going to cause a transportation nightmare. That left Clarence with a day, maybe two, to get himself out of Paris if he was going to make it to Metz prior to the festivities starting. The French had long favored invading Germany through the Saar. That industrial zone was far too strategically tempting to bypass. With the Maginot Line fortifications protecting the border, and the good fortune of the Germans pulling almost every military asset that could be moved to the Czechoslovak border, attacking through the Rhineland was hard to argue with. So onto Metz it was.

The problem was that mobilization was going to suck up every available civilian vehicle along with every eligible male. Clarence figured it wouldn't take more than a few days before the requisition squads fanned out to seize what they could. He figured his best bet would be to check with a few of his merchant friends to bum a ride on a delivery from Paris to Metz. There would be no room on the trains for more than a week. The French call-up system was based on when a reservist finished his two-year service with the army. Today was the first day of mobilization: call it M+1. Those individuals who had most recently finished their service would leave for their regiments today. On cashing out each man was handed what the French called a fascicule, a booklet that spelled out what M-Day they were to leave and what regiment to join. Coiffard had told him that calling-up all those who had missed the partial mobilisation could take as much as eight days, which would be M+8 for all of those forty-eight year-olds. Amazing how the Czechs managed to call up one and a quarter-million men in just twenty-four hours. A much smaller country had a lot to do with it but there definitely was something to be said about being prepared.

Clarence would have left already but he was dead set on staying put until Daladier got around to addressing the Chamber of Deputies. No one was certain whether the premier would go so far as actually call for a full declaration of war. The jury was out whether such a declaration was needed. All of the domestic hacks were arguing the finer points of constitutional protocol. The French, it seemed, had never spelled out the requirements, so who knew? Clarence couldn't beat it out of Paris until that little bit of theater had unfolded. His best guess was that Daladier would speak tomorrow but there had been no confirmation from the premier's office about that yet. Clarence's plan was to head back to his apartment, pack a light travel bag – just the essentials – and be ready to depart for Metz as soon as he filed a story on whatever Daladier ended up saying to the Chamber of Deputies.

MAIN ROAD, EAST OF ASCH

It was time for Sylvie to get back into the fray. The Prieger's had tried their best to convince her to stay but Sylvie couldn't mooch on them forever when there was a war getting started. And with the Freikorps kid having been yanked back to his unit there was no one to stop Sylvie from striking out on her own. They had spent most of the night listening to the German radio stations with lots of talk about dogfights in the air over Bohemia but the news announcers were mostly coy about who had shot down whom. Frau Prieger had fixed up a great selection of snacks for Sylvie to munch on the road and they had generously given her the clothes she had been wearing the past weeks plus a little old suitcase to put them in. Frau Prieger had even slipped her some Deutschmarks... just in case. They had never been able to find Sylvie's things at the place the convoy had been ambushed. Thank God her wallet and press pass had been tucked in her jacket pocket on that day.

So with a hug, and some tears, Sylvie had waved goodbye to the people who had saved her life. Her plan was to hoof it in the general direction of Eger. The Freikorps corporal had warned her earlier that week that there had been a lot of fighting around there but Sylvie was desperate to get out of Asch. Somewhere along the way she was bound to bump into some German or Czech column and would let whatever authorities she was eventually dumped on sort out what she needed to do next. She had seen several flights of planes fly over but not one car or truck had passed her in either direction after an hour of walking. All the cute young soldier boys out there somewhere and none of them were on hand to help a girl out. Sylvie had never expected it would take this long before seeing another soul. At least she was wearing the garden hat Frau Prieger had insisted on Sylvie taking with her so glare from the sun wasn't much of a bother... yet.

It was while pulling a breakfast roll out of her knapsack to nibble on that Sylvie heard an aircraft engine coming up fast and loud behind her. Looking up and over her shoulder she saw a high-winged monoplane flying low and following the road. It zoomed past not much higher than treetop level, which made it easy to see the big black crosses on the undersides of the wing. But the pilot didn't even wag his wings when she waved. The bastard just kept on going along on his way. Putting the rest of the roll back into the sack, Sylvie started walking again. Within minutes she heard more engine noises, this time of the earthbound variety. Turning around she could see four motorcycle riders sending dust flying as they sped down the road in her direction. She had to hold tightly onto her hat as they zipped by. At least two of them looked back at her and one of those waved... she was making progress. Next Sylvie made out a convoy of troop trucks making their way through the dust with a military staff car in the lead. The car was carrying two officers in back, who signaled the driver to pull off the road next to her to let the trucks pass. Some of the infantrymen cheered at her as they went by. Sylvie thought things were finally looking up.

"Fräulein, what are you doing out here," the younger and taller of the two German officers asked after jumping out of the car.

"That's an in interesting story, would you like to here all about it?" Sylvie put on her best flirt.

11 MORPETH MANSIONS, LONDON

The rendezvous was of the surreptitious variety that was destined never to exist as an item on any of the three men's official appointment ledgers. What was to be discussed was no less vital as a result, but in fact, all the more so. The conversation within this compact study would be frank and unambiguous – virtues normally unavailable within the official halls of government. Masaryk was in the hunt for an answer to one simple question made complex by politics: what concrete military measures was Great Britain taking now that German divisions were presently invading Czechoslovakia? Unlike Paris, there had been no announcements from 10 Downing Street or the Foreign Office on war preparations. Cadogan had been supportive during their last telephone conversation yet could only offer a vague, *soon*, in response to Masaryk's direct inquiry. Secretary of State for War Hore-Belisha would likely tell Masaryk what he needed to know but direct contact would land both men in hot water. More so for Hore-Belisha who was an irritant to many on Chamberlain's cabinet who were actively searching for reasons to finagle his removal. The impasse provided perfect justification for Masaryk's continued funding of political opposition to Chamberlain. Mister Churchill was most pleased to provide the venue – his personal residence no less – and serve as the intermediary to bring Hore-Belisha and Masaryk surreptitiously together.

"What is the delay?" Masaryk prodded Hore-Belisha. "Gamelin has wasted no time in getting the mobilisation orders out, and Daladier will speak to the Chamber of Deputies tomorrow to receive legislative seal of approval for war. What is Chamberlain up to now?"

"The prime minister is unconvinced that Czechoslovak forces will hold back Hitler's army's for very long. Therefore, he is averse to rushing into military deployments until it is proven for a fact your military is up to the job. It is an argument he is losing within the cabinet, but has not yet lost," Hore-Belisha explained in detail.

"How long must we wait for this theater to be concluded? We will do our part... in spades. It is time for Britain to do her part," Masaryk was in a feisty mood.

"You and I are in total agreement, sir. Cooper will not announce this until tomorrow, but as of fourteen hundred hours today, the Royal Navy was put on full alert. The fleet is putting to sea today from Scapa Flow to cordon off the North Sea from the Shetlands to Norway," Hore-Belisha felt he had to provide something tangible to the Czechoslovak ambassador.

"That is more like it," Masaryk enthusiastically approved. "You are talking blockade then?"

"Indeed," Churchill, the old naval man, spoke up. "We will end up calling it something much less threatening but a blockade it will be. Every merchant ship heading toward the Baltic shall be stopped, boarded and searched for contraband of war. Any Nazi naval vessel attempting to break out into the North Sea will be turned back to port. If their crews resist, their vessels will be interned or sunk. Our ships will patrol from the North Atlantic to Antarctica in search of the Hun. When we find them we will chase them down and *encourage* their captains to make steam for the nearest neutral port under escort."

"But what of the German submarines? Those are not so easy to find," Masaryk suspected most of those had already put to sea.

"Oh, I believe their captains will behave themselves," Hore-Belisha predicted confidently. "One torpedo fired in anger is all the British people will require to force the prime minister's hand for good. He will either be compelled to resign or declare war."

"That is the most heartening news I have received here in London in a very long time, gentlemen. My government will be most appreciative. I must, however, pursue the question further. What other, more direct actions can we expect of your forces soon on the Continent?" Masaryk risked the appearance of ungratefulness but it was necessary. Besides, with the amount of pounds he had put at Churchill's disposal, the envoy had felt somewhat greater license to press the inquiry.

"I can appreciate your point of view but most of our potential actions are still works in progress," Hore-Belisha had so little to work with it was embarrassing. "However, what I can guarantee you, is that within days of official declaration of war, bombers of the Royal Air Force will attack units of the German fleet at Wilhelmshaven, and Brunsbutte, at the entrance to the Kiel Canal."

"So the United Kingdom will declare war?" Masaryk dug further.

"With battle joined in Bohemia, and a clear French declaration of war, Great Britain must follow shortly," Churchill selected a cigar from the humidor. "At this moment we have twenty firm seats in opposition within Parliament. If Chamberlain dallies, their number will swell to forty and beyond... enough to bring his government down."

CHERNIVTSI LETIŠTĚ, NEAR BRNO

Rough did not come close to describing the ride from Prague in the elderly Fokker tri-plane. Parts of the transport were constructed with wood that creaked whenever the wind tossed the aircraft around, which had been a lot. On the plus side the flight had been provided gratis by the general staff of the Czechoslovak army. When the primly serious captain had knocked on Sanderson's hotel room door, the reporter had feared there were complications with something he had recently written. The military often takes offense at too many details about its men and equipment being published, which Sanderson had been abundantly including in his stories as of late. As he soon found out, the Czechs wanted him for a completely different purpose – a face-to-face visit with General Ludvik Krejčí at his wartime headquarters for the *responsible* representatives of the British press. Reading between the lines during his conversation with the young army emissary, Sanderson deduced that the Czechs desired to send a message of strength to the citizens of the United Kingdom. They were even providing a photographer during the visit.

It did not take long for Ros, the busy bee snoop that she was, to miraculously appear in the hallway and insert herself into the conversation. The woman was quick on the uptake, putting on a fairly impressive campaign explaining the benefits of reaching the American public. When that line of argument seemed to lack traction, Ros protested that her news service supplied many Commonwealth newspapers with material. Sanderson suspected the captain wanted to be done with her more than he was persuaded but the end result was that Ros was successful in getting one of the eight passenger seats on the plane. They had been collected sharply at the appointed hour and rushed to Kbely aerodrome. Within minutes of their arrival, their tri-motor transport descended for a temporary landing with engines left running while the group of newspaper journalists was escorted to the cabin door. Kbely was a prime target for the Luftwaffe so the Czechs were not leaving valuable aircraft lying around as targets. The transport was back in the air and on its way within ten minutes.

There were few amenities on a military transport to offset the loud and bumpy ride to their destination: a military airfield in Moravia. That was all they were told and no more. Sanderson had learned that the Czechs had relocated their military headquarters to a safer location further east yet had been unable to get anyone to say where that was. Neither were the organizers of this excursion forthcoming with that information. Looking outside the fuselage window, Sanderson noted the placement of the sun and estimated they were heading in a southwesterly direction. The cruising speed of these Czech-built Fokkers was less than one hundred and fifty miles per hour. The best he would able to do was keep track of their flight time and make some calculations.

Upon landing, the pilot did not taxi close to the hangers. Instead the transport parked on a grass area adjacent to the landing strip where a small welcoming party of army officers was waiting next to their staff car – a Tatra if Sanderson was correct. As the reporters got off the plane there was no identification within eyesight to tell where they had landed.

"I thought these people were flying Douglas commercials," Ros complained as she stepped off the aircraft.

"That's the civil airline not the air force," Sanderson reminded yet again.

"I know that but you would think the air force guys would have stolen those by now," Ros continued her argument.

"It has only been a few days, perhaps they are still giving them a new coat of paint," Sanderson was growing irritable and responded facetiously.

"Look, here comes our ride," Ros held onto her hat against the wind with one hand, and pointed to a small convoy of automobiles approaching from the area near the tower.

"Welcome," an army major greeted them. "Thank you for coming. As you can see, we will have ground transport here for you in a moment."

"How about a bathroom?" Ros demanded more than requested.

"That can be arranged," the major promised her.

The four black sedans slowed to a stop near the party, with their engines running. An army officer jumped out of the rear of each vehicle, holding the door open while they waited for their guests to get in. Sanderson noticed black curtains covered all of the windows surrounding the back seats, as well as the space between the driver and the passengers. The journalists were not going to be allowed to see where they were being taken.

"Two guests per vehicle please," the major gestured toward the waiting cars.

"Hey, that is not fair. We won't be able to see anything," Ros objected as she headed for the closest sedan.

"Our apologies, mesdame," the major affably ushered her to the sedan. "Better for you not to know where you are or where you are going."

"I wouldn't tell a soul," Ros feigned innocence before sliding into the car.

"Of that I am sure," the major played along. "The slightest slip, however, could reveal the location of Generál Krejčí and his headquarters. We cannot be so generous to our enemy."

U.S. EMBASSY
MALA STRANA DISTRICT, PRAHA

One positive outcome from mobilizing millions of able-bodied men, and the rush of many Czechs to seek the safety of the countryside after the Germans bombed the city, was an ample supply of empty hotel rooms in the capital. As more U.S. nationals made their way to Prague the embassy staff had plenty of places to house them temporarily. Getting five thousand Americans out of Czechoslovakia was a harder nut to crack. Civil aviation and train transport out of the country had been suspended. Neither were there decent train connections to Romania. The Czech government had been funding such a rail line with their one friendly neighbor but had yet to complete the work. The problem was mostly on the Romanian side with a rail system that was designed to support the needs of the old Austro-Hungarian Empire, not transit between Prague and Bucharest. But there seemed to be good news on this front. When Bess tracked Bulloch down she told him to hightail it up to Minister Carr's office. When he rounded the corner the door was wide open. Bulloch passed Chapin on the way in.

"You have a journey ahead of you, captain," the chargé d'affaires held out on him.

"I'm always the last to know," Bulloch groused as they passed each other.

Carr was standing by the side of his desk double-checking some paperwork. Noticing Bulloch, he closed the file and looked up.

"Ah, Captain Bulloch, I am glad Bess found you. I have good news," the minister seemed quite pleased.

"Yes, I gather you are sending me out on some good deed," Bulloch surmised.

"Of the highest order. I just received confirmation that our citizens who made their way to Pilsen were finally put on a special train to Prague, thanks to President Beneš," Carr would not have been able to move them otherwise.

"That is good news. This will bring the total to over three thousand people. Now what do we do with them once they get here?" Bulloch was thinking ahead.

"Well that is where you come in, son. I have been in direct contact with Minister Montgomery in Budapest these last few days. The Poles are openly hostile, which creates a question of safety in evacuating our people through Poland. The Hungarians, Montgomery tells me, may be opportunists in this crisis but they are not in hurry to commit their small little army to the battle. Montgomery has worked out safe passage for American nationals to Budapest. I have made arrangements with the Interior Ministry here in Prague for the use of one train per day to ferry our people to Košice in Slovakia. That works out to be approximately eight hundred individuals every twenty-four hours. Košice itself is just under ten miles from Hungarian territory. Army trucks have been made available to move our citizens from the rail station to the border. Once there they will walk across. On the other side, Montgomery's people will see to it that they are safely put on trains to Budapest. Montgomery is working on civil air transport to Lisbon. The last leg of the trip will be via ocean liner to New York," Carr finished.

"Košice sounds rather a long ways to go," Bulloch remembered how far east in Slovakia the city was. That was unless you were attempting to stay way clear of the German army on the move to the south. "Excellent planning, sir. Now how exactly do I fit into this cattle drive?"

"You son are going to be my point man in Košice," Carr sounded like a company president sending off a junior executive. "We are going to send the trains out of Prague at night for safety. So you will go with the first train leaving this evening. Chapin and Elbrick are already getting the first contingent of eight hundred ready to go from those people we have already processed. Once in Košice our local consul, Ferguson, will meet you plus a representative of the Czechoslovak army. Sorry, I don't have a name for the latter. You will be in charge of the border transfers with whatever aid Ferguson can provide. Your job will be to see our people on the trucks and on their way over into Hungary for each daily trainload until everyone we have processed is accounted for. The injured that can be made to travel will be on the last train."

"Thank you for trusting me with the responsibility, Minister Carr. I'll get the job done," Bulloch was also excited at the prospect of seeing new territory.

"I have complete faith in your abilities, captain. You have proven yourself most resourceful these last months. Those are the kind of skills required here," Carr lauded his attaché. "Now go home so you can pack whatever you will need. You have a very busy day ahead of you."

"If all goes to plan, I will see you back here in Prague five to seven days from now," Bulloch estimated after running the numbers in his head.

"Let us hope the Germans do not force the rest of us to join you first," Carr's jest was a little too close to the truth.

ČESKÝ LES MOUNTAINS, NEAR PFRAUMBERG

Waiting around made Capka nervous. Now that their tanks had been refueled and restocked he was itching to move onto a safer location with better tree cover. Their current position was lacking in this regard despite the protection of the medium-sized canyon they were situated within. Orders were to stay put, however, just in case the Germans made another push through the passes. Capka thought that unlikely. The results where the artillery traps had been employed had been excellent in forcing the German panzer division to lose its heaviest tanks and quite a few more of the lighter variety on top of those. No, the enemy would not risk another push until they could alter the balance somewhat in their favor. So Capka wanted to be ready to move if the need arose. Capka had the tankers in his company watching over his shoulder as he laid out a map of the area over the front of his Škoda.

"There," Capka jabbed a stubby forefinger at a specific spot on the map. "That spot will suit our needs perfectly. Plenty of dense tree cover, and close to several strategic approaches."

"We can get resupplied easily from that location, as well," one of Capka's lieutenants, Smik, noted.

Jicha, the driver of Capka's Škoda, was first to hear the high-pitched staccato whine incoming fast on their position. "Aircraft!"

"Get those tanks started!" Capka saw several bi-winged aircraft diving on their position. "Move, Henschels incoming!"

Stuffing the map into a jacket pocket, Capka followed his crew into their Škoda. He heard the solitary 20mm Oerlikon anti-aircraft cannon attached to the company open up on the German aircraft. As he closed the turret hatch, Capka could hear the dive-bombers pulling up as their bombs fell through the trees to explode on the ground. Shrapnel banged furiously against the armor of the tank Škoda but none penetrated. It was their bad luck that the Henschels had found them but at least the bi-planes were only supposed to carry four small 50kg bombs. Rotating the turret, Capka looked through combat slit to see through the dust whether any of his crews had been hit.

"Report in," Capka called out on the radio. The responses came in quickly with only one Škoda disabled from damage taken to the engine, which caused an oil fire. The crew was bailing out hoping to extinguish the small blaze before it got worse. Capka popped open his turret hatch to listen. Hearing nothing above the racket of their tank engines, he cautiously raised his head through the opening. No sooner had he looked around then the three Henschels returned to strafe the company with their machine guns. The more horizontal vector the German pilots used on their second pass made them easier for the 20mm crew to track. Capka saw the middle Henschel take a glancing hit to the rear fuselage. The damn thing must be built like a tank itself since it was still flying... but no longer flying well. Taking damage was enough to ward the German pilots off. They veered away and departed the area.

"Let's get out of here to the new rendezvous point we just discussed before they can call in some friends," Capka commanded via the radio. "Jicha, move us out."

Capka pulled himself up to ride on top of his turret. The rest of the company began forming up behind him to exit the tree line.

"Can you get her running?" Capka called out to the disabled crew examining their engine now that the fire was out.

"Fifteen minutes and we are gone," the lieutenant raised his thumb. "A piece of metal casing from one of the bombs cut through and ignited an oil line. We'll have it patched in no time."

"Then see you soon at our new hiding spot," Capka raised a thumbs-up as they passed their comrades.

SECRET PRESIDENTIAL HQ, ZÁTIŠÍ

The widely held suspicion was that President Beneš had joined the high command of the army at their wartime redoubt in Vyškov. The truth was very different. When the procession of seven vehicles carrying the president's family and staff left Hradčany two days before, their destination had been a private villa in the secluded suburb of Zátiší. Nestled between stands of oak trees, this village of quiet meadows and holiday homes provided isolation without tremendous distance from the capital's center. The president's inconspicuous security detail would have no problem identifying those who belonged in the village and those who did not. Official communiqués and documents were hand delivered by trusted subordinates only. Generál Bláha had a military radio set installed to keep Beneš in communication with the armed forces leaders and critical ministers in the government. The location was something of a compromise. The president insisted on remaining in Praha but those entrusted with protecting Beneš would not allow him to stay in Hradčany. The castle would be one of the prime targets for German paratroops or bombers that were only thirty-five minutes away. There was great trust in the air force but it was felt the risk was far too great. So quiet and picturesque Zátiší, which was officially within the administrative authority of Praha, allowed Beneš to remain in the capital while any German aircraft flew unknowingly overhead.

The first floor lounge of the villa had been converted into the president's nerve center. Beneš had a hand in every audience that was held, every debate that broke out, and the contents of every courier bag delivered to the Zátiší compound. Nothing escaped the president's ravenous appetite for a *fuller picture*, as he called it. No one knew what infinite source of energy powered him through the late nights since hostilities had commenced. The outbreak of war was like a new life to

Beneš, who was certain the republic now was presented with circumstances that would assure the brave little nation would prevail intact. If he rested at all it was via quick naps at odd hours. The president's inner circle had decided the most infamous of these impromptu slumbers had occurred the night they arrived in Zátiší. While all in Europe were riveted to their radios listening to Hitler's Sportpalast speech, Beneš was unimpressed enough to happily collapse into the first comfy chair available and fall asleep.

Most of the day Beneš and his secretariat had been consumed with the first punches thrown between Czechoslovakia and Germany. The morning air strikes had gone better than anyone had dared hope for. Mother nature had been on their side that day. Beneš clamored for estimates of how many aircraft the Luftwaffe had lost but no confirmed numbers were available. Regardless, there was certainty that the number of planes destroyed or damaged had been significant. Almost as importantly, the strike was a direct blow to Hitler's sense of dominance. The Luftwaffe had received the lion's share of military appropriations since 1933 and was Germany's most terrifying weapon... a weapon the *upstart* Czechs had brutalized yesterday. Berlin had now learned quite harshly that they were in a fight after all.

Preliminary reports on the first ground skirmishes were arriving, as well. Once again, the results were encouraging. The army's mobile units were, so far, successful at bogging down the German advance within the first range of mountains along the main front to the southwest. The attacks to the north and south in Moravia were insufficient in strength to challenge the heaviest line of Czechoslovak fortresses. In the west, German forces were advancing into the larger buffer zone of Sudeten enclaves on the way to the main Czechoslovak defense line. In the northwest a different German army was attempting to break through the fortifications ringing the Erzegebirge Mountains.

The next point on the agenda was the disposition of the Polish and Hungarian armies opposite Slovakia. Neither neighbor was crossing their respective frontiers. Hitler's rush to commence the invasion, it was debated in the lounge, had caught Warsaw and Budapest off-guard. It was well known within Beneš' government that the invasion date was set for October first, not September twenty-sixth. But what would both of these regional adversaries do now?

Of the two, Poland was the greater worry. Colonel Jozef Beck, the Polish foreign minister, had been aggressive in demanding the ceding of Teschen to Poland. When it became obvious that Chamberlain's diplomatic initiative was failing, and the Teschen district would not be awarded as part of the spoils dealt to Germany, Beck threatened to throw in with Hitler's war ambitions. Not only were Polish tank and infantry divisions maneuvering close to the border, the Poles had mimicked the Sudeten Freikorps with their own sponsored ethnic irregulars in Teschen. At least the Polish version proved to be much less dangerous and easier to rout, Bláha had confirmed. According to Second Department agents working in Budapest, Beck also had proposed grand plans of advancing deep into Slovakia in conjunction with a similar Hungarian offensive to the south. Once both armies met, the strategy was to pivot west and advance together toward German forces.

None of those ambitions had been realized however. Forward observation units of the Third Army in Slovakia reported no change in the status of either Polish or Hungarian divisions along the border. Despite the Polish leadership openly ridiculing the prospect of a Soviet response to an attack by Warsaw on Czechoslovakia, Beneš was adamant that the Soviet threats toward Poland were causing some second thoughts in in the Polish capital.

"The arrival of three Soviet tank corps and sixty infantry divisions on their borders is causing Marshal Smigly-Rydz, Beck and the rest of that ruling junta in Warsaw some indigestion," Beneš argued. "Why else would they evacuate thousands of peasants from the frontiers with Belorussia and the Ukraine?"

"Perhaps the Soviet rout of the Japanese on Lake Khasan last month has lessened their contempt of the Red Army's chances," Bláha brought up the latest major skirmish between the Soviets and the Japanese in Asia.

"You would never know that from their diplomatic exchanges," Krofta had his hands full with the Poles. "Last week when Bonnet shepherded our last dialogue to Beck on the status of Teschen, that martinet demanded immediate transfer as the cost of support against Germany. If refused, Beck vowed Poland would immediately join Germany and Hungary in forcing their claims on us by the sword. He honestly believes the Russians are bluffing."

"Beck is over-confident, that is what I have learned from my personal dealings with him. While Beck may discount the Soviets, Smigly-Rydz controls the army. He is the reason why there is hesitation in attacking us, and the taking of precautions opposite Soviet troop deployments. As long as we hold our own in Bohemia and Moravia, no Polish division will cross our borders," Beneš directed a pencil at the map spread out on the table. "Now, what of the Hungarians?"

"Regent Horthy has been playing a dangerous game with Hitler for months now," Krofta checked his notes. "Our people in Budapest confirm that there is no desire for war to satisfy Hungarian territorial demands if those demands cannot be negotiated without cost. The message we are getting from our people down there is that Horthy and his ruling circle quite practically see Germany as imposing its diktat on Central Europe and it would be unwise to set a course against that strong wind. So Budapest has decided to play along just far enough with Berlin's ambitions to stay within Hitler's good graces, but not far enough to get into any serious trouble. Hungary too, will wait to see how well we can stymie the German invasion."

"On a positive note, I have received a communication from Generál Fajfr," Beneš had received the message via Moravec in Vyškov. "Preparation on the selected airfields in Slovakia has been progressing well. Within the next three days those bases will be ready to receive the first V-VS squadrons Moscow has pledged to our defense. Once those planes arrive, I think the Poles and Hungarians will both certainly remain on the sidelines."

32. RESISTANCE

An early model Junkers Ju 87 Stuka dives on a target

SEPTEMBER 30, 1938
KARLSBAD, SUDETENLAND

The Czechs had pulled out. The whole triangle between Asch, Eger and Karlsbad was completely open. There were a few Czechoslovak locals still on their farms huddled with their German wives hoping that family ties would protect them but the civil authorities had all fled. As for the Czechoslovak army units, they had cut off the pass between the Kaiserwald and Oberpfälzer Wald mountains to the southeast, and had pulled back just beyond the natural choke point to the northeast where the valley separating the Erzegebirge and Kaiserwald mountains narrowed. Their cannon situated on the heights had perfect firing angles that made it practically impossible to approach and clear out the tank traps that had been erected on the valley floor. Neither was any of the mobile artillery that equipped the German motorized division able to out-range the Czech guns. Before they could be set up, down poured a sheet of 150mm cannon shells. A further insult was the enemy's defence lines overlooking the valley were intact after days of aerial bomb attacks. The only positive Morgen could find in this mess was that they had good beer in Karlsbad, which the joyously liberated citizens were most happy to share with soldiers of the Reich.

With nowhere to go, Morgen's unit had dug themselves in next to a platoon of Panzerkampfwagen IV tanks attached to the lead infantry division. These new models were huge compared to the tiny Mark Is and Mark IIs that were as abundant as rats on a Hamburg dock. Good armor plating on the Mark IVs would let them get close to the Czech tanks but their short 75mm cannon was not much use against tanks. How was it that most of the equipment available to them was practically useless in this fight? If nothing changed the Czechs would make fools of them. There must be a way to land a good punch to the enemy's jaw and he was determined to find it. Morgen had talked up a lot of the locals looking for some advantage. Was there a little-known mountain pass where they could get in behind the Czechoslovak positions? None it seemed. Were there any unstable mountainsides where a couple of good cannon shots could bring down an avalanche on the enemy? Not that they knew of. Could they use the rail line out of Eger to flank the Czechs? No, that line led southeast through the mountains toward Tachau and the Czechs have defenders up there guarding the route, too. Tiring of getting nowhere, Morgen gave up with getting help from the useless Sudetens in favor of discussing options with the Stabsfeldwebel of the Panzer IV.

"Let us see," Girrbach the tanker unfolded a relief map of the area over the front armor plating. "The Eighth Army is attacking west on the other side of Erzegebirge Mountains. If they can break through, then the Czechs will be flanked and we can push forward to punch through their defensive line."

Morgen examined that mountain range on the map carefully. "That army will never get through those narrow mountain roads. Do you think the Czechs won't have ant-tank cannons up there? Once they kill a few of our thin-skinned tanks to block the path nothing will be able to pass. There has to be some low spot in this damn country fit for an attack."

"There is," Girrbach ran his finger east along the border. "A sizable portion of our manpower was assigned to a big push southeast of here below the Böhmerwald range. The elevation is not so steep there and the generals think there are better odds to force our way in, overrun Budweis, then move on Pilsen and Prag."

"So the rest of us are just a distraction?" Morgen wanted to see action not prance around like a goose in front of a hunter.

"Not if we can manage to get past these annoying Czech pillboxes," Girrbach traced their only route to Prag with his forefinger.

A happy young woman presented both men with a glass of beer from a cart pushed by an equally cheery uncle, probably the proprietor of a beer hall in the city.

"Danke," Girrbach and Morgen responded in concert.

"There are worse places to be sidelined," Morgen admitted after downing his glass. "But I don't like sitting around. They only way we are getting out of this spa town is if the Luftwaffe gets off its ass... either from ground attack aircraft taking down some of these Czechoslovak positions or Fallschirmjäger dropping in on top of their forts and neutralizing their guns."

Morgen's Rottenführer ran toward them. "Hauptscharführer! Hauptscharführer! Good news from the radio. No fog in Bavaria. The Luftwaffe is sending many more planes to bomb the Czech defense line."

"About damn time," Morgen hurled the beer glass at the tank turret, which shattered into dozens of pieces. "Let's hope they bring bigger bombs this time.

RAIL STATION, KOŠICE

On his own Bulloch could have napped during most of the long journey out from Prague, but with hundreds of fellow Americans in his charge there was no opportunity for dozing off. Bulloch had lost count of how many times he had traversed the length of the train end to end. A little bit of authority in the form of Bulloch's uniform went a long way in keeping everyone calm. Someone was watching over them and that made up for a lot of the discomfort on the tightly packed cars. From what he could tell it looked to Bulloch like the Czechoslovak authorities had taken rolling stock recently devoted to moving soldiers to the front and turned it over to Carr's needs. Every U.S. citizen had a seat but there was not much room to move around. No luxury cars for anyone to fight over and no food car either. The embassy staff had managed to give everyone snack bags with fruit, vegetables and bread rolls to tide them over.

The most direct route would have taken them from Prague to Brno, then Bratislava and finally onto a Hungarian train on the Budapest line. But the tracks between Brno and Bratislava skirted what used to be the Austrian border. There was a German army down there shadowboxing with some of the heaviest Czech fortresses. Those ground forces were not expected to break through but German aircraft could make a lot of trouble for a train so close to the front. The safest solution was head east from Brno to Košice. The main tracks, many of them dating back to the Austro-Hungarian Empire, didn't run directly east to Košice. That meant engineers were forced to use some of the more *picturesque* routes to link up with the main line to Košice. One of the benefits of a long sojourn through the center of Slovakia was sunrise falling on the Tatra Mountains. They were much smaller than the Alps but had some of the same majesty about them.

Never having been this far into Slovakia had built some anticipation in Bulloch since he always enjoyed seeing new places. As the train neared Košice, Bulloch stepped between cars so he could stretch his head into the slipstream and look forward beyond the car ahead. Leaving the last rural landscapes behind, Bulloch was surprised to discover Košice straddled both banks of a river – much like Prague. The station the train was approaching was a romantic affair with some gothic touches to its decorative spires. The structure probably dated to the last part of the previous century and was much smaller than its lofty architecture implied. It was only a first impression but Košice was looking much like a smaller and more provincial version of the larger Czechoslovak cities Bulloch was used to.

Bulloch saw a small detachment of Czech troops standing at attention up ahead on the platform. No regular passengers were on hand to get in the way. In front of the soldiers stood as an officer and a civilian. The latter was stocky fellow not more than five-foot-five that Bulloch guessed was Ferguson the local consul. The door to the car behind him slid open and shut. One of the conductors looked over Bulloch's shoulder and grunted approval.

"We will keep your passengers seated until the authorities say they are ready to receive them," the conductor advised.

"That will do nicely. Thank you for all of your help and your crew, as well," Bulloch straightened up and saluted the older man. Had to keep up appearances after all.

Donning his service cap, Bulloch grabbed the safety rail for support and swung himself down onto the platform as the train slowed to a stop. Behind him, kids stretched their heads out from open windows to watch Bulloch march up to the Czechoslovak captain.

"Captain Nathaniel Bulloch, U.S. Army, reporting with eight-hundred and ten American citizens. Thank you for your assistance," Bulloch saluted in a more jaunty fashion than usual.

"Kapitán Vaclav Janik, Československé armády, at your service," the Czech was no stranger to indulging a rakish appearance either.

"William Ferguson, U.S. Consul," the stocky man in the well-cut suit extended his hand.

"Good to meet you, sir," Bulloch discovered the consul possessed a surprisingly vigorous handshake. "Minister Carr says he hears good things about you."

"Can't imagine why," Ferguson huffed. "Compared to what is going on in the rest of this country, Košice has been a beacon of placid normalcy. No matter, glad you and your charges made it here safe and sound. No problems along the way I trust. This being the first trip out here and all."

"Outside of it being a long journey, no hitches whatsoever," Bulloch looked back along the length of the train.

"No signs of German aircraft near Brno?" Janik had worried about air attacks.

"Not that we could tell. And trust me, I was watching the skies the whole time after the sun came up," Bulloch had not relaxed until they were well northwest of Brno.

"Excellent, our pilots are keeping them busy. From the tactical reports that we are seeing the German attack has been stymied across the entire front. That is good news for getting the rest of your civilians out of the country." At least helping the Americans was something worthwhile for Janik to apply his men to while the rest of the army had its hands full.

"Are the Hungarians still playing along? The whole plan would be sunk if they got cold feet," Bulloch still found it difficult to trust them.

"The word I got by telephone from that side of the border shortly before your arrival said the Hungarians were happy as pie to be helping and were all set to receive our first shipment," Ferguson hoped that relaxed the youngster a bit.

"Then we should get started. I have a lot of tired people on that train," Bulloch knew the civilians would feel much better once they got a chance to move around some.

"Agreed. We are ready here. I have trucks and drivers parked in front of the station," Janik turned around to address his soldiers. "Let's get in position to help these people off the train and move them through the station in an orderly fashion."

"That's it then," Ferguson drew closer. "Captain Bulloch, before this Czech gentlemen offs and usurps yourself for his own devilish frivolity, will you be my guest for dinner tonight when our chores for the day are complete?"

"My pleasure, Mister Ferguson," Bulloch accepted the invitation. "Just leave some time for me to find a place to call home while I am here."

"No worries, lad... all taken care of. You will be billeted at the Hotel Rohlena for the duration of our little escapade," Ferguson said the name like it meant something in these parts.

"One of the best hotels in Košice, I might add," Janik talked the hotel up before heading off to positioning his men to help the Americans step down from the train cars.

SOUTHWEST OF KAADEN
THE SUDETENLAND

The agile Avia deftly responded to the command to break right and roll in pursuit of the next target. Bozik had barely spotted the two German ground attack biplanes below. The last couple of days these Henschels had been the first German aircraft to get off the ground. They were reported to be quite sturdy little planes that were very easy to operate in primitive conditions. Thank goodness their range seemed to be on the short side or these attack planes could be a real problem. For the moment their pilots were taking advantage of the closeness to the front to carry one large bomb to drop on the Czechoslovak pillboxes pinning down the Germans forward of Karlsbad. Bozik intended to stop this pair from getting close to their targets.

"Leader to letka... wingman and I are going down after two Henschels. If there are bad guys around, keep them off of us," Bozik began his dive. No more depending on Genrál Fog to keep the Germans on the ground for another day in a row. Some of the Messerschmitts would be held for airfield defense but Bulloch expected to see plenty of them out to cause trouble in the area. The Luftwaffe had changed tactics with a shift away from bombing civilian targets in favor of supporting their armies stalled below on the ground. The Messerschmitt pilots would be looking for targets as the German bombers made low-level runs on the Czech pillboxes. No guardians for these two ahead, however, as Bozik lined his guns up on the rear Henschel.

"I will take the wingman, you take the leader when he breaks," Bozik informed Nedoma.

Nedoma adjusted his altitude slightly and backed off Bozik's tail a bit to leave room to fire on the lead German without putting holes in the major's Avia. Bozik liked to dive at high speed and not fire his guns until the last possible second to drop enemy birds on the first burst. Playing with the mouse like a cat didn't interest Bozik. Too many Germans, too little time, he would always say. Nedoma knew Bozik's ways well now and counted down the seconds he estimated it would take before the major's finger depressed the trigger. Nedoma was off by a second. The rear Henschel exploded as the hail of 7.92mm shells pierced the fuel tank. The German in the lead broke left at the same moment Bozik zoomed through the fireball. Nedoma banked left to keep his fighter's nose ahead of the target's new direction. Still riding the extra speed from their dive from altitude, Nedoma waited three seconds then fired his guns. The burst raked the Henschel from its big radial engine back toward the cockpit. The engine was hit – sputtering oil and losing power. The pilot must have been hit too. The biplane gently veered right, losing altitude until the Henschel crashed into forested hillside where the centerline bomb exploded on impact.

"Two targets down," Bozik's voice crackled over Nedoma's headphones. "We are coming back up."

CNS HEADQUARTERS, NEW YORK

Harry Lasky had a vile habit of throwing just about anyone out of their desk chair if he wanted to take a closer look at what they were working on. Since Harry signed the checks there wasn't much stopping him. In his mind no one was as good as Harry Lasky in this business, and he felt it was his right to barge right on in to make whatever alterations to copy or paste-up that suited him. After a staffer reached somewhere between five and ten years on the job was when Harry backed off a bit. If he hadn't fired you, or you had not fled in self-preservation, Harry started to trust a person. Even with Des there were times Harry got that cross-eyed look in his eyes – like a cat wanting to pounce on an unsuspecting pigeon – when the copy from the foreign correspondents came in. But Harry gave Des some leeway. Not many editors could manage a worldwide operation like Des. It would cost Harry dearly if he ticked Des off and had to pay actual market rates to steal away a replacement. If Des said, *go away*, then Harry grudgingly marched off in a huff.

It was early, things were slow and Des needed to stretch his legs so he took fifteen minutes to indulge himself with a trip downstairs. The old guy with the cart on the corner had the warmest fresh pretzels around. Baked all personal-like by the same family. There was nothing like the taste of one of those babies on a cold day. On returning to the office Des found Harry hunkered down in Des' chair with his pudgy paws wrapped around some wire that hadn't been there when Des had left. Harry's concentration was so focused on the copy in his hands that he was oblivious to Des standing over his shoulder. Not even the aroma from the pretzel was making a dent. A copyboy walking by took one look at the situation brewing and hurried off to safety elsewhere.

"Hey boss. You realize the way you're smudging up that print means no one else will be able to read it soon," Des' tapped the soul of his shoe against the floor.

"Glad you're back, buddy boy. This is great stuff here," Lasky finally acknowledged him.

"Perhaps if I could have a look for myself," Des didn't think Harry would take the hint but it was worth a try.

"That Talmadge is turning into gold. Gold I tell you," Lasky carried on. "Do you know what I have here?"

"Not really, but I would like to find out," Des was starting to get annoyed.

"Somehow that dame got into see the top Czech general... the number one majordomo. Kretch, err Kretchie... whatever his name is," Lasky stumbled on the pronunciation.

"General Krejčí. Go easy on the *kr*, punch up the *EH*, leave the *j* alone, and add on *see* at the end: *krEHsee*," Des explained like a long-suffering teacher to the class simpleton.

"That's good! Make sure we add that for the readers," Lasky slapped the desktop.

"I'll take care of it as soon as I can get back in my chair," Des rubbed his chin while considering his options.

"Can you believe it? No one outside of Czechoslovakia knows where this guy is since the Germans started bombing and Talmadge ropes him for an interview," Lasky continued on unmindful of Des. "From what it says here, no other American outfit has got to him, just the Brits. This is huge and great personal interest. How the little guy is going to beat back the big bad Hun. Hey, we can use that line for a subhead. I still got it, I tell 'ya."

"Boss, did you get that phone message?" Des figured it was time for desperate measures.

"What message?" Lasky's eyes darted back and forth as he lowered the printout.

"The one from your wife's lawyer saying he was dropping by with some paperwork," Des lied.

"Not that scoundrel again! Tell him you haven't seen me in days," Lasky kicked the chair back and away to leap to his feet. "Tell him I headed to Idaho. Is that remote enough? No! Tell him I left for Wyoming to nurse my octogenarian aunt on her deathbed."

"You don't have an octogenarian aunt, Harry," Des refused to play along on account of spite.

"The shyster doesn't know that," Harry dropped Ros' story onto the desktop then turned to sprint down the hall toward the fire exit. "Buy me some time. That's an order!"

Des calmly rolled his chair back into position and sat himself down. After Harry hit the stairwell his hollering dropped off fairly quickly. Des' little ruse should buy the newsroom several hours of quiet. More if Harry called in to ask whether the lawyer had come and gone. A simple, *not yet*, in response might buy them freedom from Harry for the rest of the day. First things first, Des savored a bite from his still warm pretzel. Next he picked up Ros' story. The kid was a champ. Just like he had always said.

NEAR MARIENBERG, SACHSEN

The wood benches bolted onto the bed their Opel truck were pure torture when the truck was moving. At least there was the anticipation of arriving somewhere to take one's mind off your swiftly calcifying rump. But stuck on the side of the road there was no anticipation of freedom and your rump still calcified. By Endicott's wristwatch they had been stuck in this ditch for more than three hours now. As far ahead as the eye could see was one huge traffic jam of army transports. The German soldiers Endicott had been sharing the ride with were just average Joes trying to take everything in stride. Finally some officer came by and told everyone to jump down to stretch their legs. A couple of the youngsters spoke a little bit of English, which gave Endicott a chance to get them talking about their favorite sports, girlfriends and booze. When he got around to asking them what they thought about this big show none of them were getting to very fast, the bunch of them got all somber on him but they didn't clam up. There was general agreement that when your country told you to pick up a rifle and go, you went. They were hoping for the best, prayed their time away from home would be short, and when things got rough that their officers better not be assholes. Not a political peep from a one of them.

Milling around the back of the truck, Endicott made it up to them for the sensitive question by passing out free smokes. American cigarettes made up for a lot of things with these guys. Many of them had far off cousins in the States and had tons of questions of their own about whether Endicott had been to this city or that and what were those metropolises like. Endicott was slipping another cigarette out of the pack when his ears caught something on the wind. His body tensed and one of the German kids stared at him rather concerned. Shanghai in thirty-two had taught Endicott a number of things, like telling when the airplane you heard coming in your direction was a friendly or not. Friendlies just sort of cruised on by. They didn't drop altitude or change speed. But pilots about to drop a bomb on your head, or machine gun your friends into little bloody pieces, always fed gas to the engine. You could hear the change as those big nine-cylinder engines revved up. Then the pilot dropped the nose to pick up extra speed and the roar of that mechanical angel of death reverberated ever closer off the landscape around you.

Endicott looked up in the direction his ears told him danger was coming from. Holding a hand over his forehead to block the glare he saw sunlight reflect off of metal. There it was... a twin-engine job diving on the road.

"Down!" Endicott pushed the stunned kid next to him into the ditch.

Others had heard the approaching aircraft, as well. Cries of *Nach unten!* dominoed down the road. Someone with a machine gun started firing skyward. The effort was futile since the bombers were already on them. Endicott felt the blast of wind and exhaust forced back from the propellers as the aircraft screamed over their heads and the bombs dropped – exploding almost instantly. A second blast made up of heated air and shrapnel thundered over them leaving dust and debris settling all around.

Endicott rose to a crouch then leapt up to look around. "Holy shit." The trucks parked several lengths behind them and further back had taken the hit. Burning metal and rubber sent deep black smoke billowing into the air. Scorched and dismembered men – some alive, some dead – littered the roadside in bloody, tattered uniforms. The screams slowly registered to his shocked eardrums. Unlike the Japanese at Shanghai, the Czechs were not circling back to strafe the helpless... they were high-tailing it. The Japanese didn't have to worry much about Chinese fighters back then, he recalled.

The kid next to Endicott staggered up to his feet and took in the carnage. "Where are our planes!"

NEAR JONSDORF, SUDETENLAND

The narrow roads through the Erzegebirge passes were clogged with the hulks of burnt out armor and motorized transport. About the only option the Germans had to clear a path through the mess was by sending one or more of their heaviest tanks forward to push aside the detritus of battle by brute force while supported by as much covering fire from the ground and the air that could be directed into the area ahead. So far the strategy had not worked. In addition to the pillboxes with overlapping firing angles on the roads, plus artillery to the rear, the Czechs had plenty of camouflaged anti-tank guns and machine gun nests dug in.

The heaviest armor plate on a tank was usually in the front but many of the anti-tank crews had unobstructed targeting views to the sides of the German tanks where the armor was softer. It was at one of these emplacements that Srom pointed out something intriguing to Kopecky. The rear take-up wheel on the Panzer IV was vulnerable to damage. Even to concentrated fire from machine guns. Once the take-up wheel became inoperable, or was destroyed, the track bunched up and the tank ceased to move. It did not take long for the Czech gunners to kill such a lame animal. This was valuable information they would have to distribute to every frontline unit as soon as possible.

Srom had been anxious to get a first-hand taste of the developing battle in the mountains. The best enemy armor was committed to the front further south but that didn't stop the Germans from cramming thousands of infantrymen into the various mountain passes of the Erzegebirge. There was nowhere for these foot soldiers to go, however. Some of the best transport arteries in Germany fed Dresden and Chemnitz across the border – rail and roads well capable of depositing a dizzying number of reinforcements into the combat zone. Kopecky imagined the access roads leading back into Germany must be thoroughly constipated with military traffic. Which meant all was going to plan. The Czech lines were holding. How this was being accomplished was what Srom had been eager to observe and had led them to be the guests of this particular anti-tank platoon.

Kopecky peered through his field glasses at the Germans latest attempt to bust through the blocked road with two Panzer IVs was slowly making progress. The 37mm cannon beside him fired again. Kopecky had gotten so used to the boom and recoil that he no longer flinched. The standard issue helmets that Srom had insisted they wear while on the line were another matter. No matter how he adjusted the chin strap the steel pot always managed to slip a bit at the worst times. Kopecky wondered if he could get one of the things customized for his apparently oddly shaped head. The second German tank crew must have seen the muzzle blast from their cannon. Through the glasses Kopecky watched the turret rotate until the stubby 75mm cannon was trained on their position.

"Our position is being targeted by the rear tank," Kopecky sounded the alarm.

"Got it already," the closest gunner calmly adjusted his aim on the tank.

The three nearest gun crews concentrated their cannon fire at the base of the turret. Their aim was on the mark. One or more of the shells must have jammed the ring the turret traversed upon before the enemy gunner could finish lining up on them. When the 75mm cannon fired its high-explosive round in their direction it exploded harmlessly to the left. This German tank commander was persistent, however. The Mark IV soon began pivoting in place to bring the now stationary cannon on target.

"Bastard," the Czech gunner adjusted his aim down to a section of discolored armor plate on the side that might have been weakened by a previous shot. The 37mm cannon fired before the German tank could complete the pivot. The armor piercing round penetrating into the crew compartment, exploding the ammunition cache and launching the jammed turret skyward.

"Good shooting!" Kopecky watched the scorched enemy turret slam to earth with a thud. "That was close."

Whether the crew appreciated the compliment or not, Kopecky could not tell. They were wasting no time in quite professionally turning their attention to the other German Mark IV. Above the racket of the guns, Kopecky thought he noticed something else. It sounded like a siren of sorts. But he couldn't place the direction. Srom must have heard it too. Looking around, and then up, the colonel made out the silhouettes of three gull-winged aircraft diving almost vertically from above.

"Stukas!" Srom pulled Kopecky to the ground.

BISCHOFTEINITZ, ČESKÝ LES MOUNTAINS

The Tatra T57 that had been drummed up for their use was quite serviceable to their needs. Better still the coupe was in excellent operating condition. Burda's chum in Strašice had taken good care of them. Too bad such good fortune had not extended to their safe house. When the little Tatra drove up the dirt access road they discovered the property had fallen victim to a German bomber. The singed metal skeleton of a stricken Heinkel lay in a pile of burnt rubble that had once been a home. A long furrow extended from where the German pilot had force landed the aircraft on the ground to where the wreck collided with the structure. Furst thought it must have made for a handsome bonfire. Miraculously, the stone walled cellar had escaped destruction so some of what they needed could be salvaged. But now they were forced to secure a new dwelling. There were other Second Department properties available but none as secluded as this one where their comings and goings would not be obvious and still situated close to Plzen. Furst's solution was to suggest a cousin who was a bureaucrat in the city government who could pinpoint a few candidates without drawing attention.

The cousin came through with an excellent property, which Burda and Furst spent most of the next day setting up after they had saved what they could from the cellar of the destroyed safe house. As a bonus the cousin had tipped them off to an increase of activities by Sudeten saboteurs attempting to disrupt communications and transportation close to the main front. Bridges and telephone poles to Plzen were being blown up. It was likely that local Germans would be involved, if for no other reason than to help select the best targets. The agents knew some of the inhabitants in the affected area who might help pinpoint suspects participating in this mischief. Upon making contact with the monastery in Vyškov with the wireless set, Burda got approval of his intentions to investigate further. *Investigate* was a term that possessed a rather wide latitude of meaning within the Second Department. Like his partner, Burda was in a mood to make their presence felt with the Freikorps. Which was how they found themselves parked behind an abandoned barn southwest of Plzen near Bischofteinitz.

Mixed families were more common in the border areas than many Czechs and Germans cared to admit. Furst's father had been a government surveyor. When his gymnasium was not in session, Furst often joined his father and colleagues on a surveying expedition. During one such trip to the Bischofteinitz area the young Furst had been befriended by an older couple whose rural property adjoined parcels under survey. They were good people who had lost their only son in the war. He was Czech, and she was German. This was hard to discern though since the family name Zemke had been Germanized centuries ago, probably from the Czech Zemek. A very common condition throughout Bohemia and Moravia as Furst well knew. Mesdame Zemke liberally stole from her storehouse of preserved fruits for Furst to snack on that summer while Mister Zemke enjoyed including the youngster on the daily chores. Furst's father was happy the boy was occupied and not getting into trouble when not taking instruction in the finer points of survey work.

Furst always remembered the Zemkes fondly. Whenever he was in the vicinity during later years, Furst put aside time to bring them a dessert liqueur or sweet cake, and would spend the rest of the day chatting with them. The old man had died a few years previously but Mesdame Zemke was still spry enough to keep the property up on her own with some help from the neighboring families. Furst's visits were now somewhat rare but today he had a good excuse for making the journey out to see her with Burda in tow. Like her husband, the old woman had never much cared whether the capital was in Vienna or Praha. Their people had been on this land for so long it never mattered. All they cared about was whether the local folk were treated fairly. As the Czechoslovak administration had been very fair since 1920 – making great efforts to build up the country with electricity, waterworks, schools, agricultural assistance and transportation – the old couple saw no reason to pine for German in place of Czech governance.

Years before when she had asked him how he earned a living Furst had told the old lady that he worked in law enforcement. On that understanding was how he introduced Burda as his partner. After she had received the gift of the now rare fresh vegetables and they had all sat for a while to lament the terrible crisis that had brought the sounds of war to her doorstep, Furst asked if she had noticed anything unusual around the area in recent days. These rural people knew immediately when they saw something out of place. There was no need to stray into politics or nationalities, and Furst was determined to keep it that way for the woman's own protection. Mesdame Zemke told them there had been some young men unknown to her who had been coming and going down on the old Gericke land. None of the children had stayed in Bischofteinitz after the parents had died off and the old place had fallen into disrepair. One of the daughters had told Mesdame Zemke that the siblings could not agree on what to do with the property so it just sat wasting away. She had no idea what these young men were up to but they definitely had not lifted a finger to clean up anything, of that she was sure.

Furst and Burda had what they had come for: a lead. Saying their goodbyes the two intelligence officers drove away down toward what remained of the Gericke stead, which Furst remembered in better days. They checked the house first but found nothing suspicious amidst the litter left by curious children and small animals. The family had obviously removed most items of value, which left a collection of old, scarred furniture in the mostly empty shell of a home. Nothing was amiss in the sheds either. Furst explained that the property had once been two parcels owned by separate families. Gericke had bought the neighbor out at some point in the past. That neighboring house was long gone but there was still an old barn further down the road on the other side of the property.

The booms of artillery fire in the distance were becoming more frequent as Furst and Burda circled around the structure. Both instinctively reached to their gun holsters to switch off the safeties of their service pistols. The framing appeared stable despite the weathered and broken exterior. They heard no hint of anyone lurking inside so the Second Department men pushed their way past the old wood door stuck a quarter of the way open. Beams of sunlight pouring in through countless gaps in the roof and walls provided sufficient light to see everything inside during their search yet there was nothing suspicious to be seen in the empty barn. Then something about the floor caught Burda's eye. He kneeled down to sift though the dirt in a particular spot.

"This earth has been turned recently. Hard to notice in this light but it is darker here than elsewhere. Looser too. Watch how it falls from my hand in small grains instead of hard clumps," Burda demonstrated.

"And I believe I can tell you why that is," Furst rushed over. "Until you mentioned the dirt I had completely forgotten. There is a storage pit down there."

"How does one forget something like that?" Burda scolded his partner.

"I saw it once a long time ago. They used to keep stuff cool from the sun under a large wood door," Furst recalled while squatting down to brush away loose earth with his hands.

"Watch for splinters," Burda warned as he joined in the earth moving effort.

"Yes, mother," Furst uncovered the wood trap door under about four centimeters of dirt. "There she is."

Burda went over to small dividing wall and pulled off several of the thin vertical wood planks. They came off easily from the rusted nails holding them. Handing one to Furst, Burda used the other one to dredge earth away more quickly than by hand. The full trap door was exposed shortly. Furst retrieved two hand torches from the car and they hauled the door open to peer inside.

"Looks like we found something," Burda saw protective tarps pulled over something large and uneven.

"We should find out what," Furst proposed as he jumped down into the small storage pit. "Beer would be nice."

Burda followed and together they pulled back the tarp to find stacks of unmarked wood crates of recent vintage.

"Wrong dimensions for pilsner or lager," Burda observed. Looking about he spotted several crowbars available for use. "These will work. We best have a look inside."

Handing a crowbar to his partner, Burda pried open the chest-level crate nearest him as Furst chose one of a different size on top of another stack.

"Definitely not Pilsner," Burda reported after looking inside his crate.

"Demolition charges here: Westfalit AG," Furst held up a brick of high explosive.

"Amatol in this one... lots of it. All stamped Wehrmacht issue," Burda tossed a stick in Furst's direction.

"Hey! Be careful," Furst caught the Amatol in his free hand.

"Not to worry. Amatol is very stable," Burda started a quick inventory.

"So you say. I have a better idea for these things, however," Furst gently put the explosives down. Rummaging around with his torch he discovered a wood box smaller than the rest, which he hauled up into the light for Burda to examine.

"Timers. Good idea, my friend. I didn't see anything around this barn that could get hurt, did you?" Burda pulled out a mechanical timer to examine.

"Nothing at all. Such a shame the owners of these expensive explosives managed to get an unstable batch," Furst double-checked the pit to confirm there was nothing else they would mind blowing up.

"A terrible loss. Fine workmanship on this timer, however... it will do nicely." Putting the device aside for a moment, Burda grabbed one of the spools of wire from a stack nearby. The wire appeared dry enough so he took a switchblade knife from his jacket pocket and cut off two equal strands. Selecting a second Amatol charge from inside the crate, Burda precisely attached the wires to the explosive.

"Your affinity for things that explode has always unsettled me," Furst backed away a bit from his partner.

"Bombs or bullets matters little, they are deadly consorts all. You like bullets, I prefer bombs," Burda stretched out the wire.

"We are not talking blondes and brunettes here," Furst found the ladder needed to climb out of the pit.

"All are deadly, blondes and brunettes just take longer to kill their victims," Burda enjoyed the analogy before returning his attention to the timer.

"Five minutes should be sufficient," Burda set the device.

"Plenty of time," Furst tensed as Burda attached the wires to the timer, then relaxed somewhat when no explosion greeted the connection to the timer's electrical poles.

Making the final adjustments, Burda depressed the arming switch. The mechanical movement engaged and started emitting a slightly audible *click-click-click*. Satisfied, Burda gently placed the timer next to the Amatol charge resting on the top crate.

"Let's go!" Burda followed Furst up the ladder and out of the pit.

The Tatra was hurtling down the low hill away from the old barn as fast as Furst dared push the suspension over the uneven dirt road. Every rut launched the poor coupe high into the air before the chassis fell back hard on its coil springs.

"It won't do any good if you kill us before the blast has a chance to go off," Burda was bounced up in the air again.

"You are far too trusting of German watchmakers," Furst kept speeding. "Speaking of which, how much time is left?"

Burda glanced at his wristwatch and ran the arithmetic in his head. "Actually... none."

For confirmation, Burda turned to look over his shoulder at the barn fast receding in the rear window. The structure erupted into a smoky fireball that hurled pieces of wood from the frame and siding in all directions. One, a considerable charred chunk from what could have been a support beam smashed violently into the earth beside the road closer to Furst, who instinctively swerved hard to the right. Smaller pieces fell to earth less menacingly around the Tatra while others clattered directly on the metal rooftop. With Furst reducing speed to something more comfortable, Burda repositioned himself to face forward in his seat. "That is one barn that will never trouble us again."

HOTEL IMPERIAL, KARLSBAD – SUDETENLAND

From the farm to the swankiest hotel Karlsbad had to offer in only a couple of days... life was looking pretty good. The truth of the matter was the Germans did not have a clue what to do with her. The hoosegow seemed like rather harsh treatment to the boys in grey so they stuck Sylvie into the Hotel Imperial under the watchful eyes of the dashing young Wehrmacht officers billeted there. She had already been invited to share dinner by a half dozen of these sharply dressed philanderers but settled for drinks and singing bar tunes with a relatively harmless bunch from one of the infantry regiments. The sweethearts let on that the Czechs had the only route to the interior of the country blocked so they were stuck in town too. But the next morning things looked like they might be getting serious. A colonel had summoned her to join him for lunch. It could be all business, or he could be another jerk trying to get his hands inside her blouse.

The message had said meet the officer in the garden courtyard. Sylvie had strolled through there before and it was a nice spot. There were lots of flowers and trees around the tables, all of which had colorful umbrellas. The courtyard was big, however, and Sylvie couldn't tell which of the officers was the one she was looking for.

"Oberst Wartenberg?" Sylvie flagged down one of the waiters.

The man pointed out a particular table in the middle of the lower courtyard before scurrying off.

"Tausend Dank." Skipping down the stairs, Sylvie approached the table where the colonel was sipping tea and reading a Berlin newspaper.

"Any good news? I could use some," Sylvie attempted to get his attention.

"There is only good news in German newspapers these days," the colonel folded up the paper, set the publication next to his teacup and rose from his chair. "Please take a seat Miss Anderson."

"Thank you, Oberst Wartenberg... I will," Sylvie glided down onto one of the wicker chairs.

"No, thank you for joining me. The kitchen here is quite good. If you have a sweet tooth, may I suggest the pancakes with the brandied raisins? They are quite tasty," Wartenberg was already quite fond of that breakfast order.

"That does sound yummy. You wouldn't know there is a war on," Sylvie decided to edge closer to business.

"Appearances can be deceiving, I agree," Wartenberg was a charmer.

"Aren't you afraid the Czechs might drop a bomb or cannon shell on the hotel here? There are quite a lot of German officers all in one spot." The thought had occurred to Sylvie the night before at the bar.

"I suspect the Czechoslovaks harbor designs of retaking possession of Karlsbad and it would be a waste to blow up the finest lodgings in the region," Wartenberg doubted the codes of engagement would deteriorate so savagely for a while.

"Do you think they have a chance?" Sylvie broached the possibility as a waiter dropped off some tea and a basket of tasty looking Franzbrötchen rolls.

"Fräulein, would like to eat?" the waiter interrupted.

"I hear the pancakes with brandied raisins are wonderful. That's what I will have," Sylvie wanted to send him on his way before the colonel wiggled out of the question.

"Excellent," the waiter confirmed before heading to his next table.

"Now then, where were we," Sylvie flashed some charm of her own.

"I believe you were encouraging me to make a frank strategic assessment of my opponent," Wartenberg summarized the conversation.

"If you would be so kind," Sylvie encouraged him further.

"I think you will find that most of us will agree that the Czechoslovaks will be a formidable adversary. They are well equipped, well trained and possess great natural and man-made defenses. I expect they will hinder our progress and make our lives miserable for a time but the outcome is a forgone conclusion. They are not prepared to fight the new way of war that Germany is prosecuting upon Czechoslovakia," Wartenberg poked a roll in the basket with his knife.

"Please enlighten me further on this new way of war, oberst," Sylvie gently prodded.

"It will take some time but we will clear this bottleneck in the mountains. Once our divisions are sweeping into the lowlands the battle will unfold at lightning speed. It is our new philosophy of war, a more merciful type of warfare. It surprises your enemy, paralyzes him at one blow and shortens a war by weeks or maybe months. In the long run it saves untold casualties on both sides," Wartenberg sounded the true believer.

"But the Czechs weren't surprised. They were fully mobilized and waiting for you," Sylvie reminded him. "That's kind of why all of us are sitting here sipping tea with no where to go, isn't it?"

"An unfortunate digression. Once our divisions have broken through into the interior of the country we will show them some surprises that I promise you. The Czechs are trained in the French school. They lack the strategic mentality to keep up with us as we roll onto Prag and beyond," Wartenberg paused to sip some more tea.

"That sounds like a pretty amazing show you are planning to put on," Sylvie broke off a piece of sweet roll to munch on. "Mind if I tag along to watch?"

"That is the reason why I asked you to lunch, Miss Anderson. We can do nothing about your lost passport but we will be issuing you military transit papers that will permit you to tag along, as you so colorfully put it, and to report on our progress for the American newspapers. I am sure once our columns enter Prag the American embassy can assist you with a replacement passport," Wartenberg laid out a fairly attractive proposal.

"Okay, deal," Sylvie reached across the table to shake hands on it. "You get me to Prague and I'll tell the folks back home how you did it."

LA CHAMBRE DES DÉPUTÉS, PARIS

God bless those German bastards. If they had not deeply violated Czechoslovakian airspace this melodramatic French theatre orchestrated by Premier Daladier would never have taken place. The shoddy treatment and cold shoulder he had received at Bonnet's hand was still a fresh wound to Osušky. The only solace he had was that somewhere that pitiful little worm was hiding in a dark corner shitting his pants that Generál Gamelin was wasting no time moving French troops into a position to actually get in the war. As Osušky had wired Beneš, there was no turning back for the French. Gamelin would attack in his own steady, methodical fashion, of course... but he would attack nonetheless in a week to two weeks. The Czech liaison officers attached to Gamelin's staff were quite certain of the timing and the inevitability of the French offensive in the Saar. Osušky made a point of inviting these military men to his dinner table often to discuss such matters. From what they conveyed to Osušky, Bonnet could do nothing to impede the offensive unless the Germans withdrew from Czechoslovakia before Gamelin ordered his army over the border. That was an unlikely scenario, however. Regardless, the reality still nagged at Osušky that had Hitler shown restraint and had he kept his Luftwaffe and Wehrmacht home in Germany, there would be no Mobilisation Générale sending millions of Frenchmen to their eastern frontier. Neither would Osušky be standing as a now *honored* guest in the gallery of this august chamber witnessing Daladier speaking in somber tones championing French honor and duty before the national assembly of the Chamber of Deputies and the Senate.

> *Forfeiting our honor would purchase nothing more than a precious peace liable to rescission, and when tomorrow we should have to fight after losing the respect of our allies and the other nations, we should no longer be anything more than a wretched people doomed to defeat and bondage.*

There were those in this hall that Osušky had canvassed individually, men whose minds he knew well, who were in favor of a vigorous throttling of Hitler. Yet Osušky had thought they were in the minority. His last assessment forwarded to Krofta the previous night was there was general political support for a limited ground campaign in the Saar but little stomach to go for the throat. But the words he heard shared between these legislators around him betrayed a restlessness to assert the might of France. That was the energy Osušky sensed igniting in the hall. Osušky had underestimated the mood of this Parliament and perhaps Daladier had miscalculated as well. The chamber was cold and silent as a tomb as the premier went on to proudly recite his many diplomatic efforts to reach peace with Hitler. Daladier was nothing if not an adroit politician. Osušky studied the premier's face carefully, and believed he saw the moment when the premier dismissed his prepared text entirely: a pause followed by a flash of irritation. Very subtle but Osušky had caught the expression nonetheless. When the Daladier continued, the words came from a different, truer place.

There comes a moment when we must acknowledge that all sense of morality as well as all glimmering of reason has died within the aggressors. Our duty is to make an end of aggressive and violent undertakings; if not by means of peaceful settlement, then this we shall strive our utmost to achieve by the wielding of our strength. Czechoslovakia has been the object of the most brutal aggression. Her frontiers have been violated. Her cities are being bombed. Her army is heroically resisting the invader. The nations who have guaranteed her independence are bound to intervene in her defense.

The legislators rose up as one in enthusiastic applause, cutting Daladier off. Many of the nearby deputies turned around and cheered Osušky. A French reporter standing beside him unexpectedly reached over and vigorously shook Osušky's hand in support. Such an outpouring of encouragement from these Frenchmen, nearly brought Osušky to tears. This was the France that Czechoslovaks had come to love so many years before. Osušky acknowledged the attention as modestly as he could manage with a slight bow, followed by a slow sweep of his arm. To do more would be ill mannered. When the applause had died down sufficiently for him to speak again, Daladier drew on the excess energy in the hall for inspiration to pick up where he left off with verve.

The responsibility for the blood that is being shed falls entirely upon the Hitler Government. He chose war. Our ambassador in Berlin has several times reminded Herr Hitler that if a German aggression were to take place against the Czechoslovak Republic we should fulfill our pledges. France is not a power that can disown, or dream of disowning, her signature. And indeed, gentlemen, it is not only the honor of our country: it is also the protection of its vital interests that is at stake. For a France which should allow this aggression to be carried out would very soon find itself a scorned, an isolated, a discredited France, without allies and without support, and doubtless, would soon herself be exposed to a formidable attack.

And then what of our Alsace, our Lorraine? What envious eyes are even now being cast across our eastern frontier? Herr Hitler has offered his guarantee that he has no designs on French soil. Did he not offer similar guarantees to Austria in 1935? Did not the German army enter Vienna on March 11, 1938? Was Chancellor Schuschnigg not imprisoned for daring to defend his country's independence? Can anyone today say what is his real fate? What becomes of France if we allow the same to happen to President Beneš in Prague? Who would be next? There would come a day when the Hitler Government, more powerful through their conquests, gorged with the plunder of Europe, the masters of vast natural wealth, would soon turn against France with all their forces. In rising against the most frightful of tyrannies, in honoring our word, we fight to defend our soil, our homes, our liberties.

The chamber erupted once more in affirmation of this central truth. They cheered like starving men receiving their first good meal after many long days. Osušky had not thought Daladier in possession of such eloquence, expedient as this performance may be. Regardless, the premier seemed a man released from his bonds after a lengthy incarceration. Osušky felt the wave of emotion in the chamber was so strong it was now even possible that Daladier could ask the assembly for a formal declaration of war.

Gentlemen, while we are in session, Frenchmen are rejoining their regiments. If they have answered our call, as they have done, without a moment's hesitation, without a murmur, without flinching, that is because they feel the very existence of France is at stake. Gentlemen, in these hours when the fate of Europe is in the balance, France is speaking to us through the voice of her sons. I fought before like most of you. I can remember. Let us recapture, as they have done, that spirit which fired all the heroes of our history. France rises with such impetuous impulses only when she feels in her heart that she is fighting for her life and for her independence.

We are waging war because it has been thrust on us. The cause of France is identical with that of Righteousness. It is the cause of all peaceful and free nations. To our young soldiers, who now go forth to perform the sacred task, which we ourselves performed before them, they can have full confidence in their chiefs who are worthy to lead France to victory. To the Men and Women of France. Every one of us is at his post, on the soil of France, on that land of liberty where respect of human dignity finds one of its last refuges. I know you will all cooperate, with a profound feeling of union and brotherhood, for the salvation of the country. We will be victorious. Vive la France!

In the end, Daladier had chosen not to ask for the war declaration. There was no need. So rousing was the conclusion of the premier's address, that by Osušky's pocket watch, the membership of both legislative houses stood and applauded for close to eight minutes. More importantly, the French parliamentarians promptly called themselves to order and unanimously voted eighty billion francs in war credits. To hear the words would have been agreeable to his ears but deeds spoke as loudly. Osušky thought the commitment of eighty billion francs to this war was a very clear declaration indeed.

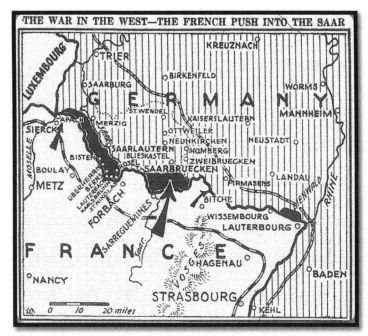

A newspaper map of the French assault on the Saar

OCTOBER 6, 1938
SPECIAL TO CONSOLIDATED NEWS
BY CLARENCE MOREL

BOULAY, FRANCE – The huge cannons of the Maginot Line here in Alsace-Lorraine are sending a non-stop hail of artillery shells hurtling over the Saar River into Germany. The French are also sending a message to Chancellor Hitler in Berlin: Your assault on Czechoslovakia will not go unanswered.

This normally quiet region between the Moselle and Saar estuaries in eastern France erupted two days ago when advance elements of three French armies poured across the border into the Saarland district of Germany. This area of Europe has passed between the two empires many times in the last two hundred years and is a reason why you can still find cities in Germany like Saarlautern, named after French King Louis XIV and where Napoleon's Marshal Ney was born. This hilly region possesses plenty of fine forestland perfect for shielding an invading force. French troops wasted no time in swiftly occupying the Warndt Forest opposite Saarbrücken, the Carlsbrunn Forest between Saarlautern and Saarbrücken, as well as taking the Bienwold Forest north of Lauterbourg and further to the east.

Directly in front of me is the imposing Ouvrage Hackenberg, one of the huge artillery fortresses making up the Maginot Line – its cannoneers participating in an intense duel with their German counterparts across the Saar. About twelve miles separates the permanent fortifications of France's Maginot Line from Germany's Westwall, the latter popularized as the Siegfried Line in British and French newspapers. Both lines are intended to protect these resource-rich lands from invasion but that is where the similarity ends. Work on the French forts was begun in 1930 and is largely complete. Germany, however, only began construction on its line in 1936. Upset at the slow progress since then, early this year Herr Hitler yanked responsibility away from his army's engineers and gave the job to Fritz Todt, the Nazi's premier engineer. Representatives of the French army tell us that despite the fever pitch in construction across the river since May, where Herr Hitler demanded eleven thousand pillboxes be finished by this fall, less than a thousand have been completed.

Another difference, the French tell us, is that while each Maginot Line fort is purpose-built below ground level to match the contours of the land as a means of extra protection from heavy guns, the German bunkers are mass-produced like Ford Model-Ts. To save time and money, most of the German fortifications have been erected above ground making them vulnerable to fire from the large French howitzers. Whatever the disadvantages Der Westwall possesses, it has not prevented their gunners from a spirited exchange of fire. What we have not seen so far are the German soldiers themselves. A few prisoners have been taken by the French yet it appears the German troops are happy to stay hunkered down in their pillboxes to let the thousands of acres of land mines, barbed wire, and tank traps they have sown along the entire border from the Netherlands to Switzerland to speak for them. French infantrymen tell of encountering a new form of land mine designed to destroy the soft underbelly of their supporting tanks from below. These defensive belts have evinced much respect from the French conscripts. So much time was being devoted to clearing these mine fields by conventional methods that the French high command ordered herds of pigs be driven into harms way to detonate the explosives in one fell swoop.

The consensus of military strategists in Paris and London suggests that most of Hitler's available men and material have been committed to the battle for Czechoslovakia, which would leave precious few to defend the Rhine and Ruhr industrial zones from French attack. The German gamble being the completion of a swift victory over the Czechoslovaks before France's fifty-six divisions in Alsace-Lorraine would be in a position to attack. Unfortunately for the German timetable the plucky Czechs have made a fight of it. German tank divisions lie stalled on mountainous terrain where Czechoslovakia's own border fortresses – said to have been modeled on, and improved upon, the French designs for the Maginot Line – have denied the attacker for nine days. Reports reaching France are that Czechoslovak armored units have fought many pitched battles with their

German adversaries in the narrow passes and valleys running through the mountains between the two countries where the heavier and better armed Czech tanks have inflicted a heavy cost on the numerically superior Wehrmacht divisions. Likewise, in the air above Bohemia, the Czech air force has made life miserable for Hermann Göring's vaunted Luftwaffe. German bombers have so far been denied the freedom to level Czech cities the way Guernica was assaulted from the skies last year in Spain.

Hitler's armies fighting in the north, south and west of Bohemia may have achieved a modest toehold on Czech soil but they accomplished this at a terrible price. With ample stocks of ammunition and supplies available, there is no evidence that the Czech lines are in any danger of buckling. For the outnumbered German soldiers here along the Saar, the longer the Czechoslovaks resist, the greater prospect that they will face the coming French offensive alone.

Much has been written in recent days questioning the veracity of France's will to fight. The French themselves readily admit that they feared the prospect of facing Hitler's recently re-armed military alone following a swift Czech defeat. For this very reason Paris has sought guarantees of British military support against Germany. But with the Czechoslovaks holding their own against everything Berlin can throw at them, the French are now more sanguine about their prospects here in the Saar. In addition to the thousands of regular army personnel stationed along the border region, the French general mobilization has deposited hundreds of thousands of citizen soldiers into additional regiments during the last week. The question is how long French Chief of Staff General Gamelin will wait before ordering his divisions to move against Saarbrücken, which lies outside the protection of the Westwall. The Germans also appear to be expecting a larger push from the French – carrying out evacuations of Saarbrücken, Trier, Aachen, and Karlsruhe.

While German military strategists have advocated a Lightning War, their French counterparts put their faith in what is called the Methodical Battle. Heavy artillery barrages clear a hole in the enemy lines by eliminating pillboxes and other fixed opposition, after which the French infantry, supported by tanks, sweep in to hold the territory just cleared. The big French guns move forward, and the process repeats itself. The strategy is vulnerable to attack from the air, however. The French pilots admit they have nothing yet to match the modern Messerschmitts recently blooded in Spanish skies and equipping many German squadrons. But no one in the Saar has yet to see evidence of Germany's feared aerial weapon, the Luftwaffe. For now, the men of the Armée de l'Air control the skies in these parts.

If there is any grumbling so far amongst the French officer corps, it is oft-heard refrain: *Where are the British?* The Entente Cordiale that has served to bond the interests of both countries together since 1904 holds no provision, or obligation, for Paris or London to go to war to protect the other. The British are quick to point out that their declaration of war against Germany in 1914 came as a direct result of treaty obligations to Belgium, whose border Germany violated. France and Germany have been at war since September 29th, yet Prime Minister Chamberlain in London has not moved for a declaration of war to support Britain's Continental partner. The Royal Navy has taken up blockade stations in the North Sea, but no British troops are being ferried to the Continent. The French are asking why?

With the Germans unable to rout the Czechoslovaks, and the French facing light resistance in the Saar, perhaps the calculation has been made in London that British involvement is not required. From this correspondent's experience here on the front lines, that argument is not going over very well with the French.

ABOVE THE WESTWALL
BEHIND SAARBRÜCKEN

What the two Armée de l'Air pilots were undertaking was not authorized. It was well known that light and heavy ack-ack belts were a design feature of the Westwall. Therefore, headquarters had forbidden low-level sweeps over the length of the German fortifications since they had far too few modern aircraft in front-line squadrons to risk on such exploits. The first of the sleek Curtiss monoplanes ordered in the United States had yet to arrive. Neither had the new Morane Saulniers made it out of French factories. Touchon thought it a crime that when the government nationalized aircraft manufacturing production output actually declined. The air force was in such a mess Touchon's escadrille was still flying Dewoitine D.510s. In 1934 this bird was hailed as radical. Four years later their fixed-gear monoplane was slower than the biplane Avias the Czechs flew. Neither could the D.510 match the Avia's rate of climb advantage. What a difference four years made. His pilots would have to pull out every trick they knew when the Messerschmitts finally showed up.

The truth was Touchon was bored. Except for four Heinkel biplane fighters that had nosed around on the wrong side of Saarlautern during their first day of combat operations, and had promptly been shot down by his escadrille, the Luftwaffe had not made a return visit on Touchon's watch. So the pilot was amiable when de Gaulle approached him the night before. The colonel had taught Touchon's younger brother, Emile, at Saint-Cyr. When they got together the kid would blather on for hours about how to employ tanks like fighter aircraft. Touchon thought it would have been much more direct for him to have joined the Armée de l'Air if he felt that way – the army was notoriously obsessed with its plodding infantry – but the young apostle would have none of this advice and ended up in the armored cavalry. Touchon had crossed paths with de Gaulle before in Metz during the last year. That's why the escadrille leader was not surprised when de Gaulle materialized at his cafe table and pulled up a chair. Simply put, the tanker desired a tree-level reconnaissance of the German fortifications. Everyone knew many sections were incomplete, but de Gaulle wanted to know which were the most incomplete sections in the zone behind Saarbrücken. The aerial photographs available were shot from such altitude that they were not detailed enough, and ground level observations delivered poor results, as well.

As fighter pilots were forgiven a certain degree of larceny, unlike most branches of the military, Touchon had accepted de Gaulle's proposal. As his wingman was as bored as Touchon that was how both of them found themselves racing at full throttle barely forty meters above the German line at dawn. The Westwall wasn't hard to find either. The earth was so scarred from recent construction that grass and foliage had not yet grown back. Then there was the odd expression of subterfuge the German engineers had employed. They had built complete dummy villages at the exact same distance from each other all along the line. Even the barns where of the same exact pattern design. Sometimes, if the light was falling right, you could pick out gun turrets intended to be hidden amongst the phony village buildings. Other portions of the Westwall had fallen victim to French cannons that had demolished swaths of pillboxes, gun emplacements and their unconvincing costumes. Then there were dugouts that were not camouflaged at all. At one section Touchon roared over a crew painting camouflage patterns over a large artillery piece. The appearance of the French fighters so stunned the men they stood motionless like statues gaping up at the aircraft. It wasn't until after the pilots had passed them that a few of the Germans waved while the rest of their compatriots dove for cover in nearby structures. Only twice did lone machine gunners fire their guns skyward in anger and no Luftwaffe planes rose to molest them.

Touchon had seen enough... it was time to break back to the French lines. He instructed his wingman to follow him home to their field. Touchon wanted to draw an illustration while his memory was still fresh. Intelligence suggested that the Westwall was densest in the vicinity of Saarbrücken. But from what Touchon has seen with his own eyes the frequency of pillboxes and gun works was light. The Westwall was an incomplete jumble and that is what he would convey to de Gaulle when the two met shortly. Touchon would give the colonel the exact locations of the pillboxes and heavy guns that could cause trouble, plus the two sections of the line that had already been leveled by French artillery during the last forty-eight hours – ruptures large enough to drive a brigade through. Later Touchon would take the full escadrille up to see how de Gaulle used the information provided. Whatever was going to happen was planned for today. De Gaulle was clear about that much. All he required was a last minute picture of the battlefield. And since the request had come to Touchon directly, and not through channels, de Gaulle must have some larceny of his own planned.

WEST BANK OF THE NEISSE
SOUTH OF GÖRLITZ

The Germans were trying something different. Their Eighth Army had been pushing hard to cross through the Erzegebirge, but had been stopped dead in their tracks. For days the Czech fighters and bombers had been wreaking havoc on the troop convoys and supply lines leading up to the mountain passes. Endicott doubted he would ever forget the daily blood and carnage that resulted from these aerial raids. How he had escaped unscathed through it all Endicott could only attribute to his lucky streak holding. Some days the German fighters were in the neighborhood and on other days they were nowhere to be seen. An infantry major finally explained what was going on. The Czech pilots were playing cat-and-mouse with the Luftwaffe. They knew the first priority of the German fighter planes was to guard the main cities and industrial centers from attack. So the Czechs raided the operational Luftwaffe airfields instead. When the Messerschmitts shifted their patrols to cover the airfields, the Czechs made life miserable for the ground troops. It was a game, and so far the mouse was staying one step ahead of the cat.

Suddenly one evening the word came down that most of the Wehrmacht units stuck in neutral below the Erzegebirge were moving out. Under cover of darkness the armor and trucks moved east. The going was pretty good too. One of the young kids with a history obsession explained to Endicott how they were on the old trade route that ran through Silesia to Breslau. That accounted for the decent roads. After crossing the Elbe near Dresden the column proceeded east until they reached the Neisse River not far from Görlitz. Endicott recalled that this was the city the actor Emil Jannings had been born in. Sounded like a nice place from what he remembered reading – somewhere he could get a bath, shave, and a hot meal. As much as he desperately needed all of those attributes of civilization, Endicott figured he wouldn't be let back on the caravan again if he slipped away now. And since everyone on the back of the truck smelled pretty bad, Endicott could bear it if they could.

From their sheltered resting place in the lightly wooded countryside, Endicott began to understand why the Germans had been so intent to push through the Erzegebirge Mountains. The multiple passes available on that route butted right up against the efficient German transportation network. But greener pastures were greener pastures and the bigwigs in Berlin obviously thought they had a better shot at breaking into Bohemia from over here. Then the infantry major dropped another bombshell. They had to get some results and quick like. The French had crossed the border in the west. Just a few villages and woodlands occupied so far but no one had expected the French to try anything aggressive. Endicott sure as hell didn't. Daladier had spent all summer long following in Chamberlain's shadow looking for a way to sell Beneš down the river... and now the French premier was punching with a forward jab? The stout

Czechoslovak defense was upsetting the apple cart. If the Germans couldn't turn the tables against the Czechs, and soon, then the usually cautious French might grow bold enough to move deep into the Rhineland. From what the major told him the high command had not left many divisions on that side of the country as a deterrent. They had only retaken the Rhineland two years before and there was real worry they might lose the region again soon.

That's when Endicott got it in his head that the story he was chasing had already flown. Back in Berlin, riding along with the Wehrmacht on their way to fame and glory had seemed like a grand idea. But poor little Czechoslovakia was stiffing Uncle Adolph going on two weeks. Maybe it was time for Endicott to call it a wash and get his paws on a telephone to tell the story he had witnessed on the road to the Erzegebirge passes. There was a ton of great copy there.

Before Endicott could ruminate further on his options, a youngish leutnant he had seen around walked up and planted himself right in front of the reporter. "Herr Endicott. I regret to inform you that the Propaganda Ministry has rescinded permission for foreign correspondents to accompany front-line troops of the Heer. Please collect your belongings. We have transport waiting to take you to a safe area."

"Well how do you like that?" Endicott's decision had just been made for him.

11 MORPETH MANSIONS, LONDON

Masaryk's hand-off of his hat and coat to the house servant was less than polite. By the time it occurred to him that his manners were in doubt, Masaryk was already half way down the hall to the study. The hired help was no doubt used to such lack of regard, but he made a mental note to make amends to the person at a later date. Masaryk was losing patience for everything British and was fast losing the control to contain his dissatisfaction. Eight days had passed since he had last visited this apartment, and despite Mister Churchill's estimations, that foul charlatan Chamberlain had not moved for a declaration of war in Parliament. Neither had the coward been sacked.

"You summoned me, sir?" Masaryk flew into Churchill's study.

"Indeed I did. Please take a seat and join me," Churchill hoped genial hospitality would help cool down the overheated Czech ambassador.

"I would rather stand," Masaryk drifted over to a nearby window.

Churchill rose from his chair to approach the envoy. "Your frustration is understandable," Events have not gone as I had anticipated."

"Minister Churchill," Masaryk cut him off. "My country is fighting for its life."

"Fighting rather well from all accounts, I might add," Churchill was not going to tolerate a tale of woe.

"That is no excuse for your government's procrastination. Your own ally France is marching into the Saar at this very moment without the benefit of British succor. By what grace does Chamberlain still hold the premiership?" Masaryk saw no reason to hold back.

"Just the matter I called you here to discuss," Churchill had sympathy for the Czechoslovak's distemper but there were limits. "Given your stout defence, and the French advance, the prime minister sees no pressing need for Britain to join the fray, and has advised a wait-and-see policy."

"How convenient," Masaryk turned his back on the parliamentarian.

"And how dishonorable! This is not how a great empire comports itself. And that is why Chamberlain's opposition in Parliament has grown sufficiently to force his hand. We now have thirty solid conservatives who are ready to push for a change in leadership. Their number will be added to Labour and Liberal party members who have shown vociferous support for taking concrete action to aid Czechoslovakia and France. Great Britain will wait on the sidelines no longer, sir" Churchill vowed.

The house servant appeared at the doorway to the study escorting a thinnish man who waited patiently behind. "Mister Alec Douglas-Home, parliamentary private secretary, to see you sir."

"Come in Mister Douglas-Home," Churchill left the Czech ambassador to greet the new arrival.

"Mister Churchill, Ambassador Masaryk," Douglas-Home nodded to both men in succession as he stepped into the room. "I have a message from the prime minister."

Douglas-Home paused, waiting for Masaryk to politely leave on his own volition. But the ambassador doggedly held his position, unwilling to yield to anyone connected with Chamberlain.

"Do not wait on Mister Masaryk's account. You may deliver your message freely, Mister Douglas-Home," Churchill saw little reason to further alienate the Czech.

"Very well," Douglas-Home bowed to expediency. "The prime minister assumes you are already aware that the honorable Duff Cooper has resigned as first lord of the admiralty."

"Quite right, I have been so informed," Churchill could not believe the fortuitous timing of Douglas-Home's arrival.

"In that case, Mister Chamberlain requests an immediate audience to discuss your joining his war cabinet as first lord of the admiralty."

OVER AUSSIG, SUDETENLAND

He had just lost Nedoma. Bozik had not seen the Messerschmitt diving on his tail from above. Nedoma did, however, and warned Bozik to break left. The kid kicked his Avia into a climb and got a burst into the oncoming 109, whose pilot chose to roll away from the incoming shells rather than diving away to certain safety at high speed. That should have been warning enough for Bozik's wingman but Nedoma chose instead to chase after the adversary audacious enough to imperil his squadron leader. Bozik had pounded into his men for months: *Do not pursue Messerschmitts!* You couldn't catch them and would only open yourself up to getting your tail shot off by a wingman coming up fast behind. But his pilots had acquired an edge that comes with winning. Nonetheless Nedoma was one of the squadron's most accurate shots, and Bozik could see where hubris would lead him to think he could down the Messerschmitt with another good burst before he became a target himself.

Bozik cursed as he saw the German Nedoma was chasing was a lure for another schwarm entering the dogfight. The diving Messerschmitts made quick work of Bozik's wingman but there was no time to mourn or confirm whether Nedoma had bailed out of his burning Avia. They were outnumbered and dancing like angry wasps to get out of this mess.

Bozik's men had been good, and they had been lucky, but their luck was starting to run short. Their Luftwaffe adversaries were finally getting smart. For a week they had behaved as Bozik had suspected by mixing it up in aerial dogfights despite their Messerschmitt's inferior maneuverability. The unpredictability of the Czechoslovak pilots in their maneuvering had thoroughly confused the German pilots and caused them to lose eleven of their own. But they were no longer playing Bozik's game. Rarely would a one-o-nine attempt to turn with his Avias anymore. Now they dove from above, concentrated on specific targets, and continued diving away while several more schwarms followed behind. When they did not follow this pattern, it was a trap like the one that had just caught Nedoma. While he had not lost a pilot until now, Bozik's fighters were getting shot up. The ground crews were keeping up, but attrition would soon become a problem. There was a finite supply of replacement B-534s available and other squadrons were not as successful as Bozik's. Soon they would be running short of serviceable aircraft to send up in the air.

Bozik looked up and caught sight of a Messerschmitt driver adjusting his dive to line his guns up on Cervena. Doing so would also expose the belly of the German fighter if Bozik timed things correctly. Bozik was not going to lose another compatriot today. Rolling right, he opened the throttle all of the way, pulled the nose up and adjusted his angle of attack. The German could not see him as Bozik made the maneuver. Depressing the trigger, the Avia's four 7.92mm guns raked the underside of the Messerschmitt from the nose to the wing root. The burst must have hit the radiator or the oil cooler. Bozik noticed vapor and oil streaming into the air from the cowling. The German pilot realized something was amiss and broke off his pursuit of Cervena. Not sticking around to become a target himself Bozik kicked his Avia in a different direction and went looking for another of his cubs to protect.

SAARBRÜCKEN, SAARLAND – DEUTCHLAND

The gaggle of swine squealed in alarm as they were rushed between the idling tanks. His men had requisitioned both the pigs and the horses to herd them with from an unlucky German farmer. The man was presented a bond for the proper value in francs, of course. The farmer was not pleased but this was war. Their orders were to test the defenses guarding Saarbrücken. While concentrated artillery fire during the last forty-eight hours had made good work of the belts of dragons teeth and other tank obstacles hastily laid by the Germans east of the Saar River, the buried anti-tank and anti-personnel mines were another matter. De Gaulle needed to be sure these too had been taken care of. Blanket cannon fire had set off some of these nasty explosives in open fields where they had been sown but many more had remained hidden. Flushing herds of pigs through suspected mine fields proved very effective, particularly in the woods where incoming shells often exploded in the tree canopy instead of the ground. This was the case for the pigs driven by de Gaulle's men through a woodlands area that had been targeted earlier by the Maginot cannons. Surprisingly, no explosions were heard. As the local population of swine suffered no further losses, neither would de Gaulle's three régiments. It was a fine start to the day.

The excellent road leading out of the woods made for a swift approach on Saarbrücken west of the Saar River by the 3éme Brigade de Chars. Gazing at the far hill line from his turret seat de Gaulle's saw French cannon shells dropping on the bunker and cannon emplacements of the Westwall fortifications behind Saarbrücken without pause. What the artillery commander did not know was that some of the specific grid coordinates he was targeting were adjacent to a new breach in the Westwall line that pilot Touchon had identified. De Gaulle wanted that rupture broadened significantly before the sun began its descent. Touchon's dawn sortie had proven invaluable indeed.

Colonel de Gaulle's own 507éme Régiment de Chars de Combat was in the lead. Equipped with the most modern medium tank in service within the Armée de terre, the Renault D2, should they meet enemy resistance it was only fitting that the heavier D2 run ahead of the much lighter R-35s filling out the rest of the brigade's complement. Under Général Delestraint's command the brigade was a unique force chosen to test out new philosophies of motorized warfare. He shared with de Gaulle a similar vision of strong all-tank units breaking through the enemy's lines and exploiting the advantage that followed. What they had come to call the Mass Maneuver. During field trials the year before, instead of getting a fair opportunity to prove what their modern tactics could achieve, the general staff hamstrung the rules so that the results delivered by Delestraint's and de Gaulle's handpicked crews were *inconclusive*. Deprived of a just opportunity at the trials, de Gaulle became convinced the only way to prove their point was on the battlefield where the vagaries of war might finally provide them the license to operate without shackles. Now they had a war, and when the order came down to test the German defenses around Saarbrücken, Delestraint had not hesitated to endorse de Gaulle's aggressive interpretation of those orders.

Entering the city limits de Gaulle's columns met no opposition. He knew this industrial metropolis well from a decade before during the French occupation. Saarbrücken was a great hub of coal, steel and iron production... and a place of great human energy. Proceeding through the abandoned avenues of the old section of the city felt most peculiar. It was known that the civilian population had been evacuated yet de Gaulle was surprised to find no defenders. His main worry was whether the numerous bridges across the river had been rigged for demolition. French infantry were already finding booby-trapped villages so the enemy may also have decided to destroy these strategic bridges. As was planned, de Gaulle ordered the 511éme Régiment to inspect and cross the bridges to the north while his own régiment drew the southern crossings. The 512éme Régiment was ordered follow in behind them to occupy Saarbrücken on both sides of the Saar.

Amazingly, no demolition charges were discovered on the bridge spans by de Gaulle's combat engineers, and soon de Gaulle was leading the dash over the river to the new city where once again they found deserted streets. Prisoners taken by scout patrols in the early hours of the offensive had confirmed that the German First Army had at most four or five regular divisions to man the entire Westwall. These were divisions with no tanks and equipped mostly with ordinance dating to the Great War. With the Westwall fortifications running behind the city, de Gaulle did not think any of those soldiers would be leaving their pillboxes to mount a counterattack without armor to shield them. Particularly given the deluge of French cannon shells raining down upon their heads at the moment. The interrogators had also learned that the five German reserve divisions were made up mostly of civilian labourers who had been drafted into military service at the last moment from their construction jobs. There was even less reason to fear harm from these *reservists*. Therefore, the brigade could secure Saarbrücken without interference.

The 507éme and 511éme régiments fanned out in a race to the city outskirts on the east side of the river. Telling his driver to park the Yorktown in the area ahead that provided some natural cover from enemy artillery still firing sporadically from the hills forward of their position, de Gaulle issued a command to pause the advance while platoons of the 512éme completed their assignment.

Since taking command of the régiment, de Gaulle had put many policies in place to build camaraderie amongst his tankers. One of those measures was a ritual christening of their Renaults after French battlefield victories. Another simple measure was that a commanding officer had to be seen as well as heard. De Gaulle pulled his tall frame out of his turret and stood in the daylight to acknowledge his crews as they passed by.

Visibility was adequate as de Gaulle raised his field glasses to scan in every direction. The individual companies were fanning out smartly in preparation for the next phase and a flight of Dewoitine fighters swooped low overhead looking for something to molest. De Gaulle suspected Touchon had something to do with the coincidence. It felt good to be working in concert with airmen for a change. This was the way it should be, he thought. Returning his gaze to ground level, two motorcycles from a reconnaissance unit were heading fast toward de Gaulle's position, kicking up a storm of dust in their wake. He wondered what were they after? His strategy counted on Général Georges taking a bit more time to figure out what the 3éme brigade was up to before de Gaulle was ordered to slow down for the Methodical Battle to catch up. Georges was in command of the Sarre offensive and not very fond of de Gaulle.

The lead motorcyclist stopped next to the Yorktown, lowered his goggles and saluted crisply. "Colonel de Gaulle?"

"That is correct," de Gaulle returned the salute and girded himself for bad news.

"Général Guérin, 12éme Division d'Infanterie Motorisée sends his compliments and wishes to know how he can be of assistance," the motorcyclist was enthusiastic to take part in the occupation of a German city.

A wide grin crossed de Gaulle's face. Delestraint had promised he would arrange for infantry support from within their IIIéme Armée and had delivered. "Please convey my compliments to the général, as well. As you just observed while riding through, the 3éme Brigade has occupied Saarbrücken and a full reconnaissance is now being undertaken within the city proper."

An approaching R-35 light tank caught de Gaulle's attention. By the turret markings it was from the 512éme. The tank braked to a stop close to the Yorktown and its commander stepped onto the rear engine deck. "Colonel de Gaulle, Colonel Lenoir instructed me to tell you personally that we have finally located the small reserve garrison defending Saarbrücken. They had not shown themselves but were amicable when we found them and have surrendered unconditionally. From what the prisoners describe the bulk of the city's garrison was previously withdrawn to fortified positions on the Westwall overnight."

"That is excellent news on both counts, thank you." Lenoir was smart. Better not to broadcast the German surrender over the radio just yet. There was more they had to accomplish and the day was still young. As the motorcycle sergeant was waiting, de Gaulle turned to address him. "There you have it. Please advise Général Guérin that an appropriate number of his men will be needed to secure and defend Saarbrücken. There certainly will be booby traps left by the enemy to annoy us after the civilians were evacuated. I will detach a company of R-35s to support his occupation. For the rest of your motorized infantry, tell him I expect to be moving forward shortly and would be grateful if they could accompany us."

NORTHERN BOHEMIA, NEAR REICHENBERG

Capka was standing on a tree stump directing traffic. The sun was already high in the sky and his Škodas were still not out of sight. The Germans had more airfields in Sachsen and Schlesien than in Austria yet the Letectvo had done a fine job of keeping the Luftwaffe off of their backs. But Capka knew that wouldn't last.

"Move, move, move! Get that tank under cover." Capka shouted above the rumbling of sixteen gasoline engines. "You're next! Speed it up. That's right... good, good."

Had the damn transport train moved faster there would have been time to get the company properly positioned not long after dawn. Capka could only hope the Wehrmacht divisions up here did not make their move until more tank companies could be transferred. Capka hoped for a break because his tanks needed field maintenance. They had been engaging both the Freikorps and regular German units for close to a month. He couldn't afford mechanical breakdowns now. Field service was something new, and mostly untested. For years they were forced to send broken down tanks back to the factory. That wouldn't do in wartime. These new mechanics squads were something of a hodgepodge of army regulars and factory technicians hurriedly pressed into service. Regardless, someone had sent a few of these technicians to Capka and he was grateful.

"Are you Kapitán Capka," a gaunt fellow in greasy overalls presented himself.

"You found him," Capka looked the fellow up and down until he spotted a wrench deep into a pocket. "I'm glad you are here to help us."

"We can't do much out in the field but we will do what we can, kapitán. Which vehicles are giving you the worst headaches?" the crew chief gestured at the lot with a sweep of his hand.

"Numbers 182 and 237 are cranky as hell. I would be appreciative if your crew would have a look at them first," Capka showed the mechanic which Škodas to look for.

"Will do, kapitán," the crew chief scratched his forehead. "We'll see what's causing the problem."

"My thanks. Let me know if there is anything you need and maybe we will be lucky enough to find it for you," Capka watched the mechanic dodging oncoming traffic as he scurried off to find the tanks that had been recommended.

At least the Germans were having worse problems, Capka reminded himself. In skirmish after skirmish Capka's crews had sealed the fate of the heaviest and most dangerous German armor. In the close confines of the southwestern mountains, with stout pillboxes and superior artillery backing them up, the Czech tankers had operated mostly in company-sized units that pressed their strategic advantage every time the Germans attempted to open a breach through the passes. It wasn't the large-scale tank battles theorized at the military academies but a succession of small and costly bludgeonings. Having thoroughly defanged the lead German armored division after a week of continuous engagements in the Český les and Šumava Mountains, the Wehrmacht still had plenty of light tanks to throw into the battle on that front but those were fresh, inexperienced crews. The dug-in Czech anti-tank guns and artillery were more than capable of holding these thin-skinned attackers at bay.

Czechoslovak generáls now had the luxury of shifting most of their own tank regiments to the north to meet a new German threat. Such redeployments had long been strategized and planned for. A necessity, really, when surrounded by hostile nations. The battlefield experience of the Czechoslovak Legion had demonstrated how swift reaction to where the enemy threat was strongest was the most successful strategy for defense. Another luxury the general staff possessed was the well-developed Austro-Hungarian military rail network the republic had inherited in 1919. So far the air force had been successful in keeping German bombers and fighters too busy to impede these rail arteries. The train journey north to Reichenberg was still too long for Capka's needs. He would not relax until his Škodas had finished scurrying to the safety of their camouflage nets. Their luck would only hold so long. Enemy Henschels and Stukas had located them before and they would find his tanks again.

The armored units moving north were being assigned to new ad hoc formations. Capka's regiment was intact, having never been broken up into ready units to fight the Freikorps. Other regiments had not been so lucky. As a company commander, Capka had been presented with an envelope upon arriving in the north. It was a briefing document detailing these new postings. The whole enterprise had Srom written all over it. Large tank regiments made up of the most experienced ready units were being created here in the north. On its face, this little bit of housekeeping could be explained away as prudent expediency. No new divisions were created, only new brigades and regiments. The generáls and plukovníks assigned to command those brigades and regiments, however, were all like de Gaulle. This was crafty indeed. What was being thrown together in the north would operate independently as the ready units had done in the Sudeten border districts... brilliant, simply brilliant.

Facing them in the north was the redeployed German Eighth Army. Most of its divisions had been committed to breaking through the Erzegebirge range. Since that offensive had been stopped dead, the briefing papers described how most of that army's motorized divisions were now shifting further east to the river valley leading to Reichenberg. It was an obvious invasion route, which likely was why the German generál in charge had originally chosen the Erzegebirge approach instead. The two German infantry divisions that had been unsuccessfully attempting to cause trouble on the banks of the Neisse were now being joined by up to three additional divisions, according to the latest intelligence. If these five infantry divisions were routed, a door would open. They could chase their retreating foe all the way to Dresden and then onto Berlin. From the briefing reports Capka knew there was no reserve army in place to protect the German capital. No Czechoslovak generál would allow a German army to retreat intact to safety. As long as there was something to chase, Capka's Škodas would be permitted to pursue. The outcome of the war would hinge on what happened before Reichenberg during the next few days.

Capka vaulted from the tree stump onto the last of his Škodas as it rumbled by. Standing beside the turret, Capka held onto the open hatch and leaned closer to the tank's commander. "There is a good shady spot to the left."

"You are in a good mood today, sir... for a man that did not get any sleep on the train last night," the porucík figured there was good news he was unaware of.

"I smell blood! The prospect of a hunt always puts me into a good mood," Capka indulged his weakness for the dramatic.

CZECHOSLOVAK ARMY BASE, STRAŠICE

There was plenty of time and privacy to get their task accomplished. With the army fully mobilized there were dozens of empty barracks buildings to choose from on the base to conduct the interrogations. For now Burda stayed a few steps in the shadows watching his partner's application of coercion. Furst had a fearsome affinity for this line of work. The cold, determined gaze accentuated by the barely controlled hostility conveyed all characteristics of a man with no hesitation of inflicting pain.

"Do you really want to anger me further," Furst paused his slow circling of the prisoner long enough to lean close to the youngster's ear. "What was your unit searching for?" Furst emphasized the point by removing his pistol from its holster. Resting one foot on a nearby bench, Furst pulled the slide back to peer down the barrel with a macabre pleasure. Releasing his hold allowed the slide to chamber a round with a well-oiled click.

"I'm only a gefreiter," the boy stammered in defense, hands bound behind the back of his chair. "Why do waste your time with me?"

"Perhaps there is no one else left to tell me what I want to know," Furst fashioned the implication menacingly.

The empty base had made it easy to separate the captive German parachutists and keep them isolated. The small squad was Fallschirmjäger, the Luftwaffe's elite airborne soldiers. A farmer's dog had raised the alarm a bit east of Klattau. Seeing the sun reflecting on some sort of metal, the farmer had wisely called the animal back and the two continued on their way to town to notify authorities of something suspicious. Only three of the parachutists allowed themselves to be taken after a Letov crew spotted the Germans from the air and the army platoon sent out to investigate caught up with them sheltering in a stand of trees.

Notified by radio that the prisoners were being held at the base in Strašice, the Second Department men rushed to take the lead in questioning the men. That they were dealing with was a reconnaissance team was obvious. What Burda and Furst sought to learn was what these men were sent to reconnoiter. The two sergeants were tough as steel plate, but the young corporal here had all of the hallmarks of someone still fresh out of training. It was Burda's idea to leave their uniforms behind. The Gestapo rarely operated in uniform and the boy did appear noticeably unnerved by his interrogators in leather long coats. If this one believed he was facing a Czechoslovak version of his own country's secret police all the better. The Nazi newspapers had been printing the worst lies for months about Czechoslovak atrocities perpetrated upon the Sudetens so no reason to waste such foul publicity.

"You realize this is only a temporary accommodation," Furst gestured at the barracks, with the pistol. "The way things are going it won't be long before they take you to a very dark place deep under the old battlements of Praha. Personally I think you are worthless and we should simply put a bullet through your temples now. But I have colleagues who wish to be sure of these things. Have you ever seen someone's fingernails pulled off? I am sure your own security people use the same technique."

"But I am a uniformed prisoner of war! There are rules," the young corporal struggled in his bindings.

"And why should I care. Do you expect your comrades or your family will ever see your poor rotted corpse again... unlikely my young friend. Too many of our comrades have met their end at the hands of your Gestapo. We have no sympathy for someone like you caught behind the lines conducting espionage. You should have had the good sense to be killed with the rest," Furst began circling the prisoner again.

"But I am in uniform," the gefreiter knew that detail cleared him of espionage.

"Such a waste of time," Furst directed the comment at Burda. "Call the guards and have this poor wretch transferred up to Praha."

Burda silently nodded his head in agreement and started to leave. The grave expression on his face weighed on the German youth like a harsh sentence from a magistrate.

"Wait, wait! Stay... please stay. I will talk to you. I will tell you everything," the frightened boy finally capitulated.

"That is more like it," Furst hovered over his prisoner in triumph. "What was your unit sent to find?"

"Supply dumps. We were dropped behind the lines to locate your army's supply dumps," the corporal could net get the words out quickly enough.

"You do not expect me to believe that tripe, do you? Your Führer has been quite clear he has every tool in his possession necessary to crush Czechoslovakia beneath his boot," Furst pressed his advantage.

"No, I speak the truth. The heer is short of ammunition and fuel. Your weapons use the same caliber ammunition as ours do. Capturing your supply dumps intact might be necessary so we were dropped behind your lines to find them," the corporal lowered his head in defeat.

"Fascinating... let's talk some more, my friend," Furst pulled up a chair to sit next to the prisoner.

CHÂTEAU DE VINCENNES, PARIS

Général Gamelin appeared satisfied with the progress marked on the main campaign board illustrating the disposition of French units committed to Offensive Sarre. At least that was the conclusion of the général's adjutants who were reliably quick to sense the slightest sign of irritation in the normally unruffled demeanor of their chief of staff. What he had wanted, Gamelin had achieved: a springboard into Germany should he choose to press the attack. Of course, Gamelin had yet to make that decision but this was something he by rights kept to himself. Colonel Petibon, the général's chef de cabinet, knew Gamelin's mind yet was just as secretive. For now, Gamelin was content to finish bringing up his reserves while allowing advance units to probe the German lines for weakness. Outside of Petibon, Gamelin's intentions were something of an enigma to the général's staff. Out of earshot there was a lively debate whether the chief of staff would turn out like McClellan in Virginia; raising a great army he was unwilling to commit to battle; or Marshal Davout, who's wise prudence never impeded his boldness of action.

"Fine, fine... everything is as it should be," Gamelin moved away from the board. "Now what of the British? Any word?"

"No developments," Commandant Huet supplied like a shipping clerk checking off items ordered yet not delivered. As one of Gamelin's primary adjutants, Huet had a full list of topics to stay current on. The British were at the top of the list.

"High time for Chamberlain to get off the pot. What more does he need? The Czechs are mounting a spirited defence against all expectations. Hitler has already been denied the easy victory he coveted. Now is the moment for us to settle the matter," Gamelin allowed his growing impatience to show.

"A shame the prime minister appears set on denying himself a role in the final outcome," Petibon coveted the sole disposition of spoils that might lie ahead.

Much of Gamelin's strategic goals had hinged on what the British did or did not do. Three weeks prior the général had sincerely believed that his freedom to choose an aggressive offensive against the Germans required, at the very least, commitment of Royal Air Force squadrons to the battle. Gamelin accepted that London was hard-pressed to raise an expeditionary corps of any consequence. Yet France's glaring need was for far more aircraft than she could raise herself. On the ground, Gamelin was in a far better position to move forward without British ground troops. The French chief of staff's analysis had long been that without the promise of fresh reserves from the United Kingdom, the depth of any French penetration into Germany should be limited. Push too deep into the middle of Germany and he risked the Wehrmacht sweeping through Belgium to outflank the French lines, which is why Gamelin had always sought British support opposite the Low Countries. But that was before the Czechoslovak's amazing battlefield success in their border mountains. The bulk of Hitler's available divisions were tied down and suffering significant rates of attrition. Those regiments would be difficult to extricate from action to shift west. That gave Gamelin more aggressive options, and he was flirting with availing himself upon them.

A runner from the headquarters wireless section hurried into the room and approached Huet. The adjutant took receipt of the message and dismissed the clerk. An eyebrow raised as Huet read the details.

"What is it?" Petibon, who was aware of everything that went on around the général, inquired at once.

"Editors from the major newspapers are calling, sir. Their correspondents are reporting by telephone from the Sarre that units of the 3éme Brigade de Chars have accepted the surrender of Saarbrücken. They seek confirmation on this great victory," Huet felt like whistling but did not dare.

"Which regiments of the 3éme Brigade?" Petibon sharply cross-examined the messenger.

"Such details were not provided," Huet answered truthfully, although there was little doubt about who was leading this attack.

"Damn that man! Those were not his orders," Gamelin pounded a fist onto the table.

"Of course, if true, it could be argued that Delestraint's regiments never operated beyond their artillery cover," Petibon thought to soften Gamelin's ire. "Which means they have not violated the principles of the Methodical Battle."

"Do not attempt to sugarcoat the matter. We both know this is de Gaulle's handiwork. That rogue is attempting to force my hand – a great victory indeed," Gamelin would not put it past de Gaulle to have delivered engraved invitations to the correspondents corps."

"Général, how would you advise we respond to these inquiries?" Huet returned to the topic at hand. "If we say nothing the editors will print whatever they wish."

"Quite correct," contemplating a plan of action permitted Gamelin an avenue to calm himself. "Until we get confirmation from General Georges' command, issue a communiqué: The campaign in the Sarre is continuing as planned."

TYRŠ BRIDGE
TETSCHEN- BODENBACH, BOHEMIA

Distant cannon fire hardly marred the serene view over the Elbe. The castle on the heights overlooking the bend of the river and homes tucked between fir trees in the woods were lovely. Several days previously a German division in the mountains was battling to open up a breech in the Czechoslovak defense line to march on Aussig, an important industrial city. They had to find a battle to eyeball in person and the one up there seemed like a good fight to shoot for thanks to excellent train connections from Prague that could get Ros and Sanderson there swiftly. General Krejčí was so pleased with the way he was portrayed in their interviews that a call from his staff had gotten the two reporters transit passes north almost to the German border. That's how the two had ended up in Bodenbach-Tetschen. But no sooner had the Ros and Sanderson disembarked the train with a reserve infantry company that it became very obvious that the correspondents had missed the fireworks. The Czech army boys had stopped the Germans dead and pushed them back toward Dresden. The big guns they heard were Czechoslovak artillery. With their plans dashed, the reporters stood on the middle of a bridge arguing about what to do next as a convoy of troop lorries passed behind them.

"There has to be a local commander who can speak to what the battle was like up here," Sanderson was looking for a way to salvage their efforts.

"It is still old news," Ros stomped her shoe on the pavement. "We're a day late and a dollar short... again."

"You and your limitless supply of odd American idioms," Sanderson dodged her point. How was he to know the Gerries would crumble under pressure?

"And I suppose that some of crazy stuff I hear out of your mouth isn't odd? *The dog's bollocks...* what in the hell is that supposed to mean?" Ros poked a forefinger in his chest.

"Don't be a difficult little bugger. I explained that one to you several times already," Sanderson's patience was growing thin with Ros never listening.

"Oh, forget it. We need a plan," Ros threw her hands above her head in frustration. "Coming here was your idea. Getting us out of this pickle is your responsibility, bud."

"Funny, I do not remember what your brilliant alternative happened to be. Please refresh my memory," Sanderson was ready to walk away if she kept on this way.

"Are you saying this is my fault? Do I have to do everything myself?" Ros' hands came to rest on her hips to accentuate the complaint.

"Quite right. Perhaps you should muddle through on your own for a spot and let's see how well you get on," Sanderson dismissed her with a backhanded wave as he marched off toward the Bodenbach side of the bridge.

"Fine! I don't need you pal. I can do just fine on my own," Ros couldn't believe she was being ditched.

"See you when I see you then." That yank was getting to be more trouble than she was worth and shedding her was giving Sanderson a welcome feeling of liberation.

"How dare he turn his back on me," Ros grumbled to herself. Part of her wanted to run after the ungrateful bore to continue the argument. Hadn't she saved his skin in Prague during the riots? But chasing after him would only give Sanderson the mistaken impression that she needed him. "You'll come running back!"

"Lover's quarrel, mademoiselle?" a familiar voice addressed Ros from behind.

"What now!" Ros whirled around to see who was so foolish to have drawn that stupid conclusion. The problem was she recognized the mustachioed owner of the voice. "Faucher, is that you?"

"None other," Faucher assured her.

"Hey, new uniform there," Ros pressed the fabric of the label between her thumb and finger. "Looks good on you. But what happened to your old outfit?"

"I resigned my commission during the shame of the Bad Godesberg conference," Faucher did sorely miss his old kepi, however. "Surprising you had not heard."

"Those were a crazy couple of days," general. "Did you hear, I was up at the castle the night the mob almost pulled President Beneš from his bed and General Syrový talked them out of it," Ros was curious to see whether the Frenchie had read her story.

"Were you now? Well then it is understandable you missed my joining the Czechoslovak army in their fight," Faucher forgave her.

"But France is in it now. I'm sure they would take you back," Ros wondered whether he had made the attempt.

"Kind of you for thinking so but what is done is done and I have no regrets. Général Krejčí assigned me the command of this reserve infantry brigade moving up to the front. Good men, they will serve their nation with valor," Faucher looked at the troops under his command proudly.

"Something big happening?" Ros called up a sweet smile to encourage the old fart to spill the beans.

"To see you here, I thought you must know," Faucher feigned surprise.

"Know what? You wouldn't hold out on a gal, would you?" Ros really did not know what he was talking about.

"The German army in this vicinity moved its divisions to the Neisse River and we are expecting a substantial attack there," Faucher gave the attractive young woman just enough to insure she would be charming company for the rest of the afternoon.

"You do say," Ros wrapped her arm inside his as a soldier riding by whistled at his commander. "How about you and I get off this ugly bridge and talk some more?"

"A shame you never got to see the lovely chain bridge that used to span the Elbe at this spot," Faucher led Ros down the pedestrian corridor. "They called it the Empress Elisabeth Bridge. There was severe damage dating back to the last war, however. Too bad the Czech authorities had to tear it down five years ago for this sturdy, if unimpressive, replacement. The old Empress was so much more romantic. I am sure your British companion would not have run off like that were she still around."

"Oh forget about him. Let's you and I have a little chat," Ros was going to show Sanderson who was on top of the heap, one way or another.

BERLINER TAGEBLATT HEADQUARTERS
MITTE DISTRICT, BERLIN

The future of the newspaper was on the line. For five years they had escaped closure by the barest of margins. In the days after the Nazis swept into power there was a certain legitimacy to be gained by allowing the paper to continue operating: *Germany does not restrict civil liberties... look there is the Berliner Tageblatt printing their liberal tripe as always.* For three years Paul Scheffer walked the tightrope as editor-in-chief. After many years reporting from Moscow he understood a few things about how totalitarian regimes operated. The Propaganda Ministry hated them but Scheffer managed to keep the doors open and the presses running while slipping as much of the truth into print as possible. But after the re-occupation of the Rhineland without a peep by Paris, even Scheffer had to call it quits in 1936 and flee the country. Since then the editors and correspondents had clung to the belief that Hitler's growing list of outrages would force the French and British to intervene. All they had to do was skirt the chopping block long enough. So far the blade had yet to fall. Then the call came in that morning from a stringer in the Saar.

"There is no sitting on this one," Culemann dropped his fist on the tabletop so hard the half-empty coffee cups rattled on their saucers. "We have to run it all... everything."

"They will close us down. Maybe they will shoot us as traitors for good measure. Some of us have young children to think about," Faber, the managing editor, jabbed a pencil at Culemann.

"Then resign before you are implicated. This is going to happen. *Saarbrücken Surrenders* is the headline on the evening edition," Culemann directed Faber to the door.

"It would be wise to get additional confirmation from our side of the border before committing ourselves," Vogt from the national desk argued.

"Access to the Saarland is now restricted. Getting someone in there from Stuttgart will take too long. My boys from the Strasbourg bureau have confirmed it. The French occupied Saarbrücken and the garrison surrendered. The city is lost," Gloeckner the foreign desk editor backed up Culemann.

"Did you ever think this all might be a fabrication?" Faber ridiculed the report from the French city.

"Number one, I trust our own people; number two, French spies are not that ingenious," Culemann ridiculed Faber in return.

"What a war," Vogt sank back into his chair with a thud. "The Chancellery has not even officially acknowledged that French troops crossed the border two days ago. None of the other papers have printed a thing."

"And that is why we will lead with the story. It is the truth. The people have a right to know," Culemann's passion was finally carrying the point. "That is the end of the matter, we tell what we know with no political embellishments."

"They will hang us for sure," Faber predicted solemnly.

"Then we hang, gentlemen."

SOUTHWEST OF KAADEN, SUDETENLAND

A bullet whooshed by so close to his right temple he felt the heat trail as the projectile passed by. Morgen instinctively dropped to lie as flat to the contours of the hill as possible. His wizened comrades followed suit without asking why. The Czech snipers up here were a terror. They had the elevation advantage and the bastards were deadly accurate shots. Morgen had already lost two men to them. More annoying these snipers were shrewd cocksuckers. This one would take an additional shot and then move onto another vantage point. Morgen pawed at his rifle that had come to rest nearby. After drawing the weapon closer to him, Morgen raised the barrel above the dirt berm protecting him from the direction the shot had come from. Another round hit the soil a few millimeters from his head but this time he had spotted the muzzle flash and had a good idea where the shooter was.

"Richter, get you ass over here," Morgen waved him closer.

"Glad to see they have not gotten you yet, sturmscharführer," Richter noted as happily as once could after having slid sideways on his stomach to get there.

"Ya, I bet you are you lying piece of scum," Morgen hated his ass getting kissed.

"I am honest as the day is long. You are a big man and I am skinny as a dachshund. Who do you think these snipers will see first? Of course I am happy you are mostly unhurt," Richter explained himself in a way the staff sergeant would appreciate.

"Wise ass," Morgen elbowed the trooper. "And what do you mean by mostly?"

"Because you are bleeding like a river at the temple," Richter found it impressive how Morgen ignored injuries.

"Crap," Morgen raised a hand up to where the wound should be. After pressing against the spot for a moment he checked his fingers to confirm they were soaked in red. "I don't even feel shit like this anymore."

Un-strapping his helmet, Morgen ripped a sleeve off his uniform shirt without a second thought like he had done the same thing thousands of times before. He then folded the fabric into a bandage-like strip that he stretched out above his ears and tied behind his head.

"That takes care of it. Now back to business," Morgen pointed to a spot above them. "Herr skinny wise ass, you are going to take Sanger and Weber to circle behind that rock up and to the left. I want that sniper dead before we blow open the pillbox with Amatol. And remember, he probably has one or two friends guarding his rear end."

"Affirmative. We will take care of them," Richter did not sound too happy at the assignment as he crawled in the direction of the other two troopers.

Morgen actually liked Richter quite a lot. He was sending the man out to deal with their sniper because Richter was good, not because Richter had made Morgen the butt of a joke. Humor was welcome out here. For the last week they had been making slow progress in the direction of Kaaden – pillbox by pillbox, mortar nest by mortar nest, machine gun by machine gun. The pillboxes were the worst... tough nuts every one. It was nigh impossible to get behind one. There always were snipers and other sources of supporting fire to deal with first. And once you got close to one, each was set in the ground in such a way to allow only one clear route of approach. Tossing four or five Amatol charges at a pillbox at the same time was about the only way to get the gunners inside nervous enough to duck for safety. Those few seconds would be the only chance to get around or on top of the casement. From the top you had a chance to drop more Amatol down an exhaust vent or some other opening.

Every pillbox cleared translated into some progress made on the road below. It was long, slow work, which meant no big breakthrough to collapse the Czech lines. If the rest of the way through this valley was as thick with Czech defenses as his men had already faced, they might arrive in Prag by 1940.

LETIŠTĚ SPIŠSKÁ NOVÁ VES, KOŠICE

The last trainload of evacuees had passed through and Bulloch was itching to get back to Prague. There was a whole lot of action that he was missing while seeing fellow Americans off on their roundabout way home. So many grateful faces, especially the kids, were fresh in his memory. It was an important mission yet Bulloch was equally happy all those folks were off his shoulders for good. During each transfer of American citizens the Czechs and Hungarians made a point of staring each other down and Bulloch got the feeling that many on the Slovakian side would have liked for the Hungarians to try something. Captain Janik had pretty much as admitted that sentiment a few nights previously over dinner. Košice was a sleepy place and Janik's soldiers would have enjoyed nothing better than to rough up the Hungarians. They were doing an important job yet it was hard to compare with their comrades up to their necks with German divisions in Bohemia and Moravia.

Berlin may be putting a lot of pressure on Budapest to open another front in the war but the Hungarians had no stomach for putting their small army on the line when Germany was not in possession of an imminent victory. If the Czechoslovaks were not going to get a chance to cold cock someone around these parts it was time Bulloch headed west to where he could see their buddies throw some punches.

One complication in Bulloch's exit plans was that nowhere in Carr's thorough preparations had any provision been made for how to get him back to Prague or anywhere else. Bulloch had been so busy with hustling civilians through town that he never thought about how the hell he was supposed to get out of Košice either. When Bulloch asked Ferguson the local consul, he said he always thought that the matter had been taken care of since no one had asked him to assist. Hindsight was golden but Bulloch should have brought the BMW out with him. At this rate he would have been happy to hitchhike on the back of any truck bed heading west. With no civilian transport scheduled, Bulloch was faced with the prospect of cooling his heels for a while until Janik arranged for a seat on a courier plane heading to Prague via Bratislava and Brno.

The morning of the flight, Janik pulled up to the Hotel Rohlena along with Ferguson in a Škoda Superb Cabriolet to spirit Bulloch off to the military airfield nearby at Spišská Nová Ves. Bulloch was anxious to see the base, which he had been told was constructed only a few years previously. The design and layout of the airfield would reveal a lot about what kinds of aircraft the Czechoslovaks intended to operate in the coming years. The drive out there was a hoot. Ferguson had invited himself along for the ride to see the attaché off and point out some of the major sites along the way. Although Bulloch suspected Ferguson's true motives were simply to enjoy motoring about in such a fine car. Janik wasn't forthcoming whom the army had relieved the vehicle from but Bulloch had no complaints as they rode out to the airfield with top down and Ferguson stowed in the back seat. It was a lovely fall morning and visibility extended for miles.

"Listen son," Ferguson leaned forward to be heard over the wind. "You can still stick around here. I could use a competent lad such as yourself in these parts as a good right hand man."

"Thanks for the offer. This is really pretty country and all, but I have to say that I prefer Prague for now," Bulloch tried to let Ferguson down easy.

"Ahhhhh... that's what they all say," Ferguson let the force of air push him back onto the rear bench seat.

"He's quite serious, you know. Keeping foreign born staff here can be a devil of a chore. Košice has a very provincial feeling not to everyone's taste," Janik included himself part of that group.

"Well, the Poles could still kick up some dust. That certainly would liven things up. Unfortunately, you would also be invaded by a far worse a scourge than the Poles: newspaper reporters. I personally know of a few I would love to get out of my hair," Bulloch would pay good money to be rid of that Talmadge woman. "I'm surprised none of the vipers stowed away on the evacuation trains."

"Foreign correspondents I can do without. But I would quite enjoy the privilege of smiting the Poles should they try something stupid," Janik veered off onto an access road to the air base.

"Almost there... and so soon?" Ferguson deplored from the rear seat.

Bulloch grabbed the top of the windshield frame to pull himself up for a better view of the airbase.

"Larger than I expected," Bulloch judged from a distance. As the cabriolet sped along he realized the field was clogged with parked warplanes. Many more than there reasonably should be. Bulloch was oblivious to the shadow that was overtaking the car from behind. A shadow cast from a very large airplane.

"What the hell," Bulloch finally noticed the shadow as darkness passed over them. "That silhouette is huge!" Bulloch craned his neck looking up to identify what sort of behemoth was capable of blocking out so much of the sun. Unfortunately, the glare reflecting off the skin of the low-wing monoplane kept Bulloch from making out the markings on the lower wings.

"That's not one of yours," Bulloch directed at Janik.

"No, it is not," Janik kept his attention on the road.

"Here comes another one!" Ferguson pointed at the sky behind them.

This time Bulloch looked up with greater care and was clearly able to make out large red stars on the underside of the broad wings.

"Soviet! That bird is V-VS! Must be one of those Tupolevs I've read about... bombers," Bulloch lowered himself back into his car seat."

"Cargo plane," Janik corrected him. "Our Russian allies need to bring a few things with them."

"You've been holding out on me, friend," Bulloch backhanded Janik on the arm.

"And on me too," Ferguson leaned forward to chime in.

"Apologies... orders. But I did tell you that you would enjoy the drive out here," Janik reminded them.

"So you did, lad," Ferguson slapped the back of Janik's seat.

"Transport jobs, eh? Transporting what? The cat is out of the bag now, don't hold out on us," Bulloch watched the Soviet plane land.

"Spare parts and ammunition," Janik kept the answer terse.

"Parts and ammo for what? Fess up" Bulloch was too close to give up now.

"Those," Janik pointed to the right at a flight of three modern low-wing fighters flying low and fast across the field.

Bulloch swung around in his seat to look at what Janik was pointing at. These aircraft he recognized from the newsreels: fat, stubby little monoplanes that reminded him of air racers. The same planes American pilots were flying over Spain against the fascists.

"Polikarpovs. Dammit, those are Moscas," Bulloch felt like a kid at a carnival.

"And quite a lot of them too, by the looks of it," Ferguson could see dozens more parked on the grass.

"I thought it was all a bluff. I never believed for a second that Stalin would actually come through," Bulloch was astonished at what he was seeing with his own eyes.

"Neither did we," Janik was in complete agreement. "I am still not sure how much I actually like the idea myself but I discovered I can live with it. Something tells me Hitler thinks like you do. That means our Soviet friends here are about to deliver a very sweet surprise to the Germans.

SULZBACH, SAARLAND – DEUTCHLAND

Thick, black coal dust covered everything in the valley: the trees, their uniforms, the Yorktown and probably their lungs. De Gaulle had forgotten the dark soot churned out by the coalmines, steel mills and factories producing everything from plate glass to phonograph records. The poor women in the Saar never saw a holiday from endless scrubbing and now they had dust and debris from days of high-explosive detonations added to the mess. The most amazing revelation on their drive north from Saarbrücken was that the factory managers had been ordered to stay in production despite the French invasion. How well the German authorities knew the shortcomings of de Gaulle's own superiors that they did not fear injury or disruption to their industry. Such a shock then for the plant supervisors when the motorcycle scouts de Gaulle had sent to their gates ordered production to cease and workers sent home until further notice. De Gaulle wished he could have seen some of their faces but there was no time for such pleasures. Everything rested on how much they could accomplish in this one day. Nothing could be allowed to delay the brigade's steady press forward.

Touchon's reconnaissance had proven most accurate. Their artillery had indeed blasted open a substantial breach through the German defense line at Sulzbach. But in getting there they were taking much greater enemy fire than de Gaulle had anticipated, much of it from the heights within the Köllertaler Forest to their left. The good news was that most of the anti-tank shells were deflecting off the armor of his Renaults without penetrating. The bad news was they were forced to waste time suppressing these nests of defenders the entire eleven kilometers up from Saarbrücken. As for the dug in German howitzers in the hills, Touchon's pilots were doing a fine job of spotting for the French heavy cannons, which were harassing the enemy gun crews into their foxholes. German shells were still falling sporadically but this was a minor nuisance. De Gaulle was scanning the way ahead through the thin viewing slit in his cupola when an enemy 37mm anti-tank shell clanged against the Renault's side armor. De Gaulle had heard that distinct note so many times since Saarbrücken that he could now identify the caliber of these rounds by the sound they made when glancing off the D2's armor plate.

"Looks like we have another one knocking at the door," de Gaulle announced with minor concern. The Yorktown was not the first Renault leading the advance. This German gunner had picked them out as a command vehicle. The only difference between the Yorktown and the other D2s was the second wireless aerial. This gunner was too smart to be allowed mercy.

Swiftly lowering himself down into the middle of the one-man turret, de Gaulle rotated the gun to the left in the direction he estimated the shot had come from, while Vauban worked the radio to alert the rest of the company behind them. De Gaulle peered through the diascope gun sight and caught the muzzle flash from the anti-tank gun as it launched a second projectile. This one also was deflected away, but de Gaulle now had the range. His fingers depressed the trigger and the Yorktown's loaded 47mm cannon recoiled. De Gaulle waited just long enough to see the high explosive shell hit close to target.

"Going to give them another round to be sure," de Gaulle told his crew as he heard the cannon on a nearby Renault firing.

Loading another 47mm HE shell into the gun reminded de Gaulle of the idiocy of politics. Every APX turret on every French tank was a one-man affair. The tank commander had to instruct his driver where to go, rotate the turret, load the cannon, aim the cannon, fire the cannon and repeat the process. This handicap seriously depressed the potential rate of fire severely. A highly accurate gunner could make up for some of this impairment but putting all of these tasks on one man was asking too much. Why was this design choice made... simply because it lowered the cost of each tank. The Czechs, Germans and Soviets were not so shortsighted. When the enemy tanks someday matched their own in armor thickness and cannon size, there would be hell to pay on the battlefield. Of course, the politicians who howled about every single franc allocated to the war budget could care less. And why should they? The Methodical Battle presumed tank-to-tank engagements would never develop against a well-defended line. Fools, they had forgotten Napoleon and Ney. The only way to change them was by shame, or by defeat at the hands of the enemy. De Gaulle was determined not to allow the latter prospect to decide the matter.

The French shell had come close enough to hitting the target for the detonation to disrupt the brush that protected the German gun crew. De Gaulle now saw grey metal paint showing through. Adjusting his aim, he fired another HE round at the same spot. The shell hit on target and exploded the crew's ammunition supply. The anti-tank nest erupted in a red ball of flame that was followed by a shockwave carrying shattered pieces of wood and metal in all directions.

"Target eliminated," de Gaulle confirmed through the diascope. "Inform the rest of the company."

"Where to, colonel? The way ahead looks clear," Arnoult picked his way through the last of the crushed tank obstructions.

"Straight by Sulzbach. Aerial reconnaissance shows the pillboxes and gun pits intended for Sulzbach are still under construction. Once we clear that village then we head the final four kilometers straight for Friedrichsthal where we will wait for the rest to catch up," de Gaulle grew confident they would accomplish their goal.

"As you like it sir," Arnoult shifted to a faster gear. Faster was a relative concept for a French infantry tank, however.

"Vauban, inform the other regiments, and the 12éme Division d'Infanterie Motorisée, that we are pressing on to Friedrichsthal as planned," de Gaulle moved away from his radio operator to head back up to the turret cupola."

At his insistence, they were using a non-standard radio frequency. De Gaulle wanted neither the Germans nor Général Georges' command headquarters to have an easy time keeping tabs on what he was up to. This way all protestations would have to go through Delestraint, who would shield the brigade from abuse. Later they could argue an unfortunate mishap in communications had led to Georges command receiving an incorrect frequency. After all, they were still developing protocols for these wireless sets and there were bound to be growing pains.

Delestraint and de Gaulle estimated they would have just enough freedom of action to allow newsmen they could rely on to publish news of the advance. Advancing fifteen kilometers into Germany in but one day would set public expectations for this offensive. Back at the brigade command post, Delestraint had a sequestered cadre of reporters at the ready to explain the modern strategy employed by the most advanced tank regiments in the army to achieve such a significant incursion.

Likewise, de Gaulle had hijacked a few more correspondents who he had riding at the rear of the advance. Their eyewitness reporting would present a momentous victory to the good citizens back home. Delestraint and de Gaulle would sing the praises of the strategic foresight of Générals Gamelin and Georges to box their reluctant superiors into a corner with the public. If this ploy was unsuccessful, Delestraint and de Gaulle could easily be sacked of their commands.

De Gaulle already had set his sights on Homburg, twenty kilometers further east of Friedrichsthal. From Homburg, the three armies assigned to the offensive could fan out and secure the entire Sarre. The Westwall was breached... there was nothing to stop them. De Gaulle had no illusions, however. Gamelin would be inclined to dig in while the occupation progressed and he brought artillery and supplies forward from the Maginot Line. There were too many pillboxes, minefields, bunkers and artillery positions to mop up. Securing the Sarre would take additional precious weeks and de Gaulle would have to wait patiently at Homburg.

The potential was so much greater. As they had seen, the Westwall only faced west. There was no protection from French units attacking from their rear. Infantry regiments could swing back around the Hunsrück highlands to surround Trèves. Hitler had no reserves to prevent the loss of the Sarre. If he continued to bleed his best divisions on the mountains ringing Czechoslovakia, then there would be nothing to send to plug the Sarre Gap and a French advance into the Rheinpfalz also became a possibility. If the winds of fate permitted it, Kaiserslautern lay only thirty-nine kilometers in the direction of the Rhine – easily in reach of the 3éme Brigade. Take Kaiserslautern and the Germans were unquestionably routed and the way would be clear to Worms on the Rhine. What mischief de Gaulle could perpetrate from the banks of that mighty river if he were fortunate enough to have a full army at his command, while supported by another pushing north from Lauterbourg. For now that was wishful thinking... machine gun rounds were pinging off the exterior of the Yorktown.

"Light machine gun nests to the right," Arnoult called out from below.

"More delays," de Gaulle did not have time for this. "Let's make sure these brave foes are not leading us into a trap of anti-tank mines. Vauban, order all stop to the column, we'll engage these hornets from here: Chatellerault's in concert with suppressing fire from the cannons."

HOTEL IMPERIAL, KARLSBAD – SUDETENLAND

The telephone lines were up again. How long that would last was anyone's guess. As soon as Sylvie got the word she rushed to the telephone bureau around the corner from the hotel and called the Berlin office collect. Finally things were popping around here, but not the way she had predicted. That morning while she was on one of her eavesdropping strolls around town, Sylvie had overheard two junior officers arguing by their staff car. Something about the French causing trouble back home – something substantial enough to cause the army higher-ups to consider pulling some of their units out of the Sudetenland. This was big but the two hauptmanns got into their car mid-discussion and rode off before Sylvie could glean anything more. Neither was that scoundrel Wartenberg anywhere to be found. It didn't matter that the phone line was probably tapped on the Berlin side Sylvie needed to know what was shaking.

"You say the French have invaded the Saar? There is nothing in the German press or radio about that. Absolutely nothing. Are you sure?" This was sensitive information but Sylvie had previously checked that no one around her was speaking English. "Really? Our people in Luxembourg went down to the border and could hear the gunfire and they interviewed German refugees? Okay, that's good enough for me. Damn... I wish I could get some of the British papers. There is nothing but German rags available in Karlsbad. Listen, I am dead in the water out here. The American consul got me temporary documents but I need cash to get on the move. There are only so many wheels you can grease with charm alone. Where are the greenbacks you promised me? Fine, fine... well he ain't shown up yet. All right, forget it for now... get ready. I'm going to dictate my story before the lines go dead again."

Sylvie had been at this a long time and knew that sometimes it was best not to put anything down on paper. Taking notes immediately put a reporter under suspicion. Especially with these security-minded Gestapo types running around looking for someone to hustle. So everything she was about to say came straight from her noggin. "Here's the gist of it. The German offensive in the Sudetenland remains stalled. The Czechs are making the Wehrmacht fight for every inch of hillside. Tens of thousands of German soldiers are bottled up in this picturesque valley. Now military channels are humming with news of a big French offensive far to the west in the Saarland. Herr Hitler has bet everything on his invasion of Czechoslovakia, but the question is being raised in military compounds around Karlsbad whether some of these soldiers and their equipment might be shifted back to protect the Fatherland... got that? Hold on a second, I need to check something."

Sylvie looked over her shoulder to see if she was drawing any undue attention but she caught no one listening in. The other customers were too preoccupied with their own calls and the staff was busy about their duties. The only people who were paying attention to her were anxious folks still waiting in line to get at a phone. Satisfied she was not drawing a crowd, Sylvie was all set to continue when the line went dead in a crackle of static. "Damn. Here we go again."

44TH FIGHTER FLIGHT, POLERADY – BOHEMIA

Bozik was taking additional time fussing with his Avia. Chief Soucek had watched him proceed from nose to tail three times already. There was not a mechanical linkage, lubricant reservoir, or surface area that had not been checked, filled or cleaned. Best to give the squadron leader room the chief had told his mechanics since Nedoma's plane had not come back with the rest. Cervena was the first to explain that the youngster had acted bravely yet had wound up in jeopardy as a result. The chief was surprised more of these boys had not been lost. Sure, a few of them had gotten their precious aircraft shot to hell but they had not lost a one until Nedoma. It was too good to last, of course. They were good boys who Bozik had trained remarkably well. The final measure was they had sent many more Germans to their fate before losing one of their own. Still, losing the first comrade was a serious blow and all of the pilots were taking it hard. It was time he kicked Bozik back to the barracks, if you could call those makeshift sheds barracks. The closest village possessed less than one thousand citizens and few establishments to drown one's sorrows at.

"Kapitán," Soucek wiped his oily hands with a rag as he approached Bozik. "There's not a bolt on that fighter you or my men have not already examined."

"Sorry old friend," Bozik straightened up and backed away from the fuselage. Many hours had passed since Nedoma's plane had gone spiraling down and there was zero word on his fate. Bozik's head was filled with visions of the boy's broken body prostrate over a crag of mountain rocks being pecked to bits by carrion birds. He had read once that this was a noble burial in Tibet but that remembrance brought little comfort. "You have been through this before. This is my first time."

"Losing one of your own gets easy," the chief had little wisdom to offer. "Was there anything differently you could have done to have saved his skin?"

"Not a thing. He made a cocky mistake. But the part that kills me though is that he made a cocky mistake while protecting my ass." It was difficult for Bozik not to feel responsible for losing Nedoma. "The sky was thick with Messerschmitts. They had altitude and we were outnumbered. There was no margin for judgment errors."

"Sounds to me like you were lucky only to lose one cub. How many Germans did you send to hell today?" Soucek held up five fingers spread apart.

"Three... it was the only way we could convince them to break off and call it a day. Otherwise they would have chased us all the way home," Bozik's modest attempt at humor was a good sign.

"You see, the German squadron leader has it worse than you. He had more planes, an altitude advantage and what was his reward... three dead men. Right now he is sitting in some shed, on his airfield, downing another schnapps and thinking about you... the devil that cost him three pilots to one and got away to boot," the chief offered far better counsel than Bozik would have given the old mechanic credit for.

"When I am dead I want you to write my obituary," Bozik patted him on the shoulder like an old drinking buddy. "Amongst other things, you have given me an idea. Would you share some whiskey with me?"

"That would be against the rules, kapitán," Soucek reminded him.

"I really do not care," Bozik would pommel anyone would objected.

The chief had stopped paying attention to him, however. There was dust billowing into the air from the far side of the field where the access road to the base came in. Squinting into the distance he could see a small convoy of trucks heading their way.

"What is that all about? There is no resupply scheduled for today," the chief hoped Bozik knew something he did not. Soucek made a point of knowing everything that happened on the base.

"Perhaps we are finally getting the extra anti-aircraft guns we requested," Bozik guessed.

"No, I would have been told about that," Soucek shook his head. "Let's find out what this is all about," the chief stuffed the rag into the back pocket of his overalls and marched off to the supply pits he figured the trucks were heading toward. As the lead truck got near, Soucek flagged the driver to pull over. "What are you carrying?"

"Ammunition," the driver leaned out of the open side window.

"Let me have a look. I want to make sure it's dry before accepting delivery," Soucek ordered as three of his mechanics dropped what they were working on to watch.

The chief climbed up onto the back of the truck and untied the tarp covering the load, which he pulled back to reveal neatly stacked crates. Strangely though, there were no identification markings on the wood.

"Someone is getting lazy at the munitions factory," Soucek groused. Knowing his boss well, one the mechanics climbed up next to him with a crowbar for the chief to grab. Prying off the lid of the nearest crate, Soucek reached in and collected a metal link belt of machine gun shells to look at the stampings on the bottom of the casings. "These are all wrong! What are those idiot quartermasters sending us? I don't believe this... 7.62mm? There is nothing in our inventory that uses 7.62mm. These are Soviet rounds."

"Indeed they are," no one had noticed Commander Luža approach from the base headquarters "Our numbers are about to be bolstered by fresh pilots and we must be ready to receive them and their aircraft."

CHÂTEAU DE VINCENNES, PARIS

Throughout the day reports in the zones assigned to the 4éme and 5éme Armies streamed in, every one much like the last – *cautious probing toward Schweix, minefields encountered while reconnoitering north of the Bienwald*

Forest, taking fire from enemy howitzers behind Pirmasens – were the most recent that stood out in Huet's mind. Not a one of these communiqués told Général Gamelin what he desired to know: where was the 3éme Brigade de Chars? Général Georges' headquarters should have known the answer but all they could report was that they had been unable to raise the brigade directly by wireless. Either de Gaulle was ignoring these radio communications, or as Georges' radio operators speculated, the 3éme Brigade was making use of a different radio frequency channel. Huet had experience with de Gaulle, who was not the kind of officer that ignored a direct order. Then there was the hypothesis of Général Delestraint that the fragile ER52 wireless sets may have broken as a result of the rigors of battle. Possible, yet Huet thought it unlikely that every radio had been disabled. Huet had his own theory, however. The ER52 had a maximum radius of two kilometers, with de Gaulle's Renault equipped with an enhanced model featuring a longer range of three kilometers. The simple answer to Huet was that de Gaulle had the 3éme Brigade operating more than three kilometers beyond Georges command headquarters.

For his own part, Delestraint had been very forthcoming, yet not very helpful. Colonel de Gaulle had reported to him that Saarbrücken was vulnerable and Delestraint had approved of seizing the city. Similarly, de Gaulle had advised the clearing out of enemy positions that could endanger forces occupying Saarbrücken. Delestraint had thought that advice prudent and endorsed the measure. In both cases Delestraint had arranged howitzer support, plus requesting the assistance of a motorized infantry division. Aside from these facts he had no idea exactly where the 3éme Brigade was operating, as he no longer could raise the brigade by radio himself. To remedy that deficiency, Delestraint had sent motorcycle couriers out to ascertain de Gaulle's position and return with a report of the brigade's status. All very reasonable and efficient, but the lack of exacting knowledge was annoying Gamelin and Petibon to distraction.

"Where are the grid reports from our artillery in the vicinity of Saarbrücken? I want to know what they are targeting," Gamelin hit upon a new way of locating de Gaulle.

"Here sir," Huet had been perusing the recently delivered file.

"Very good," Petibon joined in. "Anything appear odd to you?"

"There is a great deal of concentrated fire falling behind Saarbrücken," Huet approached the large campaign map with his notes. "That would make perfect sense given what Général Delestraint has told us. What is intriguing is that suppressing fire was requested, and delivered, for the hills all the way to Sulzbach."

"Sulzbach... that is ten to twelve kilometers further away from Saarbrücken," Gamelin swatted the map with a pointer.

"Perhaps because the German defense line runs through Sulzbach? Pummeling the enemy's artillery positions overlooking Saarbrücken would be a thorough measure," Huet rather liked what de Gaulle was up to but dared not speak such a sentiment.

"Overly thorough for prosecuting an impromptu target of opportunity, as has been represented to us," Petibon's arms went behind his back where he pounded a fist into his palm. "Especially without consultation with theater command."

A messenger burst into the room through the double doors. With every set of eyes suddenly staring at the enlisted man, the fellow suddenly felt very self-conscious and stopped dead in his tracks. "Apologies for the interruption, général."

"Yes, yes, what is it soldier?" Petibon inquired.

"Premier Daladier sends his compliments to Chief of Staff Gamelin at the taking of Friedrichsthal," the messenger held out a folded piece of paper.

"What are you talking about? Let me see that note," Gamelin walked over to the boy and snatched the paper away.

"Dismissed," Petibon curtly sent the messenger away while Gamelin read the message.

"Well gentlemen, it appears French arms have pierced the Westwall and captured Friedrichsthal for the glory of the republic. The premier has been informed of this on good authority and he is very pleased," Gamelin returned to the campaign map. "It seems we at last know where Colonel de Gaulle is situated."

"Such rank insubordination. This is too much," Petibon was interrupted by the arrival of a second messenger through the double doors.

"Report from Général Georges, sir," the second messenger saluted.

"Let me have that," Petibon commanded – seizing the typed page as soon as it was within range. "Georges has received communication via motorcycle courier from the 12éme Division d'Infanterie Motorisée currently in support of the 3éme Brigade de Chars. Having dispatched sufficient men to occupy and hold Saarbrücken, the division continued northwest as the 3éme Brigade exploited disarray behind enemy lines, which included breached Westwall fortifications at Sulzbach through a gap established by the 507éme Regiment de Chars. To facilitate neutralizing enemy bunkers and other defensive emplacements, the 106éme Regiment d'Infanterie Motorisée was dispatched to establish forward bulwark at Friedrichsthal with 507éme Regiment de Chars. Bulk of division concentrating on eliminating remaining German presence behind Friedrichsthal where they are encountering light resistance and taking prisoners. Georges advises diverting additional regiments from the 4éme Army to join ongoing pacification branching out from Westwall breach at Sulzbach, and awaits confirmation."

"Well then... I believe Monsieurs Delestraint and de Gaulle are making a point about the efficacy of the Mass Maneuver," Gamelin stopped Petibon before he could critique the message. Anger was pointless at this juncture. Even Georges saw that. Better to declare victory and exploit what had been gained.

"You realize de Gaulle is fashioning himself another Marshal Ney: *le Brave des Braves,*" Petibon had no patience for such intrigants.

"Of that I have no doubt but for now I cannot argue with the results. The genie is out of the bottle, gentlemen. The premier is pleased and the newspaper editors are surely trumpeting this momentous success," Gamelin was far more sanguine than Huet and the other staff members expected.

"De Gaulle will take even further license in the future unless we cut him at the knees now," Petibon stepped next to the général.

"No, the citizens will have our heads if we discipline Colonel de Gaulle. Perhaps the premier would join with the citizens, as well. Within reason, and as long as we are meeting little resistance, I'm inclined to indulge de Gaulle," Gamelin knew that everyone loved a hero no matter what the cost.

"De Gaulle will want Homburg next," Petibon pointed at the campaign map where the city appeared.

"Of course he will. It is only logical and again I will permit this. From Homburg we can seal off the Sarre and separate it from Germany. But it will take time to accomplish this. De Gaulle is no fool. He leads the one tank brigade trained for mechanized assault. Circumstances allowed him the opportunity to show off in the Sarre. Circumstances will just as surely keep him planted at Homburg while we digest what has been gained. His Renaults will need an ample supply of fuel before any thought is given to further advances. And quite reasonably, it will be a while before our supply lines catch up to him," Gamelin ended his lecture. "Now then, let us stake a claim for this great triumph before Monsieurs Delestraint and de Gaulle grab it all for themselves. Call the editors at the major newspapers and announce that I will be available for questions."

KREUZBERG DISTRICT, BERLIN

At first they were furtive whispers off to the side. Questions between friends or relatives: *Had you heard the truth about what is going on with the Czechoslovaks?* The government had very little to say. Victories would have been broadcast swiftly but going on two weeks with nary a word about progress on the ground led Berliners to fill in the blanks for themselves. In the absence of a successful narrative to tell, Goebbels' propaganda ministry had concentrated on promoting personal interest stories showing soldiers bravely performing their duties. Heroes they may well be but there was no mention of fighting at the gates of Pilsen, or Aussig, or Saaz or Prag – let alone the capturing any of these cities. Yet the wounded were coming home and they told a very different story of trial and sacrifice. Now when Heiden stalked the streets in pursuit of the latest newspaper editions, whispers had given way to open debate.

Heiden had built his own modest network of informants, which he had kept unknown to Ottke and other colleagues at the Abwehr. Possessing additional sources for verification of intelligence was always useful yet Heiden also knew there would come a time when he would need to operate in complete shadow with no communication with his superiors. It was the nature of the work. They all had secrets from each other. This was Heiden's secret. Yesterday morning he had made a short telephone call. The pre-arranged code was innocuous. That evening Heiden ventured by the grimy newsstand located under the elevated trolley superstructure to purchase his usual three newspapers. Tucked inside the Berliner Börsen Zeitung should be a blank envelope with the details Heiden had requested. There were other informants, and different drops, but this was Heiden's favorite. He appreciated the irony of receiving factual digests on the battlefield results wrapped in a propaganda organ sponsored by the Reichswehrministerium.

Normally Heiden could walk right up, deposit the correct change in the seller's hand and be off in seconds. This evening, however, there was a crowd of locals hovering over the stacks of newspapers.

"Can you believe it? We are doomed," a thin fellow wearing accountant's spectacles commented while reading from a broadsheet.

"Never, even if this were true, the Führer is too crafty for the French. He will find a way to make them pay for this," a loitering deliveryman in dusty overalls opined.

Heiden pushed his way close enough to the newsstand proprietor to collect his papers and pay the man.

"Oh, you save a copy for him and not for me? All these years I have come to your dingy stand and no loyalty from you," the deliveryman complained.

"This one is a regular... and he pays," the proprietor dismissed the complaint.

Heiden let the argument go on without him while he slipped away into the crowded street. There was no benefit in commenting or being seen.

"Regular? Let me look for myself. I don't remember seeing this kerl before," the deliveryman glanced over the shoulder, then pushed other people aside to peer up and down the street. "Hey, where did he go?"

Well out of sight of the newsstand, Heiden opened up the Berliner Tageblatt to see what all the commotion was about. There, in huge type across the top of the front page was: Saarbrücken Surrenders! Heiden was aware the French had confiscated a modest number of trees on the border from which they were cautiously probing German defenses. In no way did he expect they would actually accomplish something constructive. The opportunity was open as wide as a whore's legs so it appeared there was at least one French commander with the good sense to dive in. Scanning the article, Heiden noted the editors had confirmed the surrender and the occupation from numerous eyewitnesses. Good reporting, as was their nature. Then again, in their circumstances, factual reporting was essential to survival. The loss of woodlands in the Saar could be ignored. Not the loss of German cities. The party was now caught in a quagmire that would pull it deeper with each day. Tonight Heiden would tell his men their patience had been rewarded and their time was near.

34. CONSEQUENCES

Škoda LT vz. 35 tanks charge the enemy

OCTOBER 14, 1938
PERSONAL JOURNAL
TOMÁŠ KOPECKY, REICHENBERG

The Germans attempted a new offensive five days ago at the River Neisse. Having thrown their best-equipped divisions against us in the south without success, the enemy high command well knew we had responded to them with our most experienced armored brigades and motorized infantry in the Český les and Sumava Mountains. So the Germans embraced the sound military doctrine: attack where your foe is not. Their six, largely intact infantry divisions, four of which had been bottled up at the entrances to the Erzegebirge passes for weeks were repositioned east where the Neisse snaked into Czechoslovakia near Reichenberg. Had our enemy been able to move so many men and guns without notice, perhaps the outcome may have been different. But our airmen did notice and there was no surprise to exploit.

We had always trained for shifting our motorized regiments wherever they might be needed, which made defense of our rail network a top priority for the air force. Our pilots had given more than they had gotten, but attrition was thinning their numbers. German aircraft were getting past our diminishing aerial gauntlet to raid targets deeper inside the country with greater success and could have seriously disrupted our railways as we had done to theirs in Austria. There was no question that the recent arrival of Soviet fighters and bombers came at the most critical moment. The Luftwaffe never attained command of our skies, our rail network was intact, and our motorized ground units were transported to Northern Bohemia in time to blunt the German Eighth Army's attack toward Reichenberg. The next seventy-two hours saw fierce fighting, and much bravery, but the Wehrmacht divisions could not breach our lines. The same outcome as every other parcel of our territory the enemy had trespassed upon.

Not long after the enemy was thwarted at the River Neisse the most amazing thing happened. After weeks of continuous artillery barrages the German heavy guns started going silent, first in the south and then in all sectors. The Second Department subsequently distributed an alert to all commands that the enemy had exhausted its stocks of artillery ammunition and was facing a serious shortfall in the supply of rounds for rifles and machine guns. What chance did German infantry have in routing Czechoslovak fortifications without howitzer bombardment? So wherever the foe had made small gains of our territory they set themselves to digging in to hold what little they had gained. There was also the matter of our French allies for them to contend with. We greeted the dispatches telling of France wresting the Saarland from Hitler's grasp with shock and joy.

As General Gamelin repositioned his three armies at the gates to the Rhineland our own reconnaissance scouts noted that several divisions from the German Tenth Army were packing up and moving west away from our border. To bolster defenses west of the Rhine, we assumed. Gamelin's successful drive presented numerous possibilities. There was a proposal before General Krejčí to invade Germany in the direction of our French allies. It was an audacious strategy made possible by the knowledge the enemy was nearly out of ammunition plus further revelations that he was dearly short of fuel to feed his remaining armor and lorries. Another factor in favor of the proposal was the knowledge that the German Twelfth and Fourteenth Armies were mired in Austria, their one rail link west continuously cut by our bombers. The prospect of separating Bayern from the rest of Germany in concert with our French allies was tantalizing. When presented by our staff liaison attached to the French general staff, the proposal was well received yet Gamelin thought the strategy too ambitious.

This was what we learned when Srom and I had gone to Racická Castle to brief General Krejčí. It was now clear to us conditions dictated that the next step lay in our hands alone. We had just delivered a severe beating upon the German Eighth Army, whose soldiers were both weakened and vulnerable. The decision had been taken to counterattack against them in force. By cutting deep into Sachsen we could chase the lot back to Dresden, as well as cut off the enemy's Second Army in Schlesien. The latter would have its hands full with our own Second Army in Northern Moravia. Once these two German armies were dispatched, the enemy would have no other divisions in the north to face us... and there are only 195 kilometers between Dresden and Berlin.

NEAR BAUTZEN – SACHSEN, DEUTCHLAND

The snub-nosed Soviet fighters swarmed in for another pass – low, fast and risky... just the way the Russian pilots preferred – strafing anything that moved. The lucky convoy drivers were those who looked in their rear-view mirrors, saw the lines of machine gun fire speeding toward them and adroitly drove their trucks into ditches to avoid getting hit. The weary German soldiers in the back of the trucks jumped for their lives – hoping the next patch of earth they landed on was softer than the last. The unlucky had a 7.62mm bullet pierce a major artery. Given the ongoing abuse repeatedly inflicted upon the German columns on the roads below, Bozik found the skies were astonishingly empty of Messerschmitts. But a great deal had changed in one week.

The arrival of the Soviet squadrons had given them air superiority over the Luftwaffe for the first time. Bozik well knew that the early success the Czechs had achieved in the air against the enemy had been achieved mostly by out-foxing the German pilots. But their enemy had learned quickly and the costs had been dear. The force of numbers the Soviets brought to the fight had turned the tide, not necessarily the skills of the V-VS pilots. In Bozik's estimation the lot of them were crazy – completely fearless... but crazy all of the same. Too often they took the easy bait that had been laid for them and were pounced upon by several schwarms of Messerschmitts. But our new Soviet friends learned swiftly too and scored many victories in Bohemian skies. After four days it was obvious the Luftwaffe pilots were on the defensive for the first time in the war.

The V-VS squadron that had been assigned to Polerady had literally been attached to Bozik as a personal responsibility. His Soviet counterpart, Major Novikov, had proven to be surprisingly deferential in this regard. Whether it was Novikov's doing, or simply the nature of his Polikarpov pilots, Bozik found their appetite for knowledge on German tactics to be voracious. What they did with that knowledge often left Bozik scratching his head in wonderment yet all of them were dead set on doing their part. Bozik found he enjoyed this arranged marriage. Especially when Novikov offered his own Polikarpov to Bozik to test fly. Upon accepting the invitation Bozik found the aileron control was very light and responsive, which gave the little monoplane a wild ability to roll and loop. The rate of climb was also amazingly swift and the fighter had excellent maneuverability for a single wing aircraft. The Mosca had its quirks though, chief among them Novikov had warned was landing the little bitch. No cutting power at the end to let the speed drop off and allow the aircraft to drift down onto the grass. That might get you nose down in a ditch with a Polikarpov. Novikov explained how the Ishak, the Russians affectionately nicknamed the plane after a donkey, had to be flown down onto the ground fast to avoid a stall. All that time Bozik had thought, mistakenly, that the Soviet pilots were trying to show off. To return the favor Bozik had presented his own Avia to Novikov, who put the biplane through an impressive display of acrobatics. Impressive enough for the Chief Soucek to place Bozik's fighter under a magnifying glass for stress fractures to the struts. None of this fraternal sharing would have been possible had the V-VS political commissars made the journey with the Soviet pilots. Novikov confided that the Czechoslovak military had accepted every request made to them by the Soviet side for the operation of their squadrons... sans one. It was insisted no political commissars set foot on Czechoslovak soil.

Today he had most of the Soviets strafing the German troops reeling from the main Czechoslovak counterattack. It was Bozik's intention to draw out the Messerschmitt staffels. The Polikarpovs were better suited to strafe the roads, as each carried more than double the ammunition as Bozik's Avias. He hoped the one-o-nines would come in slightly below the altitude he had set for his own squadron that was acting as cover for the ground attack below. For insurance, Novikov was higher still with a flight of Moscas. But the Messerschmitts were not biting, at least not here. Perhaps the B-71s and Soviet SB-2 bombers attacking nearby German airfields and retreating tank regiments were keeping them away from defending their infantry comrades dying on the road below.

Bozik wagged the wings of his Avia to signal to the rest of the letka that he was about to bank left to stay over the patrol area. He wanted to stay off the radios as much as possible. As he led the squadron into the turn, six sleek green shapes dived through their formation at high speed – evading the Czech fighters without firing.

"Shit," Bozik had flown them into three schwarms of Messerschmitts on the way down. "Leader to letka... six one-o-nines diving fast on rapiers. Angels, cover us. We will give chase."

Bozik pointed the nose of his Avia down and opened up the engine throttle. He had no hopes of catching them before they reached the ground but Bozik's pilots would give the Germans something to worry about before they could do much harm to the Soviets below. In his headphone Bozik heard Novikov yell a terse command to his pilots on the deck to break off and disperse. It was a tactic the two squadrons had practiced. As the Avias engaged the Messerschmitts, the Mosca pilots would be freed to zoom climb to altitude so they could roll over and dive back down into the dogfight. Seeing that they were outnumbered, the Luftwaffe pilots would attempt to use their speed advantage in level flight to escape. It would be up to the Reds to use the extra velocity from their descent to take away that advantage from the Messerschmitts and bring as many of them down as possible. He would have to adjust the strategy with Novikov in the coming days to keep the Germans off-guard. The more one-o-nines they could dispatch now, the better. Bozik doubted the Germans suspected that the order had been given to clear the skies between Bohemia and Berlin. When the Luftwaffe realized what was going on, their pilots would prove especially fierce opponents. Bozik intended to thin as many of their number as possible before then.

NEAR LÖBAU – SACHSEN, DEUTCHLAND

Czech and Soviet aircraft were buzzing about overhead all morning without reprieve like angry bees looking for a victim to sting. The Russian fighters were annoying enough but the twin-engined bombers were devils. Both enemy air forces used the same plane. They came and went so fast it was hard to tell who had just forced a bomb down your throat. On reflection, Oberleutnant Gärtner found it easier to pick out the red stars of the Soviet planes. So far his Mark II tanks had not been spotted underneath the tree cover nestled next to a low hill they had discovered the previous evening. His was the only Mark IV left in the regiment. The other two had been lost in action to anti-tank gunners during the attack along the Neisse. Gärtner's regiment had been left with the modest instruction of slowing down the oncoming Czech armor long enough to allow the infantry to retreat to Dresden. What a disaster... there was only one big gun in the entire company, his lone 75mm cannon, which was practically useless as an anti-tank weapon. If his company could stay concealed long enough for the heavier enemy tanks to come into range, there was a chance Gärtner's crews could pounce on them from behind as the Czechs passed on the road and actually do some damage straight up their asses. The tactic had worked before and was about all the 20mm guns on the Mark IIs could manage. After weeks of futile engagements he would happily settle for severing the treads of the Škodas. Get in close, disable the bastards, and then get out with as few dead Mark IIs as possible. There was no use in dueling with that Czech 37mm cannon.

Even if his men were completely successful, unless someone laid their hands on shells for the artillery, their efforts would all be for naught. Everything depended on the attacking Czech tanks being greeted by a barrage of heavy cannon when they reached the outskirts of Dresden. From what Gärtner had overheard, the stocks of 20mm and 7.92mm rounds were nearly as scarce as shells for the big guns. No one, it seemed, had learned a thing since March when they had rolled into Österreich with an appalling lack of everything – ammunition, spare parts, fuel, mechanics, engine oil – the list was longer than he had patience to recite. The Czechs appeared not to be afflicted by any such shortages. Having beaten back the invasion, now they were free to pour out of their fortress lines to chase an adversary that would soon be reduced to throwing stones in defense. Someone should pay dearly for this incompetence.

Gärtner felt the change before he heard the approaching devils – like the shift of the wind prior to a storm. The inline engines of the bombers and the Czechoslovak fighters produced a more refined growl that was harder to discern at a distance than the staccato roar of the big radials used by the Soviet fighters. Three of the twin-engined bombers coming on fast was what Gärtner heard now. They swooped down low and zoomed just above the trees. Banking into a turn, Gärtner saw them lining up to come in for a bombing run. The fighters would be next.

"Turn over the engines! " Gärtner commanded his compatriots. "Gunners, open fire!"

They had picked up a motorized machine gun platoon looking for protection on the retreat from the Neisse. Now it was their turn to defend the panzers. The gunners opened up on the swiftly approaching aircraft, hopefully with enough ferocity to distract the aim of the bombardiers. Drowning out the sound of the machine guns, Gärtner heard the Maybach engines of nearby Mark IIs stutter, catch, and roar into life. If the bombers could be driven off there was just enough time for them to run to a new hiding spot Gärtner had already scouted. Days of continuous aerial attacks had taught the men to secure their hatches without delay. As the company commander, taking that last visual check of their progress meant Gärtner was the last to latch his own turret hatch.closed. He never sensed the aerial bomb explode before the shock wave jolted the Mark IV sideways and tossed the crew onto the metal deck.

"No, I am fine," Gärtner shrugged off assistance from his loader. "Thank God those Tupolevs cannot carry a large bomb load."

"You are bleeding," the obergefreiter alerted his commander.

Gärtner removed his right glove to do a quick check, discovering a deep gash on his chin. "No time to worry about that, I do worse shaving. Get on the radio to see if anyone got hit while I take a look around." Gärtner raised his head up into the command cupola to see what the situation was outside the safety of their armor plate. Pivoting around in a circle, all he could see through the dust and newly shorn wood chips were the Mark IIs nearest his own tank.

"Kalb is reporting engine damage, sir," the obergefreiter relayed the message. "No other damage or injuries reported. Enemy bombers are moving off and the machine gunners are standing down."

"Ha! I am going to kiss those gunners," Gärtner unlatched the top hatch and allowed fresh air to flow in. Having learned caution as a practical matter, he listened for a bit, but could only hear the rumble of the Maybachs. Satisfied, Gärtner lifted himself half way out of the cupola to get a good look around. Before he could make one full turn, the high-pitched howl of a Czech 37mm AT round pierced through the familiar din of the Maybachs. That calling card was now very familiar to Gärtner. On instinct, he kicked his feet off the foot stand inside the turret and let himself fall inside. Within seconds the incoming shell caught the Mark II on the right squarely between the turret and the hull. The round penetrated the light armor easily, set off the ammunition inside and blew the turret completely off its hull ring.

Capka released the tension on the firing trigger while he waited for the wind to clear smoke away from the target.

"That's a hit! Signal the advance. Fire at will," Capka waited as another AT shell was shoved into the cannon's chamber. He felt Škoda lurch forward as gears engaged and engine RPMs increased. Peering through the targeting scope he caught movement to the left of where he had just aimed. It was one of the big German infantry tanks on the move. "How did I miss you... you fat bastard?"

Good fortune the B-71s had spotted the German tanks under the dense tree cover Capka's company was about to pass. The whole area was heavily wooded and the enemy was not visible from the road. It was only after watching the bombers lining up for their attack, and hearing the German machine guns opening up, that Capka ordered the attack. The Germans had camouflaged themselves well from prying eyes at ground level. The exploding bombs had blown off enough of the foliage masking the enemy armor for Capka to see sunlight glinting off metal. Now they had to deal with the big fellow their first shot had flushed out into the open. He grabbed the radio microphone. "Panzer Four moving in our direction. Concentrate fire."

The crew was jolted backward as a heavy cannon round hit the front armor of the Škoda. Capka pushed himself forward to his targeting scope. "Smart boy. You found me. Looks like the big fellow wants a piece of us. He is a little over-anxious though. We are beyond his four hundred meter sweet spot. All stop!"

Capka wanted to keep range. There were plenty of spots on a Mark IV with less than 30mm plate that the Škoda's cannon could pierce at nine hundred meters. The German's low-velocity gun was only dangerous at a third of that range. As long as he was intent on lashing out at Capka the rest of the company could close on the enemy commander. Making allowances for the Panzer IVs forward movement, Capka squeezed off a response. The shot hit dead between the hull machine gun and the driver's view port.

"Direct hit! No penetration," Capka noted as another shell was loaded next to him. Before he could fire again Capka saw the short 75mm cannon on the German tank recoil. "Back us up!"

The Škoda moved into reverse, bringing its nose down slightly. The German anti-tank shell sailed low and grazed the front plate – deflecting harmlessly into the ground. "Good... good. Let's give him something to chase. Full throttle forward, take us left."

Capka saw the rest of the company converging on the German commander – shell impacts now peppering his hull. Still the Panzer IV was focused on Capka's Škoda. Furiously rotating the turret around by hand, Capka lined up another shot for the same spot he had hit before. That plate had to be weakened, he reckoned. When his target dipped forward into a rut, Capka seized the opportunity and fired.

The German gunner got off another shot a moment prior to the Czech 37mm shell reaching its target. With the Mark IV nosing into a rut, the upper hull plate was almost vertical. With no chance for deflection, the anti-tank round bored right through the weakened armor into the crew compartment as the German shell fell into the earth short of Capka's Škoda and exploded harmlessly.

The Mark IV driver must have been injured. Capka looked through his scope and saw the panzer chewing up dirt moving in a circle. A shell from another Škoda caught the German in the engine compartment, which started a fire. Another round severed the track. The infantry tank ground itself to a stop. In the thick black smoke Capka could not tell if any of the crew had got out. It did not matter. The tank was dead. That's when it hit Capka that no other German tanks had ventured forth to back up their leader's charge. He reached for the radio microphone. "Enemy command tank down. That little show was to give the light tanks a chance to escape. Move around the trees and give chase."

Laying prone face-first in the sod, Gärtner heard the engines on the Czech tanks open up as their drivers increased speed. They would be pursuing his Panzer IIs now. At least he had given his men some distance to escape. If those devil bombers had not spotted their position his company would have had surprise and an advantage. There was no need to waste them in a futile engagement nose-to-nose with the Czechs. Gärtner had lost half his crew in the rash lunge at his adversary. One thing he had observed since the start of the war was that Czech unit commanders were very comfortable in operating in small formations and had a habit of being the first to open fire. Rushing the commander would draw the full attention of his comrades. And that was exactly how the ruse had played out. The cost was still high though. Only his loader made it out of the burning vehicle with Gärtner. Taking advantage of the dense smoke from the fire, they had dashed to the high grass growing in a deep furrow and pressed themselves as far into the damp earth as they could. Trusting that his ears could still register the diminishing rumble of the Škoda gasoline engines accurately, Gärtner risked raising his throbbing head sufficiently to see the enemy departing for himself.

"What next? I don't envy a long stroll through the country in these boots," the loader kicked his feet around to sit on the dirt.

"Did you hear any gunfire stabsgefreiter? Gärtner did not trust his hearing.

"No sir. The Czechoslovaks are out of range," the gunner was sure.

"Well, then... that means they didn't notice Kalb's tank in the thick of the trees, or they decided he wasn't going anywhere and could be dealt with later. Go grab the toolbox off the side of our deceased tank. Maybe working together we can get their engine running and ride out of here.

SECRET PRESIDENTIAL HQ, ZÁTIŠÍ

The president and his wife were taking breakfast in the conservatory. In adjusting to their new routine at the villa the couple had come to find mornings in the cozy sunroom to be some of their favorite moments on the property. There were no resident flowers in the room on their arrival, as was often the fashion in Britain yet the staff was able to locate a good supply of fresh cut flowers at Mesdame Beneš' direction, which livened up the atmosphere in the conservatory substantially. Generál Bláha rarely bothered them during breakfast unless it was absolutely necessary. Today proved to be one of those exceptions. When he intruded into the room it was understood the reason for the interruption must be of importance.

"Good morning, generál," Mesdame Beneš' tried to be cheery as a courtesy to Bláha.

"What has happened? Our briefing is not for another forty-five minutes," the president sensed a problem and sat alert. The war had been a relative stalemate for weeks... a stalemate he had been *persuaded* into breaking by Krejčí and the other generáls. Launching a counter-offensive into Eastern Germany went against Beneš' nature. There was the distinct possibility, however, that the generáls would not have heeded his wishes if Beneš had decided against the venture. The military leadership had already sidestepped their president numerous times during the crisis, but the president's hands were tied politically. Wide swaths of the public had branded him defeatist in succumbing to the French and British coercion when the army advised resistance. Circumstances had proven them correct and Beneš wrong. He could not overrule their counsel now because the public would not stand for it.

Krejčí's position was that Hitler would not fall from power despite an economic collapse. Therefore, Hitler must be toppled by force. With the enemy's ammunition and fuel supplies depleted the advantage was on the Czechoslovak side. They could dictate the peace and such an opportunity should not be wasted. Beneš did not dispute the merits of the generál's argument, only that such a military excursion was blatant aggression that would dangerously over-extend their resources. Had they forgotten what had happened to Greek generáls at the gates of Ankara in 1921 and the blood that flowed in Smyrna thereafter at Atatürk's hands? It was Moravec who had won the president's approval. During the heat of the debate Moravec had taken him aside to explain that a counterattack toward Berlin was essential. Moravec showed Beneš evidence of opposition to Hitler. Yet these individuals were not likely to take action unless a Czechoslovak army provided the prodding. Furthermore, Moravec was positive that any occupation of German territory would be short-lived while they waited for an acceptable provisional government taking the reins of power. Convinced, Beneš acceded to the adventure.

"Good news Mister President," Bláha relaxed somewhat. "Advanced units of our First Army broke through the German line and are pursuing the enemy west. Dresden is under eighty kilometers away from our motorized brigades and they are facing light resistance."

"A very encouraging report that puts my mind more at ease, generál, thank you. Now what of our army in Moravia? Far fewer of those divisions are mechanized" Beneš wasn't going to allow success in one part of the front to distract him from the goings-on elsewhere.

"True, we can expect the going there to be slower. On the other hand, our advantage in artillery and air power is pronounced. The Second Army launched its attack from the foothills near Königshof as planned. We caught them napping, sir. The bulk of German forces are further east. Our troops are making progress north deep into Schlesien. Generál Krejčí estimates it will be difficult for Generál von Rundstedt to prevent us from cutting his army off from retreating west, Mister President."

"So it is your evaluation that our forces in the north have not only exploited the lack of fuel and ammunition vexing the German military but have successfully leveraged the element of surprise, as well? Answer truthfully now," Beneš was laying an ambush for Bláha the generál would not expect.

"Absolutely correct, sir. Our adversary was not deployed to resist a determined counterattack, so yes, we have caught them by surprise," Bláha was intrigued why the president was pressing so hard on this point.

"That is all I could hope for. Thank you very much, Generál Bláha," Beneš' put his hands on the table and stood up. "Now then, if we have the enemy on his heels in the north, as well careworn and depleted everywhere else, I see no reason why we need hide here in Zátiší any longer."

"There still may be a danger, Mister President. I would not advise a return to Praha just yet," Bláha stumbled for words realizing he had been tricked by Beneš.

"Nonsense my good generál," Mesdame Beneš looked up from her teacup having listened politely yet diligently to the conversation. "You said so yourself, the Germans have much greater worries to consider than attacking our capital. I am sure the people would appreciate the return of their president to Praha at this momentous time. We must think of our fellow citizens who deserve every positive sign we can give them."

"Well put, my dear," Beneš appreciated his wife's intercession. "There is no more to be said. We will return to Hradčany immediately. That is my decision. Please proceed with making the appropriate arrangements."

"Yes sir, at once sir," Bláha knew when he had been out-gunned and when to make a timely retreat. He should have seen this coming. The president possessed an agile mind and had been chomping at the bit to leave the confines of the villa. He had given the wily politician exactly the ammunition needed to support that decision. It was too late to put the chicken back in the sack now. "I will inquire on the status of the castle immediately and will have that information for you when we reconvene."

"Very good," Beneš agreed. "Would you also send Drtina in to see me as soon as possible?"

"At once. With your permission, sir and mesdame," the generál bowed his head respectfully and returned to the main residence.

"I will miss this villa, Edvard. Such a lovely property," Mesdame Beneš had waited for the tapping of the generál's boots on the wood floor to grow distant.

"Yes... I know, Hana," Beneš cupped his hand affectionately over hers. "Let us finish our breakfast before there is too much commotion."

NIEDERGRÜND, NORTHERN BOHEMIA

The train conductor was probably still laughing it up. No civilian riders beyond Niedergründ he said with several soldiers standing behind him for added emphasis. What he neglected to say was that there was no way out of this quaint little village on the left bank of the Elbe except by rail or river. No road... to anywhere, just tall cliffs in every direction on either side of the river. The letter of transit from General Faucher meant nothing to the conductor. What good is a letter signed by a Frenchman, he had scoffed, while pushing Ros and Sanderson off the passenger car short of the border. So here they were... stranded. The frontier with Germany wasn't far but as the friendly locals quickly pointed out the direct method was by river or rail. The alternative was walking out and the reporters had not come prepared for a hiking adventure. Neither could they buy the needed provisions or equipment to hoof it. The military had already taken anything useful. They would never catch up with Faucher now. Days went by with no northbound riverboats docking. Every train that pulled in was the same story: no space or a stern refusal to allow foreign nationals on board troop trains heading toward the border. The great scoop Ros had cajoled Faucher out of was a total loss. Sanderson suggested they build a dingy since there was no watercraft to be found or purchased in these parts. That ditzy idea of his was sounding better all the time.

Having given up, Ros was sitting on a tree stump snacking on a few carrots she had bought in the village. It was a fine stump located in the foothills right above town with a grand view of the narrow river. The Elbe looked like a snake, and was much smaller than its reputation suggested. The waterway may be long but it often was only three hundred yards or less from bank to bank. Sanderson had been scarce all morning. To economize they were sharing a small room at the inn. She got the tiny bed and he had the floor. But when Ros had awoke that morning the Brit was nowhere to be seen. His stuff was still piled in the corner so Sanderson hadn't played the cad and ditched her. The thought of doing the same to him had tempted her a few times though. As a practical matter, Sanderson was a good egg to have around in a pinch. Ros would never tell him that though. Speaking of the devil, she caught sight of Sanderson trudging up through the weeds toward her.

"Hey stranger," Ros waved her hand. "How did you find me?"

"Surely it was you I remember claiming that knotty roost for God and Franklin Delano Roosevelt. Where else would I look after such an ostentatious ceremony?" Sanderson kidded with her.

"Thank goodness I am upwind. You're looking kind of gamey, friend. Looks like you haven't changed clothes since last night. Maybe you should jump in the river and wash off," Ros pinched her nose.

"All in the pursuit of journalistic glory, I assure you," Sanderson was in the finest of moods and slurring his words.

"You've been drinking, haven't you?" Ros' olfactory senses protested as he sat next to her. "Here, have a carrot, it will help clear the whisky breath."

"Bourbon, actually," Sanderson snatched the carrot.

"No! Not your special reserve? You were saving that for a special occasion... or bribe," she recalled.

"Closer to the latter," he bit off a generous portion from the vegetable. "Last night after you nodded off I heard a diesel boat docking and ran off to check out who it was."

Ros' body went from relaxed to alert instantly. "Tell me more! I didn't see any boat this morning."

"Well, it is not a very big boat really. Only room for two light recoilless cannon bolted on. You cannot see the vessel from here. That shed down there by the water gets in the way," Sanderson raised an arm to level his hand in that direction.

"Come on! Spill! Get to the good stuff already. What have you been up to all of these hours?" Ros felt like shaking him by the shoulders to get him to focus.

"What I heard was a Czech river patrol boat coming in. There was too much fog for them to go further than this little backwater last night. The vessel is quite the economical little craft. It has to be really since only a shallow draft boat is any use with the river depth of only two to three meters," Sanderson was caught up in his exposition.

"Oh for then love of Pete, get to the good stuff, Robin," Ros pleaded with him.

"You called me Robin... how charming," Sanderson beamed. "Onward then. I chatted up the crew. They had just started shooting dice to pass the time like all good conscripts do. A spirited match ensued in which I did rather well. The stakes got somewhat high though. I do not know what possessed me to bring the aged bourbon along but thank the good graces I had. Everything came down to a final wager. If their champion won, there would go my bourbon. But if I won, however, the good crew would transport us north into Germany to where the Czech infantry divisions are pushing north."

"You unlucky chump. You lost! You popped the cork. I can smell the liquor on you," Ros was crestfallen.

Sanderson cocked an eyebrow askew. "Far from it, my dear. I won smashingly. Having taken their hard earned pay, I couldn't be a scoundrel. So I shared the bourbon with the good fellows."

"That was darned upstanding of you," Ros slung an arm around his shoulders.

"Why thank you for saying so. We should be going, however," Sanderson rose to his feet. "There is just enough time for us to pay our bill at the inn, collect our belongings, and make it back to the patrol boat before they cast off on their way upriver."

KAISERSLAUTERN
RHEINPFALZ – DEUTSCHLAND

The Yorktown slid to a sloppy stop on the loose, rich soil in concert with the rest of the Renaults in the régiment. Chasing after the swifter German light tanks was a waste of time. The rear hatch on the back of the APX turret dropped open to forcefully meet the engine deck with a clang. De Gaulle pulled his torso through the narrow opening to sit on the open hatch and look around. Three Dewoitines – their engines at full throttle – sped low overhead after the retreating enemy. De Gaulle had already seen ample evidence of how well the 20mm Hispano cannon firing through the nose spinner on the fighters peeled open the armor on these poorly armored adversaries. Better to let the fighter pilots harass them, de Gaulle concluded amicably. The 3éme Brigade had done enough damage this morning. The Germans had attacked before dawn, as was becoming their fashion since these enemy régiments had been recalled from the Czechoslovak campaign. The booms from the fighter cannons ricocheted their way back to the stationary French armored vehicles. It was a race to the safety of the Pfalz Forest for the enemy. Through the middle of the Rheinpfalz ran a mountain range that extended eighteen hundred kilometers and three-quarters of those mountains were covered in forest. If the German tankers made it to the safety of those trees, they could elude strikes from the air and wait for the darkness of night to regroup.

Kaiserslautern lay at the foot of that forest. De Gaulle had reconnoitered the area thoroughly between 1927 and 1929 when he served as part of the French occupation of the Rhineland. The wooded area was huge and afforded many locations suitable for assembling attacks from. At the moment Kaiserslautern was the furthest penetration of the French offensive with a defensive line than ran south of the city. French troops held much of the lower third of the forest but the rest was sheltering the enemy forces regularly harassing Kaiserslautern. The Germans had artillery back in there too, which they were wisely moving about on a regular basis. Their modern and fast Messerschmitt fighters were somewhat scarce though, which was good news for Touchon and the other Dewoitine pilots.

The reality de Gaulle was forced to admit was there were limits to how far his military could extend itself. One brigade could accomplish only so much as the front line grew into hundreds of kilometers. He had fought ferociously for permission to lunge for Kaiserslautern... if the twenty-three kilometer per-hour top speed of their Renaults on these good German roads could constitute a lunge. There was only a solitary infantry division facing them along the way, which put up a good fight but was dispatched without much hardship. Within days, however, Wehrmacht armored reinforcements began showing up to make their hit-and-run night counterattacks. The Germans in their light tanks kept trying to flank and get behind the slower Renaults. A very competent strategy made futile by inadequate equipment. The German vehicles were swift but their armor was easily blown open by French anti-tank shells. Yet the lack of speed of the D2 was an inadequacy as well. Dispatching enemy light tanks was much like swatting flies – an exercise in discipline and annoyance.

As the enemy could be bloodied, but not eliminated, de Gaulle's brigade was tied down and there was no other comparably trained heavy tank force in the entire army suitable for breaking through the German line. So while Gamelin had given Kaiserslautern for de Gaulle to take, the chief of staff had also assigned elsewhere the motorized cavalry régiments that could have adequately pursued and dispatched the German light armor in the area. If those cavalry régiments had been here, de Gaulle's brigade would be freed to break open a corridor to Worms. The lack of such reinforcements kept de Gaulle pinned down in defense of Kaiserslautern, which was likely Gamelin's design all along. The chief of staff was more than content with the territory captured so far, while the premier and his cabinet, were surely in shock at their good fortune so far. The people, in their celebrations of victory, would not know that their future security lay on the banks of the Rhine. It was a matter de Gaulle had considered a great deal. The Germans were too much trouble and the natural geography of their shared borders put France at a strategic disadvantage. A new frontier on the Rhine would tilt the geographic advantage to France's side. Better that they hold the territory west of the river to force the claim, however. Sitting halfway through the Rheinpfalz merely signaled Paris intended a temporary occupation.

More Dewoitines flew overhead in the direction of the retreating panzers, drawing de Gaulle's attention skyward. The colonel shaded his eyes against the sun with his right hand. Scanning away from the sounds of cannon fire ahead, de Gaulle spotted three biplanes approaching from the left and low to the ground in a tight wingtip to wingtip formation. The sesquiplane wing configuration was unmistakable.

"Dive bombers!" de Gaulle shoved himself back down into the turret. Without a word, Vauban issued the alert to the rest of the régiment, as de Gaulle wasted no time rotating the APX turret to line up the machine gun on the fast approaching attackers. The Châtellerault was mounted coaxially with the main cannon. Aiming one was the same as aiming the other. The intention was to fire upon enemy infantry, not aircraft. The German attack bombers coming in fast at low altitude would only be in the machine gun's arc of fire for a short while. Once the Henschels got too close the gun barrel would no longer elevate high enough to track the aircraft. De Gaulle waited patiently, one eye glued to the gun sight, for the lead biplane to reach the one thousand meter effective range of the Chatellerault.

The machine gun on the Yorktown's turret and those of the other D2s spitted a stream of bullets at the oncoming Henschels yet the German pilots were not intimidated as they swooped in on the French tanks. Aerial bombs slipped cleanly off the lower wings of the Henschels, falling upon the Renaults with almost no delay. Concussions from the ensuing explosions slammed the French tankers down onto their hull decks – injuring some, dazing most. One of the Renaults, the Solférino, took a direct hit on the engine hatch. The crew of the Montmirail had the misfortune of a German bomb glancing off the dirt in front of the tank – deflecting under the hull where it impacted on a rock and exploded where the armor was weakest. Survivors from both crews bailed out just as the Henschels banked around to strafe the French position.

These airmen were proficient, de Gaulle admitted while cranking the APX turret around to face the attackers. Depressing the trigger nudged the fast-firing Chatellerault back to life. But there were no obvious hits on the biplanes in the short window of opportunity available. German machine gun shells pinged harmlessly off the exterior armor of the Renault. De Gaulle heard the powerful radial engines on the aircraft distinctly as they passed overhead with none betraying any damage.

"Come back one more time and we will see," de Gaulle challenged the German harassers. The colonel knew it was an idle threat on his part. These enemy pilots were good. They did not loiter long as ground spotters likely already had more Dewoitines closing in to give chase. The German light tanks could not do much damage to his Renaults but their Luftwaffe comrades were another story.

"Montmirail and Solférino are disabled, colonel," Vauban leaned over from his radio.

"Journée de merde," de Gaulle allowed a rare curse to slip from his lips. Pulling himself out of the still open turret hatch, de Gaulle confirmed that the Germans were indeed departing before planting his boots firmly on the deck. The colonel's tall frame would have made an easy target for a sniper yet he would not let such matters deter him. De Gaulle spotted his incapacitated, smoldering vehicles and jumped down to the ground to hurry to the nearest of the two wounded tanks as a flight of Dewoitines sped by in pursuit of the Henschels.

Casualties were unavoidable yet every single engagement since Saarbrücken proved to de Gaulle that his army could not take their success against this diminished foe as an endorsement. Swatting at annoying flies had made his men vulnerable to angry bees. There should have been a gun mount on top of the turret for the spare Chatellerault to fire freely at attacking aircraft but these simple additions were still being authorized despite years of requests. The turret ring should have been larger to permit a turret where two to four men could work comfortably but that would cost too much in appropriations, leaving every tank commander in the army to do the work of three men. The main battle tanks in the army could only go as fast as the infantry could advance... by design. If this army had to face large numbers of the improved tanks and aircraft now coming out of the German factories, it was obvious to de Gaulle that most French tank regiments would find themselves too lethargic and hobbled for their number not to become separated from each other, encircled and then decimated. De Gaulle assisted the commander of the Montmirail in pulling the unconscious radio operator from the burning tank and vowed this state of affairs must change.

ALTMARKT, DRESDEN – DEUTCHLAND

An army truck loaded full with sandbags hit a pothole in the road at speed, which sent a half-dozen of the filled sacks flying into the air with all six falling back to earth in-between unsuspecting pedestrians on the sidewalk.

"Hey pal, watch the road! Can't you see people are walking here?" Endicott shook his fist at the fleeing transport as a sandbag missed his shoe by inches.

The whole city was in a mad rush to escape. Those German officer stiffs who had collected Endicott from the staging zone near Görlitz had unceremoniously dumped him in Dresden. Call it a grand house arrest. He couldn't leave and his transit passes were voided. Dresden was a fine city but a purgatory all of the same. In a cockeyed plan to get out, Endicott struck up a relationship with the secretary to the U.S. consul, who tried earnestly to introduce him to local bureaucrats. But none of the German civilian officials in the city would touch his case. They all said it was a military matter and appeals would have to be made with the Wehrmacht, in customary triplicate. Naturally the military was rather preoccupied at the moment. Days of getting nowhere with that bunch gave Endicott the strong urge to hitch a ride out of town and let the chips fall. Then news of the Czech counterattack out of Bohemia and Moravia hit the city like a nor'easter. Overnight purgatory had become the one place in Central Europe a reporter wanted to be. The Czech army was coming right to him. What more could you ask for? Lady luck was back in his corner.

No one knew quite what to expect from an army of angry Czechs. German soldiers, many of them recently forcibly evicted out of Czechoslovakia, hurried to erect barricades and defensive positions as more of their brothers in arms retreated into town. Those good citizens who had not yet fled scurried about like Chicken Little. Then there were the good American businessmen flooding the U.S. Consulate concerned about protecting their trade and personal investments. Would the Czechoslovaks starve out the populace or reduce the city to rubble? This was all new territory in the long history of European squabbles.

Czechoslovakia had been around for less than twenty years, after all. Who knew what to expect?

When Germans or foreign expatriates found out Endicott had spent months in Prague he was broadsided with the same laundry list of questions amounting to how severe a grudge these neighboring Slavs were going to hold against their attacker. The government's news reports about how the Sudetens were persecuted made many nervous. Sure it was all propaganda but wasn't there some truth in every exaggeration? Being the go-to guy had an upside though, as it gave Endicott a chance to return the favor to ask what other people were hearing. The answers were all over the place and not very reliable, however. Some folks were sure advance units of the enemy army were already streaming into the Neustadt side of the city. That's what the locals called the newer half of Dresden on the north bank of the Elbe. One young woman was sure she has seen Czech gunboats edging up the river as she was heading into the city from the countryside. The rumors flying about were simply wild but they made for good copy.

That morning the consul secretary sent Endicott a note requesting a rendezvous at the Germania Monument in the middle of the old market square. The why wasn't exactly clear. There were still a few vendors in the square with stalls selling convenience items but most of the open-air area had been usurped for use as a parking lot. Endicott bought one of the local German papers at a stand on the edge of the square. If the consul secretary was late he wanted something to occupy the time since his German was getting pretty good now. Scanning the front page, the take on war misfortunes was getting serious. Oh there was still a strong employment of euphemism in describing the full retreat as *the strategic redeployment of ground troops*, but below the fold there were a number of useful pieces on preparing for emergencies and shortages. Endicott folded the paper up and made for the statue while dodging between anxious citizens and parked cars along the way. The tide of humanity and sheet metal parted long enough for Endicott to spot the consul secretary.

"Mister Holdren! Good to see you," Endicott waved to his contact standing beside the little iron fence that encircled the monument to victory over the French in 1870.

"Very good of you to meet me out here, Mister Endicott. Things are very hectic back at the office," Holdren was shocked he had been able to sneak away at all. "We are not used to such hordes and I am unsure if I am young enough for this excitement."

"Sounds like you haven't been around here long," Endicott teased the modestly portly fellow with the look of a banker.

"Why would you believe so? I have been in Dresden several years now," Holdren was intrigued.

"Let's see," Endicott pondered a moment. "Around ten years ago someone shot at the guy with your job. Winged him good enough for a trip to the hospital."

"No one told me about that," Holdren was startled. "Forever why?"

"Who knows? At the time they explained it away as someone unhappy about Sacco and Vanzetti. But that's not all. Back in thirty-one a bunch of reds marched on the consulate to present a petition calling for the release of the Scottsboro Boys down in Alabama. When someone told them to take a hike, the mob started throwing bottles through the windows. Little chance that bunch will turn up again but Dresden has had its share of excitement," Endicott could tell he had rattled the man a bit.

"I never would have fathomed knowledge of those unfortunate negroes would travel so far from home. Such an embarrassment for the entire nation," Holdren was determined to check thoroughly into the consulate's history. "You certainly are well informed, Mister Endicott."

"I've been in the news business for a stretch. A long memory comes in handy," Endicott ended the history lesson. "So what do you have for me?"

"The consul has it on very good authority that Czechoslovak forces will reach the city by tonight at the latest," Holdren passed the tip along.

"Forgive my doubting nature but how good are these authorities?" Endicott had been burned before and preferred to be careful.

"There are no guarantees, naturally, but the first notice came from internal channels. The Foreign Ministry in Prague alerted our minister there of the progress of the Czechoslovak army. That progress was later confirmed by German employees working for the consulate. They have no reason to exaggerate the situation," Holdren vouched for his sources.

"Good enough for me. Thank you for the tip," Endicott was more than satisfied. "This is going to be a big coup for me. Can I buy you lunch for your troubles?"

"Maybe later. Panic is going to set in soon and I should be back at my desk," Holdren politely declined.

"No lie there. My bet, by the looks of these poor tired kids in uniform, is that we're looking at a short scuffle," Endicott gestured at the soldiers of a bedraggled platoon hurrying by in front of them. "They look a bit on the scared side."

BÖRNERSDORF – SACHSEN, DEUTCHLAND

The BMW almost slid out from under him on the last turn. Too much loose gravel and the laws of physics made for a nasty combination. He had already put the bike down twice since pulling out of Teplitz. This old post road was not much of a thoroughfare. Little of it was paved and much of the rest was either dirt or gravel. Dangerous conditions for the speeds Bulloch was pushing but the route had the virtue of being direct. When Bulloch had shown Otto his road map at the embassy, the well-traveled old hand explained that the road was a centuries old imperial leftover built specifically for mail coaches to operate on. The path snaked all the way from Dresden to Teplitz to transport the mail over the mountains to the small villages along the way. Other folks could use these roads but the mail coaches had the right of way and everything else was expected to clear out when necessary. The way Otto described these coaches they sounded a lot like a stagecoach in the American West. That made sense since the condition of this road was in about as good as some sagebrush trail in New Mexico. To complete the picture, most of the Czechoslovak troops he passed along the way were horse cavalry units. Lots of people laughed at the use of horses in this day and age but on a narrow road like this crossing over the mountains, horses made a lot of sense. They probably were easier on the rear end too.

Upon descending into German territory, Bulloch crossed paths with a bunch of Czech motorcycle reconnaissance platoons. Despite wearing a leather jacket in place of his uniform coat, Bulloch blended in just fine. It helped that the CZ bikes those boys were riding looked a lot like his old BMW R11. Poor fellows had to make due with engines that put out a third of the power, though. After returning to Prague from his Košice adventure, Bulloch had searched all over for Petra but she was nowhere to be found. At the hospital he learned she had been discharged to make room for wounded soldiers. No one had seen the girl at his place, which was exactly how he had left it before leaving for Slovakia. When Bulloch checked out Petra's flat she wasn't there either and her uncle's hospoda in Dejvice was locked up tight. A neighbor told him the family had left for the country but didn't know where that might be. Days went by and none of the messages he had left for her had been picked up. There wasn't much else he could do.

Without Petra to distract him, Bulloch found things were seriously dull at the embassy. Lots of cables flying back and forth but not much to occupy him. Then Bulloch got a curt message from Truman Smith: *All hell breaking loose in Berlin... wish you were here.* While contemplating whether he should ride north to see for himself what Smith was talking about, word came up from the main lobby that there was another message waiting. Bulloch hoped it might finally be some word from Petra. When Bulloch ran down to fetch the message he was informed it had been delivered by a Czech military messenger. This one was even shorter than Smith's missive and was from Faucher of all people: *Meet me in Pirna.* The note was dated two days before. When Bulloch checked the map he found Pirna was very close to Dresden... tantalizingly close. That sealed it. Bulloch headed straight for Minister Carr's office to request permission to undertake some *field research*. The attaché sensed Carr wasn't completely sold on the idea of letting him freelance during a shooting war yet authorized the request in the end. With the BMW tanked up and tuned, Bulloch headed up to Aussig. From there it was a short ride to Teplitz where he picked up the post road.

Another half-mile marker flew past as Bulloch sped down a straight portion of dirt road with the BMW kicking up a wall of dust. The distance markers in these parts were tall stone columns that were tough to miss.

Bulloch did not trust them though. These old German miles predated the metric system. They also seemed way longer than the American mile he was used to. So Bulloch just paid attention to the instruments on the BMW and noted the town names as he passed them. The further north into Germany he moved the thicker the Czech traffic on the road got in both directions. Needing a break, Bulloch pulled over next to a broken down lorry whose crew was under the hood attempting a repair.

Bulloch propped the BMW on its kickstand and lowered his goggles. "How bad is it?"

"The water pump gave out. You never know with these civilian vehicles the army took over," the četař groused as he retreated out from the engine bay to get a look at who had just pulled up. "Hey, you are not one of ours."

"No, I'm the military attaché at the American embassy in Prague. Thought I would get up here and see how you boys are doing," Bulloch was hoping to get a good report on the area.

"Some of us, not so good," the četař brandished a wrench at the truck and laughed. "But if you had told me a month ago we would be pushing north on both sides of the Elbe while our tanks pounded the Germans west all the way back from the Neisse, I would have called you crazy. So busted water pump, or no, we are very happy men."

"Anything I can do to help you guys get moving? It is a little too exposed out here for comfort," Bulloch gestured at the landscape with his arm.

"Since it does not look like you have an extra water pump handy on that motorcycle of yours, not really. Thank you for asking though," the sergeant eyed the BWM with envy. "We have already sent word ahead. Someone will eventually come back for us."

"Good luck then," Bulloch pulled his goggles back up over his eyes. "Watch out for enemy planes. I have spotted a few here and there."

"Yeah, we have heard some fly close by too. After a while you can recognize the sound of their engines. Luckily they had better places to go to than bother with the two of us," the četař had already had his fill of visits from the Luftwaffe in recent weeks.

Bulloch sat down on the motorcycle seat and started the engine. The BMW turned over without hesitation. After revving the engine a few times, Bulloch pushed off and fed the throttle. He waved goodbye to the Czech soldiers a final time and was gone in a cloud of dust.

Rolling into Göppersdorf the whole town was one stalled traffic jam. Bulloch was worried one of the military policemen would take the opportunity to stop him to check papers but instead the American was waved around stopped transport traffic. Bulloch guessed the poor guy had enough troubles to deal with. By his calculations Bulloch figured Pirna was now less than twenty kilometers away. He hoped the Frenchman was still there. Bulloch had heard a while back that the Faucher had taken command of a reserve Czechoslovak infantry brigade.

At the time no one had a clue whether Faucher would see action. With Pirna so close to Dresden, that question had been answered. No way Bulloch wanted to miss out on whatever action Faucher was marching on.

PUBLIC TELEFON BUREAU
WARSZAWA, POLSKA

Oh what he would not give for a proper telephone booth. Some Poles could be unmercifully rude when it came to foreigners attempting to conduct business over the telephone at these public offices.

"Hear me clearly, madam. I waited in the queue the same as anyone else and my złoty are as good as anyone else's," Roland turned about to admonish the portly woman who kept bumping the back of his chair. "Now shoo!"

It was obvious the Polish national spoke no English but she understood the meaning of shoo well enough. Sufficiently well for her to back away a few paces in a huff.

"Sorry about that. Sometimes the locals get a tad uppity. Maybe the woman will focus her attentions on someone else," Roland made the situation clear to the editor on the other side of the line. "Now then, where was I? Oh yes, Foreign Minister Beck. Here's the following from my notes:

> *Moving onto the matter of Cieszyn, the disputed city divided between Czechoslovakia and Poland since 1920, and known by the Czechoslovaks as Těšín. In this exclusive interview with the Times, Minister Beck was adamant that his government reserved the right to take whatever measures it saw fit to support ethnic Poles there, claiming the non-Czech citizens of Cieszyn have suffered as many deprivations at the hands of the government in Prague as the Sudeten Germans elsewhere in the country. But as Herr Hitler's campaign to liberate the Sudetens has not met with much success, and divisions of the Red Army romp up and down Poland's eastern border waiting for any perceived outrage to lunge westward, the foreign minister offered scant details on what his government was prepared to do about the long simmering territorial dispute. But as both nations share strong alliances with France, Beck said he had been moved by recent diplomatic initiatives from Premier Daladier in Paris to maintain the peace between Czechoslovakia and Poland.*

Roland paused for a moment for the editor in Stockholm to get everything down. The Swedes built the Polish phone system so there were very good connections to the Swedish capital.

"Did you get that? What about the proper spelling of city names? Good, good. What was that?" Roland listened attentively to another query. "No, I could not get anywhere close to either half of Cieszyn. Kraków was the furthest south Polish authorities would allow me to travel. Damned unfortunate. Now then, here comes my big finish:

As a former army officer, Józef Beck still exhibits a cool, deliberative directness in conversation – every word, every phrase chosen to secure a specific objective. Among Europe's more congenial diplomats socially, Beck is often described as calculating or unscrupulous, and sometimes simply coldhearted in negotiations. Yet all would agree the onetime army colonel is very effective in his dealings with other envoys. Something of an asset when your next-door neighbors are Nazi Germany and Soviet Russia. And Moscow is very much on Minister Beck's mind. Whatever disagreements that exist with Czechoslovak President Beneš, a former diplomat himself, the matter that roils Beck the most is the close military cooperation against Germany now on display between the Czech and Soviet militaries. Beck openly dismisses the existing defense treaties binding France, Czechoslovakia and the USSR, and bores directly to the heart of what he sees as the larger issue. Yes, Germany can be considered the provocateur in disturbing the peace in Central Europe yet Beck argues this disruption pales compared to the danger of permitting Soviet troops a western foothold in Bohemia. Beck believes that soon enough President Beneš will suffer a cold betrayal at the hands of the communists on his own soil but his grave error will also plunge all of Europe into a spasm of political chaos and violence. That is the grim prophecy Józef Beck is communicating fervently to the other capitals of Europe.

Roland pocketed his little leather notebook inside his jacket while waiting for the okay from Stockholm.

"You are amazing," Roland cheered the colleague on the other side of the line for getting every word he had spoken. "Yes indeed. Landing the Polish foreign minister was a coup. Not a bad comeback from what looked like a botched misadventure a few days ago. Not sure what comes next but I think Mister Beck here is onto something. The centers of gravity in Europe are shifting. That will surely keep our ilk busy. I will ring you again when I have something substantial. Cheers."

Roland hung up the phone. Checking that he had everything he had come in with, he rose from the chair and straightened his suit. When Roland turned around the same Polish woman was glaring at him from the front of the queue.

"Hmmm, our munter is still in residence. Well then, perseverance pays in the end, my dear," Roland jauntily tossed in her direction.

In return, the woman's face displayed an expression of absolute scorn as she rushed to the empty chair Roland had vacated. As they passed, he furtively stuck out his tongue at her in the best schoolyard tradition. Satisfied with the chuckles this display elicited at the woman's expense from others in the queue, Roland walked out into the warm fall sunlight. The days were starting to get chilly he noted. Much the same could be said for Continental relations.

OBERKOMMANDO DER WEHRMACHT
BENDLERSTRASSE, BERLIN

Urgent dispatches from Sachsen and Schlesien flooded in without pause like the runoff from some equatorial torrent. Nary a quarter-hour elapsed without the arrival of a courier with a description of some new battlefield reversal. In all the worst-case scenarios for Fall Grün that had been proposed during the summer, and there had been many, no staff officer had predicted that the Czechs would mount a counter-offensive into the Reich. No sooner had OKW successfully orchestrated the shift of divisions to the Rheinpfalz to stymie the French advance than Keitel and his staff were confronted with a Bohemian-Moravian incursion to deal with.

"The Führer orders we send reserves to bolster the defense of Dresden," General Keitel announced before he was through the Operation Room doors. On the way to the situation map he tossed his service cap onto a hat hook without breaking stride. "Such a mess. What I see here is worse than when I left."

"Which begs the question, what reserves? There are no reserves to send," Colonel Alfred Jodl swept the back of his hand over the map. "The Eighth Armee is in full retreat, much of the Tenth Armee was redeployed to the Rheinpfalz and the Second Armee is cut off in Schlesien. The Führer ordered us to commit every reserve division to the battle. Did you apprise the chancellor of these facts?"

"To do so would have been of no use," Keitel scanned the updated disposition of their forces on the map searching for a solution he had not noticed before. "Hitler receives all of the action reports. His order stands regardless. Now then, update me on what has happened since I left for the Reichskanzlei."

"The remains of von Bock's rearguard is still straggling into Dresden just ahead of Czechoslovak advance units," Jodl's second in the operations directorate, Colonel Warlimont, demonstrated with a pointer. "They have been under continuous aerial attack the last three days."

"That and mechanical breakdowns have taken a toll on their armor and transport vehicles. I got an observation plane up this morning. The route east of Dresden is littered with Eighth Army tanks and lorries," Jodl did not see the need to mention the numerical estimate.

"Where is the Luftwaffe? What excuse does Göring have now? This is getting ridiculous," Keitel was handcuffed in this regard since there was little pressure he could exert on the Führer's chosen successor.

"The feldmarschall claims the front-line squadrons are short on ammunition like everyone else. The deficiency is keeping many of his planes out of action," Warlimont shared the result of his phone call to the Air Ministry earlier in the day.

"We are facing a disaster. As much as I hate to admit it, von Brauchitsch and Halder were correct about this war," Jodl gripped the edge of the table tightly. "The Czech army center broke out north of Trautenau and has gotten behind von Rundstedt's army. Eastern Schlesien is cut off and the only way von Rundstedt can come to the defense of Dresden is if he can fight his way through two Czechoslovak armies."

"General von Rundstedt might not be able to garrison Breslau before the Czechs get there first," Warlimont anticipated the worst. "I wonder if the Poles would allow von Rundstedt transit through their territory west of Poznań? Surely the Czechs would not violate Polish territory in pursuit."

"That is a very good idea. But having the Red Army at their backs might be a deterrent for the Poles," Keitel considered the option. "Another possibility if Breslau is cut off is to get von Rundstedt to the rail junction at Kreuzburg. If there is sufficient rolling stock, it may be easier to get the Poles to allow a one-time transit on the old Imperial line north to Poznań, and then west to Frankfurt an der Oder. That would be much less obtrusive than having our troops marching through Polish territory and very much swifter. I will contact von Ribbentrop to propose it through diplomatic channels."

"If we could pull off such a thing, getting von Rundstedt's divisions relocated to Frankfurt an der Oder relatively intact would make the defense of Brandenburg a reasonable wager, plus we could regain some tactical surprise over the enemy," Jodl worked the possibilities through in his head. "Herr Warlimont, go find out what locomotive assets we still have available in Eastern Schlesien. We need to know whether what we are hatching here is at all possible."

"I will have you an answer within an hour," Warlimont was already on his way out of the room.

"Of course, the strategy we are suggesting means abandoning Schlesien entirely," Jodl doubted the Führer would allow it."

"Herr Hitler dictated that we send reserves in support of Dresden. We will carry out this order and let the chips fall where they may. If von Rundstedt's army is encircled and lost, all that remains between Dresden and Berlin is the garrison here in the capital and the garrison at Potsdam. It would be a brave defense, but the outcome is a certainty: Berlin is lost," Keitel could see no other choices. "In the meantime, I believe there is an SS infantry regiment holed up in Nürnberg. Himmler wanted in on this fight on an equal basis so let's see if we can get those men moved north. Leipzig would be a good staging point. By then we will know what the Czechs intend, and where their front line is."

"There is another matter. I strongly recommend we evacuate the chancellor immediately by air while we still can. North to Hamburg would work. The communications are good there, and if worse came to worse he could be put on a U-boot and spirited to safety. Innsbruck to the south also has its merits. Italy is close by and Il Duce could provide sanctuary for the Führer," Jodl already had a transport aircraft fueled and ready to fly.

"Very prudent. I will champion that proposal at the earliest opportunity. We are swiftly losing air superiority in this theater. All we need are Soviet paratroops dropping in the dead of night on the Reichskanzlei," Keitel suspected the chancellor would not leave Berlin but the attempt had to be made.

WEHRKREIS III HQ – GRÜNEWALD, BERLIN

General Erwin von Witzleben's attention had been focused on the latest battlefield reports since he had arrived before dawn. Rubbing his eyes did little to relieve the headache that was diligently working the area between his temples. Part of him appreciated finally having something tangible to contemplate. For a month Witzleben had tensely sat on the sidelines as the nation had been plunged into this futile war while waiting for the command that would permit him to do his part to save the country. Days and then weeks passed without that communiqué arriving. Now the war was heading straight in his direction and Witzleben had to decide what to do. As commander of the Berlin Military District it was his duty to safeguard the government. As such, he was one of the few generals with some freedom to operate independently. With the Erzegebirge and Sachsen fronts collapsing there would not be much left between the Czechs and Witzleben's garrison troops. For now the enemy had not tipped his hand on how far into Germany he intended to penetrate.

"Special delivery for you, sir," Witzleben's aide had entered the room without the general noticing."

"More bad news? My eyes might not have the strength to read more," Witzleben leaned back into the old wood-backed desk chair. At his age one needed firm reminders to encourage good posture.

"More like a gift from what I can tell. My best guess is a book by the way the item inside the envelope is wrapped," the aide's job was to open all envelopes and packages first to see how important the contents were. In this case, he had not interfered with the wrapping believing the general needed a small distraction after a long morning.

"A gift? Who sends me gifts these days?" Witzleben took possession of the package.

"No name that I can find. Perhaps the sender put a message inside the wrap," the aide suggested.

"Well then, let's find out," Witzleben removed the wrapped item from the heavy envelope. As he untied the string and removed the smooth brown paper, Witzleben found a copy of Deutschland Baut in his hands. Witzleben turned pages dedicated to the buildings erected by the party since 1933. "Someone knows I appreciate architecture. No note though to say who sent it. I'll let you know if I find anything. Carry on."

"As you wish, general," the aide turned to leave.

No sooner had the door to the outer office closed than Witzleben's expression turned gravely serious. He returned to the title page where there was a short Latin phrase written in pencil: *a posse ad esse.* Witzleben took out an eraser from his top drawer to rub out the handwriting. *From possibility to actuality* was the literal translation of the phrase. Well suited for a book presenting the architectural achievements of the party. The phrase was also a pre-arranged code. The operation would commence in three days: October seventeenth. Witzleben's role in the mission was clear. He had been replaying every detail in his head for weeks with growing impatience. At least now Witzleben could get the whole matter over and done with.

Much preparation had already been completed. At Witzleben's instruction, General Brockdorff-Ahlefeldt had been shifting companies of troops to Berlin from his infantry division in nearby Potsdam. There was a war on and adding troops to defend the capital was a logical precaution. Witzleben had these troops stationed at strategic control points throughout Berlin. The exact locations had been painstakingly reviewed during the previous weeks. He would feel more secure, however, to have several additional companies in reserve that could be applied where needed. Those extra troops would bring the number of soldiers under Witzleben's direct command in Berlin to more than a regiment. He would arrange for this final transfer within the hour. Brockdorff would be expecting the order, as he should have received his own coded message simultaneously with Witzleben.

Witzleben was less sure of von Helldorf, the Berlin police president. The general did not trust rank gamblers, of which von Helldorf was a notorious example. It was a question of reliability. Men with obscene debts were a distracted lot when it came to performing their responsibilities. But seeing to it that von Helldorf performed his duty three days hence was Witzleben's responsibility. The solution was to assign a motivator to the good prefect of police. Gisevius had already proven invaluable to the mission preparation and was already in contact with von Helldorf. Witzleben would set Gisevius to the task. Certainly the Abwehr would approve of the measure. The decision was made.

OBSERVATION PLATFORM
FRAUENKIRCHE – DRESDEN

Strong winds buffeted the Wehrmacht officers high above the ground as they scanned the horizon with their field glasses for evidence of the enemy their rearguard warned was fast approaching. The observation platform perched above the massive dome of the imposing Eighteenth

Century Protestant church provided excellent views of the entire city from nearly seventy meters high, especially the Neu Stadt north across the Elbe. That was the corridor the Czechs would be coming through. He could already hear the booms of cannon fire thundering in the distance from that direction.

"They are late," General Hans-Gustav Felber raised his voice above the wind. "Has anyone been able to contact the airfield at Klotzsche?"

"No Herr general, neither by wireless nor telephone. The air base does not answer," a young hauptmann stepped forward to the sandstone railing.

"Are the phone lines north intact or have they been cut?" the oberst standing beside Felber lowered his glasses.

"The connections to Hellerau and beyond are intact as of a half hour ago, sir," the hauptmann reported.

Felber lowered his binoculars. "Not for long. Czech tanks are visible on the far end of Hansastrasse. If the airfield does not answer we must consider it lost."

"Impossible. There is a full regiment defending that base. Reinforcements should have arrived by air transport to support them, as was ordered," the SS standartenführer on the platform stepped forward to protest.

"In case you have not noticed, there is a difference between what Berlin orders and reality," Felber had little patience left for SS theatrics.

"Your attitude is not constructive General Felber." On this basis the standartenführer saw an opportunity to remove the officer from command.

"No one asked you for your opinion. Klotzsche is lost and no reinforcements ever came by air transport. That infantry regiment was wasted." Felber's argument was interrupted by anti-aircraft guns along the river bank firing skyward. Three Czech monoplane bombers were racing at full speed above the river near the Baroque church.

"No explosions. They are just having a look," Felber determined their time was up. "Major Holtzmann. Issue the command to our remaining rearguard units to withdrawal back across the river to old city. Then order the engineers to be prepared to blow up the bridges on my order."

"Immediately general," Holtzmann hurried down the access stairway.

"Those bridges should already be destroyed," the standartenführer made the accusation like an indignant prosecutor.

"Not if I decide to surrender the city," Felber resumed observing the Czechoslovak armor taking up position in the distance.

"Surrendering this city is forbidden. If you disobey your orders, I will relieve you of command to carry out the Führer's will," the standartenführer did not hide his anticipation at the prospect.

"With what, fool?" Felber turned on the black-clad officer. "Look for yourself, we are cut off. Czech tanks and infantry will soon ring the city. Their artillery will not be far behind. The airfield at Klotzsche is lost. Yes there are ample food stores but only enough ammunition for perhaps three days of battle. It would take longer than that to float a barge down from Hamburg with more munitions, which I doubt are available regardless. And even should the miraculous happen, the chances of any barges getting here intact and unscathed by Czech or Soviet aircraft are nil. If those are not enough reasons, look around you, these men have been under forced retreat for nearly a week. The ones that can walk are exhausted. The prospects for a valiant defense are not good."

"None of that matters. The enemy must be resisted. There is no other course of action permitted. You will carry out your orders from Oberkommando der Heer, or I will," the SS officer moved a hand over his pistol holster. "It is our duty to defend the Fatherland at all costs."

"To hell with this. Major, confiscate the standartenführer's side arm," Felber raised his arm in a blunt gesture directed at the source of his annoyance.

"Are you crazy?" the standartenführer was suddenly accosted by a feldwebel who had moved in close behind. As the SS man struggled unsuccessfully to twist out of the strong grip on his upper arms, the major wasted no time in slipping the Luger pistol out of the standartenführer's side holster.

"Thank you for helping me make up my mind," Felber came close to ordering the feldwebel to throw the SS loud mouth over the railing. "I won't imperil the population when we can only hold for three days. To do otherwise is pointless. There was no time to properly evacuate these people. Your kind neglected to tell them the enemy was approaching. It is our duty to protect these citizens, not spill their blood needlessly. Neither will I see this city burn when we cannot hold it."

"You are a coward!" the standartenführer fought the feldwebel's grasp. "General von Bock would have never surrendered. He would have fought to the last man."

"You are correct about something, at least. But von Bock already died for the Fatherland, machine gunned back on the road to Dresden by Soviet fighters. I am in command now and this is my decision. I will suffer no more insubordination. If you do not wish to be tossed into the river chained to a block of stone, you will be silent," Felber's tone was sufficiently severe that the only thing audible on the platform was the approaching cannon fire carried on the wind.

Felber grabbed his second in command by the arm and pulled him near. "Oberst, you will lead a delegation to the enemy commander. I wish to know his terms."

35. EXPIRATION

**The Old Reich Chancellery cabinet room
at Wilhelmstrasse 77 in Berlin**

*OCTOBER 16, 1938
NORTH OF CALAU, DEUTSCHLAND*

The Polikarpov careened wildly out of the morning sky as it rolled end over end in an uncontrolled death throe. Whether by his injuries from combat, or the strain from being pulled inexorably to the earth at hundreds of kilometers per hour, the pilot lay wedged back against the side of the cockpit oblivious to the fate rushing to meet him. The Soviet fighter impacted the ground with such force the fuselage and wings crumpled into a loose mass of metal and wood as the crater was formed around them. Separated from the frame at the moment of the crash, the aircraft's big radial engine catapulted back into the air, eventually coming to rest twenty paces closer to the Czech motorized infantry column moving up the local road. The soldiers were now well acquainted with the warplanes of their Soviet allies. Observing another one felled right above their heads likely meant trouble. The barrels of a half dozen vz.26 light machine guns rose skyward on makeshift truck mounts as their wary gunners prepared for the likely strafing attack by the enemy that had just shot down the Polikarpov.

The crews of the armored car reconnaissance platoon parked to the side of the road were less concerned. They were sure the friends of the dead pilot were doing their best to keep the Messerschmitts busy.

"Damn reds lost another one," Stanek drew deeply from a cheap cigarette standing next to his Tatra OA vz.30.

"The German pilots must be a bit testy this morning," the rotný who commanded the platoon's second Tatra ventured a guess.

"Want to perform last rights on the poor heretic?" Stanek gestured at the broken Polikarpov with his cigarette hand.

"Do I look like a priest? We probably should take down the squadron number, and look for a construction number. The Soviets are not good about putting much else on their aircraft, the staff sergeant spoke from previous experience. "Whatever we find we can pass along to headquarters. Someone will want to know."

"I think you are right," Stanek flicked the last of his cigarette to the dirt.

Down the road the throaty exhaust of a motorcycle engine could be heard approaching... a loud one. Stanek squinted in that direction but could only see dust rising from the rural road. A lone motorcyclist out here this close to the front was odd, and that raised his suspicions. Stanek drew his service pistol from its holster and stepped to the edge of road. The rotný climbed onto his armored car and instructed his driver to pull the vehicle close in behind Stanek as back up. Jumping into the hull compartment, the NCO rotated the machine gun turret to line up on the road. The lone motorcyclist finally rose up the little hill before the spot where the reconnaissance platoon had parked. It was a big German bike. Stanek needed to check into this one. He waved his pistol at the rider, using the weapon to point the interloper toward the side of the road. The motorcyclist slowed as instructed and came to a stop beside Stanek. While Stanek got a good look at the man under his compatriot's watchful gaze, the rider cut the engine and waited.

"You are not one of ours," Stanek lowered the pistol slightly.

"I get that comment a lot," Bulloch lowered his goggles.

"What kind of uniform is that?" Stanek ignored the rider's flippant manner.

"United States Army... mostly," Bulloch wished he had attached a small Old Glory to the BMW.

"Is that so? You are rather far from home," Stanek slowly circled the motorcycle. "I have seen a lot of strange things the last month but I never expected to see an American soldier passing by on a German motorcycle. This is a restricted zone. What business have you out here?"

"Official embassy business. Captain Nathaniel Bulloch. I am attached to the American embassy in Prague," Bulloch calmly reached into his jacket pocket to retrieve his credentials. "Here you go. I was sent to observe the progress your army is making."

Stanek examined the paperwork carefully. Along with the identification he had a letter of introduction of some infantry general with a French sounding name. Nothing was amiss yet the circumstances were odd. He wanted to know a bit more before he decided whether or not to confiscate the fine machine the American was sitting upon.

"A military attaché is it? Where are you coming from, kapitán?" Stanek continued with his questions.

"Dresden. You boys are moving too fast and I am having a hard time catching up. Wish I had a front row seat while you took the German air base at Klotzsche," Bulloch had just missed that fracas too. "Looks like you guys don't mess around."

"Ah... thank you, we were not part of that battle though," Stanek's company was already well forward of Dresden when the airfield was stormed but he couldn't say so to a foreigner. Better to change the subject. "Where did you get that BMW?"

"Bought it from a mechanic in Prague. You can see the plates and I have registration documents," Bulloch kept his tone chummy, well mindful of the machine gun trained on him.

"No, that won't be necessary," Stanek had already taken account of the plates but wanted to see whether the American's story held up.

"Hey, I could use a smoke. Will you join me?" Bulloch calmly unfastened his leather jacket to grab a pack of Lucky Strikes in his shirt pocket.

"American? Sure," Stanek could not restrain his enthusiasm. The American even lit the cigarette for him. Stanek took a deep breath – savoring the excellent flavor. "We do not see good cigarettes very often out here. Thank you."

"My pleasure," Bulloch smiled, waiting for the next test.

"Where are you going, kapitán?" Stanek asked in a much more friendly tone than before.

"Where the action is. That's my job. I'm trying to catch up with a tank regiment. I know one of the company commanders. I would love to watch them roll into Berlin. That seems to be where you folks are heading," Bulloch saw no reason not to be honest.

"Could be for all I know, not that I am allowed to say one way or the other. You do realize the Germans still have teeth," Stanek holstered his pistol then pointed at the still smoldering Soviet fighter.

"Yeah, I noticed," Bulloch stared at the downed Polikarpov a moment before glancing down at the handle of the M1911 Colt holstered on his belt. "I can take care of myself though."

"Yes, I noticed," Stanek had been eyeing the American army pistol since it became visible. He had made up his mind so Stanek handed the paperwork back to officer. "I do not see a reason why you should be delayed on your journey. Just stay close to the main roads. Bad things can happen for those who stray."

"Good advice, thanks." Bulloch put his goggles back over his eyes and started the BMW's engine. Before fastening up his jacket, he pulled the pack of Lucky Strikes back out and tossed them to the Czech. "I have another, why don't you enjoy those."

"I am glad I pulled you over," Stanek smiled at the gift.

"So am I. Maybe we'll see each other again," Bulloch put the bike in gear, waved and opened up the accelerator.

Stanek acknowledged the American's gesture by raising a forefinger to his eyebrow the way actors did in the cinema. With the motorcycle well up the road, the rotný climbed down from his Tatra in search of a smoke. "Who was that?"

"The American military attaché. He wants to see the war for himself," Stanek thought this Bulloch fellow must be a little cracked to risk his hide to ride out here. That was Americans though... they all were a bit crazy.

"Is that allowed?" the rotný wondered, not really sure.

"As long as you have these, most certainly," Stanek flicked the pack of American cigarettes with his wrist so one popped up for his comrade to take.

PRISONER OF WAR CAMP
THERESIENSTADT – SUDETENLAND

No sooner had the battlefield fortunes of Hitler's armies soured than resistance from the Sudeten militias withered away. The worst offenders who were fortunate enough to be close to Bavaria or Austria slipped over the border as the Czechoslovaks were not pursuing retreating German units in those areas of the front. The unfortunate ones buried their uniforms and weapons in some nearby field and returned to their homes feeling disgruntled as to their fate. What to do with these rebellious ethnic Germans once government authorities began re-assuming control of their towns was a question of serious debate between the president and his ministers. In time, civil responsibilities could be turned over to the democratic Germans who had supported the republic during the crisis. But the openly defiant Sudetens had proven to be a problem for more than twenty years and there was general agreement that they would continue to be a problem in the future. The fact was integrating these people into a democratic republic had simply failed. Although a few of Beneš' ministers passionately advocated leniency and reintegration behind closed doors, Moravec had confided in Burda that too many hearts had hardened during this terrible summer. For those Sudetens who had taken up arms against the republic, forced expulsion into Germany would be their fate. The president's mind was made up. When the war was ended it would fall upon the Second Department to weed out which Sudetens were culpable from those who were innocent.

All that was for later. For now, Burda and Furst were posted at the old Austro-Hungarian fortress at Theresienstadt. The Sudetens could wait. The main challenge at the moment was the growing numbers of German prisoners of war. Temporary camps had been set up all over Bohemia and Moravia to process captured German soldiers and airmen. Most of these enemy prisoners would be relocated to more permanent camps situated in Slovakia as soon as those facilities could be erected. The officers and senior non-commissioned officers were immediately diverted here to

Theresienstadt, in the shadow of the Erzegebirge Mountains. The Austrians had used the walled fortress to contain political prisoners during the Great War, which meant the ancient stone complex was already well suited to holding their growing collection of German officers. Thousands could be interned, if need be, within the small secondary fortress inside the perimeter. With a strong command of German between them, Burda and Furst were swiftly reassigned to Theresienstadt to assist in interrogating the flood of enemy officers arriving at the fortress. For twelve to fourteen hours a day they questioned a steady procession of war prisoners in the small brick-walled room deep in the small fortress.

"Very well, Herr Stürmann. I respect your decision as a fellow officer." Burda saw the German tanker sitting across the table from him was not going to discuss any details concerning the enemy's Tenth Army. Burda recognized the firmness underneath the man's polite manner. An honorable combatant deserved honorable treatment. "Now then, one last matter to discuss. I am charged with following up on your condition while in our care. How are your chest injuries mending?"

"Well. Your doctors are excellent. The places where the shrapnel fragments entered still hurt to the touch, or when I breathe, but less so every day. My wounds are checked often and the dressing is changed regularly. You have my thanks," Stürmann hoped his own side ended up providing such professional treatment.

"How exactly did you get these wounds, it does not say on the documentation here?" Burda flipped through the forms on his clipboard under the single light bulb hanging by a wire from the center of the ceiling.

"Artillery barrage. We got caught in a small valley in your southern mountains. I recognized the trap too late. We lost the better part of a battalion in there," Stürmann saw his interrogator was a crafty one in choosing his questions but there was little of value in how his final engagement had concluded that would come as a surprise to these Czechs.

"You are lucky to be alive in that case," Furst spoke up from the back of room where he had propped himself against a wall. Burda's partner had said little during the interrogation. Every morning they decided which of them would take the lead on each of their assigned prisoners that day. In this instance, they had decided Burda's personality was better suited to getting the tanker to chat.

"I completely agree," Stürmann looked over his shoulder to answer the cold and silent one. "None of my crew survived."

"You may not be aware of this but our armies are now operating on German soil," Burda shifted topics again.

"That does not surprise me," Stürmann had spoken with recent admissions to the prison infirmary. They had described the Wehrmacht's latest misfortunes in great detail.

"There might be opportunities in the near future for us to share prisoner information with your side. As a professional courtesy, is there any family or loved ones we could deliver a message to on your behalf?" Burda proposed in full sincerity, pushing a sheet of paper toward the German.

"My wife would appreciate knowing of my good luck to be alive," Stürmann could not resist the offer, although part of him suspected the motivations.

"Good. Please compose a short note and then provide an address for us where your message can be forwarded to," Burda explained while handing over his pencil.

Stürmann pondered his thoughts for a few seconds then wrote them down as legibly as he could manage. The act of handwriting was painful. When the note was complete, Stürmann folded the paper. On the top panel he added his wife's name and address.

"That will be enough to assuage her fears. My thanks for your consideration, gentlemen," Stürmann pushed the folded sheet back to the Czech.

"Our conversation is complete. You can return to the courtyard now, leutnant. Best of luck," Burda concluded their business.

Stürmann gingerly rose from the simple wood chair. As soon as the prisoner had exited and the door had shut, Burda read the message and noted the address.

"Nothing special, as I expected from him. That one is much too careful. But the address he put down is a very good one. Much better than what a leutnant should be able to afford," Burda gleaned from what he had read.

"Another fine family pedigree then," Furst stepped forward. "Strankmüller will find a use for that information down the line. The next one is mine, I think."

"Right you are. Morgen the SS non-commissioned officer," Burda checked his clipboard. It would be his turn to stand and observe.

"I might actually enjoy questioning this guy," Furst pushed open the door to call out to the line outside. "Morgen!"

An oversized brute of a man stepped forward with a severe limp. Burda thought whatever had felled this giant must have been severe. The right arm was immobilized in a full cast, while the head was wrapped tightly in a bandage.

"Took you people long enough to get around to me," Morgen examined the two interrogators thoroughly.

"Sorry so many of your countrymen decided to surrender instead of the alternative. Now we have a backlog," Furst indulged his grim sense of humor while securing the door.

"Ha! Just what I would have said," Morgen shuffled his busted legs toward the chair the other Czech was gesturing to. "But get your records in order. I did not surrender."

Despite this beast's many injuries, Burda recognized he would need to be watched carefully. The prisoner's eyes had meticulously scanned the room searching for a weakness, or an advantage. Burda was sure this Morgen could easily fight through the pain of employing that arm cast as a bludgeon. While the German looked Burda up and down, in the eyes was the same anticipation youngsters displayed shortly before separating beetles from their wings. Burda respectfully stepped back out of man's reach to observe the interrogation from a safe distance.

"All right tough guy, what got you then?" Furst circled around his subject slowly, handing Morgen a lit cigarette, which was gladly accepted. The smoke also kept the big man's free hand occupied, which Furst preferred.

"High-explosive round. The impact brought down the hillock above me. The falling rubble spun me around like a top and slapped me down like a cheap bitch. They say my head cracked the boulder when the two met," Morgen recounted proudly... pausing to puff on the Gauloises cigarette waiting between his fingers. "French again... at least they are strong. Too much to hope for that you Frankophilen could possess a pack of Mokri so close to the Reich."

"A good brand. I have smoked those many times," Furst admitted sitting down opposite Morgen at the table. German cigarettes were plentiful in the Sudeten districts, and it was good cover to be seen smoking them. "You know how it goes, you get sent to a country to attend their military schools and you develop a taste for their women and cigarettes."

"Not really. Everything I learned about killing I was taught in the streets," Morgen leaned forward menacingly during the boast. "My kind got their education in places like Altona."

"Hamburg... now I see why you are still alive," Furst fed the brawler's ego.

"You had to be tough to survive those days," Morgen clearly relished the memory. "And if you fight with me you have to be tough in the SS."

"Unlike the regular army," Furst supplied the other part of the implied insult.

"No question. The heer is good with its mechanical toys but close in, when you can smell the other fellow's lunch on his breath, I will take my men any day." Satisfied that he got his point across, Morgen leaned back in the chair to take another long drag from the French cigarette. "You Slavs have my respect though – hard fighters... very tough."

"So when you and your men were taking out our pillboxes one by one, were you operating on your own, or taking instructions from some privileged son of a Prussian aristocrat?" Furst primed the fuse he hoped would light.

"Ha! Those lilies want nothing to do with the SS. We are unclean in their eyes. The Wehrmacht leaves us alone as long as we get things done.

And we got plenty done," Morgen took the bait gleefully. "Now what else would you like to know?"

"What are you going to do after the war, Sturmscharführer Morgen?" Furst had one more hunch to play.

"Slit the throats of the worthless fucks that found a way to lose us this war. The things I have heard since I woke up make me wretch. For five years the factories have been running overtime. How could there be a shortage of bullets? Trust me, those who did this to us will pay," Morgen left no doubt about the fire that raged in his gut. "After that, maybe we will see each other again. This time you got lucky."

"Man to man," Furst rose to his feet with the measured deliberation of a heavy gun elevating on its carriage, "you may not like the outcome."

Their talk obviously completed, Morgen raised his plaster cast centimeters above the tabletop and then crashed it down, denting the wood finish. Using the contact with the table for support he pushed himself up to stand. "We understand each other, Slav. Good, you I will remember. I can let myself out."

Burda stepped forward as Morgen hobbled out of the room with the dignity of a wounded Hercules.

"Good job getting that line of command information out of him. I think the SS hate their own army worse than we do," Burda shared after the door had shut. "But I believe he rather likes you."

"Only as much as he enjoys a challenge when he kills. Perhaps I have his respect, but I do not think there is room within Herr Morgen for anything more than avarice and butcherly. He should be put down," Furst regretted their superiors would never allow such advice to be carried through.

PREMIER'S RESIDENCE
HOTEL MATIGNON, PARIS

Success on the battlefield had its rewards. Osušky was in a position to dictate terms to the French premier. The Czechoslovak ambassador had received instructions from President Beneš to brief Daladier directly. Such an arrangement provided no difficulty as the war was going well for both allies. Osušky well remembered the foul treatment he had received at the hands of that vile Bonnet at the Quai d'Orsay only a month prior. Now, however, Osušky had some weight to throw around. The envoy had chosen to use his elevated stature to make certain one Foreign Minister Bonnet would be excluded entirely from both the meeting, *and* the property. Osušky was certain the slight would sting Bonnet terribly. That thought brought Osušky much delight as he waited comfortably for Daladier to make his entrance in one of the more intimate salons in the Rococo mansion. The elegant gold-trimmed wood paneling, complemented by mirrored walls reflecting light from the crystal chandeliers, could only be described as intimate when compared to the still grander opulence found throughout the rest of the estate.

"Ambassadeur Osušky, so good to see you," Daladier swung open the double doors, followed closely by his personal stenographer, who promptly shut the doors.

"Thank you for seeing me on such short notice, premier," Osušky rose gracefully from the red and gold chair to greet Daladier.

"Please, seat yourself," Daladier motioned to the set of chairs at the center of the room's parquet floor. "You said you had important news from your president."

"Indeed I do. It is my pleasure to deliver President Beneš' fond regards, and the news that yesterday the Czechoslovak First Army accepted the surrender of Dresden. He wanted you to be the first to know, sir," Osušky let the enormity of the message speak for itself.

"How magnificent! This is the best news anyone could bring to me. Général Krejčí and his staff are to be commended on their perseverance and skill to achieve such a prize. I am sure President Beneš is both proud and relieved this day," the politician laid on the charm a little too thick for the Czech envoy's taste. "Was there a battle? Were the German troops caught in the noose or were they able to retreat intact from the city?"

"The remnants of the German Eighth Army surrendered their arms and stores without a fight. No siege was necessary and no harm came to the civilian population. It was a bloodless occupation. There was a fight for control of the aerial base just north of Dresden but the infantry regiment in residence was badly outnumbered by our forces and subdued. Repairs are being made and we anticipate putting that landing strip to our purposes within a day at most," Osušky was keen to include that point. A forward airfield inside Germany was crucial to tightening the screws on Hitler.

"An entire German army surrendered? Even for a decimated force, that is most unexpected," Daladier vividly remembered his own experience during the Great War.

"From prisoner interrogations we have learned that the Germans have expended nearly all of their available ammunition stores. This is true across the entire front. When cornered, they surrender. Their supply of petrol is also low. At this very moment another of our armies is well into Silesia with the intent of cutting off and eliminating the retreating German Second Army. As we chase them, our airmen are reporting cases where entire motorized columns are pulling off the road and stopping in place. If there are no pack horses available, enemy troops are leaving their heavy ordinance behind and taking to foot," this last detail was not in the president's message but Osušky delighted too much in the telling to leave it out.

"That is an astonishing development. We have yet to witness that particular ailment in the Rhineland. You say your forces are chasing this other army? Will you be able to catch them before they can escape to the west?" Daladier was eager to keep those troops bottled up far away in Silesia.

"The enemy is under constant aerial attack by our pilots and Soviet aircraft. We have slowed them down sufficiently yet the Germans have not swung west into our trap. They continue retreating north in the direction of a regional railway hub. Since we have already cut the tracks heading west, their intent seems to be seeking sanctuary in Poland. Which brings me to the next part of my president's message. My government's relationship with the Polish leadership is strained, as you well know. However, the bond between Paris and Warsaw remains strong. President Beneš implores you to apply your influence with the Poles to deny those German troops entry onto Polish soil. Under no circumstances should that army be allowed to reach Kepno intact. If no other solution is possible then internment could be lived with," This Polish question was another reason Osušky had desired Bonnet excluded. He had learned if Daladier was persuaded on a matter first, then it was much more difficult for Bonnet to dissuade the premier of that course later.

"On that I am in total agreement. I was not aware of this development. The necessary entreaties will be issued to Warsaw immediately. Better those enemy troops are left in Silesia for your army to deal with. Internment would be a risk because that could be construed as allowing passage to East Prussia. Our navy is not yet operating in the Baltic in force, and there are far too many merchant ships available up there to ferry those German soldiers where we do not want them to be. Neither can we depend on the Soviet navy to do the job. Their two new modern heavy cruisers are still not even operational. I will communicate with Foreign Minister Beck personally on this matter," Daladier was rising to the occasion as Osušky had hoped.

"Nothing more could be asked for, Premier Daladier," Osušky showed the proper deference.

"Now then, it is a matter of much debate in my cabinet as to how far Czechoslovakia intends to push its military advantage," Daladier shifted to his own political needs. There was great concern as to what would be the end game of this war and wrapping it up quickly without too much cost.

"Most certainly. First, our air force has recently severed for good the solitary railway in Austria that could be used to redeploy more enemy divisions west to the Saar," Osušky chose to lead with the sweet as opposed to the bitter.

"That is most excellent," Daladier was delighted. "Please continue."

"The Germans committed everything of value to the invasion of my country. With the capitulation of their Eighth Army at Dresden, and the hoped for removal of their army in Silesia, the enemy will possess no sizable reserves in the northern states to resist us. To force Hitler to end this war, we are prepared to occupy Silesia and Sachsen west to the Elbe and as much of Brandenburg as necessary to lay siege to Berlin," Osušky presented a Daladier with an envelope containing Beneš' demarche.

NEUES RATHAUS, DRESDEN

Somehow the Czechoslovak military administrators had talked the Dresden city fathers into operating the electric trolleys. People still had to get around and most civilian automobiles in good condition had been swept up by the Wehrmacht weeks before. What cars that remained were truly dilapidated machines that stayed parked where they were. There were little or no fuel stocks left in the city before the surrender and it would be some time before the Czechs were in a position to transport in surplus fuel. Food to eat and coal to keep the power stations operating had priority. Word was the first cargo barges would arrive via the Elbe in a day or so. The rail lines south were already completely taken up with sending captured German soldiers to internment across the border until the war was over. A nighttime curfew had been instituted but during the day people could pretty much go where they wanted within the city. Once again some deal had been struck with the civil authorities to keep the police and firemen on the job. For their part, the Czechs simply took over the key defensive positions previously occupied by the German military... and watched.

The Dresdeners obviously had their feathers ruffled by this state of affairs yet Ros sensed from the conversations she had already logged with a few of the locals that they would have liked their lovely city used for target shooting a whole lot less. But while the Czechoslovak soldiers garrisoning Dresden were falling all over themselves to cause the least disruption possible to average folk, they were turning out to be downright pesky about investigating how Sanderson and her had turned up in the city without German border entry stamps or Czech exit stamps in their documents. The two reporters were constantly under suspicion every time they had tried to talk with the troops. Sanderson finally put his foot down and commanded her only to talk with Germans until they could straighten things out somehow with their respective consulates. Normally she wouldn't take such huffing and puffing from him too seriously but the advice was sound and Sanderson was too darn precious for words when he got all worked up.

"What is so funny? Do I have a tear in my trousers again?" Sanderson was starting to get self-conscious.

"While interviewing the city fathers? Oh that would be good fun too. I had forgotten about your experiment in ventilation," Ros giggled.

"I haven't. You did not tell me for hours about my tailoring misfortune," Sanderson signaled for her to follow the path through the garden leading to the entrance.

"You were being a snit that week, and deserved it," Ros reminded him as she trotted to catch up. "And how many hours did I have that bird poop on my new hat back in Vienna without you saying a word?"

"Pardon me. I thought that was just another gaudy sequin. It fit right in with all of the rest," Sanderson thought it was high time he had some fun at her expense.

"That's low, buster," Ros felt like tripping his feet so Sanderson could take a tumble down the stairs.

"Takes one to know one, my dear." While enjoying his small victory Sanderson almost collided with some fellow exiting the city hall doors.

"Well look what the cat's dragged in," Endicott wasn't surprised the pair was too preoccupied with their squabbling to watch where they were going.

Ros lunged to the top of the stairs. "You little rat. You have been in Germany all of this time, haven't you? Godesberg, the Sportpalast speech... what else?"

"Read 'em and weep, doll. Oh, you missed the last couple weeks of dispatches from the front lines did you? That's the luck of the draw," Endicott embellished that last bit since there were plenty of dispatches he had been unable to send.

"Good to see you in one piece, Charles," Sanderson felt less mercenary about the way things had worked out than his excitable companion.

"The same. That was some pretty good reporting from Prague during the protests. I got the feeling the mob was going to lynch Beneš and any stray limey they got their hands on. Great idea masquerading as an American," Endicott had almost wished he had been there at the time. What a story it would have been if Beneš had been yanked out of the palace.

"That was my idea, you know. I saved his skin... again," Ros corrected the record.

Endicott laughed so hard he dropped his notebook the pavement. "You two should just get married already."

"Oh please, I have enough troubles," Sanderson raised his hands up in mock terror.

"Forget that nonsense," Ros leaned in closer to Endicott. "Where the hell is Sylvie?"

"Don't ask me. Don't you have her? I ditched Sylvie back in Asch. The broad wouldn't budge from that backwater so I took off. Same day those Freikorps goons nabbed me. You telling me she didn't turn back up in Prague?"

"No, she did not," Ros did not let him off the hook. "How could you just leave her like that?"

"Sylvie is a big girl. She can take care of herself. Odd though that no one has seen her in a month. Come to think of it, I haven't seen her byline anywhere either." Admittedly Endicott had not thought about Sylvie much the last few weeks, which led to a tinge of guilt... but only a tinge.

"Now I am beginning to worry. Sylvie is not one to disappear willingly during a war. She is too good a reporter," Sanderson spoke from knowing Sylvie a long time.

"Look, let me tell you from personal experience. Despite the conventional wisdom, the Krauts here weren't very well prepared for the can of worms they opened up when they sent the Freikorps into the Sudetenland. There was no policy or plan about what to do about a foreign national who got caught up in the mess. I got lucky that my eventual jailer saw less trouble in cutting me loose than keeping me locked up. But if Sylvie got thrown into a different jail she might still be waiting on someone with half a clue about what to do with her," Endicott threw out the best hypothesis he could come up with.

"That sounds terrible. What can we do? I can't stand thinking Sylvie has been locked up in a cell, or worse, for more than a month," Ros was desperate to find her friend.

"I know a standup guy at the U.S. consulate here in Dresden. If Sylvie got dragged into Germany like I was, she probably is in Bavaria somewhere. He's our best bet to get one of the other consuls down there to snoop around for a woman matching her description, Endicott proposed. "How many loud mouth American broads can there be in Bavaria, anyhow?"

"Now you're talking, chum. Point us in the right direction," Ros slapped her hands together. Perhaps Endicott wasn't such a bad egg after all.

11 MORPETH MANSIONS, LONDON

Conservative parliamentarians had been recoiling for weeks against their party's leader. Honor and pragmatism demanded that the United Kingdom join its ally while she responded to naked German aggression. The discord was not all altruistic. As the fortunes of war tilted in favor of Prague and Paris there was a real sense that an opportunity to shape realpolitik on the Continent was slipping away. Neither could Neville Chamberlain escape the wolves nipping at his heels within his own inner cabinet. Many long debates had been tabled in deadlock and frustration, leading Duff Cooper to resign from the cabinet. Cooper's resignation provided Churchill a path out of the political wilderness. Chamberlain hoped elevating Churchill to first lord of the admiralty would assuage the fiercest critics in Parliament. To the contrary, the concession only fed their thirst. As the prime minister teetered in this gale of opposition, Churchill and his guests were contemplating executing a good and firm shove to knock the prime minister over the edge.

"There are enough votes to win a vote of no-confidence," insisted Robert Cranborne, who had been under secretary for foreign affairs under Anthony Eden, and had gone with Eden when the latter resigned as foreign secretary earlier that year. "David Margesson just performed a sounding. If the government's chief whip says there are the votes then it must be true."

"That tidy bit of information has not been shared within the cabinet," Churchill remarked mischievously from his comfortable study chair.

"No I don't suppose Chamberlain would want to share those findings in the least," Eden joined in. "How did you learn these results, Robert?"

"Halifax knows, so my confidantes back in the Foreign Office were quite pleased to share the results with me," Cranborne was very pleased with himself.

"Yes, Halifax *would* know. Chamberlain, the Crown and most of the Conservative Party would back him to succeed as PM," Eden knew the political calculations well. "The question is how to derail that locomotive?"

"Lord Halifax is a man of principles who knew when to draw the line on appeasing Hitler. Yet he still lined up with the prime minister at the start," Churchill reminded them. "One backs Halifax if one assumes the crisis is about to end. No gentlemen... gelding Herr Hitler is not the end. This is only the beginning. Stalin will not ignore the opportunities political chaos in Germany will offer. The Poles are already having kittens. Hostile Soviet armies in the Ukraine and Byelorussia, V-VS squadrons operating from Czechoslovak airfields and the prospect of Moscow encouraging a communist resurgence in Germany... who can blame them. And let us not forget the Spaniards. The Ebro battle still rages. Both sides are inflicting terrible carnage upon each other. Franco has the upper hand but doesn't seem to have the punch to end the contest. Without Germany to resupply their current losses it is doubtful the Nationalists will be able to put the Loyalists away, even if Italy increases her support. Either the civil war goes on for many more grueling months or the combatants will have to agree to a negotiated settlement to end it. But who would want to wager on hotheaded Spaniards giving up the cudgel for a civil alternative? Not I. The peace that lies ahead for Europe will not be very peaceful. That is our point of leverage. Great Britain no longer has the luxury to wait and see how things turn out. Regardless of how principled, that is the leadership Halifax will give us. No, we must be in the forefront... forging the outcome."

"A brilliant message, Winston, but I fear too few of Halifax's supporters can be swayed from their allegiance to him," Eden knew the majority of conservatives were comfortable with the foreign secretary. Yet they were most uncomfortable with Churchill and his methods.

"I would not capitulate the debate so quickly, Anthony. I grant you the task is an uphill climb yet we could still peel away the support of enough party members to force Halifax into a more aggressive policy should he win." This wasn't the first time Cranborne felt the need to pump up his friend's response to a challenge.

Churchill had listened intently to their political strategizing. Both of his colleagues were correct in their reasoning. Yet neither of them had focused on the weakest link in the chain. He casually lit a cigar while pondering his next words.

"In battle, one never engages the enemy where he is strongest," the impish twinkle returned to Churchill's eyes. "We do not need to convince four hundred conservative members of parliament, gentlemen. To win, we only must convince one man: Halifax himself. Upon the foreign secretary is where the full weight of our energies will be directed. We must convince him, in good faith, that he is not the man best suited to grapple with the challenges the next prime minister will face. When the time comes for Chamberlain to step down, Lord Halifax's vote is the only one that will count."

WEHRKREIS III HQ – GRÜNEWALD, BERLIN

The last of the dispatches were signed and sealed. Witzleben had spent most of the night reviewing the final placement of his troops around the capital. Every critical intersection was manned and fortified. All of the major access arteries were under guard. Now was the time to lock the doors. Witzleben straightened his uniform and then pressed the button that rang the buzzer in the next room. The general picked up the dispatches waiting in a stack on his desk and waited. Ten seconds later his adjutant opened the heavy wood door and entered.

"Here, see that these are delivered immediately," Witzleben flicked the envelopes against the junior officer's chest on the way out. "We are sealing off the city. No one gets in or out without authorization from this command until further notice."

"Yes general, at once," the adjutant was happy to finally get rid of these field instructions. Witzleben had been doting over them like a mother hen for hours. "Where can I find you sir if there are requests for clarification?"

"Personally inspecting our defensive preparations around the city. I will call in regularly for anything you might need me for," Witzleben was already in the hallway.

In truth, the garrison commander was off to rendezvous with Gisevius. The Abwehr man had eluded contact for days. That was to be expected for an intelligence officer but it was still particularly inconvenient. Witzleben required von Helldorf to fall in line now. Gisevius was the only person with the leverage to assure that happened.

U.S. EMBASSY
TIERGARTEN DISTRICT, BERLIN

The rap on the door was polite, thank goodness. Smith was not in the mood for another emergency. He had way too many to account for as it was. "Come in," the attaché glanced up from his paperwork to see who was entering his office.

"Truman Smith. Do you have a few minutes for another old hand?" Bill Shirer announced himself.

"For you Bill, sure thing," Smith rose from his desk to properly greet the now very influential Berlin correspondent for CBS. "Great to see you. C'mon on in. What brings you to my door?"

"Here to see Ambassador Wilson to get his perspective for my report this evening," Shirer chose one of the plain metal chairs fronting Smith's desk. "I got here early so I thought I would see if you were in."

"Great timing. I just brewed up some Hobo Coffee on the hot plate," Smith poured two cups of the strong refreshment, which he served before returning to his desk chair. "I haven't been outside all day. How do things look out there?"

"Tense, very tense. Lots of soldiers are setting up shop on almost every street corner. Plenty of rumors are flying around but there is a paucity of facts. People on the street are getting a little scared," Shirer was so desperate for details he was left with few options other than sounding out the diplomatic community.

"That sounds about right," Smith felt it couldn't hurt to throw the man a bone. "What was the last big nugget you got, and when?

"That the Czechs had launched a counter-offensive. That was a couple of days ago though. I haven't been able to get an international call out or in since then. Doesn't seem telegrams are making it through either."

"How the hell are you still broadcasting? I would think Goebbels would have turned off the microphones by now," Smith thought the situation odd.

"Maybe he's too busy to notice. Then again, I have very little to report lately so there is little reason to take me off the air," Shirer was sure the latter was the case.

"That might change after what I am about to tell you. The Czechs just took Dresden. What was left of a German army surrendered without a fight after a forced retreat from Bohemia. Our consular people in Dresden are reporting the German troops were almost out of ammunition," Smith gave Shirer the facts he possessed.

"That would explain it. The officers I have spoken to would say nothing but they were anxious. I thought it was the Saarland debacle. That's all Berliners on the street were talking about since the Berliner Tageblatt broke the news on the loss of Saarbrücken. But surrendering Dresden... that is much juicier," Shirer grew excited as he put more of the pieces together in his head.

"The Rhineland is old news, Smith got up for some more coffee. "Yeah, the French push out of the Saar surprised them, no doubt about it. But the German officers I talk to all believe Gamelin is incapable of quickly exploiting his success. Now that they have shifted several divisions from the Czechoslovak front into the Rhineland, the Germans feel they can depend on French caution to stall the advance indefinitely. No, what's got them rattled is the way they lost Dresden. That and there ain't much available between Dresden and Berlin to keep the Czechs from coming straight on in. Up to you to choose whether or not to broadcast that information. But if you do, I'd recommend you get the story out tonight. I don't think you'll get another chance."

HOTEL MONOPOL
KONIGSTRASSE, NÜRNBERG

Lunch got cut short. Something noisy was happening on the main street outside the hotel. Sylvie gulped down the rest of her order of Schäufele, which was the best slow roasted pork she had tasted in a long time. No rest for the wicked, she figured. Pushing her way past out of the hotel lobby Sylvie saw what the commotion was all about. A whole bunch of SS boys were marching themselves in the direction of the train station to the rapt attention of the locals. Something about those jet-black uniforms didn't seem to fit in this charming Renaissance city. At least not down here in the old part of town. But there they were anyway, goose-stepping their way somewhere and Sylvie was determined to find out where.

"Hey handsome, where you boys off to? All of you look so sharp," Sylvie called out to the nearest uniform that seemed to have any rank. German insignia always confused her and these new SS badges were even worse.

"North! Those damn Czechs must be taught a lesson," the squad leader answered as he passed the woman at the front of the crowd.

"Berlin? Really?" Sylvie acted on a hunch that came to her suddenly.

"Ya! The Führer needs us," was the last she heard from the uniform as he goose-stepped out of earshot.

That terse exchange told Sylvie all she needed to know about how the war was going. Now, what was she going to do about it? Upon getting herself out of Karlsbad and into Germany proper, the plan had been to head west by whatever guile necessary to make it to Mainz. That strategy had been hatched when the Germans were stalled in the Sudetenland and the French were on the move in the Rhineland. Now the French were moving slow and the Czechs seemed to be making strides. What the hell should she do? Nürnberg was dead center in the middle of the country far away from all of the action. Sylvie stomped her right shoe against the pavement in frustration. She seemed destined to miss the entire damn war. Continue heading west or chase after these SS chumps? What to do? Mainz it was. Berlin was the juicier choice but the bureau there could handle the war arriving on their doorstep. Better to be where the rest of the hacks were not... covering the Rhineland battle. Who knew, maybe the French had something more up their sleeves. That didn't mean Sylvie couldn't get her name added to someone else's byline in the meantime. If she could get a working phone line to the Berlin bureau, she could tell them about the SS regiment heading in their direction. Decision made. Now she just had to talk her way onto someone else's telephone.

ALTEN REICHSKANZLEI, BERLIN

The double doors to the chancellor's office rattled violently in place. The Führer was in the foulest of moods, screaming at the top of his lungs and throwing heavy objects in the next room. The fine old Rococo palace, so beautifully constructed in its day, may have served Bismarck well yet could not mask the fury of Herr Hitler's tantrums. Thank God von Ribbentrop had spared him from having to witness this latest display of outrage in person. It was bad enough having to sit in the adjoining anteroom, called the Ambassador's Room, where he could still hear every word shouted by the Führer. Platen attempted to cancel out the noise by playing thought games. How many envoys had waited on the small settee Platen was seated upon? When had the electric crystal chandelier been installed? Where did the huge Oriental rug come from and had it been a state gift from a Middle Eastern monarch?

This was the second in as many days that the foreign minister and General Keitel had personally attempted to convince the chancellor to authorize an emergency trade mission to Poland. Hitler was in the foulest of moods at the reports he was receiving. Worse than Platen had ever witnessed before. Every new slip of paper bore terrible news and his closest advisors were pleading with the chancellor to escape Berlin. Keitel and von Ribbentrop were brave to try persuading Hitler again. With every entreaty the chancellor was fixated instead on how the Reich had been betrayed by the army's incompetence. Keitel forged ahead in his arguments undeterred. The western portion of Poland had been carved out of East Prussia in 1919. The new Polish state therefore inherited numerous munitions factories and had wisely decided to standardize on the same calibers of ammunition long in use in Germany and Austria-Hungary. They could supply the Reich with emergency stocks of bullets and artillery shells. Again and again Hitler vetoed the proposal. The Reich would not go hat in hand to the Poles he kept screaming. Keitel and von Ribbentrop would not accept no from the Führer, however. Göring should have been lending his voice to their effort but had contrived other pressing matters to keep him away. The coward. Suddenly, the storm broke and the screams subsided.

"Do it! But do not let Beck and Smigly-Rydz rob us blind," Hitler commanded. "They must properly appreciate they earn my favor if they assist us in this purchase. That should be payment enough."

In seconds the double doors opened for the general and the foreign minister. Neither was losing any time in leaving the chancellor. Platen thought that was smart as the Führer could easily change his mind. Platen jumped to his feet as Keitel passed by him and then fell in line beside von Ribbentrop.

"You both were successful. Congratulations foreign minister," Platen was relieved to finally be fleeing the left wing of the chancellery.

"Wait until we get back from Warsaw and then we will see if congratulations are in order," von Ribbentrop cautioned. "Is the aircraft ready to go?"

"Yes sir, the Condor is fueled and awaiting us at Tempelhof," Platen confirmed.

"Excellent. We are heading to the airfield straight away," von Ribbentrop was anxious to get in the air. "The pilot will need to divert north to escape meeting any Czech or Soviet aerial patrols, which will cost us still more time."

DERELICT CATHOLIC MONASTERY, VYŠKOV

Moravec had to admit a part of him very much enjoyed conducting the department's business from within this religious edifice's stoic stonewalls and vaulted ceilings. But the president's return to the capital meant the military establishment that served him would need to follow soon. The nation had survived Hitler's fury and was soon to be in a position to dictate terms. The army's return to Prague would be a clear signal to the people that they could begin to celebrate. These thoughts could wait, however. Moravec was allowing his mind to wander, which was a disservice to Major Strankmüller's latest report.

"What preparations have been made to evacuate the governmental organs from Berlin?" Moravec interrupted Strankmüller's rundown of where each German politician and officer was last seen.

"No such preparations are in evidence as late as yesterday... much the opposite in fact. Additional companies of infantry are being trucked in from Potsdam to bolster the defense of Berlin. That is what the latest wireless reports are saying. The way these soldiers are being deployed we could be facing a battle street-by-street should we be forced to wrest the city from them," Strankmüller had had a hunch about these deployments but could not yet corroborate his suspicion.

"I doubt we can count on another pleasant surprise such as Dresden," Tichy had mostly listened during Strankmüller's presentation inside the old chapel. "These are district garrisons with intact ammunition stores. We cannot afford a prolonged siege of Berlin. There are too many Germans and far too many variables that will come into play. This Nazi snake must be decapitated swiftly."

"Agreed," Moravec continued to massage his chin. "What do we know of General Witzleben's will to continue the fight?"

"He is a tough old warhorse that one. Fought at Verdun, seriously wounded in battle and decorated for valor," Strankmüller recited the

German officer's biography from memory. "Witzleben is a career officer who has been openly critical of the regime since 1934. He also is of the breed where fidelity to country would outweigh politics."

"So while he might be inclined to shoot Hitler himself, Witzleben would not be deterred from defending Berlin. Do I have that right?" Tichy summarized.

"Yes, that's the profile we have of him," Strankmüller decided to discuss his hunch. He reached down into his satchel on the floor and pulled out a map of Berlin, which he unfolded. "There is something else. Look here. These are the locations where we know troops have dug in. All the major arteries into the city are covered, as are the major intersections and governmental ministries, just as you would expect. But look at these notations I have made. Those are addresses where major party members carry out their activities from. That strikes me as a bit odd. Why would Witzleben protect them?"

"Perhaps he was instructed to," Moravec was very intrigued with where the conversation was going.

"That is possible, but a man of Witzleben's nature would just as soon devote token resources to defending the party. Yet the reports we have received during the last seventy-two hours show Witzleben is putting equally strong detachments in such places. These deployments would be very useful if your intention was to assume complete control of the capital, however. I have no proof Witzleben is preparing for anything other than a thorough defense of Berlin. All I have is a hunch," which Strankmüller knew he could not verify.

"A very delicious hunch at that. Good work. I suspect we will not know for sure until after the fact," Moravec saw a completely new endgame unfolding in his head. "Let me know immediately if we receive any further information that may sway our understanding of what's going on with the Germans. For now, I must discuss the implications with the chief of staff immediately."

OCTOBER 18, 1938
HENSCHEL FLUGZEUG-WERKE
SCHÖNEFELD, DEUTSCHLAND

Twenty kilometers to the northwest lay Berlin. Kopecky had assumed he would be able to see some landmark magnified through his field glasses from the top of the metal tower but there were too many trees in the way. His first responsibility was to this airfield, however, not the German capital. The airfield itself was quite a gift. Except for the private guards, the facility had been entirely undefended when a company of Czechoslovak armor split off from the forward advance and rolled through the main gate.

"More machined components in the side structure to the right," Hruska returned from another foraging mission to watch his major climb down the tower ladder. "Crates full of them stacked four and five high."

Kopecky had grown very fond of his driver since their encounter with the Freikorps. Hruska was a very reliable man with an odd sense of humor. It was just the two of them to document what was captured on the airfield while a solitary infantry platoon guarded the perimeter. The army's advance north had been so rapid no one else could be spared. Much of the credit went to the Germans themselves for providing forty-one kilometers of beautiful new highway between Dresden and Ruhland. Government engineers in Prague could learn a great deal from these new highways the Nazis were laying down.

North of Ruhland was another forty kilometers of partially constructed highway all of the way to Calau that also made for very swift travel by Czechoslovak motorized regiments. The worst part had been the fifty-eight kilometers along the old rural roads between Calau and Teupitz. The German authorities had organized road construction crews into impromptu reserve companies, issued them Mauser rifles and instructed the workers to defend the Fatherland. Not much of a challenge for soldiers with months of experience rooting out Henlein's militias but thousands of lightly armed workers could not be bypassed and left in the rear to hinder army supply lines. As few as possible were slain until the rest happily laid down their arms. Precious time was lost rounding up the survivors, confiscating their weapons and sending them south. Once that task was accomplished the advance columns were greeted with another twenty-three kilometers of virgin pavement north of Teupitz. At the end of this splendid stretch of fresh highway was the town of Schönefeld and its brand new airstrip.

"The Henschel Company must have spent hundreds of thousands of Deutschmarks on building this installation and no one thought to station a garrison to protect that investment?" Kopecky scribbled more notes on his clipboard.

"The factory and machine tools alone are precious. Do you think we will be able to keep it all?" Hruska preferred to see this valuable catch dismantled, trucked home and put to good use.

"The Germans certainly would keep everything if the situation was reversed. We probably should as well." But Kopecky knew they might have to leave the base intact in order to get a better peace deal.

"Just look at this place," Hruska swept his arm wide. "Every building is a self-contained operating unit separated by big grassy areas. Not one of those structures is in a straight line. If a bomber damages one building, manufacturing in the others won't be directly affected. Who the hell were they expecting? You would know better than a factory worker like me but I don't think our people wasted their time planning attacks on German soil. The only reason you build a factory in such a fashion is when you are expecting to piss other people off and worry they will want to get back at you. I say take it all."

"At moments like this I appreciate having you around, desátník," Hruska had hit on a valuable point Kopecky had not considered. Only industrialists complicit in the malice their government was contemplating would design an aircraft factory the way this one was built. "I will make a notation for our people about what you just said. I think the negotiators will find it useful when the time comes."

"Won't be worth a damn if command doesn't get some anti-aircraft batteries in here. How long do you think that will take, sir?" Hruska didn't like the thought of hours of inventory work going to waste.

"No earlier than tomorrow if we are lucky," Kopecky realized that estimate was optimistic despite his urgings to command.

"I hope you are right. There is a lot of high-octane fuel in ground storage. Wouldn't take much to set it off," Hruska hoped he had found all of the underground tanks.

"At least there is no danger of ground attack," Kopecky knew Capka's company was in the area. Exactly where was anyone's guess. Capka was cunning that way. "As soon as those anti-aircraft crews get in here we can start putting that petrol to good use. The air force is already operating out of Dresden. We need our planes flying out of here as soon as possible. Let's get back to work," Kopecky slapped his comrade on the shoulder.

NEU REICHSKANZLEI, BERLIN

The convoy of six Opel trucks pulled up to the construction entrance at Voss Strasse near Hermann Göringstrasse where there already was the customary morning queue. So many deliveries of material and men had passed this guard post during the past year that six more transports full of construction workers and their tools was part of the routine. After the Führer had decried the last annex to the old chancellery was suitable for a soap factory and little else, he gave his architects one year to build a grand edifice suitable for the government of the new Reich. Not even an approaching enemy army would be allowed to interrupt the final construction.

The entire northern side of Voss Strasse was given over to the demolitionists during 1937. From the dust of those fine homes and structures grew a monument to the party, one befitting an empire with ambitions of European domination. Heiden had watched the new complex of buildings rise with interest. He was not a fan of the bloated scale or modernist styles employed but it was fascinating to watch what thousands of workers could accomplish when labor laws were ignored and construction continued unabated twenty-four hours a day. No, six more trucks would not raise any eyebrows.

"Papers," was the guard's perfunctory demand as Heiden's driver in the lead truck inched up to the stop line. Vogt handed the documents over for the expected cursory review. "Purpose?"

"Finishers," Vogt answered with disinterest. "We are here to clean up the shoddy work by the main crews. Make everything shiny and pretty for the paper pushers."

"We will be seeing plenty of you fellows then," the guard had heard plenty about foundation cracking and leaking plumbing. "Says here you are supposed to head for the buildings of the early phase close to Wilhelmstrasse. Do you know the way?"

"Yes, some of us have been here before on other jobs," Vogt affirmed. In truth, Heiden had surreptitiously toured a half dozen of the team individually through the construction site during the previous months. They had to know first hand what to expect inside the compound.

"Good. I hate giving directions. Let me see what you have in back," the guard informed them.

Heiden slipped his hand instinctively over the FN Hi-Power pistol hidden inside his work jacket as the guard headed back toward the rear of the truck. His primary concern was the guard's compatriot in the small shack and how to handle the man should something go wrong with the inspection.

"You there, let me see what you have back here," the guard lowered the rear gate and pointed to the first of a half-dozen worn canvas seabags he saw lying on the bed. One of Heiden's men reached over and tossed the bag to him. Unzipping the top revealed nothing but the various tools all of these construction workers brought with them... the same boring result every day. The guard zipped the bag back up then lifted and secured the bed gate like a thousand times before.

Heiden relaxed as the guard's footsteps grew close to Vogt's open window. They could have easily drawn a martinet obsessed with opening every duffle according to rules but not today.

"You boys are fine. Too crowded now to allow trucks very far in these days. See that open area over to the left. Drop these workers off over there. They all will have to walk the rest of the way in," the guard instructed.

"That is what we were told to expect," Heiden leaned over closer to the driver's window. "The pay is the same regardless."

"A man after my own heart. Whiners piss me off," the guard met far too many whiners on this job. "Be back here after your scheduled shift is done. The trucks can pick you up at the same spot."

"Ya. Sounds good to me," Vogt put the transmission in gear and gave the truck some gas.

"As the trucks moved past the gate into the site, Vogt glanced at Heiden. "That unfolded just as you expected, major."

"*That* was the easy part. Ten months of monotony works wonders. What comes next will be far more challenging," Heiden reminded him.

RUDOW, DEUTSCHLAND

They had done in three days what should have taken five. None of the generals in Berlin or Paris could imagine in their wildest dreams how fast a Czechoslovak army could move... but Capka knew. His tankers were tired and their Škodas were worn but here they were sitting in the southernmost suburb of Berlin. The accomplishment had netted him a field promotion.

"Get those tanks out of sight," Capka directed above the engine noise as he ran between Škodas to get their driver's attention. It was their good fortune there were plenty of places to hide within the area around the train station. "Yes, yes, right in there. That's good. If the Germans run a train through here, they won't see you until they have already slowed down."

The airfield at Schönefeld was six kilometers behind their position. Holding that base was important, which meant waiting for other regiments to catch up before there would be enough manpower to hold the corridor they had punched open from Dresden. Until then, Capka's company was sitting right where they could blunt an enemy attack heading toward Schönefeld.

"We are so close to Berlin I can smell Hitler," Capka boasted to one of his platoon leaders, Zelenka, who was climbing out of a nearby turret.

"That bastard had better run while he has the opportunity," Zelenka jumped down to the gravel to look around the station. "Any idea how long we have to stay put here, boss? Hell, we own the tracks between here and the border. How hard can it be to run a troop train or two north?"

"Can't say the same for the engines or rolling stock though. From the last response I got from brigade, in every town our boys took the German railroad companies had already sent the engines north. Our trains are too busy transporting German prisoners south. Another reason that air base has to be protected. It could come in handy soon. All I know is we might be here a couple of days," Capka would rather be advancing up the Wilhelmstrasse at the moment.

"Oh well, this is a nice town at least. Looks like a lot of rich Berliners have built vacation homes in the area. I wonder if we can borrow one to clean up in and relax at," Zelenka suggested. "I saw a few lovely candidates nearby on the way in. I read about this once. As long as you give the owner a bond for payment in our koruna, everything is legal."

"I thought I had promoted a soldier, not a lawyer," Capka poked his rank badge. "Now I suppose you will tell me you can create some of these *bonds* with writing paper and pen."

"Well think about it. We can't just take things we need without paying, can we? When the general mobilization was announced and all of the cars and trucks were requisitioned, every owner was given a slip of paper, right? Same idea," Zelenka was dead set on getting a bath and sleeping on a soft bed that night if he could get away with it.

"Remind me to hire you if I ever run afoul of a military court," Capka shook his head in disapproval. As the final tank engines were shut down, Capka's ears picked up a familiar sound off in the distance. "Quiet. Do you hear that?"

"Yes I do. Sounds like a battle," Zelenka listened carefully to what the wind was carrying toward them and leveled his hand toward the west. "Coming from that direction."

"Not close though. Get on the wireless with brigade. Right now. See if they know what is going on," Capka pushed him along.

Zelenka sprinted past his crew back to the Škoda, lifted himself back up on top of the turret and slid inside through the open hatch. Rather than wait, Capka trudged in the direction of the cannon fire. The rest of his tankers heard the booms too and paused what they were doing to pay better attention. Capka paused in the shade of a tree near where one of the anti-aircraft crews was setting up their guns. Something was not right with what he was hearing but he could not put his finger on it.

"Major! I got through," Zelenka returned in a rush.

"Good. What did they tell you?" Capka was growing restless.

"None of our units is engaged with the Germans. Brigade is in regular contact with all forward regiments and they don't know what we are talking about," Zelenka relayed the news.

"Somebody is fighting with somebody, dammit," Capka stabbed his forefinger to the west.

"Major," the second lieutenant from the anti-aircraft unit had snuck up close behind them.

It took several seconds for Capka to pay attention to the interruption. "What, poručík?"

"We are used to hearing battles off in the distance, not like the rest of you tankers who are right in the middle of things," the second lieutenant did not want to offend the cranky company commander. "That doesn't sound like our guns at all."

DREWITZ, DEUTSCHLAND

Another high-explosive shell whistled by a few centimeters above his head to detonate against the rail car behind them. Not too many screams this time so at least more of the troopers were dug in now. Sturmbannführer Daecher had been lucky. When the sabotaged section of track had exploded forward of the locomotive engine, his car had braked to a stop beside a low rut next to the tracks when many of the other rail cars had derailed. Most of land in this vicinity was completely flat but thanks to the rut there was some cover when the men had leapt out of the train car. Incoming small arms fire had started up immediately as they had jumped through the doors and they had pinned them down ever since.

"I was able to grab a few of these," one of Daecher's squad leaders dropped to safety nearby with two 50mm light mortars and the men to operate them.

"Now you are talking," Daecher slapped the man on the shoulder. "How many bombs do you have? The area is too hot for me to get range on the dogs pinning us down. You are going to get range by trial and error."

"We have plenty, although it took a while finding everything in the wreckage," Wirtz the squad leader had lost a man during the search. "I just hope those bastards are in mortar range. There is no way we can get the artillery off the train. It takes too long and anything that moves is getting fired upon from both sides. We are completely surrounded. Some of the guys on the other side of the train had the same idea and are setting up mortars over there too."

The thunking sound of mortar fire by the other crews lifted Daecher's spirits. When their train had been ambushed it was a devastating surprise to find their transport assailed so close to Potsdam by a dug in enemy. The Czechs were not supposed to be this far north or west. Then medium artillery rounds began to drop on their position and Daecher knew for certain that they were being attacked by the Potsdam garrison. His regiment may still have been forming at the start of the war but Daecher knew exactly what a 10.5cm cannon sounded like. Dynamiting the tracks was a deliberate act to stop his regiment from reaching Berlin.

"Go!" Wirtz ordered his two comrades who had set up the mortar. The bomb dropped into the tube and then launched in the direction of the traitors. "That was a wild guess on the range."

"I will have a look," Daecher crawled up the dirt rut with his field glasses. At least there was tall grass to mask him from view of the machine gun nests firing on their position. The first mortar rounds were falling close between gun nests. "You are dropping near to the machine gun pits. Increase elevation and adjust to the right slightly."

The corrections were made and the firing resumed. Daecher watched as the some of mortars bracketed the targets, and others came down right on a machine gun position. Like lightening, two mortar rounds never fell in the same spot.

"You got one! Good job," Daecher praised the trooper's deft work as a cheer went up around them. This was the first positive news since the tracks had blown. "Next position... about eight meters to the left and a bit closer."

Daecher scooted down the dirt wall and grabbed Wirtz by the arm. "When you went for the mortars did you see if any of the motorcycles were in one piece?"

"Hard to say. The train braked so hard almost everything back there is a mess But no, I saw no obvious damage when we ran by, sir," Wirtz wished he had taken a better look but getting shot at had distracted him. "What do you have in mind?"

"There is little cover and too many of our men are pinned down under the train cars. It won't be long before these bastards come in for the kill. We have to get someone out of here to alert Berlin what is going on. We were derailed for a reason... they must be after the Führer. A warning has to make it to headquarters on Wilsnacker Strasse," Daecher had a small chance to get a trooper out of this mess and on the road while the attackers were thinking about incoming mortars. "Who is the best rider we have?"

"Foerster, sir. He rides like a devil," Wirtz had seen first hand the crazy things the man did with a motorcycle.

"Is Foerster still with us?" Daecher hoped his luck was holding.

"Last time I looked," Wirtz had seen Foerster taking quick shots over a low berm nearby.

"Excellent. Go get him--" Daecher heard a 10.5cm shell dropping on their position. "Everyone take cover!"

Daecher had just enough time to push Wirtz to the dirt. He sensed the artillery shell detonate a few meters away on the ground above the rut they were protected by. The next sensation was the weight of loose earth pressing all around his body, accompanied by a blanket of total blackness.

COUNTER-INTELLIGENCE OFFICE
REICH MINISTRY OF WAR – 72-76 TIRPITZUFER, BERLIN

Ottke returned to his office to find the day's mail sitting on the edge of his desk the way he liked it. The war was shaping up to be a disaster, just as Canaris and the generals at OKH had feared. Pandora's Box was already open and the devils were loose upon the land. Which led to the question: where the hell was Heiden? He had gone to ground with his team and no one had heard from them or seen them since. That one was too resourceful and headstrong. Losing track of him was like losing an errant torpedo in a busy harbor. The torpedo was going to hit something eventually, the question was what. So Ottke had sent Gisevius out to track Heiden down. There were few others in Berlin with the connections that Gisevius possessed. Surely he could find Heiden. Then Gisevius had disappeared for days until he was seen that morning with Witzleben. Ottke sent two leutnants to fetch Gisevius back without further delay.

Ottke picked up the stack of envelopes from his inbox to distract the thoughts that made his head throb. In the middle of the stack was a postcard of a trolley rolling down Potsdamer Platz. Turning the card over Ottke found a single sentence written in hand: *What the lion cannot manage to do the fox can.* It was an old German proverb. There was no signature yet Ottke knew at once it was from Heiden. While Ottke was fixated on the fateful postcard, Gisevius rapped his fingers lightly on the open door and walked in.

"You called me in, director?" Gisevius wondered what was so important that he had to be pulled off the mission. There was still so much to do.

"Heiden is on the move," Ottke cut him off sharply.

"I know," Gisevius let a rare flash of annoyance show.

"What do you mean you know? I just found out myself," Ottke waved the trolley postcard above his head.

"As soon as I got back to Berlin from Potsdam, Witzleben contacted me and said the go code had been issued. I've been working on von Helldorf ever since," Gisevius was growing confused. "How could you not know? The operation is in progress at this very moment."

"You did not think to check with me first?" Ottke stood up.

"If Witzleben had his instructions then everything must be in order. There was no need to bother you," Gisevius defended himself.

"You do not understand. Heiden has issued the go order on his own authority," Ottke's mind raced to figure out what he needed to do. "The admiral is in a staff meeting right now with Hitler. Get over to the old chancellery immediately. I don't care what you have to say, get Canaris out of that briefing and back here at once. Tell them the truth... there is an emergency that demands his attention. We will go over everything that needs to be accomplished after you return here."

NEU REICHSKANZLEI, BERLIN

There was no rush. A construction worker in a hurry would only draw unwanted suspicion. Steady, methodical progress is what was expected and that's exactly the picture that Heiden and his team projected as they meandered through the length of the site. If there was scaffolding ahead, they weaved through it for opportunities to pause and direct attention to visible flaws in the framing or concrete work. Bad welds and seals were also good excuses for them to play their parts.

"There is another one," Heiden reached up high to a steel beam with a long slice of cheap wood that he had broken off a pallet. Fiery embers fell all around them from someone cutting metal high above as two uniformed guards passed the group watching attentively. "That weld there is going to fail under stress. The welds we can see will all have to be checked. Let's move on."

"What do you think they will use this room for," Loewe was stunned by the scale as they moved into a partially finished hall of huge proportions. "It is like a cavern."

"Exactly right. Architect Speer intends all foreign dignitaries to cower at the epic sweep of the new Reich," Heiden had read a copy of the official decree.

"My God, how much is this costing us?" Metzger wondered aloud while he adjusted the shoulder strap of his seabag.

"The estimates I have seen go as high as one-hundred million Reichsmarks," Heiden recalled from one of the briefs Ottke had shared with him.

"That could buy a lot of artillery shells," Schwab punctuated the comment by spitting at a support pillar.

"Enough chatter. There are more ears and less machine tools at work once we get into the next section," Heiden cautioned them.

They were lucky that construction on the new chancellery was incomplete and Hitler was still in residence at the old chancellery using Bismarck's cabinet room for his war briefings. The rooms in the old palace on Wilhelmstrasse were of moderate size, with lots of twists and turns in the hallways and stairwells. Very few long lines of sight to betray their number unlike in this new construction. With a degree of cunning, Heiden's team could mask their approach on Hitler's location without drawing much attention. Heiden was well acquainted with the layout of the Wilhelmstrasse palace, as well as the cheaply built annex directly ahead of the team that had been grafted on during the last decade. The annex was the structure Hitler loathed so much. The empty rooms in one of the recently vacated staff floors of the annex would do nicely for Heiden's purposes. They could assemble their Steyr MP34 machine pistols in less than five minutes. Disassembled, the weapons blended in well with the worker's tools in their seabags. Assembled, these beautifully made weapons were accurate and deadly. Thousands had been taken over from Austrian stocks and re-chambered for 9mm Parabellum cartridges. These particular machine pistols had officially been allocated to the Sudeten Freikorps by the SS and that is where the trail would end if the mission went awry and the weapon serials were traced.

"Look at the size of that crack," Heiden stopped at a five-meter long separation in a recently finished concrete wall. "We likely have a foundation problem here. That will not do. If things are this bad, we had better inspect the electrical and water connections to the old annex."

PAŁAC BRÜHLA, PLAC PIŁSUDSKIEGO
WARSZAWA, POLSKA

A deal had been made... at very favorable terms to the Polish Army. What were a quarter-million Reichsmarks here or there in such perilous times? With each hour the news from Brandenburg grew worse. If von Ribbentrop had not agreed to the prices that Beck was quoting today, then tomorrow the premium to release artillery and machine gun shells from Polish stocks would balloon a half-million Reichsmarks or more. Immediate delivery also cost extra, naturally. Platen felt sympathy for von Ribbentrop. It was a thankless mission. He would be scolded for paying too much but there was no alternative. The Polish ammunition had to be procured at any price. The foreign minister and the ambassador to

Poland, von Moltke, were in total agreement as they hurried to the courtyard of the former palace where Beck made his headquarters. Saying nothing and following close behind the diplomats, Platen found himself melancholy that negotiations in Warsaw had not taken longer. He had already sent his wife and children north to stay with family near Rostock. Platen had no desire to return to a war zone. What if the Germany lost and the Czech spies came looking for him to serve them? Platen would be marked as a collaborator for life. Eventually his throat would be slit, or worse. Much better to be stranded in Warsaw... the city seemed quite charming from what Platen could tell.

"To be honest, I am surprised Beck did not inflate his margins higher," von Moltke spoke from his long acquaintance with Herr Beck. "He is a most difficult man to negotiate with when possessing the upper hand. The only way to read his agreeable nature is that Beck is sympathetic to Germany."

"Thank you for that insight, Hans. I doubt the chancellor will see the agreement made today as a bargain, however," von Ribbentrop weighed the ambassador's words carefully. A sympathetic Poland was a valuable tool if a ceasefire was to be called and regional negotiations ensued. Hitler would see the value in that.

"Now we must get you back home as soon as possible. I will oversee matters here," von Moltke would make sure the Poles did not dawdle in shipping the munitions.

"You are confidant Beck is sincere then?" von Ribbentrop knew there was a possibility the Pole was so agreeable because he intended to betray them.

"Beck is very capable of such malice but in my experience he is a man who keeps his word," von Moltke felt sure of his conclusion. As he pushed open the door to the courtyard where the embassy car was idling there was almost a collision with a smallish man making his way into the Foreign Ministry. "Mój pan przeprosin."

"Not to worry, accidents will happen," Roland answered instinctively having no idea what the tall balding fellow had blurted out. While adjusting his suit jacket, Roland recognized the other man as Joachim von Ribbentrop. What luck, he had just bungled into a German diplomatic mission.

Platen looked around von Ribbentrop's shoulder to appraise the cause of their near collision. He recognized the little man. A reporter he remembered but the publication escaped him.

"Herr Ribbentrop," Roland extended his hand. "Roland Simons, The Times of London. I interviewed you while you were with us in the United Kingdom. What good fortune to run into you here in Warsaw. Do you have a few moments for our readers worldwide?"

"Yes, yes... I remember you, Herr Simons," von Ribbentrop stuttered momentarily while he decided how to terminate the interruption without generating bad press as a result. "That was a fine interview as I recall."

"What brings you to Warsaw?" Roland moved right in without waiting to be turned down.

"During a time of crisis, one consults with one's neighbors. You can understand the Polish government is quite concerned with the current state of hostilities between Germany and the Czechoslovak Republic," von Ribbentrop made his appearance on the doorstep of the Polish Ministry of Foreign Affairs seem as ordinary as going to one's barber.

"I am sure you can appreciate that the foreign minister is on a very tight schedule during his stay in Warsaw, Herr Simons. With other pressing commitments to attend to, I apologize that we cannot give you a full audience at this very moment. Call me at this private number and I will schedule an exclusive interview with you," von Moltke deftly interceded. Handing over his personal card to the reporter, the ambassador then directed von Ribbentrop to the waiting Mercedes.

"Good day, Herr Simons," von Ribbentrop bid his goodbye in passing.

Platen had placed the Englishmen finally. He had seen the reporter with the rest at the airport in Köln for the Godesberg negotiations. Platen tipped his bowler to the man as they hurried by.

"That would be excellent, ambassador von Moltke. Thank you. I will ring you up shortly," Roland raised his hand in parting while watching the German mission get into their sedan and putter off.

"Well now, what were the good Germans up to?" Roland was most curious. Opening a second front was most unlikely. But the Germans wanted something very important or they would not have sent von Ribbentrop in person to ensure getting it. Most intriguing. War material was a good possibility. Or something to do with their army cut off in Silesia. By the time he made it up the stairs Roland would have to choose one of the possibilities. The Poles had a new photograph of Beck that they wanted to appear with all future news pieces highlighting the foreign minister. While he retrieved the image from Beck's secretary, Roland would see what morsels about the Germans he could chisel away.

KREUZBURG, SCHLESIEN – DEUTCHLAND

Soldiers from the infantry regiment garrisoned in town had descended on the rail yard like locusts the day before. One oberst in particular was prancing around like he owned everything. The company had told Gerste to get all of his locomotives and running stock out of the region and through Breslau before the Czechs cut off the west bound tracks. They almost had the first of these outbound trains on its way when that oberst showed up and pointed guns at Gerste's crews. No trains were leaving until an inventory could be made. An hour later Gerste had new instructions. His crews were to decouple and rearrange every available car into troop transports, the kind with flat cars interspersed throughout the length to carry tanks and big guns. Those soldiers that were not assigned to help were busy setting up anti-aircraft guns throughout the yard.

"Where the hell do they think they are going with my trains?" Gerste watched an engine back several freight cars into their places. "Breslau was just on the phone. The tracks west and north have already been severed."

"One of the leutnants told me," Gerste's yard supervisor, Ackermann, whispered back. "These trains are for what's left of our Second Army. They plan to head north through Poland. Not west."

"You are shitting me, right? The Poles? We will never see those boys again. They will end up dead in some hole. That's the Poles. Better to go out fighting or surrender to the Czechs," Gerste well remembered the Polish militias that tried to take over the region back in twenty-one.

One of those hand-cranked sirens the troopers had set up started wailing from the southern end of the yard. Gerste whirled around to look as sirens closer to him wound up as well. Nothing to see yet but he heard them. Aircraft engines.

"Hurry up! Get those cars coupled," Gerste yelled at the men assisting the engine driver. "The best way to stay alive is to keep moving!"

Bozik pushed the Avia's nose into a steep dive and opened up the throttle. His new wingman, Dolezal, and the rest of the letka were close on his tail. They were only five thousand feet up but he wanted to have as much speed heading down as possible. Instead of clearing the skies between Dresden and Berlin they had been temporarily reassigned to unfamiliar territory to the east. If they had gone higher in altitude Bozik couldn't be sure where they were. This far out from their temporary airfield the squadron could not waste fuel meandering around in search of the target over German territory. That meant he needed to be low enough to see landmarks. Their job was to go in, hit the train station and get out on the first try. His pilots did not need to hit much. They were mostly a distraction for the Soviet bombers coming in low close behind. If there were any guns down there, Bozik wanted to be going as fast as possible to avoid getting hit while the SBs got a chance to drop their bombs relatively unmolested.

The controls were stiff, arguing with him like a cranky old donkey. Pulling out of the dive was a chore but the Avia held together. Laid out like Sunday dinner in front of Bozik's fighter were tracks full of rail cars. Kreuzburg was a regional rail junction going back to Imperial days so there were many tracks feeding into the yard. There was no time to count but Bozik had no doubt there was enough transportation below his nose to carry a retreating German army. Tracers were arcing skyward in his direction from the ground so no more time for sightseeing.

Bozik switched on his wireless microphone. "Target is hot. Try and hit any of those machine gun nests you can going by." He overshot the first anti-aircraft position but was able to line up on another. Bozik sent several short bursts into the sandbagged gun nest, which encouraged the loader to jump over the bags for safety. Dolezal's burst got the gunner, who had bravely stayed with his weapon. Good kid that Dolezal. He was a quick study with young eyes. So far Bozik had found little about the kid to worry him.

The Avia's fuselage shuddered... reminding Bozik of the perils of too much daydreaming and not enough watching where he was going. He was taking ground fire. Rolling the fighter to get a better look, Bozik caught sight of another gun nest to the far right firing at him so he kept the Avia hopping around like an angry rabbit to ward off further hits to his fighter. They had gone through too much and Bozik was not about to lose the plane now. Quick glances over both shoulders confirmed the squadron was all still behind him. They had done their job. In seconds they would be past the rail station and out of range of the machine guns on the perimeter.

Gerste stood in the middle of the yard, both fists clenched tightly against the side of his waist. The damn Czechs were not firing on his trains... yet. They seemed more interested in the army's machine guns. Then he noticed Ackermann cowering close to the ground nearby when they had trains to protect.

"Get on your feet, man!" Gerste reached down and yanked his subordinate up. "You have no gun, they are not firing at you. We need to get these trains out of the yard... now. You take Track Five. I will take the engineer on Track Three. Move!"

"But what about the army?" Ackermann worried.

"They are busy. We can reverse the trains back into the station later. Right now we have too many bunched up in one place. If we lose an engine the one next to it will likely blow too," Gerste sent his man on his way with a firm shove in the back.

Nearing Track Three Gerste realized the little biplane fighters had all passed overhead and gone. The annoying pests were not all that deadly so Gerste felt a little hopeful. Then he heard loud droning approaching from the south. Since those fighters would not have had time to come around for another run that meant Gerste had more to worry about.

"Shit," Gerste stopped to look back. He saw dark green twin-engine bombers – lots of them – flying just above the trees. Fast bastards too. "We are done."

Gerste stood his ground, livid at what he was watching. The bombers broke up into groups and lined up on the different tracks. The army machine gunners wheeled their weapons around but it was too late. The lead bombers let loose their bombs from the open fuselage bays. One by one the locomotives it was his job to shepherd exploded into flame. Fragments of hissing metal and wood were blasted in every direction. As the first three of the green bastards zoomed by right over his head, Gerste shook his fist at the big red stars painted on the undersides of the wings.

KABINETTSAAL, ALT REICHSKANZLEI – BERLIN

Keitel's argument was echoing off the round arches leading up to the Rococo ceiling. He rarely raised his voice in cabinet meetings but the stakes were too high. Bismarck had held court in this grand old room but he never had to face a state of affairs as confronted them today. The Führer rarely assembled his full cabinet, preferring to summon only those individuals who had a specific connection to the discussion to be held. At Keitel's insistence, Hitler had called the meeting of his principal war lieutenants. Only Admiral Raeder was preoccupied with an emergency of sufficient importance to be absent. Keitel could have done without the presence of Goebbels and Himmler, however. Those two always complicated matters with their endless supply of political stipulations. Having wrested the floor away from Göring's latest attempt at waffling between both sides of the issue, Keitel planted his hands on the long table and pushed himself into the air.

"We cannot risk the Führer's life. The Czechs are already in the outer suburbs. They have taken Schönefeld. A report has just reached me that the Potsdam garrison is now engaged northeast of Bergholz. There is no more time to argue, the Führer must be moved... now," Keitel felt like slapping his palm on the table but restrained himself.

"I will not run like a dog," Hitler muttered while slumped down in his chair. He trusted Keitel but some things a man could not bear. Hitler leaned forward and pounded his fist on the table. "Do you hear me? The leader of the Reich does not run like a dog. Nothing will pry me away from my duty."

"Conditions are not that dire," Himmler undercut Keitel once again. "One of my reserve regiments is moving up from Bayern. The Czechs keep hitting our rail lines north by air, which is slowing their progress. But these troops should not be far from Potsdam by now. With some luck my people can get a message to have them stop at Bergholz and join the battle. That should slow the Czechs down long enough for von Rundstedt's divisions to transit through Poland and arrive in Brandenburg. We can stabilize the front around Berlin. There are not enough Czech divisions available to dislodge us if we stand firm now."

"You see! Deutschland is not finished yet," Hitler thrust his arm out in a wide arc over the table. "That liar Beneš has neither the will nor the stomach for a long fight. We can outlast these Slavs."

"For how long, sir?" Keitel again attempted to steer the chancellor back to reality. "Suppose everything goes as Herr Himmler proposes. We still do not know whether fresh stocks of ammunition are forthcoming. Lack of shells is what led to the Eighth Army to surrender Dresden."

"I will see von Bock hang for that. If all he had left to fight with were dinner knives, then he should have fought with those to the last man," Hitler seethed at losing the city.

Canaris had stayed out of the debate so far. There was little to gain by taking a side. But he could not let the reputation of a good man like General von Bock to be stained. "Chancellor, von Bock died in an air attack prior to the surrender."

"Yes, I have learned the actual culprit in the surrender was von Bock's chief of staff, Felber. When we get our hands on him, Felber will pay for his treason," Himmler left no question of his seriousness on the matter.

Germany was paying dearly for General Franz Halder's indecision. He knew the country was not prepared for war. He had it in his control to remove Hitler from power. At the crucial moment, however, he had done nothing. That ass licker Göring, who had been sensible back in March, had leapt at the chance to launch the war with his Luftwaffe. And so they were at war within twelve hours after those stupid Heinkel crews had managed to get shot down deep into Czechoslovak territory. To order a coup to prevent a war was one thing. To arrest Hitler with the war already started was unprecedented for a loyal German officer. Halder had wavered and here was the result: Berlin almost surrounded and his brave armies hobbled by a shortage of munitions. Now he had been dragged in to sit in this cabinet room like a trained monkey and argue about the best way to save Hitler's skin. He had failed miserably. Worse, across the table from Halder sat Canaris. Canaris knew every detail of Halder's failure. Each glance from the old fox held the same accusation: *You brought us to this.*

"What does my chief of general staff have to say on defending the capital?" Hitler roused Halder out of his stupor.

"The Twelfth and Fourteenth armies are bogged down in Österreich. Czechoslovak and Soviet bombers have severed the single rail line west at multiple locations," Halder wanted to make it clear those divisions were unable to redeploy.

"Then fix the tracks! We have thousands of trained engineers in the army. Are all of them sitting on their thumbs?" Hitler failed to understand why such easy things remained undone.

"The tracks *are* repaired, chancellor. The problem is the enemy never stops bombing across the entire length of the route. As soon as our engineers get one section repaired, more sections are blown up," this was not the first time Halder had explained the situation.

"Whose fault is that?" Hitler was getting testy again.

"I suggest you ask Feldmarschall Göring, air defense is his responsibility," Halder was happy to shift Hitler's ire to his favored successor.

"The air arm is suffering the same ammunition shortages as everyone else," Göring defended himself. "You cannot expect me to send my pilots up without bullets and bombs."

"Had they been able to hit the Czech air fields while they had amble supply of both, we would not have to worry about their bombing that rail line now," Halder did not want to leave Göring off the hook so easily.

"We can get back to all of that later," Himmler broke in to steer them back to the original question. "What are your recommendations for defending Berlin, General Halder?"

"I have already shifted available divisions from the Tenth Army to bolster the Rhineland defense. If the Führer is to remain in Berlin, I propose the evacuation of Karlsbad, Eger and Asch to bring the rest of what remains of the Tenth up to protect Brandenburg," Halder saw the blood race to Hitler' face and braced himself for the coming storm.

"Enough of this defeatism! I will not abandon the Sudetenland." Hitler smashed his fist upon the table again.

"To do so would only encourage the Czechs to follow into Bayern. That would only complicate matters," Himmler understood Halder's logistical problems but was violently against giving up what little Czech territory they still held.

"Admiral, your staff has studied the matter carefully," Keitel turned to Canaris for a counter opinion. Like Halder, he knew they needed additional troops in Brandenburg and Sachsen right now. "Is there such a danger?"

"No, I would estimate little danger of enemy ground units launching a new front from Asch," Canaris saw no harm in sharing the truth. "So far Beneš has not allowed Stalin to contribute Soviet troops to the battle and he will not accept such assistance as long as Czechoslovakia remains intact. Therefore, Beneš only has so many troops to commit to battle. Our agents tell us the Czechs have proven very adept at shifting their forces at the regimental and battalion levels from one side of Bohemia to the other. For over a month these units – many of them pulled out of divisions in Moravia and Slovakia – have been operating very effectively in ad hoc formations of various sizes as required. We also know that what Czechoslovak armor and motorized infantry available for offensive operations inside the Reich are already deployed between Brandenburg and Bohemia. There are no more to be spared to invade Bayern or anywhere else."

"Well then, this is all very simple," Hitler's mood had totally reversed itself. "When we stop Beneš here in Brandenburg there are no more Slavs to be sent. Herr Himmler's strategy is the correct course. Between his SS regiment, the Potsdam regiment and the Berlin garrison, we can hold until von Rundstedt's divisions can arrive. Have you noticed how well Witzleben has cordoned off the city? We will stop Beneš here and push the Czechs back to whence they came. Can no one else see these things but me?"

One of Keitel's adjutants quietly appeared next to the general with a message. Keitel read the note swiftly, nodded, then instructed the junior officer to pass the message to Canaris. The admiral looked at the note then rose to feet.

"My apologies, mein Führer. Something urgent requires my attention," Canaris' voice was full of concern.

"What is so important that you must leave at this very moment?" Hitler grew suspicious.

"A matter pressing enough the subject could not be consigned to paper. Therefore, only by departing to learn the reason may I report to you promptly as is required," Canaris played to Hitler's ego while he gathered his paperwork to go.

PRAŽSKÝ HRAD, PRAHA

Beneš insisted on a personal inspection tour of the palace grounds as soon as their automobiles had pulled in through the main gate. The palace was a symbol of both his government and the republic. The German bombers had mostly been foiled in their efforts to wreak mass destruction but damage had still been done to the capital, as Beneš had well seen for himself on the roundabout course in from Zátiší that Bláha had insisted upon as a security measure. Their procession had grown to about twenty by the time Beneš entered the second courtyard on foot. There was the ever vigilant security detail that accompanied the president and Madam Beneš everywhere since the war started, as well as members of the presidential staff and several photographers that had joined them to document the moment for the newspapers. Beneš had been firm about not sneaking back into the castle and neither would he skulk behind the safety of thick walls once he returned. The people had to see their government was unafraid. He made a point to personally thank each member of the anti-aircraft crews they passed in the courtyards.

"Oh my God," Mesdame Beneš held her hand up to her mouth as they came closer to the Chapel of the Holy Cross and she saw all that remained was a charred shell. The whole upper portion of the chapel was gone, as well as the interior.

"No one told me of this," the president was saddened. "What else have we lost?"

"Lobkowicz Palace took a bomb as well. The damage was relatively contained to a single wing, however. It was a small bomb," Drtina thought the news should come from him.

"Still... a tragedy," Beneš knew the destruction could have been so much greater. "We owe our pilots and anti-aircraft gunners a great debt for protecting us so well. I realize Maximillian Lobkowicz is one of the richest men in the nation. But he is a great patriot and if the government can be of any assistance we should make the effort."

"Lobkowicz will likely refuse but I will see to it Mister President," Drtina made a notation in a small book he was carrying.

"Look! There are broken windows at St. Vitus," Mesdame Beneš pointed at the cathedral.

"There are a great many broken windows throughout the city. St. Vitus sustained only superficial damage, thankfully," Bláha hoped to calm her concerns.

"I would rather see for myself, generál," Mesdame Beneš was sure they were not getting the full story on the matter. "It took nearly six hundred years to complete work on that cathedral and I could not bear to see scaffolding go up again. Will you accompany me, dear?"

"Of course. I was thinking the same thing," Beneš looked toward his wife warmly as they ignored the clicking of camera shutters on their way to the cathedral's majestic bronze doors.

"Generál Bláha, please have an accounting of which structures in the capital have sustained damage of any kind on the president's desk by this evening," Drtina thought it best to get the request in earlier than later. He knew his friend well enough to know the president would only petition for the information later from his office.

PSCHORR-HAUS, POTSDAMER PLATZ – BERLIN

All good military attachés had their haunts. Joints where other men in uniform could let their guard down for a while, and if they happened to bump into the likes of Truman Smith, they had a round of drinks bought for them. Pschorr-Haus was a huge establishment that had the benefit of being smack in the middle of the most important section of Berlin that was flanked by government and military ministries in every direction. The owner was a well-known brewer in Munich. When the place was full the noise was deafening, which made it perfect for conducting a conversation on a delicate subject. Most nights recently the cavernous interior was mostly empty. Those who had not already fled the city were too busy setting up fortifications. But at lunchtime, Pschorr-Haus was a quick walk away for thousands of harried military officers and civil servants. Some of them were still able to get away to find some small solace in a quick beer with their meal. Between the recently added guards and sandbags that were setting up all over town, waltzing in unannounced into places like the Ministry of War had gotten much harder. So dropping into Pschorr-Haus was worth a try.

"Major Smith," Klaus, the long-time afternoon host put on his best smile for the American officer. "Can I get you a table?"

"No thanks. Just looking for a friend," Smith made his usual excuse. "Mind if I go on in, Klaus?"

"Not at all, be our guest," the American rarely took a table but Klaus had to ask regardless.

"How long you folks staying open? Things are looking rather serious out on the streets," Smith had several reasons for asking.

"Until the bullets start firing or until we run out of barrels of beer," Klaus made it sound like he was not much worried at all.

"You get the wife and kids out of town?" Smith leaned closer.

"Oh yes... last week. They are with my mother in-law," Klaus whispered back.

"You are a good man, Klaus," Smith patted him on the shoulder as he walked onto the main floor of the restaurant.

There weren't too many tables occupied inside. Berlin was going quiet. Smith kind of hated to see that happen. Berlin was one of the few cities in Europe that had that kind of brash energy that made New York or Chicago something special. If Berlin got ravaged in the coming days, Smith would cry right alongside the Berliners. Working his way through the restaurant, Smith didn't recognize anyone he had met before. There wasn't much use in striking up a conversation at the one table with a group of dour junior army officers wolfing down their lunch. Doing so would be too obvious. Smith decided to pass them by.

"Amerikaner! Ya, you sir," one of the captains yelled after Smith. "If everything goes to hell, how many Germans can go to Amerika?"

"About sixty thousand per year," Smith stopped to turn around. He knew the immigration quota by heart.

"That is not so many. So much for that idea," the officer laughed.

"Well, there are always exceptions. I do work at the embassy, after all," the attaché returned to the table and slid his card along the top to the man. "Truman Smith, U.S. Army."

REICHSKANZLEI ANNEX, BERLIN

The two clerks hurried into the third floor hall heaving document boxes that needed to get moved to the first of the new chancellery buildings. Construction was ahead of schedule so their agency had already made the move to new offices. Now the archive files had to follow. They did not expect to stumble into a gaggle of workers blocking their way. The clerks almost dropped the files in the collision.

"You idiots are lost! What are you doing in here? Can't you hear the construction is back in that direction," the senior clerk fumed. "Get out before I report the lot of you to your superiors."

"Calm down now," Metzger suggested in a firm voice as he relieved the senior clerk of his boxes. "Sorry we got in the way. Let me help you with those."

"See that?" Heiden pointed to a separation of the plaster running along the top of the wall in the hallway near the ceiling. "Stress. No one likes this shabby structure but it will do no one any good if the walls crumble. My crew has been sent in to fix things up. As I suspected, this extension took some damage as the first new building went up on the other side of the wall."

"Well then, that is different," the senior clerk felt a little embarrassed. "But this floor is still not empty. We cannot have you in the way."

"And we do not want to be in the way," Heiden was close to shooting the petty bureaucrat and his companion to be done with them, yet restrained himself. "What floor is already clear?"

"The second floor is completely vacated. It would be best if your men got started there," the senior clerk suggested.

"Thank you for your help. We will head down there immediately," Heiden would have preferred the floor they were on but could not afford further encounters with government employees.

"Very well, continue with your duties," the senior clerk dismissed them curtly.

"Our pleasure, sir," Metzger dropped the document boxes back into the senior clerk's possession without warning.

"Might as well see what we will have to fix later as long as we are up here," Heiden projected his voice down the hall.

Heiden's team went about examining rooms while the clerks took their files and left down the hall. After they had gone down the stairs, Heiden motioned for his men to draw in close to him.

"Very well, we will take over the second floor. Same procedure, check every room to make sure we have no unexpected guests. If you discover anyone, send them on their way. If they will not go, gag and bind them securely. I do not want to be thrown off schedule," Heiden felt energized. They were close... so close to their objective at last.

OVAL PARLOR, WHITE HOUSE
WASHINGTON D.C.

Hull had verification that von Ribbentrop was in Warsaw. The reason was still proving elusive, however. What did Hitler want so badly that he needed to send his foreign minister to parlay personally with Beck? Hull ventured the subject was munitions. Contact had finally been made with the Dresden consulate and the staff was very clear that the German army there had surrendered because they had used up most of their reserves of ammunition in the retreat from Czechoslovak territory. As Poland produced the same gauge of shells the Germans used there was motive, means and opportunity. It all made perfect sense to Hull. Beck had invested far too much in playing Hitler off against Stalin to see his efforts evaporate in a German loss to the Czechs. Hull would wager good money that Beck would sell bullets to Hitler. Had Roosevelt gotten wind of this? All the secretary of state knew was that he had been summoned and the subject was Poland.

Feeling out of breath, Hull took the elevator to the second floor, which opened up right across the hall from the library. The oval room far away from prying eyes and was where Roosevelt conducted his most pressing business and audiences. Mac, Roosevelt's valet, was waiting for him in the hallway.

"Good to see you again, Secretary Hull," Mac greeted him warmly. "The president says go right on in."

"Thank you, Mac," Hull stepped through the door as McDuffie opened it.

"Anything we can have sent up from the kitchen for you?" Mac always liked to make important guests comfortable.

"Some mint tea would be nice," Hull's throat was a little scratchy today.

"Straight away, sir," Mac closed the door softly as Hull passed into the library.

Every time he visited this room the secretary of state always expected another ship model had been added to Roosevelt's already huge collection. Sail or steam made no difference. After five years it was difficult to find a cranny that wasn't filled with an oil painting or miniature of a naval vessel. The president was seated behind his desk with General Edwin Watson standing stiffly upright by his side. Watson was both military advisor and appointments secretary to the president, as well as a firm right arm that Roosevelt leaned upon when he needed to stand at state functions. With all that was happening in Europe these days it was not unusual to have the general in attendance for meetings with the president.

"Cordell, please have a seat," Roosevelt gestured to the sofa facing the desk.

"Why did you call me in today, Franklin? Carr is sending in some fine reports. He's off touring the countryside again. Seems like Beneš' people are having a hard time accommodating all of the prisoners of war they are collecting," Hull was still heartened by the diligence their Prague envoy continued to apply to his posting.

"You are not going to like it but I sent General Watson here to convey a personal message to Count Potocki last night," Roosevelt thought he might as well be direct.

Hull let a curtain of calm control his expressions. One of the president's most infuriating habits was sending personal emissaries to deliver diplomatic notes or to go on fact-finding missions. Another trick of Roosevelt's was to establish direct connections with American envoys across the world to request direct reports from the field that bypassed normal Department of State channels.

"You are correct, I don't like it. But that is an old argument," Hull decided to let the slight go in the interest of satisfying his curiosity. "So what was the nature of the general's visit to the Polish ambassador?"

"This German/Czech war is going to end soon. Prague and Warsaw have never been on the best of terms but they need to play nice now. There has to be stability in Central Europe... no more petty squabbling. I want that ruling troika in Warsaw to patch up their differences with Beneš at the earliest opportunity. To that end I will pledge the full participation and influence of the United States. That was the message I had Edwin deliver to Potocki," Roosevelt stubbed the top of a pencil against the desk blotter.

"There is no reason we could not have delivered that communication formally in the proper fashion," Hull gently scolded the commander in chief.

"You know the Poles... they are never inclined to do what you ask of them when you put the request in writing. Doing so seems to insult their sensibilities and they become obstinate. That is why I chose the personal approach," Roosevelt explained his rationale.

"Well then, what did the ambassador have to say in response?" Hull would clean up any messes later yet needed to know what had been said during that audience.

"What I came away from the conversation with is the count believes we have a lack of understanding for the realities in that part of the world," Watson summarized the harangue he had been subjected to.

"Did Potocki say as much? That is very important," Hull knew the Polish ambassador was not dissuaded from delivering lectures when he felt the need to do so.

"He went to great length to explain the finer points of Polish-Czechoslovak relations since 1919 and how the differences are irreconcilable as long as President Beneš talks out of both sides of his mouth. That last part is a direct quote," Watson found these Eastern Europeans more trouble than they were worth.

"Franklin, the ambassador's comments are a fairly accurate reading of sentiment in Warsaw. An appreciation for reality may sink in during the weeks to come regarding the benefits of a more cordial relationship with Czechoslovakia. But it will take time. The two countries are competitors with a good deal of bad blood between them. We should revisit this initiative of yours when the dust settles a bit. I am sure the French would be pleased to assist in getting both parties to discuss a rapprochement," Hull decided to shift to the weightier topic with Watson. "General, did Potocki discuss the Germans at any length?"

Roosevelt's eyebrows arched up sharply at the change of context but would wait a moment to see where the conversation went.

"The ambassador is very worried, Mister Secretary. Their intelligence agents are telling them the war is going very badly for the Germans. What worries them more is that the Soviets have a military foothold in Czechoslovakia. V-VS squadrons are operating in force from Czech airfields and they find that fact seriously destabilizing. The Polish perspective is Germany was a grave danger to peace while the Soviets are a grave danger to all of Europe. He said a defeated Germany leaves a severe security vacuum and Poland will now be alone on the front lines against bolshevism," Watson recalled to the best of his memory.

"What prompted your question, Cordell?" Roosevelt's deft mind always zeroed in between the lines.

"We have verification from our folks in-country that von Ribbentrop is in Warsaw for talks with Beck. Although we do not yet have any idea what the two are discussing," Hull decided to leave his own suppositions to himself for the moment. The president was a keen study, however, and might come to the same conclusions on his own.

"Edwin, what is happening with that German army in Silesia?" Roosevelt looked up at his aide.

"The last time I checked they were getting bottled up in the north-eastern corner of the province. A fighting retreat, but a retreat all of the same, sir," Watson still questioned what von Rundstedt was attempting to accomplish with his divisions.

"You don't suppose that German army is contemplating a von Lettow-Vorbeck approach to their situation?" Roosevelt well recalled the German East Africa campaign during the Great War. "That would be serious enough a contingency to send von Ribbentrop to Warsaw."

"Violating Poland is not like marching into Portuguese Mozambique... but I had not thought of that possibility," Hull rose to his feet as his mind raced through the implications of Roosevelt's suggestion. "It is conceivable the Germans are seeking an escape route through Polish territory. That would create a nasty complication for President Beneš that the Poles would relish. Mister President, this line of thought begs further investigation. I will let you know what I find out."

REICHSKANZLEI ANNEX, BERLIN

With several of his men stationed in the hall to watch for unexpected interlopers, Heiden's team used the privacy of several second floor rooms to assemble their machine pistols and prepare themselves. Knives and side arms were retrieved from hiding places while spare ammunition clips were distributed to each man. Their workmen's clothes were well endowed with useful pockets that easily held everything that needed to be carried. Heiden wanted to avoid a prolonged shootout but intended for their weight of firepower to win any fight they could not avoid. Without having to call them, Heiden's six lieutenants appeared at his side.

"Each of you has your assignments. Take your seven man squads, secure your section of the old chancellery, and hold. No alarm must be sounded. I want no interference or surprises. Subduing guards and staff is preferable but not essential. And no bullet holes through the guard's uniforms allowed. We need our people in those uniforms at all of the customary guard posts. You have eight minutes to get in position. On the tenth minute, my nine men and I will seize the cabinet room. Any questions?" Heiden saw only determination in their eyes. "Very well, check your wristwatches."

Heiden straightened his arm so to better view his wristwatch. They were specially purchased for the purpose with one given to every man on the team.

"And mark," Heiden's free hand set the minute hand to zero. "Let's go."

WILHELMSTRASSE 77, BERLIN

Adler Kfz 13 armored cars sped down Wilhelmstrasse past the chancellery compound with machine guns loaded and ready. Following fast behind them were Opel troop trucks carrying infantry of the Berlin garrison. Some of the Adlers continued further to turn onto Vossstrasse while others braked to a halt outside the main gate of the old chancellery. The two army guards stationed at the gate raised their arms in confusion.

"What is going on?" the senior guard approached the closest Adler.

"Don't know for sure. We have orders to seal off the chancellery grounds," the armored car commander informed him. "No one goes in or out without permission until further notice. Load your weapon and wait for further instructions."

"At once, hauptmann," the guard unslung his Mauser to slide a shell into the barrel.

Soldiers jumped down from the back of the trucks to assemble at the gate. A major appeared with them, his Luger pistol drawn. "My good men, help us secure the courtyard," the major pointed to the closed gate with the pistol.

The guards hurried to unlatch the gate, which was swung open immediately by the waiting platoon of soldiers as more garrison troops continued to arrive. While the soldiers poured into the courtyard orders were given to form a ring around the chancellery perimeter. Few took notice of the small convoy of trucks with covered beds that pulled to a stop on the opposite side of Wilhelmstrasse. The squeal of tires as several black sedans turned onto the avenue at high speed were drawing all of the attention. The cars dodged soldiers waving their arms in protest to park behind the armored cars and trucks. Police detectives leapt out of the sedans to surround one of their own wearing a rakish officer's uniform.

"I am Wolf-Heinrich Graf von Helldorf, president of the Berlin police," the man in the center led his police entourage toward the major. "Where is General Witzleben?"

KABINETTSAAL, ALT REICHSKANZLEI – BERLIN

Hitler rose from his chair in a rage. The recipient of the outburst was Keitel, who had just delivered more bad news. "So you are telling me the reason Raeder is not present is because the French have mined the approaches to Wilhelmshaven? How could this happen?"

"The French have a class of mine-laying submarines. Each one can hold more than thirty nautical mines. The last report that I saw was these boats were operating in the Mediterranean but they must have been moved into the North Sea. We will know more once Admiral Raeder can investigate," Keitel had shared all he knew.

"How is it that no one in this military seems able to prevent such outrages from happening? Am I surrounded by dolts?" Hitler was beside himself.

Two loud thuds interrupted the chancellor's lecture. Something heavy had fallen against the closed doors to the cabinet room on the opposite side. Keitel nodded at Hitler's army adjutant, Rudolf Schmundt, to go and check what had made the noise but the doors flung open before the colonel had gone three steps in that direction. Eight men burst in dressed like construction workers with leather jackets over work bibs. More critically each one was leveling a machine pistol at the Führer and his war leaders. One of them hit Schmundt in the jaw with the butt of his weapon. The officer dropped to the floor unconscious. Göring and Keitel had jumped to his feet at the violent entry but the rest were too shocked to move from their seats. Halder recognized the one in the lead as that Abwehr hothead, Heiden. Canaris' premature departure now made perfect sense. The intelligence director did not like staring down the barrel of a machine pistol any more than Halder did. Heiden locked eyes with Halder for the moment it took two of the assailants to drag the dead SS guards from the hallway into the cabinet room. Like Canaris, Heiden was aware of every ounce of Halder's failure and shame.

"Who are you? Get out now!" Hitler ordered from the other side of the room as if construction workers armed with machine guns were an every day occurrence at the chancellery.

"Sit down, chancellor," Heiden dipped the nose of his Steyr to further make the point.

The blunt instruction shook Hitler's confidence. His arms began to shake but he did not return to his chair.

"Adolph Hitler," Heiden decided to go on whether the chancellor sat or stood. "You are under arrest for gross crimes against the Fatherland."

"You are insane!" Hitler lurched forward. "Traitors, I cannot be arrested!"

Heiden noticed Himmler taking the opportunity to reach for his sidearm. He would leave the SS chief for Loewe or someone else. The Führer was Heiden's singular focus. Heiden adjusted his aim.

"Have it your way," Heiden pronounced judgment and depressed the trigger... pleased to do what he had wanted to do in the first place.

The short burst of 9mm bullets from the Steyr caught Hitler square in the chest and held his body held upright momentarily. Before Hitler crumpled and fell to the floor, Loewe's machine pistol had released Himmler from his worldly burdens before the man's Walther could clear its holster.

"You are madmen," Dr. Goebbels leveled an accusing finger at Heiden as he rose to his feet like a professor about to lecture a class. "Look what you have done. You have cursed us all--"

Heiden emptied his magazine into the propaganda minister's bony frame without hesitation. While he replaced the empty clip with a fresh magazine, Halder took the opportunity to cautiously stand up.

"Enough," Halder commanded authoritatively. "No more killing is necessary."

Heiden had been conflicted for a long time about which would give him greater pleasure: killing Hitler or killing Halder? One was dangerous and the other worthless. Heiden decided to answer the question definitively. The bullets from his Steyr knocked Halder back to his chair. Heiden found shooting Halder was more satisfying.

"That is for all those who had to die because of your incompetence," Heiden focused on Halder's limp body bleeding out onto the floor.

There was more business to conduct. So far they had not been interrupted. The well-built walls of the old palace, plus the nearby construction noise, were working in their favor. But Heiden was aware they needed to complete the job and move out. He looked Keitel dead in the eye then tipped the barrel of his Steyr in the direction of Hitler's body lying on the floor in a heap.

"Would you die for him?" Heiden wanted to know for his own sake.

"Ya," was the simple, calm reply from the senior officer standing at attention.

"I appreciate the honesty, general," Heiden reached for the Browning pistol, aimed, then but a bullet through Keitel's forehead. The OKW commander's body shuddered and collapsed to the carpet.

Keitel's demise jolted Göring, who was the last participant from the meeting left alive. Feet no longer frozen in place, he slowly began to back away to the other set of doors on the far side of the room.

"As a loyal officer I was only following instructions," Göring's eyes pleaded with Heiden. "I cannot be held accountable..."

Knaak disliked groveling intensely and had no patience to listen to the feldmarschall humiliate himself further. The 9mm bullets from Knaak's Steyr forcibly knocked Göring back off his feet and the one-time aviator's head hit the floor with a nasty smack.

Heiden's men moved deeper into the room to check the bodies without need for instruction. Satisfied that each of the targets was lifeless, they used handkerchiefs to pick up the dead men's pistols. After firing several rounds from each pistol through the wall and doors the team had just entered through, the guns were placed in the palms of their dead owners, whose fingers were then wrapped around the pistol grips. Loewe nudged the unconscious adjutant with his work boot.

"What about this one?" Loewe could leave the man or kill him without reservations either way.

"He saw nothing. Let him be," Heiden was growing anxious to leave. He checked his wristwatch. They were still on schedule. "The job is done, let's get out of here."

POTSDAMER PLATZ – BERLIN

Maybe one of the young army officers would contact him some day. Smith usually had good luck in that regard. He wasn't a spy and the local authorities expected the attaché to chat up the military in the host country. Smith never asked for delicate information, however. Mostly he just let people talk about their jobs. In those small details was a wealth of useful information that could be pieced together with the fruits of other conversations. One just needed a good memory since keeping notes was a no-no around these parts. Having gleaned as much as he was going to at the Pschorr-Haus, Smith said his good-byes and decided on a stroll down Potsdamer Platz. He really wasn't sure where to turn next when he heard the sirens. Three police cars rushed up from behind and sped past. But what really caught Smith's attention were the army armored cars hot on the tails of the black sedans. Bringing up the rear were a half-dozen Opel trucks carrying soldiers in the back. Up ahead, Smith saw the cars turning onto Prinz Albrecht-Strasse. That was the street where the Gestapo headquarters was located. Someone was having a party and Smith was going to find out the particulars.

Jogging the rest of the way, Smith rounded the corner onto Prinz Albrecht-Strasse and was stunned to see Gestapo agents being escorted out of the building at No. 8. Most streamed out with their hands behind their heads but a good number were being carried out on stretchers, too. The black-clad Gestapo men that could move under their own power were shoved into the back of waiting police vans. The contingent that had just passed Smith by on Potsdamer Platz was back up to an operation already in progress. Smith joined a crowd of Berliners who were watching from a safe distance.

"Wow, the police and the army arresting the Gestapo. You don't see that every day," Smith let out a long whistle.

"No you do not," a thirtyish woman turned and addressed the American in accented English. "The army must be taking over."

Smith perceived there was an unsaid, *at last*, that belonged at the end of the woman's last sentence but she was being cautious regardless of the events transpiring ahead of them. Smart girl, he thought. Who knew how things would eventually turn out? But an army take-over was a major deal. If you had asked Smith the day before he would have bet against it but his eyes were not lying. If the local garrison had the cops in their pocket and was showing this much muscle here in Berlin, what was happening in the rest of the country? Smith hurried back the way he came. He needed to get back to the embassy.

WILHELMSTRASSE 77, BERLIN

Soldiers pushed back the doors at the courtyard entrance to the chancellery and ran with guns drawn inside ahead of Witzleben and von Helldorf. The enlisted men had no idea what they were there to accomplish but their general and the police president proceeded with such clarity that orders from both were accepted without question. The lead squad turned down the first hallway and almost collided with ten army guards escorting a large group of chancellery staffers and construction workers.

"Are these prisoners?" a leutnant challenged the hauptmann in the lead.

"No, just non-combatants we must get out of the building," the hauptmann responded without stopping.

The leutnant was not sure what to do but was saved from making a decision by General Witzleben appearing on the scene.

"Let them pass," Witzleben ordered, having immediately recognized Heiden as the man wearing the hauptmann's badges. "What is going on?"

"We heard gunfire," one of the scared civilians called out, followed by murmurs of agreement from the other office workers. Heiden had rounded them up as a diversionary ruse to better mask their exit.

"I can confirm that," Heiden agreed in a gravely serious tone as he paused beside Witzleben. When he continued it was in such a whisper that von Helldorf barely heard the words. "They resisted arrest."

"Understood, we will take things from here," Witzleben waved them through. "You may go."

"As you wish, sir," Heiden saluted. Falling in beside his men he urged the group in the direction of the courtyard. "Keep it moving everyone."

It was a relief that the general was punctual and their weapons could stay unnoticed in the seabags. Heiden's team soon exited the chancellery building to the courtyard. These soldiers and police guarding the area had not heard the general pass the procession along so Heiden needed to sound authoritative without delay before questions were asked. He chose the first police detective to stare at him.

"You there! Herr police officer, come here please," Heiden called to the man, who hurried over at once with his partner.

"What do you want? We are busy," the detective did not take well to orders from army personnel.

"These office workers from the chancellery require debriefings," Heiden commanded. "Your police president instructed for these people to be placed under your control. We will handle the construction men ourselves."

"Fine by me," the detective was happy not to have more paperwork than necessary. "You people, follow us."

The chancellery staffers fell in line after the detectives without argument. Heiden wasted no time in motioning his contingent forward in the other direction toward the Wilhelmstrasse gate.

"Make sure you have all of your tools and follow me," Heiden instructed his men. No need to throw off their ruse just yet.

As they neared Wilhelmstrasse, Heiden saw his six trucks waiting on the other side of the street with their engines running as he had instructed. No one bothered them as they exited the gate. He even waited for traffic on Wilhelmstrasse to clear before they crossed the road. Without drawing any further attention to themselves, Heiden's men threw their seabags onto the back of the trucks and climbed up. With everyone where they were supposed to be, Heiden moved up to the lead Blitz, opened the passenger door and got in next to Vogt.

"Everything go as planned, sir?" Vogt asked while easing the truck into gear.

"Affirmative," Heiden replied curtly. He would not relax until they had disposed of the Opels and dispersed the team.

Vogt pulled the Blitz out onto Wilhelmstrasse without a further word and the convoy disappeared from sight.

DREWITZ, DEUTSCHLAND

There was the real possibility that he was lost. Bulloch's gut told him he had traveled so far west he had outrun the Czech advance units. That left the question of who was fighting with whom. For a long time when he switched off his engine Bulloch could hear big guns to the west. The trouble now was that the guns had gone silent. Having travelled this far, Bulloch didn't want to turn back so he pushed on. When he saw black smoke wafting up over the trees ahead, Bulloch took the BMW off onto a dirt road through a field of grazing cows. Closing the distance on the source of the smoke, Bulloch noticed train tracks leading into the same area. Clearing the top of a small rise the attaché skidded the motorcycle to such a sloppy stop on the loose dirt that he almost put the bike down. Below him were thousands of dead soldiers strewn about around a derailed train. This was where the battle had been all right.

The smell of charred flesh was thick on the air. Exploding artillery shells or mortars had left some corpses whole while shredding many more into much smaller pieces that were strewn in every direction. Bulloch switched off the motor. Nothing moved or made a sound save for the birds circling overhead or the flames still consuming the train cars. He could hear no calls for help. Bulloch had been right, he had outrun the Czech advance columns. The uniforms of the dead below were all German. By the looks of it the northbound train had been carrying an SS unit, perhaps as large as a regiment. They were the bunch that had been ambushed. It appeared like they had taken most of their casualties while being pinned down. The end had come when the ambushers had charged in to mop up those who were still putting up a fight. Bulloch could see where the last hand-to-hand fighting had taken place by where the

Wehrmacht uniforms of the fallen attackers had come to rest next to the defending SS troopers. That close up there could be no mistake who was fighting whom.

Bulloch was sadly reminded of old photographs showing dead soldiers were they fell on the battlefield during the War Between the States. His grandfather had once told him that he had killed twenty-eight men up close for the gray. The old man had never wanted to say anything more despite much prodding from his grandson. Taking in the fatalities below, Bulloch felt he understood the old reb a lot better now.

COUNTER-INTELLIGENCE OFFICE
REICH MINISTRY OF WAR – 72-76 TIRPITZUFER, BERLIN

The admiral's office had become a command center out of necessity. As soon as Gisevius had returned Canaris to the safety of Abwehr headquarters the spy chief pulled in all of the section heads available to give them emergency instructions. Soon they got the message that Heiden had pulled off the operation successfully. But the bastard had done so in secret so there was no succession plan in place. Hitler was dead, thanks to God, but who was going to step in to run the country now? As Canaris reckoned, they had twenty-four, perhaps forty-eight, hours to install a new government acceptable to both the military and the public. Chaos would take over after any longer than that and they would not be able to regain control of the country for weeks.

"My apologies, admiral. Heiden was my responsibility. I should have put more effort into keeping him on a tether," Ottke's subordinate had let loose an avalanche above their heads.

"No, the responsibility is mine," Canaris sifted through papers in a file. "I authorized the weapons, ammunition and explosives. Whatever the result, the blame resides with me. In fact, we owe Major Heiden a great debt. Our plan could not survive the change of circumstances from the hasty onset of the war and Halder's subsequent indecision. Heiden cut through all of that inertia and brilliantly pulled off the operation. Hitler is out of the picture... with greater finality than I preferred but out of the way nonetheless. I assume there has been no word from the major?"

"None sir. Heiden has slipped back into the shadows as far as we can determine," Ottke very much wanted to find the man for his own reasons.

"That is to be expected and very wise, actually. Better to watch from afar to see the response to his handiwork," Canaris had chosen the man well.

Gisevius dodged past junior officers rushing in and out of Canaris' office to reach the admiral and Ottke. "I just checked with von Helldorf. The city is completely locked down. They have rounded up most of the remaining high party members starting with Hess. Around ninety percent of known Gestapo personnel were arrested and put under lock and key.

Some of the SS departments put up a fight but Witzleben's troops cleared out the resisters in short order."

"Excellent. What about Bormann? That one is dangerous," Canaris reminded them.

"He is still missing. There is no reason to believe he has escaped Berlin, however," Gisevius knew Hess' second in command had his fingers on much of the party's resources. If Bormann escaped, he could complicate matters significantly.

"I learned earlier today Himmler had ordered an SS regiment to Berlin by rail. Do we know where those troops are? They could prove very inconvenient," Canaris moved onto the next loose end.

"That regiment has been neutralized, sir. The battle reported near Potsdam was von Brockdorff's garrison intercepting the SS train," Ottke had already received confirmation from the general.

"Excellent," Canaris put the file folder down to focus on his officers. "My original preference was to install a military government but that proposition supposed we had moved on Hitler prior to the start of the war. Heiden's elimination of Halder, as well as Keitel, also complicates matters for us with the other generals. Oberst Ottke, how far did you get in your conversations with Prince Wilhelm? I believe both the army and the people would accept the return of the Hohenzollern if it were in the form of a constitutional monarchy. There has to be some authority for the country to rally around, at least as a temporary measure during the transition back to civilian rule."

"Our discussions were very advanced. The prince is willing and ready to take on this duty. I dispatched some of our people to bring him and his family here safely from Schloss Klein Obisch as soon as Czechoslovak units crossed into Schlesien," Ottke could not afford to allow Prince Wilhelm Friedrich Franz Joseph Christian Olaf to become a prisoner of war.

"Very prudent of you. Let me know when the prince has arrived from what was likely a harrowing journey," Canaris would have to explain the ground rules to the prince so there was no misunderstanding.

"But Wilhelm renounced his right to succession five years ago after his marriage. Does that not prove to be a problem?" Gisevius still had severe reservations to any return of the Hohenzollern dynasty.

"We are discussing a constitutional monarchy. The old rules don't apply. Wilhelm is an heir and he is well liked. He will do. We are forced to be expedient," Canaris ended the argument. "I have already been in contact with General von Brauchitsch. He will take over command of OKW, as well as see to putting the rest of the nation under the army's control. Admiral Raeder has pledged his support for these measures and will assist by securing our major port cities. As for the Luftwaffe, Stumpff has agreed to assume command of the Air Ministry, as well as accede to the authority of von Brauchitsch."

"Well done sir," Ottke was impressed with how quickly the admiral had sewn up the three major branches of the military. "With the capital secure, and cohesion between the heads of the military, there is little risk of opposition in the northern states. Bayern is another story. We will have to pull the rest of the Tenth Army out of Bohemia to defang SS units between here and Munich."

"Agreed. General von Brauchitsch is putting together a plan of operation for Bayern." Canaris was already on top of that issue.

"Orders should also go out to Wehrmacht field commanders that all SS units in their areas of operation must be disarmed and put under quarantine until the rank and file can be safely discharged. Officers will have to be dealt with on a case by case basis," Gisevius was not sure how many of these SS recruits joined for personal aggrandizement versus how many were political extremists. It would all have to be sorted out, hopefully with the help of the Gestapo's vast repository of personal dossiers.

"But we cannot wait to complete the full pacification of the party," Canaris cautioned. "As soon as Prince Wilhelm is installed, overtures seeking a cessation of hostilities will go out to Prague and Paris immediately. This insane war must come to an end as soon as possible."

"Reporting for duty, admiral," a man called out as he squeezed through the doorway into the small office. He was still young by Canaris' standards, wearing a grey wool suit that was obviously tailored for his trim frame.

"Ah, Paul. So glad you were able to make it out of Dresden without complications," Canaris greeted the agent. "Come here, no time off for you I am afraid."

"Good work, hauptmann," Ottke made room for the agent. "What was the journey like?"

"Hard not to get shot at by our side or theirs. The roads were chaotic and the Czechs were right on my heels all the way to Schönefeld. Getting into the city was rather chaotic, as well." The agent had entered Berlin only that morning thanks to a transit pass with Witzleben's signature adorning the page. Looking around at all of activity in the building, he hazarded a guess. "I gather the chancellor has been dealt with by the look of things on the street?"

"Yes, the opportunity finally presented itself," Canaris saw no reason to be chatty about Heiden's personal initiative in the matter since the fewer individuals who knew the truth the better for posterity. That is why I am sending you back into Czechoslovakia straight away. It will have to come through Asch though, which we still hold for the moment. There is no time for getting you through any other point of access."

"What do you require of me on this trip, admiral?" the agent was already calculating what he would need to do to travel once inside the Czechoslovak border.

"You have means to contact Moravec's people, yes?" Canaris knew the war made such matters difficult yet his man was very resourceful.

"Yes sir, it can be done through their field office in Pilsen. That would be the most efficient method," the agent was sure contact could be made there.

"That will be sufficient. You will be carrying a personal communiqué from myself to Oberst Moravec. He must know it comes from my hand. The subject is to establish terms for the ending the hostilities between our nations," Canaris was placing an enormous trust in the man František Moravec knew by the name of Karl.

ESTERWEGEN CONCENTRATION CAMP
EMSLAND, DEUTSCHLAND

All morning long there had been a flurry of activity at the camp's administrative buildings with lots of goings and comings by mid-level camp guards. The same series of events were playing out at the vehicle shed and at the camp storehouse. To Krisch it looked like the SS administrators were very hastily packing up personal effects, weapons and supplies to move out. Yet none of the prisoners were allowed close enough to confirm that assumption for sure. Krisch knew there was a war between Germany against Czechoslovakia and France. He had read the party-affiliated newspapers while working in the office but the articles were always vague about the details of the war. Could an invading army be near the camp? Krisch saw these developments as possibly the best news his fellow prisoners and himself had seen in years... or possibly the worst. There were three options facing them that Krisch outlined when he called the leadership committee to order. The SS was either going to move them, kill them or abandon them. Right now the first option was not the likely course. The guards would have already forced the prisoners to labor on dismantling needed materials around the camp. So it was either going to be a bullet to the head or the SS was going to save itself and leave the prisoners to their own devices.

No sooner had they broken up the committee meeting than two guards came searching for Krisch to escort him to the administrative building. They would not tell him why, only that Krisch had been summoned. When they deposited him on the front steps Krisch could smell smoke. Approaching the door he saw open fires in the metal trashcans where documents were furiously being burned. A rottenführer inside the door made to bar his entrance but Achtziger waved Krisch in.

"Krisch, I have news for you. If you have not already guessed we are shutting this camp down," Achtziger was standing by his desk feeding paper to the flames.

"What becomes of me now?" Krisch decided to play the collaborator worried about his future.

"Be happy. This is good news for you leftists. You are on you own now," Achtziger never ceased getting enjoyment from tormenting this red. He would miss that.

"On our own?" Krisch continued to play dumb as Achtziger preferred.

"The camp commander just got a... let us say there as been a sudden change of authority in Berlin and it would be prudent for my comrades and I to fade into the scenery," Achtziger had been around long enough to know when it was time to run. Somewhere there was a knife with his name on it and he had no wish to make it easy for someone else to thrust the blade into his back.

"We are free to leave?" the obersturmführer was in a good mood and Krisch decided to risk getting to the point.

"Leave or stay, that is up to you, Achtziger went back to clearing out his top drawer. With nothing else he needed to pack or burn the obersturmführer tossed a nearby grey seabag over his shoulder, stepped close to Krisch and grabbed him by his shirt lapel. "Remember Krisch, when they ask, I was good to you."

With that admonition, Achtziger released hold of Krisch and walked to the door where his comrades waited for him. Turning around, he tossed a full pack of cigarettes to Krisch.

"Remember what I said now," Achtziger looked back for a moment before leaving with the rest.

Krisch watched them all board the waiting trucks. Within minutes their convoy made its way out of the camp with all of the working vehicles. His people may be free but he had no desire to wait for rescue. There was no telling who would show up to replace the SS and Krisch did not want to wait to find out. He knew there was a couple of broken down flatbed trucks in the repair shed plus a tractor. They had some good mechanics among their people. If there was fuel left in the storage tanks they might be able to get these vehicles operating with enough petrol to carry the weakest of their number. Those in good health could walk. The food stores would have to be checked as well. With the SS leaving in such a hurry there would be plenty they could not haul away with them.

With the last guards gone there no longer was a reason for the camp inmates to deny their curiosity. Leading a contingent of the ragged, Gohler stepped through the dust cloud kicked up by the departing SS trucks and cars. "They are all gone! Why? What did that bastard Achtziger tell you?"

"Nothing much. It was more of a twisted *au revoir*." The thought of Achtziger's kind crawling back out into the sunlight ended an argument Krisch was having with himself. "Someone has finally kicked the Nazis out of power. I do not know the specifics yet whatever happened it was significant enough for these rodents to run off."

"I hope it was Stalin who taught Hitler a lesson. Imagine... a thousand Red Brigades marching on the chancellery," Gohler had been shepherding that dream for years after the socialists had failed in keeping Hitler from power. "Soon they will come to liberate us."

"Don't bet on Stalin saving our hides. He might prefer keeping all of us right where we are. Remember, it was Stalin who instructed the kommunists not join with the socialists in the election. No, the only people who are going to liberate us are ourselves," Krisch was resolute about not waiting on others to get the job done. As Krisch pounded his fist time after time into his palm, his compatriots gathered closer around him. "We must seize this opportunity. The first step on that path is getting out of this hole and organizing our people on the outside."

Scholl listened in the crowd and remembered the Krisch that had arrived through the camp gates so long ago: lost, disoriented and rudderless. This person speaking on the steps was a different man. Somehow Faulhaber had known what would sprout from the kernel.

"We must forge a Deutschland that protects every man and woman from being thrown into camps like this to languish and die," Krisch's words flowed easily. "Will the Prussian elite guarantee the rights of every German? No! Do the autocrats and their conglomerates care one whit for anything other than their capital? No! Did the church speak up when you and your family were torn from their homes and sent to the camps? No! And at the crucial moment, when unity could have stopped Hitler and sent him packing, did the Comintern implore German kommunists to stand together with German socialists? No! That is our truth. That is why we must stand together as free Germans to be free Germans."

Feeling his fellows lifted by Krisch's address, Scholl sealed a pact with himself that he would abide by as long as his lungs continued to draw air. Scholl would follow this one to hell if necessary. He would take the bullet that would one day come so Krisch may continue. These were dangerous words young Krisch spoke yet he was correct. Everyone standing there on the camp dirt understood the same truth: those who had been forsaken would have to stand together. That was the only way to keep camps like these from ever rising again on their soil. Scholl stepped forward, grabbing Gohler by the arm as he went. Together they stepped up beside Krisch. It was time they all got to work.

"A new Deutschland starts with us," Scholl took Krisch's arm and lifted it skyward in a show of support that drew a cheer from their compatriots. "We need good men to start working on the disabled vehicles in the repair shed. I watched them carefully and the guards did not have room to lug away the tools."

"Next we need an accounting of everything that the SS left behind," Gohler added. Scholl may have acted first, but Gohler felt no less committed to this kid. "Food, fuel, clothing... as much as we can carry."

"I will inventory the available tools and any ingredients we can use to make explosives. They will be our only weapons to defend ourselves," Scholl was looking ahead. There were those who would not take kindly to a large group of former leftist prisoners moving through their communities.

"There will be no looting," Krisch had a heavy burden to keep their desire for revenge in check. "Whatever has been done to us we will not steal and wreak chaos on others. We shall defend ourselves but that is all. Next, I will need men to go through the offices to check for any files and evidence they have not burnt. We will need such evidence later for the trials that we will hold. Let's get moving."

Those who had been mechanics moved onto the vehicle shed. Former factory workers and carpenters created groups to go out and inventory what raw materials were left that could be fashioned into something useful. Onetime bureaucrats set themselves upon the SS administrative huts.

Krisch drew Scholl and Gohler close to him. "With you two by my side I know we will succeed."

"You realize the challenges of the path you chose today, don't you?" Scholl rested his hand firmly on Krisch's shoulder.

"Not really. I do not much care anymore. I only see what must be done," Krisch was running on a determination he was unfamiliar with.

"We will be with you every step of the way," Gohler pledged himself as well.

"Thank you, my friends," Krisch would allow himself no further delay for sentiment. "The three of us must chart the safest course possible to the safety of Bremen. Once there, we can breathe a little easier and plan our next steps."

EPILOGUE

Crown Prince Wilhelm (C) and family

News of the army coup d'état arrived first in reports filed by radio correspondents in Berlin. What fate had befallen Chancellor Hitler was difficult to verify, however, since no one with first-hand knowledge would come forward or could be located. In the days after October 18th, bedlam ruled in Germany and conflicting accounts spread regarding the fate of the dictator. In some versions the chancellor had been deposed and was being held prisoner. Other reports popped up that said Hitler had resisted arrest and had been killed in gunfight with the Berlin army garrison and police. Finally, there were statements that the chancellor had been summarily executed. No one could say for sure and there was no longer a government in charge to approach to petition the truth. What was known for certain was that a purge of national socialists in positions of power was under way in the country. With their own eyes reporters observed that purge moving from north to south across Germany. Soon there was a flood of articles documenting the progress of German troops and police as they rooted out Nazi party members in municipalities large and small.

In his quest to seed the SS prominently into the war, Himmler had dispersed most of his trained soldiers into the field where they were either captured, dead or too far away to intervene. As the purge of the party expanded inside the country there were only a few SS companies available to stand in the way. Isolated from their command structure, these men resisted bravely yet were quickly subdued by regular army units. Ferreting out local members of the Gestapo proved a more difficult proposition. But after it became obvious the army was fully behind the coup d'état, there was no lack of good citizens in hundreds of communities who were happy to point out the hiding places of those they had recently feared.

Faced with too many unknown variables, President Beneš and Generál Krejčí agreed that it was best not to interfere with the spasm of change sweeping across Germany. Sensing a political opportunity in the chaos, Stalin signaled he too was willing to pause the hostilities. The fiercest opponents of the *watch and wait* order were the battlefield professionals such as de Gaulle. The French colonel viewed Germany as a perennial threat regardless of government and argued vociferously that France should seize and hold the entire Rhineland as a matter of prudent defense. Such sentiments were not shared in Paris or by the other governments involved, however. There was a strong conviction in these capitals that the coup in Berlin was proof enough that further fighting was unnecessary. De Gaulle countered with the recent example of Alexander Kerensky giving way to Vladimir Lenin, and while he had a sympathetic ear of ministers in Daladier's government like Paul Reynaud, the orders to stand down were not withdrawn.

During the ensuing days, much of the confusion about whom was in charge in Germany started to clear. Moravec received a message from his star operative, A-54, requesting an immediate audience. The meeting took place near Plzen. As Strankmüller had long argued, it was now indisputable that *Karl* was a member of the Abwehr. What was unexpected was that the man had been operating under the complete authorization of Moravec's opposite, Admiral Canaris. The agent carried an official overture directly from Canaris, von Brauchitsch, and Raeder seeking an armistice that pledged the immediate removal of all German military units still on Czechoslovak soil as a precondition. The overture was endorsed by Beneš in Prague and forwarded with favor onto Daladier in Paris. The French agreed completely with the proposal and negotiations got under way in Geneva without delay. A Soviet advisor was accepted, but as only Czechoslovak and French troops occupied German territory, Prague and Paris would negotiate the peace terms alone. The German representative, however, was Konstantin von Neurath. Joachim von Ribbentrop had made the spontaneous decision to stay indefinitely in Warsaw upon the mysterious disappearance of his transport aircraft and the news of the removal of the party from power. A capable representative for the talks in Geneva was needed post-haste and von Neurath had the good fortune to have been sacked by Hitler.

As the Geneva talks got under way, evidence was made public that Adolph Hitler had indeed died resisting arrest. Photographs of the dictator dead in his chancellery cabinet room were made available to news organizations to publish. But the chancellor's final resting place was never revealed in the interests of maintaining public order. With certainty as to the fate of Hitler, the German delegation at Geneva announced that Crown Prince Wilhelm would head a constitutional return of the Hohenzollern monarchy to unite the country. This new government established by the army would subsequently dedicate itself to establishing the peace. Paris and Prague approved yet pressed that any peace agreement must also dictate legal prohibitions against the Nazi Party in Germany. Knowing full well the complicity of the German military classes in the rise of Hitler to power, the French and Czech negotiators also dictated that the Wilhelm government be established as a transitionary body only, in lieu of national elections to follow after the country could be stabilized but no later than 1939. Such coercion rankled von Neurath yet the reality was Germany was in a position of weakness. Knowing this, Beneš ordered his delegation to insert one final requirement to eliminate the seed that had brought on the war. All ethnic Germans who had taken up arms against Czechoslovakia, or had actively supported Henlein's Sudeten Deutsche Party, would be repatriated to German soil at the earliest opportunity. Any physical property that could not be taken with them or transferred willingly to democratic German relations would be purchased at a fair price by the Czechoslovak government. To assure a swift peace agreement with provisions for the eventual return of conquered territory to Germany, von Neurath was instructed to agree to these demands despite the added burden of millions of refugees... and move on.

The peace agreement that resulted was well received by most Germans, Czechs and French alike. There were arguments that Germany got off easy but they were in the minority. The prevailing wisdom was that the Germans would pay terribly for the Nazi's reckless ambitions. Sudeten Germans argued they had lost the most of anyone but the general feeling was the Sudetens had rolled the dice with Hitler and lost. They would have to live with the result of their actions. The issue that was left mostly unresolved by the peace treaty was the status of Austria. The people there had voted overwhelmingly for anschluss with Germany, which complicated matters and made it difficult for France and Czechoslovakia to rip Austria away now despite forceful Soviet arguments. The one nod Paris and Prague made to the future of Austria was demanding a free and fair election be held within the pre-1938 Austrian borders before the end of 1940 to decide the matter.

Freed from their incarceration, German political prisoners returned from the camps to their homes with the intention of rebuilding their lives and playing an active role in the future of the country. Hitler's government had emptied the nation's coffers to fund rearmament and public work projects. When that spending ceased the economy collapsed and ground to a halt. The Wilhelm government had no monetary instruments to prevent factories from closing and businesses going bankrupt. Berlin could not find international investors for its bonds and no loans were forthcoming from Europe or the Americas. Germany once more found itself in a terrible depression. In the severe economic chaos that resulted, the newly freed labor leaders and workers took over shuttered factories and operated them collectively. Bartering their products with other worker occupied and operated enterprises, production started again slowly and a lifeline was thrown to the wider economy. All this was accomplished with one eye upon the promised future elections. As they worked to bring some small amount of stability to the country, this new labor movement prepared its own political slate. One name, a relative unknown, stood out among the rest: Krisch.

END NOTE

Thank you for reading. If you enjoyed Sudetenland and would like to know when the sequel is published, please visit this page at the website address below.

www.sudetenland.georgetchronis.com/send-us-a-message

Made in the USA
Charleston, SC
14 May 2015